Andrei Bitov

PUSHKIN HOUSE

Translated from the Russian by
Susan Brownsberger

COLLINS HARVILL
8 Grafton Street, London W1
1990

COLLINS HARVILL
William Collins Sons and Co Ltd
London· Glasgow · Sydney · Auckland
Toronto · Johannesburg

BRITISH LIBRARY CATALOGUING IN PUBLICATION DATA

Bitov, Andrei 1936 -
Pushkin House.
1. Fiction in Russian, 1945 - English texts
I. Title II. Pushkinskii dom. *English*
891.7344

ISBN 0-00-271088-9

© Andrei Bitov 1978
English translation © Susan Brownsberger 1987

First published in Great Britain in 1988 by
Weidenfeld and Nicolson Limited
This paperback edition first published
by Collins Harvill 1990

Printed and bound in Great Britain by
Hartnolls Limited, Bodmin

PUSHKIN HOUSE

ANDREI BITOV, novelist, short story writer, poet and travel writer, was born in Leningrad in 1937 and graduated from the Mining Institute there in 1962. He published five collections of stories between 1963 and 1972 and this early fiction won him a reputation as one of the Soviet Union's most gifted stylists. He has also published novels, travel writings (including essays on Georgia and Armenia) and poetry, but in the 1970s and early 1980s his work came under official criticism for its "excessive subjectivity" – partly for securing the publication of *Pushkin House*, which had failed to find a Soviet publisher, in the West in 1978, and partly for taking part with Vasily Aksyonov in an attempt to found an uncensored literary almanac, *Metropolis*, in 1979. Written between 1965 and 1971, *Pushkin House* first appeared in an English translation in 1987 and in the same year, as a result of glasnost, it was at last published in the Soviet Union in *Novy Mir*. Andrei Bitov's work now appears in major journals and in book form. He lives near Moscow with his mother, his wife and their child.

CONTENTS

This is what will be: we, too, will not be.

PUSHKIN, 1830

(Draft of an epigraph for *The Belkin Tales*)

Pushkin House! A name apart,
A name with meaning for the heart!

BLOK, 1921

PUSHKIN HOUSE

WHAT IS TO BE DONE?

(Prologue, or A Chapter Written

After the Rest)

On the morning of July 11, 1856, the staff of one of the great
Petersburg hotels near the Moscow Railroad Station was perplexed,
even somewhat alarmed.

N. G. CHERNYSHEVSKY, 1863

SOMEWHERE NEAR the end of the novel we have already attempted
to describe the clean window, the icy sky gaze, that stared straight and
unblinking as the crowds came out to the streets on November 7. Even
then, it seemed that this clear sky was no gift, that it must have been
extorted by special airplanes. And no gift in the further sense that it
would soon have to be paid for.

Indeed, the morning of November 8, -196–, more than confirmed
those premonitions. It was awash above the desolated city, amorphously dripping heavy streaks of old Petersburg houses, as if the houses
had been penned in dilute inks that were paling with the light of dawn.
And while the morning finished penning this letter, which had once
been addressed by Peter "to spite his haughty neighbor" but now was
addressed to no one and reproached no one, asked nothing—a wind
fell upon the city. It fell as flatly and from above as if it had rolled
down a smooth curve of sky, gathered speed with uncommon ease,
and landed tangent to the earth. It fell, like a certain airplane, when
it had had enough of flying. As if that airplane yesterday had expanded
and swelled in flight, gobbled all the birds, sucked up the other squadrons, and when bloated on metal and sky-color had plummeted to the
earth—still trying to glide down and land, it had plummeted into
tangency. A flat wind the color of an airplane glided down on the city.
The name of the wind was the childhood word "Gastello."

It touched down on the city streets as on a landing strip, bounced
when it hit the ground somewhere on the Spit of Vasily Island, and
then raced off, powerfully and noiselessly, between rows of now damp

3

houses, along the exact route of yesterday's march. Having thus verified the city's emptiness and lack of human life, it rolled onto the parade square, swooped up a broad and shallow puddle to smack it against the toy wall of yesterday's grandstands, and then, tickled with the resulting sound, flew through the Revolutionary wicket and took off again, soaring steeply, sweepingly, up and away . . . And if this were a movie, then across the empty square, one of the largest in Europe, the "toss-me, catch-me" that a child had lost yesterday would still be chasing after the wind. Now utterly drenched, it would fall apart, burst open, as if to reveal the wrong side of life: the sad and secret fact that it was made of sawdust . . . But the wind straightened out, soaring and exulting, and high over the city it turned back and streaked away on the loose, once more to glide down on the city somewhere on the Spit, having thus described an inside climbing loop.

It ironed the city flat, and right behind it, over the puddles, dashed a heavy express rain—over the avenues and embankments so well known, over the swollen gelatinous Neva with its countering, rippling patches of crosscurrent and its mismatched bridges; later we are mindful how it rocked the lifeless barges near the banks, and a certain float with a pile driver . . . The float chafed against the partially driven piles, frazzling the wet wood; across from it stood a house of interest to us, a small palace, now a scientific institute; in that house, on the third floor, a broken window was flapping wide open, and both wind and rain easily flew inside.

The wind flew into a smallish hall and chased around the floor the handwritten and typewritten pages that were scattered everywhere. Several pages stuck to the puddle under the window. And indeed this whole room (a museum exhibition hall, to judge by the glass-covered texts and photographs hung on the walls, the glass-topped tables with open books in them) was a scene of inexplicable devastation. The tables had been moved from their geometrically suggested correct places to stand here and there, every which way. One had even been tipped wrong side up, in a sprawl of broken glass. A cupboard lay face down with its doors flung open, and beside it, on the scattered pages, his left arm crumpled inertly beneath him, lay a man. A body.

He appeared to be about thirty, if one can even speak of appearances, because his appearance was horrible. Pale as a creature from under a rock—white grass. The blood had clotted in his tangled gray hair and on his temple; mold was growing in the corner of his mouth. Gripped in his right hand was an ancient pistol, the kind seen nowadays only in a museum. A second pistol, double-barreled, with one trigger re-

4

leased and the other cocked, lay at a distance, about two meters away. Inserted in the barrel that had been fired was the butt of a Northland cigarette.

I can't say why, but this death makes me want to laugh. What is to be done? Who should be informed?

A fresh gust of wind slammed the window violently, tearing off a sharp splinter of glass and stabbing it into the windowsill, then crumbling it like a shower of coins into the puddle below. Having done this, the wind dashed away along the embankment. From its own viewpoint, this was not a grave or even a noticeable deed. It dashed onward to whip banners and buntings, to rock river-bus landings, barges, floating restaurants, and the busy little tugboats that were quite alone, this frazzled, lifeless morning, in their flurry of activity around the legendary cruiser sighing quietly at anchor.

We have said much more about the weather than about the interesting event, for that will occupy pages enough in the future; the weather, however, has special importance for us and will play its part in the narrative again, if only because the action takes place in Leningrad . . .

The wind dashed on like a thief, its cloak streaming.

(Italics Mine. —A.B.)

We are inclined in this tale, under the roof of Pushkin House, to follow in the hallowed traditions of the museum, not shying away from echoes and repetitions—on the contrary, welcoming them in every way, as if we even rejoiced in our lack of inner independence. For that, too, is "in key," so to speak, and can be understood in relation to the phenomena that have served us here as theme and material; namely, phenomena utterly nonexistent in reality. So, if even the container we must use was created before our day and not by us, this fact also serves our purpose, as if closing the circle.

And so we are re-creating the hero's contemporary nonexistence, the elusive ether, which nowadays almost corresponds to the very secret of matter, a secret that contemporary natural science has run up against: when matter is split up, articulated, and reduced to increasingly elementary particles, it suddenly and totally ceases to exist because of our attempt to divide it further: particle, wave, quantum, each of them and none of them and not all three together . . . and Grandma's nice word "ether" floats up in memory, almost reminding us that the secret was well known even before our day, the sole difference being that no one ran up against it with the vacant surprise of those who think the

5

world intelligible—people just knew there was a secret here, and accepted it as such.

And we pour this nonexistent ether into Grandma's nonsurviving phials, surprised that for each vinegar, in her day, there was its own corresponding purposeful shape; gladly we wash the word "cruet" in lukewarm water, gazing with pleasure on the idea of the cut glass, until a ray of childhood, sparkling with soap and crystal, shines an iridescent light on the yellowish tablecloth crocheted in someone's distant and inconceivable needlework childhood, on the anise drops, and on the thermometer with its antique color of mercury, unchanged as yet only by virtue of its devotion to the table of elements and chemical fidelity . . . And this iridescent ray will shine on someone's delicate bundled-up neck, Mama's kiss on the top of his head, and the great novel The Three Musketeers.

And how surprised we are at a sudden, so unaccustomed quality in our own movements, deliberate and tender, mysteriously interrupting and halting our flurry of activity, and prompted only by the shape and cutting of these phials . . .

A museum novel . . .

And, at the same time, we will try to write so that even a scrap of newspaper, if not used for its ultimate purpose, might be inserted at

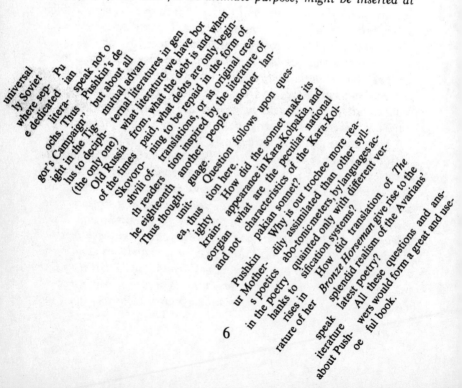

universally Soviet literature, where sep- e dedicated . . . Pu[shk]ian litera- ochs. Thus speak not of Pushkin's de but about all mutual advan[tages], [in "I]gor's Campaign", ight in the Tig- lus to deciph- (the only one) of Old Russia of the times of Skovoro- shvili of- he eighteenth th readers Thus thought unit- ea, thus ighty krain- eorgian and not . . . ternal literatures in gen[eral] what literature we have bor[rowed] from, what the debt is and when paid, what debts are only beginning to be repaid in the form of translations, or as original creation inspired by the literature of another people, another language. Question follows upon question here. How did the sonnet make its appearance in Kara-Kolpakia, and what are the peculiar national characteristics of the Kara-Kolpakian sonnet? Why is our trochee more readily assimilated than other syllabo-tonic meters, by languages acquainted only with different versification systems? How did [the] translation of The Bronze Horseman give rise to the splendid realism of the Avarians' latest poetry? All these questions and answers would form a great and useful book. Pushkin ur Mother- s poetics in the poetry hanks to rises in [lite]rature of her speak literature about Push-oe *any point in the novel, serving as a natural continuation and in no way violating the narrative.*

So that, on putting aside the novel, you might read a fresh or stale newspaper and suppose that what is happening now in the newspaper—and consequently, to some extent, in the world at large—is happening in the time of the novel. And, vice versa, on putting aside the newspaper and returning to the novel, you might suppose that you hadn't broken off reading the novel but had reread the introduction once more, in order to clarify a few trifling points about the author's intentions.

Since we hope for this kind of effect, since we count on the inevitable collaboration and coauthorship of time and environment, there is much that we probably will not spell out at length or in detail, believing that all these things are mutually known, from the experience of author and reader.

SECTION ONE

FATHERS AND SONS

(A Novel of Leningrad)

Supporting each other, they walk with burdened tread; they draw near the rail and fall to their knees. Long and bitterly they weep, long and attentively they gaze at the mute stone under which their son lies . . .

TURGENEV, 1862

FATHER

FOR LYOVA ODOEVTSEV, of *the* Odoevtsevs, life had brought no special traumas; in the main, it had flowed along. Figuratively speaking, the thread of his life had streamed rhythmically from someone's divine hands, skimmed through the fingers. Without undue haste, without breaks or knots, that thread had remained under steady and moderate tension, showing only an occasional slight sag.

In point of fact, even his belonging to an old and famous Russian family is almost immaterial. If his parents had ever had to recall and define their attitude to their surname, that was in the long-ago years when Lyova did not yet exist or was in the womb. For Lyova himself, ever since he could remember, there had been no need of it, and he was rather a namesake than a scion. He was Lyova.

His infancy, it is true (Lyova was conceived in a "fateful" year), had brought some disagreeable relocations for him, or rather for his parents, to the land of their notable ancestor—"deep into the Siberian mines," as it were. Lyova vaguely remembered this: it was cold, Mama bartered her kimono (huge silk flowers) for potatoes, and he, little Lyovushka, once ran off to the pond and found three rubles on the shore. That little stretch of water, the stretch of blank gray fence, and the stone on which he painfully stubbed his toe in his joy were fixed in his memory, along with the color of the three-ruble note. He could neither remember nor understand that his father had "really been lucky," that such "mild" measures were most unusual and what had happened to them was great good fortune and a happy accident, if only because

Lyovushka's grandfather had been "taken" the year his parents got married, almost ten years back, and all those years they hadn't been "touched." (That Grandfather had been taken back then was "lucky" for Grandfather, too, because it was "in time"; later he would have been "dealt with differently," but this way he migrated from exile to exile, nothing worse.) That there was no news from Grandfather might also be as bad as you could imagine, though not for Grandfather— for them: you never knew what he . . . Not to mention the other relatives "over the border"—you could expect any dirty trick from them. On the whole, it "might have been worse." But these favorable calculations were beyond Lyova. He could neither remember nor understand this—even later on, when he might have been able, if not to understand, then at least to remember—because Grandfather had not been discussed in his presence for a good ten years, and everything that had personally happened to him, Lyova, had somehow turned into a so-called wartime childhood. Indeed, the war had begun soon after they were exiled, evacuees had appeared in their remote backwater, and there was no longer anything exceptional about their family's situation.

In the end, for reasons that were hidden from Lyova even longer than the existence of a "live" grandfather, everything turned out happily, and after the war they returned to their native city as if from evacuation, all three of them, without casualties. Papa began to lecture, at the university as before, eventually defending his doctoral thesis and occupying the chair in which his father had shone (the only fact Lyova knew about Grandfather); Lyova himself studied and grew up, eventually finishing school and entering the university under his father; Mama didn't seem to do anything and got older.

Lyova grew up in the so-called academic milieu, and from childhood he dreamed of becoming a scholar. Only not a philologist, like his father and apparently his grandfather; not a humanist, more likely a biologist . . . biology was a "purer" science, he fancied. He liked the way Mama brought strong tea to Father every evening in his study. Father paced the dark room, softly clinking the spoon against his tea glass and saying things to Mama in a voice as muted as the lamplight, which picked from the gloom only the desk with its papers and books. When no one was home, Lyova would brew himself some nice strong tea and drink it through a stick of macaroni, and then he fancied he was wearing on his head the black professorial skullcap. "Like Father, but bigger than Father . . ."

That was the pose in which he read his first book, and the book was *Fathers and Sons*. It became a point of special pride for him that the first book he ever read was a thick and serious one. He bragged a bit about never having read skinny little children's books, no Pavkas or Pavliks (not realizing that he got second credit: the Odoevtsevs simply didn't have those little books in the house. The reason was neither stated nor explained—it was acted on). What most impressed him, perhaps, was that he read this thick book with absorption and even enjoyment. The reading of thick books, a labor that was due such major honors as he conceived it, turned out to be not so hard after all, not even boring (the latter, in his childish mind, had somehow seemed a necessary condition of elitehood). What also impressed him in Turgenev was the word "maidens" and the fact that now and again these maidens drank "sugar water." Imagining this and forgiving Turgenev for it, Lyova supposed his own time to be better than Turgenev's in that one had to be so great, gray, and bearded back then, just to write what could be so well mastered in our day by a boy as little (though very gifted) as Lyova, and further, his own time was better in that he had been born now, not back then, this was the time that had borne Lyova, so gifted at understanding everything so early . . . Thus for a long while the concept of the serious, in Lyova's mind, coincided with solidity and an imposing appearance. But after he had read "all" of Pushkin and done a report in school for the poet's sesquicentennial, he really had no idea what more could be required on the path that had opened so easily to him: everything was already within his grasp, and he had just as much time left ahead as in childhood. To endure this waiting, one needed "willpower," a magic spiritual category of those years, almost the only one Lyova picked up outside the family citadel. In this very armchair, sinking into it so deep that the only thing visible was the black skullcap, he taught himself the first lessons in courage, because the willpower that Meresyev had plenty of in the absence of legs, Lyova had too little of in the presence of arms. Was this when he announced that the natural sciences attracted him more than the humanistic? . . . but that would be too psychoanalytical. His parents, privately noting their son's humanist bent, did not block his naturalist leanings.

In the newspapers, Lyova liked to read the obituaries of scholars. (He skipped the obituaries of political figures, because politics was never mentioned in the family, neither damned nor praised, and he regarded it as something very external and exempt from criticism, not even so much out of caution—they didn't seem to have taught him that, either—as because it was totally irrelevant to him. This side of his upbringing, his "apoliticality," should also be recounted in detail, but for the time being we merely note it.) In obituaries for scholars he would find an unusually pleasant tone of propriety and respect, and naturally he would imagine himself an old man already, surrounded by his numerous pupils, a member of numerous scholarly societies, his life a sort of sustained celebration. The obituaries also mentioned tireless labor, unbending will, and courage; these were somehow a matter of course, even little Lyova understood that without the "labor" it was "nothing but shallow daydreaming"—but, nevertheless, chief in those dreams were the strong tea, the skullcap, and all the many forms of idleness to which a man of merit (or, as it was customary to say for some reason, "emeritus") was entitled, apparently by right.

Their house, which had been built after a design by the well-known Benois, with the elegance and insouciance typical of pre-Revolutionary modernism; a house in which no two windows were identical, it seemed, because the apartments had been built to order (a "cooperative" of those years, in its own way) and everyone wanted something different— some wanted a bay window, some narrow and high, and some even round—beyond all symmetry, and yet somehow with an easily grasped sense of the whole; a house with a predominance, insistent as child-hood, of the seaweed lines of Liberty silk—in the molding, in the grillwork of balconies and elevators, in the occasional surviving World of Art stained-glass windows—this dear house was populated by a numerous tribe of professors, their dying-out elders and currently-dean sons and graduate-student grandsons (although not in all families had the succession been built up so effectively), because three institutions of higher learning and several scientific research institutes were located in the vicinity. The house stood on a deserted and handsome old street, right across from the famous Botanical Garden and Institute.

Lyova had always liked that quiet vale of science. He pictured people working selflessly and nobly in the great white-columned building, as well as in the ancient wooden laboratory cottages, dating back almost to Elizabeth, that dotted the beautiful park. Far away from noise, from all this thundering technology, people were busy with their serious business, their plants . . . During elections to the Soviets his parents' voting place was at the Botanical Institute, and as Lyova climbed the broad carpeted staircase with them he respectfully scrutinized the portraits of eminent graybeards and pince-nez wearers of botanical science. They looked at him dryly and without enthusiasm, as at an infusorian, but could they know that someday they would have to move over and make room for Lyova's portrait? His heart sweetly stopped and skipped a beat with delight over his own future.

Since the chapter is titled "Father," we should mention this: it seemed to Lyovushka that he did not love his father. Ever since he could remember, he had been in love with Mama, always and everywhere there was Mama, but Father would appear for just a minute, sit down at the table, an extra without a cue, his face seeming always in shadow. Ineptly, awkwardly, he would try to start playing with Lyova, take a long time choosing and shuffling things to tell his son, and end up saying something banal—and Lyova would remember nothing but a feeling of awkwardness for his father, remember neither words nor gesture, so that eventually every fleeting encounter with his father (Father was always very busy) amounted only to this awkward feeling, awkwardness all around. That is, Father didn't even seem capable of tousling Lyova's hair correctly—Lyova would cringe—or taking him on his lap—he always caused his Lyovushka some sort of physical discomfort—Lyovushka would tense up and then be embarrassed by his own embarrassment. Father wasn't even any good at "Hello" and "How are things," somehow it was all shy and false, so that Lyova lowered his eyes in confusion or felt glad no one was looking. Lyova vaguely remembered that Father had once been good at trotting him on one knee—"A-riding he will go, a-riding he will go, a-gallop, a-gallop, a-bumpity, *boom!*" He used to have the strength . . . But even here, Father never knew when to stop, he didn't tire of it (he was so glad to be good at it, perhaps?), and Lyovushka would have to be the first to end the game.

So all through his childhood, seeing his father often and little, Lyova didn't even know what his face was like: was it wise and kind, was it handsome . . . One day, suddenly, he saw it for the first time. Father had been lecturing for almost three months at a branch institute somewhere in the south, Mama had decided to wash the windows that day, Lyova was helping her. They had washed one window and started on the second. The room was illuminated half and half: a dusty, swirling light, and open, washed, spring sunlight. And now, creating a wind with his extra-wide tussah slacks, Father burst in, flourishing a brand-new briefcase with a little engraved plaque from grateful people. The sun flashed on the plaque, and Father's white shoe stepped in the small puddle around the basin . . . So Mama and he were standing on the dusty half of the room, and Father, consequently, on the washed spring half . . . He looked like a negative, like a tennis player, like the cover of *Health* magazine. Too tanned and white-haired (he had turned white early), with a young smooth face, a big loud man in an apache shirt as snowy as his hair, setting him off and so becoming to him . . . at this point we're supposed to describe the open collar, the strong, masculine, desirable neck . . . we're repelled. He had a neck. Lyova stared too hard at Father's shoe: the tooth powder on it was quickly getting very wet. Lyova too vividly pictured Father wetting the toothbrush with saliva and scrubbing the shoe . . . And that was how Father was fixed in his memory, so that for the next ten years he didn't notice what he was like *now*, but pictured him just as he remembered him *then*—tanned and confident—as if they had since parted ways forever. Even so, he probably remembered only because Father was mirrored in Mama, at that second, by a discomfiture Lyova did not know, by a weak smile, by the way she grew young again and in the same second utterly old right before his eyes, an old little girl on the dusty half . . . and most importantly, Lyova at that instant did not exist for her. Lyova was jealous, and he remembered. The window was left unfinished that day . . . But how instantaneously the life of an alien, secret love, someone else's, is mirrored in us, wordlessly and unconsciously; discomfited by the alien brilliance, we stumble against our own buried love, then withdraw into ourselves: too late, not for us . . . But we're skipping ahead. This was not for Lyova yet—though he was all the more able to sense it.

And now, too, the "story of the ruble" framed and glassed that chance image of Father's tanned neck, beloved by someone (heaven knows whom) and confident of that love . . . The ruble was almost irrelevant, but for a long time Lyova thought of it as a note of large denomination, larger than ten. A neighbor from their courtyard, fifth-floor stair landing, old hag, bitch sucked dry by three children—and Lyova hated her long after for that ruble!—she stopped him, pinned him in a doorway somewhere, and, while Lyova filled with shame for her, told him (and she didn't recall now whom she happened to hear it from) how his father had been seen in the Park of Culture and Rest, apparently at the restaurant, with a young lady—and Father had given a beggar a whole ruble! The hugeness of the ruble was especially hateful, insulting, and scandalous to the neighbor . . . A park, a beautiful young woman, a restaurant on the water, a ruble for a beggar— such a lush quantity of other life dazzled Lyova, too, and he went home overwhelmed. Well he might; times were still hard, it wasn't long after the war . . . Ah, but he found out, Lyova did—later, much later, a quarter of a century—that they hadn't been old then: they had all been young! Father was under forty, Mama was thirty-five, and the damn neighbor not even thirty.

He said nothing for three days, would not speak to Father, until Mama said, "What's the matter with you?" He held out a while longer, only to crack, almost eagerly confessing to the whole immense ruble. The story must have made a considerable impression on Mama, too, for she pulled herself together immediately. Her face took on an expression of pinched severity toward Lyova himself. A punishment followed, harsh and able, and this—how clearly he saw it now—relieved her greatly. The impeccability of her logic, the rhythmicity of her justice, the lucid form of her accusations were proof of her relief. For both of them, things became transparent and flickeringly calm, like breath on a mirror. Then the breath evaporated, dusk crept over the mirror, all was dim.

Yet no fresh image of Father arose in place of the one at that homecoming, and there had been no previous one except the wedding photograph, where he had loved Mama . . . darling Mama, not even twenty, her big round eyes, a sort of turban on her head. Comparing these two photos, Lyova could not help marveling at the change. The handsome calf with the bowler and cane, with the corners of his mouth round like berries, with an Esenin-like purity and doom in his eyes, and this sated, tanned bull in the tussah bell-bottoms ("a fine figure of a man")—supposedly they were one person. As though his father had been born in two eras at once, in both yesterday and today; as though the epochs themselves had faces, while a man did not.

Lyova reached a decision once: that he was very different from Father. Not even his opposite—different. And not only in character, as was already clear, but also in his person—totally different. He had grounds for thinking so with respect to the actual dissimilarity of their features, their ears, hair, and eyes. Here they really did have little in common. But the main thing, of which he wanted (perhaps even secretly from himself) to remain somehow adroitly unmindful, was not this, the formal kind of resemblance, but true family resemblance, authentic and elusive, which is not a resemblance of features. In adolescence and youth his growing irritation with this or that gesture or intonation of his father's, his increasingly frequent rejection of Father's most innocent and trivial impulses, may even have signaled this developing, implacable family resemblance, while his revulsion at the inevitability of recognizing his father in himself may have been merely a way and a means of forming and establishing character . . .

Mama, too, plays quite a definite role here: although constantly irritated by Father's inability to shake his habits—such as standing there eating from the knife or drinking from the teapot spout—she hardly noticed it if Lyova did the same thing. Her insulted love was manifest here, for what she loved in her son was practically the same as what made her pretend (and from long years of training she no longer had to pretend) not to love Father. But if Lyova caught himself in a gesture of Father's—drank from the teapot spout in the kitchen, let's say, glancing over his shoulder—it meant that his inner irritation at Father had grown some more, and he evaded remarking to himself on the resemblance.

People seemed to remark equally on Lyova's striking resemblance to Father and on his striking lack of resemblance. But when it's fifty-fifty, we choose what we want. Lyova chose the lack of resemblance, and from then on, all he heard from people was how different he and his father were.

It reached the point that one day, when he was already in college and suffering through his first and ill-starred love, he caught himself thinking (a case of belated development) that he wasn't really his father's son. And one time, transfixed by his own acumen, he even guessed who his real father was. Fortunately, he disclosed this secret to just one person: turning to the dark window to brush away an involuntary tear, his face all distorted, he used the story to try to exact one more consent from his cruel love . . . However, she wasn't much moved. But we're skipping way ahead again.

But if we skip even further ahead, we can say with confidence that when Lyova, too (by about the age of thirty), had been run over by life, though in its exclusively personal peacetime forms, and Father had grown utterly old and transparent, then through this transparency, with pity and pain, Lyova more and more distinctly discerned a kinship with his father so ineradicable, so vital, that at some absurd and trivial gesture or word of Father's he would truly have to turn to the window to blink back a tear. Sentimentality, too, was typical of them both.

In sum, only by that distant time, which brings us near to the sad end of Lyova's tale, only then could Lyova grasp that Father was his father, that he, Lyova, *also* needed a father, as it turned out Father had once needed *his* father, Lyova's grandfather, Father's father. But the story of that important "also" must be told separately.

If we were to set ourselves the more detailed task of writing a famous trilogy, the *Childhood, Adolescence, Youth* of our hero, we would grind to a halt before a specific type of difficulty. Although Lyova remembered something of *Childhood*—the resettlement of the ethnic groups at age five; his own seduction at six; fistfights, going hungry; a few hovels, cattle cars, and landscapes—and these details might be used to reconstruct the atmosphere of a child's perception of the national drama, even lend density to that atmosphere by saturating it with poetic vapors of barefootedness, of fragrances and dappled light, grasses and dragonflies ("Pa, Pa, our nets hauled in a dead man!"); although his *Youth* passed before our very eyes, distinctly and in detail, and separate chapters will later be . . . ; still, Lyova remembered almost nothing, in any case remembered the least, of *Adolescence*, and we would have trouble, as it is now the custom to say, "with the data." For those years of his life, all we could do is substitute historical background. But we won't do that: everyone already knows as much as we'll need here. So Lyova had no adolescence—he studied in school. And he finished.

So—let's narrow the trousers, thicken the shoe sole, lengthen the jacket. Let's knot the necktie small. Daring young men came out on the Nevsky, to give the historical time greater precision of detail. Let us be fair to these men. They had a share in the common cause—and a share in the common fate. The first is underestimated, like every historical task; the second never did arouse the sympathy or pity it deserved.

One way or another, they did put themselves on the line. The best years (the strength) of what was not the worst part of our younger generation—the part receptive to unfamiliar forms of life—went into the narrowing of trousers. We are obliged to them not only for this (the trousers); not only for the free possibility, which followed years later, of widening them (the trousers); but also for the difficult public adjustment to the permissibility of *the different*: a different image, a different idea, a different person from you. What they confronted may be called a reaction, in the immediate sense of that word. The liberal sneers from the right, apropos the frivolity, pettiness, and insignificance of this fight (trousers—big deal!), were themselves frivolous, while the fight was in earnest. Even if the fighters themselves didn't recognize their own role: that is the point of the word "role," it's ready-made, written for you, and you have to play it, perform it. That is also the point of the word "fighters." So what if they just wanted to please their dolls and chicks. Who doesn't . . . But they endured persecutions, picketings, exclusions, and evictions so that two or three years later

Moscow Garment and Leningrad Clothing would independently switch to twenty-four centimeters instead of forty-four. In a state the size of ours, that's a good many extra trousers.

But we're beginning to sound mawkish. Let's hasten to mention their other "share" in life, not their piece of the common pie, but their fate, their fortune. You won't encounter them on the Nevsky anymore, those pioneers. They were routed and sent flying—and they grew up. Whether more or less, they contribute their mite by some sort of service to the modern day as well. Were they to appear now in that heroic form, how pathetic they would be amid imported clothes with such elegance of line, amid foreign currency, black-marketeering, Terylene, Dacron! If we recall their fighting youth, we can say we get all this for free now. As veterans, they have a right to beat their breast with their drunken stump of an arm over having shed blood to get Soviet vodka for the Finns and Finnish polyester for the Soviets. Here again I'm looking over my shoulder, from the age I'm telling about, into the age I'm writing in.

Several years ago, for the last time, I happened to see one of them again—forty years old, his face rutted by life, but still true to that better, heroic era, his own.

It was impossible not to notice him. He stuck out. People stopped and turned to stare and were so startled they didn't even laugh; not a hand was raised to point at him. He shuffled proudly by, signifying that—good Lord!—ten, maybe even fifteen years had passed since he vanished into thin air . . . because he was the same as ever. Fifteen years, well, that was nothing, but what had happened in those fifteen years—that was something! That was an epoch. How gradually, how instantaneously it had passed—no one had even noticed, being in it and moving ahead with it. And suddenly, in the present, here came the past, shuffling by, or as they said then, "shagging along," foolish to the point of pride and unsurprised at the changes.

He was that same famous hepcat of the early fifties. The very same trousers, that same green jacket drooping from shoulder to knee, apparently the same shoe soles glued on by an enterprising craftsman, the same necktie tied in a microscopic knot, the same ring, the same pomp hair, the same walk—straight caricature, even for that time, straight out of *Krokodil*, a style long since passé even on circus clowns. "Vyatkin . . ."a little old man recalled, but no one remembered even Vyatkin anymore. And the thing was, the man was walking along like that in *earnest*.

Well, he got his share of the street's sympathy and shame. People didn't laugh, they were all embarrassed—he was a madman. He was disabled. Good Lord, I thought, how loyal people are, forever, despite all, to the time when they were loved, and most importantly when *they* loved! Unbelievable . . . Yes, if they won't hide behind a new style, they're loyalists, like this madman.

This veteran of fashion, this little gumdrop soldier of History who for some reason had never dissolved on her tongue, signified day-before-yesterday's taste. Oh, it's too easy now to devalue that taste! He may have defended "merely" the freedom of the secondary male characteristics, yet he had borne the full weight of something (if only the big shoulder pads) and there had been something he could not bear, to which we were now witness, yet he had stood his ground, leaving to subsequent generations the struggle (but a much easier one!) for a subsequent widening of the trousers, yet even he had not stood his ground, forever turning his gaze to the youth that was over for us all.

This one-of-a-kind urban madman is not seen at all now, for some reason, so we no longer have any chance of verifying that experience. But one day, well along in our own time, almost twenty years after *that* time, we'll encounter a small group at the corner of Nevsky Prospect and Malaya Sadovaya Street, three or four men. For some reason our glance will linger on their faces. We definitely have never seen them and don't know them by sight, but they're the ones—the most famous men of the Nevsky of that time! Benz, Tikhonov, Temp . . . No, we didn't know them, but we remember their names, as every generation remembers willy-nilly the names of *the* goalies and *the* center forwards. Now they, too, glance into my face, slightly dubious, and avert their eyes.

Where have they been all this time? Why haven't I seen them, even once, in all these hectic years? And where have *I* been? . . . Here they stand, unrecognizable, balding, flabby, fortyish—and *elegant*: after all, they developed their taste before others did. A light whiff of black-marketeering can be detected with a little effort. The tingle of a cognac-and-lemon from the Soviet Champagne Shop around the corner still lingers in the mouth. Oh, take care, lads! What haven't you seen in your time . . . They stood there, gave the Nevsky a barely prolonged glance from out of their past, did nothing to distinguish themselves from the crowd, got into a Volga with private plates, and drove off, leaving me ulcered in spirit over so many years of someone else's life and mine.

No, the years had not passed in vain, we were better dressed, it was worth a life . . . Dear God! It's intolerable to humiliate people so!

It was in this historic time, to which we have alluded by means of the narrow trousers, that Lyova successfully finished high school and entered the university under his father. No, he wasn't one of those, the desperate, he didn't go to ridiculous extremes—but he, too, profited by the fruits of their defeats, gradually narrowing his trousers at the lawful rate, though also to the utmost limit. Not ridiculously and not dangerously . . . we can't say with any confidence what educates us or when. At the university, in the era of *Youth* (the magazine), he was training himself to cope within maximum (optimum) but permissible (permitted) limits: to fill the available space.

But somehow it has taken us forever to tailor this new suit, which we've all been wearing now for quite some time. Let's get Lyova dressed in it, and move along . . . Even Lyova's father, after playing it safe and enduring his wide trousers for another five years, was forced to dress like everyone else. Admittedly, even now his attire evidenced a certain sincere lag, three years, let's say, and a loyalty to "durable" fabrics—heavy wool, cheviot.

Lyova had his first suit tailored in 1955, from an English magazine for '56, and this suit was so becoming to him that he won his first heart, or rather, this first heart won him. Faina . . .

So, when he entered the university, Lyova seemed to have approached his childhood dream of science—but he immediately lost interest in it. Not that he declared his veneration false or naïve (Lyova was still uncritical). He simply became lazy. And it was high time he began, if not to understand, then at least to detect that things weren't quite right with these professorial skullcaps and that if the creator of a cosmogonic theory also played tennis and liked to make excursions to the lap of nature with his sketch pad, it didn't prove his theory was worth anything . . . Although Father had never enlightened Lyova in this regard, had not initiated him into any backstage machinations of academe: perhaps he was protecting Lyova, perhaps himself. Otherwise, Lyova might have understood sooner. But if Father knew how to keep from his son the secrets of his time, secrets dangerous to himself, the very time no longer kept them. Now, even in Lyova's house, for all its restraint and caution, something began to stir, perhaps the air shifted somehow, or they replaced the curtains, or they washed the dishes and dusted the vases an extra time, they finally unstacked the ceiling shelves and put them together again—a sort of excess energy, an added light.

(Thus, in the movies later on, the hero, in a wordlessly lucid interval, will often go to the window and fling it open with one decisive gesture, and beyond it "the brooks will sing, the rook's on the wing, and even the stump . . ." The director himself won't know why he does this whenever the script calls for the paralytic to get back on his feet or the new production line to be started up at last. But it's because, from this time on, it became *all right* to fling windows open in films.)

The time was getting more and more blabby. Once in a while it would suddenly remember, and then be scared and look over its shoulder, but when it saw that nothing had happened, no one had noticed or grabbed its arm or caught it talking, it started blabbing away with fresh, uncaught force. Even Lyova's father, schooled by the time, though he didn't blab with everybody, would come out to the kitchen and listen to his son for a brief while, swaying and emitting occasional puffs of smoke, when Lyova came home from the university and told anecdotes. He would listen briefly, narrowing his eyes merely as a mannerism, and go off to his study: to smoke his tobacco, sip his tea, and tap at his typewriter. So he neither consented to this talk nor objected, he merely puffed smoke and narrowed his eyes, but that meant nothing—it was a mannerism.

The time began gathering in company—as though there had previously been no friends, no guests, no birthdays. Now they didn't even seek an excuse to flock together to enjoy a supposed spiritual kinship and marvel at their neighbor, how good, clever, or talented he was. They loved him for their own pleasure. The time blabbed, and people floated up to the surface of it and happily bobbed around as if in a warm sea, on vacation at last—those who knew how to float . . .

Now a drunk appears on the scene, an old man we have mentioned in passing. We wouldn't need to tell about him, except that all the participants were mirrored in him in their own ways. (But what if he's the only one we "needed" . . . ?) At some time, before Lyova existed, he had been a family friend, he had loved Grandma and Mama—and now he returned. Being a man with no expectations, lucid, venomous, and free, he secured permission to move into his old apartment and became again, as ten years before, the Odoevtsevs' neighbor.

Lyova came home one day from the university—both leaves of the apartment door were wide open—and saw an unfamiliar old man, striding about angrily and coldly as he directed the removal of things familiar (things we've had a relationship with) since childhood—namely, a mirror, oval, in a frame of gilt-and-black grapevines; a table lamp with two little carved Negro cupids (they were augurs); and a long, polished mahogany chest on which Lyova had played tiddledywink soccer as a child, and the little buttons had skimmed along especially wonderfully . . . The old man swore foully at the janitor, who had carried the chest to the door incorrectly; he fluttered the chest around, emphasized with trembling and angry hands how it should be carried through. Joyously and stupidly the janitor obeyed him.

Now Lyova saw his father and mother, who were bustling around willingly and joyously, almost like the janitor. They appeared to fawn on the old man; his foul language, so forbidden in the family, seemed to caress their ears. Their faces were smoothed, clear, almost as in the wedding picture, the way faces seem to become, with relief, at the first possibility of love. That love, in no way hidden or suppressed, undistorted by relationships—that pure reflection—was what struck Lyova in his parents' faces. That possibility was youth. And much later Lyova understood that their love for the old man was so suddenly accessible and joyous for yet another reason, that given the purity of its selflessness it might be the means of love within the Odoevtsev family, almost their sole means of love for one another.

"Well, Lyova! This is Uncle Dickens!" Lyova felt a hard and hot hand, saw a white, porcelain cuff, an agate cuff link. "Hold this!"— and Lyova was holding the oval mirror in his hands, conveniently grabbing a golden grape cluster. For a second he was reflected in the mirror. His reflection affronted him by its clumsiness and health, and now he honored the old man with a word forgotten through disuse, "elegance." But if a word has been forgotten or doesn't yet exist, there is a mute sensation, a stammer, a catching of the eye: the unnamed is surprising.

What surprised Lyova in this old man was the absence, despite his utter freedom, of anything repellent—his attractiveness. Everything about him was attractive: the fastidiousness, the coldness, the harshness . . . the thuggish aristocracy. And the blue pinstripe dangling on the dried-up body like a smock—an outdated prewar suit that must have lain in the trunk all these years folded in four, like a letter, and those four crosswise creases were mostly all the crease it had left—so elegant was that suit, he thought, it would come into style only in a future season (Lyova's English suit was tailored to a cow, for cows). And the wine-red boots with creaky patent-leather toes, the antithesis of stylishness. And his shirt—good Lord, you have to *be* somebody to wear a white shirt, they never quite come clean. And the stickpin in his tie (and this wasn't a tie but a four-in-hand)—to Lyova's eye it had the flash of a diamond, first water. A personage . . . Lyova had already fallen in love with Uncle Dickens. He was uncommonly clean, Uncle Dickens. And it wasn't just that he had scrubbed up; that sort of thing is obvious right away. He was *always* clean, the visible absence of any smell . . . which was strange, considering where he had returned from. He was uncommonly skinny and swarthy; his last little silver threads were so painstakingly parted (Lyova subsequently spotted a special silver brush for this purpose at Uncle Dickens's apartment); his mouth folded into an extraordinary satirical accordion—Uncle Dickens hadn't gotten around to having his teeth made yet. And the almond eyes, thrown wide even though Mongolian: the eyes of a snorting, shying horse, there's no other way to describe them. To this pile of a portrait we should add that Uncle Dickens's person was withered and miniature, yet he could not be called small. "Where do you think you're going, you stinking bastard!" he shouted, jabbing his tiny fist into the janitor's ribs, and his voice was as Russian as a saint's.

The things, although so much the family's as Lyova saw them, really turned out to be Uncle Dickens's. That is, his life had been such that he still had things, yet he had no home.

Uncle Dickens (Dmitri Ivanovich Yuvashev), or Uncle Mitya— nicknamed Dickens merely because he was very fond of him and reread him all his life, and because of something else that hadn't been put into words—had fought in all the wars, and had spent the rest of the time, except for short intervals, in prison. In the First War, as a youth, he was a lieutenant, which is to say an officer of the czar, but in the Civil War he suddenly became a Red officer; he got demobilized later than everyone else and was about to join the administration of a scientific institute, but shortly before Lyova's birth he departed for Siberia, from where he was recalled to the front as a regular officer, and fought all through the Second War. After being demobilized, he either found somewhere or even brought from Germany (that would have been like him) these three pieces of furniture. But he didn't have an apartment yet, and he let the Odoevtsevs "keep them for him," since they still had nothing after returning from "evacuation" except their empty apartment and the grandmother who had somehow survived in it. One day he felt very sentimental, very generous, and gave them outright to the Odoevtsevs—but suddenly he received his apartment. Then he told the Odoevtsevs, who by now had provided themselves with a few things, to let him keep his gifts for them "temporarily." But at that point they came to get him, in the empty and not yet livable little apartment, and he returned to where he had spent the prewar years.

Now, upon his final return, Uncle Mitya didn't even mention that he had once made a gift of the furniture. All those years he had been remembering how he'd never gotten around to furnishing his apartment, and the first thing he did when he saw the Odoevtsevs after their long separation was to list the property he had given them for temporary storage. The list also included a suitcase with his suspenders and toilet articles (a Gillette razor, a set of hairbrushes), and a few reproductions cut from old magazines. When he had stated his list, and foully cursed Mama for ironing on his chest and thus damaging its impeccable surface, he took back all this property of his and carried it one floor up.

Really it made Mama happy, telling how Uncle Mitya had in fact taken back things he had given. Uncle Mitya's stinginess, even his greed, which had other petty excuses for manifesting itself—these, too, were the dearest traits in the world to the Odoevtsevs. Besides, Uncle Mitya himself, venomously folding his toothless mouth, loved to emphasize that yes, he was stingy, and as the son of a Kazan innkeeper—here he would ascribe to himself the famous anecdote about the cabbage soup and the raisin fly, this had supposedly happened to his father—he was quick to get tipsy, and when soused on the home brew of life he exaggerated about the tavernkeeper. Lyova continually marveled that even shortcomings were a trait in Uncle Mitya, and that they could be loved. An individual.

The air in their apartment shifted again, as though there were a certain piled-up little room, which they had always remembered but forgotten, and it had been shoveled out, the ragged bentwood chairs had been taken away to the dacha and looked so right there, standing out in the yard in the rain, while here the little window had been washed, and it turned out to face the other side—directly onto the garden . . . In the evenings Uncle Mitya came with his little decanter (the monogram an N with the crossbar low), and they all gathered in the kitchen. Lyova didn't even remember such a thing as their ever having been together, although there were only the three of them. Even Father—and apparently eagerly—abandoned his study, the dark bridgehead of his pacings, and listened to Uncle Mitya's sharp and idle talk with visible enjoyment. It was as though, listening to his own pacing, he had all his life concealed in his study a secret idleness, and so had grown weary with longing. In Uncle Mitya's presence, Father almost ceased to narrow his eyes. Mama gazed at Uncle Mitya with smiling love, and when she turned her glance to Father or Lyova, across the sugar bowl or the teaspoon, she failed to change her expression, and its light poured on them, too. All of them, briefly shifting their glance from Uncle Mitya to one another, failed to cancel their expressions and were made happy by these half expressions of half warmth in halfway glances. Neither understanding nor recognizing this happiness, they winked lovingly at one another, as if to say: What a fine man Uncle Mitya is . . . Lyova's house thawed out, and it was as though homeless Uncle Mitya had created a home for them. To Uncle Mitya they permitted much; more than to anyone else, and more than to themselves. Why do we need this—to permit another to know everything about ourselves . . .

One time, when Uncle Mitya said something very apt and exact—when Mama burst out laughing so happily, and Father so unnaturally, and Lyova felt so unhappy (from jealousy; Faina again, as always)—he glanced at Father with hatred, and thought that his real father was Uncle Mitya.

Mama turned out to have a "young" picture of Uncle Mitya, a prewar picture with a loving inscription. An Adonis, an *élégant*, a noble ladykiller . . . Lyova stood in front of the mirror with the photograph, made faces, and became totally convinced. Uncle Mitya was only about ten years older than Father, and if his teeth were gone it was no wonder, Lyova reasoned, as though he were entering an unequal marriage. And the truth was, in his thinness, brownness, and wiriness, and chiefly in the transparency of his malice, Uncle Mitya was younger than well-fattened Father, who had escaped it all. Lyova tried on the patronymic: Lev Dmitrievich . . . no worse than Nikolaevich.

It wasn't that Uncle Mitya said anything in particular. What made him attractive when he got drunk was his increasing definiteness and soberness toward the world. "Shit"—that was the sum of it; yet when Uncle Mitya summed it up that way, the sun practically came out, because each time there could be no doubt: he was accurate and right. Like every out-of-the-ordinary alcoholic, he possessed the particular humor of gesture, smirk, humph. It totally replaced speech and was always clever. He would seem to be considering both this and that in answer, and we were witness to his thought, knew what he wanted to say, but then he said neither this nor that, because neither this nor that nor the other was worth it—he humphed at the right time, and everyone laughed a happy laugh of mutual understanding.

Once, in his presence, Lyova hinted that he had made a mistake by following in his father's footsteps, and heaved a sigh for "pure" botany. Uncle Mitya dispelled these remnants of Lyova's veneration of academe, because this, too, was "shit." It turned out that after the war Uncle Mitya had found himself a job at just such an institute. Therefore, he knew for sure that "this Botanical Institute of yours" was shit, a jar of spiders: the quieter and more aesthetic it was at a superficial glance, the surer you could be that inside, in the quiet at the bottom, there was such infighting, such a spiderish turmoil. He, Uncle Mitya, had taken a walk to Siberia. "I'm an economic planner. So what do I care about Mendel and Morgan?! But the director, what a stinking bastard, he thought I wasn't saying hello as a criticism of him for hounding the Morganists—and he got me sent up. I'm just not in the habit of shaking hands with scum. What's Mendel got to do with it, when you can see by his ugly mug that he's scum! So he gave me a bum rap, the shit!" And because both that institute and its director and poor Mendel, who had nothing to do with it, and even the weather had become shit, Lyova was feeling free and gay, I can't even begin to explain the effect.

ON DICKENS
INDIVIDUALLY

FAMILYLESS UNCLE DICKENS could so *easily* become essential to the familied Odoevtsevs for a further reason: he did, although alone, have a home *of his own.*

Lyova liked it at Uncle Dickens's. He liked it when Uncle Dickens seated him on the settee, thrust some sort of "pornography" at him to peruse, and went out to the kitchen to brew *chifir* tea, leaving Lyova by himself. This was a room made to be sneaked into by children despite a ban. A book forbidden in childhood—that's exactly what Uncle Dickens's tiny apartment was like.

Everything about it was droll. An individual apartment carved out of a large one ("subdivided"), it was so small, it had gotten so little of the so-called common area (which hadn't been part of the division authorization), and it so emphatically had *everything* that had been impossible to fit in but was essential to a bachelor gentleman like Uncle Dickens. It so emphatically had everything, and things had been so impossible to fit in, that they all seemed to have moved over, crowding each other out: the bath had given way to a tiny kitchen, the "latrine" ("lavatory" is a more unseemly word than "latrine," Uncle Dickens said) to a shower; the toilet, left for last, had nowhere to go, and it stood in the foyer under the coatrack (how Uncle Dickens persuaded the engineering inspector is a mystery, but he knew how to talk to *them,* they gladly bowed to his will). So the first thing we saw as we walked in was a toilet, but of extraordinary whiteness and elegance—that same Liberty line, Uncle Dickens's favorite, was evident in its languorous morning curves. Who had sat on it? Famous personages, Uncle Dickens claimed; and now he himself, by his own account, sat there draped in an old, moth-eaten, lordly fur coat that had also come to him through some chance. But we never caught him at this pastime. He seemed to perform no natural functions at all: neither slept nor ate nor anything else. He took this to an extreme: "Don't spit when you brush your teeth!" he admonished Lyova once. He himself only drank and washed. "Uncle Mitya is cleanglorious," Mama joked.

Indeed, the old alcoholic's entire apartment was noteworthy for the incredible cleanness of conscious egoism: the floor was scrubbed in the country manner, and Uncle Dickens often went barefoot at home. One time when Lyova expressed admiration of this spotlessness, he made a characteristic frown and said, "You just don't know what it means to wake up in the morning." And truly, if you ever once caught Uncle Dickens early in the day, gray-stubbled, pacing his cramped little apartment barefoot, wearing snowy long johns, with an Orenburg down shawl thrown over his shoulders, endlessly drinking his tea (he never got high on it and didn't touch vodka before evening, before "eighteen hundred") and endlessly sniffing the air—"Don't you think something stinks in here?" was the first thing you heard as you walked in—then you might understand what Uncle Dickens's cleanness meant to him, though he never spoke of trenches or barracks. But this was one thing he needn't have worried about—there was never any stink at his house. It was a kind of standard for the absence of stink. Lyova merely felt constrained to sniff for his own smell.

Uncle Dickens had everything—he even had a "fireplace." Actually, not a fireplace but a tiny stove, though a very fine and sensible one, which he had carted around with him almost all through the last war. Because the only thing Uncle Dickens was unable to tidy up and bring into line was his blood vessels. He never had enough air and he was terrified of a stink, therefore the windows were wide open; and he was always improbably shivery and cold, therefore his "fireplace" was kept roaring ("A robin in winter," Mama said, "Uncle Dickens is a robin in winter"). Half the time he went around the house barefoot, half the time in thick felt boots. He never was able to reconcile his blood vessels to the environment.

So that was how you might catch him in the morning in his study: barefoot, with his window open, wearing the Orenburg down shawl and long johns, his back to the flaming "fireplace," an open volume in his hands—Dahl's *Defining Dictionary*, or *Bleak House*, or *War and Peace*—and he was so attractive, it was so *all right* to love him (he was so undemanding of this), that Lyova always had the childish idea he was reading a different *War and Peace* from everyone else, not in the sense that he was reading it his own way but that he really had a different book by the name of *War and Peace*, with a different Natasha too, a different Bolkonsky, also by Tolstoy but a different Tolstoy. And this was true: it couldn't have been the same.

Absolutely everything associated with Uncle Mitya underwent an unexpected regeneration for Lyova. Even what belonged to all men—for example, history, the instant he substituted Uncle Mitya in it—would take on an extraordinary optical effect: Lyova would begin to see it as though it had really happened. As though nothing around Uncle Dickens grew dim—he was like a silver coin dropped into the water of time . . . Grandma used to propagandize on the benefit of silver water, Lyova remembered. He would begin to see as though he had never written any school papers, never watched any movies, as though his lessons had covered no history. It can't be said that Uncle Mitya told a lot of stories—he didn't tell any (not out of caution, but because it had become "all right")—yet, strangely enough, Uncle Mitya had only to use the words "Civil War" or "Patriotic War" or "Kresty," and Lyova himself would seem to see Uncle Mitya there. Uncle Mitya—bluntly put, the rare outline of his soul—created the fact alongside him by his plain use of words. And Lyova would swallow his saliva, tasting in his mouth the metal of authenticity: it had happened, but it had, all of it had happened. As though Uncle Mitya, by being rare and fantastical himself, by his own exceptional example (in the sense of being an exception), underscored the considerably greater reality and possibility of even the most remote things, even the most impossible, because you could imagine anything more easily than Uncle Mitya himself—but here he was, before your eyes. This was the thing: Uncle Mitya seemed to have no memory of the effort to overcome, no petty detritus from the indignities, the times of exhaustion, of utter rage; all that remained was the outcome, the conclusion, and one need think no more—it had happened, it was done, it was gone. The wind blew through Revolutionary wickets, it blew the crests off sand dunes, the horses pawed the ground and neighed, Uncle Mitya turned up his collar, the bullet went right through him, life was over . . . There is no sweeter platitude than the one that belongs to you, there is no greater man than the one who invites us to believe in what we no longer believe in but, it turns out, would so like to. Because, my God, how many times can you fall in love on this earth! But over and over again someone manages to speak those same words, but in that very, very same sense . . .

War and Peace—the very same one—in Uncle Mitya's hands was different.

By three o'clock he would begin to come alive—shave, wash, perfume himself, tie his necktie. It was a delight to watch; there was no one to see it. Lyova once had the honor of being present at Uncle Dickens's toilette, and could not forget it: the spectacle had a polish and a ritual beauty of its own, though Uncle Dickens was no fetishist. His toilette was a tale of the nature of things, and he appeared to deal with the very concept of each thing, not its material form. When he put on a shirt he seemed to be *understanding* the shirt; when he tied his necktie, he was understanding the tie. By five o'clock he was all ready. By 17:30 he was approaching the Hotel Europe (on foot; he did not recognize public transportation and economized on taxis). Greeting everyone (they all "knew" him), he went up to the "roof" and was exactly on time for the evening opening (after the afternoon break)—arrived to find the room empty, just-spread tablecloths pale blue in their whiteness, waiters not yet overworked or rude, the afternoon light flooding evenly through the glassed roof. Here he dined and drank his first vodka. He finished his drinking at the Odoevtsevs'.

His life was understandable to all. He lived on really very modest means—"a pensioner of the *réhabilitance*," he said of himself. And as a matter of principle, he lived without need. Of anything or anyone. "Need and shit are synonyms," he said.

So the heart of this funny little apartment was the study—not in the same serious, industrious sense as Father's, but in a sense now lost and unfamiliar: a study where a man, a gentleman, spends time by himself, writes a letter, turns the pages of a novel, or simply lies still— and Lyova loved to be left there for a moment by himself, on a settee created for uncomfortable sitting, to leaf through a monograph sweet and small as a childish sin, about Beardsley, let's say, but also to examine the forbidden little room he had missed out on as a child. And the books that he borrowed and returned to Uncle Dickens (which served as the occasion for his visits) were also a *filling in* of his childhood: *Aphrodite, L'Atlantide, The Green Hat.* When could he have read them, except under the bedcovers by flashlight?

He was *right* to take his things from us, thought Lyova, with difficulty discerning his own congealing image, far in the distance in the oval mirror, as if it reflected the former, little Lyova. Above the long, low chest that was buffed to a constant gleam, on the pink wall with the wide white stripes (wallpaper from some sort of play), there were two little pictures by Puvis de Chavannes ("puiedeshaan"—like that, a child's all-one-word), Uncle Dickens's favorite artist; they could be studied vacantly and at length, like the cracks and the wallpaper studied from his bed during tonsillitis holidays . . . Near the window was a small upright piano, on which Uncle Dickens would softly play a medley of Griboedov waltzes ("Uncle Mitya has absolute pitch," Mama said). In the far corner was some junk already hidden in shadow: a three-legged spiral washbasin stand, with basin, and crookedly sticking up over it a little mirror; leaning behind it, right in the corner, folded up like a centipede, was a camp cot, which (like the basin) Uncle Mitya had carted around with him starting in the First War, and which he slept on to this day. How Uncle Dickens coped with it all by himself Lyova did not understand, because he absolutely had to help with it if he was present—prop it up, hold it back, stretch it out—and the two of them together barely managed. "Not like that, fool!" Uncle Dickens flared, angry not at the camp cot but at Lyova. That it did unfold after all was a kind of childish miracle: when from the armful of sticks, accordionlike, there suddenly extended a many-legged construction, finely wrought as a vaulted bridge, flickery and wavery as a campfire, and over it, on the sticks and little hooks, was stretched a Kiplingesque tarpaulin consisting of patches whose painstaking care would make any widow weep.

Even to list the really very few things standing along one of the study walls—that is, opposite Lyova, still sitting on the settee—seems a challenge, because we could easily and involuntarily become absorbed in each of these few objects. They were all "things belonging to one man" (which of those words to italicize is uncertain: they're all accented); namely, to Uncle Dickens (Dmitri Ivanovich Yuvashev). The old man had taste. Not in the widely current sense that his taste was better than others', or no worse than the Joneses', or to avoid being ridiculous or backward; not the modern classless-intellectual taste that strives to break into a higher social group while at the same time remaining indistinguishable, dissolving and blending with the level that has been attained—he had his own taste, *his*, in some respects high, in some respects low and decadent (his weakness for Liberty silk), and it was unashamed, self-respecting; that is, not slavish, not snobbish. He *liked* the things he had around him—that was the basic premise of his taste. And that was how they lay, tastefully and every which

33

way, his things gave no impression of being sentenced to their places. It was as if they had been carried in one by one, and Uncle Dickens had said: Over here, no, put it over here, and this one here, not like that, you shit! Sideways, sideways, bastard! And where'd that piece of junk come from? Mine? Let it stay. What about putting the cupboard over where the piano is? Maybe it's better like this? Ahh—good enough, stay put! . . . And had gone off to wash his hands again, returned fastidiously shaking them, and found the towel already hanging on the tripod over the basin idled by peacetime . . .

(Let us recall the urban madman we mentioned above: the fashion plate of '53 or '54 who lingered over his own "golden age" of the Nevsky and preserved that appearance, with enviable fidelity, into the sixties. Here's a contrast for you, here's a comparison! Uncle Mitya, too, is a loyalist of a departed time, a golden age . . . and a lot more time has passed since then. But what a difference!)

. . . Where's the lamp? The lamp, where is it? Lyova thought belatedly, and found it on the left, behind him. Of course, next to the fireplace. Then he looked toward the door: it was time Uncle Dickens returned. And in he came, carrying a small silvery kettle of piping-hot *chifir*.

FATHER

(continued)

. . . AND SO IT WENT every night. Uncle Mitya finished his drinking and left with the empty decanter, which by now was all yellow because his vodka was flavored with tea. "Mitya's specialty," Mama christened it. Uncle Mitya went away quite drunk, swaying and somehow preserving his elegance. Father and Mama talked a while longer about what a "terrible" time it had been (Father felt so shattered by Uncle Mitya), how the old man had suffered for nothing, such a noble person . . . so they said, while the glances cast after him cooled, their warmth faded . . . and "justice triumphs in the end," they said, by now entirely cold. Suddenly they yawned in a preoccupied way and went off to their beds.

"Justice" triumphed further—Uncle Mitya had been the first swallow—they permitted themselves to remember Grandfather in the family. All these years, Grandfather had been alive! This was traumatic for Lyova. He reacted childishly: had a tantrum, shouted impertinences. How dared they hide it! How skillfully, how long they had hidden it—it was mind-boggling. So that he'd have an easier time in school, so that he wouldn't say too much . . . Lyova resented his childhood weakness for old men, when he couldn't walk past a gray beard without emotion (he used to ask to give a kopeck to poor old men, but not old women), which apparently meant that a child's soul has a place for everyone: he still had a grandma, she had survived to see her grandson and lived with them for three years after the war, but he did not have a grandpa, and without noticing, Lyova missed him to make a complete set, to have *everything*. For this purpose, children—slightly more than animals do, more than a place to sleep and something to eat—need to have everyone *be*, that's all. And now, when he learned about Grandfather, Lyova resented his childhood. Not to mention that this has the absolute value of sudden death, it is equal news—to learn that a man always dead is alive. A bad dream.

The news has the same absolute value, but the opposite sign. Perplexed and discomfited by Lyova's explosion, Father admitted that it wasn't good, but he, Lyova, must also understand, et cetera, and besides (Father cast down his eyes), he himself hadn't known whether his father was alive, because he had received no answer to his letter about Grandma's death . . . At heart, Lyova probably wanted to believe his father and did not realize that in our country, one way or another, we are always notified of a death. He believed, and from that moment on was more occupied with the fact that Grandfather was alive than with his insulting resurrection.

Really, that was more important. Little by little, Lyova learned to regard one more person in his life as alive, as family. There was a secret game in this. At the thought of Grandfather, in remote corners of his consciousness heaped with all manner of junk—notebooks, dusty globes, ski poles—he fleetingly glimpsed an inexpressible little scene, quite irrelevant to Grandfather of course, from his wartime country childhood: a shed, a log, a hen, the meadow beyond; or a little river in the woods, flood grass in the bend of the river, on the grass a drowned body, a still man . . . A scene like this would instantly rise up at the word "Grandfather," and Lyova would banish it as trivial and groundless; he would go on to discuss Grandfather *logically*, put two and two together.

A photograph of Grandfather was unearthed from Mama's hiding places. (A suspicious number of photographs had been found in the house lately, whole boxes of them! There used to be only the one wedding picture.) Grandfather stared at Lyova, the narrow face so unthinkably handsome that it seemed evil—this is who he really was! This is who he *was*, it turns out . . . Grandfather stared straight and unblinking, and it was as though the smooth cheeks had actually sunk into that gaze, as though the fine perfect nose were actually intrinsic to that gaze; the eye sockets, the brows were the caryatids of a high and narrow, upwardly focused forehead (the gaze came from there, behind the columns); the dark little beard, mustache, sideburns (wherever the gaze had nothing to shape)—all these melted blackly into the also-black background, all these were where the face, the gaze, stared at Lyova *from*. And Grandfather was young—they were all young, these photographs . . . Where had all these marvelous faces gone? They no longer existed physically in nature, Lyova had never encountered them, not on the streets or even in his own home . . . Where had his parents put their faces? Behind which cupboard, under which mattress? The faces were hiding in miscellaneous little boxes; with astonished eyes not yet paralyzed by the object lens, they studied the flowery name of the owner of the studio where the cousin next above had had his portrait done . . . they had been laid away face up, as in a coffin. A common grave of faces, on which we can no longer read any challenge but which pique us by being unquestionably different from us and by indisputably belonging to a person. Yet he had seen this face somewhere . . . A dream face, encountered in a dream, not in nature . . . Suddenly he knew: in the Hermitage, in a painting by somebody, five hundred years had passed. Terrifying.

Whenever he portrayed Grandfather to himself now, he substituted Uncle Mitya, trying him in Grandfather's place. And it became easier. After all, he had no other model.

One night there was excited talk that in the "transactions" of some provincial university, in a certain article, there had been a favorable mention of Grandfather. He had been inconspicuously "sneaked in" in a list, and in some thick journal. Grandfather's name was floating up from nonexistence.

It came out, there in the kitchen, that this name had been undeservedly and unjustly forgotten; Grandfather had been the creator of a new branch of science and the founder of a whole scientific school. His work had been picked up in the West only ten years later, and now we were behind the times in our own area of primacy . . . Father grew excited, strangely bold and pale, took the glass away from Uncle Mitya. Expectation rose.

And was answered. All their talk turned strangely hollow in memory: someone else got Grandfather out, not they. They were behind the times at home, too . . . Father went to meet Grandfather in Moscow.

He returned the next day, alone, pale and dismayed, rather shaky. He locked himself in the study. Then he let Mother in. They whispered about something for a long time, very loudly. And Father kept pacing and pacing, making his turns more often, as though the study had become shorter, narrower.

Even without them, Lyova grasped roughly what had happened. He was able to turn away now in silence, aware that his face was pale and long. The idea was strikingly absent from his mind at that moment, only to perturb him later in private: in his own face, Lyova was proudly aware of Grandfather's.

Father abruptly drooped and aged. He would come home tired, lost, to conceal himself in his study. The apartment shrank and darkened, you couldn't get by in the corridor. They hid things from Lyova, timidly relying on his gracious tacit permission to hide them; they pretended nothing was happening, but so clumsily and uncertainly that it merely called his notice to how they had declined, his old folks, and what's more, how *backward* they were. This he discovered with suddenness. Though what was backward about them Lyova found it hard to say. Their good form, probably. They held now antiquated concepts of truth, honor, and falsehood and were always trying to hide things that no one hid anymore, which was how they gave themselves away. Everything else was out in the open. There was much of the naïve and touching in these old traitors.

Uncle Mitya came more and more seldom; it had ceased to be cozy at the Odoevtsevs', and the loving atmosphere he habitually bathed in had disappeared. The pond had dried up. Uncle Mitya loved comforts and was in the habit of habits. And without this, without his ration of love at the Odoevtsevs' (hand it over, and don't make any trouble), even Uncle Mitya could get tired of *being* everybody—both Lyova's secret father, and Mother's selfless worshipper, and Lyova's grandfather (as a model), and a father to Father (and this was partly true, as Lyova understood afterward, too late). Uncle Mitya stopped coming to see them.

But even without them, Lyova had understood. Without them . . . and he swallowed a lump of childish tears. They found themselves behind the times with Lyova, too, in exactly the same way. Life turned to Lyova, he stood in her presence for the first time. Her face proved a whisper, a shadow, a patina, a ripple . . . To walk toward each other down a narrow corridor, squeeze past with your backs to the wall, meanwhile cope with the inevitable glance, drop and raise your eyes— this is life? The whisper at your back, the turning around to look— try it, turn around yourself: nothing there, nobody. An army of people, corridor columns that have no business with you but they know *about* you—so you are no more, you're dead, as in a childish war of Greens and Blues . . . If they *know*, in your presence, that means you're dead. To discover that you also exist in the third person, for others, in another time and space, where you no longer are, where you will not be— and to endure the trauma, to go on living, with them, accepting the game, joining in, to await what follows . . . Lyova walked the gauntlet.

That is the way it happened in fact, but metaphorically it happened like this. From his parents' awkward behavior, from the way people several times made slips of the tongue in his presence, as if by chance, betraying themselves by a sudden glance in Lyova's direction, people he hardly knew at all, it developed that a definite and unseemly role had been played in Grandfather's drama by his son, Lyova's father: in his youth by renouncing him, and twenty years later by earning himself Grandfather's chair through criticism of his school—so that the chair was still "warm." (This little word, too, Lyova overheard: how could it have been warm, if it had been cooling for twenty years?) . . . So that Grandfather, it was whispered roundabout, for almost thirty years had . . . he didn't want to see his son, or hadn't even shaken hands, or had even spat and said the hell with him, in front of everyone . . . He had to swallow it.

Everything had changed . . . and not even a month had passed. All glances and conversations had begun to seem filled with hints and cool curiosity, as if something were expected of him.

And one day, the first time ever without knocking, Lyova flung open the door of his father's study, to clarify once and for all what it was really about and how matters actually stood.

Lyova heard out his father's muddled and scarcely audible speech, again rather shaky, full of limp parting injunctions to attach no importance and not to take literally, or rather, Lyova was already a grown man, and there was no reason, of course, to explain it all to him, in due time he himself would understand and get it all figured out . . . Father emphatically rejected the main accusation, but the mere fact that he didn't scoop Lyova up by the scruff of the neck and fling him right out of the study was very noteworthy. Lyova remembered forever Father's long handclasp on the threshold of that study, unchanged from his childhood, as always half dark, as always it made him want to speak in a whisper . . . For a long time Father clasped Lyova's narrow, cool hand in his own hot, dry ones and said things; Lyova, aloofly observing the movement of his lips, no longer even heard. Father was blocking the desk lamp, the light struck the back of his head, his flyaway hair shone and seemed to stir in an invisible draft, and as Lyova studied this martyr halo he suddenly compared Father to a dandelion. And because the tremor of Father's handclasp was transmitted to him, he also had the thought that a dandelion will fly apart if you blow on it. For a third time Lyova fixed his father in memory . . . this time forever.

Father's strong, hot handclasp suddenly seemed weak and cold to

Lyova, and therefore broke apart. A sense of aching pity stirred within him but never came through; at this moment he sensed much more keenly a certain vague triumph over Father. Here, on the threshold of the very study at whose door he had ever since childhood switched to a whisper, he said unexpectedly loudly: "Very well, Father." His voice sliced through all that cozy stillness and darkness and seemed disagreeable to Lyova himself. Turning abruptly, he stepped over the threshold; Father somehow lurched awkwardly forward as if to close the door behind Lyova, Father's shadow was cast under Lyova's feet, and it seemed to Lyova that he had stepped over Father.

That memorable day, Lyova walked in on Uncle Mitya with the despair of last hope. We go for help pretending to ourselves that we don't even believe in the possibility of help anymore, we're just simply going; we arrive at the very place where we can still expect it, arrive with hand outstretched, like beggars—and receive a handshake, some-one *gives* us his hand. Natural as it is (a form of greeting!), the hand-shake ("Is that all!") disillusions us the minute we walk in. "Even he," we think bitterly. "He, too . . ."

So with Lyova. He was expecting something, although the nice thing about "Uncle Dickens" was that you knew ahead of time every-thing you could expect from him, he as much as began by warning you thus, thus, and so. "And *that'ss it*," as he would say. But Lyova let his imagination run. It seemed to him like something from the theater, something in the Stanislavsky method. As though he were worn out, sunken-cheeked, the kind who had endured all and held his peace, and they were two of that kind, who had been through it all, they had never asked help of anyone . . . And Uncle Mitya, who never displayed his feelings because nobody's troubles were serious, understood that Lyova had real trouble, he offered his hand, a wise word (the only one "Uncle Dickens" could have spoken), a spare male tear . . . *pah!* Then, with the welling of the tear, with that sympathetic tingle, it also emerged that Uncle Mitya was in fact Lyova's father . . . after that came such an uproar, such an apotheosis, such an adagio that it was beyond the power of even the Moscow Art Theater.

Indeed, Uncle Mitya did understand something, the minute he saw Lyova in the doorway; a subtle man. He even seemed unwilling to let him in. Then he did let him in, probably because he couldn't think how not to. "But I'm going soon," he said, from the inertia of some previous unspoken sentence, and probably hated himself for this spoken one, too, because he hastily turned away, hesitated, plunged into the room ahead of him. Except for that swift and instantly frightened first glance in the doorway, Lyova never once succeeded in catching his eye. Uncle Mitya was very nervous, this was clear, and Lyova had never seen him in such a state. His glance darted about vacantly and shiftily, somehow contriving always to bypass Lyova, not meet his eyes, and Lyova was struck that it was leaving around the room a twisting, eye-white trail, a rubber tourniquet. Uncle Mitya, of course, was neither able nor ready to go anywhere: he was in his dismantled morning state, and for technical reasons, the soonest he could collect his creaking parts would be two hours from now—but he wasn't even thinking of collecting himself. The more so since the "fireplace" was roaring, and tossed on the settee was an open volume of Dahl, Uncle Dickens's daily reading (he loved to admire the conciseness, the "definitiveness" of "that Swede's" definitions). Catching Lyova's glance, Uncle Mitya was still more discomfited. He bustled over to Dahl and made an attempt at their usual game: "Tell me, but as concisely as you can, what's a lorgnette?" "Well," Lyova responded limply, "it's something halfway between binoculars and eyeglasses, you held them to your eyes at the theater or a ball . . ." "That's concise?!" Uncle Mitya said furiously, and peered into Dahl. "Eyeglasses with handle— and *that'ss it!*" He ran angrily around the room, and perhaps he thought Lyova was about to open his mouth, because, frantically and grasping at anything, he began to talk, quite fast and interrupting himself, losing the thread, as was not his style either. In brief, he didn't know how to behave, which had seemed inconceivable, at least to Lyova, for whom Uncle Dickens was deportment itself, the standard. He could easily have told Lyova, as he so well knew how to do, in the only tone appropriate to the case, "You're a shit, Lyova," or "So he's a shit!" (meaning Father), and thereby calmed the troubled soul. But he didn't say even this; he began to curse *"them"* (Lyova didn't understand whom), moreover in a way so insistent, obtuse, and dirty that it made Lyova uncomfortable, almost ashamed, he almost wanted to defend *"them"* against Uncle Mitya, they were so defenseless. But even Uncle Mitya, apparently, was finding himself more and more disgusting and unbearable. He broke down and at last said the long-awaited "It's all shit!" But even this sounded false; he fled to make tea, and disappeared, seemingly forever.

Lyova cast an indifferent glance around the study that had always been dear to his heart—nothing touched him this time. Everything looked boring, like a book read in childhood. He himself seemed lonely and old. For some reason, it suddenly occurred to him that

Uncle Mitya had never in his whole life been anyone "big," except to him, Lyova. For all his exceptional qualities . . . "Eyeglasses with handle . . ." *Uncle* Dickens . . . the nickname suddenly struck Lyova as very exact, expressing something else, beyond what he had suspected in it. Precisely: not Dickens, but Uncle . . . Here Lyova forgot what he meant by this. Because all of a sudden he remembered the first frightened glance Uncle Mitya had met him with. And now, distinctly, in a way that had never happened to him in his life, not with anybody, he pictured Uncle Mitya as existing *individually*, apart from him. It was an astonishing sensation—Uncle Mitya stood before him in the doorway, an old, unhappy, destroyed man, who spent his day's strength, to the last drop, on never again being humiliated, or rather, never being humiliated for others to see, never once being dependent and pathetic. Dignity, the yearning for dignity, was Uncle Mitya's last passion, the last possibility of his life, and he barely had strength to preserve even an appearance of it. To do so, it was essential for him not to need anyone, so that no one would need him either, because the smallest dependence, the smallest obligations of love, would have sent him straight to the bottom like a heavy, water-soaked log. He couldn't have endured even the smallest burden of feeling: he would have exploded, disintegrated, smashed to smithereens—the dry, sharp, fine smithereens he had trouble consisting of. Not quite in this way, not quite in words did Lyova sense this, but very fully, somehow in a coalescent space, as though he were no longer Lyova but Uncle Mitya himself—such yearning, fear, and bewilderment did he sense within himself, as he examined the image that rose up in memory, that he might have been seeing it for the first time now, not a half hour ago. But, my God, thought Lyova, what a terrible life he lives! And he, Lyova, was coming to him for love, wisdom, pity . . . how dared he, a full, fat, husky, young, obtuse nonentity! Lyova went to the other extreme: Uncle Mitya's egoism struck him as noble. At the least, it was so much better and purer than the unseemly emotional sloppiness to which Lyova had just abandoned himself . . . In this appraisal Lyova was partly right. Can I really subject *another* man to the danger of not being able, not enduring, not coping with the burdens placed on him? Haven't I burdened him enough as it is? Uncle Dickens, Father, Grandfather—Uncle Mitya played them all, alone . . . Entering into the role, Lyova imagined how humiliating and nauseating it had been just now for Uncle Mitya when he lied that he was in a hurry (for the first time! how frightened he'd been, poor thing), when he was avoiding Lyova's eyes and babbling . . . Don't worry, Uncle Mitya, I won't do it, I will not dump my burden on your weak little sickly shoulders, nor will I subject you to the danger of being humiliated by your own helplessness and inability to cope in a dignified way with what happens . . . I'll look after you . . .

Lyova was talking to himself almost this way, unfortunately already mugging and feeling moved by his own words. Indeed, to give him his due, he had never in his life been so subtle, exact, sensitive—so intelligent. For about a second, Lyova was a truly mature person, only to forget this too, shortly afterward, for many long years, almost forever. It may have been an insight of rare common sense for Lyova, outstripping his experience and therefore teaching him nothing, although that is strange . . .

Uncle Mitya entered warily, eyes downcast. Lyova was right. Convinced of it, Lyova cruelly stood up and said, "Goodbye, it's time for me to go"—and this very moment, of smugness over his intelligence and pleasure in his deed, was probably when the experience of his recent insight was stripped from him, almost forever, as being premature, undeserved. He had already received his reward.

Uncle Mitya looked up at him, eyes wide with an inner light of surprise, stared at him thus for a moment, and said nothing. Walked him to the door.

Besides, how could he be my father . . . how could he possibly be Father, Son, and Holy Ghost? Lyova told himself, like an upperclassman, smiling wryly at his own recent folly. My father has to be *exactly* the way he is, no different. And I'm his son. Terrible—but true. As for Uncle Dickens, how could he have sons! He died a hundred years ago. Eyeglasses with handle.

It seemed to Lyova that he had stepped over Uncle Mitya, too.

But there he exaggerated.

Was he incapable of imagining that Uncle Mitya's shame or disgust might have been . . . not for himself?

We titled the chapter "Father," mindful, however, not only of Father but of the time itself. Father has turned out somehow double: one moment he's a timid, neurotic man who can't even do a good "Here comes the billy goat" for little Lyova; the next moment he's confidently and powerfully pacing off his academic, cultish study, feeling that he is solidly a part of the epoch. But even though we hadn't programmed this contradiction from the outset, we don't consider it an error. In the first place, such things do happen. In the second place, much more in this novel will be double and even multiple, rendered consciously this time, and if not very artistically, then at least openly and frankly.

After all, life itself is dual right at this indivisible instant. And the rest of the time—which doesn't even exist from the standpoint of reality—life is linear and multiple, like memory, because, except for this second, which has just this second vanished, except for this one which has replaced it, there is no time in the present. And the memory that replaces the vanished time also exists only at this instant and according to its laws.

Therefore, Father is double once again, on the next day of memories, which aren't even about him—they're about his image (after all, we made him up). By the next day, his image is double in a different way: on the one hand, a "fine figure of a man," a success, and the object of a teenager's jealousy of his mother; on the other hand, readily submitting to the influence of an outsider, a man whom his wife evidently prefers.

And Father is once again double when retribution begins, when he is crushed by his own treachery, when the image of Uncle Dickens expands and masks Father. Because, although the author may snicker at Lyova's youthful fantasy, he himself hasn't made a final decision that Uncle Dickens is not Lyova's father. Anything can happen . . .

So it's possible that our hero has a different family altogether. The author very much wants to present here a second variant of Lyova Odoevtsev's family, a variant that would produce, in the author's belief, the exact same hero all over again. Because the only thing that interests the author is the hero; the hero, as a research topic already selected (however unfortunately), is the only thing he doesn't want to change. But the author will postpone, for the time being, his desire to disclose the second variant.

We had planned to tell about Father and about the time. In the upshot, we have said just as little about Father as about the time. But we believe that two unlike objects, in this instance, can be added together. The time itself was Father. Father, Papa, the Cult . . . what other synonyms are there?

FATHER'S FATHER

On Brühl Terrace in Dresden, between two and four o'clock, the most fashionable hour for a stroll, you may encounter a man of about fifty, already quite gray and apparently suffering from gout, but still handsome, elegantly dressed, and bearing the special imprint that is given a man only by long sojourn in the highest strata of society.

EITHER LYOVA COPED with life, or life with him: he ceased to agonize about his family, in very short order. Being young, after all, he didn't so much know his various feelings as presuppose he had them. Yet the presupposition that one has feelings is very agonizing (which is why we can maintain that our young people are "very emotional"), because it has no foundation except nature itself, and that is the one thing it doesn't presuppose. These hypothetical feelings are vigorous for the further reason that young people have a good deal of vigor. Lyova had worked off his "second father" hypothesis, there remained the "grandfather hypothesis."

Father had been born to the son. Grandfather is being born to the grandson.

. . . When the family started talking about Grandfather, back before his return; when Lyova scrutinized those handsome photofeatures and quarreled with Father, proudly and silently turning away his own long face, which seemed to bear the same features; when he felt childishly resentful that Grandfather had been alive all along, and this "all along" was replaced in his mind with fleeting scenes of his wartime country childhood; when he just as childishly disguised Uncle Dickens as Grandfather in his imagination; when he was schooling himself to the new kinship and hypnotizing himself with the idea of "blood" . . . then, inspired, Lyova bypassed his father and obtained on his own, displaying unaccustomed initiative, from rare booksellers and archives—obtained and read—several papers by Grandfather, inasmuch

45

as they were now relevant to his future specialty, though very remotely. Grandfather had been a linguist—that is, he had *known* something—and so had been engaged in something more exact than the philology to which Lyova devoted himself; moreover, he had been something of a mathematician and almost the first to . . . but here again we enter the precarious domain of "primacy." Lyova read, some of it was over his head, but he managed to get a feel for the unaccustomed freedom and authenticity of Grandfather's thought, and to marvel at it.

Grandfather proved to be not alone; there had been other men with him and before him—Lyova had known of them only by hearsay, from survey lectures, as men who had distorted, underrated, perverted, misunderstood, et cetera (and those were the mildest words). Lyova found it hard to believe they had misunderstood anything, because to him, for example, what they had misunderstood was obvious, a snap, whereas what they had understood, since they wrote about it, Lyova often understood not at all or with great difficulty and strain, so that he seemed to hear the roar of his overtaxed brain parts grinding in his head. But again, what stayed with him was chiefly this feeling of authenticity, so unaccustomed . . . Finally Lyova found himself someone slightly easier, a man he worked at with enjoyment: this one was flashy and formal, easy and brilliant (by the way, he was the first to begin being resurrected, very shortly after Lyova's illegal reading, and Lyova could pride himself on knowing *already*, having known for *ages*).

So Lyova became fascinated by an integrated and still half-forbidden research method, and now, whether he meant to or not, he used it in his studies, to check everything. It convinced him. After the mental overstrain of reading Grandfather—that is, after he had *worked* his mind for the first time—everything that concerned his studies was suddenly so crude and easy; the syllabus monographs, which terrified his classmates with their thickness and scientific-looking language, became schoolboy prattle for Lyova. And although it was still impossible to pursue his captivating method consistently, Lyova hoped to use it, to some extent at least—he was terrifically pleased with it—in an upcoming term paper. So he had already derived one profit from the family drama . . . Thanks to this positivistic effect, the "Grandfather hypothesis" was established even more firmly in Lyova's mind. He no longer had any doubt, Grandfather was unquestionably a Great Man, and that rank made "Grandfather and Grandson" sound very good.

Lyova was already planning a pilgrimage to him, an independent, secret one, as if against the will of his dictator father, and he outlined numerous and varied scenes, which soothed him by their tearful sweet power and postponed his intention into the continual future . . . why so suddenly? . . . why tomorrow, exactly? . . . The first impulse had long been lost, and Lyova was already in the habit of thinking he would do this someday, of course, later, later . . . when suddenly Grandfather telephoned.

He had no wish to speak with his son—he talked to Lyova's mother. All her artless pleas to forgive and come home, she just hadn't had the opportunity to tell him what she was telling him now, et cetera . . . all this he heard in silence, and started talking only when Mother could dream up nothing more to say, she had even decided the phone was out of order. Grandfather said he wouldn't dream of being angry at her, he had no grudges, he was no scullery maid, to go holding grudges; she (Mother) had always been a fool, terribly pretty though, he remembered her as a bride and he had liked her then—what could he expect now, after thirty years. Let his grandson come see him, tomorrow, he wanted a look at the galoot. That was all. Mama said she wasn't sure, but he had sounded a bit strange to her, a bit drunk.

That Grandfather himself had called, the great man himself wished to see him, was extraordinarily exhilarating for Lyova, and he promised himself a great deal from this meeting. He no longer noticed his parents. Didn't hear what Mama said to him. Didn't look at Father.

Lyova got everything for free.

He walked to Grandfather's with brand-new beating heart. Something that was distant and fresh but seemed always to have been present in him had opened its shell a crack. He peered lurkingly into those dark recesses, but could discern nothing.

He was dreaming of the sudden friendship that would spring up between them at first sight, bypassing Father, over his head, a bridge over a generation . . . and in that case it wasn't just grandson on his way to grandfather, but specialist to specialist, pupil to teacher—gratifyingly for Lyova. Absorbed in his daydreams, he seemed to forget completely that he was on his way to see his very own grandfather for the first time. Though in slightly altered form, it was the same old fantasy of the strong tea and professorial skullcap.

But it wasn't just that. There was something naïve and idealistic behind it. That shell inside him, which had opened up a crack and in which he couldn't yet discern what was there—Grandfather would see and understand it right off, he thought, and then he and Grandfather would be man and man! Grandfather would help open it (the shell) even wider, he would explain what was there, and a completely new life would begin for Lyova—actually his real life, but, until now, painstakingly concealed from him.

And yet it *was* almost the same fantasy: they would walk down the broad carpeted staircase at the Academy of Sciences, for example, the old man and the young, and everyone would applaud them from the boxes.

Suddenly it seemed to Lyova that he was late. He wanted to be punctual. He flagged a taxi and arrived much earlier than necessary.

Grandfather had been given an apartment in a new district, the last buildings. Lyova had never been here. With surprise he caught himself thinking that he probably hadn't left the old city once in his whole life; he *lived* in that museum, not one of his day-to-day routes lay beyond the museum's avenue-corridors and hall-squares . . . strange. He knew by hearsay about the projects on the outskirts, that they existed, but their names were confused in his mind—he had forgotten the name of the district he was in. Maybe Obukhovka, or Proletarka . . . he reached for his notebook again.

He felt as if he had arrived in a different city.

Lyova dismissed the taxi, deciding to take a stroll around this city in the time he had left.

. . . The sun was setting, an ice-cold wind was blowing, and the air had a sort of dangerous clarity. To the west, three long, sharp clouds stabbed the horizon. They glowed a faintly violet red. Out into that void stretched a wasteland, with weeds and trash dumps; at the near end, right in the field, was a streetcar ring—really, a ring (Lyova had thought the expression was figurative, not literal). It gleamed in the black grass, and there was no streetcar. The houses seemed to stand abandoned, so absent was human life and so chiming the stillness. In the sunset rays, against the blue background, the sparse, frost-covered house cubes stood detached and sugary, their smooth windows blindly and lifelessly reflecting into the sunset. It was like something dreamed.

Crossing this dream space, with chill drafts gusting through it from all sides, he was inexplicably unaware of his own movements. A breeze, an aura . . . He found Grandfather's entry and stood under a frivolous red awning, beside a wretched holey green wall. A blue and yellow bench nearby for old women to sit on. He stood and froze. Time dragged. He thought his watch had stopped—but it was ticking, and the second hand moved reluctantly around the circle. Lyova's excitement was strange and mysterious to him, unfamiliar, as though he had never been excited until today. Soon, however, all sensation was concentrated in his feet: he had put on new shoes for the occasion, and they pinched. His feet were frozen, they ached, and Lyova seemed to be standing not on his own feet but on prostheses. At last, he had the sense to go inside the entry. The stairway was warm. Lyova snuggled up to the radiator and hugged it. Now the door flew open, and a scruffy young man ran in, his coat all undone and flapping. As he ran by, he glanced sharply at Lyova, taking him in (Lyova had no chance to jump back from the radiator), and disappeared, flying upstairs two at a time, showing a ragged heel. Lyova stood there a while longer. Now at last the watch hand crawled to the long-promised mark, and he started upstairs, frozen solid, clumsily stamping his artificial feet.

He had almost reached his landing when one of the apartment doors opened slightly. The same young man came flying out, pierced Lyova with a glance, and went pounding downstairs, four at a time now. In the doorway, someone loomed darkly behind him for a second . . . and after the door shut and the locks began to clank, Lyova realized that this was *his* apartment. Lyova was upset that he hadn't hailed him in time, hadn't asked him not to bar the door, although on the other hand it was good, he thought, because their first meeting couldn't be like that . . .

. . . A queer-looking stranger opened the door to him and stared with level nonrecognition. What if—? Lyova went cold at his surmise. Impossible: so different. That shaven skull, quilted work jacket, very indeterminate age—from fifty to a hundred—but worst of all, the red, stubbly, hardened face was staggering in its unspirituality. And it was silent, blank, too lazy to unstick its lips.

"Excuse me, I've got the wrong door," Lyova said plaintively, and in his mind he was flying down the stairs four at a time, pounding down like that young man, slamming the front door—and choking as he gulped at the cold air. How embarrassing! All had been thought through, variants sorted out, formulas learned by rote . . . but the fact that he would have to greet him, say something, recognize him by sight, had not occurred to him, as if there were only a cloud beyond the threshold.

"Who d'you want?" the face said, rolling out the muffled *o*'s with difficulty: *Oo-oo wan?* And when the mouth came unstuck, the face was suddenly long. It could be Grandfather.

"Modest Platonovich . . ." *Moesto*, almost Maestro, Lyova thought, mimicking himself: his mouth was thick with horror. "Odoevtsev," he pronounced ringingly, in outright despair, reddening in the darkness.

Something swept past under the skin of the old man's face—confusion, recollection, panic, reassurance—very swiftly. The face expressed nothing.

"Come in." The old man let Lyova by into the corridor and dithered for a long time barring the door, bumbled and clanked in the darkness—the locks were giving him trouble. Lyova wanted to say, haltingly, sincerely, that he had recognized him, recognized him! Just in the first second he hadn't, but then he recognized him immediately! (So that Grandfather would realize things weren't so terrible after all, he was *recognizable*—etiquette learned on a train, from a disabled vet's song about a burned tankman and his bride.) Lyova was inwardly so prepared for ecstasy that even the incongruity of Grandfather's person had enchanted him on the spot. Already he was practically glad that Grandfather had turned out to look like this.

"Why don't you go in? Go on in," Grandfather growled thickly, throwing across his shoulders the shawl that had fallen off while he dithered with the locks. He shoved open the door into the room.

Lyova's ecstasy faltered again—there was yet another old man sitting in the room. As they entered, he glanced at them attentively (Lyova had an impression of "goodness"). This man seemed more cultured, he looked more like Uncle Mitya (so Lyova had been right in substituting him!)—ecstasy mounted anew in Lyova. This man really did look something like Uncle Mitya, only not so clean and elegant. Good, good, Lyova quivered to himself. Good thing I didn't say—

"You're Lyova," the first old man said, as thickly as ever, but more as a statement than a question, as he closed the door of the room carefully behind him and walked to the middle. He was dragging one leg.

Lyova's mind rushed about like a rabbit. No, it can't be!

Yes, yes! he would have liked to say joyfully—and he nodded, swallowing.

"Please sit down." Dragging a chair as well as his leg, the old man came toward Lyova; too late, Lyova rushed to help, when he was already wiping the seat with newspaper. What are you doing, there's no need, Lyova wanted to say imploringly, and he took away the chair. The effect was awkward and rude. The old man staggered. He hadn't been just wiping—as he wiped, he had been leaning on the chair, on the paper. He glanced at Lyova.

"Do sit down. *He'll* be here soon." The old man's face twitched twice, and again expressed nothing. The man who looked like Uncle Mitya turned his attentive gaze on them for an instant and then lowered his eyes.

What *is* this? What *is* this? Lyova thought feverishly. His feet were thawing painfully, and his face burned.

"The place hasn't been picked up . . ." the first old man said guiltily.

Again, Lyova was taken aback and slightly distracted: it really hadn't been picked up. On the table lay greasy paper, crusts, an open tin can—very unappetizing. The whole room was uninhabitable and dormitory-like to the point of weirdness. As though they had just moved in, hadn't yet washed the floors or windows after construction, hadn't brought over the furniture. The table covered with leftovers, the haphazardly made bed on which Uncle Mitya's look-alike was sitting, three straight desk chairs, and a keg. No books. Admittedly, there was a crucifix standing in the corner. Not Orthodox, painted.

No one said anything. The room had grown almost dark, but they had not turned on the light.

Am I in the right place, Lyova wanted to shout. But he only squirmed.

The first old man made an attempt to clear the table. He shifted things around with minute gestures, picked up a dirty knife and looked at it. Flung it angrily back on the table.

"Damn it! Will *he* get here soon?" He plunged about the room like a shadow, all gray by now in the twilight, plunged about the room dragging his leg.

"Uncle Mitya" raised his attentive eyes. "But he just left," he said apologetically.

With a sigh, the old man settled down on a chair. "Sorry," he growled to Lyova.

Where did he go, Lyova wanted to ask, but decided that the question would be foolish.

Maybe I should leave and say I'll drop by a little later? Although on the other hand, why didn't I say that right off? Now it's too late. Lyova's head was muddled, his face burned (in the dark, fortunately), his lips were dry and seemed ready to burst—the blood was pounding so in his head. Maybe he's one of them after all, Lyova thought deliriously. The resemblance to Uncle Mitya and the attentive ("good") eyes corroborated that this could be Grandfather: If Uncle Mitya looks so much like Grandfather, there's no doubt that he's my father! Lyova all but laughed aloud at himself. But how do I get that? he taunted himself, mentally shaking all over with bitter laughter. Seems that if Uncle Mitya's my father he automatically becomes Grandfather Odoevtsev's son, but I don't cease to be his grandson! Fool! Ha-ha! Having had his fill of self-mockery, Lyova thought okay then, there was no doubt: the first old man really was his grandfather . . . he was just testing Lyova. How he must be agonizing over the fact that Lyova didn't recognize him. "Will *he* be here soon?"—how could this be understood to mean anything but "When will he, Lyova, guess?" That is, when would he, Lyova, arrive in reality, not just physically. Of course the first one is Grandfather. He's the more important of the two . . . The fact that his behavior showed him to be the "more important" one in the room almost convinced Lyova, but here too, just in time, he remembered not to confess to his discovery. Because . . . My God! I must have a fever. Lyova felt his head, his hand was just as hot as his brow, or just as cold: he couldn't tell whether he had a fever. How can I be such an idiot! He asked me clearly whether I was Lyova, and said, "Sit down. *He*'ll be here soon." What a fool I am! Mentally Lyova was guffawing, shaking his head, wiping away a tear. But he could not reassure himself. The old men said nothing, though "Uncle Mitya" had lit a cigarette, and from time to time the ember illumined his attentive eyes.

Why don't they switch on the light!

The first old man had turned away to the window. Rigid, he was whispering toward where a faint pink still glowed, a fine little ash-coated thread of sunset.

Maybe they've killed him! Lyova suddenly thought piercingly. Maybe he's lying in the other room! Lyova remembered the young man plunging out the door and pounding down the stairs, and for some reason this became the final proof of his conjecture.

They've killed him! They've killed him! Lyova sobbed to himself. He was walking behind the coffin, a light snow was falling—

A sharp ring pierced the darkness.

"Oh! Oh!" Lyova jumped up and could not shout; he started flailing his arms, as in a dream when you're falling out of bed.

"Thank God!" With ease and agility, on his one leg, the first old man had loped to the door, flipping the light on as he passed, and was already clanking his many locks in the corridor. Lyova frowned in the light and in his shame. He was still standing in the middle of the room, and "Uncle Mitya's" attentive eyes were watching with slight surprise: What have we got here, a psycho?

Lyova went weak. He sank onto the chair in a cold sweat.

In walked the same flapping young man, looking frozen and disgruntled. He gave Lyova a long stare—how did this guy get here!—and gently plunked a heavy knapsack on the table.

"Couldn't you have cleaned up?" He began to clear the table, angrily and rapidly. Now the first old man finished clanking his locks and cheerfully came back in.

"The store's a very long way," he explained to "Uncle Mitya."

The young man grinned, swung around to the old man, saw him— and his homely face lit up. He fished in his baggy overalls and handed the old man a bottle of beer.

The old man hunted for an opener and didn't find one.

Again the young man tore himself away from his work. He solic- itously took the bottle, skillfully opened it, filled a beer-stand mug to the brim, and handed it to him.

The old man sat down, still unbelieving of something, embraced the mug in both hands, and pressed his lips to it . . . He drank long, delved deeply, choking, sucking in, soaking in, breathing in, sinking in, withdrawing entirely into the mug, he bumbled over it like a bee over a flower, and when he leaned back with a happy sigh Lyova noted with horror that the beer had not actually diminished in the mug— there was as much left as ever. The word "thirst" seemed written before them in the air, in all its fullness, with all its snakish hiss. Long afterward, forever, this mug, nowhere near finished, nowhere near, despite such effort and passion, was linked with the image of Thirst, the concept of Thirst as such.

"Now, that's nice!" said the comforted old man, and he looked around at everyone with eyes that had warmed and were already ex- pressing some sort of life. He caught the disgruntled glance that the young man threw Lyova.

"Oh, I haven't even introduced you . . . Rudik, this is my grandson Lyova."

"Why's he just sitting there like a stranger!" Rudik said, taking vodka from the knapsack, bottle after bottle.

Good God, Lyova managed to think.

. . . .

"So you didn't recognize me at first!" Grandfather laughed, and his face wrinkled contentedly, but only on one side. "And you froze to death, in order to get here exactly on time?" He swung his gaze toward Rudik and "Uncle Mitya": his face laughed in halves.

Lyova still continued to regard this as "rough kindness." He still felt the lively sense of joy and community that had brought them all sociably together around the table: Grandfather clinking glasses sep- arately with his grandson, "To our meeting," a look straight into his eyes. Lyova could not help drinking with these men, he had been so miserable until now, had so wished the earth would open up and swallow him—he downed his drink at one gulp (Grandfather had mixed in something else, it was not unlike "Mitya's specialty") and after downing it tasted how revolting it was. He choked, but Grandfather, providently, was already holding a cucumber on a fork. And then, chewing the cucumber, with his mouth full, through crystal tears that refracted a world where the faces of his new friends hung on long shining needles extending from the naked light bulb . . . he felt rewarded by liberation and happiness, for an instant found thanks for the world, and the world thanked him. The general laughter was inoffensive, the table beautiful, the faces bright, the world was true— and at that moment it seemed so natural, so easy, to declare his love for this world, sincerely making fun of his own naïveté and simplicity, as if inviting everyone to laugh lovingly at little Lyovushka, because look, he'd cried a minute and was laughing, it all had the image of the sun peeping out after pouring rain, with a gleam of droplets on blades of grass; reconciliation with a beloved woman, the gleam, again, of teardrops on long lashes; the drying off, the tautness of fresh, washed skin; the lightness after tears and rain. Thus he invited them all to love him, under the probing "warmth" of their eyes, in the sympathetic silence, before he was destined to realize that the probe was a probe and the silence a silence . . . Until Lyova became so warm and full that he himself lost the thread.

"But I'd even forgotten you were supposed to come, Lyovushka. Let alone what time. Actually, I never meant to call—must've been too drunk to know what I was doing. Afterward I completely forgot. Well, it's okay. Tell me this: Why did you freeze? What did you think I'd be like? So why shouldn't you get here early, since you did—or be late? You didn't have to come at all. Why come exactly on time?" Grandfather had suddenly taken shape somehow, come into focus, he spoke almost distinctly, or at any rate without difficulty. His eyes, direct as the jabs of a skinny little fist, saw absolutely *everything*, not in the sense that they distinguished and separated all physical objects from one another, but what was behind things and under them and around, and where they all fitted, and what else in addition they were part of—he saw everything whole and as a whole—and there was no place to hide from his gaze, you went back, back, back to the wall, shielded yourself with your elbow, as if from a blow. Lyova did not know why they were doing this to him, but Grandfather's inexplicable rightness penetrated to him even through the screen of childish resentment, he was ready to obey and submit, if only they'd encourage him sometimes, like animal trainers, with a pat or a stroke, a sugar lump. But they didn't.

"What image made you freeze to death? The hypnotism of the watch mechanism working? Happiness at the hands coinciding? What slaves you've become! Him, too." Grandfather nodded toward Rudik. "But he's at least a poet and a know-nothing, a natural talent . . . Why must your face always be twisted into some sort of feeling? You can't believe yourselves at all without 'feelings.' Which is why you need for everyone to love you, and that's what all your sufferings—such sufferings!—your *agonies* are about. What's the necessity?"

Lyova couldn't bear it, ceased to understand what Grandfather was saying, looked around as if seeking support. The salvation of "Uncle Mitya's" gaze—he grasped at this last hope. But Grandfather pursued him, wouldn't let him alone:

"Oh, why gaze like a dog into his dog eyes!" he said furiously. "What makes his eyes so remarkable, do you think? Right this moment, your version of the facts is at work accommodating your feeling, right this moment you're explaining the origin of his gaze by its convenient consequences, precisely by its consequences. You're explaining it to yourself as goodness, attentiveness, understanding—that's what you need right now. All you f—ing humanists—people are supposed to understand you! But he really does understand you, he's got you figured. Because he has a flawless *method*, and it's all he uses, it makes him sharp and clear; he's not looking at you—he's reading you, he's a professional. His method is simple: he looks at you and sees what you'd be like at an investigation or an interrogation—because he's seen thousands, thousands like you. He's the Mendeleev of human souls. To him you're calcium or sodium, nothing more. He knows all about you ahead of time, from experience—your first movements are enough for him to know your every next one. He has just a single flaw—he's gone mad, like Hermann: three, seven . . . he keeps running through it. He can't escape. It's beyond him to rest for even a second from the automatism of anticipating your movements and comparing them, the mental ones, against the ones you produce for him as proof at that same second—and keep in mind, they always match up. That's all there is to his gaze. For you, understanding is already sympathy. You're accustomed to think so because, in your life, understanding is an accident, or indeed not an accident, but a kind of functional, periodic misquote of the situation—like a physical function, only not so honorable or necessary . . ." Lyova looked once more into "Uncle Mitya's" eyes. He was in fact listening and hearing Grandfather and watching Lyova. The attentiveness and sympathy of his gaze had not changed: he observed the effect of Grandfather's words, anticipated the effect with an idea, and checked the idea against the too slowly developing reality. It could be as Grandfather said. Lyova was terrified . . . "But he's my former camp commandant. A good man, Koptelov: he twice *didn't kill* me."

Koptelov burst out laughing and looked at Grandfather with pleasure.

"He's tickled that I told a lie and he didn't see it coming. After all, he checks me too, if not my every word, then at least the movement as a whole, the vector. Only he thinks too much of me, overvalues me—which is why he never expects I can pull a fast one. Well then, a rare pleasure for him: it didn't tally, and he's amused."

"Modest Platonovich . . ." Lyova said plaintively.

"Modest Platonovich! Modest Platonovich . . ." Grandfather mimicked. "Come on, call me Grandpa, say it."

"Maestro Plato . . ." Rudik teased.

"Quiet! You're just envious," and Grandfather tousled Rudik's hair. "Pour another round."

Grandfather was right: Lyova could not have uttered the word "Grandpa." The shame and hypocrisy would have turned his stomach. Then why did I come here? he thought with sudden shrewdness. To see whom? I didn't come to see *him* . . . He looked at Uncle Mitya/Koptelov, at Rudik. They *loved* Grandfather, he realized suddenly. But did he?

Everyone drank.

(Italics Mine. —A.B.)
We have always wondered, since our earliest, most spontaneous childhood, where the author was hiding when he spied on the scene that he describes. Where did he so inconspicuously put himself? In the setting described for us there is always a certain secret corner, with a dilapidated cupboard or trunk that has served its time and been put out in the vestibule, and there it stands, just as inconspicuously and needlessly as the author, who has seen all as if with his own eyes, only concealing from us where those eyes were . . . There he stands, in a buttoned-up frock coat, dim and invisible as a Japanese ninja, not breathing or shifting his weight lest he miss any of what is happening in someone else's life, which withholds no information from him, out of trust or shamelessness, or habit and disdain for him.

As we read and check against life, we will be struck that the spirit of the dormitory and communal apartment, before its incarnation in the real world, arose in literature, in the author's similar relationship to the scene. He is a communal inhabitant in it, a neighbor, a new roommate. Probably one reason why Dostoevsky excels at managing a large "kitchen" scene is that he himself never conceals his status as the heroes' new roommate: he inhibits them, they don't forget that he can see them, that he is their audience. The remarkable candor of his spying does him an honor ahead of his time. A major and openly declared convention of this sort is true realism, for it does not exceed the limits of realistically permissible observation. The first-person narrative is least reproachable in this regard—we have no doubt that the "I" could have seen what it describes. Nor is any particular suspicion aroused by a scene that is worked out through one of the heroes—in the third person, but solely by the process of his seeing, feeling, and comprehending— where only the visible behavior and spoken words of the other heroes enable us to build any hypothesis as to what they think, feel, mean, and so on. That is, subjective scenes (written from the standpoint of a subject—the author or the hero) are the very ones that arouse no suspicion of the depicted reality's reality.

But then how dubious, precisely in this regard, are the objective realistic solutions revered by realism proper, where everything is passed off as being "like it is," "the way it really happened," by eliminating that little crack or chink the author spied through—carefully caulking and curtaining it. This is exactly what forces us, and no longer in a childish way, to doubt the reality of a literary event. If the conventionality, the subjectivity, the particularity of the solution are not declared to us, we may still read it, out of condescension, as we applaud a bad singer, but we find it difficult to share and believe by living through it. How does he know? What makes him think so? And if we don't know how it really happened, then experience suggests that it couldn't have happened. After all, no man has ever had an experience in which he was not a direct, even if passive, participant.

Consequently, for no man, ever, under any conditions, has an action occurred of general, objective, neutral significance. It is quite presumptuous to pass off a strained "objectivity" as reality. God alone, if it is first agreed that He exists, can see from above. But only Lev Tolstoy has permitted himself to write from God's standpoint, and we won't even discuss here the extent of his competence in those efforts. Especially since our hero was named Lev in his honor, whether by us or by his parents . . .

Interrupting our running start, we wish to stress once more that literary reality, in our view, can be apprehended as reality only from the standpoint of a participant in that reality. And, in this sense, what is customarily thought of as the optimum realism—namely, everything "the way it happened," seemingly without an author—is the extreme of convention, and moreover insincere, not to be trusted, formally formalistic. That is, what declares itself to be realism is not, as a rule, a quest for reality, but merely an accustomed use of literary forms and even norms.

Despite being so laudably convinced of the right way to do things, we now find ourselves in a considerable quandary over the pursuit of this conviction in practice. Since we are working everything out through Lyova, and since what happened to him in this scene and what he participated in and witnessed cannot yet, in accordance with the maturity he has attained, be either recognized or heard or understood by him, then drawing a prolonged, consistent picture of him not understanding, not hearing, and not seeing is both too complex and too technical a technical problem. We have already highlighted his condition sufficiently. But what matters to us in this chapter—matters for Lyova, even though he was incapable of digesting the event to the degree that it mattered for him to do so—what matters to us is Grandfather Odoevtsev. He matters as a sign. Therefore, we will have to depart somewhat from a purely Lyovian "prism" and, without passing the depiction off as reality (but without repudiating reality either), frankly give only a sign, without attempting a live man . . .

Especially since Lyova's unpreparedness isn't our only obstacle. Everyone in this scene also drinks a whole lot. From experience, both our own and our precursors', we can assert that the things most doubtful and controversial in verbal transmission are: the world of the child, the world of the drunk, and the world of the false or talentless man. None of these three has ever had authentic self-expression, and memories play tricks on everyone. We will each always have our own view on these things, because we don't remember ourselves as children, don't make a point of remembering ourselves as drunks, and don't recognize ourselves as false and talentless.

"That's not how children talk, that's not how children think" is such a widespread rebuke to those who try to write seriously about children. It's pointless trying to prove that yes, children do talk like that, do think like that—grownups are all so convinced they know. At best, grownups take seriously their own care of children, but not the children themselves.

Because "grownups" are already in too much trouble with life to have the strength to be as serious as children. A full understanding of children's seriousness would greatly dishearten, disarm, and debilitate them. Did nature herself, perhaps, take care of this barrier? But it's true: no matter how much you deal with children, you're unlikely to know any more about who they are.

Surprisingly, it's almost the same with drunkenness: no matter how much you drink, you won't learn any more about getting drunk than you already knew.

In the scene we have undertaken to describe at Grandfather Odoevtsev's, there was no one who could have described it soberly. But almost no one ever has that experience, though many have been drunk: our attitude tomorrow to what happened yesterday is rarely fair. No company will tolerate having someone observe and listen, but not drink— and rightly so, because descriptions by sober people are always repulsive and, needless to say, show no talent for conveying the palette of a drunk person's feelings. But people who have been drinking cannot convey to us the sober facts of how it all happened, and they have almost no recollection of, or can't find words for, the festiveness of their feelings. It is beyond our power to reconcile this contradiction in the data.

So, with many reservations, we announce: "This is how drunks talk!" Whatever may be said to us later, we will have to stand our ground.

You yourselves, therefore, should put in wherever you please, as your experience suggests to you, the stage directions possible in such scenes (these, by the way, will be things that Lyova himself might have noted): where and how and after which words of his "performance" Grandfather Odoevtsev coughed, sneezed, and blew his nose, knitted his brow, puffed up and deflated, where he lost and caught his high, where he grimaced and forgot the point and where he gave up on it, where he rubbed his bald spot, rolled himself a cigarette, spat, turned up his eyes, and jabbed a companion (mainly Lyova) with his finger, and at which points he repeated, "For all I care, you can . . ." (Remainder indeciph. —A.B.)

FATHER'S FATHER

(continued)

. . . RUDIK WAS RECITING poetry, obscure but powerful.

"Do you like it?" Grandfather asked Lyova.

"Yes," Lyova said uncertainly, under the jealous and disdainful gaze of Rudik, the attentive gaze of Koptelov. Could he possibly have said no? But yes hadn't worked either. He didn't stand a chance of giving "them" the right answer. In Lyova's mind, the three of them had already become "they."

"He doesn't know much, but he can catch a high," Grandfather said. "An attribute of youth . . . Funny thing, by the way: 'to catch a high' isn't a prison-camp expression at all, it isn't only modern. Dostoevsky at seventeen, long before jail, wrote his brother that he was finished: 'What have I done in my lifetime? Nothing but catch a few highs . . .' Recite some more." Grandfather liked poetry, he was nicely drunk, and he didn't have a care in the world. His half faces were smoothing out and growing young.

The inspired Rudik very nervously recited a new poem that he thought especially powerful, prophetic . . . with the evident intention of striking them dead.

This time Lyova liked it very much.

Grandfather was incensed.

"F— your chickenshit predictions! Who says it'll happen like *that*? Who says anything at all is going to *happen*? Don't feel moved by your own lousy stuff, Lyovushka." (Lyova pouted: the poem wasn't even his, and he was to blame all over again.) "What West, what Russia! In your sense, the ideal sense, there's no life either place. They have the conditions, we have the possibility. How can anyone be a Sla-vophile or a Westernizer these days? People in either camp these days are nothing but uneducated. To say that the past is ours and the present is in the West, voiding the present here and the past over there . . . What you kids like is the nineteenth century, not Western democracy. You'd swap the centuries for the four directions . . . even our precious regime can't cope with that kind of task. Much as you might like something more ideal, everything will submit to the logic of progress, the logic of consumption and obsolescence. Humanity was born poor and few in number. It was inscribed that way in the perfect circle of nature and being. I'm an old man, I've lived attentively, and I can judge with some certainty, based on the end of some contemporary events and the beginning of others, what will happen to your con-sciousness ten or fifteen years from now, before the next big change. And so, ten years from now, when all the newspapers begin to write in apparent alarm about what we're doing to nature, begin to exploit the rich vein of honesty in this theme, then somebody's going to write about how perfect the primordial methods of agriculture were, with respect to the way they were 'inscribed,' intercalated, in the closed, supremely economical, perfect chain of natural processes. Man was poor and fed himself by laboring, not by blasting open the dome of nature. He stood humbly at her door and never contemplated burglary. By going slightly hungry he could fill the bellies of a few princes and churchmen, there weren't even that many of them, and the social 'injustice' was negligible considering that this *differentiation* is essential to humanity as a foundation for culture. By accumulating surpluses they were unintentionally creating an image of *possibility*. No equality will raise temples and palaces, paint them, decorate them. After eating, or feasting (let the schoolteachers have it their way), they could listen to a little poetry or music. From material comfort came preparedness; from preparedness, the ability to appreciate; from the ability to appre-ciate, the level of culture. Absolutely not vice versa. Culture needs a base, wealth. Not to satisfy the artist's needs—to create an authentic economic demand. It's too late now to understand this passive, almost biological role of the aristocracy, obvious as it is. For some reason the idea doesn't occur to anyone that the oddball from a petty principality must have known a lot about music if he had Haydn or Bach 'working' for him. That the Pope knew painting, if he was choosing between Michelangelo and Raphael. Despite all, these were enlightened men. Yes, they were . . . And this unthinkable, dizzying difference in human potentials, from the peasant farmer to Rublyov, was effected on an

61

energy base so infinitesimal that it strikes the present day funny. The meaning and possibility of man survived—at the cost of mere social inequality. That is, the economicalness of human culture, when at its height as a condition, is just as striking as the economicalness of natural processes in the cycle of being. Almost mirrors it. I say 'almost' because nature surpasses any society in its aristocratic principles, if only in that same 'potential difference,' accumulated on minimum amounts of energy. Nature isn't interested in intra- and interspecies equality, she's interested in expediency and perfection. All are equal before God. That's equality enough for her . . . I say 'almost' for another reason: even then, of course, in the era of the highest forms of aristocracy, people devoured and trampled their living spaces. In Juvenal, a freedman makes the following complaint: 'He (the patron) gets red mullet, which has been almost entirely fished out in the Mediterranean Sea, while you (i.e., himself, the freedman) get the horrible snaky eel.' Even in those far-off times, you see, a certain mullet was in the same situation as the eel is now . . . So man stood humbly at the door of the so-called storehouse of natural riches. Have you noticed the crassness of this expression 'natural riches'? As though the 'riches' were a surplus of nature's, not nature herself! Until our day, man was not devoid of humility or even shyness, although he should get no credit for that—it was the conditions. Technical progress, meanwhile, moved quietly along, at the level of improving the accuracy of the clock mechanism and adding yet another wheel to the pulley block, one per century . . . until it built up to the point of producing, not master keys, but jimmies, the tools of housebreaking and burglary. They had to be used—and they were, to force the doors of nature. People didn't discover nature's secret, they didn't open her door in order to enter her, they forced it without even seeing which way it opened—maybe there wasn't even a lock, and the door just opened out!—they pushed, shoved, if you've got brawn who needs brains, and fell inside with the door. They had lost patience, the way a child does over something beyond his understanding. They found themselves really among mountains of riches—more than they could take! Snitching, spitting, pie-eyed on piracy, they straggled off and multiplied chaotically over the face of the earth. Ali Baba, who throws out the coppers because he has found a chest of silver, only to throw out the silver for the sake of gold, and the gold for the sake of diamonds—and all this before the owners come home to chop off his head and fit a new lock on the gates! That's progress. Man is commonly thought to have found the way of progress, whereas he has *lost* his way. This is evident from his whole history. The point where he branched off can be determined with an accuracy of a few decades—that's a micron for history—the fork is still visible to the naked eye, if anyone had time to look back, but no, everyone's running. Had he not turned off, maybe he didn't have far to go—he might have entered by the same door—a light push and the gates would have swung open—but he wouldn't have flung himself on the riches with the wantonness of a looter, he would have known how and what to do with them. Those same laws, that same secret, are bound to be discovered when it's too late, when no one can be persuaded to listen and no one will be the first to stop. That will be the last possible moment to stop and think, so that nature can rest, lick her wounds, regenerate. But man, egged on by the age, will not agree to any kind of sacrifice today, even for the sake of tomorrow morning . . . The momentum of consumption and propagation will be so massive and great that even if you realize what's happening all you can do is consciously observe the moment of fall, the instant the avalanche breaks loose from the crest. And the coil won't spring back again, it will stretch into a wire and snap. Nature will unravel like a laddered stocking, and this won't be a descent of the same ladder you climbed—it will be instantaneous and in full view, vaporization, an evil bald spot left where someone has suddenly jerked off the wig for all to see . . . disgraced before all. —This is the 'progressive paralysis' of the earth—pardon the pun . . . An avalanche of consumption and propagation based on the looting of nature—a parasitic exploitation of nature—a substitution of mere performance for all forms of creation—a swift, fantastic fall under your own self, where you yourself will crush yourself under your own weight, break your own bones with the full tonnage of what you have consumed, taken, not produced, not returned—zero from man—that's the path of progress. Perhaps—and this is the most optimistic view—what's happening in the world now, not on the social surface of the processes but in their invisible depths, is a struggle, a rivalry, between human intellect and progress (God and the devil, to the old way of thinking). In that case the task of intellect is to succeed—at all costs, before the critical point (of irreversibility) when earth is destroyed by progress—to succeed in discrediting all false concepts, to be left with nothing and *suddenly* grasp the *secret*. Here a revolution takes place in consciousness—and the earth is saved . . . Desirable as that may be, it's a utopian fantasy. If there really is a secret force of intellect opposed to progress, it works parallel to progress—this is a race with a reverse start and massed finish. Intellect may well catch up with progress, but if so they'll arrive at the finish together, chest to chest (the critical line of irreversibility will be the finish line)—too late to profit by the spiritual revolution, it won't have time to bear fruit, its ovaries will burst in the cosmic cold, irreversibility will set in: retribution. Retribution becomes possible, after all, only from the moment of awareness . . . That's what it comes down to."

Grandfather sighed and took a sip. Half his face stayed always alive, half his face dead. He continued:

"This is just as graphic, just as obvious, in culture, language, the spirit: progress as the consumption and elimination of all the words and concepts that comprise our moral and civil structure. First the small and concrete ones, then the fair-sized and false, then the large and abstract. Any idea, once it has occurred to you, will strike you as salvific. Words are selected—first whichever come along, and then the ones that are left (all the best are left)—and spent forever. The whole strength of the human spirit, in our century, has been redirected to the mere spending, voiding, unmasking, and discrediting of false concepts. All the positivism of contemporary spiritual life is negative. False concepts are wiped out and replaced by nothing. You had one stroke of luck: for thirty years (exactly while I was gone) the hunting of word and concept was forbidden, words ran wild and at the same time ceased to fear man, they wandered off—plenty of room—and they're roaming unrecognized, uncaught, unpronounced. Now, you think that '17 destroyed, devastated our previous culture. But it didn't; it canned and preserved it. What matters is the break, not the destruction. The authorities froze there untoppled, unmoving: they're all in their places, from Derzhavin to Blok—the sequel won't shake their order, because there won't be a sequel. Everything has been turned upside down, but Russia is still a land off-limits. You can't get there. Life, not as it had been but any at all, began only in '17, but there came to be a lot of it, and they put a stop to it. And that final stop, that prohibition, which everyone curses now, will nevertheless give you a semblance of spiritual life for ten or fifteen years. In demolishing the 'false' and trapping the 'true,' you will seem to experience enthusiasm and ecstasy and labor . . .

> "So-orrow, joy, great labor too,
> I am ready, love, to share with you . . ."

Grandfather sang suddenly, in a faint, true voice. ". . . but she's bound to abandon you, don't flatter yourselves . . . It won't be long, because

64

all this has already happened, already taken place in the world, and no matter how you resist, it will all return to you, with the swiftness of a dream. You will put the liberal mill to work unmasking false notions, allegedly for the sake of the 'true' ones that are now still forbidden but so much desired. But let just a few years pass and you'll get hold of those too, the ones that seem true to you today, and they will quickly disillusion you, because, before concepts, before they were possible, culture had already been permeated by the specter of progress; i.e., of a consumer's rather than a creator's attitude toward spiritual concepts and values. That specter is what goads, what incites all this inchoate and gleeful hustle. Mark my words: the most advanced of you, those who bowl along ahead of progress . . . ten years from now, you'll hear all your most treasured words and concepts used with erroneous and falsified meanings, and it won't be thanks to bad people seizing and distorting them, but thanks to you yourselves, your very concepts themselves, on which you rest your hopes. Still forbidden and unpronounced, they already contain within them the very same untruth that so exhausts and drives you. Ten years from now, you'll be hearing at every turn all the words from Rudik's rhymes. Russia, homeland, Pushkin . . . the word, the nation, the spirit . . . all these words will be heard again as if in their first, natural, unofficial meaning, they'll strip naked—and that will be the end of these concepts. Next will come an era of 'new' ones, which you will have tracked down among concepts even longer forgotten. This will be a kind of industry— the 'mining' of the word (one poet has already put it that way, I think). Exhausted words will be dumped in slag heaps. Like in a mine . . . Ever work in a mine, Lyova? . . . Now you're going through Tsvetaeva and Pushkin, next you'll go through Lermontov and somebody else, and then you'll stumble on Tyutchev and Fet: you'll make the one a genius, the other a great man. You'll drag up Bunin . . . This inflating and devouring of reputations will pass for the growth of contemporary culture. It will all exist, it already does exist, all of what you so passionately thirst for, all of what seems to you to explain and rectify everything. In your ignorance you will guzzle each succeeding permitted concept individually—as though it alone existed—guzzle till you're revolted, vomit it up, and firmly forget it. What does not and will not exist is an intelligent, nonconsuming relationship to reality. The spirit would be in that condition, perhaps, at the founding of a new religion. But it's hard to believe in what does not yet exist. For the time being, I assure you, be grateful to the cult."

65

In the spirit of this reactionary speech, perceived by all as having been spoken with aptness and inspiration, they drank another round.

. . . .

Grandfather frowned, writhed—and interrupted Rudik:

"But everyone, everyone's already Soviet! There aren't any non-Soviets. You're for, against, in between—but only in relation to the system. It's the only stake you're tethered to. What freedom are you talking about? Where's this word? You're not free yourselves—and that's forever. You want to speak on your own—you can't speak a word on your own. You can speak only in the name of that same regime. And where else will you find that regime? The conditions for you are nowhere to be found: if you export yourselves, you won't be able to take with you the only thing relative to which you have any existence, in your own view. Unleash you and you'll start applying to come back, your necks will freeze without the dog collar . . . You'll discover that the likes of you don't exist without this regime. Only here do you exist. Nowhere else. You don't like this life . . . but I do! What do you know? You can't appreciate this. Rudik here . . . I gave him a lousy crumpled scrap of paper and he disappeared, vanished into that waste-land—he was just gone, gone!" Remembering, Grandfather was incensed again. He snorted. "Why, judge for yourselves—it's impossible! Where did he go? Nothing but rock, flatness, blizzard . . . and suddenly he's back out of nowhere: he brings bread, wine, tea, sausage, even tobacco! From where? For what? . . . When I think I'm going crazy, it's always because of what's considered completely natural, self-evident, what needn't be understood! This place where we're sitting right now—most likely it doesn't even exist on this earth, can't exist. An island of nonexistence. Yet turn on the faucet and water comes out! Oh, electricity, gas—you can still resign yourself somehow: that's beyond understanding, boggles the mind. But water! How did the water get here? Yet you can even taste it: water! Even more than taste it— you can drink your fill, slake your thirst! Isn't that staggering . . . Let's agree, water is the most surprising thing in the world. Transparent, tasteless, odorless—and you drink it! Pure relief. What runs down your chin is already riches . . . It's almost air—so surprising and so unsayable. If you're really thirsty, it *is* air. I said a lot to you about progress . . . forgot the main point. The threat comes not from where things are gotten by labor, even if by the labor of thieves. Not from where things are expensive, where there's a cost, where everyone needs and everyone grabs—where there's a price, a declared value. Oh, of course

66

we'll eradicate the forests, waters, fishes, soils, animals . . . the animals, the animals first, so as to be left in private . . . but all that comes later, we won't even quite have time. Because, above all, the threat comes from what is free, from what is God-given, from what never cost anything, neither money nor labor, from what has no cost—here's where our ruin will come from—from what we have put no price on, from the *priceless*! We will breathe up and burn up the air, we will drink up and throw out the water. That is, the first thing we'll destroy is what's *free*, while the gold, the diamonds, oh, what else?—all of that—will lie safe and sound when we're gone . . . Still, obvious as it is, it's amusing that what will disappear first is what was nobody's, communal, from the very beginning. We can work out a rather exact cost progression from air to diamonds—and that will be the sequence of loss and disappearance. And they'll be—what's the phrase?—inversely pro-por-tional! But that's not what I . . . I was talking about how I like everything. I like the earth, being on this earth, I even like the way you've fixed things on it for yourselves . . . Whatever I may have said, however I may have complained—that's all stupid. Because the essence is the order of things, and that's how everything happens, according to its essence, inevitably. Only we don't always understand, and then we *want*. Or maybe vice versa, we want, that's why we don't understand . . . So, about water: I want it and don't understand it and don't want to understand—that's happiness. Okay. Someone can still explain to me, taking water as a given, that there's a spring, a pump, a tower, a pipe—plumbing. I'll understand the man wants to explain something to me, this I'll understand. But why does it flow to *me*? The explainer will fuss and fume, bug out his eyes—explain as he may, he'll never know what it is that he finds as understandable, as clear as chocolate. Never mind water, he finds chocolate understandable, you see! Not for the world does he want to be a madman like me. He doesn't want to not understand. He's as good as anyone! So he'll keep surrounding the concepts with a blather of words, till he piles them so high you can't see them, flings his torn net of words over the phenomena, covers them somehow—okay, he's caught them . . . People like that are very fond of explaining how they've understood and appreciated this world: such pleasure, such clarity and efficiency! Now, dear, you take a saucepan, better this kind, not that, you light the fire, tha-at's the way, you put in so much salt, you chop up this and that, this way and so much, you put this in first, then that, don't get it mixed up, and—borscht! If you do it all the way I told you, they'll lick their fingers and praise you to the skies . . . How they love to list the things they understand! how splendid to think in terms of borscht, where everything's arranged as it should be! why, what a pleasure it is to live in this world, when everything turns out so smoothly . . . What saucepan? where do potatoes come from? why soup? . . . No, a world without prayer is utterly hopeless with respect to intellect. Remember in Turgenev, *Fathers and Sons*, in the epilogue I think, about the servant Peter: 'He has gone quite rigid with stupidity, says all his *e*'s like *u*'s: *I'm wull provided at prusunt.*' Everybody's wull provided at present . . . at prusunt . . . I walked into a store, the same 'nowhere' that Rudik brought all this from." Grandfather gestured sweepingly, blessing the table. "There was a woman there, oh, just a woman, a crummy old woman, fat and bearded, she's rasping away, shaking her beard: There's nothing in the store, says she. I was just giving thanks to God—buying a split of vodka—and that's the moment she says such a thing to me. Pah! And what's this, I thought. What's this, I ask you! This isn't merchandise, in your opinion? You think they didn't have anything to put in the window—so they put the trash on display? And I was right, because the windows were piled high with all different kinds of ugly Russian merchandise—which can be eaten. What do you think, woman, I said, nobody eats these little processed cheeses?! They didn't have her kind of cheese, you see. What, people don't cook kasha? They don't eat canned goods, flatfish in tomato puree? They eat and cook everything. What, in your opinion, does all of Russia eat? These purple pebbles, what do you think they are? They're gumdrops, very edible . . . Gingersnaps too, nice and fresh, only a week old—you don't even need teeth! Eh? At this point a police officer gets me by my little white arms. Not rudely either, just takes hold of me seriously and fairly, the tartar. He doesn't hit me, just leads me out nicely and sees me home. And he didn't take away the vodka—he understood, then . . . just folks, then. No, they're wonderfully well fixed, these people! Everything adjusted, no excesses, exactly so much, and *just*! Notice, just in the extreme! The only thing you mustn't do is break the law; you must *observe*! Oh, they're very strict with the lawbreaker. The fact that he doesn't have everything, all the conveniences, so to speak—that's logical, understandable. Everyone else can live with it, why can't he? But the main thing is, this system provides happiness for those who are *in* it and don't stick their necks out. Who's making him stick his neck out? . . . Yes, everyone's wonderfully well fixed—and confident of it. Notice, the system even suffices to impart confidence. It's strong! . . . Here I was, on my way home, there was a man standing in the middle of a field, just standing, nothing for him to do there. Next to him there was a post, the plaque on the post was swinging in the wind. Nobody around, nothing. 'Are you sure of it?' I asked. 'What?' He was even frightened. 'Why, what you're expecting,' I said. 'What are you talking about?' He looks at me as if I'm crazy—and rightly so, what could he be expecting? 'The bus,' I prompted, 'are you sure the bus will come?' 'Oh . . .' He was reassured, he took it his own way. He looks at his watch for some reason, not at the road, and he says, 'Why wouldn't it? It'll be here in five minutes.' 'But why are you so sure of it?' I implored. 'You know, Gramps,' he said, 'you're soused to the gills. Get lost. You should be ashamed, bothering people at your age.' He wasn't a bad guy, he wasn't mean, or else he might have beat me up, he was so sure . . . So, I haven't lost the capacity to be astonished or quietly surprised at the world; this is a serene surprise, so to speak, prayerful, healthful, nurturing. But if there's one thing that drives me crazy, it's that people consider everything in this life natural, self-evident. Where do you get that idea? I was walking along here recently, I looked and they'd excavated a big cellar hole beside one of these apartment buildings . . . maybe ten meters away from the foundation, they rarely dig so close . . . by itself the building's a bit taller than the others, too . . . and here it was, standing over a precipice—such an enormous box! I looked and it was just set on the ground, oh, just like a matchbox . . . but no problem—it stands. How very quiet and patient our earth is, I thought. She doesn't even flick her skin, she doesn't move a muscle, we're crawling around on her. And we're confident: All's quiet . . . go ahead! And everyone lives in this building that's made out of trash, set spang on the ground, they live just as unerringly as they lift a spoon to their mouths, and such order they've introduced! They get up at the same time, come out at the same time, the bus picks them up and takes them not where it needs, where *they* need to go, they do something there, who knows what, and ride back—public transportation again, it plays no tricks this time either—they arrive and immediately figure out who lives where, they have this designated by special little numbers, they re-member them, the numbers tally with what they remember, and they don't get mixed up; twice a month, for riding there and back, they get scraps of paper handed out to them and everyone understands how many he'll receive, then for these scraps of paper they unerringly buy merchandise and disperse to consume it; they enter under one number, then under another; they light the lamp and it's light, outside the window there's a blizzard—but the radiator's warm . . . And not only

69

are they well fixed in life, but they've been so slick about fixing up their world! With the care and coziness possible only in childhood, playing dolls. Notice, they've built the world for themselves—not for you! You've built nothing for yourselves! So you've got no f—ing complaint. You look down your noses, you call it: sublimation, substitution, ex-is-tence! Yes, perhaps—but it's *exactly* what they want! You haven't even dreamed such exactness! You *yourselves* are unhappy, like fools. Anybody will tell you you're fools . . . You think *you're* spiritual and therefore free. But your protest and your boldness and your freedom are measured out to you, as if by ration cards. You all discuss in unison the bones they toss you from on high. In your opinion it's impossible for "them" to have either spirit or even intellect—yet only in relation to what they permit are you allowed to discover the self-sufficiency and freshness of your independence. In 1980, you'll read *Ulysses*, and argue, and think that you have won this right . . . I tell you this in the 'late fifties'—but you verify it. At that point the end of the world will arrive. Imagine, the end of the world, and you haven't had time to get Joyce. Your modernity will have been more permissible to Joyce than to you. The extent of your dependence is beyond your understanding. You're enviers, you're losers, you haven't happened, in either the past or the present or the future . . . I, at least, have learned not to believe that what I don't like doesn't exist. Not for me, but it exists. And my heart just sinks at the slickness, the sweet expediency of human world-building . . ."

Everyone drank to this, God Himself so ordered. Rudik said: "Now I understand how you got lost that time. When you were speaking so angrily a minute ago about the numbers on people's quarters—"

"I was not angry, you do not understand! Those numbers are necessary, what fool would deny them—how could you do without them! I got lost myself, through my own stupidity, and . . . Lyovushka, you don't know, why are you nodding? I'll have to give you an idea what we're talking about. I went out for bread, not so long ago, and I got lost. The buildings are identical. I forgot my address—clean forgot it. I walked and walked. It was cold, and I started to cry. I had voided the hardships in my life, decided there would be no more—and here I'd declined so. I went back to the bakery, sat down and cried. They called a policeman. He said: The old man's not drunk, he's lost his memory, this is the doctors' function, not mine. They called the ambulance. The doctor said: The old man's not sick, he's forgotten his address, taking him home is a job for the police. They argued a long time. Finally the doctor, he was an intellectual after all, young, kind of a nice kid—he spat in anger and went to work. He drives up to an apartment building. 'This yours?' he says. 'Might be,' I say. 'Pah!' he says. He gets an idea, starts asking the children: 'This your grandpa?' 'No,' they said. Then at some building or other I was recognized—and it did turn out to be mine. I don't go out of the house anymore."

Lyova all but wept: what had they done to the man! But he contained himself and started talking about something else, in a very roundabout way.

. . . .

. . . Grandfather cut Lyova short.

"But why undeservedly! Why undeservedly?" He attacked like a rooster, turning his head sideways to Lyova—the live half of his face. His voice sounded almost resentful. "I suffered *deservedly*. What a word! De-serv-edly! They put me away for what I *did*. I was never a do-nothing, never frivolous. I don't pride myself on this: it's vulgar to be always serious. But I was and still am. If I weren't serious, I wouldn't be talking to you now! I'd have thrown you out on your mother-loving ear . . . My God, they're still asking and wondering. *When*, they say, did all this begin! The first time an intellectual entered into conversation with a boor in a doorway, began to explain himself—that's when it began. You've got to throw 'em out on their ear!" Grandfather's ears actually turned red in illustration. Lyova began to worry about a second stroke, but needlessly: Grandfather was no longer serious, he was performing. He had tried-and-true listeners, and Lyova was live bait. "This regime is all square with me. I'm not one of those worthless, prideless people who were first put away undeservedly and have now been released deservedly . . . The regime is the regime. Had I been in their place, I'd have put myself away. The only thing I didn't deserve is this affront of rehabilitation. They're not afraid of me anymore: I'm slag. They threw me out into retirement—I've served my time as a prisoner and I'm no good for anything else. That's how capitalist countries treat workers in the textbooks. I'm no danger. I'm not needed. Here's your apartment, here's your pension. As a present at that, as compensation, in order to degrade me once more by reminding me I hadn't been able to do anything to them . . . as though I hadn't earned such things by my labor. I used to think I was too proud to be broken— I myself used to change. The way the girl who sees that resistance is useless and she's going to get raped all the same may take her own clothes off, precisely out of pride . . . I've only just now been broken,

7 1

after my 'liberation.' I had never been sick, but the first thing that happened to me here was a stroke. I started falling apart. I couldn't reconcile myself to this, and I deliberately began to drink—I can't—in order to fall apart myself. So I can do at least one thing myself—what I can't. I can't live. I'm not surviving, Lyovushka. I'm another person. By now I have exactly no relationship to the person you came to see. This is cruelty, to do it to a person twice! Rape me first—then darn me up and declare me a cherry. As a result—at seventy years of age!—having wasted them all on making life be *my* life, whatever it was—I can say that I haven't coped with life . . . When they took me I went with them myself, so as to avoid rape, so as not to be *taken* (like that girl). I gave up on my past as hopeless, gave up on my work and profession. As I understood life, and thus understood myself, everything fate did to a man must become his life. This became my life. I did an excellent job, I was a good construction boss, I knew how to think in terms of the material of life, no matter what kind: the word, or soil and building materials. I became another man and was he for all those twenty-seven years, I am another man! I don't give a f— for the kind of justice that would force me to become again the man I was thirty years ago! I was forty then, I'm seventy now—there's a difference, isn't there!—but even had I been seventy then and forty now, I couldn't make this life a third time *my own*. How dared they, these same people, after perpetrating one injustice, turn around and reproduce it! This is cynicism, at best: it turns out they *knew* all along what they were doing. They knew even *then* that after a while, after my life, they would void it! That's just what they did, they voided thirty years of my life, by returning me to the previous point. It's a mistake, they say, that I lived those thirty years the way I did. I'm not about to live them over again differently. By hook or by crook: it didn't work to void your life by putting you away, we'll void it by releasing you. Here's a two-room apartment for you—mockery, a clean-shaven smirk . . . Suppose I wanted to stay there? Suppose I left a woman back there, a stubby, illiterate fool? She's a criminal, see, she can't go into the big cities . . . At first this was all fate—by now it's retribution. Too much, I can't take so much. Execution—by all means. Retribution—leave it to God! You people have always remembered me only as I was when they sent me up!" For a long time he had been addressing himself only to Lyova, and now he was jabbing a crooked finger right in his chest. "And that's the way you want me now, you swine, after thirty years, because those years of mine didn't exist *for you*! Yours did, but mine didn't! I was supposed to return as that

72

man—brilliant, forty years old, in a turndown collar . . . knock the women dead . . . but now am I disappointed to have you see me another man? Here, look! what's left . . ." He reached to undo and show them but hunted too long—they stopped him.

Lyova felt frightened and sobered: he was tired of being tormented by Grandfather's torment, not the torment in his words but another, which was over his words, *because of* his words. Grandfather was sickened and shaken by the nothingness of his own words. He knew what he meant and could not say it. He heard his own vulgarity before anyone else, even if no one heard it he was vomiting—and not outwardly.

They stopped him. He went slack. A pitiful old man who had voided pity toward himself, and just now had forbidden it once more. He could not be touched, there was no way, no gesture, none left, by which one could have done it, no one who could . . .

"There's no one I can even tell about my life—you wouldn't understand," he said sorrowfully and quietly, but not even melodramatically. "Him?" He jabbed Koptelov. "He knows anyway. Him?" He jabbed Rudik. "He's an orphan, he wouldn't understand anyway. You? You—don't know anyway . . . It's stupid for me to be angry at your father" (he did not say "my son"), "I just don't have the strength."

They poured him a drink, but he didn't drink it.

. . . .

"Well, and how is he?" Grandfather asked. He had subsided and grown calm, even sober and guilty.

This shift, such a change, no longer surprised Lyova: he had already witnessed several like it. Grandfather's behavior had such a uniform and obvious amplitude that it could probably have been expressed mathematically, if desired, in the form of a curve. Two trials would have sufficed—the third would already be a test. The curve might be drawn in different ways, merely by shifting the starting point, the coordinates of the graph, where the quantity of vodka is plotted on one axis in milliliters, and the "high" on the other, in thought units of some kind (choosing such a unit is the hardest part), expressing the degree of independence, of rebirth, and its slope.

At first there seems to be nothing: pulsating tremor and immobility. The whole world—in its scattered and excessive diversity, with no possibility of preference, no freedom of choice—is a pure nerve field. The needle trembles near zero: hangover. A dose is taken, but its effect is not instantaneous, and the condition is already critical and intol-

73

erable. It is discharged in a burst of irritation and aggressiveness—a way of prevailing over time and the wait for the effect; anything at all may serve as the excuse for venting irritation, the first thing that comes along. A short time goes by in this still-dull irritability, and the high overtakes it. Gratification leads to a momentary relaxation, a loss of logical sequence ("What was I talking about . . . ?"), the failure of a vague half smile . . . And then the growth of "first high" into the high proper takes place: Grandfather's performance, the condition when Grandfather is Grandfather, when the hitherto diverging heart and mind are fused, the thoughts and feelings seem to have come into focus in this restored center of reality. His discourse develops and broadens—and breaks off as suddenly as though a windup mechanism has stopped. And so it has. Decisive proof of the "chemism" of the alcoholic's spiritual processes: "the effect has worn off."

Grandfather was not only intelligent enough but "conscious" enough to understand this. The affront by alcohol, the sense of degradation at the "chemism" of his own thought (that is, in any case, its conventionality, relativity, unnaturalness), the inability to regain a state of waking thought—these were the subject of especially severe, especially intolerable agonies for Grandfather, which in turn were also degraded and also by "chemism," the chemism of hangover.

He was affronted and degraded, and his thought was degraded in the literal sense of the word—it did not achieve reality. And if his audience could feel gratified and even delighted by his performance, then their delight in the splinters, the provincial rubbish, of the bygone edifice of Grandfather's spirit served as an added affront, by now past bearing. He grew wrathful and had another drink and grew wrathful all over again, waiting for his high.

"Well, and how is he?" Grandfather asked. He seemed quiet and guilty.

Lyova had been presented with another chance. Unmanned from the very beginning, and now downright frightened by Grandfather, by his stormy attack, his harshness, his accusations (after all, Grandfather was really more to blame for Lyova's fate than Lyova for his), he tried once more to interpret everything according to his own lights, in a way that he could understand and accept, in a way that it really was not . . .

In Grandfather's sudden quietness and guilt, and in the fact that he had asked Lyova about Father, about his son (and Lyova had immediately noted, with a certain pleasure in his own powers of observation, that Grandfather did not call Father "my son"), Lyova had seen "how the old man was really suffering," how empty and lonely he felt without them: without the family, without any son whatever. Shakespeare's role in Lear's tragedy . . . Lyova's nose even began to tingle from hypothesizing these feelings. It was misfortune and injustice that had made him (Grandfather) so difficult and mean, really he was kind (Lyova's elementary-school teachers had made a strong impression on him, after all: "You're not really mean, you're really a good little boy. This is something you've acquired. Tell me who wrote the bad word on the blackboard and you'll be a good little boy"—and a couple of pats on the back, the first corruption), really, Lyova thought, all this was only a challenge, something "acquired." He could almost picture it: despite all, very gradually, very subtly, he would find an approach to Grandfather, a key, he would thaw the ice of resentment and woe, and, though in the sunset of his days, love and home would smile on Grandfather . . . but now, when he practically had them all seated at evening tea, he caught sight of Grandfather next to Father and across from Uncle Dickens. For an instant he felt sick at the impossibility, and lest he lose his deep feeling he immediately erased the scene from the inside of his forehead, first thinking, by way of transition, that yes, *different* people (Grandfather and Uncle Dickens) used to be able to exist, and had existed; and then once more, this time like a final decree, that really Grandfather was a gentle soul, as was proved by his coarseness.

Since he must now tell Grandfather something about Father, tell father about son—and what is more, in the light of all manner of emotional subtlety, because of the "thawing of the ice"—he became so busy choosing what to say and what not to say, but most importantly how to say it, he found he had so much of this emotional subtlety, which lay in the evenness of his voice, the certainty of his tone, the honest frankness of his gaze—that he was very much carried away by it all, and no longer seemed to be doing the talking. With the very attentiveness and sudden collapse of tension, the very relaxation that he had meant for Grandfather, he himself listened to Lyova talking—his soulful and appealing voice falling from somewhere—and did not hear at all the thickening, chilling silence that suddenly hung in the room and did not thaw.

"Look at you, old fellow—mugging again!" Grandfather said, quietly but somehow very audibly. Lyova was left with half a word on his lips. "You're a strange kid . . . Are you all like this now, perhaps? You never seem to be utterly sincerely—do you hear, Lyovushka, I don't doubt your sincerity, being sincere seems to be important to you—but

75

you're never utterly sincerely *yourself*. The present-day system of education must be a more serious business than I thought. I thought it was just crass and ignorant. But no! Try to teach a person not actual understanding but the concept that he understands and grasps what's happening—now *there's* a staggering pedagogical phenomenon! Neither facts nor conditions nor reality exists for you—only concepts of them. You simply have no suspicion that life exists! But do you at least digest your food? Do you shit? Sorry, Lyovushka, I didn't mean to offend you . . . You're impossible to talk to nicely, you know, because you have a prior concept of what's supposed to be said to you, and an attitude toward that concept—and you feel hurt that they didn't coincide. You're going to hurt a long time and in vain, Lyovushka, if that's so . . . The unexplained world throws you into a panic, which you take for the emotional suffering characteristic of a man with subtle feelings; you're unable, I see, to explain anything yet; then the single happy remedy for you (and somehow you use it with a paradoxical prudence) is to have had an explanation for what happened before it happened, that is, to see only the part of the world that fits your premature explanation. What makes you think, for example, that no matter what I say aloud I'm secretly suffering (subtext? is that the word now?), almost secretly from myself? Why do you so confidently differentiate what's 'natural' and what's unnatural? Who read you a ukase that if you fall in love you love all your life? That the development of a feeling is good and the loss of it bad? Who succeeded, and when, in convincing you that everything is exactly thus: a grandfather loves his grandson, a grandson respects his grandfather? . . . That way you'll never come face to face with life. But I'm afraid it's no remedy, she's going to kick you in the ass—another painful, strange, and unexpected event for you. Apparently, the people you think intelligent are the ones who say what you've recently understood to be intelligent, and the ones you think foolish are those who still say what you've recently devalued as being unintelligent. That way you'll keep on achieving a higher level than the one you were at, you'll always be climbing one rung up to yesterday. But what distinguishes the intelligent man from the foolish? That, by the way, is a question to which it's very difficult to formulate an answer. As a rule, I for one can't give myself an answer to it. But I was struck, just now, that what distinguishes the wise man from the foolish, exactly and precisely, is not the level of his explanations of what is happening but the 'unpreparedness' of those explanations in the face of reality. Do you hear me? Or are you eating tomorrow's again and digesting yesterday's? Do you know what that is, what you ate yesterday?"

Lyova knew well—Uncle Dickens had explained this to him. But he had not been hearing Grandfather since the moment the word "foolish" was uttered. He could do nothing about his lips; they swelled, stuck out, and quivered. I seem to have been called a fool, Lyova thought.

Lyova was not hearing, but Grandfather was no longer talking to him. He had turned to "his" audience and was already talking to them, because something about these notions fascinated him.

"Intelligence is zero. Yes, yes, the zero is what's intelligent! A void, an absence of memory, of preparedness—the perpetual ability to mirror reality at the instant of reality, at the point of its effectuation. Intelligence is more than brain, more than heart, more than any knowledge or education . . . Intelligence is of the people. Intelligence is the capacity for the birth of a mirroring thought, synchronous with reality; it's not quotation, not recollection, not preparation according to any model, even the highest—not performance. Intelligence is the capacity for reality at the level of consciousness. For anything but a live life, intelligence isn't even needed. That's the way it is."

With satisfaction, he divided the last bottle among the glasses.

"One thing I haven't encountered"—Grandfather grinned—"is people who consider themselves foolish. By the way, this may be one of the secrets of power. People are easily governed, if they are incapable, under any circumstances, of conceiving of themselves as foolish. Therefore, one must flatter them, admire their intelligence, so that they never take a new direction. In this respect, it's a good thing to give them all an education, so that they can never again count themselves more foolish than others.

"The basis of intelligence is ignorance. Therefore, no one who has ever been to school will become intelligent. Zero is still intelligent—a grade of 5 is already foolish. There is no life where life has already been; nor must one seek now or here the life that once was or somewhere is. The here and now is precisely here and now. There is no other life. Let's drink! You drink, too, Lyovushka, don't be upset. That's the main thing, Lyovushka, don't be upset . . ."

Lyovushka was upset. He drained at one gulp his full 125 grams; Grandfather knew how to divide so that each got no more and no less. And now a strange thing happened to Lyova. He felt himself sobering up. His sad situation struck him funny, without his remembering what

77

that situation was—the sadness itself struck him funny. He burst out laughing. The whole of this ungraspable evening disappeared somewhere, and he seemed to have just come in from the cold, with all those same worn-out intentions from the "Grandfather–Grandson" hypothesis, which was quite unimpaired and in no way undermined. And Grandpa had put on a little black skullcap for the occasion . . . Now Lyova caught sight of two strangers he didn't know or like. They were laughing.

"Why are you laughing?" Lyova said. "We're not drinking—we're sobering up. In a broad sense, the sober man is really drunk, and when he drinks he sobers up."

"Good for you!" said Grandpa, straightening his skullcap. "So tell us about yourself. I guess you'll be following in your father's footsteps?"

"No! No!" Lyova ejaculated, as if he had seen a ghost.

Now, most urbanely, he asked Koptelov for a cigarette, inhaled with the serious air that inevitably and unaccountably comes over people before they jab the butt into the ashtray, and . . . from somewhere muscular oarsmen came running, someone said "Cast off" and shouted "Farewell" to someone, the galley picked up speed to the harmonious sighs of the shining oars, the wooden woman on the prow took the blows of the waves on her bare tits, and somehow he contrived to see them although he stood on deck commanding the oarsmen . . . The deck listed again . . . An attack of seasickness . . . Darkness fell upon his eyes and lifted. Lyova sat there in the room and realized that he had been talking for a long time now and everyone was listening. He heard himself speak the word "literature," but he had no idea what came before it. Literachoor-poor-boor, he thought, but his tongue rescued him by speaking some sort of coherent phrase, the sense of which he didn't understand, but it had the word "culture" in it.

The room had grown hot, he undid a button. It seemed odd to him that they had drunk nothing for a long time and yet he was getting drunker with his every new word. But no, I'm not drunk, he told himself in astonishment, how could I be drunk? . . . The difference between history and geography, he thought, apparently still continuing to talk, is like the difference between the old and the painted . . . He inhaled so deeply it hurt—the air was full of smoke, reeked of snack foods—he tensed all his muscles, and for an instant the room came into focus, he sharply and separately saw Grandfather standing in the middle of the room (he was emitting his cheap tobacco smoke, and the two halves of his face seemed to have become equal), and Rudik,

78

motionless and scornful, staring a bit upwards and sideways, and Koptelov, twisting the glass in front of him and no longer staring attentively,
as if he already knew all to the end . . . Lyova held his breath and
preserved this scene before his eyes for about a second; then, of itself,
came the exhalation, and again everything scattered—both Grandfather and Rudik and Koptelov, a keg from somewhere, a crucifix,
colors and sounds, words and thoughts—all these again swirled before
him, lightly dancing. And all this time he continued to talk.

At last his galley spurted through this narrow, nauseous strait and
shot out to bright, smooth, open water—count the sails and the holes,
exchange dead men for oarsmen . . . But better she hadn't shot out
to this smooth water! Memory began returning to Lyova, unwinding
backward, and ever more swiftly: here was the word spoken a minute
ago, here was the sentence, and here, suddenly, his whole speech, a
miscellaneous mass in the indistinguishability of its run-together words—
but like a blow in the clarity of its whole meaning. Lyova even squinted
in the blinding light of irreparability.

For Lyova had talked a lot about something, about which it was
already abundantly clear he categorically should not have talked: about
Grandfather's works, about the members of his old school, about how
he, Lyova, himself, by his labor and his own efforts (a gnashing of
teeth now from shame) . . . how he, Lyova, wanted recourse to their
methods, to some extent at least, in his own work . . . Lyova remembered how he had bent every effort to flatter Grandfather, waited for
an encouraging reply and even a clap on the shoulder, hinted that he
must show surprise and delight at his grandson's so obvious virtues (a
mute howl, a cold sweat) . . .

This sobering-up process, ever accelerating, progressed by a kind of
simultaneous clearing up and clouding over (from the unbearableness),
and Lyova turned cold, because out of the murk of the room Grandfather's congealed face appeared before him, and the chilling thing
was not the finally established sharpness of his own physical vision,
not the sharpness of the features of that face, but the sharpness of its
whole meaning—and this again was like a blow, and a blaze of irreparability.

But that was just what he should not have done—repair his error!
It was right that because of his hopeless feeling that all along, from
the very first, he had been out of step here, out of phase, the harder
he tried to get in the more *out* of step he would be, he was already
doomed because they were expecting him to be out of step (Grandfather—okay! but what had he done to *them*, to *them*?? what was he

guilty of before that pair! why this injustice, too?), and even if he miraculously guessed and got in step, it would be all the more out of phase!—because of this feeling, Lyova wanted to run, shrink, diminish to a point and vanish, crawl far back in time so that nothing, nothing at all had ever happened, almost be sucked back into the womb, go whistling through the womb, too, and dissolve in a milky, ghostly shudder . . . He wanted to go flying out of this room with a prolonged whistle, just as he was, chair and all, backward out the window—this, too, would have been right. He just shouldn't have corrected his mistakes . . .

The word "Father" flew through the room, and Lyova convulsively grabbed it on the wing, gripped it in his fist like a fly. Yes, yes! This was precisely where the chief mistake had crept in, as he now thought, glimpsing salvation. He could no longer repair everything—but he could at least not ruin everything. It was precisely when speaking of Father that he had made his chief and unforgivable blunder: he had told Grandfather everything all wrong and not what Grandfather *wanted* to hear. He had tried to do it as if telling a father about his son, but he should have told Grandfather about Father, that is, about what he, Lyova, saw and felt about all this. This was the "mistake" that now seemed most important to Lyova, but it may have seemed to him most important only because this was when, in his opinion, he had been called a fool. Why this was so offensive to him had perhaps been explained by Grandfather, but Lyova did not remember. It's a strange thing: for no other insult would Lyova have lacked the dignity or the pride or even the self-esteem, but he categorically had no wish to be— or what was still more hopeless, to be seen as—a fool.

And having plucked out of the air the word "Father," black and frock-coated like a fly, he started talking about him rather too rapidly, groveling in proportion to that rapidity, and ever more intensely aware of his own groveling. About how he had found out, how he had reacted, what he had found out, and what he had done—and now there was more and more untruth and calumny: he was disengaging, ungluing Father from himself as if with a special trowel, peeling him off, picking him off, trimming the edges of the rupture. He and Father had always, since the day of his birth, been turning into opposites; the alienation had been progressing instinctively when Lyova still only felt without knowing what, but felt so correctly, he was such a born wonder that he had recognized later why he felt that way . . .

Lyova suffered as he groveled, groveled as he suffered. Oh, how he would have liked to go back to being drunk! And he almost achieved this, from the backbreaking weight of the burden he had loaded on himself and the force of it crushing him. Why had he himself, voluntarily—no one had been tugging his hand—scraped his whole day into a heap (it turned out to be a lot) and wanted to carry it away? He could not move the burden of this day's life. He was almost drunk from the weight, his eyes clouded over with a stifling myopic invisibility, and he began to tangle his words, no longer understanding what he said, and even experiencing a sort of uplift from handing things over to someone, handing over everything—Father, himself, Uncle Mitya—and all this almost with pleasure, even an unfathomable joy. As if one were to drop a backbreaking and precious burden in the mud, failing to carry it all the way, and nevertheless feel relief . . . Drop his mother, too, if he only could, his sister, too, had he had one—it was almost delight . . .

Something shocked him awake, his eyes seemed to open, he saw hanging over him Grandfather's too large face. Something whistled across the dark red face, the mouth was crookedly open—Lyova realized that Grandfather was shouting. He realized it but at first didn't hear it, a shout like a pealing bell broke through at midsentence, as though someone had abruptly switched on a radio.

". . . Gh-gh-*him*! Gh-gh-gh-*him*! Talking about your *father*! To me! *His father* . . . Gh-gh-ghe-oo-oo!"

Here's the one. He was shouting, but somehow indistinctly again, as if the tongue were too thick in his mouth, wouldn't obey, wouldn't fit.

Lyova was getting up, snagging his foot on the chair, the chair was swaying and not falling. Rudik, too, had jumped up and was standing somehow wrathfully and aslant and violating the laws of equilibrium. Even Koptelov's gaze had violated its own attentive equilibrium with a kind of emotion, quite unrelated to Lyova.

"In the seed! There's treachery already in the seed!" Grandfather bawled, half moaned, sitting on his chair. "Disinterested already, abstract . . ."

Lyova was snatching his coat, hat, scarf from Rudik's hands. Backing out, arm in one sleeve, dropping, picking up, hugging both coat and hat. Hitting his back against corners and doorjambs . . .

Lyova stood on the landing, dropping his hat for the last time and picking it up for the last time, still feeling Rudik's weak and clumsy but insulting blow, which had landed just behind . . . and the door, it seemed to him, was still quivering from the blow, and "Sold out! Sold out!" rang in his ears like a record stuck in the groove.

He went downstairs in a quiet stupor, carrying himself carefully and slowly as if swaddled and touchingly light. The freezing wind, which had sprung up toward midnight with special violence, lashed his cheeks instantly, before he walked out the gate. Or, rather, there was no gate, as there was no street either—all was one big yard, over which the wind was rushing about, coiling in evil little dry twisters. It had plenty of space here, nothing to bound or direct it, in a sense it had nowhere to blow to—and it blew everywhere. Snow was already beginning to cover this wilderness, rustling as it swept across frozen puddles of asphalt. Dim spots of light swung back and forth under sparse lamps arranged according to an unfathomable system. There were no people, there were no cars, there was no street—there was no path.

Lyova trudged along in this failed space, tumbling out into holes of light and disappearing again. He shook with a gross, implausible tremor: the expression "his bones rattled" would be no exaggeration or image, it would be literal. Suddenly, up ahead, out of nowhere, a green taxi light blinked on. This was hard to believe—a mirage, unthinkable happiness. Lyova started to hurry, seeing nothing now but the tiny rescuing green spot. It was motionless—it couldn't be real—it should drive off and rush away the moment he ran toward it, as soon as he got within two steps. And when the spot went out and blinked on again, Lyova had no further doubt: he was going crazy, he had cracked, gone bonkers . . . The taxi was quite near, but those few steps that he took seemed endless to Lyova. He was oddly aware of time flowing through him. It was uneven and seemingly fitful: it dragged, stretched out, thinned like a droplet, forming a little neck— and suddenly broke. Thus, he walked toward the green light for a long time, thinking now of absolutely nothing, then started to run after all, flailing his arms and shouting—nothing had changed for the moment, the light stayed in place, getting no nearer . . .

Suddenly he was already sitting in the taxi and riding. The driver, even en route, continued to fiddle with the light, adjusting the connection. The plausibility struck Lyova as horrible.

He warmed slightly and stopped shaking. He felt a little bushed, and then acutely resentful. How come, he thought fuzzily. This is maybe just the first time I've felt all this, the real thing, nobody taught me this, so I should get credit for it, I went in all sincerity . . . and that's how they treat me! They shouldn't have done it! Thoroughly enraged, he wiped away a tear with his sleeve. Imagine, the old blab-bermouth, the fool . . .

He felt more reassured, and thought with greater firmness, as a final resolve: He's not at all intelligent—meaning that had Grandfather been an intelligent man he would have understood Lyova's condition . . . even certain awkward contradictions in Lyova's behavior were quite understandable and justified by the excitement of the meeting; even his own incongruities with himself were natural and permissible. Curiously, although that was how he reasoned, claiming that someone else's mind should certainly discern Lyova's excellent essence through the very imprecision of his behavior, Lyova ascribed to Grandfather himself behavior that was definitive and precise, taking his every gesture and word at face value, for full congruity of thought, feeling, and their expression. And then: "He's not at all intelligent," Lyova told himself.

He felt more reassured—and more bushed . . . Everything began sailing smoothly, the glowing instrument panel shifted somewhere to the left, his head lurched and fell on his chest, he returned it to its place with an effort. At this point they flew up onto a bridge and down. Lyova's gut plopped and heaved, and he vomited.

On the dark and empty street, the driver walloped Lyova, then stepped hard on the gas and drove away, swearing. But this was already quite near home.

No one at home was asleep—they were waiting up. Lyova grinned a loathsome grin and walked past into his own room without saying a single word, as if it were almost a pleasure to turn aside the plea in his father's eyes and the entreaty in his mother's. As he undressed, he had the feeling he'd gotten worse that day. He told himself as much: "I've gotten worse." This was a new, unexpected feeling. He could not have said why he was worse, or worse than what. Before, he had never seemed either worse or better; he was Lyova. But today—"I've gotten worse," he told himself, and for some reason found it almost gratifying. He had become worse than something, it was unclear what, and shuddering at the cold sheets he as much as threw up his hands, gave up on himself, on everything. "Well, that's that," he told himself. And once again, for completeness, did in fact throw up his hands, again not quite realizing at what; he closed his eyes, and his head started to spin, the bed turned a couple of times as if around an axis . . . And Lyova disappeared, he was gone.

Lyova woke up strangely empty and free and apparently unable to remember anything. If any shadow of a scene suddenly appeared in his brain, he was almost sincerely unable to say whether whatever the scene and the shadow came from had really happened, or whether it was a trace of a half-forgotten dream, a nightmare, or whether nothing had really happened.

This was a lesson he could not yet assimilate.

He had extracted no lesson, but something in him had shifted. He dulled, filmed over. One time when Uncle Mitya showed up with his little flask, Lyova went off to his room or even outdoors. To Father he once said rudely that he couldn't care less about the Rehabilitation, that he had to laugh at this fashion for those who had "suffered" when in fact it had simply been *permitted*, this fashion.

He had extracted something, after all . . . By now he understood perfectly that Uncle Mitya was essential to Father for the further reason that he frequented their house not only in his own person but also a little bit "in exchange"—in exchange for Grandfather. Lyova understood this perfectly, but had no wish to be "just." He did not need justice.

VERSION AND
VARIANT

GRANDFATHER SOON failed to survive.

He fled back to his place of exile, but on the way he was caught, sent home, hospitalized, placed under guardianship—and did not survive.

Or, having fled, he came down sick on the way, like Lev Tolstoy, and died in the Pechora Railroad Infirmary, without ever reaching the village of Syr-Yaga or Voy-Vozh.

Or thus. Grandfather was hospitalized involuntarily. He fled, and made it to Syr-Yaga, where his old woman, having no reason to expect him, had taken up with a locksmith by the name of Pushkin (no relation).* The old woman promptly left Pushkin, and he racketed under the windows every night, drunk. But Grandfather Odoevtsev soon failed to survive, because the "second" return to a "former" life sapped the last of his strength. He departed this world, to the wails of the old woman, in the arms of Pushkin the locksmith.

There are several legends, differing in emphasis, about how Modest Odoevtsev died. Yet in all versions, despite their utter inconsistency, one observes a series of shared words: involuntary hospitalization, flight, Syr-Yaga (also known as Voy-Vozh and Knyazh-Pogost), and death. This last tallies in all variants and always stands at the end of the series.

* There is nothing improbable in such a coincidence. A friend of mine works at an institute where Lermontov is head of maintenance, Pushkin is the janitor, and Nekrasov is the plumber; he saw them once at the store, chipping in on a half liter. Curiously, Lermontov is senior to Pushkin here in his official position.

The remaining words get transposed, which also changes the plot, and fundamentally at that. More is known by the Odoevtsevs themselves, but they confide in no one. The word "guardianship" is excluded from their lexicon.

We, too, will avoid being any more specific. This vagueness is important to us as a color, as an imaginary value in the presence of the absolute value of death. Something of the sort, at any rate, happened to an acquaintance of ours.

The funeral was quite a ceremony. Clean-shaven professors took special pains being courteous with each other, took special pains getting past in the narrow aisles, not quite shaking their heads, significantly dropping their gaze. They all knew *something* about the fate of Modest Odoevtsev, who no longer knew anything about himself. They all knew what they weren't talking about. This communality intoxicated them a little, and they could ascribe their intoxication, in turn, to an ennobling association with death. There was much in common in the faces, a certain constitutional resemblance . . . Words were spoken, hints were voiced—they stimulated the mourners still further by a sense of commitment and involvement with the brave few who confront the numberless forces of evil. Voices shook with excitement on approaching a hint, the guaranteed peril brought everyone still closer together, and death no longer had meaning . . . No one here had come to weep over the old body that only yesterday had been alive, no one was here for the man who had lived his life and lost it—they had all come for a man who once had written something, and their grief savored of enthusiasm that he would never write anything more. An orator who had managed a more transparent hint would lower his head, as proudly and sorrowfully as though this were his own funeral, and descend from the pulpit. There was no pulpit, but still he moved his leg as if to descend a stair. He stumbled slightly as he took that faltering little step, and for a while afterward, despite his best efforts to control himself, he cast triumphantly beseeching glances at the audience, for a while did not hear the next orator.

For all of them there was already more advantage than danger, both in praising Grandfather Odoevtsev and in voicing a hint. Odoevtsev was beginning to be the fashion—they were its priests. Like beetles putting out their locators and antennae, clapping each other with their feelers, they instinctively tested their circle of support and backing. A new era was beginning.

Even before Odoevtsev's death, his name had been established in mentions and references; a series of provincial reprints of his old papers (short ones and not fundamental, for the time being) had nevertheless been noted and read in the right quarters. There was persistent talk of publishing the papers in book form, but despite the friendly attitude of the management of the publishing house, this was held up for the time being. Everyone was lacking his death—and he died. That seemed to be what they had been waiting for, there was definite progress on the book, they had all but sent it to the typesetter. A specialized journal ran a long obituary—without reservations—placing the name of Odoevtsev among his *peers*.

Modest Odoevtsev's son and his still young but able grandson, as everyone remarked, played an important and noble, almost selfless, role in bringing order to his legacy and popularizing it. They did indeed go to work on it with zeal and will. It looked like work, it had objective reality, with this difference, that it had already been done, and more-over long ago, by another man already dead. They were now painting the trellis, watering the flowers, negotiating with a progressive Moscow sculptor. At this point our mouth is no longer twisted in a sneer: we have often had occasion to see a Russian minding someone else's business with gleeful animation and will. For example, telling a sighted man the way, even escorting him solicitously by the elbow to the streetcar stop, and moreover in the other direction from where he himself had been in a great hurry to go. Or aiding a drunk, at length, with pleasure . . . or, having found no better use for himself, punc-tiliously taking a man who was still sober to the drunk tank. They were all drunk on their own "exemplariness." In any case, the will with which Odoevtsev's son and grandson took up his work, I stress once more, depended not primarily on profit but on the fact that it was someone else's work, a thing that undoubtedly needed doing, and moreover had already been done. The father after hours, the son even at the neglect of his studies, dug in the archives, wrote letters, compiled and recompiled. There was a yearning for real work in all this; their hands itched like those of master craftsmen after long compulsory or custom jobs.

A reverential, familial cult of Grandfather sprang up and flourished within the household. The photographs hung on the walls with in-creasing confidence and size—and already seemed to have hung there forever.

All this had a positive effect on Lyova—for a second time he derived a benefit from the family drama, admittedly the same as the first. He learned. He was taught by the same agitated people who had buried Grandfather—but he assimilated something other than what they recited: he assimilated them . . . While still at the university he managed to define his own creative strivings by sounding out an area, planning a topic; he thereby distinguished himself from the common student mass advancing sluggishly toward the diploma and succeeded in stepping directly from college to graduate school.

His father, too, was a considerable help to him. By that time, the turbid wave of revelations had settled somewhat and begun to abate. Father had managed to separate slander from blame and to shed the blame along with the slander; he coped fully, consolidated his position, and even grew younger.

He was very pleased with Lyova, almost proud of him. Lyova's attitude toward his father was peaceable and indulgent.

The fathers-and-sons conflicts were smoothed over and substantially obliterated. The moat between the generations had been filled by the previous generation.

The ten years promised by Grandfather Odoevtsev passed.

Lyova had lived, and no one of his had ever died. He hadn't been present at Grandma's burial, and besides, that was too far back in childhood. Now they were dying one after another, as if by prearrangement. Thus one's school friends, all in concert, get married and have their first babies: all Annas or all Andreis. And suddenly there they are, just as concertedly dying off.

Uncle Dickens was found in the cold clean apartment, by the extinguished "fireplace," with his hand at his throat—he had been tying his tie. He was all dressed for dinner, lying there arrayed and ready for the coffin. No one had to do a thing, no one had to "fuss," as he himself would have remarked. One more aspect of Uncle Dickens's mania for cleanliness had been discovered: readiness for death at any moment. An old officer . . .

His funeral in no way resembled the ceremonial mockery of Grandfather Odoevtsev's. Despite the poverty of it and the few people, it made a very moving and unshadowed impression. The weather was exceptionally clear, and Dickens had been allotted a bright nook in the cemetery. There was almost no one at the funeral, only the Odoevtsevs and, to Lyova's surprise, Koptelov. Koptelov whispered to Lyova that he had served under Dmitri Ivanovich's command during the war; however, they said nothing more. Mama cried hard. Late and out of breath, a beautiful tear-stained woman arrived with a wreath from the waiters at the roof. He had been "one of them," Uncle Dickens, and he had enjoyed that.

88

In sum, it was the first time one of Lyova's own people had died. With Grandfather, things had been all wrong: the death was overshadowed by enthusiasm for the birth of a great man. This is the price always exacted for greatness—human regard. No one was interested that Grandfather had been a man. Grandfather had been a dolphin, what you will, but not a man. With Uncle Dickens, it was the reverse: nothing had died with him but a man, yet nothing was left afterward either, nothing was born, and this void between death and birth was filled by nothing, was *unfillable*. With Uncle Dickens's death, Uncle Dickens was gone.

This was a loss. Only now could one fully imagine what Uncle Dickens had been to the Odoevtsev family and what they had or had not been to him. Uncle Dickens was not a great man at all in the conventional, "weighty" sense, but we want to stress his special and very rare greatness, the greatness of recognizing his own size.

He was not a strong or a large man, he had very little, yet he appropriated nothing to himself and infringed on nothing belonging to anyone else or to the public, as men customarily do. But all his life he remembered *himself*, and at a time when everyone was forgetting everything, he never forgot the little he had. There was no reason to prefer the Odoevtsev family to many another, including a possible family of his own, but this was the family that *happened* in his life, and such being the case, he did not exchange them. This devotion was a devotion to the self, which makes it higher than, let's say, a dog's. In a sense the Odoevtsev family consumed Uncle Dickens, used him up with their love, at the same time taking full advantage of his love, too. As we have already said, he had only a little, but that was everything. So he was used as cement for their nest. They, being strong and robust, expended him easily, without noticing how or when this happened, supposing that they were relieving his loneliness by their love. On the way from the Civil War to prison camp, the stout and invisible fish line of his fate had landed him in the Odoevtsevs' pond, and there he stuck, as a man imbued with true nobility. On his rare vacations of freedom, he no sooner took them his little knapsack of accumulated warmth than he was arrested, it was already time . . . So he had spent himself in dribs and drabs, as happens in a family. There was nothing left to him. He had no cache of treasures. But the Odoevtsevs would nod, yawning a little at bedtime as Uncle Dickens's departing footprints cooled, and say yes, every man needed "a place to go . . ." They were well-read people.

* * *

89

Uncle Dickens and Grandfather Odoevtsev, men correlated by history, lived out this historical fate in different ways, opposite but grown from one root, like two branches. Nothing makes them kin, it would seem; these branches do not see each other, separated as they are by their common trunk. But the trunk makes them kin . . . Both men tried to "preserve dignity." Both men found their own solitary paths to that end, unique impossible paths characteristic of no one else. But the word "try" and the word "preserve" already preclude the notion of dignity. "Dignity" in Russian also means "worth"—that which is, face value. Hence, if one "preserves dignity," he is preserving his own worth, and what matters in that case is the word "his." They displayed the religiosity and ferocity of the kulak, but their property was their identity. Dickens displayed religiosity, hiding what was his and hoping to preserve it, and then trying to preserve even what was left. Grandfather displayed ferocity, the moment they found what was his and took it away. Possibly it was easier for Dickens to preserve what was his because he had less property. Possibly . . . All the same, we would like to point out that Grandfather was too serious about his life (what was his). What tripped him, after all, was something within himself—infringement and appropriation, though in their highest forms, the ones hymned and placed on a pedestal by humanity. But one must not infringe, must not appropriate, ever, anything—that is always bad.

Possibly. Possibly these developments were quite a bit tamer than described, without the violent pathos and drama of a Gorky play. Especially since there has already been a kind of casual promise made, a hint given, that possibly our hero had "a different family altogether," that we had in mind a "second variant of Lyova Odoevtsev's family, a variant that would produce the exact same hero all over again." There followed an insincere apology for our unfortunate choice of the hero himself as hero. But we are not convinced that our every promise should be kept with immutable consistency. Occasionally we might do better to skip one, rather than persist in our empirical ("vampirical," as Uncle Dickens would say) experiments with the narrative. Especially since we have persisted far longer than anticipated. We do not, in brief, feel like telling the second variant right now.

But no; out of greed, we'll jot something down, after all—two or three awkward but self-confident lines . . .

What matches in both variants? First of all, we want to keep the surname, the hint of noble birth, in the remote and obsolete sense of the word. Why this is so important to us we ourselves can't quite explain.

Possibly, like Lyova, we were impressed by our high-school discussions on the "nature of the typical" in literature; specifically, that even the individual phenomena of life may become objects of typical representation, if the writer examines the phenomena behind them which are merely individual now but for which a future has been ordained (Rakhmetov). We, too, are guided by something of this kind, although in reverse: no future has been ordained for Lyova, even though he is individual, like Rakhmetov. It is also important to us that Lyova's celebrated ancestry seems to have no meaning for him, he is more "a namesake than a scion," he seems to be a thoroughly contemporary young man (whether better or worse than our typically wonderful young contemporary is another question). But his family is important to us for the furtive and secret atmosphere that makes his existence somewhat unique.

And it still seems to us that the individual and unique examples—the so-called exceptions, which (by definition) are supposed to prove the rule—are precisely the ones where we may discover many extremely contemporary and typical phenomena; individual experience is precisely where the time common to us all is formulated with special clarity. By the same token, if we took typical examples, in order to achieve the same effect of contemporaneity we would have to place them in plot situations so unique that the authenticity of the narrative might seem doubtful. The problem of the typical in literature, to our mind, has been put through a revolutionary transformation by history itself. If in a clearly demarcated class society the hero necessarily bore formative class traits (the character's family origin), and if these in combination with personal and contemporary traits produced a literary type, which perhaps really had to be spied on, picked apart, and generalized, then in our time the hero is almost devoid of this ancestral substrate, or there are flashes of it in the form of certain relict stimuli that he himself cannot recognize or understand. But each and every man from the general, almost classless mass got run over by the time itself, so emphatically and violently that any man with personality traits marked in the slightest by nature became a *type*, in which, as the saying goes, the whole world was reflected as in a drop of water, the whole sea expressed as in a drop of the sea. Here our discussion is getting into the very specialized problem of the social and historical aspects of character and personality conducive to a rebirth of the literary method of realism, provided that realism wants to keep on being realism . . . and we put on the brakes.

That is why even our Lyova is a *type*, despite his belonging to an extinct breed. (It is curious that right up to the present day—and especially, judging by literature, right after the Revolution—the word "type" has been so widely used in Russian conversation to mean "oddball," with reference to people who have, as it seems to us, yielded especially easily to the formative influence of the time.)

But if Lyova belongs to our time and is separated by historical time from his own ancestry, then his parents, although they belong primarily to our time, are less separated from their ancestry; they even belong to it, through their early childhood. Grandfather is not separated from his own ancestry at all, but on the other hand he is separated from his own children, and especially from Lyova. Hence the family microclimate in which our hero is being raised.

In personal life, as a rule, people measure the absence of falsehood in a relationship by its plausibility and freedom from revelations—the absence of any facts revealing a lie. Proof of the truth is entirely unneeded, the facts of truth are not obligatory in a relationship. A revealed lie is no longer a lie, it is drama and nothing more. But the unrevealed lie, i.e., the seeming truth, *is* a lie—and it is tragedy. Where a man flounders agonizingly on the turbid surface of a legal, factual lack of proof, a lack of confirmation for his own sensations and emotions, and is forced, as if by law, not to trust his own inherent, naturally precise sensations and emotions, and loses the art of being guided by them in his deeds, that is, ceases to commit them—*his* deeds. This leads to the withering away of the naturally moral human substrate. It is a classic example of the *disorientation* of man as a biological species.

And if you asked us at this moment what the whole novel is about, we would not, at the moment, feel bewildered but would confidently reply: Disorientation.*

Thus Lyova too, since childhood, had been shaped in an "unproved" atmosphere. Regardless of the possibility of proving this, we can assert that we have all been shaped, not by the obvious biographical facts that we can show as proof, but by the very facts that are agonizingly unprovable, often seemingly quite nonexistent, "given to us only in sensation," mute and eyeless—white, like cataract. Especially in child-

---

* When a man has been concentrating on a subject, everything is about that one subject. Just now I opened a book at random—and what a remarkable sentence! ". . . More striking still, they pursued falling leaves of various sizes, shapes, and colors, and even their own shadows on the ground" (Niko Tinbergen, Animal Behavior). This is about moths.

hood is it hard for us to say what has really made an impression on us—we will find this out much later. In childhood, all is shameful, mute, disguised, and too scary.

So it all begins, not at the moment when Lyova finds out about Grandfather, about Father, about the time, but much earlier, when he cannot yet know about and does not suspect the existence of these facts, yet the facts nevertheless exist independently and also exist, after a fashion, in his ignorance. The scary thing is not that he suddenly finds out these facts so late, as a youth, as a half-grown man, but rather that he recognizes in them what he always knew but didn't know what it was, and now he has been told its name: the organs have been pointed out on an anatomy chart and he has been told what they are for. He has received proof.

Strangely enough, our own time has a tendency to idealize and justify the aristocracy.* Not all of them were ethical monsters, it is said; there were also intelligent, honest men; more than that, not all of them were even *enemies*. This is a sated, cannibalistic, liberal fairness toward an adversary safely defeated and even digested: the poor stiff didn't taste bad.

Yes, there were intelligent men, and honest, and ethical—even more of them than any ultra-liberal will admit—but there is no justification for the aristocracy themselves. They themselves are guilty of their own death, and there is no justification for them because they have no justification in their own eyes. They turned out to have existed only in their class affiliation, they lacked an *idea*—the idea had become the property of upstart intellectuals. There was nothing left to them when their class affiliation was taken away. Nor does it speak well of the aristocracy that they were not all enemies. They had no supreme idea because their supremacy of position was a given; repelling an alien idea was repellent to them and beneath their dignity. Therefore, we did not have authentically *ideological* enemies in our battle with them. They were incapable of party commitment. They yielded haughtily and with distaste, in the literal battle only, by the rules of dignity and honor, never suspecting how long a life lay ahead. And for this the author scorns the aristocracy with the whole essence of his plebeianism, which gained nothing.

* Here and below, we are discussing precisely the aristocracy, and not the intelligentsia. Moreover, we are discussing only the none too large part of it in respect to which the following discussion will be completely accurate.

93

They had not supposed that any life lay ahead of them—the fact had to be confronted. And now became manifest a certain remarkable aristocratic trait, only superficially at variance with prevailing concepts: vitality. The aristocracy are customarily thought of as effete, nonvital, unfit, unable to endure deprivation and hardship, incapable of labor. In point of fact, aristocracy in its highest interpretation is the highest form of fitness, and the most vital. Because only he who has had all is capable of losing all without losing heart: only he who has possessed can know that having is not the point. He who has not had cannot not have, because he *wants* to have. True aristocracy does not want to have. It *has*, as a given. In losing, it knows it has *possessed* something to which, without entering into discussion, it had a right. It is accustomed not to enter into discussion of urgent mundane issues and therefore has been able to develop inner qualities "as such." In losing all, it can believe that it is not losing its aristocracy, since it preserves those "as such" qualities. That is why the aristocrats, when first confronted with hostile circumstances, could suddenly manifest those qualities (When would such qualities become manifest if not at the first and unexpected confrontation? Training and experience are not qualities, experience is a bourgeois phenomenon), could surprise us by their fortitude, patience, dignity—that is, by their fitness, because authentic aristocracy is the ability to do without all and preserve oneself to the last.

But that is the ideal, spiritual essence of aristocracy, so to speak. A peasant may have such aristocracy as a trait; the aristocrat merely by birth may not. In practice, everything was naturally otherwise, and the aristocracy's adaptability became manifest in their ability "not to enter into discussion" and "to serve." The intellectuals did the discussing—the aristocrats manifested an unexpected capacity for labor. They may once have known how to sit in the saddle and kiss dainty hands, but it must never be forgotten that they were a class, they had a class nature. Their philosophy, their morals and ethics were inherent in them by birth, and if they belonged to their class they had no need to waste either emotional or physical energy on developing convictions and principles, which result from being individually and severally beaten down by life. They were able to serve and to perform, guided by concepts of honor and duty, without entering into any conflict with conscience.

That capacity became manifest. They had accepted none of the changes, but they stayed on to live in the changed world in order to preserve, within themselves, at least those traits that were inherent and made their lives coherent, traits that might have been common to all men, such as: honesty, principled conduct, fidelity to one's word, nobility, honor, bravery, justice, the ability to keep one's temper. They had lost all, but they would want to lose these traits last: these were their nature. But even these traits had no possibility of surviving outside their class essence, abstractly, outside the meaning of what happened and with their very foundation gone, taken away. To follow these principles consistently, to follow them at all, threatened them with immediate death, yet to betray them was unthinkable—it would be moral death—and thus was generated the marvelous psychological phenomenon that allowed them to survive. One might call it "absolute apoliticality," and that would be close, though not quite it.

They had to shut their eyes to their betrayal of their own class, to the fact that they had avoided becoming our enemies in order not to die: the awareness of such a betrayal would immediately deprive them of the opportunity to bear the traits that they supposed or felt to be their steadfast essence. Duty, honor, and dignity, like virginity, are used but once in a lifetime, when they are lost. They had to pretend unconsciously that there had been no betrayal, and never touch this question again, lest, God forbid, they blast it open and set free the genie of conscience, which incinerates the Russian soul with the speed of light. And they became as non-Russians . . .

The ones who succeeded in this were primarily those who, while possessing all the positive qualities of the class, did not possess powerful intellect. Such men—possessing magnificent emotional qualities but not intellectual ones, at least in the modern interpretation of the word—proved more than abundant in their milieu. Intellect, after all, is not an aristocratic but a natural property, and in that sense belongs to the people. Having thus escaped moral death the first and principal time, they sealed up a sort of wall in their consciousness with blank boards and nevermore looked back, as if it were really so—a wall. Then life spun them around again and yet again. They walled up more corners and windows of their consciousness in the same way. Ultimately they had nothing left but the blindered view in front of them—all was boarded up, except those two tiny holes in the fence. Like a man who has broken his neck in the wonderful wide-flaring gallops of youth, they could no longer turn their heads, but the constant corset gave their bearing still greater erectness and nobility . . .

Family, family! . . .Of all the causes of this phenomenon, we have forgotten to add in the main one. There were children, for their sake one had to survive, one had to raise them, and an aristocracy, by definition, must have an extremely strong family instinct.

They had accepted nothing—and they accepted all.

That is, in order to produce Lyova Odoevtsev again, we could have portrayed another family altogether, considerably more positive and attractive, perhaps even exemplary, a family one could only feel touched by, marvel at its existence, and hold up as a model. It was quite unnecessary to grow up in an atmosphere of secret treachery in order to be Lyova.

So, this is a House, this is a fortress, inhabited by friendly, loving people endowed with many increasingly seldom-met qualities. They are handsome and well bred, they don't lie to each other, they bear willingly and without complaint all the burdens and duties that they have voluntarily assumed for the sake of the family; there is no crassness or filth here at all, people love each other. Lyova, the little rascal, fat and cute, runs down the corridor away from Mama—stomp, stomp!— and loving hands catch him, catch him, catch him. He goes flying up, to a large handsome face—Uncle, Aunt, Grandma!—and he laughs, so right is the world, so answering the big smile from above . . . They live bravely, cleanly, and virtuously, while around them on the stair landings and in the courtyards people are quarreling, separating, single mothers are "bringing them home," drinking, brawling, and the children increasingly seldom recognize their own fathers on sight . . . — they live *well*. There are lots of them, and together they're a large family, the kind now encountered only in novels. They live for the sake of the family, they live within the family, the family is the form of their survival.

Lyova has a childhood. In any case, he is not deprived of his early childhood, it's a classic, it can be bound in a little volume. Are those the late thirties and early forties of twentieth-century Russia out there beyond the window? Halloo! But by now it's the postwar era, Lyova is able, "if not to understand, then at least to remember," yet the only place nothing seems to change is their family; to notice this difference between family life and life outside means to ask oneself a question. Lyova assimilated "from the air" the only way of not asking himself a question: he ceased to register the outside world.

The outside world was also a book, of which there were many in Father's library and which Lyova was allowed to snitch and read on the sly, with his parents' tacit consent. The outside world was allusion, manner, style, it stood in quotation marks, all it lacked was the binding.

Lyova, of course, was friends with the caretaker's son. He longed to go downstairs, to the cabbage smell; he felt hurt when he didn't understand something there among "them," or when they didn't accept him into the group or laughed at him for not understanding; here he experienced the first pangs of desire and jealousy. But, for lack of a manor house, these were manorial outbuildings, and Lyova's parents weren't at all opposed to having him "learn a bit about life." It was already safe: Lyova had assimilated the lesson of inattention taught by the family.

But already the time was fully recognizable even in the canned air of Lyova's apartment. It came right up close with its boundless face and breathed its hot stifling breath. It pressed up against the window at night, slouched against the door, flattened its nose against the black night glass, and stared eyelessly into the bright insides of the apartments . . . Self-control is a family trait, however: nothing was expressed in the family's way of life, nothing affected the relationships or conduct of the members of the vast Odoevtsev clan. If shadows did fall obliquely across their faces, they were noticeable only to a very observant and specially intent person—not to Lyova. Yes, once again, very close, before Lyova's unseeing eyes, life came right up to the Odoevtsev family, she was ready to put her question in a form so distinct that they would have to answer it—and the miraculous psychological phenomenon might not work this time. There could not be a single misstep, a single slip. *Irreproachability* was the only way out. They must be irreproachable in form, at work and at home, lest, once again and for good, they confront life.

Lyova was twelve years old. The family controlled themselves, did not look back as in the story, did not turn into pillars of salt. How did they do it? How did they adapt? By what surprising method did these people conceal their own life from themselves!

In this family, people had aged only once, when they were reunited after the war. Since then, they had always been so much in each other's sight that they literally stayed handsome and young, aging just a tiny bit when separated during summer vacations.

They did raise Lyova. On their personal example of irreproachability. He was being taught beautiful abstract models of the form of the soul, thought, and behavior. Exactly why this kind of trait, why exactly these traits, where and when these traits, was painstakingly concealed. It may already have been concealed, and not only from Lyova but also, above all, from themselves. These people wanted to teach Lyova at least what they knew how to do, since they had no wider opportunities for educating him, for shaping Lyova, the new Odoevtsev. They taught him what they knew how to *do*, concealing all of what they knew. By now they themselves almost didn't know, but they brought him up in the best traditions and principles—as far as the "material base" allowed (and it allowed them almost nothing but personal example)—and tried to conceal life from him, even more of it than they themselves didn't know. Lyova grew up as the infante in this childhood republic of adult and handsome people . . . Ah, but if we add to these formative influences Lyova's primary and secondary education, where they in turn taught the cart not only before the horse but without wheels so that it couldn't go . . . then we get the bouquet, then we get the dessert, then we get that pink little cutie in the blunt-toed shoes, in the little zippered jacket homemade by Mama, with the Komsomol pin on the little fake pocket!

They taught him—he didn't even have to be taught, he himself assimilated—the phenomenon of ready-made behavior, ready-made explanations, ready-made ideals. He learned to explain everything very competently and logically before thinking. Both family and school bent every effort to instruct him in all that would not be needed later on.

Seeing around him no example that approached their family in loftiness and beauty, Lyova also learned an abstract and inarticulate elitism and exclusiveness. But since he was being taught—again, by personal example—simplicity, modesty, a secretly arrogant democracy, his elitism was not the slightest hindrance to his contacts and inter-course with the outside world. It merely closed the lid on him tighter, this time letting in no air. A self-perception of elitism is also a means of isolation, and consequently of defense—this, too, he assimilated, and just as unconsciously.

Thus they swam, in their fortress aquarium, all through Lyova's *Childhood, Adolescence. Youth*, however, would be subject to time. They were like deep-water fish: under the pressure of the conquering class, in total darkness, in a closed self-sufficiency system: with their phosphorus and electricity, with their internal pressure.

Lyova, then, would be hauled to the surface and blown to bits by the intolerability of his own internal pressure! Nothing but a plumpish soul (starchy food, no vitamins), slightly pale from lack of light but beautiful and tender, as if raised on prematurely discovered hydro-ponics (primacy!)—that's all there was to him. Lyova did have a soul.

He was pure and untaught, subtle and ignorant, logical and unwise when he finished high school, fell in love with Faina, and at last met Grandfather. Until that time, he did not know (and this is literally true) such words as: betrayal and treachery, repression and cult, Jew and kike, MVD and GPU, penis and clitoris, humiliation and pain, prince and zhlob.

Yes, in this second family of Lyova's they were all exceptional people, who had never forsworn duty, honor, or conscience. Until such time as it threatened their lives, let us add. But, in keeping with their intellectual attributes, they quite honestly and sincerely failed to see in this life those conflicts in which the possession of duty, honor, and conscience would inevitably have led them to a tragic end. Had they but seen, had they ever been placed in a position where a decisive yes or a decisive no would decide not only their own fate but also the fate of another, they most certainly would not have forsworn either honor or conscience, they would have answered the yes or the no that corresponded to their ideas of the truth. But, in practice, no such situation befell them. This was the phenomenon of "honest good luck."

So, honesty and safety. There can be no treacheries in this family. Grandfather returns. (This we also want to keep, this matches in both variants.) But no one in the household is in any way guilty of or sullied by his fate. This is a family celebration, his return. Grandfather is handsome and unexpectedly young. He has withstood all his ordeals firmly and virtuously (in that case, let's shorten his sentence by ten years or so). He has returned with a clear mind, having preserved all and lost nothing—the professorial skullcap suits him. Everything would be perfectly wonderful, but Grandfather is homesick for his last place of exile (somewhere in Khakassia, it seems) and goes back. He teaches there for a while in a pedagogical institute and manages the local history museum. Not for the world would he want to go to either Leningrad or Moscow, despite the numerous invitations; for his name is beginning to surface, many people remember and know him, and he has a burgeoning reputation as a "great man with a great destiny." Then Lyova, who is in college by now, goes to see Grandfather—and it all comes clear. A certain old and pretty maid out there has fallen in love with Grandfather, and they have had a son! At his time of life! Everyone is proud. Grandfather looks like a young man, he answers their compliments with a compliment to himself—takes from his watch pocket a little black figurine: a very rare thing, a Khakassian fertility idol, he who owns it is himself holy, to gain possession of it men will conduct raids and wars; it came to Grandfather under extraordinary

99

circumstances, when a great Khakassian Negro lay dying on his bunk, the last German shaman of the Kham-Kham Indian tribe. At the Odoevtsevs' table, this flattering story draws an intimate chuckle. Lyova sends off to Grandfather the proofs of his old articles, which appear with increasing frequency; Grandfather wordlessly returns them but does not protest their publication. As before, they invite Grandfather to come home, to the family. He says that his home is *here* now. They tell him, Our home belongs not only to you but to *yours*. By now this is turning into a family game with a well-regulated ritual . . . And then Grandfather arrives with his son and the eternal maid: a skinny little woman, narrow pigtails done up in a small bun. At first they are slightly standoffish with her, though very tactful, but then, having reached agreement, they come to love her with all their hearts . . . Grandfather, however, fails to endure, doesn't make it, and dies lamented. His funeral takes place amid the same ceremony and commotion—and here we are, back at the same point in the novel.

But it nearly turned our stomach to write all that. Quite frankly, we like the first variant of Lyova's family better. It's more to our taste. Lyova's first family almost strikes us as more honest, more "plotworthy" than the second. Then, too, we've grown accustomed to Uncle Dickens, and he didn't fit in here. All in all, these psychological phenomena where a plus is repelled from a minus in defiance of the laws of nature, these mutations of the soul . . . We're doing our best to write bravely, but we don't have the patience. If you're a realist, you have to pick a realism commensurate with your strength. God love them, these mutants, for theirs is the kingdom of heaven! They're fine people.

So we settle on the first variant.

. . . In conclusion, we seem to enter a large and empty classroom, we approach the blackboard, and from under the rag we take the sodden chalk, which writes so poorly and faintly, in a way so repugnant to the skin. And we draw on the board all manner of formulae, taught to us by fences, barns, and stairwells.

And among them, in particular, we write:

FATHER − FATHER = LYOVA (Father minus Father equals Lyova)

GRANDFATHER − GRANDFATHER = LYOVA

We transpose according to the algebraic rule to obtain a plus:

LYOVA + FATHER = FATHER

LYOVA + GRANDFATHER = GRANDFATHER

But, after all:
FATHER = FATHER (Father is equal to himself)
GRANDFATHER = GRANDFATHER
What does Lyova equal?
And we stand at the board in Einsteinian reverie.

THE HEIR

(MAN ON DUTY)

ON THE BANK OF our famous river there is a place not yet clad in granite and paved with asphalt, even though almost in the heart of the city. A few barges lie there forever idle, rusting and crumbling. At the water's edge is a narrow sandy strip littered with bark and other trash. Half-rotted piles, black and sharp, stick up from the water. The houses on the embankment are mansions, mostly very remarkable and ancient. Some of them have memorial plaques, and some are guarded by the state.

There, too, is a former palace, now an institute, a research center of world importance. In it, carefully preserved, studied, and so on, are the manuscripts and even certain personal effects of men long deceased, whose mere names set every Russian heart to beating. The place seems especially suited for quiet, deep, and solitary occupations inspiring all kinds of respect. In the big noisy city, the second capital, it's hard even to imagine any other place like it, any place as appropriate. The embankment has almost no traffic in this spot . . .

About a year ago a large construction crew arrived here, all kinds of equipment came floating up the river, and it looked as if the work of reconstructing the embankment had begun. For a while the institute scholars were distracted from their studies and watched out the window. Piles were being driven. This spectacle, in its rhythmicity, seemed especially intended to be scrutinized. Life, which until now had skirted the embankment and the institute, seemed to have burst in with its ebullient energy, as it bursts in upon us everywhere. But the piles began to be driven more and more seldom, and the workers mainly seemed to eat lunch or breakfast, seating themselves under the upraised crane and unwrapping their parcels and taking out bottles stopped with paper corks. They ate with such appetite that any scholar who ran past in the corridor at this time would be unable to resist going down to the snack bar—he would get some tongue or a puff pastry and gulp it with disappointment.

Then, even the workers disappeared somewhere and could not be seen eating breakfast. The equipment lay idle. But the traffic along the embankment, which had been halted in conjunction with the start of work, did not resume. So, as a result, the place became quieter than ever. Except for the filmmakers who sometimes turned up. They couldn't stay away from this place, apparently because its cobblestones had been preserved. They would set up their equipment and run in all directions; a stupid black horse-cab would appear, hitched to un-likely old nags, and there would be a take of a young terrorist clan-destinely meeting his fiancée, or some other revolutionary episode.

This, too, entertained the scholars, and they would have their sci-entific discussions by the window, in twos and threes . . . A jet plane would trace a line across the sky, and this would be the very scene that had to be cut.

Lyova Odoevtsev, too, worked here. If it befitted anyone to work at such an institute, it befitted him. If only as Odoevtsev's grandson. Lyova worked hard, no longer with the enthusiasm of his undergrad-uate years but without boredom either, and was reputed to be very promising. He was writing a dissertation on "Certain Distinctive Traits or Features of . . ." It was an interesting elaboration on a small twig of the tree Grandfather had planted, and he was making rapid progress. In "scholarly" conversations, Lyova had learned to differentiate easily when people were using the name Odoevtsev to mean his famous grandfather and when himself; he did not get muddled, as he used to, or blush like a little boy.

Especially since he believed in his own mind that he had no reason to blush. When he looked over his shoulder, he discovered a conve-nient absence of competition: no one could do anything, no one knew how to, and no one wanted to. Lyova knew how and could (by com-parison), but did he want to? He once had wanted to, in any case.

While still in the master's program he had written a long article—very unexpected for his time, level, and situation—called "Three Prophets," on three poems by Pushkin, Lermontov, and Tyutchev. The article was not published, but it created an "internal" stir: many people read it, and it made an impression. The paper wasn't strictly scientific, perhaps, but it did seem to have talent and was written in good Russian, in such a flying, soaring style, but the main thing that struck you, that made an impression . . . it was inwardly free. We saw it once at the department, already yellow and dog-eared. It was apparently being preserved there as an unprecedented case. They were proud of it, although they didn't reread it, and they showed it to a few people on the sly. That was how we read it, too. The article itself is naïve in many ways, over the years it has *become* naïve in many ways, but it's as fresh as ever in this respect, that it's not about Pushkin, not about Lermontov, and especially not about Tyutchev, but about him, about Lyova . . . it bespeaks *his* experience. We would very much like to recount it right here, but just now that would dreadfully disrupt the composition of the book, which is already beginning to worry us. Someday, however, we'll try to find a moment.

Lyova's role in developing Grandfather's legacy, together with his own article "Three Prophets," which everyone read, his article "Brilliant Latecomers," which no one read, his article "The Middle of the Contrast" (on *The Bronze Horseman*), chapters of which some people read, and a few plans, intentions, and opinions that he expressed aloud, had played an important part in creating a *reputation*. Lyova possessed one.

Lyova had a definite reputation; that is, the very indefinite thing that everyone instinctively strives after but not everyone possesses. It's very hard to express neatly what a reputation is and what it consists of. But we will try to surround the concept, with many fuzzy words, in order to close in on it gradually. That is, we want to try to deal with the task, not in words—no words exist for defining a phenomenon as curious but elusive as a "reputation"—but in a style reminiscent of its surface texture . . .

So Lyova had this definite and indefinite thing. He deserved no special credit for it, it seemed to have come about of itself, but having discovered it already extant, Lyova seemed to utilize it and try to consolidate it. His efforts in this direction gradually became more and more conscious. It was as if he were maintaining a steady flame in a hearth that had been lighted without his knowledge. This required no special energy or exertion, and for a time it even smacked of a game. On the whole, this reputation boiled down to the fact that Lyova never did the dirty or easy work (which were the same thing at this particular institute), only the clean and skilled work.

That is, he didn't hop on board one or another advantageous ideological fad to come out with an article or a speech, just in order to make it visible and clear to everyone what the author was for and what against, and to get this candid obviousness noticed at once in the right quarters and make it work to that author's advantage. No, in such situations Lyova preserved a certain sober clarity of thought and didn't rush to support one person and criticize another in the heat of the moment, if only because it was clear to him that he could not withstand this competition, which also required definite qualities. Moreover, it doesn't take much intelligence to realize, all things considered, that the gain here is small and temporary and it's still up in the air whether it *is* a gain, more likely it's not, because having to express yourself so definitely, even though with complete security, may later, or even sooner, have very disadvantageous consequences in the event of a change in the security itself, and then all those who didn't express themselves so definitely will start gleefully rubbing your nose in your own definiteness, and your falling banner will be caught up in a jiffy by other ready and willing hands. Lyova understood all this, or maybe he didn't—because even to understand such a thing is much too candid and cynical, and Lyova can't fairly be accused of that—but in any case he was well aware of it.

He studied his own unsullied antiquity and did not betray it, and his definiteness won him the trust of a definite intellectual milieu sometimes called liberal. This cleanliness of his, because of which he never took unfair advantage, being completely unmindful of ways to grab anything that was out of turn or excessive, though he quietly got his own way in the end, winning because he would make do without a big win but without a loss either—this cleanliness of his wasn't cleanliness at all, it may have been merely an instinctive or familial reluctance to go in the bed, just a certain cultured habit of sanitation, but it was what created that reputation for Lyova.

As a rule, such a reputation is considered progressive and disadvantageous, but this view is most likely spread by the very people who bear the reputation. It does have its advantages, because when a man possesses it he finds himself in quite a definite though inconspicuous support group, as if through an ethnic characteristic, and he cannot perish. These people, who are always the most highly skilled, protect and maintain their own necessity to society, and you yourself then seem to be necessary, too. In general, Lyova didn't want to be numbered with people who have just said "white" and by the next day are asserting "black" on account of a sudden change; nor, especially, with people who would like to be as mobile as the first though they don't succeed at it, they always start saying "black" instead of "white" a little later than the first, reorganize themselves a little later, and therefore make a spectacle of themselves; nor, especially, with the complete losers, who pick up the universal fad too late and finally get around to saying "white" after "black" has already become imminent, when the sharpest people have already sensed this and are already proclaiming "black" again with eye-catching self-abnegation. Nor did Lyova want to be numbered with the maximalists, the most liberal group, who always assert the reverse of the official opinion, while emphasizing what they are losing; here he eagerly supported the opinion that you gain nothing by such extreme measures, rather the contrary, you ruin everything. In general, no matter how strongly people asserted A instead of B, or vice versa, Lyova preferred, for example, his own C, or even W, which may not have been very topical but kept their significance and were almost impervious to devaluation. Proceeding from this reputation, Lyova did not try to advance himself at the institute along social lines; i.e., he avoided community work, a policy that basically just suited his own inclination, his familial and bourgeois-intellectual but nonetheless defensive inertia. At moments of drastic change, people like this move up, since they are steady and honest and on the other hand don't frighten anyone by being extreme. Lyova had quietly moved up in this way two or three times, the last time quite recently: he had been made general editor of a certain important joint work, he was all but promised a chance to study abroad as soon as he defended his dissertation. The best of it was that no one could object to his candidacy. Lyova left no tracks, so he had a wide, smooth road opening up ahead of him, the road he could travel the farthest without being noticed.

As has already been said, he maintained the steady flame of his reputation, and for a time this even smacked of a game, almost an art, wherein the artist constantly makes use of chance events that he himself has not anticipated, they crop up only in the process of creation, but his management of these chance events gives rise to a fresh coloration. This was a game until such time as his reputation was so firmly established and had gathered so much force that it almost ceased to be subordinate to Lyova, because by then it was too powerful a determinant in all his actions; that is, it had gotten out of control and sometimes forced him to act in a way he did not want to. Briefly, one time a situation arose in which Lyova's reputation forced him to act in a way that was absolutely definite, absolutely disadvantageous, and moreover jeopardized everything. Lyova, who until this time had experienced no special difficulty with his reputation, did not know how to handle it now, and panicked in a frightening way. He was trembling in the cross hairs, with two machine guns aimed simultaneously—one at him, the other at his reputation—the only thing required of him was a yes or a no, but he had absolutely no idea what to do. That is, on one hand he knew very well it was yes, but that pulled the trigger of one machine gun, so it was no, but that fired the other. His reputation, which until today had seemed to exist of itself, free of charge, now required payment—a *deed*.

The affair concerned an old friend, very intimate (so far as that was possible with Lyova), the situation was wretched, the investigation very painful and highly charged (the friend had maybe written something, or signed something, or printed it, or said it aloud . . .), Lyova was either implicated or indirectly involved . . . Something was required of him. He utterly lost his composure and went around totally blank-faced and tongue-tied, did nothing but mumble, and of course it would all have ended badly if things hadn't suddenly converged in a most surprising way: Mama fell gravely ill, his vacation came due, he was urgently called to a conference in Moscow, Grandfather died, simultaneously, Lyova won a trip abroad in the lottery, his old flame returned to him for a while, and he came down with the flu and grave complications. In brief, he was deprived of the opportunity to be present at any of those investigations, and when he was able, everything had already been decided and his friend was gone. That is, he was around, but no longer at the institute, and when they met once on the street he did not offer Lyova his hand and seemed not to notice him. Lyova reacted almost calmly, discovering with surprise that perhaps they hadn't been such good friends as he thought, because he found in his heart no bothersome impulse, either toward or against his friend. Though he'd worried a lot beforehand about how they would meet . . . The whole incident aroused a troubled and disagreeable memory in Lyova—Grandfather's shade—and he drove that shade away. Lyova's reputation wobbled and slipped a little, especially in the minds of extremists, but to the rest it remained almost the same, because too many objective uncontrived circumstances surrounded the incident and almost excused Lyova. Anyway, time marches on and all is forgotten, and you know how it is . . .

On the whole, now that it was less overblown, his reputation was even more convenient, placid, and safe. It existed—and also seemed not to. People didn't count on Lyova too much; so far as they did count on him, he didn't let them down. But Lyova had become wary of too close and binding friendships, and the ones he kept up were mainly social, neither close nor binding.

He suddenly had a great many friends.

In Lyova Odoevtsev's personal life, too, everything could be said to be satisfactory. He lived as before with his parents and was not yet married. Mama speculated on this point without success. Lyova had three girls, whom Mama called his "lady friends." (She could not pronounce their preposterous names, so typical of Lyova's generation.) It had gradually worked out this way, that he had three, and precisely these three. Ever since his school days, he had been hopelessly in love with the first. He ran after her, she ran away from him. Lyova even lost his head and "did heaps of silly things," as Mama said, but despite those "heaps," everything stayed as it was. This woman even came to him now and then, but mainly she kept leaving. She had been married and divorced and was now planning to get married again—but Lyova was at her side as before and wasn't leaving. Both he and she were used to this. Scrambling for her every capricious phone call at all hours of the day or night, Lyova would think with surprise that he was doing this precipitately perhaps, at breakneck speed perhaps, yet at the same time almost calmly somehow.

The second lady friend, by contrast, had been hopelessly in love with Lyova ever since his school days—but he did not love her at all. Now an apparent equilibrium was setting in: as if Lyova were at the center between these two women, as if he never moved. Every time Lyova made a final break with the second lady friend, she submissively disappeared, existed somewhere in obscurity, and, with astonishing instinct, showed up again whenever the first lady friend turned Lyova out. She was like lotion on a scratch, took away Lyova's humiliation to some extent by accepting her own from him, and he allowed her this.

The third lady friend wouldn't need to be mentioned at all, except that the author is picky about details. She and Lyova were bound by no strong feelings. They seemed not to demand anything from each other, although they did receive something from each other; they made each other no promises and felt no obligations; but this relationship had a constancy and fidelity such as could not exist in the others. It too, then, had its unwritten rules and limits.

Thus his life came to have, in this matter as well, an equilibrium, a rhythm, even a regimen, so measured and habitual in its intolerability that it seemed easier to accept than to change. Plead with one woman, not love the second, have the third . . . They existed separately, and from each he received what was his, but together they constituted some one thing: the one woman who was not, and could not be.

We are accustomed to think that fate is fickle and we never have what we want. Actually, we all get what is ours—and that's the most terrifying thing . . . Since childhood Lyova had dreamed of scientific work in a quiet, solid institute, like the Botanical Institute across from his house. It could be said, of course, that this was a childish daydream, shallow and even silly. Lyova never gave it a thought when he tried for, and got into, his institute on the embankment. But, for all its absurdity of form, this dream had nevertheless existed, and it had come true: Lyova was working in just such an institute, just as academic, in just as ancient a building, in just as quiet and beautiful a corner of his native city, his thesis was already in the last stages of gestation, and he hadn't even hit thirty . . . Lyova had loved and wanted one woman only—also almost since childhood—and although she did not love him, she didn't hide from him either, and in his own way he had even gotten her, although in triptych form. It would be wrong, of course, to say that this dream, too, had come true—but something of the sort had happened: a rhythm, at times peace of mind.

In general, Lyova got what was his. Not that he prized it or supposed it held happiness . . . but this was no longer Youth, it was *his* life. And that is the whole point.

Such was the state of Lyova's affairs on the eve of the October Revolution holidays of 196–.

On those ritual days Lyova's solid reputation was fated to suffer the gravest of tests: to wobble so suddenly, almost collapse, and nevertheless stand its ground. This may, or rather should, be the main incident in the novel, the crux of its plot. And the curious thing is, this menace will threaten Lyova without any political or ideological error or blunder on his part. Pure chance, it would seem; a grimace of fate, a sudden darkfall . . .

Lyova had been left on duty at the institute for the holidays. Such was the custom there. For various reasons, one of which was his upcoming thesis defense, Lyova had been unable to get out of it this time.

His first evening on duty, before the holiday, was spent in utter and ever growing melancholy. One minute he would phone Faina, the next minute grab his dissertation and become despondent over it, and in his despondency start looking through his miscellaneous "secret" notes. They would strike him as brilliant, and then, feeling even more depressed because he had abandoned them, he would call Faina again, trying to clarify the relationship after all and thereby complicating it even more. Although how it could be more so . . . Faina stopped answering the phone.

Lyova fell asleep there on the director's couch, the telephone receiver practically in his hand. He dreamed a horrible dream, that he had to take the Komsomol swimming test, right by the institute, in the November Neva.

A call from Mitishatyev woke him . . .

. . . .

(Italics Mine. —A.B.)

And—stop! We stand on the shore of the story we have longed for from the very beginning, it is swelling before us like a breaker—but there's no ford, it turns out, we can't cross here: we are swept backward, toward the beginning of the narrative, and cast up on the same bleak shore, at almost the same point where we began our journey.

We thought we had dislodged the boulder . . . But it's in the way again. As if we hadn't been over Lyova's whole life, from his casually mentioned birth right up to the death that we spotlighted back at the very beginning; for we are separated from his death now by only a day or two. But what have we actually told about Lyova himself? Well, his grandfather . . . he's more likely our desire, not a grandfather. Well, his father . . . more of an uncle than a father. Father's almost not there. Delete a timid hint and he's not there at all. And Lyova himself . . . only by a slanting ray through a random crack—the rim of an ear, a deep shadow under the chin—we've made do without a portrait. His voice is barely audible on the other side of the wall: what is he doing there, whom is he calling, whose number does he know by heart?

Faina who? Where did Mitishatyev come from? What are the "secret" pages? More than once we have said that we would tell about something later; we never had time, and now we no longer have a place. It is sad to discover that by proceeding sequentially we have skipped so far ahead that we've lost touch with our own narrative.

This kind of incompleteness may have arisen from the mere fact that we have a different past now from what it was then, when it was the present for us. If we look at a single constant point on the plain, first from one summit and then from another, we see a varying landscape. Each of the two depictions is incomplete, and they are not compatible.

We have told Lyova's whole life from out of today, imagining Lyova as a full and equal participant in the historical process. Possibly he himself now remembers his past in just this way and would recognize himself in our depiction. But if he had read all this while it was happening to him, he would never have recognized himself in the hero, for it is extremely doubtful whether people attest to their own participation in the historical process from within the process. So, although everything described here happened to Lyova, he had no notion of it. In his own mind, very likely, he had just one notion . . . and did not know that his love was historical.

So, having told all, we have told nothing. We've told all that we could about the "fathers"—and almost nothing about the "sons." The heroes that we managed to tell about have died, and the main heroes of the chapter that we've finally gotten ready to write are still absent. Anyone else would bypass that pit where the boulder recently lay—but we want to climb across it. There's a natural divide running through here. Before we succeed in continuing our story, we will have to tell it all over again, in order to get a clear idea how it seemed to the hero while he was alive in it.

This will be a different story. It will be about love alone.

Although people are within their rights to reproach us (they already have) for being capable of telling things only in order, "from square one," we consider this correct; i.e., we can't do it any other way. For we, too, have a right . . .

First, because there is no sequence more correct than the temporal, after all: it contains not only our revealed patterns but also the ones that we do not yet detect. And secondly, the epoch to which Lyova belongs in part one and the time to which he will be subject in part two make it possible, we think, to tell about almost all the features of our environment separately and in turn, as not belonging to each other. Life is separate from history, process from participant, heir from clan, the citizen from the man, father from son, family from work, individual from genotype, the city from its inhabitants, love from the love object. The curtain has been dropped, not only between the country and the world, but every place there's anything to hang it on. A fluttering multitude of gauze curtains, and one of them curtains man from himself.

Just think, it's only been a little over ten years, and already we have to explain how such a thing could have happened, how there could be such a Lyova! But segregated education, have you forgotten? As everything else is separate, so are the boys and the girls. As Lyova doesn't know that he's a prince, so he doesn't know why he has a kind of ideal image hovering in his soul like a wisp of smoke. Naturally, the image will therefore pass to the first woman he meets. And so it does: after quailing for but a second at her utter incongruity, it promptly and completely coincides. Already Faina is the one he has cherished in his dreams and under the school desk, and a complete reconstruction has taken place in his underdeveloped clan memory—history has been cleaned up, scraped off, to look like Faina.

So we will have to tell his history anew, parallel to the first one. That is, the forthcoming second part of the novel is only a version and variant of the suddenly concluded first part. Which of the variants is the more accurate? We think the second, for it's the more real. Then again, the first variant is the more true. Yet if we have used the words "real" and "true" in that relative form, what else is there to talk about? . . . It seems to us that Lyova will be more real in part two, but he lives in a maximally unreal world. In part one the world around him was much more real, but there Lyova was utterly unreal, incorporeal. Does this mean that man and reality have been severed in principle? It's a bit difficult . . .

Perhaps what we should have done is begin the novel with the second part and continue it with the first? But—let's submit to the way things work out; in the end, that, too, is a principle. Without ever getting a clear idea of the sequence of the parts—which is the second and which the first, i.e., which of the parts is basic and which its version and variant—we proceed to our next part blindfolded, like the Lyova who will live in it, knowing nothing of what lies in store for him. (In the first, we already knew what would happen to him.) We will continue his existence and take it to the same point in time and space where he was left to wait for us in part one. Our parallels will intersect, and we will let time run together, in the happy hope that the hero's time will acquire a fullness of flow as if at the absolute now, the very moment of writing. We will then behold the Present—directly before us, not from out of the past, not from out of the future—we will see before us the variantless present, and it will not be a blank wall.

We don't know which part is more burdensome for the hero, the first or the second. Perhaps the second, although it's about happiness alone . . . Because a historical evaluation of his personal past does, despite all, ease every man's lot, by the solemnity of his belonging to the rumble of the historical process, but real life is sunk in timelessness, where man does not know the future and is deprived of the opportunity to evaluate himself, where man inherits all the torments measured off for him *forever, torments independent of country and century, even though it may occasionally seem to us that a universal quality-control stamp has become visible in DNA.*

END OF THE FIRST PART

APPENDIX TO
THE FIRST PART
Two Prose Styles

THEY DIDN'T THINK Uncle Dickens had anyone, but, although she was too late for the funeral, his sister, a retired schoolteacher, arrived from Yoshkar-Ola. Someone even vaguely recalled that Uncle Dickens had said something once about having a sister . . . they even had an argument over whether he had said it or not. But here was the sister, she sat in the Odoevtsevs' kitchen and drank her tea from the saucer, noisily and self-consciously: her fingers were thick and stubborn. Everything but tea she flatly refused. She acted timid and shy, and Mama was especially considerate—Lyova grinned to see them. She was "another breed," as Mama said later. Really, it did look like a pointer having a dachshund sister. She probably took after Uncle Mitya's grandmother, or maybe it was his mother, who had been a Bashkir, or maybe a Chuvash. Uncle Mitya had said something once about that, too . . . the Odoevtsevs had another argument over whether she was a Chuvash. But the Chuvash finally got into Uncle Mitya's tiny apartment and was now photographing the material valuables with her tenacious and frightened gaze . . .

The retired schoolteacher relinquished nothing, she took every last nail to Yoshkar-Ola. Hard as the Odoevtsevs tried to tell her to leave the piano at least, they would buy it, it wouldn't survive the trip, who needed it in Yoshkar-Ola—her lips drew tighter and tighter, and she would not let herself be tricked: the piano sailed off to Yoshkar-Ola. Apparently that's just what it did, it sailed, because that turned out to be cheaper, and she wasn't in any hurry. Curiously, she, too, had no family.

Even the Puvis de Chavannes—hard as Lyova tried to explain to her that it was only a reproduction, not worth a kopeck but precious to him as a memento, she kept wincing at the word "kopeck" and wouldn't give this, either. A memento, indeed. He might remember Uncle Dickens's tales of the family greed. The Odoevtsevs did remember them later, ruminating about the schoolteacher.

Lyova's only success was to pilfer *L'Atlantide* while she was watching Lyova's mother, on whom she had been inexplicably intent from the very beginning. He reread it and was moved. "On that still and moonlit night, de Saint-Avis killed Morange . . ."

But, on the other hand, she readily gave Lyova Uncle Dickens's papers. Mama took them away, however, and locked them up. Lyova wasn't sure she didn't read them sometimes, when left in solitude. One day she turned over two notebooks to Lyova, "as an expert": Take a look, you might be interested . . . They were the works of Dickens.

One notebook was entitled *Poems*; the other, *Novelle*. Lyova experienced the shame and pain of love as he read them. Inevitably, he devalued Uncle Mitya in relation to the childish concepts he had cultivated. Yet this devaluation was not altogether crass. It was multiphase and complex: his despicable gratification at the semi-downfall of an idol gave way to disappointment (not with the idol but with its downfall), and disappointment to a lasting tenderness. His pain at the ruin of the old image proved to be mild and swift, while the formation of the new one was bright and joyful, confident and conclusive: seemingly true. In sum, Lyova merely came to feel a stronger love for this image, which now ceased to acquire new traits.

The poems were uncontroversial—weak and naïve to the point of implausibility—but even here the unsullied Dickensian soul filtered through. (With prose, the problem of evaluation is more complex. Prose is harder than poetry to evaluate categorically. Poetry or nonpoetry—there seems to be no middle ground. In prose, there is always something expressed: the author's intentions, or the author himself. If only as a document, it always offers private interest.) But there are some things we even like in Dickens's (the uncle's) prose, and we place a higher value on it than does Lyova, who still isn't quite free of snobbery. In this instance Lyova should not be held to account, although he is a more professional expert in the field than, let's say, we are.

He cannot judge objectively because, for him, reading Dickens-the-uncle's prose is more of an immediate, personal experience, rather than one that is mediated, readerly. He makes other connections, beyond the ones expressed by this prose. For example, there was trauma for him in the slight lifting of the veil between the generations, a veil that always exists . . . Thus, after a young man has himself reached the age of private life and is up to his ears in it, he suddenly asks himself a naïve question: I wonder, can it really be the same with other people? And in his search for an answer he remembers his own parents (whom else can so young a man remember?) and discovers that he knows nothing about them in this regard. Did they love, did they suffer, what were they like or maybe even what *are* they like, in their own minds and in each other's, let's say when he isn't there? Can it be that they, too . . . and so on. That is, when he is already a grownup man, it would seem, he is allowed to comprehend everything for himself in forms suggested to him by the time, because the previous generation grows old and departs without ever having shown him its cards—has it lived at all?—leaving him to make do all his life on his supply of childhood images and experience of the life of grownup people. This is surely remarkable, and there is a secret here, inviolable and holy—a safe-conduct. For even an absolute logical conviction that it's the same with other people remains empty and lifeless, unfertilized. This may be what allows a man, at the cost of suffering, to go on living his *own* life.

Well, when Lyova read the works of Dickens-the-uncle, it was as if a breeze had stirred that veil and very slightly turned back the edge. He found no "details" there in the vulgar sense, but on the other hand, his image of the wise old man with a kind of hyper-experience, expressed in behavior alone— where every gesture is final and summary, concludes a profound series—that image slipped badly, revealing an infinite childishness, naïveté, sentimentality, a want of taste and force. But, to make up for it, the image was instantly plastered afresh and painted in poignancy: people used to be purer and nobler, people used to be different, they used to be more naïve, more timid, more idealistic—this is individuality in the true, not the professional interpretation ("to become an individual"). All these *people-used-to-be*'s equaled only the departed Uncle Dickens.

There was a certain effect observable here, and it leads us to a certain frivolous thought on the nature of prose. We can't refrain from this hint . . .

The effect is this: if we suddenly stumble on a page by a man we know well or even intimately but of whom we hadn't known that he "wrote a little," and if, with inexplicable greed, we read it, we immediately begin to know many times more about him than we ever knew from associating with him. And it isn't a question of any jealous or secret facts. The conclusive example would be one in which we find on the page no such facts for curiosity or jealousy. In this case nothing blocks our view, and we learn even more about the author. The invincible curiosity with which we pick up such a page, when we have the chance, is nothing other than the thirst to learn an "objective" secret—a secret "in our absence"—and such a secret is the brilliant cloud on which we live. But what do we learn from this sheet of paper if it contains no gossip? Style. The secret of which we speak is carried by the style, and not the plot (the jealous facts).

Beyond the problems and facts presented by the author for exposition, the resulting prose will always reflect more than he intends, since it has emerged independently of the author, irrationally, almost mystically, like a kind of substance. (We have had the experience of unexpected surprises with it.) The man who has taken pen in hand for the first time and is still embarrassed by this unexpected urge, still protecting himself against possible fiasco with a scornful sneer (although no one sees him—he has found this moment), but in fact instinctively scared (his health!) of what is about to happen—not to it (the prose), but to *him*—this man has already confronted the phenomenon of literature: like it or not, he will betray his secret. From this moment on, he can always be unmasked and recognized, caught—he's conspicuous, he's visible, he's in the public eye. For style is the imprint of the soul, just as precise, just as unique as the fingerprint is the ID of the criminal.

Here we arrive at an idea long dear to us, that there is no talent—there's only the man. No separate "talent" exists, like height, weight, or eye color. People exist: good and evil, wise and foolish—people and nonpeople. Thus the good and the wise are talented, and the bad and the foolish are not. And if a man has intelligence of the heart, and wants to disclose to the world what he has, then he will inevitably be talented in his words, provided he believes himself. For the word is the most accurate tool inherited by man, and never yet (which constantly comforts us) has anyone managed to hide anything in a word: if he lied, the word betrayed him, but if he knew the truth and told it, the word came to him. Man does not find the word, the word finds him. The pure man will always be found by the word—and if only for an instant, he will be talented. In this sense there is but one thing we clearly know about "talent": it is from God.

That is the reason it's so awkward, so scary, so shameful and dangerous, to find out of an intimate friend that he "writes a little." It is also the reason we unfailingly take advantage of our very first chance to find out . . . Writing is always shameful. The professional is at least protected by the fact that he has long been going naked and is toughened and tempered in his shamelessness. He has already told, blabbed, and betrayed so much about himself that he seems to have canceled out the total surprise of information about a man, which is literature. We, again, know nothing about him. A man's goal in everything is to be invisible to others (defense), and there are but two means to this end: absolute reserve and total openness. A writer is the latter. We know all and nothing about him. That is why, after his death, we try so intently (with the same uncontrollable greed as in glancing at someone else's sheet of paper) to establish just who he was—letters, memoirs, medical records—and have no success. This man who lived so openly, so on display, so in the public eye, turns out to have been the most secretive, the most invisible. He has carried his secret to the grave.

For this to be true, writers must be geniuses, and hacks crystal-pure and sincere.

The notebook *Novelle* contained as many as ten miniature pieces. They had all been written at the front in the summer and fall of 1944. The shortest was hardly more than a hundred words, the longest no more than three pages.

Here is a novella whose pivotal event apparently also inspired the whole cycle—"Loneliness." The hero ("He") arrives in a city on leave and comes to his beloved ("She"), to try once more (without hope or infringement) to convince her of his love. " *'I know,' she said quietly. Controlling his agitation, but in a calm voice now, as if attaching no importance to his words, he added: 'I came from the front—and I'm leaving for the front again.' He spoke—and left the room.*"

Then he wanders all day around the city, stands all night on a bridge . . . "*And only at noon, when the sun had climbed high in the sky, did he board the train and leave for the front.*"

A very lonely life Uncle Mitya led! We will be the more respectful in our attitude toward his independence. Here he is, encountering a little orphan ("The Girl") on the roads of war: " '. . . *but I have no bread, not a kopeck, probably just like you, I have no loved ones, no family who might shelter you . . .' 'My poor little one! Come, let's walk down this straight road. We'll turn neither right nor left . . . Is there nowhere we can turn, my little sister? We have neither friends nor home—not even a little copper kopeck.'* "

Next come little novelle attesting that this man had become no skeptic or cynic as he yielded to life. So sincere and simplehearted is his hatred of the Germans: "*There is no bird of passage, no starving beast that will eat this filth.*" Or: "*What was this sneaky cur of a vile German fiend thinking, as he carried out the assignment of his hangman masters?*" So unconditional and supra-personal are his sympathy and pain: "*I stand by the window and look at these ashes—and my heart bleeds.*"

And the two together, fused: "*. . . This is still more arresting. Looking closer now, you clearly see that it is a Fritz, struck down by a bullet while doing his work.*

"*This figure, in the naturalness of its very posture repairing the wires, stuns you, astonishes you by its vitality, and ultimately arouses a feeling of disgust and deep hatred.*"

Wonderful, that "ultimately." And we believe that Dickens was a true soldier. The loneliness of his fate, his unrequited love, the everlasting war, the pain for his homeland—how pure and strong are the few lines with which his self-portrait is sketched! Sensitive and romantic . . . and for almost the first time we accept and forgive romanticism. Crystal purity was all we needed.

The prose of Dickens (the uncle) unquestionably expresses him, more than he it. Very likely he didn't even suspect how much it expressed him. But, to our mind, he himself is so appealing that he's better than any prose, even the most durable, and we are grateful to Prose for expressing him to us.

We will not begrudge a clean man clean paper . . .

Here is his longest novella.

THE SNOWSTORM

This was long ago, very long ago—in the days of my far-off youth, when I was in love with a certain girl. Her name was Nastenka. Perhaps she was not so beautiful or attractive, perhaps not even so clever as others, but I loved her, as only a young man's fiery heart can love. I loved madly, passionately, violently—loved her so much I would have committed a crime for her, as they say—and at the same time felt all the hopelessness of my dreams, all the futility of my impulses.

I was poor, even very poor—and this prevented me from realizing my hopes and being more bold and decisive. In the end, no longer able to restrain my passion and honorable intentions, I fell at Nastenka's feet, asking for her hand and heart.

Nastenka showed no surprise, no indignation, she did not fall into my arms. She only replied, "Go see Papa. I can't without Papa."

Hard as it was for me, I was forced to do this.

As should have been expected, I received a refusal. A stern, categorical refusal.

I was infuriated, insulted—I was ready to shoot myself from grief— and suddenly chance, or Fate herself, turned to face me, gave me hope with her golden rays, and started me on my way to seek happiness by another road.

My comrade, my best friend from school, gave me the idea of "stealing" my bride, marrying her in secret, without her parents' knowledge. Like a madman I seized on this idea, ran to Nastenka, and shared my plan with her. Nastenka was terribly frightened, she warned me off, but in the end she consented and even took an interest in the coming journey.

All was ready by the appointed day and hour. A covered carriage, a pair of sound horses, a reliable coachman. Here we were in the carriage, Nastenka and I, riding to a village forty or fifty versts from our city. We rode in silence, somberly, and now some rough weather blew up. Snow came whirling along the roads and blocked all the paths and crossings. Snowdrifts, wind . . . in a word, a wild storm rolled in, a blizzard. The world ceased to be visible.

Nastenka fidgeted and chewed her lips, but she kept silent and asked no questions. I sat restraining myself from fury, ready to bite the throat of any creature in our path—wild beast, horse—ready to smash the carriage windows and strangle the hateful snowstorm with my own hands.

I poked the coachman, exchanged curses with him, and raged—but the horses would not budge. Ever higher, ever more mercilessly, the blizzard drifted over the tracks and my carriage.

It was already dark when we drove into an utterly unfamiliar little village. The storm had died down. The snow had stopped falling. The moon was rising in the sky, a big, bright moon, like a silver ruble or a dinner plate.

Nastenka was crying and asking to go home. "I want to see Mama, I want to go home," she sobbed constantly, and demanded insistently that we go back.

And I . . . I understood the inconsolability of true grief, the irreparability of the situation—I was overwhelmed by unhappiness, tricked by pitiless Fate—I no longer could do anything in the face of the horror that gripped me.

Toward midnight, with difficulty, we reached the city. Nastenka climbed out of the carriage without even saying goodbye to me.

I have not seen her since. The memory of the ill-starred adventure lives in my heart to this day, disturbs me and forces me to relive the past.

Even now, as if in reality, I see Nastenka sitting in the carriage, wrapped in a fur coat and crying ever so quietly. I see her blue eyes, the distraught look on her sweet face—I see her beautiful, childishly capricious lips quivering with nervousness—and I see tears bright as crystal breaking through from under her dark thick eyelashes.

This was long ago, very long ago, when I was young and in love—and like all men young and in love I should have won forgiveness for my frivolity and violent youthful impulses. But I did not ask forgiveness nor even seek pity in anyone's eyes. And now—I am too old to change my habits and tastes.

And still, this is all very sad, my dear reader.

We have so far succumbed to the charm of this little novella that we can't refrain from citing one more, although the point is already quite clear. But you won't have another chance to read these—and we cite one more. (This is the last novella in the cycle: it all began with an arrival and ended with a return.)

THE MIRROR

After many years of roaming and wandering through wild country where you sometimes go months at a time without meeting man or beast, I ended up in a little town, where the people huddled with their meager belongings, the usual poverty and dirt.

They received me hospitably and put me up in a small cottage, which seemed to me cozy and nice.

Through some strange chance there was also a fireplace in the room, and this put me in an even better mood. At last I could rest and set myself to rights!

I lighted the fireplace and began to warm up. A pleasant drowsiness overcame me. I tried not to think, not to reason about anything, it was so pleasant to sit by the fireplace. But images of every kind woke memories; they crept into my mind, swarmed about like worms, and little by little they irritated my nerves.

I remembered the past, my friends, a beloved woman. Days of bitter disillusionments, of failed hopes, of loneliness came back to me . . .

How distant, how long forgotten it all seemed now—only my heart still beat in my breast, forcing me to relive what I had suffered.

Yes, yes! You are right, my poor, tormented heart. I still love that woman—and no long years of separation could stifle my feelings and passions.

I still want to love, to dream, to hope; I still thirst to be shown kindness by the hand of a beloved woman. After all, I am not yet so old as to have no beautiful desires. And, sooner or later, don't the roads converge on the path of life, don't the rivers overflow their banks in spring?

Everything in life changes—the times and the people and the feelings. Perhaps she whom I love to this day will yet make me happy with her smile and tenderness.

Thus I sat by the fireplace, remembering the past, and dreaming, as in bygone days, of happiness.

Suddenly I caught sight of a mirror on the wall. I took it down, and . . . my hand flinched. Looking at me was an old man's face, with gray hair, a high bald forehead, dull deep-sunken eyes.

No, no! This was not my face, this was not I. I did not believe it, did not recognize it—I was shocked by the cruel change.

A bitter, somehow malicious sneer crossed the old man's face and startled me awake.

I burst out laughing, and with disgust and hatred I flung the mirror into the fireplace.

"Let them all burn—the gilt frame and old age and the fantasies!"

I drank off my glass of freezing coffee and lay down to sleep in a warm soft bed, for the first time after my long years of roaming and wandering.

If Dickens (the uncle) didn't so much express anything by the word as the Word expressed his pure soul, then according to our hypothesis Grandfather Odoevtsev was able to express something in the Word (hide something in it), since we assume he bore within him (instead of a pure soul) traits of genius. Let us try to verify this. Two lives, two dignities, two deaths, two prose styles . . .

Rummaging in his business papers (not so many of them survive, by the way), Lyova came across the text of a singular manuscript, which had been left unfinished. It wasn't yet the mature and great Modest Odoevtsev (he would be mature for only a few years, and "great" only for us, later); the notes had a personal, diarylike character—"for himself." This work lacked the disorder of a diary, however. It was obviously meant to have an overall structure testifying to its finished design, although what that might be was still too early to judge by these pages. The manuscript had been titled *Journey to Israel** (*Notes of a Goy*)† and broken into chapters with the alternating titles "God Is Not" and "God Is." And again "God Is Not" and "God Is" . . . Six or seven chapters survive.

Such a manuscript had no chance of being published, but Lyova liked it in the same way Grandfather had written it . . . "for himself." And he copied some of it out, for himself. Here is one of his excerpts, which he marked: "From 'God Is Not.' "

That is the homeland's irradiation: though it certainly has something to suffer from, to suffer from the wrong thing. Yet how they've managed to condition us already (more to come!): that you absolutely *ought* to have something, that somehow you ought to have it *precisely* this way, other than as it *is*, that somehow you *must* have it. Why so, one

* In 1913, M. P. Odoevtsev journeyed through the Near East.

† The word "goy," like the words we have already mentioned, was unfamiliar to Lyova. By now he had learned those, but he had just one association to this one: its ancient Russian meaning of "hail," as in: "Hail, my brave hero!"

might ask? Where's your example? What makes you think that something no one else has succeeded in ought to come easily to you? Whence this swarm of false ideals, which impart to our already truly unfortunate man a feeling of groundless inadequacy as well (for he does have reason to feel inadequate)? The constant Russian preoccupation with the fate of the Tower of Pisa . . . But how dishonestly they have had to shuffle the life of society in order to achieve such an effect! What more must they do to consolidate the effect permanently? For lack of even the slightest life, introduce a consciousness that categories and ideals are accessible; perturb souls with the possibility that absolute concepts can take material form; replace the capacity for something by the right to something—what's a simpler example?— call weary conjugal coition "simple human happiness" . . . Done! The new man. But how near this is: lost happiness itches, the primal deception aches. "Yet happiness was so possible, so near . . ." Quite recently, it seems, "happiness" was understood to mean only an instant (*sei-chas* 'this instant,' *schas* 'now,' *schast'e* 'happiness' . . . I insist on this etymology!), a butterfly's-age of happiness bothered no one, it was understood that happiness merely *is* (or is not), but does not continue, is not extrapolated, *will not be.* Let's promise it ahead, but this time forever, for keeps. The deception of instinct is not difficult— it is called "corruption." Insinuate the possibility of a year-long spermatorrhea, such as even elephants don't have . . . and immediately it develops that only a random and evil coincidence has prevented you (because who was born for this, if not you?) from achieving the abovementioned effect. And lest you hold any grudge against fate (you alone were destined for this, so you alone have not succeeded), a materialistic, vulgar attitude should be inculcated toward fate itself, as being a prejudice, a nonobjective factor, nothing but a mere word. Toward the Word, above all, a new attitude must be inculcated, it must be moved to the end of a mundane series, and "In the beginning was the Word" must be given back to the poets, as a metaphor. In brief, Vulgarity must be turned over to the people for their use in perpetuity and free of charge—not being land, vulgarity doesn't need to be fertilized, it fertilizes itself. Then again, vulgarity is not "accessibility" per se but an attitude toward what is accessible, as we have a vulgar attitude toward water and air, let's say (i.e., that they are free). To consider the laws of nature an insult to high and mighty Man (the highwayman); to conquer Nature and its gravity . . . to introduce a material attitude toward abstract categories, while simultaneously inculcating a romantic view of reality—that is the methodology of Vulgarity. Its foundation had already been laid, the channel for its stream already plowed, by those who warred against it, "the prophets of a new life"—"amiable Chekhov," "the complex figure Gorky."

And yet you have an aching feeling that *your* life is over . . . that *you* have disappeared into the gap . . . that *you* have had bad luck with the age . . . This is Vulgarity.

A strange feeling, this. Time! Either we have already written this, or someone has already read it . . . Lyova had read it. It was, it became, it came true. What is the point, if you have come to know something, of learning that everyone knew it long ago? Why the zeal? This is a pleasure we don't understand. So what if they knew independently, so what if even before we did, so what if in 1919, so what if before the Revolution even . . . Primacy— it will no longer move us.

We are touched by a different consideration: however seemingly destructive the changes that have happened to a man, his inner personality, if he had one, remains the same along his whole lifespan, perhaps even at the expense of the distortion, the deformation, even the disfiguration, of all the other parameters enveloping it. The later Grandfather, the earlier Grandfather— by now there is no difference for us. He was. He was he.

Lyova is another matter. Exactly what he liked so much about this passage is hard to say. Grandfather was twenty-seven when he wrote it; Lyova was twenty-seven when he read it. But that still does not mean that what he read was exactly what Grandfather wrote. More likely the opposite. Lyova copied this text with much too much enthusiasm. A gleeful yes-yessing directed his hand. Opposite the word "Gorky" stands the copyist's *Sic!* But the momentum of this enthusiasm thrust Lyova onward, to the chapter "God Is":

Lord, by what silence I am punished! I grope in darkness, emptiness, blindness, and do not hear myself rustling. This is proof that there is nothing around. When you do not exist. Searching outside yourself is futile. The world is invisible in your absence. The Divine punishment, the Divine reward of the world, of existence around you . . .

When conscience speaks the lips are silent. About what? . . .

"Am I serving God or the devil?

"When I fight, am I not admitting the reality of the thing I fight?

"When I feud with progress, am I not serving it by perfecting and honing its mechanism?

"When I drive out the devil, am I not yielding to temptation?

"When I bring to people's attention, in living language, what was not accessible to them before; when I put into effect ideas that are perhaps very noble and, as it suddenly strikes me, pleasing to God— am I not acting as a servant of progress, enlarging the Sphere of Consumption by yet another New Appellation? So, rather than extract 'use and benefit' from the Spirit, isn't it better not to enlighten the consumer?

"That is, is what I do pleasing to God? Or am I using it, do I steal it from Him and market it?

"For God, for people, for myself? For my own god?

"The answer 'For God alone' will not enlarge the 'sphere of consumption.'

"But do I know what is pleasing to Him? Can I know? Can I know what Is, and what I have attributed to Him in temptation? . . ."

That is the prayer of silence.

If a man cannot create, he can give an example. But wait, Lord! I am not ready.

Lord, give me words! I am night-blind to the word. Let me finish speaking! My eyes are in darkness, as if I had looked long at the sun. My heart is so empty, so mute. Lord! Like the sky . . .

Lyova evidently tired of copying. His letters became more regular, more bored, lost their tremor. Recognition is another strange thing: who's wearing what, who has gotten what . . . The copyist fell asleep.

It was not God but Lyova who did not hear.

Sorry . . .

SECTION TWO

A HERO OF OUR TIME

(Version and Variant of the First Part)

For a long time I lay motionless and bitterly wept, not trying to hold back my tears and sobs. I thought my breast would burst. All my firmness, all my composure had vanished like smoke; my heart was faint, my reason silent, and had anyone seen me at that moment he would have turned away in contempt.

LERMONTOV, 1839

(Italics Mine. —A.B.)

We wrote out the title of the second part, in large, careful letters on a separate blank page, and winced: why, that's effrontery . . . that's Lermontov . . . one must know one's place.

Yes, Lermontov has certainly been promoted from lieutenant to general in the last hundred years. One must approach him in accordance with his rank, through his more and more subordinate superior. And his doubtful "Hero," in the same hundred years, has moved up the career ladder, too. Very likely you couldn't get past to see him, either . . . I can hear it already: "Well, but he's Pechorin! Who, may I ask, is your hero?"

"Our public is still so young and naïve," Lermontov wrote in his foreword, "that it does not understand a fable unless it finds a moral at the end."

But reread that foreword in full. It's worth the trouble; we're even taking a risk, encouraging comparison with a text that has the historical advantage over ours. All the same—reread it. We cannot deny that our time (especially!) has a tendency already apparent a hundred and thirty years ago.

And while you are reading, we will furtively and hastily write out a few words of self-explanation and justification.

A strange, telescopic, spiraling justification this is. Lermontov justified himself to the public for conferring on Pechorin the rank of Hero of Our Time. A mere century goes by, and already we're apologizing—

to himself, to Comrade Lermontov!—for allowing ourselves the temerity of quoting him.

Casting about for justification, we again hit upon the newspaper.

The newspaper backs us up by its experience with the use of "ready-made" headlines. In almost any newspaper we may discover an article or essay under a title already well known to us from literature or films, sometimes barely changed—and as a rule the content of the article has nothing in common with the original. But it isn't only journalists. Serious writers too, in our modern age, have a tendency to a similar practice. They use the slightly changed titles of famous works—but changed in such a way that the earlier title is immediately recognized, whereupon the author, apparently, ceases to be lonely and lost in his intentions, establishes a "tie with the past," and stresses his modernity through a graceful distortion of emphasis (analogy and contrast), thus annexing to his own strength the tried-and-true strength of his predecessors. The work cited isn't always a classic; sometimes it's a best seller. For example, in a small regional newspaper we once happened on a satirical piece with the headline "Shield and Board" (this was just when the film of the same name, Shield and Sword, after the novel of the same name, was playing everywhere)—about a certain construction boss's opposition to a certain type of lumber. Or just now, trying to recall another typical example, we have opened a magazine . . . and here's "A Moveable Car"—on how to build yourself an amphibian mini-car (the author has been reading Hemingway, a car is his idea of a feast).

Thousands of such examples could be cited, perhaps less droll but more straightforward. One could even write a slight but original structuralist paper on this topic.

But the problem is that even Shield and Sword is already a quotation, a rephrasing. The result is quite curious: "I came not to send peace, but a board." This has no "shield," though. Well, perhaps the author of the famous novel had in mind the aria "Either with my shield or on it," which everyone has heard. But this has no "sword." Anyhow, it's a quotation from somewhere. The Hemingway title is a quotation, too, from an American poet, whom we haven't read.

(Hemingway's titles are almost all quotations: For Whom the Bell Tolls, To Have and Have Not, The Sun Also Rises. Thus, the epigraphs of the nineteenth century are the titles of today. Anna Karenina, à la Hemingway, would be called Vengeance Is Mine or I Will Repay.)

That is, a lesser familiarity with the subject breeds a greater directness of address: "Hey, you!" instead of "Dear Sir." When we encounter in a newspaper the headline "A Time to Live!" we may confidently say *that the author of the item alluded to Remarque, not the Old Testament.*

It is curious what and how we recognize, and when, and at what hand, so to speak.

And before progressing, we digress . . . We recently saw the film The Gospel According to Matthew. *It was being shown to professionals—directors, actors, scriptwriters, editors. Opinion was divided: some people were deeply impressed, and others "liked it, but . . ." Such a division is normal, but the puzzling thing was that both camps, in approximately equal numbers, included people who were: wise and foolish, with taste and without, right-wing and left-wing, old and young, sincere and insincere, given to ecstasy and habitually apathetic. That is, there was no way of assigning their ecstasy or moderation according to some criterion, as one usually can: "Oh, he's a fool," or "Oh, he's a swine." Each of the camps preserved in miniature the overall makeup of the room. We would simply have left without unraveling this phenomenon, had not one of the ecstatic advocates shouted in a temper, apparently as an argument in the film's favor, "But the Sermon on the Mount?" Now it dawned on us, and we did a few experiments to test our surmise. We approached people, and after first extracting a terrible oath that they would answer our question honestly, we asked, "Now, have you read the Gospel?" And here's how it came out: the people in absolute ecstasy were those who had not read the Gospel. Those familiar with it responded more objectively and severely. A simple conclusion, or question, comes to mind: Which made the impression, the Gospel or the picture? the quotation or the film? The honest ones blushed and agreed that yes, it was the quotation. The dishonest ones agreed without blushing. Thus, many were first deeply impressed by a Gospel read to them in literal translation by an interpreter sitting in the dark.*

So it matters—at whose hand. It does make a difference.

The overall influence of such quotation in our education is hard even to assess. Sometimes it seems that only through quotation do well-read people know the names of "Christ, Mohammed, Napoleon" (Maxim Gorky), or Homer, Aristophanes, Plato, or Rabelais, Dante, Shakespeare, or Rousseau, Sterne, Pascal . . . and a few of their popular sayings.

The title of this novel is stolen, too. Why, that's an institute, not a title for a novel! With nameplates for the departments: The Bronze Horseman. A Hero of Our Time. Fathers and Sons. What Is to Be Done? *And so on, through the school curriculum. A tour of a museum novel.*

The nameplates guide, the epigraphs remind . . .

FAINA

*. . . the idea of evil cannot enter a man's mind without his wanting
to apply it to reality . . .*

FOR LYOVA ODOEVTSEV, of *the* Odoevtsevs, life had brought no
special traumas; in the main, it had flowed along. Figuratively speaking, the thread of his life . . .
   This is appalling: we now have to tell all over again everything we've
already told. We should begin with . . . But that's very arbitrary. Let's
skip his birth and early childhood, to which we devoted no more than
a dozen pages even in the first part. We will leave them with the same
meaning: in some sense, a man's earliest years always have the one
meaning for him. From those years, let us stress his love for his mother
as his firstmost love, preceding his first. And let us move on, past
Father, past Dickens, past Grandfather—hurry on, to Faina. As for
his adolescence, the remark has already escaped us that he had none.
And having begun to tell Lyova's story a second time, we will again
skip his adolescence.
   Let us begin at the end of it. Lyova appears to be lucky: his age
boundaries mark historical boundaries. His birth and his hinted death
are both dates, both landmarks in the nation's history. Skipping adolescence, beginning youth, we again coincide with a date. The very
date that determined all of part one, all the departures of the heroes,
and most importantly their returns. The trousers . . . There the date
was not named, perhaps precisely because it was causative. But here—
how else to begin a story of first love?—here we will name this non-
causative date. On March 5, 1953, you-know-who died.
   Much as we would like to avoid, in this part, the unappetizing

embrace of the historical muse (marble, eyeless), much as we would like to avoid the school, we do seem to have to stop in for a moment, precisely on that memorable day.

How short of light the school is! The days have been drawing out for more than two months now, but all is dark. Very, very dark in the mornings—that will be Lyova's only lasting memory of school. On the frosty morning dash to his office he may think again of Peter: What could be more absurd than a northern Palmyra? Palms—like hell!

Nine o'clock, pitch dark. In the school assembly hall, Lyova has been ordered into a funereal line. There he stands in line, a "senior class student," a plump, rosy boy with a bass-voiced look, the seducer's dream, although at that time even the seducers had disappeared . . . there he stands. He is not quite sure of himself—his grief is supposed to be very, very deep. This is hard to describe . . .

It's hard, indeed. Just what we so wanted to avoid by beginning the second part, actually the reason why we began it . . . and here we are again! How to depict the past, if we didn't know then what we know today was happening then. The significance we now attach to this death is precisely that we seem to understand it. But Lyova has no understanding that this death, for him, will also be a sexual emancipation. A wilder idea cannot be imagined: I guarantee it could not have been in anyone's mind. As it happens, this death is the end of segregated education, hoo-ray! But these fruits are not for Lyova to enjoy, because he is just finishing school. The fact will remain in his biography for life: that women are found not in space but in time, outside the age of sixteen, after he gets his passport . . . So there it is. Just what should we attach significance to: the fact that people don't know they're being dragged along like grains of sand by the glacier of historical process? Or the fact that they don't care a fig for the process, because they think it's they themselves who are creeping along? Is this tragedy or comedy? Only a backward glance will register the historical turning point. On the ship of the present, nothing moves—all moves with the ship. A miraculously revived fly is buzzing around the light bulb . . .

All is deathly still. Lyova deliberately avoids looking at the fly. He stands and has no idea how much this matters to him personally, the fact that he is now standing in this line. He does not know that at this instant his sweet reads in Father's study come to an end, the door opens, and . . . in walks Faina. He experiences this death quite differently, not at all as a liberation: he is embarrassed. He is embarrassed by the insufficiency of his shock, the shallowness of his woe.

He is afraid. He is afraid that this insufficiency is evident on his face. For, what impresses him in all the other faces is precisely the sincerity and depth of their grief. The principal has eyeglasses full of tears. The portrait wreathed in black ribbon—Lyova feels a bit sorry for it: it's the portrait of a man no longer alive. This is a strange feeling, that the portrait is no longer alive, for the portrait is precisely what had been alive, because no one had seen the living man himself. Lyova wants to understand what has disappeared from the portrait: it seems to him to have changed, although clearly it can't have changed over-night . . . Again Lyova avoids looking at the fly.

There is a smell of freezing pine needles. In Lyova's mind it's the literature teacher who is being laid to rest: good thing the teacher didn't outlive the Leader, he'd be sobbing now, outdoing the principal. Lyova is absorbed in recollections of that funeral. Then, too, it smelled of pine needles; then, too, he avoided looking to the right, where the coffin stood. Lyova risks looking to the right—and sees no coffin. He is surprised and suddenly remembers, tries to drive a mournful cloud over his pink and kindly face. Like a voluptuary, he wants to experience grief, and cannot.

(No, he does not know, unlike the others, who exactly don't know and for that very reason are so deep in their grief . . . no, he does not know the true face of the deceased, his parents have managed not to initiate him. So the nature of his apathy is quite special, and obscure to Lyova: he has never doubted the divinity of the Leader's genius, yet here he stands and feels nothing, except for the fact that he feels nothing. This is a different problem, Lyova's own.)

He cannot grieve so intensely as Valya Spokoynov, the prettiest and stupidest boy in the class. What tears are welling on Spokoynov's long, curved eyelashes! How attractive he is . . .

The whole nation has frozen in five minutes of silence. But Lyova is thinking that first period is physics, a quiz he isn't ready for, and he can't help feeling a blasphemous joy that in the meantime the period is going by, it's a good bet they won't have the quiz.

He is very embarrassed to catch himself in this petty, bad thought. He thinks he is the only such emotional freak, amid all these people who know how to feel so deeply. How they would shun him, what hatred they would feel for him, what scorn . . . if they could just see his thoughts. But societal development hasn't come that far yet, and at this moment Lyova blesses his behind-the-times human trait of having nothing written on his brow. Only the hateful physics teacher, that dim peasant, stunted person . . . He alone—is he ever dim!—

has nothing but lethargy written on his face. I bet he's feeling bad we've missed the quiz, Lyova thinks venomously. The physics teacher could not withstand Lyova's stare and tried to slip out of the hall unnoticed. Now everything somehow came to an end. They heard the principal making the solemn oath to study forever . . . his voice shook, and at this moment he was as handsome as Spokoynov, who could not, in the end, suppress the sobs breaking from his chest. The fly lighted briefly on the math teacher's bald spot; he was afraid to make the blasphemous gesture of shooing it off. It flew away. They all went off to their homerooms, carrying grief in their souls as if in overfilled vessels, afraid of spilling it.

They retreated to their homeroom without exchanging a word, without stirring up their woe. Quietly they let themselves down at their desks without slamming the lids. Spokoynov buried his uncommonly handsome face in his hands. Many took advantage of the same pose. The room hadn't been this quiet the whole ten years. They could hear the fly buzzing. But it had stayed in the assembly hall . . . Meanwhile, they had obviously missed the quiz . . . Lyova had read somewhere that the deepest grief lacked any form of expression, that it was sometimes replaced by very strange behavior and sensations. If this meant him . . . he doubted the truth of the observation. He would have liked to explain his apathy in just this way, so as to become like everyone else and not be a freak, but in all honesty he could not so explain himself at this instant. Spokoynov remained an inaccessible ideal. His beauty seemed so justified, and not superficial . . . Lyova was embarrassed.

They couldn't all be thinking, as Lyova was, that it was lucky he died, if they'd missed the quiz? This was an assumption that Lyova, chastising himself, could not make about the others. All the others, heartbroken, had just forgotten outright about such trivia as the quiz. This was the reason why one and all were still sitting mournfully in the classroom, not going up to the physics lab. One and all—and Lyova the only one alone. It was lonely for Lyova to be so self-aware amid this elemental popular woe.

Of course Lyova couldn't suppose that they had all pretended in some respect. Well, maybe one, or two, Lyova thought, with a detective's logic. But they couldn't all have pretended the same thing . . . ?

So, this death hasn't always been understood as it is now. But they were not to sit out their whole lives like that, in the mournful classroom. Beyond the window, it was even getting light. Let's try not to attach one particular meaning to this world event. Let's leave Lyova in his quandary over his own sincerity. Far more important to have a good attitude toward history, a humane scorn: I didn't care at the time, didn't care about the march of history—when she trod on me, I remembered the ridges on her boot sole.

Of course it's impossible to assume that they might all have pretended the same thing, without prearrangement. But what, then, is society? It's too early for Lyova to suppose that society *is* collective insincerity.

Especially since the physics teacher will burst into the room any minute now, all fired up: Why the devil aren't they on their way to the lab? "So he's dead—that's no excuse!" this coarse, dull-witted man will snap. How indignant they will be! But Lyova will have trouble restraining the idiotic, scandalous, out-of-the-blue laughter he feels within: they've missed the quiz. He doesn't know that this is the guffaw of History herself, if she does, after all, exist. He doesn't know that someday he will come to remember with warmth the physics teacher he has hated throughout his school years, and will shudder to remember the principal, his idol and dominant influence. The physics teacher doesn't know that he will finally have his cottage with a little flower bed and vegetable patch; the principal doesn't know that he will become vice president of the Academy of Pedagogical Sciences; Spokoynov doesn't know that he will arrive at the Russian idea through the Komsomol; Lyova doesn't know that Faina is passing on the other side of the door . . . No one knows anything of what we all know now.

So let us try to change our omniscient tone, and take up the cheerless restoration of Lyova's past. Let us try to get used to the windy plywood shack of the present, in exchange for the comfortable and magnificent ruins of the past. Let us prepare for an abrupt change in the narrative: we will find ourselves in the rarefied, blind world of Lyova, as he was when he was . . .

Now must be told the story of the ring. If only as a symbol, it is extremely revealing.

Because the plot of Lyova's life coils lightly in rings, forming a hank of rope or a sleeping snake. And if our tale was begun with a handsome phrase about Lyova's thread streaming rhythmically from someone's divine hands, then at some moment, as it seems to us, this divine being either wearied or fell asleep outright, bewitched by the rhythmic monotony of Lyova's thread flashing past without knots or breaks. The clew slipped from his hands, and the thread, unwinding, began falling in circles on the imaginary floor, loop after loop, loop after loop, as in the childhood pictures where Grandma has gone to sleep and the kitten is playing with her ball of yarn. Granted, the kitten is missing. But one may easily mistake for it Lyova's first and eternal love, or his friend and enemy Mitishatyev, as a kind of collective image embodying a force opposed to Lyova.

And it's a ring for a further reason, that all three in the triangle seemed to grab hands and go whirling around, stamping with unnatural glee, and a circuit began, along which, if one of them played a dirty trick on another, that one immediately transmitted it to the third, and the third returned it to the first, and at last everything was spinning like a record stuck in a groove. Very likely no one of them, trying to remember back to the starting position, could have said for sure that he was or was not the one who had started it, and by now it looked as if they had started it simultaneously—besides, it was somehow even better that way, since things were equal and no one got hurt more than the others and no one was offended. That way, at least, in his own masculine self-perception, Lyova won.

The incident of the ring is especially revealing in that, although naïve, it was the severest of the first, or the first of the severe, symptoms of the way in which the very mechanism of a relationship affected Lyova (he extremely quickly and easily fell under the sway of anyone who knew how to manipulate this simple mechanism), and also because it shows how anyone who catches a blow in life has already "caught" the very mechanism he hates; i.e., not only has he been hurt, aggrieved, or defeated, according to the plot, the situation, the turn of events, but he has actually been *struck down* as one is struck down by illness.

Besides, without claiming to be the primal source, this incident simply launches the count, it's number one, if not in significance then at least in order. If we exclude a vague something about Father, which at that time was entirely unknown to Lyova but nevertheless somehow existed, like a little cloud, in the air that Lyova breathed without yet noticing this component, not lethal but dangerous enough that if it didn't poison you it would at least leave you with a tendency to get poisoned subsequently, a certain imperceptible constitutional predisposition . . . Well, if we exclude this faint smell, of which Lyova, by and large, was unaware, then the incident of the ring really is number one, if we take things in order.

A series of these rings will also extend through the tale, reflecting a particular segment of Lyova's life, namely, the one when the divine being dozed off, and the thread, slipping from his hands, began falling in rings, with the top one falling on the one before, just as that one had on the one before that, just as they all, piling up, lay on the first ring. We can only hope that someone will suddenly poke the being in the ribs, he will rouse himself with a start and take up the neglected thread.

Moreover, this story really is about a ring, a very ordinary wedding ring ("of yellow metal," as a detective would put it), a round, hollow little ring that Faina wore on her finger.

Only about a ring.

We should begin, though, with the fact that when walking out of the classroom where they had taken the final exam for their diploma— when walking out of the classroom after their grades for this final exam had been announced to them—they all at once lit up cigarettes. Lyova hadn't even supposed that the whole class smoked. It turned out there had even been an agreement that they would all light up, but by some accident Lyova had not been included in the agreement. Each got out his own pack and lit his own cigarette, most of them awkwardly. Mitishatyev shook his pack of Northlands and offered it to Lyova. Lyova took one.

The exam was "History of the U.S.S.R.," and Lyova got a perfect 5, while Mitishatyev, alone in their strong class, got a 3, because he was keen on history at the time and had spent the whole exam period reading the ancient Solovyov and Karamzin but hadn't finished the *Short Course,* so that he knew only the third questions, and those in a form quite the reverse of what he should have; but Lyova had read only the *Short Course,* and they didn't ask him a third question at all. So, still experiencing a covert truimph over Mitishatyev, Lyova also took a cigarette. When he managed not to choke on the first puff, he was seized with a certain pride, as well as dizziness, and now suddenly he was aware that he was through with school—at last.

Thus, the end of school and the sensation of the first puff were united in his memory for life. Everything started swimming before his eyes, he suddenly experienced an unusual lightness, and it seemed to him that he didn't walk, he flew, over the sunny, trampled school-yard and found himself on the street with Mitishatyev. "We should get drunk," Mitishatyev said, gloomy over his 3. "Why not, it'll do us good," Lyova said gleefully, and felt surprised—he never drank. It was as if he had found himself for the first time in a wide-open space and immediately exposed himself to all winds.

Mitishatyev promptly agreed that Lyova should buy for both of them, because Lyova had money and Mitishatyev didn't. "There'll be real women," he said. "French." "What do you mean, French?" Lyova choked. "Coeds from the Foreign Language Institute." But "coeds," too, sounded like "courtesans" to Lyova. One of them, Mitishatyev said, had even been married.

By this time, Lyova wasn't so much lending money to Mitishatyev as becoming indebted to him for life. Because, naturally enough, all this had been much on Lyova's mind and he knew nothing about *it*, while Mitishatyev, although he had begun to forge ahead in all these matters much earlier than Lyova, had never before made such a proposition to him. He had smirkingly evaded Lyova's hints and rare timid questions, thereby offending him and leaving him isolated in his virtue, which by that time Lyova was almost ready to sacrifice.

Now—the whole situation was different. They arranged to meet that evening, and after lighting up one more of Mitishatyev's cigarettes, Lyova walked home, but again he didn't walk, he flew, as if borne homeward by all the suddenly revealed winds.

He spent the whole day scrubbing and shaving, and an hour before the agreed-upon hour he was already fluttering, circling, puffing at newly purchased gold-rimmed cigarettes. He flew around the same block a hundred times before Mitishatyev came strolling up.

There were three girls in the rather bare room—let us label them the dark girl, the light one, and the blue one. They were speaking Russian (Lyova had been sure they would speak only French—there he could shine, because his parents' efforts had made him fluent in this family dialect). Somehow or other, the time was still filled, as long as Mitishatyev was greeting them himself and introducing Lyova, and Lyova was shaking the unaccustomed little hands and enduring the stares; then he drew out his bottles, two muscatels he had heard were so loved by the ladies, which now struck him as ridiculous, although he himself had bought them; time emptied, and he was suddenly self-conscious.

Mitishatyev promptly left him to his own devices, right away starting a conversation with the dark girl and the light one in a cozy corner. Lyova ventured nothing, he was too self-conscious to start a conversation, and for the time being he justified this by the need to decide on one of the three girls; moreover, not Mitishatyev's. Which of them had been married, Lyova wondered. For the time being, it appeared that the girl in blue was meant for Lyova: like him, she was somewhat apart from the rest. Lyova flipped through a magazine without seeing anything in it, occasionally glancing at his blue girl. She really was blue; her dress was blue, and her hair somehow had a blue sheen. The light girl—the hostess—kept coming and going.

Actually, Lyova had no preference: they were all somehow the same to him, even though different colors. Or perhaps his seeming indifference, his lack of a specific interest in any one of the three, was a displacement of his indecision and embarrassment. Instinctively he had already started seeking the inner strength to like the blue one best, and little by little he began to succeed at this, finding virtues to set her apart from her girlfriends. But now Mitishatyev threw everything off: abandoning his little group unnoticed, he suddenly turned up talking to (Lyova even became indignant) the blue girl. The dark one began bustling around: "Well, why don't we have a drink? But where's Faina? How much longer are we going to wait for her!"

Which one is Faina, Lyova thought belatedly. And why do we have to wait for her, when they're all here . . . Just then the door opened, and in walked a new girl altogether, tossing back her damp, wild hair with one hand. Not a girl—a woman! In the most genuine sense of the word, from Lyova's point of view. Yes, she was a woman—that was how she walked in. Without realizing it, Lyova had swiftly crossed the room while she took barely three steps from the doorway, and he stood before her like a statue, his mouth hanging slightly ajar as if he were saying "Oh!" Faina—because this was she, and she was the married one, there could be no doubt of that—Faina, as if only because something had blocked her way, lifted her eyes to Lyova standing frozen before her. Smiling as if from the same surprise as Lyova, she, too, said "Oh"—moreover, in such a way that Lyova even thought he could hear her approval, he did hear it. "Faina," she said, in a husky voice that immediately enraptured Lyova, and offered him her hand— Lyova was aware of her hand as both pliant and assured at the same time, cool and tender—the handshake sent a most voluptuous chill down his back. He was still holding her hand in his when he heard, "And your name?" "Yes, yes . . ." he said as if trying to recall, and hastily let go of her hand. "Lyova. My name is Lyova," he declared, as if trying to convince himself of it.

In sum, this was love at first sight and on the spot. Lyova never even noticed the muscatel being drunk, the table being moved out of the way, the record player turning on by itself, and Mitishatyev starting to dance with the light hostess. Although Lyova did not know how to dance, he did know French, and as he talked to Faina he alternated

Russian phrases with French ones, in which, as a specialist, she couldn't help appreciating his pronunciation. He was unashamed. They had found a spot by the wall, in the aisle between two beds, they were clutching the nickel-plated bedsteads like handrails, they were riding this bus to somewhere far away, and there were no other passengers . . . Their compartment was rather cramped, there was only a small nickel-plated ring between Faina's hand and his—Lyova gasped at the closeness, he gripped the ring, and his knuckles whitened handsomely. Mitishatyev was dancing with the dark girl now. The blue one walked over to Lyova and artlessly offered her hand, drawing him into the circle. "No," Lyova said, for some reason even crossly. She shrugged, half in scorn, and walked away.

Mitishatyev took the rap for Lyova by dancing with the blue girl. He danced as if getting more and more wound up, as if in a frenzy, but even though Mitishatyev carried it off well on the whole, Lyova mistrusted his frenzy. In Lyova's opinion the effort of this unaccountable convulsion was too visible, it overstated the frenzy of Mitishatyev's nature. Lyova himself, in contrast to Mitishatyev, was talking easily and spontaneously—so it seemed to him. Faina for the most part said nothing, gently nodding assent, but very correctly, cleverly, and in rhythm, so that Lyova was more and more convinced of her exceptional intelligence. The coffer of her virtues, in his conception, was already becoming too great for any possibility of appreciating and endowing this woman in full. Moreover, even though she said little, Faina somehow managed to keep Lyova from feeling the awkwardness of his immoderate talkativeness, and because she was so sympathetic and tactful, Lyova was becoming all the more grateful to her and all the more violently in love, if that was still possible.

When he finished his dance with the blue girl, Mitishatyev came over to Faina and started to introduce himself, blushing a little and acting extremely prim, as if in contrast to the frenzy of his just-ended dance. Lyova was slightly surprised that the ubiquitous Mitishatyev turned out not to know her, and this made him feel almost superior. After introducing himself, Mitishatyev asked Faina for the next dance. Lyova gave him such a menacing look that although Mitishatyev did dance one dance with Faina—and, to Lyova's special displeasure, even whispered something to her—at any rate he didn't ask her again, leaving her entirely to Lyova.

The gaiety, meanwhile, had gone flat: the dark girl had left altogether, while the light hostess came and went from the room incessantly, with or without need, and as if making some point. By all indications, Faina was staying with the hostess tonight and didn't intend to leave at all, but Lyova should have left long ago, as Mitishatyev morosely hinted by putting on his raincoat, and there was no time for the resolute actions Lyova had been working up to all evening, which would consist of securing and guaranteeing himself his next meeting with Faina, so that she wouldn't hide from him anymore (for he was weirdly haunted by that very feeling: that she had already vanished from him once, as though he had known her a long time)—there was no time at all left for these ill-planned actions. Hastily now, out of the blue, as if shutting his eyes and jumping (but he had wanted to do it smoothly and casually), he invited Faina to go out to a restaurant. Lyova panicked at his own audacity, he choked in certain anticipation of her refusal and even outrage. But Faina consented surprisingly readily, right off, as if there were nothing so phenomenal about it; Lyova had not expected this, and his audacity dangled in the void. "But when?" Faina asked, and her tone sounded businesslike. "Why not tomorrow!" Lyova exclaimed ecstatically. "No, but the day after," Faina said. They agreed to meet day after tomorrow, at eight in the evening.

And Lyova stumbled homeward, by now completely aflutter. Mitishatyev went in the opposite direction, with the blue girl. Lyova wondered once more about his being with the blue one (for some reason, he had thought Mitishatyev was with the dark one), wondered—and promptly forgot. Because, frantically taking wing like his fluttering heart, soaring and dipping, he was at his house in an instant, quietly fumbling at the lock lest he wake his already sleeping parents. And all around was the flare of a weird flickering light, where it came from he didn't know, because the bulb on the landing was not burning.

How Lyova made it to the day after tomorrow, how he found within him the strength to overcome this fathomless time, is something of a marvel—but now he was sitting in a very sumptuous restaurant (Faina had chosen it), at a table with two embezzlers from the provinces, and talking to Faina, mainly in French because his conversation (they had already had a fair amount to drink) was of a kind not meant for outsiders, and Lyova was flying higher and higher because—so far as he could judge by Faina's silent and therefore, from his point of view, increasingly eloquent nods and glances—things were obviously going well.

They sat until closing time. They were left almost alone in the room, alone at the table in any case, and Lyova hardly saw beyond it: in a fog. The waitress—a very amiable woman, for whom Lyova felt a growing affinity because of what seemed to him the special care she extended to their table—stood by the wall and kept glancing in their direction with a soft, almost motherly expression. Lyova was enjoying everything, moved by everything: he caught her glance, and then somehow specially straightened up and spoke louder. Faina listened to him, looked down, twisted the wedding ring on her thin finger.

Now there occurred a quite symbolic scene, which left Lyova in utter ecstasy. The waitress came over to them and said, opening her notepad, "You must be newlyweds?"

Lyova flushed in confusion. But all of a sudden, just as readily as she had agreed to come to the restaurant with him, Faina said, "Yes." Then Lyova too, realizing suddenly and choking, said, "Yes, yes." "I could tell right off," the waitress said. "The nicest couple today. Have you been married long?" Lyova looked at Faina in dismay. "Six months," she said. "And three days," Lyova joked, thrilling with happiness, and immediately felt very annoyed with himself. "I could tell right off it's a good marriage," the waitress said. "That's so rare nowadays." "Yes . . ." He sighed absurdly. "Well, would you like to sit a bit longer? You can have another five minutes or so," she said benevolently, and dropped her notepad into her pocket. As she left their table she asked, "Do you live with your parents?" "Yes, our parents," Lyova said, this time confidently. Now, somewhat to Lyova's surprise, Faina called her back and whispered something in her ear. The waitress shot a quick, bright glance at Lyova and returned her whisper. Lyova leaned back in his chair in a well-bred manner and pensively looked away, as if he heard nothing—but, strain as he might, he heard nothing. The mere fact that there was some other understanding between them, inaccessible to Lyova, made him tensely alert: they were at home with each other, the waitress and Faina, and then this strange laughter, and then the waitress left, still smiling over what they had been talking about, and the last exchange of glances—Lyova glimpsed in all this something carnal and unclean, but he promptly tried to forget it, which he succeeded in doing. After a while the waitress returned carrying a small package and handed it to Faina. Now they settled the bill. Lyova left a big tip, and frowned because he caught himself recalculating the tip in terms of movie tickets.

But what happened next was altogether a miracle: the walk home coalesced for Lyova into sheer flowering, blaze, and fragrance. Never had he talked so marvelously as when they suddenly paused at the canal to lean on the parapet and look at the black water and he finally dared to take Faina's arm. Later they kissed in the front entrance so decorously, so uncontrollably, that beyond the window it treacherously grew light. Faina spoke such words to him, such words, that he could not repeat them even to himself, because they would cease to mean anything, they would wither on the spot, leaving nothing but disillusionment.

He did not suspect, at the time, that Faina's bundle contained six pastries; that she understood not a word of French, because she had never even studied at the Foreign Language Institute, having gotten married right out of typing school; that although Lyova had already switched to Russian, back there by the parapet, in the speech that he thought had conclusively confirmed his triumph and without which he would not have attained her love, she remembered nothing of this speech either, being fully content with her excellent understanding and knowledge of his condition, and nothing else; he had no idea of the degree to which the unique words he first heard from Faina between kisses, there in the front entrance, were as natural and obligatory for her as the kisses, and meant almost nothing: it was simply that she knew how to give him joy and had no reason to deny it to him. (Although we shouldn't so vigorously deny sincerity to Faina either. Because we, too, are surrendering ourselves to insincerity. At any rate, she surrendered herself to it fully.) But Lyova knew nothing of this— it would have been disgusting of him even to suspect it. He knew nothing of this, and there was only one thing that poisoned his intoxicating happiness unbearably, one small need, which blanketed the world with its dimensions. (Later, when he told her about his comical torture of that night, expecting a certain tenderness on her part at the revival of their first, so joyful memories, Faina merely shrugged her shoulders. "You could have stepped outside. I'd have waited," she said.)

Again, their next meeting was the day after tomorrow. Lyova did not live through this time, he broke through it by force, and found himself that morning in Faina's room. At last there was nobody around, and with an unexpected show of audacity he promptly possessed her. She, however, put not the slightest hindrance in his way. Lyova practically went crazy, though not from his divine delight—which hadn't proved so great as he expected, and for the first time he drew the boundary line between desire and delight—but from the fact itself, which blasted open his consciousness with a happy crash and could not be fitted in. Not knowing how to thank her, how to balance what she had given him, he showered her with kisses and jubilantly confessed, in hopes of flattering her, that she was the first woman in his life (prior to winning her, he had tried, on the contrary, to appear experienced). But Faina would not believe him: either he had in fact been terrifically slick and smooth, or she, too, meant to be flattering.

The next day Lyova was rather more emotional about it all. And now, in his intoxication, it seemed to him that things would go on this way, ever higher and higher, until the pealing bell was unbearable in its sweetness—on and on, all his life . . .

But he noticed almost immediately that something changed in Faina, as though she were surprised to see him back again; that she averted her eyes and said nothing when he ardently chafed her hands and demanded the old words; that despite her being dedicated to this kind of thing, as Lyova had already noted, she surrendered herself to him with a kind of indifference, all but reluctance.

Then one time she was away from home. He kept watch for three days—she was still away. Finally he caught her, and she was gayer and kinder than usual. Now he was tortured not only by her three-day disappearance—where to? with whom?—but also by the fact that she had returned so contented. Lyova was beside himself and kept wanting to understand what was the matter, wanting her to "just explain" what he lacked and what more he had to do to make everything be "as before"—because it was obvious to him there was nothing he wouldn't do for Faina or, more precisely, wouldn't do to keep her.

He decided to have a "candid talk" with her (by "candor" he unconsciously meant just one aspect of it—the restoration of her old words and confessions). With this in mind he took her to a café, partly because he wished to repeat that wonderful evening in the restaurant and felt more and more convinced that it would certainly be repeated tonight. (I should have done this long ago, Lyova reproached himself. I should have done it earlier, before Faina cooled.) But he took her to a café, not the restaurant, because he had little money (thus we always suppose, as we give less and less, that we are giving our last, and in return for our last we demand from another his all). Still, even the café, by Faina's admission, was one she had always liked very much: cozy special lighting, you could "be alone together" there, and so on.

At the café he asked, bluntly because of his despair, what more did she need? She was not annoyed (because she was still in rather a good humor after her disappearance) and said, also bluntly, "You ought to let me feel your strength." What she meant by this was hard to guess, but strangely enough Lyova understood her at once, and his heart contracted in anguish and despair. It simply meant that he was too good to Faina and that all would have been better had he been worse.

Lyova talked for a whole hour, with just as much beauty and inspiration as that evening by the parapet, about how she didn't understand that it was disgusting, this game of "who wins." He, Lyova, simply didn't want to play this game, he couldn't play it, unlike some people, unlike, for example, that fellow Mitishatyev ("Mitya who? Oh, the one that danced. A nice boy!"). He believed, Lyova continued, that outside this game there could be truly beautiful relationships, of a kind most people never knew, this was precisely the way he loved her, and it was a rare love, or not even rare, but the one love worthy of the name. ("There . . ." she said, and even stroked his hand caressingly. "You just love me too much, and it's hard for me." Lyova was surprised and horrified by this simplicity, although one must give Faina her due: never after did she speak so purely and honestly.) But, said Lyova, he didn't want to be, he couldn't be, on a level with everyone else, and in that case, in that respect, someone might even think him weak, but it wasn't weakness at all, it was strength, his strength! it was the rare gift that comes to a person once in a lifetime . . . And how could she turn away (from the gift and from Lyova) when harbored within (the gift or Lyova?) was the highest happiness, such as could only be given to one person by another person! Turning away from this gift was even a crime . . . (But sure enough, Faina was turning away, she had long since let her mind wander from Lyova's speech, because she had also long since known it, basically and as a whole, and all that she could say to Lyova in this regard she had already said very frankly. She was turning away, her glance following a tall, mustachioed young man who had just walked in.) Now, it was the very lack of strength, a lack of the strength to feel and truly love, that she meant by strength . . . said Lyova, and went limp, weak, slack, could not utter another word.

"I'm awfully hungry all of a sudden," Faina said (on arriving at the café, she had refused to have anything). "Would you please order me the *petits filets*. This place does them very nicely."

How would she know about the *petits filets* at this place, Lyova wondered.

They continued to "see each other" (it would have been hard not to see each other, even if Faina had wanted that). Without ever having shown his strength, Lyova pined and suffered greatly, and somehow it all took more and more money. His father looked askance, and after reaching a certain limit—chosen according to considerations of his own—did not increase the subsidies. One time Uncle Mitya came to the rescue, although Lyova, after hearing so much about his stinginess, had had no thought of asking him. "Here," Uncle Mitya said, with a sigh of farewell for his note, "you need the money." Dropping his *porte-monnaie* into his pocket without the note, he said crossly, "You're not a man, Lyova, you're a catch." Lyova did not take offense and felt moved to tears. Another time it was Albina, perhaps the only girl Lyova had known even before Faina (by a coincidence in real life, not the novel, she was the daughter of a longtime lady friend of that same Uncle Mitya). Lyova considered her homely and felt shy whenever he met her: she always tried to be pleasing, and he never knew what to say to hasten their goodbye. This time he complained of living in penury, and she promptly offered him a loan. Feeling terrible, dropping his eyes, Lyova took advantage of it. Took advantage, also, of knowing that she herself would never remind him of the debt. He perceived his considerable baseness only as abasement, however, and only until he had disappeared around the corner with the money. And that was it. The end of the Samaritans, the beginning of "need." And its synonyms. Lyova filched books, sold his truly valuable coin collection (from Peter to the Revolution—passionately accumulated over his school years) to some swindler at a real giveaway. But even this sum, a very substantial one for Lyova at the time, flowed away instantly, as if into sand.

So the problem that began to interest him now, almost on a par with clarifying his relationship with Faina, was how and where to raise money (thus, he was imperceptibly growing accustomed to buying love). He was learning to economize (this was the domestic percentage of their relationship). By now he thought of restaurant going as too unprofitable, because there were far more urgent expenses (stockings, cosmetics, electricity and gas, pins, thread, don't forget to buy two meters of grosgrain belting, ask for it that way, "groh-grain") . . . If only he'd buy flowers someday! Lyova smiled wryly.

It was at this time that he participated in a "bring-your-own" party (which is cheaper than a restaurant). The party was being arranged by a school chum of his and two other boys of the same age but very advanced in their diversions, one of whom was Mitishatyev. Somebody's apartment had been freed up (his parents were away somewhere), and they could do what they liked there. Mitishatyev thought of Lyova and invited him "with guest." Having long since exhausted all available alternatives for diverting Faina, and feeling sorely perplexed on this account, Lyova was very appreciative, even touched.

Faina griped for a long time and refused to go. "A kindergarten," she said frowningly. Then she spent just as long getting dressed, taking even more pains than usual.

What is irksome to us, after the fact, wasn't yet the least irksome to Lyova—he wasn't the least bored observing her preparations, he even took pleasure in them. He found a peculiar beauty and charm in Faina's studied, mechanical, almost instinctive movements before the mirror. Precisely in these movements—not at all calculated for an onlooker, for effect, not aestheticized—he now found, precisely and above all, beauty.

He was made glad by the smoke-blackened iron fork that Faina took to the kitchen to heat on the gas and came running back with, waving the red-hot fork at arm's length (she used the fork to wind a lock of hair, effecting a final and most expressive ringlet), and the table knife that she used with stunning adeptness to curl her eyelashes after she made them up. This to-do with objects that cut and stabbed (right by her eyes!) seemed risky and dangerous to Lyova, but the calm and efficiency with which Faina did all this both delighted and frightened him, like the daring of a circus artist. Again, he was both attracted and frightened by Faina's eyes in the mirror when she was busy with all this—absent, cold, aimed, a sharpshooter's expression. The studied, undeviating sequence of movements and operations that Faina carried out during her preparations did not lose their charm for Lyova, despite their uniformity: he felt a definite pleasure in the mental anticipation of Faina's movements, and a kind of joy when an imagined movement tallied with the real one a second or two later.

(And while he so timidly observes and uncomplainingly awaits Faina, we have time to study his gaze . . . How does he manage, while not taking his eyes off her, to see so little of her? To see so little of her that even we, looking through his eyes in this story, do not see her?)

He especially liked it when she washed off her old makeup and looked bewildered and nearsighted for an instant, as though she might easily be insulted now and Lyova would defend her. In general, he increasingly loved and prized this unremarked beauty in Faina. Her face sleep-swollen or tired, any carelessness in her dress, an awkward uncalculated movement would inspire in him a blissful sense of permanence, belonging, and gratitude, which in other situations Faina allowed him to experience increasingly seldom.

Thus it was that when Faina complained of looking bad she seemed to Lyova most beautiful, beloved, and close. If this had been fully conscious, one might have said that it gladdened him when she was exhausted, weak, and unhappy (thus, he especially loved her when she got sick), and vice versa, it frightened him when she was "at her best": beautiful, confident, cheerful. In the first instance, Lyova had the illusion that she was dependent on him, she hadn't gone anywhere and couldn't hide anywhere. In the second, she was gone from him eternally, forever, gone the more hopelessly the more beautiful she was, gone even if she was beside him and they were alone together: his reach no longer seemed to extend over her, he was lagging behind, gasping in despair.

There was a paradoxical muddle here, in the concepts of closeness and distance, in the designation of these concepts by the words "usually" and "sometimes," "naturally" and "unnaturally," "as a rule" and "in exceptional cases." What was usual and natural for Faina, what brought her ease and pleasure, was the state of being "at her best," and what was exceptional, undesirable, rare, was the reverse state: fatigue, lack of confidence ("I'm not at my best today"). For Lyova it was the other way around—her "best" periods seemed increasingly undesirable, unpleasant, and unnatural, and it was precisely the "not-at-her-best" state that seemed usual and natural. In Lyova's consciousness these two states of hers were in growing antagonism. When "at her best" Faina struck Lyova as unnatural, malicious, false, callous, egoistical, endowed with all the vices; when "not at her best," as sweet, natural, tender, and so on. Precisely when not at her best was Faina herself, it seemed to him; and when at her best—alien, not his kind, a stand-in. Although he lacked the power to vary the correlation between these two hypostases, although Faina strove mainly to reduce to a minimum the very states that were, more and more, becoming dear to Lyova—that is, she strove to be "not at her best" as rarely as possible—nevertheless, it seemed to Lyova that Faina, albeit slowly, through endless sufferings on his part, was drawing near to, advancing to, the state which Lyova supposed was natural to her, her essence, and which, if one were to unshroud the phenomena of Lyova's unconscious, would be called "the state of belonging to Lyova." And since Lyova had no real grounds for supposing that she increasingly belonged to him—rather the contrary—he succeeded in seeing what he wished by a means that may seem strange but at the same time is completely natural; namely, he increasingly recognized just one side of Faina, he kept amassing and collecting these "not-at-her-best" states that were so dear to him: he simply saw and recognized them better, focusing his attention on moments that were extremely insignificant in Faina's image overall, perhaps, but seemed to increase and grow precisely because of his growing attention to them. That is, it was a purely psychic or even optical phenomenon, but it lent him strength and helped him to survive the most disheartening situations.

Had Lyova recognized the groundlessness of such logic, however, he would have been a most unhappy man, because he did not possess the strength to be equal to this knowledge. Thus, the more time he spent at Faina's side, the less he knew her. This must be what is meant by "love is blind." The Faina who could be seen by anyone and everyone, all and sundry—the real Faina—he never saw once.

The moment when Faina was putting on her makeup and getting ready, although it gladdened Lyova, was nevertheless ambiguous. She was with him and wasn't leaving, inasmuch as she wasn't ready, inasmuch as the most unnatural of women could not be called unnatural when she was before the mirror. Yet she *was* leaving, leaving in prospect, she would find herself at last quite ready, beautiful, at her best, and with a final sigh of relief or pleasure, with a final glance in the mirror, at some one instant would immediately and utterly enter the state of readiness, be at her best—and thereby be gone from Lyova. But while Lyova sat and observed this transition, he was still happy to be observing. If any slight choppiness or haze moved in over his love-shattered soul (increasingly often as she approached the end of her toilette), he put it off, brushed it from his brow with a light hand movement, as we brush off a cobweb in the autumn woods. A gesture faint as a sigh . . .

Of course, it's inaccurate to say that Faina at the mirror was alone with Lyova—no, at the mirror, of course, she was utterly alone in all the universe, like any woman—but neither was she with anyone else; this was enough for Lyova, and the definiteness and consistency of her movements engendered a feeling of stability in him. It would likewise be stretching the point to say that Faina always reenacted her ritual before the mirror in the same manner. The sameness was rather a qualitative phenomenon than a quantitative one. She behaved differently at the mirror depending on where she was preparing to go: whether the occasion was average, important, or exceptional. She could get dressed hastily, with ordinary care, or—with inspiration. It was as if there were a small, medium, and large kit of operations and movements, with different amounts of physical and spiritual energy invested. (At this moment, heaping abuse on the brats whose party she had to go to because there was nowhere else to go, and accordingly heaping abuse on meek Lyova, she was nevertheless getting dressed by the most comprehensive system, the maximum.) But all of these systems, small, medium, and large, were constant within themselves, which was why Lyova loved to suffer through these moments with her.

Lyova had no right either to protest her reprimands or to observe her openly—no good would come of it. But by now he could see Faina perfectly with a sort of side vision, which had become unusually keen where she was concerned, especially in company. He could even see her with his back, though he saw nothing of what was under his nose, in the magazine whose pages he was turning with apparent interest.

In the upshot, they arrived a little late, to find the excitement and animation that are called the first, or light, intoxication. That is, they had missed the mysterious moment when the coldness, constraint, and discord of half-acquainted people has built up little by little and approached its height, when they are all assembled and the table is ready, and now they're all taking their places, already growing excited and slackening their tension; a round of vodka is being poured, and somehow, though it has not yet been drunk, it has already begun to take effect; and then, after the first round, a hasty second—and by now they all know each other, the brakes are off, and someone is talking loudly, and someone is laughing hard, and it seems to everyone that the gaiety has been going on for ages, though if anyone with an idle bent for detective work were to note the time, it would turn out to be all of ten minutes since they've sat down at the table, fifteen at most; but already the first intoxication is beginning its smooth and implacable escalation into the second—and the more aloofly, primly, and decorously the guests have awaited this moment, the more rapid the escalation.

When they arrived, someone opened the door to them with an immoderate smile already on his face, jacketless, his collar undone, his necktie at half-mast like a flag, saying with quite unwarranted joy, At last! everyone's waiting for you—although they weren't acquainted at all. Such an open welcome is always timely, however: you leave something outside the threshold, a sort of heaviness, like a fur coat on the coatrack. But since it was summertime and there could be no question of any fur coats, the heaviness was that of an invisible garment only, which Lyova threw off then and there, in the foyer. He even seemed to track its fall with his glance: his glance fell on a trunk.

The foyer of an unfamiliar apartment, especially a communal one, is also mysterious: a small purgatory before gaiety, but darkish, crammed, and junk-filled—more like a bathhouse dressing room. The trunk, above it a bicycle, above the bicycle some antlers, below the antlers a horseshoe—all these things imperceptibly entered Lyova, in the moment when he had taken out his bottles and handed them to the host and was waiting for Faina, hurrying her with an inner effort, while with a movement so light that it seemed all but needless she touched her hand to her hairdo as if very slightly encouraging it, changed her shoes, and again pierced herself with an incorruptible glance. Now she seemed to be quivering all over, drawing herself erect; her face was becoming cold, as if chiseled, almost majestic—all this was reflected for a moment in the mirror—Faina was turning, and without looking at Lyova lest she lose her expression she was walking to the doorway, and Lyova had the impression that this was no longer Faina, her reflection had stepped out of the mirror and started to walk, an inanimate thing. His heart very slightly contracted.

To continue the simile, after the cold, dark dressing room they found themselves directly in the steam room; or, to recall the simile of the fur coat left in the vestibule, it was like coming in from the intense night cold into a warmly heated and lighted cottage, when the steam comes rolling out of the open door in a great shining ball, and then, when the door slams shut behind you and you begin to see, you find yourself in a pocket of cold, which emanates from you; or, more simply, they were bowled over by the noise and smoke and laughter, and a certain pause and scrutiny, neither conclusive nor universal but quite perceptible, like a touché—and then the same noise again.

They were seated separately—this was a principle of the group. It struck Lyova as silly, and he felt annoyed, but there was nothing he could do, and he was placed next to a pudgy girl in a transparent blouse with very pink underwear showing through it. She burst out laughing when Lyova sat down. Lyova stiffened and again felt annoyed, because the girl couldn't compare with Faina—this was as ridiculous as boarding a bus going the wrong way. But by now he was able to get his bearings. Actually, he had begun to take his bearings even before he sat down, because his keen side vision where Faina was concerned had immediately switched on.

She was next to Mitishatyev, and this gave Lyova a certain satisfaction: at least it was someone he knew. She had been able to preserve her expression, or rather her reflection, which she had carried out of the mirror, so decorous and cold, and after taking her seat she looked around unhurriedly but keenly. This was the same apparently absent but sharpshooterish gaze that she aimed at the mirror while handling, for example, the eyelash-curling table knife. Lyova would not have seen anything outside of Faina, but he tracked her gaze. It was turned first on the girls: they were all very young, still children really, although "well developed," as they say (in those years that was still an infrequent phenomenon, a merit of sorts). Her gaze was instantaneous, intent, and piercing. It appraised the girls in a flash and was reassured, having ascertained that there was no hint of any dirty trick: she cast them aside, she was unexcelled. Lyova mentally agreed with her, there could be no comparison. Faina was a *grande dame* in this hen coop. Reassured and seemingly softened, her gaze ran over the boys secondarily, this time more slowly, lazily, and good-humoredly, although it didn't seem to linger on anyone. Well, Lyova knew all the boys, there was no point in his studying them, and after tracking her gaze he reached for the vodka. All this scrutiny had occurred in the briefest of intervals, however. The speed with which Faina managed her reconnaissance testified to experience, but this was the very thing that Lyova did not think of.

Mitishatyev was already pouring for Faina. Lyova raised his glass, waiting for Faina's answering glance, wanting to establish a bond across the table, invisible and so sweet, telepathic (if they could just draw this thread tight and hold it all evening) . . . and saw Faina run one more apathetic glance over the assembled young people, then inconspicuously slip the wedding ring from her thin finger and hide it in her purse. Then she raised her glass and responded to Lyova with a nod. Lyova's whole being went out to meet her but discovered no answering desire to establish that invisible bond: Faina did not seem to notice his outstretched hand, and turned to clink glasses with Mitishatyev. Somewhat unnerved, Lyova thirstily drained his drink and immediately had a second (the "latecomers' penalty" came in handy), instinctively wanting to hurry and accelerate to the same speed as everyone else at the table, not be an outsider, an excruciating loner, which is always unpleasant, both for you and for the others.

Now a segment of time flashed by unnoticed. He suddenly discovered himself hastily chewing something, in his hurry to displace the unpleasant taste of his last drink, and at the same time saying something to his tablemate, as she positively dissolved in laughter. This (the fact that he was both chewing and talking at the same time) somehow surprised him. He swallowed and stopped talking. Leaning back in his chair with satisfaction, he realized that the sprint was already over. He had caught up. Waves of pleasant warmth ran through him, blissfully pushing farther and farther, to his fingers, his fingertips. Lyova looked at his fingers and thought he wanted something; there was still something missing, some simple thing—but what was it? A cigarette, he thought with sudden joy, how could I forget that? When he lighted up he felt good at last, as if until then he had been excruciatingly torn in two, and now the parts had joined, fused—not a stitch, not a trace of the tear—and he was again the person he had always been, whole. Now that he felt more alive, leaning back and puffing at his cigarette, he was able to take his bearings of the table a second time, completely differently, he even seemed to see it for the first time. Everything had gained in attractiveness, the girls were even nice. But all this pleasant oneness in his soul lasted for just a moment or two, between the first and the second puff, because as he surveyed the table again he couldn't help also seeing Faina, who had been placed in the far corner, diagonally across. This in itself was strange, that he saw her not right away but at second glance.

Now he caught Faina's eye and realized from her expression that she had been watching him, apparently for some time. Her glance was faintly derisive and at the same time surprised. Lyova instantly recalled how he had jammed his fork into his mouth, simultaneously saying whatever it was that had made his tablemate giggle so. Something in him contracted, and he immediately felt within him again the disjunction, the splitting of these two excruciating parts: they were separate again, independent, and began biting at each other. Fleetingly, like a sensation, the thought raced through his mind that Faina was in neither of those disjoined parts. Consequently, she had not been there when the parts were together just now—she especially hadn't been, even couldn't have been, perhaps . . . so Faina was the very fact of the split, the break itself, the void that separated the two parts. She was an abstraction, she wasn't there—but then why was she tangible, if all of her fitted in the gap?

It would be wrong to suppose that when he caught her eye he was frightened by Faina's jealousy. Jealousy, had there been any, could only have gladdened him, as a safeguard and guarantee. What frightened Lyova was that she had been able to take prompt advantage of this (his having forgotten her for a moment), what frightened him was not her glance but the change in it. Because he too, in his turn, had caught her glance slightly unawares, and had seen in it only a cool surprise and curiosity; but when their glances met and Faina realized that Lyova saw hers, she hastened to change it to one that was almost offended, and now, having thrown Lyova that offended glance, she turned toward Mitishatyev. Lyova was thoroughly flustered, ready to put on an expression of utmost guilt and entreaty, but he was left with this expression, as he had been left with his extended glass, unanswered.

Apparently Faina and Mitishatyev had only briefly interrupted their conversation, which was, moreover, very private, even intimate: they continued it intimately now, leaned toward each other intimately, smiled and nodded. This made Lyova tensely alert. But they didn't know each other, he thought, startled. Lyova remembered his surprise at finding they didn't know each other, that first evening—but now they had an obvious look of *long* familiarity. Their unclear degree of familiarity, this utter muddle in time and his own ideas, set Lyova's mind whirling. Maybe they had known each other, back before Lyova? And Mitishatyev's introducing himself to Faina so emphatically had merely been his idiotic notion of a joke? But Lyova could not remember whether Faina had smiled in reply—he didn't think she had. Or maybe it wasn't even a joke, but a sort of emphasis intelligible only to the two of them, maybe Mitishatyev had been expressing his displeasure, or even jealousy? Or maybe they had met afterward, conversed, and come to know each other more intimately?

In sum, Lyova got muddled; he even lost interest in the issue, being too disturbed by the very fact of their conversation *now*, this evident intimacy, interest, special animation. What were they talking about? He would never know . . . Again his everlasting powerlessness to know anything about Faina came over him in full measure, and at this moment his strongest desire was to have some fantastic bugging device, so that he could hear all this, unnoticed. Lyova's upbringing, in which eavesdropping was considered the ultimate degradation, was absolutely irrelevant at this moment. The desire was too passionate to be resisted by upbringing. But he had no bug. Lyova would also have been glad at this moment for a tiny little TV, because he could not see their hands and feet, only their inclined heads—and what if Mitishatyev was already holding Faina's hand, or their hot knees were touching? But he had no TV either. What were they talking about for so long, so engrossed in? Maybe even—him? Were they snickering? Here was Mitishatyev, laughing at something Faina had said, raising his glance to Lyova as if to make sure of something—as though Faina were a tour guide and he, Lyova, an exhibit—that kind of glance. He made sure, seemed to grin even more broadly once he was sure—and again was all engrossed in Faina, saying something to her, and now Faina was laughing . . . All that time she had never once turned toward Lyova! No matter how Lyova reached out with his mute entreaty, no matter how he called mentally for her answering glance—not once.

Lyova's pink tablemate was saying something to him, trying to continue their interrupted conversation. He was answering distractedly, in monosyllables, and not to the point. The change was so abrupt that she even took offense and fell silent. But when she followed Lyova's dismayed glance, she immediately put two and two together in a feminine way, despite her youth, and burst out laughing. "Jealous?" she said, leaning toward him. "Better have a drink." Lyova blushed an excruciating red. He was ashamed of having been so unable to do anything about himself or his face that he betrayed himself completely. Second only to his desire for an eavesdropping device had been the desire to make his face as aloof as possible, unconcerned, even cold. And now the face he had so vigorously perpetrated on himself turned out to be what most betrayed him. "No, what foolishness, of course not!" Lyova told his pink tablemate, crossly and hastily, and realized at once that if he wanted to change her opinion, this kind of answer wouldn't do it. "You don't even want a drink?" his tablemate said, derisively twisting his words. "No, I didn't mean that, I meant"— Lyova was utterly confused—"I'd be glad to have a drink." They had a drink. Lyova was even able to be somewhat diverted again; he successfully recouped, in his tablemate's eyes, by saying something that sent her into another peal of laughter. "You're pretty good, you're witty," she said. Witty, but no sense of humor, Lyova thought in anguish.

His urge to turn toward Faina and Mitishatyev was excruciating, and he was restraining himself with his last strength. And of course could not resist. And then, again, caught Faina's glance. This second glance was like a second warning notice, and the gist of it was something like: "Well, if that's what you want . . ." It even seemed to Lyova that he had seen Mitishatyev—admittedly at the last moment—nod slightly in his direction, which was why Faina, too, had turned to him. It seemed to Lyova that they were all observing him—Mitishatyev, Faina, his own tablemate, the whole table—he was discomfited. But Faina turned back to Mitishatyev, so definitively, so emphatically forever, that Lyova wanted to tip the table over on them. His whole body was braced for the effort. But of course he didn't tip it over, and then, also as a demonstration (but who needed his demonstration? after all, Faina wasn't looking at him), he turned back to his tablemate, catching her observant glance with annoyance. Although she was good and drunk by now, his tablemate. Giggling, she poured another drink for herself and offered the bottle to Lyova. Aware that this drink would have a powerful effect on him, he nevertheless drained it with a very resolute air, and got high.

Now came a scraping of chairs all being pushed back at once, and at last Lyova heard what an uproar there was in the room. Until this moment, there had been something wrong with the sound, there hadn't seemed to be any. Faina and Mitishatyev had been there, and the act of listening to them, which reduced all other sounds to nothing— though he had failed to hear Faina and Mitishatyev, too—and then the sound would burst in for a second, like the roar of the street through an opened window. The sound had been like that, one moment on, the next moment off . . . And suddenly the chairs rumbled, someone put out the overhead light, everyone stood up from the table at once and, seemingly also all at once, started saying, "Dancing, dancing! Why aren't we dancing!" That, it turned out, was why they had all stood up. Lyova, too, stood up, lurching slightly.

They dragged the table out of the way. Lyova dragged too, or rather, he chased after the table foolishly, still looking for a place to get his hand through, because they swarmed around the table on all sides as if it were hugely heavy: such fun for all, dragging the table. Someone even fell down—sheer ecstasy!

Just when he was looking so foolish, chasing the table and trying to find a handhold, Lyova discovered Faina and Mitishatyev, two steps away. They were having no part of this enterprise, merely observing, the only sober ones there. Lyova hastily straightened up and fell back from the rest of the group, making a stony face and feeling excruciatingly silly. "Lyovushka," Faina said caressingly, "how funny you are!" Lyova was both unnerved that she had said such a thing in front of Mitishatyev and overjoyed at her caressing tone, which he had not expected. He cared more about the caress. "Funny? Really?" he said, as though he would stop if it was bad, but he could be even funnier if Faina liked it: he would do whatever she wanted. Faina laughed and patted his arm. Lyova melted.

They danced. Faina herself asked Lyova. Lyova danced joyfully and clumsily and made Faina laugh hard. He realized at last that all his fears about Mitishatyev were utter nonsense—he was simply her tablemate, she had naturally conversed with her tablemate. So, in a general way, she had been with him all along, with Lyova. This filled him with joy, and pride, too, when he looked at the others: but of course she was the best, no one else had a date like her.

The dance ended. Smiling broadly, Lyova himself led Faina over to Mitishatyev, as if returning her to her escort—such a joke. Just then Lyova was grabbed by his pink tablemate. She kept laughing, and was unsteady on her feet. Lyova looked at Faina in dismay, finding himself in the strange posture of a man who is being pulled by the hand and, after taking one step in surprise, begins to pull in the opposite direction—to Faina, Faina! But Faina nodded at him with a smile: It's all right, go ahead.

And now Lyova was dancing with his pink tablemate. She was hot and soft, she melted in Lyova's arms and kept giggling, and her eyes swam, unable to focus on one point. To Lyova's surprise, this even had an effect on him. Now he caught sight of Faina's back—she was dancing with Mitishatyev. It struck Lyova that they danced very beautifully, and then he himself became utterly clumsy. His tablemate didn't mind at all, she even liked it when he bumped into her. But somehow Faina was dancing so that her back was to Lyova the whole time, he simply couldn't find a moment when she would turn around, all he saw the whole time was Mitishatyev's face, smiling a smile borrowed from the movies and continuously saying things to Faina in a soft (so that you couldn't hear without a bug!) whisper.

Striving to repair the situation, Lyova rushed to ask Faina for the next dance, but again it was as if a stand-in had taken her place. "You're all danced out," she said coldly and spitefully, as if alluding to his tablemate again, and refused him.

But the dance did not take place at all, because suddenly someone turned on the light and knocked the needle off the phonograph. "Let's play Spin, Little Bottle!" he cried. "Spin, Little Bottle! Spin, Little Bottle!" everyone cried. Lyova recalled that he had heard of this: a kissing game. A circle was formed. Mitishatyev and Faina were in it, so Lyova crowded in, too (his tardiness reminded him of the table-moving, and he frowned). In the center was a large champagne bottle. "Spin it, spin it!" they cried. Someone tried to spin it, but nothing happened, and he fell down. "You can't, you can't. Let go!" they shouted to the man, who was on hands and knees. "It won't spin," he said, aggrieved. "Why not?" Lyova asked, to his own surprise. "It just won't," he said reasonably, getting up from his hands and knees. "We need a little bottle," he told Lyova crossly, "and this is a big one! We need a little one, a flask!" "A flask"—they guffawed—"a flask!"

Someone spun it more adeptly, and the silver bottle neck fixed on Faina as the compass arrow fixes on the north. An *O-o-oh!* swept the circle. "Spin for who gets her! Hurry up, spin it!" someone shouted impatiently. Lyova stood stock-still and turned white. Me, come on—me! he ordered the bottle mentally, even moving his lips. The bottle pointed to Mitishatyev. Lyova went numb. "Kiss, go on, kiss!" they cried. Mitishatyev looked questioningly at Faina. Lyova fastened his eyes on her. Faina laughed oddly, glanced at Lyova, and shook her head. "How do you like that!" someone drawled in annoyance.

They spun the bottle once more, but it pointed to the least interesting girl. Everyone lost the desire to kiss, and the game somehow broke up of itself. They put out the light again and began kissing whomever they wanted, with no particular excuse. Lyova's pink tablemate captured him again and pulled him away somewhere. He kept dragging his feet and looking around, but nowhere did he find Faina and Mitishatyev, not in a single dark corner. They were gone.

"Yes, yes . . . I'll be right back," he told his tablemate thickly, and jumped up from the couch on which she had just managed to sit him down.

He stood for some time, pale, all stimuli and impulses, like a pointing dog—his nostrils even flared (or did he hear in the distance the summoning sound of the horn?). "But why are you leaving?" his tablemate asked caressingly. He made no reply. "Oh, I know—looking for her again?" she guessed. "*No!*" Lyova growled angrily. "Why should I?" With long, straight strides, which nevertheless seemed unsteady, he headed for the door.

He saw Faina and Mitishatyev so instantly, as he plunged out of the room, that he was even thrown off balance and seemed to stumble: he had been coming too fast, braked too sharply. Faina stood by the trunk, leaning back against the wall, and Mitishatyev was in front of her, with one foot planted on the trunk and one hand braced against the wall above Faina's shoulder. They seemed to have been just standing there without touching each other, even before Lyova arrived, but Lyova imagined a rustle, some movement on their part that he hadn't caught at first. (And for some time afterward, whether he was watching *A Husband for Anna* with Silvana Pampanini in the lead role, where she stands on the stairs and her sailor somehow draws up his leg in a peculiar way, or reading the famous line in Hemingway, "Like any man, I couldn't talk about love very long standing up," he could neither see nor read it calmly—he was always haunted by the trunk in that vestibule.)

They both looked at him calmly and without apparent embarrassment. "Well, Lyova," said Faina, "how's your tablemate?" "All right." Lyova gulped, unable to fight down the spasm in his throat. "We're out here talking," Faina said. "It's stifling in there." "Oh," Lyova said. Mitishatyev gave a faint nod, and only now changed his pose a little. He pushed off, and removed his arm from the wall, but kept his foot on the trunk—made it all look as if he had nothing to hide from Lyova: there had been nothing special in his pose, it was all right for two people involved in conversation to stand like that (in our era of unconstrained and natural movements). To think anything else, he was saying, would be silly of Lyova, and what could be funnier than unwarranted suspicions . . . But that was exactly what Lyova was thinking, and all his strength went into not letting anyone notice it. Still, he sensed that he could do nothing about his face. "I'm off to piss," he said then, as if excusing himself with a joke. "Good grief, Lyova." Faina laughed, almost approvingly. Lyova paraded past without turning around. He stood for some time in the kitchen, furiously smoking a cigarette, and went back. Mitishatyev and Faina were no longer by the trunk.

They were in the room. "How are you?" Faina inquired sympathetically. "How! You know how," Lyova said in exasperation. "Oh, I didn't mean . . . Silly, did you think—? But that's funny." "I don't think anything," Lyova declared proudly. "Good for you," Faina said. Mitishatyev came over. "Should we have a drink, perhaps? Call your tablemate," Faina suggested. "The hell with her!" Lyova said. "Why say that? It's not nice," Faina said. Lyova woke his tablemate, she roused herself and gladly consented. Lyova had to help her up from the couch by main strength. They had a drink. Lyova came to life again and started to talk, all the while feeling awkward because his pink tablemate was hanging on his arm. He held his elbow at a lifeless angle, trying to seem separate from her. "Look, she's not at all well," Faina said. "Go with her." "Ah, hell!" Lyova almost howled, and he looked at Faina with hatred.

He led his tablemate to the couch, but it was already occupied: someone was petting. He seated her on the bed and wanted to leave her there, but she wouldn't let go of his arm. Incapable of rudeness despite all, Lyova sat down beside her in anguish. His tablemate cuddled up to him softly and affectionately, nuzzling his shoulder and murmuring. Lyova went completely numb. Faina and Mitishatyev were standing where he had left them, with their backs to Lyova. His tablemate suddenly began to groan and suffer. That does it, Lyova thought in anguish, drawing back slightly. He saw her face, her open pudgy mouth—she was nothing but a child. Suddenly he was overcome by an excruciating, squeamish pity for her. "Come on now, come on now," he urged her. "Come on now . . ." He was dragging her, and at this point he again discovered that Faina and Mitishatyev were not in the room.

They weren't by the trunk, either. He dragged his pink tablemate—her face by now altogether white—down the dark corridor, looking around in torment as if he might spot Faina in some crack. He knocked at the shower room. It was locked from inside, light showed from under the door. He all but shoved his tablemate into the lavatory, then rushed to the kitchen. They weren't there, either. He rushed back to the shower room. It was locked as before. He even stooped down, put his head to the floor, but did not see or hear anything. I'm losing my mind, he told himself, hastily jumping up and dusting off his knees.

He returned to the room and looked around foolishly, again as if hunting for Faina in a crack. She was not there. He discovered only her purse, which she had stuck behind a table lamp. For some reason, he grabbed the purse and darted out into the corridor with it. In the doorway he bumped into the couple who had been petting on the couch. The door to the shower room was open; nobody in there now. Then, at his back, he heard the stair door slam. He stood for some time in grave perplexity, his mind a blank. He rushed to the stairway. Voices were audible below. He ran down the stairs three at a time. Nobody. Nobody in the yard, either. He was suddenly struck that it was snowing.

He went back and sat dully on the couch, opening and closing the purse, snapping the catch. At length he glanced inside: a compact, a pencil stub, a handkerchief . . . It was tied in a knot. He undid the knot and discovered the ring. He recalled how she had quietly slipped it off her finger. He tried it for fit. It wouldn't go on a single finger. Well, she told me herself it's worth five hundred rubles,* he thought, somewhat dryly. We can go out to dinner three times—the thought spun neutrally in his mind, as in an adding machine. What can I do,

---

* The price scale before the reform of 1961. Money was different then, larger in format but of lesser value. So when Lyova agonized over getting fifty rubles, it wasn't like fifty rubles now. It was nothing—five rubles in today's money. But the fact that five rubles today is no serious matter for anyone, while fifty back then might be extremely serious—you'll never explain this to someone who doesn't remember it. Time! (Herein lies the secret of whatever age a man has achieved: If I just remembered things aright, as they were . . . I wouldn't want to go back, not even for a day!)

if I haven't any money . . . And he stuck the ring in his pocket. He retied the knot in the handkerchief. Closed the purse. Took it and put it behind the table lamp. As he walked away, he took one more look—exactly right. He sat down to wait, strangely calm.

How can you do this, Faina! he said mentally, even moving his lips. Do people really behave this way? Even if I was mistaken and suspected you wrongly, how can you jeer at me this way! What am I guilty of? Can't you see when a person is suffering? That doesn't even take love—anyone would have pity. But you're like a vivisectionist. It's unimaginable to me that one person could do such a thing to another. And do it to one who loves you. To the very one who loves you—but not to Mitishatyev? How could you, Faina . . .

Softly he coaxed Faina, and she appeared. She ran up to him. "What's the matter, you poor little thing?" Lyova was silent, fingering the ring in his pocket. "We've been for a walk. You know how nice it is on the Neva!" Lyova silently stroked the ring. "Oh, what's the matter, silly? You mustn't be so silly! Did I offend you? But how else can I deal with you . . ." "Well, how else can I deal with you . . ." Lyova echoed. "Let's go out, hurry up, let's go! How can we stay inside! It's so nice outdoors. It's light already." "But for some reason I thought it was snowing," Lyova said. "Snow in July? You *are* weird!" And Faina headed for the table, drew her purse out from behind the table lamp. Watching her do this, Lyova felt an obscure satisfaction. Something within him relaxed, and he sighed.

All three of them left together.

It really was beautiful outdoors.

Lyova walked along, his blood rang with a high small jingling, he was unaware of his body and even seemed to be flying; the three of them were all talking at once, and it seemed to Lyova that there was something faintly flaring beside them. He even turned his head to watch it. There was nothing there, yet it flared again, more to the side, a little farther off . . . From time to time he felt for the ring in fright—but it hadn't disappeared, it was there. He would sigh with relief and stroke it a little, and the flaring would become brighter. "Like Aladdin," he suddenly said aloud. "What's like Aladdin?" Mitishatyev asked. "The spire," Lyova said. Hastily pulling his hand from his pocket, he pointed at the famous gilded spire across the river. "I want to rub it with a rag and make everything disappear." "Now that's what I call an image," Mitishatyev said. "What are you talking about?" Faina said.

Then they were a long time saying goodbye at Faina's house, as if waiting each other out: who would go home first, and who would stay. Lyova waited silently and patiently, studying three dislodged bricks (they were just at his eye level), and finally they all took their leave at once: Faina entered her front door, he and Mitishatyev set off together.

Lyova felt relief and joy, and with his every step the strange flaring around him intensified. They walked to the streetcar stop, his suspicions fell away like stifling garments, and there at the core, naked and clean, surrounded only by the flaring white light, was Lyova—the kernel, the seed! He inhaled with his whole chest, he heard sounds and smelled smells, and the stars came out clearly for him. At the streetcar stop it was already quite light, another two steps and Mitishatyev would be home. Amiably, candidly they shook hands, and Lyova jumped on the running board of the morning's first streetcar . . .

THE FATALIST

(FAINA, *continued*)

*"You will die today!" I told him. He turned swiftly, but his answer
was slow and calm: "Maybe so, maybe not . . ."*

HE HAD EXPECTED to hear about the ring the minute he walked
in. But Faina was gay, unexpectedly affectionate, and cordial, and he
was amazed. Let him wait a minute on the stairs—she'd get dressed
in a jiffy and they'd go for a walk. He waited.

Faina reappeared instantly, pale as death. "What's the matter?"
Lyova exclaimed, conscious of what a poor actor he was. Within
moments he was repenting his deed—never had he seen Faina in such
unfeigned distress! His loving heart bled. He would have been glad to
return the ring right now and comfort her, but his insides knotted in
terror the instant he imagined himself confessing. Faina would banish
him at once, and he would never, never see her again! "All right,
don't cry now, I'll buy you another!" he said, as in a fairy tale. "Not
an ordinary one, but gold. Maybe not so expensive . . . But this will
be *my* ring. It's the ring itself you care about, isn't it, and not that it
was from *him*?" he asked with fright and hope, already sweetly moved
by this potential happiness. The ring his—then Faina, too, forever
his. "The ring itself, of course! Who cares that it was from him!"
Faina said, very bluntly. "Well, then you shall, you shall have a ring!"
Lyova said almost tearfully, clutching her thin hands in ecstasy. "Just
don't be upset, just don't cry!" Very quickly, all of a sudden, Faina
regained her composure: "You mean you'll really buy one?" "Really,
really," Lyova said, conscious that he was regaining his composure
along with her, and somewhat distressed that she had regained hers
so quickly. All right then, I'll sell this ring and buy another, he was
already thinking, almost indifferently. If that's how she wants it . . .

164

"You know," Faina was saying, "you can buy a ring comparatively cheaply. Two hundred rubles, even a hundred and fifty if you look. And then we'll be engaged," she said. She kissed him as tenderly as she knew how.

Lyova melted again, and stayed to wait while she got ready. All right then, he reasoned, I'll sell this one, I'll buy another, a cheaper one, and there'll be something left over, we can go out to dinner a couple of times. No, three times—again the thought clicked dryly through his mind, as in an adding machine—what's the difference. And as for buying her the ring, there'll be another compensation for that, he thought grimly. At last she'll realize how I love her. She *knows* what a hard time I have getting money.

At the resale shop the clerk turned the ring this way and that in his hands and said, "Fifty rubles." No, five hundred! Lyova all but shouted. No, it can't be! A swindler, well of course, he's an old swindler!

And he raced to a second resale shop. At the second shop the clerk was not a man but a woman. She tossed the ring on the scales, such accurate scales. (Well, but of course the other was a swindler, Lyova thought joyfully, he didn't even weigh it!) Painstakingly, interminably, the clerk nudged the delicate balance, weighed the ring, then clicked her abacus. Lyova's insides knotted and froze. "Forty-nine rubles," she said at last.

He stood dumbfounded, holding the ring in front of him, and it tarnished before his very eyes. "My God! Brass!" he exclaimed. In a fit of anger he almost threw it in the trash can, but something suddenly stopped him, some obscure thought. The clerk was watching him curiously from her cage. He gripped the ring in his fist, thrust his fist deep in his pocket, turned abruptly, and hurried out.

The long, narrow, empty sky of the avenue stretched into the distance. Not a single bird traversed that strip of sky, watch as he might. If only a bird would fly over . . . Lyova understood that he had no one. Neither father nor friend . . . Almost happiness—such grief!

It was this emotion that led him . . . his feet themselves went . . . his aimless path chanced to pass . . . and he didn't notice how he came to be in that entrance, on that landing . . . pulled the polished brass button. Far inside, the bell tinkled anciently. Uncle Mitya opened at once, as if he had been lurking behind the door, unshaven, in his shawl, without his teeth. "I won't do it," he said through the chain. "I won't give you a loan."

Lyova went back to the stores, simply to make the time pass. He stared at the rings: smash the display case, ask them to show him one, snatch it—and run, run! He would have time before they collected themselves . . . His heart was hammering above the counter. The rings were all very expensive, there weren't any for even two hundred. And where would he get the two hundred? But most of the rings really did cost five hundred or more. Faina was right, Faina had lied correctly . . . Suddenly the obscure thought that had kept him from throwing the ring away popped into his mind and became so clear that Lyova nearly jumped up and down, or at any rate he let out an inarticulate exclamation, something like "Eureka!" A sense of malice and even triumph stirred within him.

By the time he arrived at Faina's, the idea so possessed him that he could not drag out the game and think up some reason why he must measure her thin finger. Instead, he got right down to business, no longer taking care to make it all plausible. He still felt within him an inexplicable, unaccustomed strength and malice.

"Give me your hand," he told Faina. Faina was somewhat surprised at his unaccustomed tone but gave him her hand, somehow submitting at once. "Shut your eyes," he ordered. "Oh, darling!" Faina guessed suddenly. "You didn't—!" And she threw her arms around his neck. "But how were you able—?" "Shut your eyes," he repeated, "and don't dare open till I tell you." "All right," she agreed obediently. "Which finger do you wear it on?" Lyova asked, suddenly realizing that he did not remember. Faina cocked her ring finger. The ring went on easily, as was to be expected. "Now you can open," Lyova said.

He was still holding her hand in both of his, so that the ring was not visible. "Oh, Lyova, it just fits!" Faina exclaimed, blissfully wiggling her finger in his hand. Never had Lyova seen Faina's face so unself-conscious, so happy. She jumped up and down to kiss him and missed, clumsily getting him on the nose, the eyes, the forehead. Lyova almost hated her.

"It fits just right!" she exclaimed, and Lyova took his hand away. "How did you know . . ." Faina stopped short, peering at the ring. Possibly Lyova had never seen Faina's face like this, either. Between the first face and the second lay a vast distance—it had been traversed instantaneously, with the speed of light. "Where did you get this ring?" Faina asked in a changed voice.

"I bought it," Lyova said calmly. "Where?" "From somebody," Lyova said. "This is my ring," Faina said. "It can't be," Lyova said, going numb with a satisfaction he had never known. "Mine. I know my own ring," Faina said. The life seemed to drain from her face.

Can it really hurt her so much to learn that I'm the one who did it, Lyova thought almost wonderingly. As if the ground had slid out from under her feet, as if she had already lurched into a fall—that was the expression on her face.

"It can't be yours. How much was yours worth?" Lyova asked. "Five hundred," Faina answered automatically, dully. "But I bought this for a hundred," Lyova said, "and paid double at that. I had it appraised afterward, it's really worth fifty." Faina was silent. "If you don't believe me, let's go check." In his triumph, Lyova was tightening the screws.

"I don't want to," Faina said, and her face even came back to life a bit. "I don't want to wear a ring that somebody's already worn." Lyova was slightly disconcerted: "What makes you think anybody's worn it?" "I could tell right off." Lyova was even more disconcerted: "You should go shopping yourself—you'd see there aren't any cheap rings at all. Where would I get that kind of money? I was lucky to even find this one." "All the same, I won't wear somebody else's ring!" Faina said insistently, with growing life and fervor. "I'd have put on a new one, because it would have been *your* ring, from you. But this one—no."

Faina slipped the ring from her finger and held it out to Lyova, staring at him vacantly. Lyova looked down, went rigid, forcibly gripped the ring as if he wished to crush it. And again something flared to the rescue in his mind, he didn't even have time to clearly grasp what. "Is that so!" Lyova shouted suddenly. "Then I don't need it, either. No one needs it!" He swung his arm with unnatural force and ran to the window. He was already winding up for the throw, yet he was gripping the ring tighter and tighter, conscious that he would never really be able to throw it away. Suddenly he felt Faina seize his arm. He turned and gave her a haughty glance: Now what? He turned— still rooted to the spot by the voluptuous hatred that so utterly filled the space of his bitter passion, still holding the little ring in his upraised hand—and was astounded by their instant equality. "Don't," Faina said. "Give it to me . . ." she said, softly and submissively. And Lyova suppressed a sigh of relief.

Much later, when the issue was long dead, so to speak, Lyova glanced at her ring one day (Faina never took it off now)—and suddenly it all came back to life and started spinning before his eyes. The feeling of that night with Mitishatyev revived, too, and of all the days that had followed . . . He remembered the feeling as powerfully, as exactly, as can sometimes happen at a forgotten smell or music. (They were riding on a little old streetcar, on the rear platform, through the wasteland on the outskirts, and for a long time before he *suddenly saw* the ring Lyova had been watching the rails running from under the car into the wasteland . . .)

Lyova suddenly remembered it all so vividly that he could not refrain from asking (ever since that time, they had mutually avoided bringing up the incident of the ring, but now he asked), "Listen, Faina, how much was your old ring worth? Tell me the truth."

Faina glanced at him in surprise and puzzlement. "Why old? It was always this one. It's worth five hundred rubles."

"No, it's worth fifty," Lyova said insistently.

"Oh yes," she said, "in the new price scale, it's worth fifty."

(Notably, after the incident of the ring they had what was perhaps the most prolonged and peaceful period of their relationship. In a real sense, all sciences are natural, Lyova thought, apropos of this. Even philology . . . And that may have been when he went and paid his respects to Grandfather. Without, however, attaching all that much significance to the step.)

ALBINA

*"Either you despise me, or you love me very much!" she said at last,
in a voice in which there were tears . . . "Isn't it true," she added
in a voice of tender trust, "isn't it true, there is nothing in me to
preclude respect . . ."*

IN ALL CLARIFICATIONS of a relationship—especially if it has
long been undergoing clarification and has acquired its own period-
icity, its own ritual and rhythm—no matter how complex and well
developed the superstructure of accusations and arguments, the participants are basically interested in one question only: Who started it?

And placing his hand on his heart, as he theatrically did at these
moments, trembling with despair, Lyova was convinced, naturally
enough, that it was Faina and only Faina, he hadn't done even the
least little thing. Whereas she—! Really and truly, only Lyova could
have borne the flagrant injustice of her stubbornness, anybody else in
his place would have . . . oh, all right, he wasn't the first, he wouldn't
be the last, the fact itself he could endure, he said . . . but this wall
of falsehood he was beating against, what was this for! a man could
go out of his mind! That's just what she wanted, to drive him out of
his mind. What is "truth" after all, Faina? Truth is surgery, an operation. You lose something, but you get better. Everything will be
all right with us again . . . but in order to leave the past in the past,
we have to leave *all* of it there. You understand, ALL of it! . . . Oh,
Lord! *He* would endure, he would endure all for her sake . . . but—
his heart!

This really is a wonder, how our poor heart endures! It does. Every
time.

But if he actually had placed his hand on his heart, or rather, if he
could have placed his heart on his hand, then there at the bottom of

it, in the barely divinable vascular distance, lurked some small thing, indistinguishable, very terrible, to which he would never have agreed, to which he would not have confessed under any torture, as if the edifice of his irrefutable rightness, erected in the forests of logic according to a standard quarrel-plan, were his only piece of real estate securing any continuation whatever of their life . . . his rightness was his one saving support, the only shore in the ocean of her treachery. But there at the very bottom—which he did not bring closer for scrutiny, because he already knew what was there—he did not know who had started it. Faina, of course; she really was deeply culpable, whereas he—well, it was trivial, no involvement, didn't count, but still . . . if he remembered that trifling matter, his stance began to waver and collapse.

It hardly needs saying that Lyova loved Faina. Even if we doubt the "truth" of his feeling, still, he had always loved her in his "nontrue" way. Even before she appeared on the scene (he had been friends with Mitishatyev back in school . . .). But once upon a time (let this sound like a fairy tale) Faina, too, loved Lyova. Not exactly loved him, but anyway, that was how it worked out or came across. It may have been the same "peaceful" period with which the incident of the ring concluded . . . More precisely, it may not have been love, just a kind of interim period for Faina—she just didn't have anything else, so that, although he was well aware of this (we are all well aware of it), Lyova was serene; like any man alive, he did not entertain the notion that his every feeling of confidence would be paid for by a subsequent lack of confidence, far more intense. Here is the whole difference: some receive confidence as if in reward for their previous lack of confidence, others receive a lack of confidence as punishment for their previous confidence. All this is indivisible and barely distinguishable, however, all of a piece. In brief, Lyova was serene, but strange as it may seem (perhaps it's strange only to Lyova), the steady, infinite happiness that might have been imagined here did not materialize. What developed was simply a kind of void, seasoned with a certain amount of satiety and complacency, which may have been, not the substance, but merely the form of the bewilderment peculiar to people of Lyova's type when they don't know what to do. They never do know, but sometimes that is suffering and sometimes satiety. Lyova found himself facing a void of gratification—and he was either bewildered or sated.

At this point Albina emerges as a possibility. Although from Lyova's standpoint Albina would never pique Faina's jealousy; to cheat with her would always mean exactly nothing and could establish no equi-librium. If Lyova did sometimes notice women, he noticed them only from Faina's standpoint, noticed only those whom Faina might look upon as her rivals (thus we acquire the tastes of the enemy and begin to whistle *Rosamunde*).

But now for Albina. She was poor, and Lyova was very ashamed of his debt (which he never did pay back). They met again on Uncle Mitya's birthday. Lyova was surprised to see Albina at Uncle Mitya's. (When inviting him Dickens had said, "But without your wench"—he did not like Faina, and he was the only one Lyova forgave for this.) Lyova was also surprised to note Dickens's special considerateness and gallantry in conversation with this "nobody." It made Lyova pay some attention to her. Besides, he had been laying into "Mitya's specialty"; the rusty *chifir* had started humming in his veins. Uncle Mitya, still admiring his guest, even got out a Ghirlandajo reproduction and in-vited everyone to mark the resemblance. At this point Lyova had the temerity to squeeze pale Albina's hand under the table. He petted her soft little hand for some time, and she did not take it away.

The next morning Lyova forgot to even think about Albina—he just had a splitting headache. But she did not forget. She telephoned him endlessly. Lyova, to his shame, remembered how he had squeezed her hand and talked about getting together. She was calling about this rendezvous. And the voice in the receiver was such that he could neither refuse nor, especially, consent. He cursed himself roundly for this. He remembered Uncle Dickens—there was a man! There was a gentleman . . . he would never feel ashamed of a fellow human being. How considerate he had been with her yesterday! But even Uncle Dickens's example did not inspire him.

(It's time we admitted it to ourselves: we very much wish Uncle Dickens had first turned up in this part! As a variant of Grandfather, instead of Grandfather—he would have been very suitable and very ornamental [in the role of Lermontov's Maxim Maximych]. Especially since he was the one whom Lyova perceived, and remembered, in the colors of youth. But it's too late. We wasted Uncle Mitya in part one, and we don't have another like him. Still, he was essential in that part, to offset Grandfather's unattractiveness. He was more "needed" there. [What would he think of that little word now!] He is always there, wherever he's more needed by someone [than by himself]: by Lyova, by the country, by me . . . He is always and obediently there—with humble pride on his face.)

Anyway, Lyova did not want to go to this rendezvous. His inner boorishness may have been an involuntary expression of his shyness (segregated education), or of Faina's tastes (which is more likely), but in either case he could do nothing about it. What stopped him was not that he had no need of this rendezvous at all, so much as the necessity of meeting with, and being with, Albina in public. Although she was far from homely. She had something . . . And something else good and pure, as the saying goes—she could not tell a lie, for example—but Lyova was supremely indifferent to these virtues, however rare, including her sudden devotion, however undemanding of him. He couldn't for the life of him appear with her in public. Yet his kind heart not only was irritated but also bled, every time he heard her voice in the receiver, heard her painstakingly concealed and therefore so obvious entreaty. He would gladly have consented . . . He was already coaxing himself: her face wasn't bad, and she dressed with taste, he alone was so ashamed of her, others were not . . . and as for mind, heart, all the inner qualities, there was no question—the absolute ideal. But, and here we can understand Lyova, something in her far from ugly face betrayed a dependence on the same mechanism in which Lyova himself had been so passively involved until now. She was like Lyova—that was the trouble. But Lyova was no longer the same . . . And at last he set off to this rendezvous.

They had windy, slushy, ink-black weather. Fine day he'd picked! They immediately turned away from the center of the city, onto unfrequented old side streets, almost totally dark. It was Lyova who turned, saying he couldn't bear the crowd, he felt positively faint. In this instance he was not lying. He really did feel almost faint, because of the crowd's seeming attention to him and Albina. (Might this have been, after all, a fear of meeting Faina by chance? Although Lyova believed in mathematics: the probability of meeting her in a big city was so small. But even that probability might have frightened him.)

They turned onto these little streets, Lyova was cold here, but at least it was dark and there were no people. She listened spellbound no matter what he said. If he said he couldn't bear the crowd, she simply accepted it and consented willingly. She seemed to keep waiting (Lyova was well aware of this) for him to remind her of the other evening, that he hadn't just squeezed her hand by accident, and if it wasn't by accident, then for him to squeeze it again and for everything to go on, develop. But Lyova tried not to notice this silent plea. He said boring things about his work in a snappish voice, as if it had been an exasperating day and he couldn't get it out of his mind. He seemed not to notice her reaching out to him again and again with her entreaty (although he saw only her), he felt very bad, ashamed, ill at ease—never had he known himself to be such a scoundrel that he could not respond to a feeling so absolute.

Albina listened spellbound anyway, even though she could hear nothing. But now her shoelaces came all untied. She flushed, excused herself ruefully, and began to tie them. In her desire to get it done quickly, she took such an awkward stance that tying them became quite impossible. Lyova stood over her, fidgeting with impatience, unable to do anything with his wind-frozen hands, saying nothing, a malicious moron . . . but what could he say, contorted as he was with shame for a fellow human being and with shame for that shame! And God forbid, a man walked by, all alone in this empty lane, so of course he had to turn around with a curious stare.

Albina straightened up at last.

They walked a little farther, her shoelaces again came untied, and again the whole thing was repeated. She stood hunched in the wind, off balance, getting tangled in the laces in her dithery haste, and apparently forgetting completely, in her despair, how she had been doing this all her life: left loop on right, right on left?

Mean weather, what horrible mean weather it was! Albina, in her wretched little coat, was already shivering violently and could do nothing about it, any more than she could about her laces. But Lyova was almost happy that the weather was like this, it seemed to set a natural limit, and he began coaxing her: she was so thoroughly chilled, she'd get sick yet, they'd had such bad luck today, better next time, when the weather wouldn't be like this—next time without fail, Lyova promised. But Albina said that she couldn't understand why she was shivering, because she was warm. You must have a temperature already, a fever, said Lyova, and what a shame it turned out this way . . .

Anyway, with the help of the weather, things somehow came to a relatively swift end. Lyova gathered his last courage and patience to get her home, and the minute the front door slammed behind her he was already flying as if shot from a sling, aware of an unusual lightness, almost happiness, shameful though it was. He flew around the corner so fast that Albina, who immediately opened the front door again to ask or ascertain something more from Lyova, saw no one in the empty street, only the wind, plastering her face with wet, heavy snow.

And Lyova was flying back, to Faina, he was even singing with joy, vowing to himself that he would never again get caught in such a gruesome farce. Who enjoyed feeling like a pig?

But when he returned, he did not find Faina home. He waited and waited—but she had disappeared somewhere, no one knew where, without even leaving a note, without warning him. But hadn't she planned to be home all evening? . . . And she didn't even call. Then again, it was already one o'clock in the morning, he told himself, and she was afraid of waking the neighbors.

Lyova did not sleep all night. Then—retribution! Faina appeared, not even early, but late in the forenoon. The minute she walked in, she offered poor shivering Lyova a fantastic story, along with a kiss on the forehead (for which Faina was forced to stand way up on tiptoe, because Lyova, in his effort to look stony, cold, and imperturbable, would not bend his head; Faina was never moved by this look, however).

Her story was about how in Lyova's absence an old friend of hers had arrived quite unexpectedly and invited her to go for a ride: the car was waiting downstairs . . . (but she knew, Faina said, that Lyova himself had gone to meet someone, even though he tried to conceal it he didn't know how to, he should never try, so she had decided why couldn't she, too). Anyway, they had driven out of town . . . no, they weren't alone together, the friend had a friend along, also a university lecturer, he was the one who drove the car, because her friend hadn't gotten his license yet . . . So beautiful! Everything's melting here, but out there the firs are all snowy, real winter. They arrived at the dacha, no, not her friend's, the friend of the friend's, also a lecturer, they had supper there . . . Well, yes, they had a little to drink, she hardly had anything . . . Now wait, this is where it all starts . . . the friend of the friend, the one who was supposed to drive the car, suddenly got drunk, dead drunk, and they couldn't leave . . . but what did they do all night? played cards, Kings, believe me I was never so bored . . . yes, we did . . . you think I don't know that two can't play Kings? the three of us played . . . so what if he was drunk, he could *play* . . . and besides, that wasn't the problem—he was out of gas—and besides, that wasn't the problem—the car broke down—oh, leave me alone, please, don't badger me!

On her arms, her breast, her neck, Lyova discovered the kind of marks that—forget the chauffeur! Faina was slightly rattled for a moment, shed a few tears, but Lyova was adept at catching her in this shallow water. His sharpened logic where Faina was concerned quickly drove her into a corner, and with unexpected, excruciating readiness, she confessed all. And having confessed, unfortunately for Lyova, told no more lies. Lyova instantly sprouted horns. Moreover, she might at least have lied about who it was, because it was his best friend, Mitishatyev, and Lyova himself was practically to blame: how would she know why Lyova had gone to meet someone? yes, if you must know, it was jealousy . . . Lord, what Lyova's rendezvous had cost him!

And then it began, they were off: how many times, and did they undress? . . . Of course it wasn't Mitishatyev . . . Oh, what do you care who it was—what does it matter! Well, once, and they hadn't undressed at all. Oh, he believed that—ha! All right, they *did* undress! yes, stark naked, and then what did they have to lose? Well, and suppose it was Mitishatyev . . . She was drunk, that's how it happened. Oh, leave me alone! He was right about you: a martyr! But no, it wasn't him . . . Swine yourself!

Let us leave them.

Lyova retired to his father's dacha to nurse his grief. To Faina, who felt very sorry for him on the whole, he said that he could not see anyone and wanted to be alone. To his father, that he had an urgent piece of work to complete. But he passed the time there in a dreadful state of dither and decay, endlessly playing a stupid solitaire game, the only one he knew, and drinking. At this point Albina paid him a visit. Someone had told her the address over the phone (Faina perhaps?) . . . yes, a woman's voice.

Albina brought him some silly chocolate-covered pastilles and a bottle of vinegary wine. Coldly, dully, Lyova put out the light and *possessed* Albina, strangely feeling nothing, nothing but power. As though studying himself from above, as though suspended from the ceiling and vengefully observing the mechanical rhythm of his deserted body. And in response to her passionate questions he merely reiterated, supposing it a kind of honesty on his part, that no, he could not lie, he did not love her; that is, he liked her as a person and thought very highly of her—but didn't love her.

In the morning Albina hurriedly left for work, timidly trying to wake him. He was far from asleep, but he mumbled as if unable to rouse himself and would not unstick his eyes. Out of tenderness she stopped trying to wake him, since he was so soundly asleep. She scribbled warm and pathetic words on the pastille box, stroked him one last time with trembling hand, murmured something like "my precious"—which made Lyova blush wildly, although by now he was snoring for effect— and finally left.

Lyova sat up in bed and began to howl. That is the word for it, without exaggeration. He howled a long time: at first from the heart, then listening with surprise to his own howls, and then for no reason at all, in stupefaction. "So much for your pastille! What a swine," he told himself indifferently. "But so what?" He quickly got ready and left the dacha. On the empty train he drank a split of vodka and slept the whole trip.

He knew that he had done this after Faina. And besides, could he really consider his betrayal a betrayal? But it was enough of one to make everything shift, fluctuate. He wasn't absolutely pure now: he'd traipsed off to this rendezvous, hadn't he? And no matter what explanation he found now, his absolute rightness was gone—none of that seemed relevant to the investigation any longer . . . a second bottom had been revealed, and what else might be lurking there, in the depth of the depths? What lurked there was true vertigo: now Lyova wasn't even sure of the sequence. This time—yes, he had gone to a rendezvous that could not wittingly have led to a betrayal. But then why, after all, had he gone? There had, it seemed, there had after all been—though unnoticed, or rather unremarked by him—a certain episode, which might have left Albina puzzled in her own mind and caused her to show such persistence. Of course he could not consider (especially!) that faded fact a fact. He wrote off that fact, but now another forgotten something flamed up, and this was Faina again: surely she hadn't even then—! He simply didn't know, did he, where she had disappeared to, either that time or that, which girlfriend she had visited in the country . . .

"Why, how can you! How can you!" Faina would exclaim at this deepening of the subject. "Why, the very first night we met, you liked another girl! Don't you remember? Stella—" "Stella who!" Lyova roared. "The girl in blue"—and Faina mimicked her so artfully that Lyova couldn't help grinning, couldn't help remembering. "You went for her first that night!" "Oh, come on," Lyova stammered, flattered by her jealousy—and Faina was his own again.

So that's how it goes, Lyova thought. All the way back to Eve (and Eve betrayed Adam before she became his wife), back to Original Sin. It vibrates like an elementary particle, ever splitting and never annihilated . . . There is a series AB, AB, AB, AB . . . Betrayal A, followed immediately by Betrayal B, followed again by Betrayal A, again by B—like a chain. Once begun, it stretches on. Drop the first A, and we get: BA, BA, BA . . . What's the difference, if the series recedes into infinity? reasoned philologist Lyova Odoevtsev in a mathematical way, gravitating toward the natural sciences.

"Well, so get out!" Faina said. "Why should *I* get out?" Lyova gritted venomously. "You get out." It was not the first time in their lives the words had been spoken, and what was Lyova's surprise when he found, instead of Faina, only a short, unusually affectionate letter. She was gone. "Don't try to find me"—and all that sort of thing. Lyova made a wild dash, but nevertheless did not follow her to Sakhalin.

Three days later, he came to. At that moment he was walking along the Nevsky. The darkening avenue somehow had a peculiarly sharp gleam after the rain—umbrellas, automobiles, asphalt, the sated swish of tires, the red flare and squeal of brakes—as if he saw it all through his drying last tears, as if it were all rushing along, braking and swerving to pass him. He was treading on air, he lifted up his face to the rinsed, blued sky and understood that he was alive, alive! . . . This was irrelevant to anything, any kind of intention: he was alive because his sorrow could go no farther, he stood at the summit of it and easily looked down at the surrounding and impending expanse of life. And suddenly he came alive and began to live—began to live steadily, rhythmically . . . as if in the past, in an earlier life that he had skipped, before the war, before the Revolution even. Day after day slipped quietly by, neither speeding up nor slowing down, and Lyova had time for everything. Mama could not find words for her joy: Lyova worked, wrote, easily passed his examinations for graduate school . . . and did not notice how. Only a month had passed in all.

And so suddenly—so unexpectedly!—Uncle Dickens died. Now this was sorrow! Lyova found himself thinking how inessential his personal squabbles were, how wrong it all was, how shallow and shameful, in the face of this thing starting with a *D*.

. . . Lyova saw Albina at the church, at the burial service, and was impressed. He had no thought or memory of anything inappropriate, he did not tell himself how becoming her black scarf was . . . but that was precisely what impressed him. When he had to throw an inexpert handful of sand into the hole, he started to cry. Immediately it was over. Rapidly and efficiently, as if furling an empty overcoat, rolling it into a bundle, Papa led Mama away, for some reason bypassing Lyova, for some reason even giving him a silent hand signal, behind her back, that he was not to approach . . . Albina took Lyova's arm.

They walked all the way from the cemetery. Albina talked splendidly about Dickens. Lyova was surprised: he, too, was thinking almost the same thoughts, but he lacked the words. It turned out Albina was not merely an acquaintance but a friend of Dickens—Lyova had no idea of this. "He was very much alone," Albina said. "He had no one, no one at all. All of his people had perished." Even Lyova had not known some of the details. "It may be better there for him," Albina said. "More of us are there." Somehow she spoke this simple thought well, somehow in a special way, as if she had a right to it.

She was thinking of her own father.

His photograph hung over the divan; Lyova studied it in the morning, as he lay next to the vacant crushed pillow and the turned-back corner of the blanket. The white, executed face gazed chastely and nearsightedly, through a pince-nez, at the rumpled half of the bed where his daughter had just lain. He had been a subject of the Lithuanian state, a builder who had erected his buildings in Paris and Bern, a European name mislaid after the war in the expanses of Asia . . . In the twilit recesses of the apartment a cup clinked, a robe fluttered: "Are you awake?"

To Lyova, Faina was always alone. Not merely because she was unique—she had no one around her. Like Albina she had no father, but she never seemed to have had one at all. Her embarrassed mother, who arrived from Rostov (-on-the-Don), promptly dropped out of sight, as if Faina had hidden her. The mother was fat and benighted, couldn't string two words together. More tenderly than ever, then, Lyova clasped to himself Faina's solitary, kinless beauty. Just once he saw on the street her ex-husband, whose shadow (wealth, success with women) she had exploited to prick Lyova's jealousy. Somewhat to his own disappointment, Lyova was reassured: except for his wealth . . . The husband was old and ugly. Lyova was better—even by the girlish, provincial criteria that had become chronic fixtures of Faina's lexicon with respect to the past (before Lyova). Such shrinkages in an image were intolerable to Faina. Only when he was alone with her was this image undimmed. Faina had no one around her.

Albina never had been and never was alone. She had the legends about her father; she had her mother, who even in poverty preserved a foreign *geste* of wealth (Lyova liked her face, liked to bring out youthful features through the "traces of erstwhile beauty"); she had photographs of villas and grandmothers; she had her cat, Gilberte, and the problem of homes for the kittens; she had her rapidly developed "shared" memories—the proximity of their schools, Uncle Dickens, Lyova's ideas and "projects." Her "past" was offered to Lyova on the spot, apparently whole and complete: the husband she had married without love (not one hard word about him), a gentle, cultured man; they had separated by her wish (after that rendezvous with Lyova, it turned out); the husband had requested—although she assured him all was over and it was impossible—requested her to wait a while longer with the divorce, he was ready to come back at her first summons . . . it was all told as if to avoid even mentioning it. ("All wives are widows," as Uncle Mitya once said.)

Lyova was more reticent. He would lie comfortably on his back beside Albina, studying the ghostly window sash on the ceiling, with its blurry network of leaves from outdoors beyond the balcony, and think dispassionately of Faina . . . This was what it came to: he had never seen, never understood, never felt her. She was not a person but an object . . . yes, an "object of passion" . . . how exact! Ah, words! (Lyova loved words.) *Ob-ject*. Only at Albina's side was he beginning to understand and see anything. Clearly: Albina was more refined, more clever, more ideal, more cultured, more complex—but all understandable and visible to Lyova, *real*. And Faina? Coarse, vulgar, materialistic—and utterly unreal to Lyova. Only his passion was real, and even in that sphere Lyova was ceasing to feel real. But although he understood nothing, not even himself, in his relationship with Faina—still, he could be confident that he knew *all* about himself. About Faina, however, he knew nothing. Only a series of incoherent, occasionally helpful manipulative skills: there's no use approaching her now . . . today's the day to find some sort of present . . . don't notice that . . . I must give that hairdo special praise ("How sweet of you to notice!"—suddenly he really would hear her voice, and turn with palpitating heart). "What's the matter?" sensitive Albina would ask. Lyova would groan and draw her to him, passing off roughness as passion.

She would go wild and climax in his arms, someone else's beloved wife, but how was she relevant, and how was Lyova? This was Faina writhing in Mitishatyev's arms, Lyova wasn't betraying Faina. Faina was reenacting it for him for the umpteenth time, and Lyova was no longer Lyova but Mitishatyev—by now it was practically a case of split personality, in the most medical sense of the word. Lyova would experience revulsion and an inexplicable delight, terrible in its power and keenness, without ever possessing either woman.

Now, suddenly, Faina came back. It turned out she hadn't gone to Sakhalin at all but to her mother's in Rostov. This was immediately reassuring to Lyova, that it hadn't been Sakhalin. You really wouldn't go to Sakhalin without a man. Lyova looked at her tanned, newly wholesome face and was glad to note a certain serenity in his soul. Despite all, he had acquired a modicum of self-awareness during this short period with Albina. He did not tell Faina about his romance, however. Not that anything was stopping him . . . then again, something was stopping him. Although he was somewhat out of the habit of Faina, he immediately realized that he wasn't at all out of the habit of the relationship, the accounts, the *enmity*. He noted this with surprise: how quickly he was becoming another person with her, the old Lyova. He told her nothing about Albina, as if keeping a trump in reserve. But Faina noticed a change. "I think I'm falling in love with you again," she said. In her lexicon this meant that she felt his "strength." Lyova despised her, and was content.

Things were more complicated with Albina. The first day, he could not bring himself to tell her Faina was back. The second, he didn't tell her but kicked himself for not having told right off. His pangs of conscience exasperated him. (Faina at least had the advantage that when he was with her these pangs were totally absent.) The third time . . . Albina already knew.

Lyova, of course, was intensely ill at ease. He was splitting in two. But what loneliness it is in our time to really find one another, thought Lyova, anguishing beside Albina. Yes, it's unbearable being doomed together, when you have beside you people to whom you can pretend you're the same as others. In an alien world it's easier with strangers than with your own kind. You don't notice yourself oinking—and no one else does, either.

But when it suddenly became clear that Faina hadn't been in Rostov either, she had gotten her tan on the beach at Makhach-Kale, then all things reverted to their previous places: the actors again rehearsed their roles, which they knew by heart as before. Faina is life, Faina is beauty, Faina is passion, Faina is fate. What is Albina!

Ah, what torture it all is . . . what murk. One woman beautiful, the other not. But try to prove even that. Beauty is such an illusion! Is Faina beautiful? Funny question—what difference does it make. Puffy, smeared with makeup, snoring (provided she's beside him), she's dear to Lyova, and everything about her even dearer. And how he will be tormented by his revulsion at the teeny little blackhead under very, very beautiful Albina's ear, as soon as this sweet and so uneternal instant fades and with his whole being he tears himself away to study her from a distance. For that matter, there is nothing uglier than a beautiful woman if you don't love her. Only a temporary illusion, an optical trick, and then—nothing but deformity and discomfiture.

How much people have rhapsodized about feminine beauty. Pure gibberish! Beautiful Albina is ugly when she isn't loved. Here she comes with Lyova, she begged for a meeting, got him to a café, she eats pastry, she weeps—what does Lyova feel except horror? Later they walk side by side and Lyova is a kilometer away, his hands are hidden in his pockets, his elbows are pressed to his sides—and there's no way she can thrust her hand under his elbow. The poor little hand prods, poor little mitten, poor separate creature of her hand, a fish against the ice, a fish with a blunt fur snout. Beautiful Albina weeps, she speaks ardent words all run together, the hot breath is snatched from her lips, her eyes peer at Lyova, they beg, but he will not look and does not hear anything—he's a kilometer away. And all he sees the whole time, with his hostile side vision, is a pastry crumb stuck on her lip, bobbing, bobbing. This pastry crumb disgusts him—and there's nothing else in Lyova's mind. That's no beauty—only ugliness! That's no ugliness—only beauty . . .

But Lyova will return to her more than once, and every time it will be after he has been hurt. He'll be back to pass on the hurt. At first his conscience will torment him, but later a convenient mechanism will develop. Albina, for her part, will believe him at once and warmly respond. As for Lyova, the minute he gains confidence he'll be gone, and the minute he loses it he'll be back again. Villainous? Villainous. But let the reader pay his own accounts.

Especially since this isn't even so. Lyova isn't such a villain, and our Albina isn't such a pauper. She suffers, of course, but she's also a "martyr." Very important, that "also"! She's convinced that even though Lyova often doesn't behave as she might wish, still, he loves her. Otherwise, why does he run, yet keep returning and returning, as if tethered. She sees manifestations of his love in everything, and collects them. He's back—he loves her. He's gone—he also loves her. He's tender—it's for her. He isn't—trouble at work. Or suppose he's sick? . . . But perhaps Lyova does love Albina, who knows? At least "in his own way." She alone can know this. After all, Lyova knows that Faina loves him. He just tells himself she's still young, or she doesn't understand, doesn't realize . . .

All lies, and all true.

In this period of his life with Albina—brief, and later so emphatically denied that eventually it seemed not to have happened to him at all—Lyova was allowed to experience firsthand the full force and horror of his own *not*-love (precisely, *not*-love: mere unlove is mere emotion), he was allowed to experience the tyranny of another's feeling, and the Christian helplessness of man.

Why do we not love? Placing that hand on his heart again—Albina was more worthy of his love. But when he placed that hand, he was placing it on—Faina. His heart was occupied. There isn't enough of us to leave room for anyone else. For this, our insufficiency, we again do not love the one who has allowed us to feel it. "It's all right for you not to love me," Albina said, after exhausting her wealth of suggestions. "But you don't have anyone now, do you? [What all had Lyova told her?] You need a woman, don't you? I am no worse than others." Lyova winced as if he had been struck—again, the full measure reached him. "You are not an *other*," he had the sense to reply. There was a grain of truth in this. And it was something else for which he could not-love her: she was one of his own kind, he was extremely sensitive to her: she was like him: her every move was projected in his soul as something recognized, understandable: they were identically constituted, and tuned to the same wavelength: he could not-love her as himself. He picked up her every signal, knew perfectly how he should reply to her—but with what?—and could not. Who indeed would love for this? And he could not-love her still more intensely for Faina: Faina wasn't gaining by the comparison—Lyova's wasted life was becoming more offensive. And, too, he could be annoyed that although Faina now knew about Albina, she didn't so much feel piqued by the fact as exploit it. But the real thing for which he did not love Albina was his first experience of discovering what he had tried so fruitlessly to ascertain from Faina: her true attitude toward him, what it was she had felt for him all their life . . . So *this* is what she felt, Lyova sometimes thought, as he squirmed in false inadequacy beside unloved Albina. What deadly anguish pierced Lyova at this admission! Especially since he could now, from his own experience, express a certain sympathy for Faina and almost admire her mercenary patience. For this, he could not only not-love but also murder the culprit (again Albina). —In sum, the feeling of not-love that we're talking about here is extremely wearisome and extraordinarily not-flattering to him who loves not. We don't know how women endure this feeling, how they deal with a success they have craved (it seems to us that at the moment of success, in order to be aware of it, they must not love anyone), we don't know . . . but a man who loves his success with women seems to us to be not fully a man. And Lyova cursed her feeling of unrequited love. But—not his own.

How violently did he not-love! How forever . . . If even ten years later (a diligent descendant can try to determine the date, by digging a little in the history of consumer goods) Lyova's heart ached with a nauseating anguish at the sight of innocent objects that he had first encountered at Albina's for some reason, such as a type of flowery elasticized slipper, which had outlined her foot so softly; or another object of the same type, a "footlet"—an invisible little sock, a "shortage item" of its time—things that were even touching, it would seem. But, for no reason at all, Lyova's hatred was also transferred to a later shortage item that had no connection with Albina, a stylish folding umbrella. All these things contracted, shriveled, shrank—without her foot, without rain. An image of formlessness, unbearable decay. Hastily slipped off her feet, abandoned on the floor, these slippers contracted without excuse, like his heart, and were frightening, like Albina, in their naked submissiveness. In later years the most enchanting of creatures might perish, in Lyova's eyes, by the mere fact of such an item's belonging to her.

Lyova tried to see Albina increasingly seldom, but even so, he was incapable of wounding her: he knew too well, it seemed to him, what she was experiencing, how she was suffering, and when he did not see her he began to sympathize with her to some extent (is such suffering perhaps flattering to us after all, from afar, in the abstract . . . ?). So he saw her increasingly seldom, freshening her wounds from purely Christian motives. One day, nevertheless, he made up his mind to a last conversation.

They met at a corner and walked to her house in silence. He irresolute, she afraid. Lyova refused to come upstairs. It turned out he was only seeing her home. She had to tell Lyova something else. "What?" Lyova asked. "Not here." "I won't go to your place," Lyova said, picturing her mother quietly disappearing in the twilight, almost managing not to look Lyova in the eye. Albina profited by the opportunity to take Lyova's arm and led him to a small public garden not far off.

There they sat in silence, as if they had already been sitting there when they arrived . . . The sky showed through the thinning leaves, it was prematurely cold, their hands were freezing. This was the first autumn cold spell, the kind before coat and gloves. With her frigid hands, Albina smoothed on her knee a maple leaf that had floated down to her. Lyova allowed himself to feel exasperated, taking this for coquetry. Coquetry was not the privilege of too-well-bred Albina, *his* Albina. It was unbecoming, pathetic. Lyova was being unfair to Albina: she really was occupied with the leaf, lest she happen to glance into Lyova's eyes, lest she read in them—

"Well, what is it," Lyova said, exasperated. A single large drop fell on the leaf. Now again Lyova felt her *full* torment in him, heaving about in his alien soul, and he could not bear it . . . He narrowed his eyes and spoke. She was silent. Lyova could not bear the pause and talked for quite a while longer, coating the pill with an acknowledgment of her virtues such that Albina was finally frozen solid by his icy compliments. A little drop hung on her nose. "But you're mine, *mine!*" she exclaimed desperately, and saw that he was looking at the tip of her nose, at the drop . . . She did not start dithering, did not get flustered, she wiped it off and said stonily, "Well then, goodbye." "You have to understand—" Lyova began, and did not continue. "Go." Lyova felt a cold jab, as if from the other side of his heart, where he had never felt pain—as though his heart, like the moon, had a back side—and realized, almost with disappointment, that he had achieved his goal, it didn't *seem* over, it *was* over. (In this, a man's heart, too, is elementary, like a woman's.) He realized that he must stand up and walk away, that this was her right, for him to leave, her last privilege (the only one in their whole time), which she was using. Now at last Lyova saw that Albina was beautiful, her lofty neck . . . that she might be desired and loved, though again, for some reason, not now, but by the remote Lyova who so generously had not loved her, by that Lyova, not this one still sitting beside her, still not leaving, and almost loving her . . . Yes, he might have loved her, she might have been his wife. (He pictured her apartment, the open doors, in the twilight he caught a glimpse and the scent of her robe, the delicate little coffee cup in her hand . . .) "I don't love you anymore," Albina said.

A little wet streak still glistened on her hand. Lyova sighed wordlessly and got up . . . But had he suddenly disintegrated, crumbled, cracked, and turned to her at last with feeling—it would already have been too late. The irreversibility staggered Lyova. For the first and last time, there arose before him the innate image of eternal love whose embodiment he had so insistently wished on the first woman to come along. This was She—and he promptly said goodbye to her forever, no longer dreaming of what does not happen in life.

(They never saw each other again. Lyova walked down the yellow path of the little park, and left, and for a long time walked with that yellow before his eyes, muttering unwritten verses like "Goodbye! Till we meet . . . No more shall we . . . Goodbye! . . . Da-da-da, da-da-da . . .")

So reads the story of Lyova under the sign of Albina: other stars in this sky, differently situated in relation to one another. Lyova does not see them, just as we in our Northern Hemisphere do not see the Southern Cross.

LYUBASHA

*Passions are nothing but underdeveloped ideas: they belong to the
youth of the heart, and he is a fool who expects to be excited by
them all his life. Many calm rivers begin as roaring waterfalls, but
not one bounds and froths all the way to the sea.*

TO LYOVA'S THIRD WOMAN we will give the plain Russian name
Lyubasha. Beloved woman, unloved woman, any woman. She plays
no role in his fate—she merely signifies something in it. Some sort of
profit, someone's loss. More time had passed. Nothing seemed to have
changed, but all had become different. Nothing was recognizable, but
all was the same. Lyova, too, looked quite different: a bit thinner in
the face, better dressed, a bit more confident, a bit more insolent,
more used to his torments, more comfortable with himself. He seemed
to have nothing to boast of, but something had already *happened* in
his life, and that in itself was something. He had acquired some of
the features he'd always had. It was as if he showed through, had
become visible through himself.

Lyova would turn up at Lyubasha's unexpectedly, by chance. She
did not have a telephone at home, though she did at work, an inconvenient one, at some distance. Lyubasha had given him that number,
but at the same time had seemed to advise against using it: apparently
he was required to ask for a certain Lida first, and Lida, a close friend
of Lyubasha's, would call her without fail. This was somehow awkward
for Lyova. He tried it once, and the male voice seemed annoyed that
even Lida had a call, and then Lida, after saying "Right away," was
gone so long that Lyova grew faint listening to the distant dead crackle.
He was sweating in the hot phone booth and kept glancing at an
impatient-looking man who stood restlessly outside the glass door but
nevertheless did not rap his coin on the glass, which made Lyova feel

even worse: he had to be stupidly silent, shifting his position and keeping an intelligent look on his face; he was getting hot, and all over his skin he felt a nibbling, which seemed to emanate from the crackle in the receiver; especially since someone had apparently come on the line while he was waiting, a man again, and asked all over again: Who do you want? And when Lyova, in a fright, gave Lida's name, the man said Lida was out, and almost hung up before Lyova thought to explain it all. In sum, when he finally heard Lyubasha's lazy voice in the receiver, he felt, along with relief, a certain embarrassment at the gross incongruity of all these difficulties and tribulations with what he must now say to Lyubasha. He held back, fell silent. "Has something happened?" Lyubasha said, very calmly. "No, it's nothing, I just wanted to drop in and see you." "Drop in, then," Lyubasha said simply. Lyova hung up. He did have Lyubasha's phone number, it turned out, but for an emergency. What kind of emergency could there be for him and Lyubasha? This, perhaps? So Lyova did not call again. Had he not waited that time, none of it could have happened. But if it hadn't, then what would have?

He dropped in unexpectedly and rather seldom, but until now had always found Lyubasha at home, and moreover alone. She appeared to be waiting for him, and although she did not pretend to be overjoyed, she was always cordial. They would sit down to a leisurely tea, and Lyova never did succeed in noticing how it all started and came about, but somehow they would manage it all and he would always leave at the right time, as required of him—the next morning or that same evening—somehow he didn't notice this either.

At first his unaccustomed good fortune in always finding her alone at home surprised him, then even flattered him, because in a relationship so undemanding Lyova would not have been surprised by anything at all. He had supposed himself outside her private life. It may have been just luck that he caught Lyubasha alone at first, but whatever it was, something suddenly changed now, became more obvious. He found someone going out as he came to the door, then someone wasn't let in when he was with Lyubasha, and then one day she didn't let Lyova in, either: her mother had suddenly arrived.

As she said this, her broad face expressed the same broad generosity. Lyova even felt as if it were a convenience that he couldn't see her today. As if the time, although he had had so much of it on his hands that he could only run to Lyubasha, had suddenly become a gift.

It is also of interest to note that Lyova was in a rare mood, for him, when he turned from his usual path and dropped in at Lyubasha's.

Not as at Faina's, where the more unfavorable were his situation and mood, the more importunate his arrival and the more he seemed to push things, to almost insist on his ever greater loss, as we prod an aching tooth or, if we're reserved, worry it with the tongue; where his attempts to stir her pity, to touch her, to debase himself, were the more insistent for being the more fruitless. Nor as at Albina's—where he showed up only in a black mood, weak, unhappy, or vicious.

In any case, it was when he was *not* unhappy that he dropped in at Lyubasha's. Perhaps still vicious, but not unhappy.

He would suddenly have some kind of success that inspired him with strength; or Faina would be unexpectedly nice to him, or even suddenly dependent; or the weather, after weeks of being oppressive in this rainy city, might suddenly turn, for the first spring-like day or an Indian summer; or an inexplicable briskness would simply descend on Lyova all of a sudden—without rhyme or reason like that rare weather—and then his nostrils would flare wide to inhale no matter what the air, he would rejoice at the life in an insignificant little leaf and feel attracted to himself, seem stronger and taller; or he would feel attracted to someone on the street or on the bus and detect a response, almost exchange winks, but she would walk on by, or get off at the bus stop, and he never could bring himself to catch up, jump off . . . Yet the sudden arousal and the surge of unexpected strength would stay with him and fill him to bursting, push and lead him to—Lyubasha.

In this unaccustomed mood, aroused, breathless, light of heart, even jubilant, his eyes almost glowing, he would find himself at Lyubasha's door and push the bell.

He would have no thought, no recollection of Lyubasha, sometimes for weeks; Faina was all he needed for this. And suddenly he would find himself at Lyubasha's door, fresh, handsome, so far from despair— and push the bell.

Or did a mechanism later evolve, whereby, when he found himself at Lyubasha's door, he would suddenly become completely different, fresh, handsome, and so forth? . . . and decisively push the bell.

That is, he may have been coming here to forget his troubles and improve his mood. It may already have been a reflex, and if so, it sounds much more trite. But even in this case it must be noted that his mood improved not merely in consequence of his encounter with Lyubasha, and not in the process, but even before the encounter, or at least right at her door, and the fact that he changed so before seeing Lyubasha tells us something, whether about Lyova or about Lyubasha

. . . She had the startling ability to define at once, without negotiating, without explaining, the extent, nature, and uniqueness of a relationship—otherwise, men apparently did not approach her, and in order to approach, Lyova had to allow for this, if only instinctively.

Lyubasha asked just once, very calmly it is true, and as if without emotion, "You like me better than Faina, don't you." Lyova was much amazed and somehow flattered. He thought about it and never did think it through. But Lyubasha did not demand an answer. She had asked, that was all. In her own way, she knew that he liked her better.

But Lyubasha was always at home, even after Lyova gave up his absurd, though flattering, supposition that he was the only one she had. She was always at home and never failed him here, having eliminated from her well-defined life the superfluous trouble of making dates and getting dressed to go out: she had perhaps repudiated in a fit of temper, or perhaps was calmly denying, the existence of any different or even slightly interesting world or way of life whatsoever, beyond the one that was, whatever it might be, her own. She was always at home or at work, went nowhere except to the bathhouse or a movie—but they came to her, and this was necessary to them, even essential.

So, to his own surprise, Lyova would find himself at her door—and push the bell.

Lyubasha opened the door to him and for the first time seemed surprised. "Is it you?" She looked at him more attentively than usual and said, as if she had decided something in her mind, "Oh well, come in. But I'm not alone." And while Lyova—as usual aroused, unexpectedly swift in his movements—was following her down the corridor and had no suspicions that could stop or dampen him in his headlong rush after slow-moving Lyubasha (because what could Lyubasha be suspected of?), while he was walking down the dark corridor and asking vaguely, "But who is with her?" and not quite catching the reply, it was all as wonderful as ever. But now he was standing in Lyubasha's cramped little room, and he felt sick.

They could not fail to meet. The meeting was so natural here.

"Well, at last!" Mitishatyev exclaimed. "I've been waiting for you."

THE MYTH
OF MITISHATYEV

This morning the doctor called on me: his name is Werner, but he is Russian. What is surprising about that? I knew an Ivanov who was German.

TIME PASSES even in the past—things seem to become more obvious and understandable than they were in the present . . . Mitishatyev had been a schoolmate of Lyova's, although by now it was hard to believe. He had gone bald and flabby before his time, but the main thing was that long ago and somehow imperceptibly he had acquired the array of trivial gestures and habits, purely superficial, by which we can always distinguish a middle-aged man, even from the back, whether he's boarding the bus or wiping his feet or blowing his nose. In their schooldays too, and Lyova was still able to recall them easily, Miti-shatyev had looked older than everyone else—he could even look older than a teacher—as if he kept varying his age as a function of his companion, so as to be always slightly older than he. If anyone new came along, especially someone completely opposite to him, Miti-shatyev pounced on that person with obvious pleasure, but he always managed to pass for one of his kind, even a bit more than one of his kind. Whether talking to a pace-setting worker, a front-line soldier, or an ex-convict, he become almost more of a pace-setter, front-liner, or convict than his companion, though he had never worked or fought or been in prison. But he never overplayed it. By and large he stayed on an equal footing, just barely implying his superiority: if he had been in his companion's trenches or prison camp, it was just for maybe a day or a month; but still, even though just for maybe a day, he'd been there. Whether from this desire to seem always a bit older and more experienced, or from his physiological peculiarities, or from the kind of inner uncleanliness that ages one before his time, Mitishatyev looked almost twice as old as Lyova.

He passed for that old, too. No one really knew what year he'd been born, and if anyone suddenly found out (a personnel manager, for example), amazement naturally gave rise to a story about the unprecedented events and traumas that must have rocked Mitishatyev's short life and left their elusive stamp and mark. One way or another, Mitishatyev immediately inspired respect and got elected to the presidium of the meeting.

Even Lyova, who had known Mitishatyev since childhood, found it implausible that they were the same age. Lyova accepted Mitishatyev's front-line and prison-camp past more easily than the fact of their having sat at the same school desk. Of course, Lyova could have no delusions on this score: it was just that the myths about Mitishatyev had long since become more real in his consciousness than the truth itself. This was why Lyova never betrayed him; it cost him no inner effort to override the truth about Mitishatyev and assent to any untruth (for again, in relation to Mitishatyev, an untruth seemed to be the greater truth). Mitishatyev appreciated this, even though he treated the paradox as something perfectly natural. In any case, he had ceased to fear Lyova in the company of strangers, didn't even fear the oblique or mocking silent glance that is always so dampening to us; and when Lyova was around he talked whatever nonsense came to mind, feeling almost inspired by his presence.

Ever since childhood, Lyova had been mystified by Mitishatyev's peculiar influence over him. It was an extremely simple thing, the very simplest—a pure and utterly uncalled-for power play, a technique that was always the same, even forbidden (below the belt), but always worked perfectly on Lyova. This naked pressure yielded to neither analysis nor logic. Lyova could not place it within his own system by understanding it, that is, he could not vanquish it or override it by reason—it simply *existed*, like a kind of peculiar physical phenomenon, and Lyova kept finding himself in its field of influence. What is more, it attracted him. He rebelled, of course, he fought back (that was just the trouble!), he put up his reason as a shield, but the enemy was unexpected and inexhaustible.

This model had been operating since childhood, like a perpetual-motion machine. After a long and futile wrangle, where the truth was conclusively on Lyova's side and his advantage indisputable, Mitishatyev would suddenly say, "Let's wrestle!" ("Let's butt heads!") And, accordingly, wrestle a moment . . . Suddenly this would turn out to be not simply coercion or physical superiority but truly—a victory! In moral, mental, all possible terms: that was how Mitishatyev presented everything, and how Lyova felt it.

Gradually Lyova could not help noticing that as long as he took any interest or tried to figure out the mechanism of Mitishatyev's influence, he always suffered defeat, but when he simply forgot about him for a while in despair and rage, walked away without having vanquished him at all, then the influence would end, and Lyova would see this as a victory. But this quite intelligent discovery didn't help him very much. Again and again Mitishatyev managed to draw him into his mechanism and subjugate him. It would begin with kindness— with friendship, with an affirmation of Lyova's virtues, with equality and recognition. Melting, savoring the flattery and his sense of superiority, Lyova would rise to the bait again and immediately be hooked: shunned, mocked, and completely under his sway.

This cycle of enticements and subsequent treachery, ever the same, so simple and always a mystery, attracted Lyova as a light the moth and corrupted his soul, gradually becoming ingrained in his consciousness. Each time the process of Lyova's involvement in treachery was repeated, the concomitant suffering seemed to traverse the same tender spot, which eventually became mere insensitive scar tissue, a kind of parade ground over which treachery marched without leaving a trace.

Lyova's relationship with his first and eternal love made this especially clear. One day (after the passage of several years) Lyova suddenly grasped that the secret of this woman's influence on him, the mystery of his eternal captivity, was humiliatingly similar in its mechanism to the secret of Mitishatyev. Good Lord! In neither case was the initiative fully Lyova's. These people, like animals, simply scented a kind of odor emanating from Lyova, which told them that they needed him. That was the trouble, they needed Lyova, rather than he them. They enticed him, he felt himself being attracted, he stood on his dignity for a while but then nevertheless opened up, uncurled his anemic petals—and at that point they spat lustily into the very core of his being. He curled, curdled, and was forever hurt and pinned, a butterfly, a badge . . . Even if such desecration brought Lyova to the limit of his endurance, as a rule he merely descended to foolish and ignominious rudeness—in which there was not a shred of mastery, might, or victory. They seized the advantage: he was immediately at fault, they had been infinitely offended in their pure feelings. And then Lyova would find himself tirelessly crawling, begging, and apologizing, falling more and more under their power.

Everything now merges, quite absurdly, pulsating all the while in the same simple and omnipotent pattern. Mitishatyev even merged with Lyova's sweetheart at some point in the monotonous plot of Lyova's life. They could not fail to meet, of course, since they fed on the same Lyova; and when one day they did meet, as though by a pure coincidence of that plot, it was as if they clasped hands and no longer could do without each other. They coalesced.

Lyova remembered forever that flickering, diffuse night, the corner of her house with the three dislodged bricks (they were just at eye level and distracted Lyova endlessly), while the three of them kept trying to take their leave and were utterly unable to do it. Someone's sentence fell apart in the middle and hung unfinished, suddenly revealing the pointlessness of the whole preceding conversation, lively as it had been; Lyova was crowded out by a passionate, even an indecent, silence; all three were shifting from foot to foot in impatience, and for a long time now had not been looking each other in the eye. Lyova still could not get a clear idea of something that was apparently clear to Mitishatyev and Faina, didn't allow himself to think it.

Finally they did separate, and Lyova felt relief and joy as he strode along beside Mitishatyev to the streetcar stop. His suspicions fell away like stifling garments, and there at the core, naked and clean, was Lyova—the kernel, the seed! He heard sounds and smelled smells, and the stars came out clearly for him . . . At the streetcar stop he took his leave of Mitishatyev (who had just a little farther to walk and he'd be home). Amiably, candidly, Lyova shook Mitishatyev's hand, and Mitishatyev, too, shook Lyova's with all his might and even kissed Lyova, suddenly and impulsively. Lyova jumped on the running board, bashfully smiling and waving, and honorably rode home.

Several years later, in the period of his most prolonged break with his beloved, when he had already begun to forget her little by little— discovering with surprise that lo and behold, he could exist without her, it wasn't bad, it was fine—and was tirelessly rejoicing over this, he encountered Mitishatyev on the street. They strolled around and stopped at a little bar, then at the zoo. Lyova was suddenly impressed that Mitishatyev had a remarkably exact way of speaking about the animals, with great intuition and insight. It revived Lyova's schoolboy notion that there was a certain originality, a hidden talent, in the nature of his enemy and friend: Lyova loved it when people spoke exactly, he opened up joyfully to language. After some sly and sentimental remarks about the animals, they had a beer.

"Say listen, Prince," Mitishatyev said, blowing the foam off, "do you have our high-school class picture?"

"Of course I do. Why?"

"No special reason . . . It'd be fun to see it now. Listen, do you look at it often?"

"No. Why should I?" Lyova said in surprise. "My mother has it lying around somewhere."

"What do you think, how many Jews did we have in our class?"

Lyova was taken aback. "I never counted—"

"Try to remember, try!"

Lyova hesitated.

"Why no," he said, "it's funny—I can't remember. All Russian names, not a single Jewish one. Perhaps we didn't have any?"

Mitishatyev burst out laughing. "Sure we did! Tell me—what do you think Kukharsky is?"

"You mean the Rat? Russian, of course," Lyova said. "Such a dumb mug. Besides, his name—"

"His name, his name!" Mitishatyev mimicked. "That's nothing! He's a Jew, a Jew. And Moskvin, you think he's not a Jew?"

Lyova laughed heartily. "Kukharsky—okay. But Moskvin! It's true we always called him Moshe. But that was nothing, a joke, it never crossed anyone's mind he was . . . If it had, we'd never have called him that."

"You had an intuition," Mitishatyev said. "Intuition never deceives you. He *is* a Moshe."

"What do you mean?" Lyova asked in surprise.

"And your Timofeev was a Jew, too."

"Timson?"

"But of course," Mitishatyev said gravely. "That's why you nicknamed him Timson."

"I suppose Potekhin's a Jew, too?" Lyova asked venomously.

Now it was Mitishatyev who roared with laughter. "Potekhin? Haha . . . Lyova, you're a born fool! But of course he is, a hundred percent!"

"Well, but Myasnikov?"

"How can you doubt it! You saw his nose?"

Lyova thoughtfully touched his own nose.

"I told you so," Mitishatyev said. "Listen, Prince"—Mitishatyev's tone suddenly became searching, confidential—"you're not a Jew yourself, by any chance?"

"Me!" Lyova choked.

"Oh, right—you're a prince," Mitishatyev said, hastily backing down. "But then why are you called Lyova?"

"My God!" Lyova exclaimed. "What's the matter with you? Even Lev Tolstoy was Lyova."

"Hmmm, yes . . . Tolstoy," Mitishatyev said, as if in open doubt. "And all your friends were Jews."

"What do you mean, all? Who, for example?"

"Timofeev, for one. Or Moskvin."

"But they're not Jews!"

"They're Jews," Mitishatyev said unshakably.

"How stupid can I be!" Lyova said, suddenly remembering. "Even if they are Jews, what do I care?"

"There, you see," Mitishatyev said with satisfaction.

"Wait." Lyova had a sudden hunch. "What about you? You're not a Jew, by any chance?"

Mitishatyev roared heartily. Afterward he went on shaking his head and sobbing slightly—Lyova just killed him.

"Sure you are," Lyova went on. "Your snout isn't what it should be either, is it?"

"My spout . . ." was all Mitishatyev could say, because he was choking with laughter again. "Teapot . . ."

"Besides, you're a friend of mine," Lyova said with inexplicable joy and delight, "and by your own admission, every last one of my friends is a Jew. I, too, seem to be a Jew. So you're one, too. We called you Myakish, remember? 'Softy.' It suited you very well," Lyova said with a pleasant, sobering harshness. "There's something Jewish about Myakish, too—"

"Myakish?" Mitishatyev seemed to wake up and even take offense. "What's Jewish about Myakish?"

"Besides, why does the question bother you so? That usually happens when people have a stake in something themselves. Well, if you're not a Jew, then a half-breed for instance, or a quadroon." Lyova suddenly discovered that they had simply swapped texts, he had begun to sound so much like Mitishatyev. "Or even an eighth—isn't that worth something, too?"

"No," Mitishatyev snapped.

"Then what is it you have against them?"

"The Jews are spoiling our women," Mitishatyev said firmly.

"How so?"

"They just are. Besides, they have no talent. They're not a gifted people."

"I beg your pardon! What about—"

"Just don't talk to me about the fiddle."

"Who cares about the violin!" Lyova said, suddenly angry, and he enumerated the poets.

Mitishatyev rejected them.

"Well, but Fet? You won't deny Fet?"

"Fet was slandered."

"Well, but Pushkin?" Lyova said, lighting up. "What about Pushkin?"

"What about him." Mitishatyev shrugged. "He's a Negro."

"But you know what a Negro is? An Ethiopian! And the Ethiopians are Semites. Pushkin's a black Semite!"

The argument was strong. Mitishatyev lapsed into a sullen silence. Lyova exulted. He became condescending . . .

Mitishatyev detected this and cheered up. He turned away as though hiding something and said with apparent indifference, "By the way, how long since you saw your Faina?"

He *would* give it to him like this—in the face, the groin, the solar plexus! Lyova choked.

"Quite a while . . . Why?"

"Oh, nothing," Mitishatyev said, finishing his beer. "I ran into her recently. Well, are we off?"

Suddenly the memory of that night hit Lyova like a wave, like a twist of the knife: the three of them standing by her house together . . . Now the question that had tormented him was on the tip of his tongue and he didn't dare ask. Mitishatyev strode along in silence, unseeing, erect.

"How about another drink?" Lyova asked timidly.

"I don't have any money," Mitishatyev said stoutly (although everything so far had been at Lyova's expense).

Lyova did have some.

He bought the drinks and all the while—feigning unconcern, talking of this and that—kept sneaking up on his goal. When at last, not recognizing his own voice, betraying himself at once (though he bent every effort to make his question indifferent and casual)—when he did ask it, Mitishatyev's lips suddenly twitched in an inimitable little smile, even though he said no, nothing of the kind had happened. Oh, that smile . . . Lyova was ready to race back to Faina and beat down her door. Mitishatyev could not resist adding (there was even something spineless about this, an immersion in vice) that to be totally honest, as he must with his best friend, so that this would be it, the whole story, and nothing remain between them . . . he *had* gone back that night, after Lyova went home, but, again, nothing had happened.

Now who could ever say whether it had or had not? Although, from another angle, why would Mitishatyev hide anything, since he knew that all was over between Lyova and Faina? Although, and from yet another angle, why would he confess to going back and hide what happened next? . . . In brief, Lyova was up to his ears again in what used to be, as though the years had not passed, one after another, and he had never left square one. Soon he put the same question to Faina.

She evaded it, because she and Lyova were at peace—having just been reunited—but she too, like Mitishatyev, could not resist giving poor Lyova a tormenting little smile. And then, apparently wearied by Lyova's hassles, throwing up her hands, she acquiesced in his proposed version. She disavowed it on the spot, however, saying yes, Mitishatyev had come back later, but she hadn't let him in, they'd simply gone for a walk and talked; yes, of course he kept after her, but he didn't get anything, no, he didn't, although he even dragged her into the cellar of his building, where he really knew his way around; it was warm there and he kept after her there too, but again, he didn't get anything there either, and—oh, the hell with it! if Lyova would just let her alone! everything, everything happened, only not in the cellar, of course, but at her place, because when Lyova left, Mitishatyev came back and spent the night with her, and another time too, once when she didn't let Lyova in (remember?)—that was Mitishatyev too, and then several other times . . . Okay then, she was saying it for spite, none of it had happened, none of it, none of it! Lyova had always been the only one (come to me, Lyova darling . . .). All right then, it did, that time in the cellar, it did, but only once, and that was pure shame . . . But no, nothing had ever happened (me, with that freak? Why, it disgusts me even to look at him!), it was just that Lyova kept pushing her, what more could she say to him? Oh, don't, darling, I love you, oh, get the hell out—you make me sick and tired!

Such sweet torture, always refreshing and revitalizing—and he never found anything out! Besides, Lyova would think wisely, what can we ever really know about another? But this held even more despair and not a scrap of comfort. He would remember his other women—and then fly up, as if from a toothache. All would be illumined with a brilliant white light: if even he had others, then what had she—! And

196

he never could really betray her, it turned out: his betrayals merely rested upon him like added cargo and dragged him straight to the bottom. In each of his other women, he saw chiefly her other man, always Mitishatyev. And this, the only betrayal Lyova knew of (her marriage somehow didn't count), turned out to be the one he knew least of all. The belated thought must soon occur to Lyova that he no longer loved, he merely dreamed of escaping from this love.

And already Lyova was trying on his cardboard armor, unsheathing his inopportunely wooden, painted sword! But although he tried to fight his enemies with their own weapon, that is, betrayed them in his turn, Lyova simply could not outplay them, outdo them in treachery. He himself would trip over his own meek and feeble little sell-out, when he recoiled from their sudden, out-of-nowhere, incredible treachery. An enormous monster, and new heads grew out every time . . . Lyova would have to put away his wooden sword. All his demonic behavior would suddenly turn out to be a forgivable childish prank that he had exaggerated to hyperbolical dimensions. He could only be mocked, condescendingly and affectionately.

Although the two of them never did let him commit true treachery and overcome them, this did not mean, unfortunately, that Lyova's pure nature came to his aid or kept him from being stained. He just looked pure by comparison with them. In fact, having been drawn into this process, this pursuit of snowballing treachery, he himself was moving toward the brink, though not of his own accord but with them, following in their footsteps. That is, without realizing it, he was on the other side, and by now he was secretly capable of doing unto others the things he suffered from himself. And this disgraceful game of "Who wins?" that they were always foisting on Lyova, while he believed that there ought to be love and not "Who wins?" (light floods in from somewhere, music plays, they walk and walk, hand in hand, dissolving and sinking and not treading on one another, and everything dances and swirls in a graceful dance, soaring up and away like the planets and worlds, widening beyond all bounds)—this game of "Who wins?", this unreality (Temptation), was more and more becoming the waking world for Lyova. Already, although clumsily and still in no position to compete, he was trying his mischievous little hand at the things that he thought (extrapolating from his own experience) everyone else did—so how was he worse than everyone else? . . . And the two of them suddenly started to divide and multiply before his very eyes, spread with the speed of experience, so that the world was clearly beginning to divide into *he* (Lyova) and *they* (everyone else).

Moving thus a millimeter at a time, with inexpressible anguish and suffering (which has never been any excuse for anyone), closer and closer to the brink, Lyova should have tumbled over it and found himself in the vast, packed, peopled hall (railroad waiting room) where the gala closing of Lev Odoevtsev's soul would take place! And Lyova would never have known what he was really like—because he would no longer have existed.

In the end, Lyova was merely a bit slow to realize that the Mitishatyevs didn't so much oppress him as he allowed them this. As it was, to give him his due, he long resisted the "Who wins?" system of relationships, until, having followed his tormentors to the brink, he discovered with surprise that he was separated from them only by time, he was already secretly selling out and betraying someone else, passing the baton, as it were, to someone who had appeared in the recent past—he hadn't meant to accept it, but here he was, already gripping the stick . . .

. . . Still, Faina did help Lyova in one respect—he got out from under the power of his friend. After the molten lead of Faina, the boiling salt water of Mitishatyev no longer burned him. Time flies.

But in this, too, he was mistaken. Naturally he must have thought it was true, because for a long time he was in no mood for Mitishatyev. But as everyone knows, a Mitishatyev is patient. He can wait for his triumph as long as you like. Lyova's vigilance had only to flag. And one time, during Lyova's calmest and fullest period, when Faina had gone off with someone, apparently to Sakhalin; when Lyova, after somehow stabilizing at last, had entered graduate school, happened on a very interesting subject, plunged into science, and was feeling proud and happy about it, experiencing a surge of strength and a certain creative potential that carried him far and away above his classmates, colleagues, and supervisors; when he felt sighted, at least in his work, when life had at last begun to bring satisfaction and he felt that nothing could knock him off his feet—Mitishatyev turned up from nonexistence. And Lyova repeated the same mistake he had endlessly repeated back in school.

Mitishatyev did not vary his basic method, though he varied his face. By now, Lyova thought, he had developed an antidote to all Mitishatyev's faces and discredited them in his own mind. Even so, he made the mistake of naïvely supposing that he would see one of the old faces in Mitishatyev, he would triumph by being armed to the teeth. Mitishatyev, as always, took him from the rear. By this day and age, it's obvious that Achilles is a very doomed man and will be almost the first to fall. Because it's silly to strike the invulnerable spots, when there's that transparent heel . . . This time Mitishatyev twisted Lyova round his finger so easily, so primitively, that later, when he left, Lyova could only throw up his hands in bewilderment. It was like getting a simple kick in the teeth, after expecting to be murdered by a rare Asiatic poison sprinkled in century-old wine.

Mitishatyev telephoned Lyova. At once, in a rush, omitting any sort of greeting, question, or account of what had happened during their whole long separation, he wrung from Lyova an immediate appointment. In the peculiar voice he used for such an occasion—Lyova knew it well—Mitishatyev said they absolutely had to get together and talk, because he must explain to Lyova something of extreme importance for everyone, which only he, Mitishatyev, had thought of. Everything was so like him, both the significant tone and his intention of communicating some unusual experience, that Lyova was practically rubbing his hands with satisfaction. How powerless Mitishatyev and his old tricks would be—against him, Lev Odoevtsev, in his equilibrium and wisdom. Mitishatyev and his ignorance—against scientific, perfect thought . . . The whole trouble was that Lyova had overarmed himself, overimagined his enemy. His enemy was simple.

Hypothetically (and this scene can be depicted only hypothetically), it happened like this.

The minute he walked in, Mitishatyev announced he was the messiah, he had reached the summit and was capable of moving heaven and earth. Prior to him there had been, to use Gorky's expression, Christ–Mohammed–Napoleon (he gave other names, however), and now him, Mitishatyev. Therefore he, Mitishatyev, would start by crushing Lyova spiritually. "Oh? And how will you do this?" Lyova said with a condescending smile. "Very simply," Mitishatyev said, "I feel the strength in me." "The strength to do what?" "To move heaven and earth, and to start by crushing you spiritually, because you're my ideological enemy." "Why your enemy? We haven't—" "My enemy," Mitishatyev said stoutly. "All right, but how will you crush me?" "Very simply," Mitishatyev answered confidently, "I feel the strength in me. There were 'Christ–Mohammed–Napoleon'—and now me. Everything is ripe, the world is ripe, all that's needed is a man who feels the strength in him. I feel the strength in me." That was all, Mitishatyev could say nothing more. Lyova artfully tripped him up, discredited him, derided him. Mitishatyev merely frowned in disdain: hogwash, intellectual trivia, you people will be devoured by your own weakness, your weakness is stronger than you are, there's no need to fight you—

you'll do it all with your own hands. He had written an article called "Confidence in One's Own Enemy," it would soon come out in *Pravda,* and then everybody would understand. But Lyova was the enemy, and he, Mitishatyev, had simply conducted a little experiment today (a small test of theory in practice) and had satisfied himself, once more, that he was right and felt the strength in him . . . Why right, what strength, Lyova thought, weakening, he's just a punk— "What of it," Mitishatyev said. "A punk is top dog now. Everybody's gotten so weak and jellylike that a punk's the only one who can even speak clearly, use four-letter words." Suddenly Lyova wearied and flagged. He could no longer make any objection to Mitishatyev, could not contradict him, could not vanquish him. There was nothing to vanquish: always the same naked pressure, naked space, a desert . . . "Let's butt heads." Lyova collapsed.

What if he really does? thought Lyova, by now almost in delirium, even backing away from Mitishatyev. He really does feel it in him. I *know,* but I'm powerless even to show him what I know. Is it because I don't feel the strength in me? But Mitishatyev does—

"Do you feel this force in you?" Mitishatyev said threateningly, as if in reply to Lyova's thought. Automatically, before he could collect himself, Lyova timidly jerked his head in the negative. Mitishatyev took a step toward him: "And in me?" Lyova almost shrank. And before his very eyes, a miracle really did happen to Mitishatyev—he swelled, became massive, and gradually filled the room, advancing on Lyova and breathing hotly. Lyova felt a strong, real current emanating from Mitishatyev, a psychic field of unusual force. He went rigid and watched with unmoving eyes—Mitishatyev was filling the room. "Do you feel the force?" Mitishatyev whispered loudly. The heat positively blazed in his words and breath, and Lyova flattened himself harder and harder against the cupboard. "Well, say something, protest, why don't you speak! Do you feel it or not?!" Lyova soundlessly unstuck his lips: "I do." "I told you so," Mitishatyev said with satisfaction, and suddenly he turned on his heel and left. Lyova stayed, feeling utterly beaten and ill. He could not explain to himself what had happened or whether he had imagined it all. He soon fell into a heavy sleep, and next morning he simply drove it all away as a mirage and vision.

But this, too, passed. He and Mitishatyev ran into each other at the institute, where Lyova was already finishing his dissertation and Mitishatyev was just beginning graduate studies. Nowadays they both gave an impression of being very solid and commonplace, they remembered everything as having occurred in their childhood, and when Lyova, not quite confidently, alluded to that strange visit, Mitishatyev laughed and flatly denied everything. He told a very tangled story about being treated one time in a nerve clinic. "I saw some real weirdos there, you know," he said complacently. "A guy will grab you by the buttons, in broad daylight, and whisper shrilly, 'See that? A little star. The green one—see it?' " But these stories, too, recalled his trenches and prisons. After taking Mitishatyev personally for so many years, Lyova could not agree that he was just a madman.

And although everything passes, and we do eventually get out from under the things and people that have burdened us (more precisely, we outlive our memories of them); although Lyova by now confidently supposed that Mitishatyev was simply a rotten insignificant little man; still, something that was, if not mysterious now, then mysterious in recollection, something sanctified by childhood, had survived to this day in his attitude toward Mitishatyev. "We are all Mitishatyevs to some extent," Lyova told himself with relief, and no longer felt obliged to see anything significant in people who were simply rotten. "As are the non-we," Lyova told himself, as if with sorrow, using Mitishatyev's favorite expression, "As are the non-we."

Notably, despite strong points that were unusually advantageous for his career, and almost because of these talents, Mitishatyev had still achieved little in life, so to speak, a lot less even than Lyova. Although they were in the same field, and according to his old pattern Mitishatyev should have yielded nothing here. But Mitishatyev seemed to have subsided, or perhaps he had unselfishly dissipated his energies—mostly on Lyova—while still within the precincts of school and college.

Mitishatyev smoked only Northlands.

Thoughts and memories not quite like these, but of this sort, would one day rush through Lyova's mind with peculiar distinctness and suddenness, and the reason would be rather remote. Especially since Lyova saw Mitishatyev nearly every day now and gave no thought to him at all.

. . . It was a frigid day, and Lyova was stamping his feet under the clock on the corner, near the bus stop, waiting for a really lovely girl, not Faina, whom at that time he was trying so hard to fool that he had fooled even himself, if only out of integrity. He had arrived a bit early—it just worked out that way, he wasn't nervous at all, since he felt sure she would come, she'd even come running—and was therefore looking calmly around, entertaining himself as best he could by watching the street.

Then he noticed a certain youth, who was standing at the bus stop, not in line like everyone else, but at a slight distance. This youth, despite the frigid weather, was coatless and hatless, and it was obvious that he went around that way all winter, he hadn't just run out to the nearest store for wine. What made it obvious is hard to say: either he didn't show the excitement and impatience that are natural for ill-clad people in frigid weather, or he was standing so calmly, not shivering, not shifting from foot to foot, that it was clear this was a matter of habit for him, a way of toughening himself; or too, he was dressed poorly under the nonexistent coat—his turtleneck sweater was unclean and a little too short, and his big frozen hands would stick out of the sleeves, tug as he might; oh, and of course his slacks were baggy at the knees, and also too short . . . His face was large and well-made, rather virile, with a grayish cast to it, one of those faces that seem unwashed or slightly depraved even in cleanly men; and, too, there was the expression not very blatantly but distinctly settled on his face—it might have been called an expression of self-esteem: the sum of traces of challenge, secretiveness, and distrust. Such was the leisurely glance he gave passersby, a secret taunt perhaps, especially for the girls—here the secret grin would get just a little bigger, and for some reason it very much betrayed him, not by the candor of the expression but on the contrary by its secrecy, by a sense of the incredible effort of will that went into that secrecy. He stood there looking quite normal, except perhaps a bit more self-sufficient and apart, holding some little books in his hand ("Pisarev" showed on the outside, in gold letters), and Lyova suddenly realized that he had more than once seen a similar youth—he just hadn't paid attention. There was one young man like this who had been catching his eye for a long time now. He had appeared in their class in second grade. His toughness evoked a re-spectful grin, and for this reason and some other reason they nicknamed him Cyclops; the girls all kept looking at him with attention and interest, but not one of them would make friends with him; he was none too regular in his studies but sometimes became masochistically industrious, taking up some very narrow and strange field of knowledge for no reason at all and wading through a monstrously voluminous literature; there was the hint of a vocation in him, but he had already cooled toward the idea of a college degree and did not come up to expectations . . . what else? . . . oh, he chinned himself on the horizontal bar an absolute record number of times (in homely long shorts, with his legs bowed in an ugly way), evoking respect without admiration, but on the whole he wasn't too athletic, though he devoted himself privately to lifting flatirons and chairs . . . Lyova had a sudden, distinct memory of his body: extremely powerful abdominals and long strong arms, very pale . . . it floated up to the surface of his memory like the body of a drowned man.

To be fair, he didn't look at all like Mitishatyev, but it was Mitishatyev Lyova remembered, and with the kind of sudden clarity and freshness that were impossible by now, their association having been so long, close, and soiled. Especially that moment by the cupboard. And one other point, which he had never recalled, moreover had never understood, and only now, looking at the youth, was aware of and understood.

Mitishatyev hadn't known how to call from a pay phone! That is, how to drop in the coin, lift the receiver, dial a number, press the button. The whole sequence was absolutely obscure to him. Very likely he had learned it only in his last year of college. Yes, yes, yes! He didn't know how it was done and couldn't ask anyone. Always when Lyova said, "So give me a call," Mitishatyev would smile strangely and never do it. Even for some trifle he would go all the way across town, totally without guarantee of finding anyone home; he could not call. But still, no one knew this small weakness of his . . . Now Lyova was so piercingly aware of this man from the inside that the tears even started to his eyes. And the strange, unaccountable conviction that this very point, more than all others, revealed the soul of Mitishatyev was also something new, and Lyova could not have explained it to himself.

(. . . Lyova stood and stared at his overthrown enemy, aware of a certain void, perhaps sad, perhaps sweet. His enemy rode away from him, athletically dangling last from the bus—he himself was already on board, but the hand with Pisarev still floated along the street.)

VERSION AND
VARIANT

AB, AB, AB . . . Lyova thought once, and by dropping just the first A, he obtained: BA, BA, BA . . .

B, B, B, B! That's the series. It's the same as saying: Lev Odoevtsev! Of course we know him, sir, we've read . . . Or: Odoevtsev, Lev! "Present!"—and snap to attention. Yet there is a difference.

Reality *is*, you know. It is, whether or not we can comprehend, describe, explain, or change it—it is. And is not, the moment we try to look through someone else's eyes. A heat haze, a shimmer, and reality shreds like rotten fabric—mere version and variant, version and variant. Not as unbridled authorial license, not as a formalistic literary device, nor even merely as the coloration of a shifting actuality, but as the bare mechanism of a so-called relationship, which you should not enter into, under any circumstances, ever again. But in no time at all, you're floundering once more in the spider's web.

Faina, Albina, Mitishatyev—already they're beginning to flicker, divide, multiply, and disappear. Faina may already be another Faina, not in the sense that she has changed (we have no hope of that), but simply another—a second, a third . . . And there certainly isn't one Mitishatyev; a dozen Mitishatyevs will pass through Lyova's life before he comprehends the first. As for the Lyubashas, we could lose count. Only Albina—his first other woman—will always be unduplicated . . . Were they this many at the very beginning, I wonder, and did I, as author, fuse them into one Faina, one Mitishatyev, one . . . in order to give at least some kind of focus to Lyova's blurred life? Because the people who affect us are one thing, and their effect on us is quite another; very often the one has no relation to the other, because their effect on us is already ourselves. To the extent that what concerned us was Lyova and the effect people had on him, our Faina and Mitishatyev are also that same Lyova: either they compose Lyova's soul, or his soul splits into two parts, three parts, them. Using the rules of the parallelogram of forces, we have substituted for the numerous forces affecting Lyova two or three equivalent vector arrows, thick and bold, which lie across Lyova Odoevtsev's amorphous soul and crystallize it under pressure. So if these people/forces, people/vectors, have a certain unreality, conventionality, and generality, it doesn't mean that they are just like that. We are seeing them like that through our semi-transparent hero. And since all the vectors are drawn across his soul, they cannot fail to meet at least once, all of them together. Lyova has only to stop and stand still . . .

Everything in the past has grown cold, and the readily available future crumbles under its blade. Red-hot shavings of the present scorch the paper. We *do not know*. Only version and variant, version and variant, riffle before the author's gaze as he approaches his hero's present.

But what does Lyova himself think, as he marvels at the way his life rides off into the past, day after day, stopping nowhere, always skipping the flag stops of the present along the way from the future—to its absence?

Reflecting on the uncertain course of his history, Lyova has lately begun to attach more and more significance to two concepts, picked up he knows not where—"vitality" and "nonvitality." It seems to him that they mean something, they explain the plot of his own life and the destinies of those dear to him. Overwhelmed by his experience, he supposes that vitality and nonvitality are something innate, a given. It seems to him lately that he is nonvital, or subvital. He is depressed by this conclusion.

Much as he wants to preserve his life, or rather his existence, there is no way he can achieve the vitality that has attracted him in others: in Mitishatyev or Faina, not to mention Grandfather or Dickens, where everything is measured differently. He would like to escape as they do, wriggle away, slip from their grasp and emerge the victor.

For what is a victor, thinks Lyova, if not the man who escapes from defeat, who at the last moment jumps from the step of a derailing train, who manages to leap from a car that is plunging over the bridge into the water—if not the rat fleeing a ship. Most likely the rat, in our circumstances. No one is to blame that vitality, in our day, is

incarnated in very disgusting forms, chiefly ignoble ones. No one is
to blame because everyone is to blame, and when everyone's to blame,
the one chiefly to blame is you. But life is already being built on a
framework designed to keep people from ever recognizing when they're
to blame; this is the method by which paradise on earth, the happiest
society, will be realized. Escape, betrayal, treachery are three successive steps, three forms, not to say of life, but of its preservation; three
ways of staying in the saddle, winning, emerging the victor. That is
the course taken by the vital. The nonvital—well, they must die out.
Their efforts to sing the same song are unwarranted and pathetic and
do not lead to success, only to defeat. They may leap from the car,
but if they do they're a little too late, differing in just one respect from
those who don't leap: they plunge into the same abyss independently
of the car, parallel to it. Nowadays life is a protracted copulation with
life, an ever postponed orgasm.

Lyova thinks he's got no place to hide anymore, he's here, pal, here
to stay.

So it suddenly seems to him, but we are not sure . . .

They could not fail to meet.

The simplest, most natural common ground for such a meeting was
at Lyubasha's.

"Well, at last!" Mitishatyev exclaimed. "We've been waiting for
you . . ." And indeed, it wasn't just Lyubasha who was not alone this
time in her parlor—Mitishatyev was not alone either.

Staring through his embrace (over Mitishatyev's shoulder), with
sudden perspicacity, Lyova recognized the third man from a photograph he had once seen briefly and casually, and thought he had
promptly forgotten. Albina's husband.

They offered their hands and introduced themselves by names familiar to the point of revulsion. There being three of them, they
"chipped in" on a half liter of vodka. The chance to run out and get
it was won, like a prize, by Lyova.

He lunged out to the street and for some time stared wildly around,
emphatically inhaling the air with his whole chest. "Madness, madness, madness!" he repeated. "All the things that have happened—
and that's all it was . . . Lord! Reality does exist. Here it is!" His eyes
grateful, brimming with salvation, Lyova gazed at the trees in the little
park next door, the asphalt wet from the watering truck that had just
gone by, the sparrows racketing on the roof of a shed, the bathhouse
opposite, and the thoroughly steamy woman who seemed to be heading

straight from the bathhouse to Lyova . . . His eyes grew wet. "Have I really escaped? None of it happened! Faster, run faster . . ."

And Lyova runs out of this version, out of this variant.

Well, but it does happen, he thinks with surprise. Yes, such variants are quite often encountered in life. Only on stage have they been compromised.

Lyova runs out—and into another variant . . .

This variant is on communal rather than common ground. Our topic will be the Café Molecule, an amateur youth café at a very large, very secret institute for scientific research. It, too, belongs to the category of places where such meetings cannot fail to occur.

The café was observing its fifth anniversary. A sumptuous party was in preparation. The invited guests were to be very famous people: poets, performing artists, cosmonauts.

The café had been built by the institute fellows themselves—young scientists—from plans by amateur architects, and had been painted by their own abstractionists. The furniture had been made from their own designs in their own workshops. Not without difficulty had all this been accomplished, not without resistance from the personnel department, on enthusiasm alone and not without struggle. But all had been overcome. The painting proved a bit dilettantish, but quite nice; the furniture a bit uncomfortable, but original; the quarters, being below street level, a bit damp, but cozy. Gatherings in the café always had uncommonly interesting speakers—people were flattered to appear within precincts so famous and secret—and took place in a lively, unconstrained setting. Coverage of these gatherings in the city's youth newspaper was also lively and unconstrained.

The anniversary party was supposed to surpass all previous ones. The invited guests were to be people like Yevtushenko, Smoktunovsky, Gagarin, and so on, people who were interesting, like dolphins. Admission would be strictly by invitation cards and according to a list— a select audience. In addition to speeches by the invitees, and their flattering companionship at table, a showing of a rare film was also contemplated, perhaps a Hitchcock or a Fellini. A Nobel laureate, the director of the institute, was supposed to tend the coffee maker; senior faculty, no less, were supposed to serve.

The ticket takers did in fact admit people strictly by invitation cards and according to the list. A police patrol pressed back the straining but ticketless mob of beautifully dressed young intellectuals. But at the last minute it turned out that Yevtushenko couldn't be there; poet X was admitted in his place. Smoktunovsky couldn't either; Y was admitted in his place, and Z in Gagarin's. Paradoxically, X, Y, and Z were also on the list, though somewhere near the bottom, so another three were admitted in their place. Exactly fifty people were admitted according to the list; names were checked off, crossed out, and written over: each in place of someone else. Behind the coffee maker stood, not the Nobel laureate, but a Ph.D., and the serving was done by lab assistants. In place of caviar they had salmon, and in place of salmon, sprats. Not to mention the film.

Curiously, it happened that the man who got into the party in place of X was also a poet, less well known than X, but still good. He read this charming rhyme, among others:

> Now a knife in slipper shape,
> Now a brooch in flipper shape,
> Now in birdie shape a dipper,
> Now in barrel shape a slipper,
>
> > Topsy-turvy, upside down!
> > Crazy madhouse all around!
> > ....
>
> > ....
>
> A thing points to another thing:
> Here's a finger—it's a ring,
> Here's a table—it's a chair . . .
> Get back! get out! and give us air!
>
> > Not life—a cave, a den of thieves,
> > Performing monstrous sleights-of-hand!
> > Create new images? Not he!
> > Clichés consumed across the land!
>
> So this is why the modish masses
> Call a tear a crystal bead
> And poems are now a salesman's passion . . .
> Home! away from poems! don't read!
> . . . .

There was more, also very nice. This poem was received with especially frantic applause.

Strange, thought Lyova, because he, too, was at the party; here they are, applauding. Their faces are all pleased, gay, and even winking. They truly liked it. They're flattered to be involved. The real reason they liked it is that this doggerel is about them, about their ghostliness at this absence of tables. They liked it precisely because it has a direct bearing on them—yet by some mysterious process that avoided wounding the soul, their impression instantly became abstract. They appreciated only the level of poetry; the hopelessness of their own existence never got through to them at all. They're pleased with the verse, with the poet who wrote the verse, with themselves who heard the verse, with the subtlety of their own perception. They're pleased with the hint at an external something that pressures everyone, a hint they've discovered jointly, exchanging winks. They're pleased . . . and have no self-awareness! How come he said, "Here's a something, it's a pistol," and no one's shooting himself!

Lyova's bleak generalizations have even more substance if we report that he was at the same table with Mitishatyev and Albina's husband. That is no mystery: Lyova, it seems, was there in place of Shklovsky, Mitishatyev in place of Z, and only Albina's husband was in his own place, because he worked at the institute and was one of the chief organizers of the party. Now, slurring some of his letters and spattering in Lyova's ear, he was relating the obstacles he had encountered in inviting So-and-so to the party, you do know he signed a certain letter . . . but he hadn't given up, he had insisted, he'd taken it all the way to the director. And see, there he is, sitting to our left . . . Albina's husband gazed at Lyova with canine eyes, and now Lyova understood Albina very well.

They sat at the same table, each in place of someone else, yet they were all themselves, and the whole thing was played out in almost the same sequence as the first variant. And it was the same game. They all knew a great deal about each other—but, at the same time, had barely been introduced. Ostensibly, they had never heard of each other before—and were not supposed to betray where they had heard of each other. Until the behavioral technique of each had been determined, the most advantageous behavior, naturally, was *none*—but then again, that was also the most habitual behavior for each. The game bore a positional character, so to speak.

My God, thought Lyova, recalling that he seemed to have seen Albina's husband briefly—at Lyubasha's. How unreal it all is! Immediately he drained his glass, having poured himself more than the others, and got very tight.

Suddenly he had a distinct revelation that they were all components in a kind of structure, components that hadn't quite acknowledged their function before but were now, all of a sudden, fused together so solidly, so tightly, that they could never again be separated. If he, Lyova, had a dowel in one side and a socket in the other, if he'd lived his life in some discomfort, snagging the dowel on passersby and carefully concealing the socket, then everything had now found its place, because where he had a dowel, Albina's husband had a socket designed for that dowel, and they matched, right off. The same was true of Mitishatyev. And everything matched, had been fixed in place, the structure had acquired stability. Now, clamped together, they could none of them budge any longer. The formulas from his high-school chemistry book came suddenly to mind. Yes, yes, exactly! he nodded to himself, almost jubilantly. Organic chemistry. Bonds. Rings. Each element is bonded to another by one or two bonds, and all are bonded together . . ..

With drunken inspiration he began to sketch something on a napkin, feeling a little like Mendeleev. At first it looked like this:

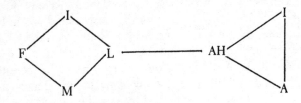

Then like this:

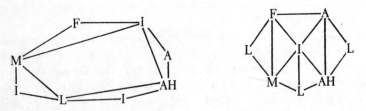

That didn't work . . .
Like this?

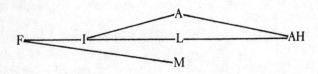

At last, like everything of genius, it all looked simpler and more generalized:

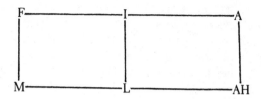

Where:
F is Faina, A is Albina, L is Lyubasha, M is Mitishatyev, AH is Albina's husband, I is Lyova himself.

A molecule, Lyova repeated to himself. A true molecule! Not one of us is a chemically independent unit. We are a unified entity. Where I have a hole, he has a dowel, and where I have a dowel, he has a hole. Where I have a convexity, he has a concavity. We've been carefully fitted and joined. Little clocks, little wheels. Lyubasha is a SHE or a HE to us, and unites us all. Wheels, clocks . . . a child's construction set. Like it or not, a cart or a crane . . .

He divided the two obtained squares by diagonals—and was dazzled by the multitude of triangles. They appeared to have exploited all the various triangle combinations corresponding to the number of participants.

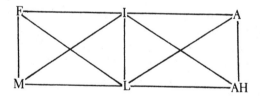

I–Faina–Lyubasha, I–Faina–Mitishatyev, Lyubasha–Mitishatyev–Faina, I–Albina–Faina, I–Albina–Albina's husband, Lyubasha–Albina's husband–Albina . . . A molecule, a true molecule. It lacked Faina taking up with Albina's husband, and Albina with Mitishatyev, but, well, that was yet to come! FAL, LFM, Lyova thought mindlessly, IFM and ILM . . .

At this point we may say that the door swung open, and in walked—Faina. This, too, is entirely realistic and admissible. She might have come here to see Mitishatyev, or to find Lyova, or for no reason at all. It's entirely realistic and admissible. "But—unbearable," said Lyova.

(In concluding our coverage of this gathering, we must confess that we've been somewhat carried away, somewhat too literal about our task, too ready to rise to the bait. This is all vaudeville, and not worth the trouble. Now it's too late. We have trampled this stretch of prose— the grass will no longer grow on it. We shouldn't have lost our temper . . .

For some reason we keep seeing before our eyes a puzzle picture, a riddle picture, from a magazine of our childhood: trees of some sort, snowdrifts, with fallen branches made of fine, superfluous lines. In this puzzle, find the bear, the crow, the bunny. Where is the little boy hiding? Something about this piques us even now: where is the little boy . . .

Our own riddle has no more sense to it:

WHO IS LYOVA?

WHO IS FAINA?

WHO IS MITISHATYEV?

In vaudeville style again, we imagine the Lord's quandary on Judgment Day. He turns our little picture this way and that . . . shrugs his shoulders. *Where are they?*

He tosses it into the file:

"UNIDENTIFIED ON JUDGMENT DAY.")

(Italics Mine. —A.B.)

While I'm arranging and rearranging the chess pieces, and everything's taking unusually long and I just can't get the game going, that is, I just can't get to the development that I've known and yearned for since the very beginning, the development for whose sake I undertook all this, hoping to get the pieces set up in the course of the first two or three pages . . . and suddenly Grandfather appears, Faina, many people . . . Suddenly, like a pawn, Albina's husband pops up, or not even like a pawn but a minus-pawn—well, little by little I'm beginning to see that if I keep on like this, I'll never get to the game itself. It will wither away and become superfluous. Either there will no longer be any need of it, or, simply from overanticipation, I will no longer feel like playing.

That is, when at last I have stationed them all in the proper array and relationship to one another, I'll go off and leave the game in combat position: all the pieces will express a readiness to charge into combat and won't be able to budge, having been woven into too rigid and hopeless a construction ("That's how it is"). And I won't be able to blow up that construction . . . For why all the fuss, why the always postponed story, if not to blow up all these things that have accumulated from within, and thereby at least shed on them a brilliant though instantaneously disappearing light: the light of an explosion! More and more I am aware, with respect to my hero—who more and more is turning into a collective hero—that even if I do succeed in writing an actual story, the explosion will be illusory. Staggering, perhaps—but everything will stay in place, the boom will merely die away, its waves fading as they spread . . . But even then I will still have hope of light, if the explosion puts a crack in even one of the heroes, delimiting one from the others anew, as at birth, and thereby cleaving their disagreeable togetherness. They're a blur to me, an authorial blank! Their faces are all one. So it's no longer they who are the heroes of this narrative, nor, especially, is any one of them (unless we treat the matter formally, taking the main hero to be the one most talked about—Lyova, let's assume).

Yes, everything has developed in a way I didn't anticipate, so that no one of them is the hero, nor are all of them together the hero of this narrative, the hero isn't even a man but a kind of phenomenon, and not a phenomenon—an abstract category (but that's a phenomenon), a category such that . . . having begun, as by a chain reaction, with someone specific and perhaps long ago, beyond the range of the story, it permeates all the heroes, entangles them among themselves, and kills them off one by one, transmitting itself, almost at the moment of one hero's death, into another's essence and flesh. Because within my muddled novel, this category is what has a story, while the heroes—who more and more are becoming "characters" from the flow of mere physical (not to mention historical) time through them—turn out to have less and less of a story. Even they are ceasing to know who they really are, and the author is having more and more trouble telling them apart. By now he sees them as clots, of varying density and stage, but always of the same category, which is the hero. But—what kind of category is this!

Nor can the author rest, or experience the slightest gratification, unless and until one of these clots, these characters, can suddenly find the story, after all, and at least blast it open, at least enter like a phenocryst into the category's story, which is already wearisome in its monotony, its primitive communication, its inescapability, and its violation of all the laws of energy—not only losing nothing in vigor but *apparently growing out of nothing, from itself . . . And if one of them finds that story, most likely as he is perishing, if all is tinged with tragedy—a man finds his story, a story finds its man—then one chain, at least, will be complete. A shining point will appear at the end of it, like an exit from the labyrinth into the blessed world, a point of light that may not illuminate but at least will give, if only to the author, the strength to reach the end; something, at least, will start to flicker like a distant star, unattainable, but still visible to the naked eye. And if this, God grant, is what happens with the narrative, as I sincerely hope and trust; if it begins to be the story, not of a category, but of one clot—if only of Lyova—then I, with jubilant cruelty, will even let him perish in the name of his story, provided we not return to the story of the accursed "category." (In ancient times, as I was recently told by an educated man, when they prepared a medicinal balsam, they would throw into the concoction of honey, herbs, and so forth a live slave, necessarily live, so that as he perished, at the instant of transition, dissolving in the compound, he would impart to it his life force . . .) Well, but what if he won't perish, won't climb into my vat, what if I fail to destroy this tiny chain, this rivulet of treacheries, and everything locks in a ring? Then the narrative will commit suicide like a scorpion, for the scorpion, too, forms a ring in this, his last moment . . . God forbid that the author strangle in his own collar! His blanket, don't you see, is suffocating him.*

The third part, the third part! Grant, O Lord, the strength to finish what I have wrought . . .

MADAME BONACIEUX
(MAN ON DUTY)
(A Chapter in Which the First and Second Parts Converge and Form the Source of the Third)

When the dew of night and the mountain wind had refreshed my burning head, and my thoughts had recovered their usual order, I realized that to chase after my lost happiness was useless and foolhardy. What more did I need? To see her? What for? Was it not all over between us?

NOW WE MUST SKIP AHEAD and relate an episode that belongs, by sequence, only to the third, future part of the novel; we badly need the episode right here, however . . .

Lyova had been left on duty at the institute for the holiday. Such was the custom there.

He was asleep on the director's couch and having a dream. A call from Mitishatyev woke him. Mitishatyev was planning to pay him a visit. A very important matter.

Enigmatic as ever. Lyova grinned good-naturedly at Mitishatyev's changelessness. He knew perfectly well what the "important matter" was—Mitishatyev was contacting people about organizing a high-school class reunion. Fourteen years already, Lyova thought sentimentally.

And woke up. He was glad to wake up a different man. Last night's determination to get some work done this morning despite all—despite his ill-starred conversation with Faina, despite his bad luck with the holidays—wavered for a second and lightly vanished. All that remained was a Lyova who rejoiced at the unexpected chance to be not alone but in company, free from the necessity to conduct a weighty dialogue with himself; a Lyova who had dismissed his eternal escort (double); a Lyova who was jumping up from the couch, stretching his awkward limbs, smiling wryly, rubbing his eyes, gathering his scattered face into a kind of individual whole at the office mirror; a Lyova who was suddenly heading for the window and looking out . . .

This was an unexpected and unwarranted move, made by an already different Lyova, who had suddenly returned. What had clicked in his mind, so easily bridging two such distant points, is hard to explain, just as, in the entire fragment about to follow, it is hard to establish the sequence—what comes after what, and what results from what—and hard not to confuse cause with effect, which are increasingly identical where my hero is concerned. But he ran to the window with a child's inner lightness and weightlessness, which no longer had any outward manifestation: he stomped hastily to the window, something urged him to hurry and look out. And while he ran to the window and looked out, a small mental picture arose before him, as if to explain his sudden childish lightness. The picture was from *The Three Musketeers*, and had the same look and feel as long ago, a good twenty years back, when he would come home from school and sit in the empty apartment—his feet up in the easy chair, his father's skullcap jammed on his head— sipping oversweet tea from a glass in an heirloom glass-holder (the monogram from the glass-holder lay at the bottom of the picture, like the artist's signature). In the picture, Madame Bonacieux, so lovely in her nun's habit, was running to the narrow convent window and had frozen in that unstopped pose, as if she were still running, on out the window and beyond, her light feet now treading the air. Standing motionless, she looked out the window, and there was trusty d'Artagnan galloping to the rescue, with his cloak streaming, and on it the cross of the Muske- teers. But it was too late: she could run to the window, she could look out—but she could stand in this headlong pose no longer than it would take d'Artagnan to shove aside the spying Mother Superior and race up the convent stairs, his dusty heels pounding. And there, with one sweet moan, Madame was still falling and falling, so slowly that d'Artagnan had time to race all the way across the room and catch her as she fell, and only then did she breathe her last in his beloved arms, and this sigh was their final kiss, so sweet that what else could she do but die! There could be no sequel . . . Faina, oh God, Faina! She was falling by the high lancet window, there was just time to catch her, but she would already be dead, dooming d'Artagnan to gallop and gallop till his dying day, his cloak streaming . . .

Lyova ran to the high window of the former private mansion, now an institute that had imprisoned him within its walls for the duration of the national holiday and celebration, and he looked out the window with aching heart.

The embankment, deserted as always, nevertheless had a kind of backsplash from the roar of the torrent of marchers passing nearby; the black pile driver, now so lifeless, had drifted to rest by an undriven pile; the cobblestone pavement stopped short of the river, leaving a strip of dirt, fenced off from the water by a tongue-and-groove board paling, and along that sidewalk, along that path, Faina was walking, with a companion Lyova had not known about before. He was tall and curly-haired, somehow surprising to Lyova in his appearance; for some reason he wore a quilted work jacket—he was no clotheshorse. They were just now skirting a puddle. They had walked side by side until now, but at this moment the puddle disconnected the two of them, slid them apart, their arms stretched over the puddle, lost hold in the middle, and dropped, with a laugh. They were alone on the embankment, separately and oddly, like actors, as though an open ZIS convertible were crawling slowly along behind and they were being filmed, while, from somewhere above, Lyova watched the scene being played—director and god.

Perhaps because of the weather. Wind high in the sky. Puffed-up wisps of clouds. Transparence. Odd weather, that it made you think they really did use airplanes to drive away bad weather on the eve of a march, so that nature herself would celebrate along with the people, as in the news reports. Mean weather yesterday, with rain and snow, the same tomorrow, even meaner, made brutish by human interference, baffled, entangled in its own malice. But today the clarity, the cleanness, the blue of torn-in-half space, torn by mysterious and mighty war vehicles, which would fly again at the parades today, easily visible to the nation, in the sky they had cleared for themselves.

Lyova stood motionless at the window, after flinging it open with one agile movement and nearly tumbling out on the street. A needle-sharp wind, seemingly the result of those implausible airplanes, blew into him. It was blowing as if down a hatchway, and in fact all this blue, transparent, empty space was perfectly like a hole striving to close up and disappear, an ice hole that longed to skin over with ice, and the wind was perfectly understandable.

Lyova stood at this window like a man who had never been asleep, and in his soul he bore an inexplicable resemblance to this torn, tattered, cleared weather.

He saw both Faina, so tormenting even yesterday, and her new companion, the very man, unknown and intangible, who had been the force behind all her actual companions, who was taking Faina, tangible and close Faina, away into the far distance—Faina was running away, her upturned flying face filled with a kind of desperate and risky hope, again like today's weather.

And her companion, so curly-haired . . . Why is it you never see curly-haired people nowadays? Lyova suddenly approved of her taste. The fellow wasn't handsome, of course. But he had something, which had been chosen by Faina, discovered by her. Which Lyova would never have seen in him, were not Faina beside him. Lyova felt something akin to the surprised respect we experience on seeing a homely man escorting a beautiful woman, or, vice versa, a prominent man with a homely woman, when it strikes us that beautiful people possess a certain knowledge or truth permitting them to be with those they love, regardless of public opinion, and have therefore mastered the secret of happiness. He recalled his quiet bewilderment over foreign magazines, with their photographs of film stars and their spouses.

Her companion walked along, filled with the strength that Faina lent him, and the sight did not destroy Lyova, as it usually would, with a bullet through the heart. Even though Lyova saw it all as he always did, he saw it—differently. He didn't even care now about the fact that usually tortured him so in respect to his beloved. Had she or hadn't she? With this man or another? What foolishness! Could it interest anyone at all? After all, it wasn't even a fact. The f- :t was Faina herself. Suddenly, for the first time in many years, Lyova had before him a real object, the real Faina just now walking past his window, along the embankment, with a companion whom Lyova did not know. For the first time in many years, Lyova saw Faina.

She was nowhere near so pretty as it had seemed to his agitated imagination. She was tired and somber, even though something about her forbade one to think she was unhappy now—a stillness, perhaps, and repose. Very likely her companion was able to lend her importance, as she did him. No, he wasn't gazing at her with ecstasy or enchantment or deep emotion; his eyes simply held not the shadow of a doubt that Faina was the only woman on earth. He had no need to discuss her virtues and failings because there was no comparison and never could be. That is probably the way happy people look, inseparable from one another . . .

Suddenly Lyova's heart stood still with love for her, just for her, for no one else—even he had no part of it. For perhaps the first time in all these years his feeling could have been called love, except for just one other long-ago moment, the very first, which he had already forgotten.

Perhaps because the atmosphere today was so sharp, even from high across the street Lyova saw everything as if through binoculars. The wrinkle on her neck, and the already slackening skin of her cheeks. An idiotic sort of hat. A button dangled by a thread. One tattered high heel (it must have been on the escalator), and her buckling gait . . . The sharpness of the image was suddenly beginning to disappear—Lyova's tears.

And what he had always imagined to be armor, a force aimed against him—her clothes, makeup, mannerisms—suddenly struck Lyova as a touching defenselessness, uncertainty, weakness: a delicate little switch against a crushingly assaultive life. None of this had either plus or minus sign, it had no vector, it was not aimed to impale him. And their recent, last conversation: Lyova kept attacking in despair and getting nowhere, he battered against her and she was like a wall, he seemed to have blood flowing down his face, a crown of thorns . . . What did she say to him? Not a word; she was silent, impenetrable, and suddenly: "But what have I done to you? Whatever have I done to you? Well, answer me. Answer me!" And suddenly Lyova had no answer for her: truly, what had she done to him? Lyova was taken aback, all his numerous, ramifying arguments evaporated, and there was just—nothing. Truly, what had she done? Lyova was dumb with surprise, and she left.

Accounts? How could they have accounts to settle!

Now they had skirted the puddle, and their hands came together again. Their faces turned profile to Lyova and began to disappear. The back of his head was funny . . . Laughter, her primeval laughter, suddenly spilled over the pavement, went bouncing over the separate little cobblestones, her terrible laughter, which had frightened Lyova all his life . . . Her pathetic laughter, faint and irrelevant to Lyova . . . It's she, Lyova thought with sudden illumination. My love! She is my wife!

Suddenly he wanted to lean out the window to his waist, start shouting, waving his arms. All joyful and excited, Lyova waves his arms at her and shouts, "Faina! Hey, Faina!" She turns around in surprise and smiles, recognizing him. "Drop in and see me! Drop in, both of you!" "Me, too?" her companion asks wordlessly, pointing at his own chest, and smiles charmingly. "Of course, of course! Together!" Lyova shouts, and waves his arms.

Choking, Lyova stood in the window and stared after their ridiculous backs. How suddenly Faina had recognized something (oh yes, she'd come to see him here, and more than once, Lyova remembered), and turned away. Her glance had swept over the building, recognizing it. And her eyebrow had lifted. Her companion paused, and swept the windows with a glance that reflected her changed face.

Lyova recoiled from the window and all but wept from the terrible awareness that he must not have her suddenly see him, because he could never explain to her why and how he had just been watching her, because he had lost the chance forever, he did not have the right to watch her, and her wrath would be just . . . Only to glimpse her.

Recoiling, Lyova stood with his back pressed to the wall as though they could see him, frightened that they would see him, and suddenly he pictured her taking her companion by the hand and starting to drag him: "Come on, let's get out of here!" "What's the matter?" said her companion, we may suppose. "Nothing, just come on," she said.

Could she really . . . from me? Lyova thought with horror. My God, how awful. When . . .? He covered his face—he did not want to see. His days raced before him in the darkness of his hands. He so wanted to find the simple little mistake that would explain everything. But his days were the continuance one of another, and that saving point from which all had started was not there, still not there. He could find no break in his thread, feel no knot. I shouldn't have taken the ring that time, Lyova told himself, without conviction.

That's why! I simply didn't let her love me. I didn't let her, he thought with relief, and took away his hands.

With strange tranquillity he looked out the window again. Two small figures in the distance, and he could no longer tell whether they were hurrying. They might even be running.

"I love her, I simply love her—and that's it. Can I help it?" Lyova said. "She's my wife. It's so."

He remembered her companion's face. "She dreamed this once, she told me. A sun-warmed field, the smell of sagebrush. That was the point. Just the field. And the smell. Something vague on the horizon, like a thing forgotten. And someone walking behind her, not hurrying to catch up.

"It's cold." Lyova shivered, and closed the window.

(He watched through the almost transparent glass, and the idea that had for so long seemed definitive in his experience—the idea that nothing but treachery had chained him to this love for so long—suddenly struck him as treacherous and banal. That is, the very idea of treachery struck him as treacherous. That was why.)

END OF THE SECOND PART

APPENDIX TO
THE SECOND PART
The Hero's Profession

I recently learned that Pechorin had died on his way back from Persia. This was very glad news; it gave me the right to publish these memoirs, and I have taken the opportunity to put my own name to someone else's work. God grant that my readers will not chastise me for such an innocent forgery!

WE HAD MEANT to find a moment . . . It seems to us that the moment not only arrived but was also let slip again, in the interest of composition.

We had meant to tell in more detail what it was that Lyova devoted himself to, what he *did*.

One disquieting thought is that he may not quite like the work we have picked for him to do. May not be quite satisfied. Although, if that's true, he conceals it carefully, even from himself. (Would that he knew what threatens him because of his insincerity, according to the plot!) There is even a possibility that Lyova's profession just doesn't suit us, but suits him fine. This is a common mistake—for a man to put himself in someone else's place and draw conclusions—but the author has no right to make it, even in relation to his own hero. We should have thought before. In the very beginning . . .

Choosing a profession for an intellectual hero is always a professional predicament for the novelist. If you want the hero to walk, see, think, emote— what profession, in our era, allows him the time for it? Night watchman? But he takes on the features of an unrecognized genius as soon as the author tries to give him ideas with any sophistication. "Truth to life," so to speak, will suffer at once, if we make such an unlucky choice. So here we are, in a malarial fever of creativity: "A certain young architect . . . no, too solemn a profession. A young physician . . . too responsible a profession, I'd have to be a physician to . . . A certain promising young bridge engineer . . . cumbersome, but okay . . . but if he's so promising, when will he have time to reflect? On the riverbank? Standing on his own bridge? Dampness and cold waft up from below, a suicide's insight . . . and then, why a bridge engineer?!" An annoying chill, we have to choose all over again. Now some unexpected possibilities turn up: retirement, the first relaxed days, the first thoughts in his whole life up to retirement . . . a bit too old for a hero. An illness, then, convalescence . . . but we want things to be all right with the hero's health, at least. Demobilization, then, release from prison. Won't do? A vacation, then. What a lot of stories like Bunin's have been written when the hero relaxes in the open air and gains insight through the author's adapted revelations! An uninhabited island—now there's a mirage of a plot! Defoe took it away from us ages ago. Most such solutions are already taken—you might say, all of them.

I'm not alone in my plight. As far back as Lev Tolstoy . . . (As far back as, or as recently as?) If I recall, he was shrewdly rebuked for Levin by a certain Soviet writer: had Tolstoy dared to call Levin a writer (call a spade a spade), he would have avoided all the hypocrisy associated with Levin. There is a specious ease to this solution, however. Had Tolstoy called him a writer, people would immediately have thought Levin was Lev Tolstoy himself. But it must be said that the chasm between the landowner Levin and a landowner resembling "the truth" would appear extremely small, compared to the chasm dividing the writer Levin from the writer Lev Tolstoy. There is a paradox here, never taken into account by the ungrateful reader in his swift reprisal. The paradox is as follows: the writer is the very person who cannot write about himself. It's merely an optical illusion that he is bringing the hero close to him. The edges of the chasm come closer together, but the chasm itself grows deeper. There's a classic example: the numerous Proust scholars in the West run into difficulty trying to track down the prototypes of the heroes and situations in his interminable novel, although it was conceived as a reenactment of his own life and gives an impression of undistorted reality. Meanwhile, in the case of Tolstoy, although he's a model of realistic typification and objectification, we have no trouble locating the numerous cousins and uncles who served as the prototypes for nearly all his heroes.

But in those days it was all right. In those days a hero who had time for all the nuances of tribulation, thought, and feeling was no surprise to anyone. Tolstoy and Proust had a milieu, which they unmasked, shall we say, but it also understood them. There were plenty of enlightened people who had not been enslaved by life, who possessed both time and money. For all that they were being "mercilessly" unmasked, a degree of sophistication or intellectualism was within their comprehension, and flattering to them. Nowadays it's considerably harder to occupy a hero in such a way that he more or less expresses the author's latest ideas. As recent a writer as Chekhov several times found graceful ways to extricate himself from this situation. In our day the process has begun to look surprisingly clumsy. Within our recollection the last writer able to get out of this professional predicament was Mikhail Zoshchenko, with his giddy sense of proportion. Let us give him the floor:

"Kotofeev was a professional musician. He played the triangle in a symphony orchestra.

"There are some strange and wonderful professions.

"There are some professions that appall you to think how a man arrives at them. How did a man ever hit upon the idea of walking a tightrope, let's say, or whistling through his nose, or tinkling a triangle?

"But the author isn't laughing at his hero. No. Boris Ivanovich Kotofeev was . . ." And so forth.

Brilliant. Not only has it become difficult to pick a suitable profession for the hero, so that he approaches the author more or less closely without our telling lies against the "truth" of life; it has also become somehow awkward and shameful. It's like being on a bus when you've got a couple of fellows bouncing ideas off one another, carrying on a loud "intelligent" conversation and throwing big words around as though the bus were empty, as though they weren't on a bus at all. Frightfully shameful and awkward. You try not to remember the last time you yourself might have behaved the same way.

This is the very feeling about which one may say that "the writer is with the people." A writer, even one who doesn't write about "the people," is very much a creature of the people. This "sense of the people" is also used in making that secret selection, where the criterion is by no means intelligibility, accessibility, or popularity. The writer, even the most super-sophisticated, is not primarily an intellectual, if of course he's a worthwhile writer. But, although in any case he has come, let us confidently say, *from the people*, the writer gains new social experience, which thirsts for its own personification. And when he checks this experience against his native sense of the people (sixth sense?), he experiences awkwardness, embarrassment, and shame. Hence we may conclude that conscience is a trait "of the people," but again, not in the sense that the people necessarily have a conscience—needless to say, the people tend to be conscienceless. And this applies with special force to those who have, precisely, come from the people. So. That's what a writer is, perhaps: someone who doesn't lose his "people's conscience" after he comes from the people.

In sum, it's awkward, embarrassing, shameful. In vain do his patrons take care of the writer—he'll always be a renegade from the stratum that he penetrates with such difficulty. If he needs a cultured, intellectual hero to express him more directly and match his level, you can be sure this hero will be unmasked.

It's awkward having a loud "intelligent" conversation on the bus. And Lyova is just the kind to get carried away and blurt out something inappropriate. Although, to his credit, I can add that he blushes easily.

But what a profession I've picked for him! Don't be a writer, but write anyway. Live by literature, on literature, with literature, but not in it. This has been convenient for me, not for him.

And really, has it been worthwhile to entertain myself with a biased description of him—to submerge myself in his familial, historical, and amorous tribulations and ordeals, developing and formulating the hero through his life itself, and never quite reaching the junction at which all the problems we conferred on him were supposed to find their bleak solution. Things seem to have started out accurately, but after a while the hero began to come through as rather unattractive, even more so than I would have liked or had intended. What is the matter? He still feels, thinks, even has some ideas; at any rate, there's nothing nasty or villainous about him . . . but he doesn't *do* anything. It has been strange to suffer this defeat to my authorial pride. After all, I reported at the proper time that he was studying in school, in college, in graduate school; here he's even finished his dissertation, just hasn't defended it yet. He may even have worked somewhere between college and graduate school, picked up some experience. Everyone can imagine that he hasn't had an easy time of it. As before, however, he isn't *doing* anything. And when an egghead doesn't do anything, then, like it or not, he becomes a bit disgusting. From time to time I've also mentioned certain secretly cherished ideas for papers, mentioned that these ideas had even elicited the admiration of his colleagues, or at any rate had contributed to his being assigned a reputation as a "man of talent." And yet the do-nothing impression remains. It has utterly sunk my hero.

But every cloud has a silver lining. If my choice of a profession for my hero is so unlucky that his labor has not ennobled him in the pages of the novel, still, as I suddenly see, it's a bit of good luck as well. Because, had I chosen any other profession, I could hardly have appended the product of my hero's labor directly to the novel—a sheaf of wheat, let's say, or a steamship, or that bridge. But here I can cite in the novel the very product of his labor, by publishing, let's say, an article by L. Odoevtsev, from among those which he himself privately considers "the real thing" or those which have elicited the warmest response from his colleagues.

We have already said that as a graduate student Lyova wrote an article about three poets. That in some ways it was naïve, and in other ways *became* naïve. That it wasn't strictly scientific, but on the other hand Lyova said a lot that was *his own*, and this is valuable in our time. That it's fresh even now, in that it's not about Pushkin, not about Lermontov, and especially not about Tyutchev, but about him, about Lyova . . . it bespeaks *his* experience. His meeting with Grandfather, his love for Faina, Albina's love, his friendship with Mitishatyev—none of it had been without consequence, after all; it showed in his experience. Interestingly, Lyova's work on this article can be dated from the precise moment when Mitishatyev "vanquished" him for the last time (the moment "by the cupboard"). That is, in the time frame of the novel, the writing of this article coincides with the chapter "The Myth of Mitishatyev" and comes well before the chapter "Madame Bonacieux," which even spurted ahead of the next part of our narrative. There's no way to bring all these things into line . . .

So the article was titled

THREE PROPHETS

Introducing the article were two epigraphs, printed not one under the other but side by side, parallel, which is somewhat suggestive of both the content and the method.

<table>
<tr><td></td><td>Nor warmth in your eyes,</td></tr>
<tr><td></td><td>Nor truth in your words,</td></tr>
<tr><td>The man envious enough</td><td>Nor soul have you.</td></tr>
<tr><td>to hiss Don Giovanni was</td><td>Dare all, O my heart:</td></tr>
<tr><td>capable of poisoning</td><td>Nor has creature creator!</td></tr>
<tr><td>his creator.</td><td>Nor prayer a use!</td></tr>
<tr><td>PUSHKIN ON SALIERI, 1832</td><td>TYUTCHEV, 1836</td></tr>
</table>

And Lyova goes on with the comparison. He takes two poems found in every schoolboy text—Pushkin's "Prophet" and Lermontov's "Prophet"—which would have been no novelty, but he found a third, and the three of them willingly "chipped in." The third one proved to be Tyutchev's poem "Madness." All three had been written in different years, but Lyova happily put his arithmetic to use, subtracted the birthdates from the composition dates, and in all three cases obtained the same result—twenty-seven. Lyova was in his twenty-seventh year, and this inspired him. Pushkin was the first of the four to turn twenty-seven, in 1826 ("Pushkin was even in time to be born in the eighteenth century!" Lyova exclaims. "That one year is very significant"), and he wrote his brilliant "Prophet." But in other years, too (and other epochs, Lyova thought, with himself in mind), men have reached that same age— Tyutchev in 1830 (he was born too late for the eighteenth century, which is also significant, Lyova notes), Lermontov in 1841 (Lyova in 196–, let us add in parentheses)—and have begun to be troubled by the same questions.

What are these questions?

Lyova asserts that in essence they boil down to the problem of uninterruptedness. What he means by this word does not immediately become clear, nor is it totally clear even later. Lyova says that people are born and live uninterruptedly until the age of twenty-seven (a year or two, one way or the other—twenty-seven is close enough, Lyova claims). They live uninterruptedly—and at twenty-seven they die. Around the age of twenty-seven, the uninterrupted, placid development and accumulation of experience culminates in this qualitative leap, an awareness of the world's system, life's irreversibility. From this moment, Lyova goes on to say, a man begins to "know what he does," and can no longer be "blissfully ignorant." Full consciousness prompts him to *solitary* acts, yet the logical chain they form is inviolable, and a single violation of it will mean spiritual death. In so cruel a spiritual system, only God survives. Man dies. This point in time is critical, specific, and very brief, not much capable of extension . . . and a man must decide, choose his further path before it is too late, and then look back no more. Like the epic hero, he has before him three paths. God, the devil, or man. Or perhaps God, man, death. Or perhaps Paradise, Hell, Purgatory* (and these images, Lyova claims, are taken from our experience: the three stages of one human life, which are eternally repeated in each life and independent of the era of history). Pushkin, Tyutchev, and Lermontov chose among the three paths, each his own. Pushkin chose God (or he had the genius to live uninterruptedly until the age of thirty-seven, which amounts to the same thing). Lermontov preferred death to interruptedness, repetition, spiritual death; Tyutchev went on living *interruptedly*. At twenty-seven, men die and begin to live as shadows, even if under the same names. Theirs is an existence beyond the grave, and a world beyond the grave. At its threshold all is decided, the entire subsequent destiny of the soul; this is why all three geniuses addressed one and the same issue, and all three chose a different answer. They all argued with the first, with Pushkin. Tyutchev even bore him malice (Lyova alone, a hundred and some years later, reached out a hand to him).

We have of course been too concise and dispassionate in conveying the question that troubled Lyova, i.e., we may have conveyed nothing. But it's a long time since we read the article, and by now we are used to wandering in that shadowy next world beyond the grave, in Lyova's definition. It's hard for us to relate to things that we have already had time to forget.

Lyova begins the literary part of the article with high hopes, making one

---

* *We wouldn't want to discard these constructs as irrelevant: they do characterize Lyova. At that age, people are impressed by the number 3, for it signifies the birth of a series, the first labor pang of experience.*

noteworthy disclaimer: that he is taking three unquestionably brilliant poems, written by three unquestionably brilliant twenty-seven-year-old poets. All three poems are perfect in form and poetic expression. Precisely for this reason, without getting into a discussion of the development of their poetic forms, he has made bold to contrast them in *content*, which has not been the custom in science recently, because content is a less-than-scientific subject. Such being the case, he speaks as a critic. I trust I will be forgiven, Lyova declares, for comparing meaning rather than form.

The article as a whole was written frankly (with all candor) in Pushkin's favor. In his name . . .

Lyova credited him with a lofty absence of the private, personal "I," and the presence of only a supreme, universally human "I" thirsting to fulfill its destiny on earth. And indeed,

With fainting soul athirst for grace . . .

—the whole poem delighted Lyova. The precision with which the spiritual story was recorded, its almost superhuman terseness, as if "from on high." And the utter insignificance of the personal, worldly "I," with its immediate interests, in the face of an "I" that is spiritual and divine.

Lermontov's "Prophet," in Lyova's view, was a complete and comical contrast. It, too, was a brilliantly precise record of a story, but that was all. Not exactly unspiritual, but "prespiritual," youthful, almost adolescent. Brilliant self-expression, but the man who's expressing himself doesn't seem to be brilliant yet. Or rather, he's brilliant, but what he expresses is totally unbrilliant. (Lyova did not wound Lermontov to the quick, because "The Prophet" is the last poem in his slender volume. It was almost a testament: next came his duel, his death, so that Lermontov could not revise.) For Lyova, the first two lines of each stanza bespoke Lermontov's indisputable natural genius; if the whole poem had been made up of these first lines, minus the second ones, it would have been just as good, almost, as Pushkin's. But then the second two . . . good God, why does he do it! The whole thing falls flat, he goes from the sublime to the ridiculous. His thesis is excellent, the antithesis nothing but childish, naïve resentment: people don't recognize him, don't show their gratitude! But these "hind" lines are where Lermontov himself is to be found. These are the lines he sets against the first two, which seem to be not his, someone else's, refuted by life itself—Pushkinian lines. Lyova broke up the poem and structured it as a dialogue. First to speak is Pushkin, as it were (really Lermontov, but in a bass voice that slides to a falsetto). Lermontov himself answers, pouting, grumbling aggrievedly, complaining about some childish injustice in a playground game. For example:

"PUSHKIN":
Since that day when the Lord on high
Endowed me with a prophet's knowledge,
    LERMONTOV:
    (Interrupting, butting in, thin-voiced and angry)
    I've read in every human eye
    A chronicle of vice and folly.
"PUSHKIN":
Love I proclaimed; and I began
To teach the Truth—simply and purely:
    LERMONTOV:
    (Interrupting again, breaking into tears)
    My neighbors rose up as one man
    And threw stones at me in their fury.

And so forth, in the same spirit. There you have it, Lyova concluded, the unworthy and pathetic behavior that inevitably characterizes every "I" personality, entering the fray, putting the world on notice of his rights. What makes Pushkin great is that this doesn't concern him. He's too lofty and *busy* to feel aggrieved by the pain (the pinch) of his own ambition. Lermontov keeps expecting recognition and gratitude, a candy, a pat. An aggrieved little boy.

"But this is mankind itself!" Lyova exclaimed next. "It has a grievance against itself, for no earthly reason. Or it trips on a stone, kicks it again in vexation—and then feels aggrieved by the stone and starts to cry." Pushkin and Lermontov, he said, launching into free analogies, are like Mozart and Beethoven. One of them still has before his eyes the whole edifice of the world, a temple, clarity. The other one runs into the edifice and gets lost, he keeps seeing some corner or beam, he wants air, light, he's forgotten where the exit is. He sees a beam and it becomes the world, he pours out on it his sorrow and anger and despair: the beam is ugly, bad. Or again, a corner, a spider in it, he feels aggrieved. In a fragmented world a man enters into each little fragment as if it were the world. The "I" appears (*"mine"*), frustrated, resisting itself, wrestling in a sudden cul-de-sac, grabbing and clawing itself, setting itself against its own shadow. Beethoven is a stormy struggle under a blanket that has fallen from a balcony and covered him, head and all.* The "I" is already shouting at the top of its voice that it's the "I," yet it feels aggrieved that it can't hear anything anymore, because everyone's bawling

* *We'll leave the "music" to Lyova's conscience.*

his own "I" at the same time and doesn't even hear himself, much less anyone else.

Lyova copes in this decisive and picturesque manner (keeping his own distance, let us add in parentheses). This is still good, pure, and intelligible— Pushkin as Mozart. But now, in addition to the noisy and unhappy Lermontov/Beethoven, a Salieri/Tyutchev appears. Even though he was earlier than Lermontov (turned twenty-seven earlier), he is later, he's closer to us, he's more contemporary to us. Although he, too, lost sight of his reference point and the edifice as a whole, he did not burst out crying like Lermontov without his Granny. He looked carefully, deeply, at all the little spiders and corners of one of the anterooms. Pushkin had not known such intentness, he stood in the light and in the open, but Tyutchev felt that he was seeing something Pushkin did not see, he felt people didn't recognize him for this, for going *further*. Now, years later, we recognize it, but they didn't then; like Lermontov, he didn't immediately get his share. But Tyutchev reacts differently, more maliciously, more small-mindedly. He doesn't need a caress, as Lermontov did; he needs a monument. He wants a *place* for himself. Look . . .

Next, by the same device, Lyova builds a parallel between Pushkin's "Prophet" and Tyutchev's "Madness." But if Lermontov speaks openly, on the same platform, and merely looks ridiculous, then "this fellow" (Lyova had no pity for Tyutchev) isn't even on the platform, he's hiding backstage, surreptitiously hissing from the wings, in a loud and evil whisper—a secret, dark word for every word of Pushkin's—he doesn't even interrupt (as Lermontov did), he nags, treading on the heels of Pushkin's words.

PUSHKIN: "The Prophet"	TYUTCHEV: "Madness"
With fainting soul athirst for Grace,	*Where, like smoke, the arch of sky*
I wandered in a desert place,	*Fuses with scorched earth,*
And at the crossing of the ways	*There pathetic madness hides*
I saw the sixfold Seraph blaze;	*To live in careless mirth.*
He touched mine eyes with fingers light	*Entrenched amidst the blazing sands*
As sleep that cometh in the night:	*And incandescent glare,*
And like a frighted eagle's eyes,	*It something seeks, and wildly scans*
They opened wide with prophecies.	*The clouds with glassy stare.*
He touched mine ears, and they were drowned	*Now suddenly it starts: its keen*
With tumult and a roaring sound:	*Ear pressed to the cracked ground,*
I heard convulsion in the sky,	*It listens with secretive greed,*
And flights of angel hosts on high,	*Complacence on its brow.*

And beasts that move beneath the sea,	It thinks it hears the roiling streams
	In subterranean night,
	The cradled murmur of their dreams,
And the sap creeping in the tree . . .	Their strident surge to light!

Tyutchev seemed to write more densely, briefly, scathingly. His poison suf-ficed for but half of Pushkin's poem. For the second, the divine, half of Push-kin's poem (no longer a process toward God—a God found), Tyutchev had no strength left: after biting Pushkin's boot, he slithered away. So Lyova argued.

Pushkin openly tells the story of his dealings with God. Lermontov com-plains quite linearly and monotonously about how things haven't worked out between him and God. Both speak from the "I." Tyutchev has no "I" in his poem. He has hidden it. He asserts his opinion about another, but he himself is not there. He is categorical in his appraisal—and puts nothing in the other pan of the scales (does not appraise himself). The impression is that he wants to wound someone, while remaining unrecognized. There is a sort of evil cowardice in his covert surveillance and his judgment that will go unanswered. He has no hope of being heard by the one he mocks, and he therefore has time to hide before he is *not* noticed. The thing most hurtful to one's pride, perhaps, is to inflict an insult—and have it go unnoticed.

Pushkin reflected the world: a reflection pure and clear. His "I," like breath on a mirror, will appear as a little white cloud and evaporate, leaving the surface still purer. Lermontov openly projects his own reflection on the world, he keeps nothing back; however dull the reflection, it is still he, himself. Tyutchev, more artful than either, *hides*. ("Be silent, be hidden, and con-ceal"—a brilliant poem, from that same year, 1830; Lyova hitched this, too, to his mill.) He is the first to hide something—the very impulse to his verse—and he curtains it, tucks it away, even cuts short the story. In the upshot, the all-controlling Tyutchev does not express himself and yet he himself turns out to have been expressed. So Lyova concludes, as he tries to formulate a kind of paradox of craftsmanship, whose boundaries unfailingly delineate a focal lesion, a spiritual ulcer, the cancer of individualism. Only openness is elusive and invisible; it is poesy. Concealment, although very artful, is visible; it is the mark of Cain, the mark of craftsmanship, which incidentally is close and contemporary to us in spirit.

But we must not suppose Tyutchev to have been "ahead of his time"—he is an exceptional occurrence of his own epoch, an occurrence that has now become universal, without his sophistication or genius. He is not a progenitor but a precedent in time, if we draw conclusions about him only in accordance with the laws of his own day. And what other laws can we judge him by?

Ours? "The law is not retroactive." Such were the paradoxes Lyova arrived at. But he went on to even stranger ones.

"Tyutchev as Pushkin's Murderer" is one of his most impressive chapters. It is part experiment in crime detection, part subject for the criminologist; part psychiatric case presentation, part material for the psychiatrist. In any event, it gives free rein to a psychoanalyst. The author of the article builds a rickety structure of dates, quotations, and references, a kind of table reminiscent of Mendeleev's, where the letters and numbers, somehow clinging to each other's tail, are held up by friction alone—builds it, however, rather impatiently and in haste to reach the point for whose sake he is building. (Naturally, we can't remember how he reckoned all this. The department no longer has the article—Lyova took it back from them some time ago and stopped showing it to people—and we don't care to consult Lyova himself . . .) Essentially, these reckonings are not a proof proper but a proof that Lyova's version is not contradictory, that it is possible. He calculates Tyutchev's "tactics" in publishing his poems. He encircles "Madness" with the dense ring of poems that Pushkin himself had accepted for publication in the *Contemporary* before his death. He discusses whether Pushkin could have read "Madness" in a certain literary miscellany, the only place it had been published. Significantly, "Madness" was not included (although it could have been, in view of its poetic standard) in the cycle offered to the *Contemporary*; significantly, Tyutchev included it in no other editions during his lifetime, as if he wanted it dead and buried. A great many more conjectures of this kind, and he tries to prove them all somehow.

And now (we recall the feel of this passage, but are unable to reproduce it) Lyova makes an impetuous, convoluted logical transition, from "there was something about" Tyutchev's attitude toward Pushkin to "there was something going on" in their relationship. There was something there, something behind it . . . there was a *theme* to this relationship, it had a *story*, and—the thing most galling for Tyutchev—Pushkin did not notice. Next Lyova names the word "duel" and rides it, long and beautifully, from sentence to sentence, stitching them together, like the bobbin in a sewing machine. We well remember that oscillating motion. A duel—a duel that was not—a duel that was—it was indeed a duel. A secret duel, because nobody knew about it except one of the duelists. An open duel, in which one of the adversaries simply did not notice anyone dueling with him (hadn't he had enough of challenges and duels?).

Over thirty years later, twenty-five years after Pushkin's death, Tyutchev *remembers*. Ah, how he remembers! He doesn't have all that many inner echoes in his poetry, after thirty years . . . but now there's a quotation. And it's something twice hidden, thrice buried. Now the very existence of "Madness" is being concealed, the poem is rewritten and readdressed to Fet,* in a tone less "injured," more epic, grown wiser and humbler (wearier?):

> Others are given by Nature
> An instinct prophetic and blind,
> They can feel, they can hear the waters
> Even in earth's dark depths . . .

"Others," you see. "Prophetic and blind" . . . the word "prophet" has been germinating. So now he agrees that it's "prophetic," but he is still jealous of, still hates the very nature of, the phenomenon "instinct," which he does not possess. "Even in earth's dark depths," with Tyutchev's ellipsis points—this is Pushkin, who, apparently from the grave, still feels, still hears.†

Contrasted to this quatrain are four weak lines, lacking in self-confidence. If the first four are about Pushkin, then the person being contrasted to him is either Fet or a generalized image of the "dedicated" poet, which includes Tyutchev as well. Amusingly, perhaps the only poet who doesn't contradict the ideal expressed in these contrasted lines is Pushkin himself. Tyutchev trumps Pushkin with Pushkin.§

As for the "water seekers" (to whom all scholars refer), who supposedly served as prototypes for both of Tyutchev's poems, what was there about these wretched and worthless people that could have inflicted such a personal, such a concrete, such a diarylike wound on Tyutchev? On such a master of *concrete* poetry, who so innovatively introduced the concrete details of personal, even private, vivid (vicious?) experience into his poetry? How had they offended him, the water seekers? The water seekers, it follows, are the innovative Tyutchevian "screen," by which the poetic experience, although expressed with extraordinary sharpness and concreteness, is fenced off from the *story* of that experience, its subject matter.

But what, in this case, is the subject?

---

* Incidentally, Lyova remarks, if Pushkin could have read the 1834 Morning Star and did not, then Fet almost certainly did not. He did not know "Madness," and regarded the poem that had been dedicated to him as a new one.
† Inappropriately, Lyova imagines d'Anthès as a downcast old man, his tone "humble and weary": "A demon made me do it . . ."
§ Lyova assumes that the bridge from this poem to "Madness" is Fet's article "On the Poetry of F. Tyutchev." Fet builds his article on Pushkin, by comparing Pushkin's "Insomnia" with Tyutchev's (the method is, thus, not new!).

The subject is a grudge. A complex one, moreover, with many facets and many turnabouts. Very secret, very deep, hidden almost from Tyutchev himself, a grudge that was all the easier to hide and all the harder to suspect, because in due course Tyutchev obviously demonstrated to everyone (and to himself?) that he, *too*, was a genius. His grudge was against nature herself, which was why he meditated on her so splendidly and for so long. (That's going too far! we exclaim.) And he would never have felt this resentment had he not had next to him, at his side, an example for comparison, eclipsing and refuting any logic of gradual increase and growth. Pushkin!

Everything was "better" in Tyutchev, the line itself was better, but even so he lacked something of what came so easily, so freely, so naturally to Pushkin. During his lifetime Tyutchev outwrote Pushkin (in the sense that he went farther, outdistanced him). But Pushkin never saw his back, while Pushkin's back always loomed maniacally before Tyutchev. And Tyutchev knew—secretly from himself, without putting it into words, but knew deeply— that he lacked "one little thing," a seemingly minor thing that was given away free but could nowhere be earned, acquired . . . while Pushkin didn't even need to know he had it, because he did have it. They were of the same class, but Pushkin was more the aristocrat, he *had* it, without pondering where it came from; Tyutchev was more the upstart intellectual, he *wanted* to have it but did not. This was overscrupulosity on Tyutchev's part, to notice that he lacked something; it never struck anyone's attention later, his job was not to blab it. And he didn't. But when he did blab it (in his own opinion), he immediately hid it, like "Madness," but he did not destroy it. Genius had been given to—a petty man! What pushed him? What was it he lacked? Had he come too late? Was he envious? Had he infringed . . . ? But his own infinitesimal deficiency, unnoticeable and imperceptible to an ordinary, normal man, yet hideous to a genius like Tyutchev, was what he could not forgive the man who had everything— Pushkin.

There was one possible remedy for this: the recognition and friendship of Pushkin himself. Their names must be linked while they were still alive. What the Lord had failed to give Tyutchev (ah! it dawned on Lyova that Tyutchev had an account with God, in contrast to Pushkin's conversation and Lermontov's grievance) he and Pushkin must share, to some extent, by supping from the same bowl, and by this bowl, which they could share only by breaking it, by this object both fragile and solid, be united through the ages. But Pushkin had other things on his mind than keeping up with the new gymnastics Mr. Tyutchev had thought up in Germany . . . he was carrying his iron cane. Nor did he notice Mr. Tyutchev's smart figure, with the biceps beautifully flexed under the fine broadcloth . . . * And now—a second insult, all the keener for resonating with the first (it might have canceled it, but it redoubles it). The year is 1830. Tyutchev has been away from Russia for almost five years, he arrives in Petersburg, and here he reads in the *Literary Gazette* the notorious article in which Pushkin acknowledges the indisputable talent of—whom? Shevyryov and Khomyakov! And denies that of Tyutchev!

They may even have met somewhere in passing (at Smirdin's, let's say). Pushkin walked by, incandescent, white, insane, paying no attention to the fear and trembling of the unknown young man (who was twenty-seven; not so young! this is the age of one's touchiest awareness of life's missed opportunities, the age of farewell to the uninterruptedness of life—no wonder Lermontov did not survive it), who was already writing his perfect and more "far-seeing" poems, although he remained in the shadow, unrecognized . . . In his own mind he always knew, in his own opinion he was never what Nekrasov defined as "minor," nor was he so in the opinion of history. But how could Pushkin have noticed anything at all that summer? When he had again been refused permission to go abroad; when the Goncharovs had finally given their consent to his marriage; when he had broken free of his exemplary and unaccustomed courtship to go to Petersburg, where "to my own shame, I confess I am living a mirthful life" (how and where did he live a mirthful life?); when he felt around him a thickening, petty atmosphere of nonrecognition and muscling-in on his fame ("reconsideration"), and the literary life had begun to disgust him in the extreme; when there lay ahead of him the autumn at Boldino—that is, when the internal pressures developing within him must have been unbearable? "There, there will he write it!" Lyova says, almost exclaiming. "A single drama, staged twice in his lifetime.† He does not have to notice Tyutchev now because he has *already* seen him, knows him from long ago and far ahead, through and through, like a bullet!" So he walked past Tyutchev, sweatily breezed past him, all unseeing, with white

* *In this connection, it seems that Lyova did not spare Bunin either. He drew a historical parallel: Bunin, a "latecomer" who wrote better, more perfectly (like Tyutchev), was jealous of all famous people. When he had finally outlived them all and found himself alone, the last and only one, he spent the rest of his life quietly distancing himself from his own contemporaries and moving closer to Tolstoy and his only contemporary, Chekhov, trying to restore historical (temporal) justice by main strength. Like Tyutchev, he had every reason to do so. The title of this digression, as we now recall, was "Brilliant Latecomers," and Lyova expressed the intention of devoting a separate article to this topic. We have not seen the article.*

† *Lyova apparently has in mind a truly striking coincidence of dates. Pushkin's tragedy* Mozart and Salieri *was performed twice in 1832, on January 27 and February 1, without success. Five years later, on the exact same dates, there was a "new production"—his duel and burial service.*

234

eyes maddened by life he looked at Tyutchev as at a thing that had not made way and therefore wasn't even alive . . . walked around him unseeing. Perhaps he bowed and smiled a bare-toothed, muscular smile . . . perhaps brazenly, perhaps clowning . . . and Tyutchev measured him against the poem he had just reread in the four-volume edition that had begun to come out (Pushkin's collected works, the first copies: what a gap, unfairly greater than their four-year age difference!)—measured him against "The Prophet," as though Pushkin, once he had written something, were supposed to go around wearing the poem all his life, like a jacket! Tyutchev tried the poem on him for size, and . . . notice, even the background is that of a Petersburg August, with the stuffy heat, the haze, a fire . . . and how much portrait detail there is in "Madness," a poem about water seekers whom Tyutchev did not know! "Its life of careless mirth"—where had he observed the careless mirth of water seekers? ("To my own shame, I confess I am living a mirthful life . . .") "It something seeks, and wildly scans/The clouds with glassy stare"—it's easy to imagine Pushkin's stare when he wants to recognize no one, see no one. "With secretive greed,/Complacence on its brow . . ." No, this is all a portrait, an ephemeral, thoroughly enraged portrait that has wounded the soul of the photographer. Reread "Madness"—what detail in its descriptions of movement and gesture! Had Pushkin perhaps stepped on Tyutchev's foot and not apologized? How could the Prophet have stepped on his foot! We don't know . . . but Tyutchev's bile breaks out in double measure, and he writes "Madness"—with the image of Pushkin the shaman, the "water seeker."

Lyova offered this and other hypotheses, finding some sort of basis for them. In particular, he attacked the legend of Pushkin's alleged special kindness to Tyutchev in publishing the famous cycle in the *Contemporary*. And contrary to the customary explanation, Lyova saw in the title "Poems Sent from Germany"—which was given to the cycle by Pushkin himself—not an emphasis on the philosophical tendency of Tyutchev's lyrics but simply the fact that they were from Germany, not Russia, and there was no need to hold them accountable in Russian. This, supposedly, was what Pushkin had in mind. But even we, although we're not an expert, don't agree with him here. *

But when Lyova states that the line "Aged Derzhavin noticed us" certainly wasn't supposed to be a perpetual-motion machine; that we must get slightly out of the habit of observing everything as in the recent painting *Belinsky and Gogol in the Bed of the Dying Nekrasov*; that their contemporaries did not live out their lives in accordance with some understanding as to their

* *Pushkin never used a word without good reason, and there is something to this title, some sort of formula. Still, the shade of meaning seems to be something more subtle and ambiguous than either naked Russophilism or deference to German thought. Pushkin is remarkable also for never having committed lapses.*

own future place and significance in literature, as it seems to us in a schoolboy way when we've become used to thinking that they had full insight into our times and in the interest of our times—all these statements are hard to disagree with. * His recent personal experience of secondary education is evident here.

But now Lyova says some really terrible things. He doubts the sincerity of Tyutchev's poem on the death of Pushkin! (Incidentally, Tyutchev never published it during his own lifetime.) Limp and stuffy, Lyova claims; a complacent poem. This is the kind of thing a man feels after a crisis, after it's over. And the telltale little words "Be he innocent or guilty" (about Pushkin's adversary), and "Peace, rest in peace, O poet's shade,/Rest in peace and light!" (which is tantamount to "Lie still, lie still"). The whole poem is like listening to one's digestion after dinner. † Only at the end is there a sincere, *converging* force:

> Let Him judge your enmity
> Who hears the call of your spilled blood . . .

It is significant that Pushkin's "enmity" must yet be "judged." And isn't there an echo of the "water seekers": hear the water, hear the blood?

> But Russia keeps you, like first love,
> In the heart's eternity!

Now, these two lines, remarkable enough in themselves, are authentic. First love! Tyutchev himself is present in this attitude toward Pushkin. His first and unrequited love. Tormenting him and making him jealous all his life. And the relief that is felt by an unlucky and single-minded paramour, along with what seems to be grief, at the death of the woman he loves: she

---

* *That he had not read Yuri Tynyanov's article "Pushkin and Tyutchev" strikes us as inexcusable in a literary critic, although Lyova's article was written some time in the early sixties, before Tynyanov's had been reissued. But hadn't Lyova gone digging for other inaccessible sources, and much earlier? Then again, this is characteristic evidence, this is typical of our time—entire obvious spheres of investigation escape attention, even as the subject is being closely studied. But if Lyova hadn't read it then, he read it later, and he must have been simultaneously distressed and gladdened. Distressed that he wasn't the first to have doubts about Pushkin's attitude toward Tyutchev. Gladdened by Tynyanov's interpretation of the epigram "Meeting of the Insects" ("Here's Tyutchev, a little black ant,/Here's Raich, a beetle in pants"), if one also recalls that Raich was Tyutchev's tutor. Tynyanov does not have full primacy, however. Lyova was perhaps the first to reverse the problem: "Tyutchev and Pushkin," instead of "Pushkin and Tyutchev."*

† Lyova also cites the complacent way in which Lev Tolstoy mourned Dostoevsky: "How can we live without him?" He gives the offhanded explanation that there wasn't room for them both in the same era, any more than for Pushkin and Tyutchev.

won't belong to anyone else now. And then there's . . . the main thing is, she can't love anyone else. Whew! But one must go on living . . . and Russia will go on living with its wife, with its mistresses, with him, with Tyutchev.

Here, without reference to Tyutchev, Lyova wrote a good many more pages sketching a psychological picture of such an emotion. He wrote with knowledge and passion. The experience of his sad love for Faina was evident here. As, in its turn, the experience of his attempt at a rapprochement with Grandfather was evident in his reckonings about Tyutchev's attraction to Pushkin, the lack of response to this attempt, and, in that case, a "devaluation" of the very object of attraction ("I didn't want you all that much," and "Fool yourself!"). We can't re-create them from memory, but there were several remarkably judicious pages of psychological substantiation (again without reference to Tyutchev), likewise testifying to the author's personal experience, to his having lived through something similar.

Here follows an unexpected line of ellipsis points, and, seemingly to the surprise of the author himself, the article makes yet another turnabout, a bold departure.

. . . Suppose there was an answering shot? After all, Pushkin had enviable reflexes—he was an excellent marksman. Didn't their shots ring out almost simultaneously? But Tyutchev knew whom he fired at, while Pushkin fired at a rustle in the bushes.

TYUTCHEV, 1830	PUSHKIN, 1831–33
"Madness"	"Don't let me lose my mind, o God"
There to live in careless mirth	*Don't let me lose my mind, o God;*
Pathetic.	*I'd sooner beg with sack and rod*
	Or starve in sweat and dust.
. . . . madness	*Not that I treasure my poor mind,*
	Or would bemoan it should I find
	That part from it I must:
	If they but left me free to roam,
	How I would fly to make my home
. . . . . hides.	*In deepest forest gloom!*
Where, like smoke, the arch of sky	
Fuses with scorched earth . . .	*In blazing frenzy would I sing,*
. . . Entrenched amidst the blazing sands	*Be drugged by fancies smoldering*
And incandescent glare,	*In rank and wondrous fume.*
It something seeks, and wildly scans	*And I would hear the breakers roar,*
The clouds with glassy stare.	*And my exultant gaze would soar*
Then suddenly it starts: its keen	*In empty skies to drown . . .*

Ear pressed to the cracked ground,
It listens with secretive greed,
Complacence on its brow.
It thinks it hears the roiling streams
In subterranean night,

But woe befalls whose mind is vague:
They dread and shun you like the plague,
And once the jail-gate jars,
They bolt the fool to chain and log
And come as to a poor mad dog
To tease him through the bars.
And then upon the evenfall

The cradled murmur of their dreams,
Their strident surge to light!

I'd hear no nightingale's bright call,
No oak tree's murmurous dreams—

．　　．　　．　　．　　．

I'd hear my prison-mates call out,
And night attendants rail and shout,
And clashing chains, and screams.

One sensed that Lyova had hit on the idea of this parallel in the process of his work, when everything was "ready" in his mind. And one can understand Lyova, who after all had made unto himself a graven image: even the honor of a duel with Tyutchev may be refused for the sake of a rendezvous with Pushkin! Lyova could never have counted on or hoped for this when he undertook his labor. A wave of emotion lapped him up and bore him far, far away from science, to cast him up at Pushkin's feet. This encounter justified all. To Lyova's credit, it may be said that he had indeed given his all.

Ah, how Lyova would have liked Tyutchev's "glassy stare" to scan Pushkin's "empty skies," how he would have liked the incandescent desert landscape to migrate through Tyutchev's "Madness" from "The Prophet" to "Don't let me lose my mind . . ."! It may have seemed to Lyova that such a crossing would dispense with all the difficulties of further proof. It always seems so to us, that the only obstacle is the one in our path . . . But this would have been too simplistic for Pushkin, says Lyova, doing an about-face. Even if one can imagine the unlikely, and moreover absolutely unattested, circumstances under which Pushkin might have become acquainted with a manuscript copy of "Madness," he undoubtedly just glanced at it, just skimmed it, without quaking. His reply would have been written from an instantaneous impression, and that impression was negative. Moreover, the negative was so exact that it had a physical meaning, as in photography: these two poems correspond in chiaroscuro like a negative and a positive. In Tyutchev the sheltering shade is in madness itself, and the flame is roundabout. In Pushkin it's backward (chronology alone permits us to express it this way, because Tyutchev was the one who had it backward, while the positive, as the true image, was Pushkin's); in Pushkin the sheltering shade is roundabout, and madness is like a flame. In Tyutchev, the secretive complacence and careless mirth of madness—on scorched, cracked ground, under a sky fused with it like smoke. In Pushkin, blazing frenzy and smoldering fancies—free to roam, in the benign cool of night, of forest, of the skies, of the nightingale's song . . . But how could there be breakers in the forest? Lyova then asks, in amazement. Although we note the formal brilliance of his construct, we are also compelled to note that Lyova is stretching a point here: he explains the incongruity in Pushkin's line as an unconscious reflection of Tyutchev's "water theme."

But Lyova suddenly recollects himself. After hastily discussing the possibility of Pushkin's first reaction to Tyutchev's "Madness," Lyova rejects this possibility for more important assertions. He begins to discuss the *substance* of these poems, their correlation of Intellect and Reason, and achieves utmost incomprehensibility. It's as if he's straining to recall something once heard, and can't—that's the impression. He prefers Reason to Intellect and proclaims Pushkin the first and only bearer of Reason in Russia. With the death of Pushkin, he asserts, Tyutchev *vanquished* him in poetry. The scope of Pushkin's official recognition by his contemporaries proves nothing in this regard; Pushkin's line has no supremacy. This was a duel in which his d'Anthès was Tyutchev. The spirit of Pushkin's poetry was murdered in an undeclared and unequal struggle. Pushkin was left with the respected regimentals of poetic form—he himself was gone. They sewed a few buttons and a more elegant braid to his coat, then stuffed it with every kind of dull, heartfelt garbage. Wholeness, harmony, air, peace—all had been done away with. Of this, too, Lyova writes lengthily and obscurely.

Pushkin he deified. In Lermontov he perceived his own infantilism, and took a condescending attitude. In Tyutchev he frankly hated someone (we don't know whom).

Lyova concludes his historical novella (we have no other name for it) by discussing the legitimacy of his own constructs. He expresses the evasively simple idea that it is equally false, if not more so, to infer a historical picture of a given age solely from data that are clearly known and thoroughly verified. Such data are few and extremely meager. The contemporary of an age and his historian move toward each other in darkness, but this is a bizarre simultaneity, for the contemporary exists no more, and the historian not yet. The few things that the historian sees when he looks back are too clear to him; to the contemporary, they are engulfed by life. Why, one might ask, if a scholar succeeds in establishing something with precision, does it seem to have become more obvious and better known in the past? The scholar, more often than the dramatist, succumbs to the delusion that every gun fires. When he recognizes something "brand-new" in a departed epoch, he somersaults for joy, and then makes a kind of logical *salto* as well: without a moment's thought, he begins to assume that the thing he has established with such convincing effect has become with the same implacability a fact, a piece of knowledge, an experience, for those who participated in the segment of the process he is studying. And however objective a scholar may wish to be, let him merely enumerate a sequence of known facts and he is already, even against his will, drawing a well-defined picture of life and an arrangement of forces in our consciousness. But since that picture inevitably lacks any sort of completeness—and especially since we have no grounds for claiming that any likeness or proportion of a once real life is preserved in the facts that have come down to us or disappeared from us—then this kind of "scientific" picture is just as inevitably untrue as Lyova's may have been, with this difference: although it may not contain a single factual error, a "scientific" work legitimizes and subsequently prescribes for everyone its own skimpiness and poverty of understanding. How often we are snared by a fact of undoubted authenticity! Almost more often than by a doubling hypothesis.

Much was probably false in Lyova's article. Even what proved true, or may suddenly prove true, was derived by accident, from false premises—a coincidence. Our opinion is that if a version like Lyova's could be as widely prescribed and propagated as the existing "scientific" version, it would rapidly become just as boring and tasteless as all the legends about progressive continuity, the friendship of great men, the relay race of thought, and Promethean fire. Perhaps it would pall even more rapidly: there is so much brashness and bluster in it. But it has one indisputable advantage. It will never be legitimized.

We may also be asked how we happened to remember all this. But, in the first place, we remembered barely a quarter of it (in terms of the number of pages); almost the entire "scientific" part has escaped us. In the second place, at the time we read the article we were already very interested in our hero. In the third place, when we returned home after reading it, we rushed to the shelf and leafed through our three volumes of the aforesaid poets, to check all this against our personal impression . . . In the fourth place, it doesn't matter how we happened to remember.

We thought Lyova's composition sound but unfounded, informative but inconclusive. Yet it was not unfruitful for us to compare the texts, refresh and reevaluate our memory of them, and we owe thanks to Lyova for this. It may be the reason we managed to retain so much. Even today, as soon as we take a volume from the shelf, Lyova's article comes inevitably and obsessively to mind. So in the end we have nearly reconciled ourselves to it. And then we've had the thought that perhaps he isn't so wrong; that is, perhaps he's wrong, but he has the *right* . . . and then his infringement on the sacred no longer seems so sacrilegious to us. It's all right to infringe on the sacred, Lyova declares. In this regard, what we like best about Lyova's article is what he began with, the *content*, leaving aside perfection of form, as an essential condition for beginning the conversation: What's it all about? Oh, so that's it . . .

Our only remaining reproach to Lyova is that the positions and principles expressed in his article, when consistently followed, preclude the possibility of the article itself, even the very fact of its having been written. What always surprises us in the nihilist experience is its apparent enviousness, its need to assert itself by overthrowing someone. A kind of Salierism in those who fight Salieri . . . If you reject, reject all. Why this yearning to occupy the place of the overthrown? He (the one being overthrown?) at least made his assertion in conformity with the place he occupied in space and time. His assertion and his place are so much of a oneness that the assertion can be rejected only along with his place. It's paradoxical to reject one half while desiring the other . . . In this sense, any extreme of rejection is surprising. When a man hates fuss and bother, let's say, he begins to castigate it, but in a fussy way. If you hate fuss and bother, why fuss? When people hate injustice, they begin to restore justice with respect to something insignificant and dead, and in the process they offhandedly perpetrate an injustice with respect to something living. If the vacuity and uselessness of human prattle makes you sick and tired, then you yourself, in rejecting it, begin to blab as if out of control . . . So it is with everything. But the worst of it is that in consequence of all this activity—nothing happens, nothing is created. O mankind!

What had Tyutchev, for example, done to Lyova? And what, after all, had he done to Pushkin? Even if Lyova was right about everything, what was Tyutchev guilty of? Of feeling jealous over Pushkin and of Pushkin? Of preserving, throughout his life, a peculiar and secret relationship with him? That's no crime. People always took a more personal attitude toward Pushkin than Pushkin took toward anyone else, and since his death this has even become a kind of Russian tradition—one-sided personal relationships with Pushkin (Pushkin established this kind of relationship only with Peter the Great). So that Tyutchev was merely a pioneer in these relationships, as he was a pioneer in many other respects. Moreover, it was he who wrote "It is not given us to foretell/The echoes wakened by our words . . . ," and many other remarkable lines (as Lyova does not deny). He is to blame only for the recognition, Lyova's recognition of himself, his impartial confrontation with his own experience. Tyutchev is to blame that Faina happened to Lyova, Grandfather happened; he is to blame for being born too late and emerging too late, like Lyova (each in his own epoch); and Lyova the latecomer, with his heart turned to another epoch, cannot forgive Tyutchev for having been its "contemporary," as Lyova desires to be and cannot . . . Oh, if only it had been Lyova! *He* would have embraced Pushkin, *he* would have pressed him to his heart . . . but enough; he has already embraced his grandfather once.

No, positively, all experience is terrible! Especially if expressed. If personified, it triumphs over its creator, even though its creator may hope that he has overcome it at last. A personified experience stings itself like a scorpion and sinks to the bottom. If you've already had the misfortune to acquire it (experience sticks with you like Bad Luck in a fairy tale: in your sack, on your back), don't personify it, because it will reenact you, rather than you it!

But Tyutchev is in his rightful place. He hasn't noticed Lyova dueling with him, any more than Pushkin (if Lyova is right) noticed Tyutchev dueling with him. But there's a difference . . .

By the same token, when you're reevaluating and overthrowing authorities, it's bizarre to raise up others still higher. To work as a loved authority against unloved ones, like a jimmy, a lever, a truncheon . . . It's the same old thing: to hate the authorities, yet sacrifice yourself for their glory. O mankind!

O Pushkin! . . .

THE HUMBLE HORSEMAN

(A Poem of Petty Hooliganism)

> Astride the marble beast,
> Head bare, arms tightly crossed,
> Yevgeny sat unmoving, pale
> With fear.
> He feared, poor man,
> Not for himself.
> The Bronze Horseman, 1833

> Otherwise, you see, my heavenly angel, this will
> be the last letter; and yet it cannot be so, that
> this letter is the last! No, no, I will write, and
> you must write, too . . . Because my style is taking
> shape now . . .
> Humble Folk, 1846

(Italics Mine. —A.B)
A spongy, round-cornered pack of cards at the dacha. What was, what
is . . . (we have spread the cards) . . . what will be. For himself, for
his house . . . (we are telling Lyova's fortune) . . . for his heart. These
cards are paired, and these . . . what is he left with? The Faina of
diamonds, the Mitishatyev of clubs . . . (this simple little method of
divination is the only one we know). What will console his heart?

A slight change of fortune, the queen of diamonds, a short journey,
worries . . . It's all true—who could deny it? What was, what is . . .
what will be? Cards are exceptionally truthful, because they tell all
and leave just one thing vague. Time. Yes, a trip, yes, a government
house, and of course a woman. But when?

I can't talk about the future. Especially since, being in charge of the
experiment, everything in the future develops with a chemical inevitability. The reaction $H_2O + NaCl =$ salt water. Tears.

As if it's this way: early morning, a young wife, we are building a
house. The shavings smell of the forest, and the forest itself is not far
off. We have love enough that it isn't work . . . To start with, we dig
a pit, the cellar hole. The foundation, the first row of beams . . . My
wife rests her head on my shoulder and whispers. We are to have a son
. . . The shirt sticks to my back, I swing the ax more and more smartly.
The future—a son, a house. Chapters, parts, outbuildings. Openings
for windows, doors. The hero has entered, he's forgotten to exit, someone
is climbing in the window. But, oh, I'm getting tired, it's all getting
tired . . . The ax is tired, the log is tired, my wife is tired, the baby's

getting tired in the womb. Already he's too lazy to be born—time itself is getting tired.

We've overreached ourselves with this life—it's long. We were greedy. We wouldn't start a temporary shack. A house right off, a big one. We're sick of it; all day and we hardly drive one nail, there's no end in sight. The day has grown shorter, the night longer, but still we don't feel like getting up. My wife's a stranger, with her everlasting belly—she has turned color, like autumn. Autumn is here: the rains have started, we must hurry and do the roof.

Or perhaps as is, without a roof? So that it stands amid the chips, its windows letting in the four directions: the southern draft, the eastern forest, the western neighbor, the northern byroad?

People will say, How can anybody live in a house like that?

I will answer, "In Pushkin House? Nobody does. One man tried, just for three days, and what happened? It's impossible to live in Pushkin House."

"You've muddled us with your allegories," the reader will say.

I will answer, "Then don't read."

So. The reader has a right to ask me, I have a right to answer him. Or, as the poet said of me:

> I will write a monstrous novel,
> A multi-volume Novel-house . . .
> I will tentatively call it,
> Say, The Falsehood or The Fraud . . .

Light at the end—we promised, we hoped . . . But we have a premonition. We won't be able to get to that end now. Just between us, there is no end. The writer made it up.

We're in a hurry. Ahead is Warsaw. September 1 is close at hand, the deadline for submission. The first autumn raindrops are dripping on my desk and typewriter—there's no roof. Ahead is Warsaw, an authorized trip to research our novel (it's important for us to study Russia within the borders of Pushkin's century). In that case, we also have Finland and Alaska in store, before we resolve to depart for Western Europe or, let's say, Japan; but that's for the next novel—Japan . . . Our sad experience with construction inclines us to the other extreme: given the hopeless upward striving of buildings, the unfortunate vertical to which we are prompted by the small area of our Petersburg lot, we would like, in our dreams, to convert it into a horizontal—to be free

246

and slack about arranging things in the space of our journey and the hotel stay of our existence.

We have far-reaching plans: we want to understand the nation at the stage of the Empire.

But we are still in Petersburg, we're moving to Leningrad . . .

Haste may be a vice, but what can you do if life and time have hopelessly different velocities: either you break free of time or you lag behind your own life. By the end of the second month, the fetus is sick of waiting to be born, and if it should appear by the end of the ninth, it will do so out of a hopeless indifference to the question of existence and nonexistence. It has failed to become a fish at the right time, a bird a little later, all opportunities have been let slip. A human being is born.

My house, with its uncapped head, is empty. The floor is yellow with leaves that the maple has dropped to me through the empty window. The heroes don't live here—no crumbs for the mice. The heroes are huddled at the neighbors', they've rented a corner.

Nobody lives in Pushkin House. One man tried . . .

MAN ON DUTY

(THE HEIR, *continued*)

AND SO, that was precisely the state of our Lyova's affairs on the eve of the October Revolution holidays of 196–.

Having lived, in his own opinion, a sufficiently long life, Lyova was an apprehensive man. That is, he worried prematurely about what lay ahead, and met it almost indifferently when it came. So he lived at one remove from trouble, always suffering it with unmediated pain. When anything finally happened to him, he had "known it all along" and felt all the more hurt because fate had obtusely failed to change her course, had easily washed away the barrier of his predictions and premonitions.

That autumn, Lyova's sufferings were especially keen. The divine thread was streaming too rhythmically, nothing had happened in too long for all this "nothing" not to accumulate and signify at least "something." Lyova felt a covert thickening above him, a design of the forces of evil. He did not know what threatened him or from where, but It was sneaking up on him, undefined and unjustified, which made all Lyova's terrors seem irrelevant and irrational, even to him, and until they were justified he had no one to confide in without fear of being misunderstood—everything was closing in on him. As before, he had no reason to expect a blow from anywhere, and he explained his premonitions by telling himself that it was too long since he had written anything of his own, almost a year already, even more than a year. He was losing the autumn, to which back in the spring he had so hopefully postponed everything, golden autumn, which in imitation of Pushkin he preferred for inspiration, October was already lost—

248

nothing. If he didn't sit down to work at last, he would be in real trouble, or so Lyova explained the oppressiveness of his premonitions. If he didn't get hold of himself one of these days, then no doubt about it, something external would happen, Lyova concluded when he studied his fate.

And it did happen. It was less a blow of fate than a sneer. Every holiday, some luckless staff member was left on duty at the institute. This time the honor went to Lyova. The choice fell on him for many reasons, the most weighty of which, albeit unstated, was that Lyova would find it exceptionally hard to refuse this time. Even though not in the Party he could not refuse, being a young, unmarried (on-the-outs) staff member who carried no particular social burdens and whose thesis defense, incidentally, was scheduled for soon after the holidays.

"You can be gone for an hour or two in the daytime, of course," he was told in an affectionate, fatherly way by the Vice Superintendent for Economic Affairs, who was also secretary of the Party committee and spoke "in a spirit of cooperation." "An hour or two. A bite to eat, that kind of thing. If you make arrangements with the doorkeeper first. But not at night. Under no circumstances!" Lyova's "reputation" made it impossible for him to object. His refusal might be interpreted as an antisocial act, as was stressed by a glance, just one glance, from the Vice SEA. His glance was peculiar: you wondered whether one of his eyes was false, but when you looked closely it was not.

Lyova would find it disadvantageous to refuse.

Oh well, he thought. He even convinced himself that it was for the better (though what choice did he have?). He was on the outs with Faina again and therefore had no plans for the holidays anyway. He would finally be able to sit down to work, and where else, in the holiday bustle, would he succeed in getting a little work done, if not here? Absolutely, it was a divine blessing to have the opportunity of working for three days in complete seclusion!

Nevertheless, Lyova's first evening at the institute, the evening before the holidays, was spent in utter and ever growing melancholy. It struck him that his bad luck with the holiday had by no means deflected the hand of fate.

He did not succeed in sitting down to work. He opened his dissertation ("Certain Issues . . .") and squeamishly turned a few pages, standing up. His pose was careless and supple, emphatically separate from the bulky manuscript . . . as though someone could see him: he was still defending himself, with abstract cunning. He turned a few pages and grimaced: a sudden mouthful of saliva, an attack of nausea. He gulped, and theatrically slammed shut the dissertation. He looked over his shoulder—but no one could see him.

He drifted through the corridors, looked in on empty rooms, rummaged in other people's desks, and found nothing of interest, just trash and junk. The weather outside the window was like dirty wet cotton batting. The building was cold, even though they heated it. They're heating a museum, he thought damply. During the workday Lyova was never this cold. It was the first time he had felt such keen distaste for his academic citadel.

He kept calling Faina. She was out. When at last he heard her jaunty, cheerful voice, his trained imagination instantly sketched certain scenes, so habitual that they were almost indispensable to him in their galling brilliance. But no, she said, he'd made it all up as always, she was just in that mood today, just in a pre-holiday mood . . . and how were things for him? She seemed to remember nothing: neither their last conversation nor the insults nor their break . . . She'd been calling him—he was out . . . Really? She had even called? Her affectionate tone and her unexpected leniency disconcerted Lyova. Melting, he eagerly began to complain of the fate that had locked him up within the walls of the institute; evidently he expected sympathy from Faina. But she was suddenly angry: things like this were always happening to him, and she had wanted to spend the holidays together . . . She hung up.

As usual, Lyova was thrown into a tizzy. He began frantically dialing, scrambling the digits, but the line was always busy. He had scarcely put the receiver down when suddenly the telephone rang. Trembling, Lyova snatched up the receiver as if it were a pistol. "I've been calling and calling you. The line's always busy!" said a jaunty, cheerful voice that never seemed to indulge in the mopes. Mama. "Lyovushka, we all feel very sorry for you, but don't you mope, Lyovushka . . ." Lyova started: What? Where did she get this "don't mope, don't mope"? "Your father, too," Mama said quickly (she thought it her task to improve relations between father and son). Lyova's gut rose and fell as in an elevator; he slumped hopelessly onto a chair. Yes, yes, he said, holding the receiver away from his ear. Had he eaten, because she would come straight over and bring him—you won't believe this—mushrooms! And cookies, she'd only just baked them, nice and fresh . . . Cookies. For some reason, that touched Lyova, and his whole body started to itch and ache. Sizzling with love, pity, shame, and impatience, he bobbed and turned like a mushroom in

Mama's frying pan. Maybe Faina was trying to call him right this minute? "No, no, I don't need anything!" Lyova interrupted, rudely and coldly.

Resolutely, then and there, he dialed Faina's number. Enough! He wanted to tell her once and for all not to make a fool of him, he knew the whole story, he wasn't a kid anymore to be twisted around her little . . . and so forth. But it was busy. Then he wanted to explain to her that it wasn't his fault he was stuck at the institute, he would ditch everything right now, both the institute and the dissertation (want me to?), and come right over . . . But it was busy. Then he wanted to tell her, simply, without explaining himself, that he loved her as before, please not to be angry at him, and then they would think what to do, because you could always think of something, if you were in love and didn't torment each other . . . And now his call suddenly went through. Lyova said who had she been blabbing with, he'd like to know, for the last half hour . . . Faina said . . . They had an utterly pointless conversation, and both of them confidently flung the receiver back on the hook. After that, Lyova got no answer, no matter how long he let the phone ring. Then he began endlessly getting a drugstore.

These telephonic sufferings had helped him while away the evening, however, and he lay down on the director's couch—but could not fall asleep.

Suddenly, resolute and sleepless, he jumped up and turned on the light, illuminating his long white face and cavernous, glittering eyes. He went to the desk and abruptly pushed aside his dissertation, almost throwing it off the desk. He took from his briefcase a slender, scuffed folder: he'd been carrying it around a long time but hadn't opened it in quite a while.

In it was the "Three Prophets" article, the same dog-eared copy. He pushed that aside with the dissertation: nowadays he felt the same way about it as he did about Lermontov's "Prophet." Next came another article, half retyped, half in shambly, soggy-looking handwritten notes. This one he pulled toward him. He turned page after page—stopped, began to read. Gleefully he smacked his lips, nodded his head. Yes, yes! Just think . . .

We will peer over his shoulder.

This was "The Middle of the Contrast," Lyova's paper on *The Bronze Horseman*. He had started it back then, in the excitement after "Three Prophets," but when he was only halfway through he had begun showing it to people . . . and had encountered something odd, a kind of bewilderment. This article, as one could already tell, was even more confident, clear, and strong. More professional, too—Lyova was learning fast. But suddenly it seemed to be nothing new . . . Lyova had written it in the same manner, with the same spontaneity and freedom from mediocrity, expounding ideas that were his *own* whether new or not new, ideas that had occurred to him independently—and his readers praised it. But without enthusiasm, as if they might have read it somewhere before, as if the article perhaps already existed: nothing new . . . It had become nothing new that Lyova was basically capable of writing something with a beginning and an end, *on his own*. Oh, you can do it . . . you showed us that . . . but we've had it. You made your mark, enough already . . . There was something of this sentiment in the glances that slid over his cheek. And Lyova cooled, wound down, lost interest, he was overtaken by a new and this time quite grandiose project. Feverishly he began jotting things down—and stopped short.

Now he was reading "The Middle of the Contrast" and fidgeting with impatient satisfaction: How true it all is, how true! He glanced around. How could he have *known everything* when he was still so young, when he understood nothing and knew nothing! He read again about the State, the Individual, and the Elements—and exclaimed aloud. Good Lord, could he, Lyova, really have written this? He jumped up and ran around the room, his impatience mounting, soaring to the ceiling, his eyes unseeing and dim. He rubbed his hands: Yes, yes . . . yes! How wonderfully he had written! The middle of the contrast, the dead zone, the muteness at the epicenter of the tornado, of the typhoon! The calm, from which the invulnerable genius sees! The principal thing, brilliantly conceived, mute, omitted, central— the axis of the poem! Wonderful!

Lyova rushed to the desk . . . No, he'd already been over these! He snatched the remaining pages from the folder. Here it is! The vault, the dome! Now, now . . . I'll seize the . . . This, *this* is mine to do! I'll write it now, here, to spite them all . . . The thought fluttered more shallowly and was left behind—he became absorbed in the pages. The image of Grandfather applying himself to the mug popped into his mind and out again. Here it is . . . the thing that makes it all . . . worth it . . . This was his great project. "The 'I' of Pushkin"— no more and no less. Actually, this came naturally to him, this kind of project. Having stepped several years back from it, he now saw distinctly that "Three Prophets," too, was essentially about this same thing. "The Middle of the Contrast" even more so—this was actually the whole point of it. The organic line had been taking shape even then! Even then . . . The unintentional unity restored Lyova's inspiration. He picked up his pen. Now, right now! The dome!

He slid the pages back and forth, evening up the edges . . . He was reading these inspired, fragmentary, *aide-memoire* notes, and could not understand what he had had in mind then. It nagged and obsessed him. He couldn't give himself over to what controlled him *now*—it was absolutely essential for him to remember what he had had in mind *then*, and he could not. He pushed away the notes and took up a sheaf of outlines for the article. There were already a lot of them—the first, second, third . . . These were the tracks of his "returns." The outlines became neater and neater, and toward the end he even found just a copy—pathologically steady penmanship, painstaking and dead.

Horror crept over him, but not quite: Lyova resolutely stood up and turned away from the thing in the dark corner, the Godunovian thickness in his mouth. "Anew! Anew!" he cried mutely, like Chaliapin crying, "Avaunt, avaunt, child!" A new outline! Begin anew, without peeking, without looking back, *now*! The only way.

There was no blank paper. The desk drawer was locked.

Still aroused—and his fright was over—he darted out to look for paper. He jerked at the neighboring door. Aha, the doorkeeper had the key.

He went downstairs then, with his sleepless face, to see the doorkeeper, and they got into a conversation. Lyova politely heard out the story of her daughter and her drinking son-in-law, and it struck him that he had already heard this story somewhere, or perhaps read it. He grew bored and wanted to talk about himself. Which he did, gradually getting carried away and lapsing into unnecessary frankness. The doorkeeper listened with healthy curiosity and a rather stupid animation on her face: Lyova was telling about his love, with great feeling. His mouth already had the horrible aftertaste that goes with being too garrulous. And the more he tasted it, the faster he talked. The doorkeeper could no longer keep up her end of the conversation— she merely listened, with evident voluptuous pleasure. Lyova suddenly frowned and stopped short. Then, quite accurately sensing her power over Lyova, the doorkeeper asked him to let her go to her daughter's to help deal with the drinking son-in-law. After all, there was no need for them both to be here, and he would manage perfectly well by himself. Lyova hastily consented, then and there, saying "Thank you" instead of "Certainly."

Lyova went back upstairs. Spotlighted and separate, the pages lay scattered on the desk, as though they alone existed in the invisibility of the rest of the room . . . as though floating. Lyova stole up to them, peered at them quietly, from one side, as if over someone's shoulder. "Well, yes, of course . . . But to whom? For whom?! Why!!!" he cried silently—and swept them into his briefcase without sorting them.

Furtively he extinguished the light and hastily lay down. He wanted not to remember the doorkeeper—but he did. The institutional couch, black even in the darkness, he pictured as boundless. Big though he was, Lyova curled up in a ball like a little boy, so as to fit on the couch in a lonely, tiny way, and deliberately began to sob. He badly wanted to cry. As in childhood, he pictured his own funeral—and even so, he almost didn't succeed in crying. But he did succeed a little, with dry, out-of-practice tears. That was the best he could do, and he had no choice but to decide that it was enough—grow up!— and that he had already regained his composure. Night is the mother of counsel, he thought wryly, and fell hurriedly, warily asleep.

He dreamed of a wide river, seemingly the same one that flowed by their institute, but also not the same. The ice had gone out unexpectedly, at the wrong time, and the river was thick as glue. A heavy vapor hung over it, and everyone at the institute, position and age notwithstanding, was supposed to swim across, in order to pass the Komsomol fitness test.

Many were already swimming, absurdly and slowly reaching out their white arms from the thick slime. Only Lyova and a senior professor—a noble old man with a long beard, whom everyone called Captain Nemo behind his back—were still huddled among the piles, hiding. Captain Nemo was shivering and kept tucking his beard into his trunks. Right by the bank, bobbing like a fishing float on the slow, thick waves, lay the Vice Superintendent for Economic Affairs, face up, fully attired in his suit and all his medals. Gazing at them with improbably round, congealed eyes, he beckoned them with cardboard hand . . .

The ringing telephone woke him. Lyova jumped up frantically, his heart fluttering in his mouth. He swallowed it and for some time stood looking around, not grasping where he was or why. At last he padded over to the telephone in his socks and got there exactly too late: it stopped just as Lyova reached for it. Lyova stood over it for a moment on tucked-in feet, with his toes curled, and unrecognizingly examined the desk as if it had a stain on it. Suddenly he was assailed by last night. But the whole thing—especially the doorkeeper—was still a dream, a shadow play, and Lyova did not remember it. He simply woke up again, with the intellectual's weird evening sensation that he had been drunk yesterday: whether or not he had taken anything into his mouth was immaterial. Who could it have been, calling so early? Faina? But it wasn't Faina: the telephone began ringing again, seemingly louder and more frequently than the first time. In the receiver he heard a splashing sound, like waves in a dishpan.

"Well, Prince, how are things?"

It was Mitishatyev, one of the closest of the new institute friends he had recently acquired. Lyova glanced out the window, at the icy-looking sky, and felt glad to hear from Mitishatyev.

"Are you rotting?" Mitishatyev said affectionately, in his solid, persuasive bass. "Well, I'm about to drop in on you. We're marching in close ranks, and we've just pulled alongside your cell."

So that was why the strange splashing in the receiver! The institute was so situated that on one side it really was a completely quiet and deserted spot, but on the other, only a block away, lay a main thoroughfare, along which the torrent of marchers always flowed as they headed for the square. Consequently, Mitishatyev was three steps away. Yes, of course.

Lyova went to the window. Faina! Oh God . . . What's that, a quilted work jacket? Ha, thought Lyova with gloating melancholy, will she bump into Mitishatyev? . . . She's gone . . . This is all I have left, Lyova sighed mournfully, once more getting out his humble papers.

Downstairs someone was knocking, ringing, rattling. This suddenly reached him. A din . . . They're congregating, Lyova thought darkly, hurrying to scoop the papers off the desk. Who set things up this way—never to let a man do anything creative? When he got to the door, fingering the keys, Mitishatyev's fat face was already there, nose flattened against the glass: he was squinting blindly and could see nothing in the dark vestibule, although he himself was well lighted. And he was not alone. At his back loomed someone else, red-haired, hatless. The face looked familiar.

Lyova himself had not expected that he would be so glad to see Mitishatyev.

"Your pass?" he said playfully, waiting for them to walk by so that he could lock up after them.

"Here it is!" Mitishatyev took from his pocket a split of vodka.

"Gottich," the red-haired boy introduced himself. He blushed, bowing primly and even clicking his heels.

"Von Gottich!" Mitishatyev exclaimed, guffawing. "My advisee. Your devotee. He considers you the Fourth Prophet."

Lyova dimly recalled having seen Gottich in the corridors of the institute.

They started upstairs, laughing loudly and slapping each other on the back. Gottich modestly stayed a step behind.

"Careful what you say," Mitishatyev said in an undertone. "He's a . . ." And he rapped expressively on the banister.

"Then why'd you bring him?" Lyova asked in astonishment.

Mitishatyev laughed contentedly. "He respects us."

They reached the director's office.

"Making yourself at home, I see," Mitishatyev said, glancing ironically at the nameplate on the door. "But I mean it. If only we had a director with a decent name. A prince! Clout!" he said as he flung open the door with a crash, burst into the office, and belatedly began stamping and brushing the snow off his feet, huffing and puffing. He tossed his coat on the couch and went running around the office with noisy pleasure, rubbing his hands as if they were frozen. "Hey, we've got glasses!" he exclaimed. "And something to wash down the vodka with." He carried a tray with a carafe to the director's desk. "And something to eat with it," he went on, grabbing the massive paperweight blotter from the desk and trying with exaggerated helplessness to take a bite out of it. "Something to soak up the vodka, so to speak. No, tell me this, Prince, where can I borrow thirty rubles?"

In brief, Mitishatyev made as much noise as if a large group had come bursting in from the cold. Why does he need more company, Lyova thought with delight and envy; he's a party all by himself. Gottich, during all this, had quietly taken off his coat and hung it where it belonged—on the coatrack—and was standing by the coatrack, smoothing his hair and squaring his shoulders. Mitishatyev meanwhile found time to run for a missing glass, and actually brought back two. He opened a can of goby fish, poured a round of vodka.

"Well, help yourselves. Potluck."

He raised his glass.

Gottich waited for Lyova to raise his and then did likewise.

"A great and happy holiday, my dear friends!" Mitishatyev cried, with a seeming quaver in his voice and even a restrained sob. "Since it's vodka, we can clink glasses," he added calmly. "Your health, Night Director . . . And yours, Gottich . . . And ours"—and Mitishatyev knocked back his drink. His eyes bulged, and he hastily stuffed a goby into his mouth. Lyova drank with dignity, but Gottich choked and dropped a goby on the rug. Having dropped it, he turned very red and started whistling *"La donna è mobile,"* inconspicuously kicking the goby under the desk.

"Tsk-tsk!" Mitishatyev said. "You didn't learn that from me." Without a trace of squeamishness, Mitishatyev picked up the goby by the tail and tossed it in the wastebasket. "Please Help Keep This Room . . . "

Having thus destroyed Gottich, Mitishatyev ran to his coat and got another split.

"Another round?" Hearing no answer, he poured.

They drank. Lyova felt a warmth and pleasantness, his eyes grew moist.

"What would I do without you?" he said to Mitishatyev.

"I wouldn't know—bring in some girls, maybe?"

"Oh no!" Lyova waved a hand. "This is lots better."

"What are we doing standing up? And not smoking?"

"Really," Lyova said in surprise. "When I drink, I always forget that I smoke. I keep thinking: What's missing?"

"Have another drink," Mitishatyev suggested, and he took out a split.

"Not another one!" Lyova said in delight. "How many have you got?"

"As many as I've got, they're all ours," Mitishatyev said.

Gottich looked at the split with dull fright.

"Okay, let's take a smoke break." Mitishatyev sighed, glancing at Gottich.

"Tell me, Prince," Mitishatyev said, "why is that word so pleasant to pronounce? Pr-i-n-ce . . . "

"When I was a child I preferred 'Count,' " Lyova said thoughtfully, glancing at Gottich.

"That's from Dumas," Mitishatyev said. "Count de la Fèr-re! But pay no attention to him," he said, nodding in Gottich's direction. "He's drunk."

"Nowadays I, too, like 'Prince' better." Lyova grinned.

"Nowadays, everyone's begun to like it. Any party you go to, you're bound to find yourself next to some ancient scion. Here we are, after so many years—and suddenly the intellectuals have such a fascination with blue blood! Barely had a drink and he's a count already, or at a minimum a privy councillor. Fascinated, just like a scullery maid before the Revolution . . . Well, the scullery maids were their servants at least. But what were these guys? I was at somebody's house not long ago, started to introduce myself, and there was this dandy, really looked like a hussar—in a polyester suit, though. Naryshkin, he says. Aha, I thought, blood tells—you can see right off! I asked everyone: Is he really a Naryshkin? They laughed. Come to find out, he was pure Kaplan."

"Yes . . ." Lyova laughed contentedly, because the conversation flattered him: he truly was a prince, and no one could doubt it. "You've spotted something real. It's extraordinary the way they've started bragging."

"They wouldn't do it if it weren't to their advantage. Why, you can practically build a career on it now! For one thing, if you're a prince, you're no longer a Jew. Though if you're a Jew, it's still flattering: you'll turn up someone sympathetic and deferential. People are bored with respecting no one and fearing everything. They're eager to show respect. And what could be more obvious—a prince. They're not afraid. Take you, for example, do you think your successes are all your own doing, it doesn't mean anything that you're a prince? Of course it does. They forgive you a lot they wouldn't forgive someone else, especially where you're so unaffected—flatteringly unaffected, from the point of view of the riffraff. They'll figure a lot comes naturally to you, where someone else has to understand and know his place. Or still has to prove—"

"But why are you so worked up?" Lyova said in bewilderment.

"Sure, what's a prince now? But still . . . People have stopped being afraid of the origin question on official forms," Mitishatyev concluded venomously. "A sign of the times, as it were. So they boast."

"But why boast?" Gottich said, prying open his lips with difficulty. "Take me, for example, I'm a baron and I don't boast, do I?"

"You'd be worth your weight in gold!" Mitishatyev burst out laughing, and Lyova turned aside to smile. "You'd be worth your weight in gold—if you had a proletarian origin. But you're a von! It's true, Lyova. So. Stand up, you two, behave as one does in high society. Imagine, candles burning, ladies waltzing, and I introduce you to each other, although that last is the hardest to imagine—I'm the son of a simple shopkeeper. So you see I'm not a proletarian either; I, too, have an origin. Anything can happen in this day and age . . . So, I introduce you to each other: Prince Odoevtsev! Baron von Gottich! Eh? How do you like that! Has a nice ring to it . . . Prince Odoevtsev is a splinter off the Empire, and the Baron's a splinter, too . . . Me— I'm *in* splinters! Ha-ha-ha!" Mitishatyev howled for a long time. At last, apparently wiping away a tear, he gave permission: "Well, you may sit down. That's all. You've imagined it; enough. You won't see any more of that, believe me. Or are you hoping for the restoration? How about it, Lyova?"

"Oh no," Lyova answered, squinting at Gottich anyway with inappropriate gravity. "What would I want with the restoration? What would I do with it? The very idea is ludicrous. What's left of the prince in me? A name. I'm no prince," he said sadly.

"But your sense of worth? Your dignity sticks out all over."

"What dignity? It's just laziness, an unwillingness to push."

"Don't talk that way," Gottich said suddenly. "That's unworthy. One must bear . . . with honor . . ."

"What must one bear?" Mitishatyev asked. "One mustn't bear nonsense, my friend. Or interrupt one's elders, either."

"I can stand up!" Gottich said, offended. He braced himself feebly on the arms of the chair and fell back into it. "I can leave!"

"How about the split?" Mitishatyev said. "We haven't finished it yet."

"So let's finish it—and I'll leave," Gottich said.

"Forgive me, Baron," Mitishatyev said after the next round. "It was a joke. Coarse and stupid, maybe, but a joke, a loving one . . . Give me your hand. There. Never again, right? Till death do us part, isn't that so? Come, let's kiss." He winked at Lyova.

Lyova felt disgusted and bored. "Don't," he said.

"Right you are," Mitishatyev said, turning serious. "Right as always . . . No, seriously, the fellow's had a remarkable career. He's a poet; imagine. He gets published. Contributes to patriotic magazines. Von Gottich, poems on Party life—"

"Nautical life," Gottich corrected.

"Oh yes, naughty life. In all of Russian poetry there's never been such a career. After high school the Baroness tearfully cast him adrift. He drifted and drifted—and suddenly got an idea. He went to a library, got the files of some old provincial newspapers, cribbed a few holiday poems, and began taking them around to the editors, appropriate poems for the appropriate holidays. Well, you know what a dearth there is. His poems began to be accepted and, accordingly, published. So he lived from holiday to holiday and carried the clippings in his pocket: showed them to the official if anything came up. When suddenly—ruin. Some idiot recognized *his own* poem. Imagine, the memory people have! He started making phone calls, proclaiming from the housetops. There was even a newspaper article: person of no definite occupation, plagiarist, and so on. Our Baron felt hurt, and he decided:

Why should I answer for all this garbage, I can do as well myself. He gave it a try, and in fact, it came out better. Ever since, he's done his own writing. Does it *better*. He gets published. A contributor . . . with his picture. And he's one up on the official—he outranks him now."

"You're mocking me," Gottich said listlessly. "I want to leave."

"Maybe we should have another?"

"Can do," Gottich said.

"Only you have to go out for it, okay?"

"Go yourself."

"You wanted to leave anyway—you're going out anyway—so what will it cost you?" Mitishatyev said pleadingly.

"Maybe so . . . That's right, I didn't think," Gottich said. "Going out anyway, you know . . ." Abruptly he pushed off and stood up, turning dreadfully pale as he did so. He stood there for some time at attention, perfectly straight and pale.

The telephone rang. Gottich fell backward into the armchair, and Lyova picked up the receiver.

It was old Blank.

When he picked up the receiver, Lyova lost his equilibrium—he stumbled a little and balanced on one foot for a moment—but mainly he was balancing on the telephone line, swaying and hovering.

On one end of the line, Lyova's end, was Mitishatyev: this was reality, they were together and drinking, Lyova and Mitishatyev. On the other end, somewhere very far away . . . (Lyova even had a strange thought about the improbability of it: since he couldn't see the man he was talking to, maybe the man didn't exist: certainly vibrations turn into electrical current, the resistance varies, a carbon plate—what gibberish! how is this related to the fact of one man's saying something to another? what does a carbon plate have to do with anything?) . . . on the other end, nevertheless, was Isaiah Borisovich Blank, a noble old man.

Mitishatyev knew one Lyova, Blank knew another.

Lyova was forced to converse with Blank in Mitishatyev's presence. He was unpleasantly astonished by his abrupt change of tone, as if someone else had started to talk: his own good manners were a little sickening. Mitishatyev kept sending ironic glances from under the receiver, as if he knew all about Lyova. This smirk too, though it was no more than Mitishatyev's habitual little mask, infuriated Lyova because it seemed so highly developed, so skilled—so appropriate to the event, whatever Mitishatyev's perspicacity.

And while old Blank, on the other end, was showering him with compliments, Lyova, on this end, was falling all over himself to reply in kind, but literally falling all over himself, for Mitishatyev to see. By now he felt ready to be rude to Blank, in order to please Mitishatyev—but something held him back. His blood would not let him . . . Now Blank began to apologize. Lyova too, inappropriately, launched into apologies. Mitishatyev, for ironic effect, played "Chernomor's March" on his teeth. Exhausted by his own duality, which had been so shamefully exposed—this *would* have to happen!—Lyova no longer heard what Blank said, he agreed without taking it in. But when he hung up he understood all and went cold: Blank would be right over.

"Blank will be right over," Lyova said to the darkly silent Mitishatyev. He was unpleasantly aware of his intonation changing in this short phrase—he seemed to surface one minute, sink the next—and if the word "Blank" was spoken in the exact same tone he had used with Blank, by the time he spoke the word "over," his tone was the one he had previously used with Mitishatyev.

"Isaiah cometh!" Mitishatyev guffawed. "Come, oh, come . . . I-sa-iah! What do you think, how about if I borrow some money from him?"

Lyova still did not want to meet Mitishatyev's eyes. "You shouldn't," he said in alarm.

"Why shouldn't I?" Mitishatyev said gleefully. He tackled Lyova out of habit, sensing a weak point. "I *will!*"

"Please don't," Lyova said, cringing at a premonition.

"Why not? He's just the man to give it to me. He'll think he's bought or humiliated me—and he'll give me the loan."

Lyova said nothing.

"Do you hear the dripping of time?" Mitishatyev asked. "Isaiah cometh!"

"Isaiah had a marvelous face," Gottich stated profoundly.

"Go on down, unlock the door," Mitishatyev said. "Don't you hear Isaiah stamping the snow off his ghetto galoshes?"

Lyova descended the stairs in inexpressible anguish.

As we descend the stairs with Lyova, we will tell a little about Blank. He is our last character.

Blank and Lyova had a peculiar relationship. Blank existed on a pension and had not worked at the institute in a long time now. He hadn't wanted to retire—he liked to hint at this, that they had "retired" him. He endured it and went on showing up at the institute, less to

261

do anything than to look and listen, mill around in his native ferment. But he had a perpetual excuse: a certain paper that he was writing. "No, no, premature to talk about it . . ." He was a brisk old man, hearty and sociable, and simply felt bored lounging around the house all the time. He could not "create" in the quiet of his study, nor did he seem to want to. Two or three times a week he came in and made his way from office to office, listening to the news, rumors, and anecdotes and carrying what he heard from one office to the next. He "couldn't do without people."

The first thing that struck one about Blank was his extraordinary personal neatness, which might almost have been considered sophistication and elegance, although it was neither. It was the rare imprint of physical cleanness; one finds it in people long rich and long civilized, but in other circumstances the trait is individual. Blank seemed able to mix easily with whomever he pleased, the lowest riffraff, and remain ever the same well-pressed Blank, without a spot. Lyova attracted him immediately, in advance—his breeding, the family name. He liked to stop Lyova in the corridor, and they conversed for hours on end. Everyone who walked by was food for their conversation, which consisted mainly of evaluations, of mutual satisfaction over their concurrence in these evaluations, and, in turn, that concurrence's concurrence with a common, seemingly absolute evaluation, which was the *opinion of the circle* (this stock exchange was precisely regulated with regard to who was a genius, who had talent, who was honest . . . and any adjustment to these "cartridge clips" was a spiritual liberty that threatened one with promotion or demotion in the opinion of the circle, as in the service). So they had their discussions, the little flame of their conversation was fanned by everyone who walked by, and in the space of an hour they had time to discuss many people. In addition to these gladly shared topics, Blank and Lyova apparently also shared a small passion for collecting. One of them had apparently collected for a long time; the other was apparently collecting, too, or intended to begin. It may have been coins, or was it matchboxes . . .

Lyova eagerly became the man Blank wished to see in him—a man of "breeding," of culture, of the decency that is in the blood and has no substitute, cannot be dislodged. He was playing up to Blank, of course, but the game afforded him the pleasure of remembering something about himself, something that had a kind of truth not yet manifested in his life. He felt natural in this role. Because he himself had not known for a long time where or who he was, he even developed quite an authentic feeling that he was indeed the man for whom Blank

took him and for whom he passed himself off to Blank. Remarkably—
and here his instinct was at its peak—Lyova never conversed with
Blank in the presence of a third person. He stopped talking and left
as soon as anyone else came along. Blank naturally took this to mean
that their conversations were not for outside ears and there was no
need to profane their true relations.

Blank seemed to be this kind of man: he could not speak ill of
people. If he said that everything was horrible, his assessment of individual people would be superlative. If he did allow himself to be
horrified by someone, he would speak of life as a divine gift. His
consciousness would travel a fantastic logical circle, spiraling up and
back, to find an explanation for any man's deed from the humanistic
viewpoint—when all was not yet lost, it was still too early to give the
man up as hopeless, and so forth. (Curiously, despite his capacity for
explanation, in Blank's opinion there existed a group of people united
by just one common feature, a group he had given up as hopeless in
advance. But this made the remaining majority all the better . . .)

This same stretchy quality, which might have been termed benev-
olence, brought Lyova especially close to Blank after the notorious
incident of Lyova's friend and his trial, when Lyova became so flustered
and lost face. Lyova was just back from the vacation that had saved
him (his friend was no longer around), he was enduring as best he
could all the allusions and innuendos of his colleagues—and now the
noble Blank approached him. Lyova shrank back, because, if the
opinion of the others was immaterial to him and could matter only
for selfish reasons—though, as it turned out, also for selfish reasons,
Lyova himself was immaterial to them to begin with and they didn't
even have an opinion—then it was Blank's opinion, which had struck
him as so insignificant in his career calculations, strangely enough it
was this one, this no-account opinion, that signified something, and
not merely in a personal way, moreover: it was the one that something
depended on. The thing that would be the most dangerous of all to
ignore . . . And now the noble Blank gave Lyova a huge advance. I
understand, he said with deep sympathy, how hard it is for you to bear
all these rumors, all this filth, especially since you cannot protest, as
a decent man, because in defending yourself, no matter how uprightly
you did it, you would involuntarily appear to be selling out your friend;
that, and only that, is unquestionably the way they would see it; you
are incapable of this, I understand you so well! but let it be some
comfort to you that I don't believe a word of all this gossip . . . Lyova
nearly burst into tears of joy and shame right there in the corridor,

and he accepted the bribe, believing immediately that all was just as Blank said. Who could have known he was such a deep man! Blank was touched to see Lyova's agitation. Again he interpreted it in his own way—nobly—and for a long time they clasped hands in sweet, moist-eyed silence. After this, their conversations became still more heartfelt. They seemed to have developed a common secret, and whenever Blank appeared, Lyova indulged in him as in a vice, voluptuously posing as Blank wanted to see him. Blank had developed a certain "right" to Lyova.

The more abrupt the contrast with the rest of Lyova's life—with what he had just been saying to his colleagues the moment before Blank poked his curly gray head in the door, before Lyova broke off in midsentence, went right out to him, and began saying completely different things, in a changed voice—the more abrupt and instantaneous this contrast, the sweeter it was, not more painful, strange to say (this surprised Lyova himself). True, the conversation never took place in the presence of outsiders.

People laughed at their attachment. Laughed at Lyova as if he had a weakness, although a forgivable one; laughed at Blank on general principles.

And now here was Mitishatyev sitting across from him, and Blank on the telephone, saying to Lyova (who was sobering with every word) that of course he could imagine how dreary it was for Lyova, sitting in that poorhouse by himself on the holidays; his wife had sent him out for bread—they were having company today, what a pity Lyova couldn't come—and here he was, on his way home with the bread, just passing the institute, he was calling from the pay phone and would be right over, if only to divert Lyova somehow and relieve the dreariness of his day . . . Lyova went weak all over. He positively could not tell Blank what the trouble was or why he shouldn't come. Mitishatyev was grinning, although he himself didn't yet know why, as he eavesdropped on Lyova's conversation. Suddenly, right then and there, the old mechanism of his influence on Lyova was regaining its strength. It seemed to be reviving, once more filling with life force. Lyova was already in Mitishatyev's power, he was torn between Mitishatyev and Blank, and neither could prevail over the other. The result, for Lyova, was a kind of mumbling muteness—and he said nothing sensible to Blank.

Mitishatyev and Blank were contraindicated for each other. Mitishatyev killed Lyova in Blank's eyes, and Blank killed Lyova in Mitishatyev's eyes. Discreditation and exposure . . . How Lyova would extricate himself—how he would speak two languages at once, act within two opposite systems simultaneously—he hadn't a clue. What would happen now? Scandal, contempt? And if he could still scrape by with some small sacrifice, what would it be? To disentangle this situation, generated by his weakness, struck Lyova as impossible.

Paling with every step, he descended to unlock the door for Blank. He felt like swallowing the keys.

They're congregating, Lyova thought.

DEMONS INVISIBLE
TO THE EYE

The demons came whirling
Like leaves in November

. . . . .

What happened next was so hideous and fast that Pyotr Stepanovich
was later quite unable to arrange his recollections in any kind of
order.

. . . . .

"*What are you doing to the wallpaper?*"
Peredonov and Varvara started to laugh.
"*It's to spite the landlady,*" *Varvara said.* "*We're leaving soon.*
But don't go blabbing it."
. . . *Peredonov went over to the wall and began kicking it with*
his boot soles.

PUSHKIN	DOSTOEVSKY	F. SOLOGUB
"The Demons"	*The Devils*	*The Petty Demon*
1830	1871	1902

IF YOU ONLY KNEW how little I wished to bring Blank in just now!
Too late: he will enter. And Gottich's been here a long time. I should
have thought before—but, from now on, everything happens in only
one way, indifferent to any attempt of ours to improve a given situation.

We know how Lyova surrendered himself to impotence in his solitude. But pathetic as he may have been during those hours, there
was something noble about him: he was alone in this condition and
had involved no one else. It was, shall we say, his own business. Lyova
was alone, then Mitishatyev arrived. He brought Gottich with him.
Blank appeared next . . . We don't know what condition these men
were in until they arrived at Lyova's. We assume, as did Lyova, that
they were just as they stepped over the threshold—just what they
seemed to be. And we've no doubt that they saw themselves just as
an outsider would. We are implying, without foundation, that they

266

saw content and expression as adequate. Quite understandably, therefore, sensing this boundary between solitude and society, standing motionless over this chasm, Lyova tried to be just like them and not betray himself in any way. The author did not notice at what moment they became a party of five. They had drink after drink, joyfully growing to resemble each other and lowering the level. They spoke as one man, glad of their own society. That is, a man might have known all about himself and therefore considered himself unworthy, but suddenly he found himself surrounded by amiable people, not one of whom thought so ill of him as he himself did. And in actual fact, upon comparison, he was nowhere near so worthless as he had deemed himself in solitude. They spoke as one man, one bulky man with indefinite clay features who had absorbed them all. And all their trite words were made new again by the mere fact that this clay mouth had never before pronounced them, no one before had heard them from this mouth . . . They spoke of the weather, freedom, poetry, progress, Russia, the West, the East, the Jews, the Slavophiles, the liberals, cooperative apartments, cheap boarded-up country houses, the people, drunkenness, vodka-making methods, hangover, *Oktyabr* and *Novy Mir*, God, women, Negroes, currency, authority, privilege certificates, contraceptives, Malthus, stress, stoolies (Blank kept giving Lyova cautionary winks behind Gottich's back), pornography, impending change, corroborated rumors, physics, a certain movie actress, the societal meaning of the existence of brothels, the decline of literature and the arts, their simultaneous upsurge, the social nature of man, the fact that there was no place to hide . . .

How strangely they talked! As though they had all been handed an equal number of equal wooden chips and were exchanging the ones that matched. As though this were some kind of childish domino game: a pear on one half, an apple on the other, with the apple to be placed against an apple, and the pear against a pear. Mitishatyev played a doublet, dreaming of making a doubleheader; Lyova passed. The lamellate path curved artfully, making a tricky turn and still not breaking. The conversation raced steadily along over this rickety planking. It was a kindergarten domino game, but what macabre little pictures were duplicated, in small quantity, to be recognized on these wooden matrices! Instead of the apple and the pear, a policeman and a naked woman. These two suits were especially in demand. The presence of Blank and Gottich raised the conversation to fever pitch. Anything not meant under any circumstances for Gottich's ears was shouted in Blank's ear, and anything not fit for Blank's ears was whispered in unison in Gottich's. The less either was meant for utterance, the more vocally and loudly it was spoken. This strange balance was very precisely maintained, however; the pans of the scales vibrated slightly, being overloaded, but neither outweighed the other. As though the "too much" that should not be said in Gottich's presence had been completely neutralized by the "too much" that was being said in Blank's presence, and vice versa. The surprisingly swollen zero of this conversation, like a magic ring, enfolded the rash fearlessness of the speakers.

They said that the weather had become totally different. Moscow used to have a totally different climate—hard winter, hot summer—but now, Leningrad or Moscow, it's one and the same. And the Caucasus and the Crimea—same damn thing, can't tell them apart. Well, what do you mean, the same! they said. Just compare Moscow and Leningrad—no comparison at all: how can that be Leningrad?

They talked about freedom of speech—it was out of the question. In the clayey maelstrom of the common voice, only now and then do I catch a phrase that belongs to someone, or distinguish someone's voice. Gottich is saying that this is scandalous, if we reason this way we'll perish utterly. Lyova observes that literature doesn't need freedom of speech, what it needs is a public, as a condition that allows its mere possibility, nothing more. Mitishatyev says they don't know what they're talking about, because what they're talking about never existed in Russia, in any kind of weather. How so, quite the opposite, claims Blank, who is not drinking, and he offers as corroboration the mere fact, the mere possibility, of Chekhov's book on Sakhalin. But Mitishatyev is quite sure that the existence of literature has never proved the possibility of its existence. More likely the opposite. Blank begs them not to talk this way in the presence of a young man who is no stranger to poetry. Gottich fully agrees that Blok is a genius, but he feels much closer to Pasternak. Mitishatyev says Pasternak isn't a poet at all. Lyova mildly coaxes Blank to change his viewpoint on Esenin. Blank makes no protest to Lyova.

In the conversation about Russia, Blank remains silent, shifting his wise and modest gaze from Mitishatyev to Lyova. As always, we remember nothing of this conversation. Lyova quotes his grandfather as having once told him personally that Russia was a preserve, the last center of resistance to progress. Mitishatyev is enchanted with this remark. Blank interferes just once, to observe that they are distorting the true meaning of the great man's private words. Naturally, this conversation is tightly intertwined with the subject of progress; Mitishatyev remarks caustically that "America is a Jewish land." Gottich mentions individual freedom as the chief value. No one in the group pursues the conversation about the camps. The conversation easily shifts to a discussion of the problem of other private accommodations. Mitishatyev brands cooperative construction as the main impetus to the renaissance of a narrow, petit-bourgeois ideology. Lyova preaches the charm of the trend from the city back to the country; it turns out Gottich knows where you can buy a house for a hundred rubles; "You'll never leave," Mitishatyev says emphatically. Lyova takes offense: "There's no need for me to be a Slavophile, for the simple reason that I'm a Slav." "Why is it you're a Slav?" Mitishatyev wonders. "By blood." "Original," Mitishatyev humphs. "No one's ever given me that answer before." "But have you asked everyone?" Blank asks ironically. "Not you," Mitishatyev says rudely.

China, artificial caviar, the High Renaissance . . .

"Venturi quotes Vasari . . ."

"No, let me tell you, here's the simplest secret of success. Have an intelligent conversation with her. You absolutely have to have an intelligent conversation with a woman—"

"Exactly the other way around," claims a new character, who has turned up out of absolutely nowhere, a product of the intelligentsia's false concepts of the people. "The important thing with women is, never have an intelligent conversation. An intelligent conversation is exactly what you shouldn't have. Let her sound off. And take her, right away. Honorably, like a soldier."

This character arouses the general admiration of the company by being able to string words together, with a subject and predicate. This is the son-in-law of the doorkeeper whom Lyova let off; he has dropped by for a roll of linoleum he left with her last week and is very disappointed not to find her in. To everyone's delight, he resolves any argument, pronouncing the last word. It convinces and reconciles everyone. He's not just a man, he's a mine of information. Another happy thing about him is that all the touchy subjects seem to become safe in his presence. How lucky they all are that he has dropped by and infused a healthy stream. By now they can't imagine him not among them. The tolerant son-in-law allows them this flattery.

"How true that is!" Lyova takes him up. "It's an astonishing thing: for all practical purposes, the woman does not exist who doesn't think she's the best of all. That's why you have to let them talk; either way, the conversation will be about their virtues. Try to mention the name of some woman you know, even in the most disinterested tone, just in passing. What will you hear? 'They say she has beautiful eyes. She does have beautiful eyes, of course, but her . . .' And there's nothing left of the girlfriend, because she doesn't possess this 'but her,' which by pure coincidence is what your companion is supremely endowed with. Her eyes aren't much to speak of, but then again her . . . This 'but then again her' will be the most invaluable and absolutely unique combination of qualities."

"I agree. Briefly put: women are their own best boosters."

"We know from literature that prostitutes are extraordinarily loyal—"

"But everyone does it!" Gottich said, taking offense on behalf of women.

"Most nobly spoken, young man!" Mitishatyev exclaimed. "Here's to women!"

We don't know at what moment they became a party of five, but when they were seven, this is what they were talking about . . .

"No, no, don't say that. Nathalie was first of all Woman. Why should she understand her husband's mission? He understood it himself. He wasn't so shallow as to need a comrade-in-arms rather than a woman." This remark was probably Lyova's.

"But all these poetesses von Gottich's been talking about—they all just want to sleep with Pushkin. That's the whole story! They can't forgive her, because they were born too late to correct his mistaken choice. *They* would appreciate his genius! That they could do. The one thing they don't take into account is that he might not be attracted to them as women." No; we thought that was Mitishatyev's voice, but it's not. Who is this dark, elegant-looking, venomous man? The author doesn't know him, but with half an ear we hear someone whisper: You mean you haven't read his remarkable article "What Pushkin Deleted"? No, the author hasn't read it.

"Yes, maybe he wouldn't even want to f— them!" the son-in-law took him up.

"Oh, Pushkin didn't miss a . . ." A general smirk.

" 'A few days ago, with the help of God.' Her sister Alexandra—"

"No, old boy, we don't know the whole story on that yet—"

"Excuse me, but what more is there to know! Did they find a cross in his bed? They did. Of course he lived with her sister. It's even funny—"

"What are you arguing about! You've forgotten what you're arguing about. You have to establish A, and *then* B." (Ha-ha-ha! He burst out laughing himself.) "So here's A: Did Nathalie Pushkin sleep with d'Anthès, or didn't she?"

"She did."

"I say she didn't!"

"But what does it matter, gentlemen—"

"She was just a fool, that's all."

"I fully agree. Vulf corroborates that she was just a silly young girl, sloppy and tasteless, not even very pretty. We can believe his testimony."

"She was a delight!"

"But how could she have lived with him, and understood so little!"

"But who understood him! Who ever understood him! What are you asking of the girl!" Lyova flared. "Vyazemsky? Baratynsky? Not only weren't they charming young girls, but they, too, didn't understand him. Do I have to repeat these truisms for you? Vyazemsky— he was just chasing her himself, he wrote to her even after the death of . . . It's all a filthy myth! Legend and myth! From what they've found of her letters, she fully joined in her husband's concerns, and she was clever about money and housekeeping. When all is said and done, she was young, pure, beautiful—"

"Innocent—"

"Exactly. Innocent. Innocent, and not guilty. Why, when all is said and done, she never had a break! Her longest interval between babies was a year and a half."

"Have it your way. But did she love him?"

" 'No, I value not riotous pleasure,' " Gottich began, with expression. " 'Far dearer to me—' "

"Brilliant lines!" someone interrupted, shedding a few tears. "No, gentlemen! In the whole of world lyric poetry, do you know anything like it for nakedness, concreteness! Everything is called by its literal name. The right words. No allegory!"

"Sex and Eros were clearly formulated, then and there!"

"Exactly! But did she love him?"

"If she didn't love him, in any case she didn't know it. She didn't know love."

"Oh yes, she loved him. She was like a cat in love. Jealous."

"Well, you can be jealous even without loving someone."

"That's right."

"She loved Lanskoy."

"By the way, it made Pushkin happy when she slapped his face for

271

Mme Krüdener. And Mme Krüdener was Tyutchev's first love; how's that for a grimace of fate!"

"Also Nicholas's."

"What, her too?"

"And later Benckendorff's."

"Notice the commonality of tastes. Pushkin's daughter married Dubbelt's son."

"Pushkin himself liked d'Anthès! He even liked the czar."

"Handsome, tall, such a czar-r," Mitishatyev said, mimicking Blank.

"Nathalie was strict with him."

"Stop, gentlemen, aren't you ashamed! Count how many men she had besides her husbands. Maybe one, maybe two—"

"Or maybe even none."

"By modern standards she's a saint."

"A saint she is."

"But Pushkin needed so much support in that last year! She had absolutely no desire to understand his agonies, his despair—"

"You're being banal, von Gottich! She endured and suffered *him*. Isn't that enough for you? Just imagine this psycho, this bilious nigger, this obscene—"

"You're about to get punched in the nose."

"Stop, stop, calm down, gentlemen!"

"Yes, yes! 'Pathetic, filthy, but not like you, villains!' "

"But here's another letter: 'A lawful c—t is a kind of warm cap with earflaps.' "

"Yes . . . exactly . . . and how everything changed! Pushkin, who all his life had mocked at horns—and suddenly he's the champion of his wife's honor and fidelity."

"Haven't you read Khodasevich's 'Cupid and Hymen'? Then what *have* you read?"

"That's all true, but we keep forgetting that things were different then, everything was different. You're measuring by your own yardstick."

"By your own centimeter . . . ha-ha-ha!"

"Listen, how big was Pushkin's?"

"Peter the Great's was eighteen matches . . ." (The doorkeeper's son-in-law?)

"Lengthwise or crosswise?"

"Ha-ha-ha-ha."

"Fie, fie, gentlemen! Enough! Shame, sin, disgrace! What nonsense we're talking! Nathalie Pushkin was beautiful for the simple reason that Pushkin *loved* her! He didn't love Akhmatova—he loved *her*."

"Bravo! She was his wife."

"The one. The only."

"Gentlemen! In honor of Nathalie Pushkin! Everyone up! Gottich, don't fall. To the most beautiful of women, gentlemen!"

Lyova suddenly felt sick. He caught himself talking. He had been carried away, and had almost forgotten how bad things really were. An unreasoning fear fell upon him, a fear so complete that the Mitishatyev–Gottich–Blank combination, which had been such a threat, no longer scared him. A sense of nausea gripped him, as if all the words pronounced here in unison had not disappeared, had not throbbed away in the air, but were stuck inside him, damming up his soul and tormenting him like a sin. How many words people have understood over the last few years, Lyova thought, remembering back. Just recently they didn't know a single one . . . how fast they've learned! And how passionate they are about cashing them in for new meanings, more and more of them. As though they've understood something—understood how to understand. People have understood, and have ignored *what* they understood. As though understanding were one thing and living another. Therefore, all of what they've understood has turned to shit, even though it wasn't shit before. They have understood nothing—but they've learned. That's why there'll be retribution—for the Word! That's the sin . . . So, he thought, the premonitions that had recently tormented him were not in vain! They were bound to come true now. They were rehearsed, deserved. Maybe they had already come true—if so, they were no longer premonitions. He was aware of retribution as a fused, dark mass of perished words, their nuclei compacted, heavy, like an extinct star; it was a dismal body of nausea, a fluctuating volume equal to the mass of the words pronounced. Blasted, wasted, tasted words . . . A critical mass . . . What would happen, what would happen!

"Gentlemen! Silence." Lyova lurched to his feet. "I must speak."

With anger and pain, Lyova delivered his speech on the wasted word. He spoke of the inexpiable sin against it, of the inevitable retribution, of Babel. The word within him was sickened, and it shot out. His speech was ecstatically received. Gottich wept. "What's got into you?" Mitishatyev marveled aloud, as if standing at his pedestal. Blank, who had been on the point of wariness, warmly shook hands with him, as being truly the grandson of a great man. Inspired by Lyova, they all started talking even more freely, vying with one another, racing one another.

"There are seven of them, seven of them—a hundred of them!"
Lyova muttered, and got drunk, as if drowning.

. . . .

You can't keep track of everything. At some point Lyova discovered
a great many people in the room. Blank was there, and Mitishatyev.
Gottich had turned up again. There were also two girls, whose origin
it would have been difficult to trace, unwinding time backward. There
was also a handsome man always half in shadow like the cupboard in
the corner, an Adonis of an outmoded type, brazenly flashing a gold
tooth. He was quietly behaved, heavy, and apparently not subject to
drunkenness—the kind of man people expected a fight from. He knew
this from experience, which is probably why he was so passive in his
certainty: go ahead and try, but you won't get away. There was a
glimpse of a shadow with him, not even enough to arouse Lyova's
suspicion—nothing, just an image, the image of Faina. She herself,
however, was not there. Lyova couldn't have sworn just when, but
Lyubasha appeared. She attended the meeting for a while, patient and
indifferent, and disappeared just as unobtrusively as she had come.
Possibly with the gold-toothed fellow—the tooth had ceased flashing
in the corner; for some reason the fight hadn't come off.
Time pulsed and space breathed, marked by pauses at the way
stations of "splits." Together, now the two of them, now the three,
now the ten, now again the five, they divided up the bottle, always
the same one, it seemed. Sequence, that most implacable of things,
changed very easily with each of these discrepant doses (what preceded
what, and what followed what?), until finally it stopped marching single
file as if on parade and took an easy, dispersed form, as though time
itself had gathered for a nice reunion with itself, where the present
awaited the arrival of the past, and the future had arrived first of all.
"Speed does not cause drunkenness. Drunkenness *is* speed!" Lyova
proclaimed.
"Bravo, bravo!" And everyone drank.
Lyova remembered the entrances—and did not remember the exits
. . . There is something exact about Lyova's definition of "drunkenness," at least with respect to Lyova himself. The more he was drained
away into immobility and bodily absence—the more inactive his substance was—the more swiftly his essence raced along, with a tapping
of heartbeats at railway junctions and switches. Everything around him
flowed together, smeared and blurred by his speed.
Ever fewer were the clearings along the sides of his movement, ever

farther-spaced the distance, and suddenly—stop! A station, an abrupt wave of momentum, a brilliant light. The pool of luminosity paused and came into focus, it had room in it for someone's new mask, rather less successful than more so, there was a glimpse of the name of the station—Osobaya, Malenkovskaya, something near Moscow—and the train pulled out, yanked rapidly away, leaving its substance behind for a second. Lyova flushed brown from the G-force, then the velocity became habitual, and both visuality and luminosity flowed together in two uniform and indistinguishable stripes.

So Lyova whirled along, where time was measured not by the distance covered but by the number of stops. At several stops he tried to get out, but somehow he didn't make it.

"No, people don't drink vodka!" he exclaimed at the next stop. "People drink time!"

"A genius!" Mitishatyev marveled, with conviction.

"Hear that? They drink hours!" Lyova's eyes had welled with tears at the word "genius."

So Lyova did not remember the legs of his own journey. They were his "condition"—velocity, distance, and time—he was drinking them. He remembered only the stations and way stations; but he did not remember which came after which. They shifted around in his head like change in his pocket: in any order, but each one separately, by virtue of its shape and nominal value.

Flashes of insight came to him. Their penetrating forcefulness moved him deeply, and a treacherous quaver appeared in his voice when he tried to express them aloud. For example, after detaching substance from essence within himself, he realized that substance was a plant and essence was an animal.

"The express life of animals and the mail life of plants . . ." he said. No one understood, and Lyova felt hurt. He had said it so beautifully! But he himself forgot the context. (I later spent a long time deciphering this phrase, which Lyova scratched on a cigarette box in order to remember it.)

He could not recall when or under what circumstances Blank had vanished. He did remember that Blank had still been there at the previous station, but he was gone at the next. At the previous station, a stunned Blank had suddenly been given the spotlight: his shaven, milky cheeks were jouncing above the porcelain collar, and he was quieting them by resting them on its firmness. The gesture was a continuation of the line formed by his puffy, very white hand on the knob of his cane—both hand and cheeks were "in repose." But this

275

repose was an expression of deepest indignation and anger; his words, numerous and unpronounced, fluttered and twined above his collar like so many ribbons in the wind. Also illuminated, but not so brightly, was Mitishatyev, emphatically distinct and economical in his gestures. But an unimaginable fuss was evident behind that economy, as though he had something jumping and running around under his skin, something small, like a tiny mouse, although invisible: such is the look of an ill-bred man poisoned by notions of form and polish. The picture had switched on when Lyova lowered his empty glass. He couldn't tell which of them had just spoken and which was getting ready to reply, Blank or Mitishatyev; in the corner, with an irony emphasized by restraint, the cupboard was flashing a gold tooth (so he hadn't left yet . . .). When Blank finished chewing, he did not speak to Mitishatyev but turned to Lyova, his anger replaced by dismay.

"Lev Nikolaevich! Why are you silent?" Blank said, in a voice made childish by the unimaginability of what was happening. His eyebrows floated up, farsightedly, as though he were holding Lyova's picture at arm's length.

"What? I didn't hear," Lyova said, with Mitishatyev's little smile on his face. It swam in his already shapeless features like a dumpling in soup.

"How's that?" Blank's eyebrows began flipping past on his forehead like a rolling picture on a television set: eyebrows . . . they're gone . . . eyebrows again.

"Now don't get excited," Mitishatyev put in. "This is all I meant. You hinted that in that case I myself might be a Jew. Right! I may be. I don't know my own father, after all. Or my mother either, it seems." Here he bared his teeth in the icy sneer of a man who has seen and suffered much. "In that case, *you* may be my papa. As in the classic segregation novel about the drop of blood. It's nothing terrible or surprising—we have to reckon with it. An original variant of *Fathers and Sons*, written by Victor Hugo in collaboration with Howard Fast . . ."

At this point Lyova's "train" pulled out and dashed into the distance, so abruptly that his whole body yielded, waiting out the acceleration.

But at the next stop Blank was already gone. What chasms of splashing consciousness had Lyova swum in that pause?

Similarly, he did not remember later what came before what: had they looked for girls while Blank was there, or after? At this station the light fell on Lyova himself, rather than on those around him. He could not see himself—but it was his own figure that was primarily highlighted for him here, by the shame and childish disgrace of being suddenly intelligible and visible to all. Mitishatyev and Lyova were making phone calls.

They had aroused each other's mettle by a previous conversation. Listen, how about calling up some girls, Mitishatyev had said, coming to life. Why, sure, what could be easier! But the more they spun the dial, the more clearly they both saw that each was not only what the other imagined him to be but also, in and of himself, something little, helpless, and homey.· Each of them, it seemed, was supposed to have a notebook stuffed with girls, all neatly expressed in six-digit numbers for purposes of portability and pocketability. But whom, let's say, could Lyova call? The same old Albina. Lyubasha, after all, had only a work number. He couldn't call Faina! Besides, it wouldn't be any use . . . This was when Lyova caught himself dialing any six digits and asking for any Anya, another Nadya, or a miscellaneous Masha—and he realized the value of multiple masculine conquests. But it was a surprise to Lyova that Mitishatyev turned out to be in the same boat. Hadn't Mitishatyev been dialing those same three numbers? Lyova peered over his shoulder. Mitishatyev slammed his notebook shut. "Blind swap?" he proposed. "No," Lyova said. So Mitishatyev had beaten Lyova again, at this telephonic poker game, but he was highly annoyed. He disappeared for some time. Humiliated by the pity of all the men, Lyova kept trying to reach Faina. In vain!

A pause came floating along and floated away. Mitishatyev—loud, a girl on each arm—burst in as if from the cold.

"Meet the Natashas!" he proclaimed, pleased and proud: he *had* managed to show Lyova how this was done!

"And over here, Prince Lev Odoevtsev!" he proclaimed. The girls giggled at his joke. "Well, how about it?" he asked smugly. "Was I gone long?"

He had, in fact, been gone only briefly. Lyova was the one who had been gone a long time—he had dozed off. Somehow he had dozed backward in time. He found himself somewhere in yesterday, and he couldn't immediately get across to now, to Mitishatyev and the Natashas, across the heap of today. He looked around unsteadily.

"The bread," he said. He saw the bread in front of him. It was Blank's bread: a big string shopping bag, filled for a big family, a big dinner. "But where's Blank?"

"What Blank?" Mitishatyev said.

Lyova wagged his head: did that mean the girls had appeared *after* Blank, or before . . . ?

The girls were two Natashas. One Natasha, a fat one, was somewhat bottom-heavy, with a remarkable tower on her head and a gauze kerchief around her immobile neck, a dull expression of unapproachability on her face; Lyova privately christened her Anna Karenina in the role of Doronina. She seemed to become Mitishatyev's. The other— a thin, wiry little thing with a shallow, seemingly pretty, asymmetrical face and spots of sharp color on her narrow cheeks—kept darting glances from her seemingly large and lively eyes. She seemed to become Lyova's; she remained a Natasha, but in the role of Audrey Hepburn. To each his own . . .

A fresh split flashed by without stopping. The girls refused it. They were embarrassed. Privately, Lyova decided that they were embarrassed to find themselves in a palace, a museum. Anna Karenina glanced at the molded ceiling. She sighed, carefully smoothing her skirt around her melon knees, and then sat motionless, her hands in her lap. Light little Audrey skipped around the room—her first ball!—on her stringy legs, in slightly baggy stockings. But, glancing at her girlfriend, she recollected herself and sat down beside her, just as decorously motionless. "Have a drink with us, girls! Come on, why be shy?" Mitishatyev said. "Then would you like some tea, perhaps?"

"Yes, we would," Anna Karenina said in a bass voice.

Karenina went off with Mitishatyev, to help him make the tea.

"Unlike Victor Nabutov, my dear," Lyova was saying meanwhile, "Vladimir Nabokov is a writer."

He told Natasha how Tolstoy had dreamed about a woman's elbow. Female companionship made Lyova sentimental. Wouldn't you know, he thought. We work with all this, and it causes us no trepidation, nothing but boredom, whereas they—

"Have you read *Anna Karenina*?" he asked.

"M-hm," Natasha said. "I saw the movie."

—whereas they may not have read a single worthwhile book; what causes their trepidation and respect? Is it just the walls? A *priori*?

Natasha breathed in his ear.

Lyova started. "What did you say?"

"Nothing." Natasha was hurt. "I blew in your ear, that's all."

"Why?"

"No reason. I always blow in men's ears."

Good Lord! What for, Lyova thought furiously.

Mitishatyev appeared with the teapot, and Karenina with an even more unapproachable face.

"Still talking?"

Lyova threw a glance at his enemy: Is he mocking me? He could not read Mitishatyev's face.

They downed another split. The girls drank tea from saucers (to complete the picture), because no cups had been found. They cocked their little fingers. Decorous. It seemed to Lyova that the train was carrying him away, with his back to them. He kept looking at the watch on Karenina's arm. The watch impressed him: golden and tiny on her wide puffy wrist, it had drowned in the folds and lay there smiling. Lyova laughed. He laughed and purposely heaved his shoulders as if sobbing with soundless laughter, as if on the point of tears.

Mitishatyev was morose. He weighed Blank's shopping bag in his hand. Suddenly decisive, the shopping bag still in his hand, he headed for the window. He flung it open. A fresh breeze swept through the hall, startling Lyova. Mitishatyev plunged his hand into the bag, took out a round loaf, and tossed it up, hefting it in his hand as if weighing it more precisely.

"Heavy bread," he said pensively and mysteriously. "Heavy!"

And he tossed it out the window.

"Heavy bread! Heavy . . ." Now he was weighing the next one.

"What are you doing? Why?" Lyova frowned, intercepting Karenina's glance.

"Where were you during the blockade?" Mitishatyev asked.

"In evacuation."

"I was here . . . My mother died here"—and Mitishatyev threw the bread out the window. "Heavy, heavy bread!"

"What are you doing! Stop!" Lyova said in fright. "Don't!"

"I'm lying," Mitishatyev said. "Put out the light, will you!"

"The light?" Lyova stammered.

"Do as I say! Put it out."

Lyova clicked the switch. Darkness bulged. Adapting, a soft twilight crept over the room. Lyova ventured to take Natasha's hand. It was rough and awkward. Suddenly a light exploded in the window, a palm tree of cold Bengal fire sprang up and crumbled away. The window showed white for another second, with Mitishatyev black against the background. After the light, it was totally, invisibly dark.

"The salute! Hooray! The salute!"

A new sheaf ripened beyond the window—multicolored. Falling, fading, dying away, the tiny stars lost color and turned completely white at the level of the windowsill, which truncated the light into night.

And again.

The flying up and the fan-shaped crumbling suddenly struck Lyova as laughter.

Soundless, blinding shouts of laughter flew up again and again outside the window.

"To the streets!" Mitishatyev called. "To the barricades!"

. . . .

MASQUERADE

You're in a fever, I see, prepared to lose all.
How much for your epaulettes?
LERMONTOV, 1836

THE FRESH COLD AIR, at first gulp, tasted like happiness and liberation, but it worked like another large vodka. Lyova was put out of action, although he more or less managed to follow Mitishatyev without dropping behind or falling down.

Once in a while, his mind cleared. Then he would notice above him the cold jab of a star, glimmering among swift clouds lined with moonlight fur. He would lose his capacity for motion and stop dead, thinking he was at the bottom of a stone well. His consciousness was unpeopled. No one jostled him, no one crossed his path. Nothing met his double gaze, and only in the farthest distance could he see distinctly—always that same star.

"Alone I come out to the hi-igh-wa-ay"

he sang. A massed popular celebration was marching toward him. The "sparry path" was asphalt.

"No, look here!" Lyova said, clutching at Mitishatyev. "What a ravishing landscape that poem has, but you know, not a single detail! It's all in that 'sparry glitter'! The very lack of detail brings out the main point: the autumnal emptiness. Did you ever see a sparry path? Is there such a thing? But this is really a very accurate weather report: late autumn, and a light frost touching the still snowless highway. What true, unpremeditated exactness! The spar is gravel, the glitter is the ice, and nearby, unspoken, the word 'thorny' . . . We'll have to check—he must have written this in November, returning home late and on foot. He'd been drunk, he'd sobered up—"

"Sure," Mitishatyev said. "Don't forget that. Where'd you lose your Natasha?"

Lyova spun around—and in truth Natasha was gone.

"What did you do with yours?" Lyova asked, because the second Natasha was gone, too.

"I let mine *go*, you let yours *slip*."

"I do not want to suffer and enjoy!" Lyova declaimed.

"Then don't," Mitishatyev agreed readily.

Lermontov could not have written those lines in the fall, because he died that summer. The wrong landscape . . .

. . . The next star Lyova saw was the one over St. Isaac's Cathedral.

At the Bronze Horseman there was a maelstrom of popular celebration.

Here we should have a Gogolian exclamation: "Do you know" and "No, you don't know" what a massed popular celebration is. Of course we all know, each and every one of us. Everyone knows everything now. The form is known. We haven't that many forms, and all of them are mutually known. Where have you been? To the celebration. What did you do? Celebrate. The form is known, the content is not.

The spontaneous holiday celebration of the elemental masses (because it's true that it's spontaneous: the celebration has been allowed for, but not organized) is a march that has lost its way. We're not sure how accurate this notion is, but we'll use it to explain something . . . We are somewhat depressed by this somber pacing. We study the crowd, peer into a face, seek to recognize it. No face! Why this somberness? What we observe in the crowd as "life" is *in* the crowd; it is not the crowd. The crowd is merely the milieu of the alive. The alive prowls around in it—hooliganism, flirtation, a fistfight. The alive is a theft from the crowd. Thieves get beaten.

In the morning, by daylight, there's none of this. We march along, irregular and disorderly but all in one direction, we all flow together into the common body of the day, we participate in demonstrating that body. We have noisemakers and little flags. We sing, not very confidently. Everything's a little too brightly lit, it's been nice out all day—we are privately embarrassed for ourselves. We look around: are others as embarrassed? Apparently not. We, too, cease to feel it. More and more confidently we stride along, and we shout an irresolute "Hurray." The Square—here's where we were going! But we go past it.

Now here's a puzzle: we have no further obligation. We've gone past.

What is on the far side of the Square? The Square is high noon. On the far side is evening. Disconcerted that we're no longer going anywhere—there's nowhere to go, yet we're into the swing of it—we come out to the streets, this time for no reason. A celebration.

This is "existence," so to speak. On the far side of the Square we ourselves must keep ourselves interested, whereas on this side we have grown accustomed to a formal, synthesizing purposefulness. So abruptly . . . In the evening we can be of interest only as law-breakers. We don't risk this, and we celebrate for no reason, to do something.

Celebrating, we will converge on the same square to which they led us, on which they abandoned us. We will wander mindlessly around the place of our loss, searching. We will find acquaintances, a drinking companion, a fistfight. We'll find nothing, and go to bed.

We will also be reproached for having spilled a lot of vodka here. But not blood! Vodka is the plot's myrrh-bearer. And the deed is becoming not *what* but where and with whom . . . We'll sober up—and discover a corpse.

The crowd overflows the Square, having found nothing there, and distributes itself over lighted areas. The darkness of the embankment is gray moth-flight, the Square is a lantern. It has pleased us to light our scenery as in the theater . . . Once something comes into style in our country, it won't go out. We find it tasteful, and in our love of doing the same thing, we'll develop to the utmost within its limits. Illuminated are: the dome of St. Isaac's; the Bronze Horseman (lighted from below, with reverse shadows, towering horseshoes and nostrils—Benois's perspective); the Admiralty spire (that it may always be "bright"); the Admiralty's yellow wall, lighted in yellow from below (a soffit? footlights?); opposite, across the black gap of the Neva, we'll throw a soft light on the university (Department of Philology). A small ship, a warship, will provide its own lights: it will outline itself, childishly, with light bulbs. Proceeding from the bow cannon will be a racing dotted line, also of light bulbs—it will race along, go out, race along, go out, as though the little cannon were firing, spitting the light bulbs one by one into the black absence of the surrounding water . . . We have thus allowed for the elemental celebration this evening, after the march, and arranged a place for it to walk, something to see. The little cannon is firing, the stage is full of extras—who wouldn't feel like a soloist, who wouldn't go out to center stage and strike up a song!

(Here we've paid our tribute to the universally obligatory carnivali-zation of the narrative.)

Mitishatyev did have a little trouble with Lyova. The fresh air made Lyova thoroughly drunk, and the crowd made him rambunctious. His rambunctiousness was gay, good-natured, an invitation to be glad for him. Harmless enough, but who knows! Mitishatyev had to restrain him.

We're not excited by all this, but Lyova was having fun. He realized, accurately, that he was dreaming it all: the soap-scrap faces (the blurred background of extras in the dream); the cracks in the scenery (wind blowing in); the cardboard horse, deliberately made to rear (from close up, right on stage, how obvious that he's a drawing!); the little wrinkles, the billowing shadow on the Admiralty backdrop; the general negli-gence, the hack melodrama, of a dream. Who wouldn't take advantage of the safety of sleep! Lyova was overjoyed at this notion, that in a dream he could do anything with impunity. He twirled, leaped back-ward! backward! and did another pirouette, the better to look around. It pleased him to have guessed that this was a dream, and now he rejoiced in deceiving the extras, pretending he believed in their exis-tence. He apologized with exaggerated gallantry for brushing against them, he bowed and scraped. Mitishatyev kept straightening him up, supporting him—he was dreaming Mitishatyev. Lyova winked at him: I've guessed that you're in my dream. A steam band was playing "The Blue Danube," a good, childish, safe background, bland and distant memories in his dream. To the accompaniment of this music, he dreamed about the writer Chubukova. A little bit drunk, she was doing a circle dance to the accordion, jingling her war medals on her bosomy soldier's blouse—ah, the fiery tease!—with the eternal memory of her regimental maidenhood in her eyes, happily aware that she was with the people again. And when Lyova was accidentally showered with melodramatic intentional confetti . . . he accepted this masquerade and rejoiced again at his ability to guess all, even though asleep. Mitishatyev's shadow had horns—aha, we'll take that into account!

"You're my Virgil!" Lyova said, lest Mitishatyev guess that he *knew*.

Mitishatyev tossed up the white ball and caught it on the black. A cap went off. There was a smell of sulfur.

"Oh!" Lyova said joyfully. "Show me! I haven't seen those since the war! Remember, we had those after the war?" he whined, like a child. "Where did you get them?"

"I saved them." Mitishatyev grinned.

He let Lyova take one toss. Lyova caught the black on the white and laughed, happy. But Mitishatyev took them away: You'll drop them, they'll break.

So they pushed on.

"See that mask? Pretty," Lyova said, leaping around. "Madame!" He clicked his heels gallantly. "What a charming domino!"

"Dominoes . . ." Suddenly it struck Lyova funny—everything started gleaming in his tears, in long sharp feelers of light. "Dominoes! What a reversal! They wouldn't have understood then what the word means now, and now they'll never understand what it meant before! Imagine, she thought I was inviting her to play dominoes! Akhmatova playing dominoes . . ." Lyova doubled up with laughter.

So they pushed on through the crowd at a rapid pace, holding the hilts of their swords. An argument stopped them. Lyova became terribly excited.

"No, no! You're thinking of the wrong lion, I tell you!" They had stopped beside the Admiralty lions, the ones playing with balls. "This isn't the lion Yevgeny sat on, absolutely not! 'Astride the *marble* beast'! Pushkin was always precise about things like that . . . How can you say it's marble? When was this marble? It's a casting! Here, look, it's turned absolutely green . . . What do you mean, black marble!" Lyova was waving his arm and growing desperate. "Poetic license? How could it be! Impossible."

Suddenly, with unaccustomed agility, to prove his point, Lyova was sitting astride the lion and rapping on it.

"Hear that? Resonant! What do you mean, marble! *I'll* show you the ones, let's go right now. They're entirely different beasts! Here, look!" Lyova scraped the beast with a coin, to get down to the metal. "Don't yank my foot! Hey, let go, let go!" And he kicked.

"Ouch! What's going on!" Lyova said in surprise. Then he guessed, and laughed heartily. "Look! He's wearing a policeman costume! Ah-ha-ha-ha-ha! But where's his mask? Oh—if he's wearing his cap, he doesn't need the mask . . . Let *go*! I'm sitting on the *wrong* lion! . .

. . . .

. . . .

. . . .

.

THE DUEL

We fought a duel.

 .   .   .   .   .

This was at dawn. I stood at the appointed spot with my three seconds. With inexplicable impatience I awaited my opponent. The springtime sun had risen, and the heat was already setting in. I saw him from afar. He was coming on foot, wearing a full-dress uniform with saber, and accompanied by one second. We started toward him. He approached holding a service cap filled with cherries. The seconds measured off twelve paces for us.

 .   .   .   .   .

"Flip the coin," the captain said.

The doctor drew from his pocket a silver coin and held it up.

"Tails!" Grushnitsky cried hurriedly, like a man who has suddenly been waked by a friendly nudge.

"Heads!" I said.

The coin soared up and fell with a clink; everyone rushed over to it.

"You're in luck," I said to Grushnitsky. "You have the first shot! But remember that if you don't kill me, I will not miss—I give you my word of honor."

 .   .   .   .   .

"I will fight in earnest," Pavel Petrovich repeated, and he went off to his place. Bazarov, on his side, counted off ten paces from the barrier and stopped.

"Are you ready?" Pavel Petrovich asked.

"Completely."

"We can advance toward each other."

Bazarov moved slowly forward. Pavel Petrovich put his left hand in his pocket and started toward him, gradually raising the muzzle of his pistol. "He's aiming straight at my nose," Bazarov thought. "Squinting so carefully, the thug! This is not a nice sensation. I'm going to look at his watch chain—" Something shrilled sharply by Bazarov's very ear, and at that same instant a shot rang out.

 .   .   .   .   .

Kirillov immediately declared that if the opponents were not satisfied the duel would continue.

"I," Gaganov rasped (his throat had gone dry), "declare that this

man"—he pointed again at Stavrogin—"fired in the air on purpose. Deliberately. It's another insult! He wants to make the duel impossible!"

"I have the right to fire as I please, so long as it's by the rules," Stavrogin declared firmly.

"He does not! Explain it to him, explain it!" Gaganov shouted.

•   •   •   •   •

Of all those present, it turned out that not one had ever been to a duel in his life, and nobody knew exactly what the seconds were supposed to say or do.

"Gentlemen, who remembers how Lermontov describes it?" Von Koren asked, laughing. "And Turgenev had Bazarov fight a duel with somebody . . ."

•   •   •   •   •

"I'd like to spit on you," Peredonov said calmly.

"Oh, no, you don't!" Varvara screamed.

"Here I go," Peredonov said.

"Swine!" Varvara said, quite calmly, as if the spittle had refreshed her. "A real swine. Got me right in the puss."

"Don't yell," Peredonov said. "Company."

•   •   •   •   •

1828	1830	1839	1862
BARATYNSKY	PUSHKIN	LERMONTOV	TURGENEV

1871	1891	1902
DOSTOEVSKY	CHEKHOV	SOLOGUB

•

. . . AT THEIR LAST GASP, they burst into their institute. They ran in, flew in, tumbled in, fell in—and collapsed. Their bodies were sheer pulse. But fear was still gaining on them. Lyova suddenly felt the keys (they were in his pocket! he wasn't even capable of surprise). He crawled over to lock the door. Crawled—because his legs were two blimplike air columns and would not support his body, and also because he was afraid of being seen through the glass part of the door. In movements taught by the movie camera, he sneaked up to the door like a guerrilla mining a train, squatted on his haunches for fear of sticking up over the edge—over the boundary between wood and glass— and in this awkward position tried to sneak the key into the keyhole. Lyova locked the door like an inexperienced thief forcing it. He was afraid of rattling the key, and every tiny sound reverberated in the world with a celestial roar. First the key didn't fit, then it fell through, then it went in but he couldn't back it out: Lyova did not remember which key. It's a bore to describe him failing to cope with this lengthy task, despairing and dying. At last his persistence was rewarded and he crawled away, jubilantly and hastily.

Now that he was sheltered by the inner darkness of the building, behind the double doors, he took the risk of sticking his head up a little and looking through the glass.

Nobody there.

"Whew!" he said, and wiped his brow with the back of his hand, as in the movies. "I guess it's over."

"Over . . . ?" giggled an insolent voice, and only then did Lyova remember Mitishatyev.

Deep in shadow, a cigarette glowed and flared.

Mitishatyev was sitting on the doorkeeper's desk, smoking.

Now at last a strange calm took possession of Lyova. He was sitting on the floor, slumped against the doorjamb, his legs out full length and his mind far away. His safe body experienced the happiness of absence. The sweat was drying, his brow tightening, his cheeks sinking— a vascular triumph. After the incandescence of his mad run, his body was contracting and congealing. The cool of a breeze . . .

"What was I so afraid of!" Lyova marveled with sober simplicity. "Why did I run so? From a policeman? It's absurd to run from a policeman, isn't it? He's not going to do anything! He won't kill you. He has no right to kill you. It's a known fact, with him more than with anybody else, what he will or won't do. He won't kill you. Why be terrified?" He recalled the childish face, pink as strawberry soap under its rustic down; the navy-blue pink-cheeked stomp of the uniform—and he was terrified anyway. But not for that reason. What terrified him was the babyish, mama's-boy face, the physical awkwardness of the soldierly body, from boots to collar, the fact that to catch a fleeing man, as in some kind of blindman's buff, was not a subject for discussion. And to run like that, forgetting everything— isn't that in itself terrifying? To sink that low, in front of oneself, has to be very terrifying. Humiliating! How could there be dignity or individuality here . . . There had been nothing. Only the one thing— the running away. A cloud is like this, a cake of soap, round, like the fear. In it, inside, was Lyova, like a fly in amber. He hadn't been running of his own volition, hadn't been running out of fear—how could he have run out of his fear? He ran with it, in it, he raced along in it under sails of horror, a dark boat in the night, driven by the wind of power. Power? That pup? Ridiculous. It was a closed space of fear, with a pulsating boundary at his back—gaining on him, dropping behind—and up ahead, the open-armed, distant embrace of the hope of deliverance. A weird building. No sky overheard, no stars. "Absence of the fear of God—what a staccato horror it becomes!" Lyova cried, opening a chink for his spirit, escaping himself. "I was in a panic—I still am. The terrifying thing is that I was so terrified, and of what! To be afraid of a policeman—instead of God! They've swapped places . . ."

These thoughts astonished him with their well-worn obviousness.

"What am I afraid of? Everything!

"Now think for yourself." He was playing house with himself, with a childish quaver in his mental voice and with the equally childish sanctimoniousness of the senior role, which he rarely had a chance at. "What danger threatened you? Climb down peacefully, present your document. We were conducting a scientific experiment. Document-experiment-excrement. Other scientific words. He's easier to scare than I am! Then why did I get scared so easily, so unconditionally, so instantaneously—and not resist? Well, you started running by mistake. Stop. What will happen to you? You'll get a beating, maximum. Is that really so painful or distressing? Compared to fear? They'll take you to the station, notify your employer. It's hardly likely you'll even be fired. On the contrary, they'll understand. They'll bawl you out, get to like you, meet you halfway . . . But how can you not know, to this day, what you've known so long? They *would* fire you. And that's a blessing! Think for yourself. What you could lose is nothing compared to what's already lost. Any variant—the very worst—is a blessing compared to humiliation and fear. What was I running from? I was choosing between humiliations, I feared the greater humiliation. And chose the greatest. If I'd just been running because he chased me—someone's chasing you! run!—that would have been right, in accord with nature. But I ran from fear! Oh, what a mistake! What a mistake! Lord, how I hate all this!"

He stood up, creaking. Erect, resolute, with a gleam in his eyes.

He passed Mitishatyev without a glance. It was all too clear how the fellow squinted along his cigarette. He groped for the switch and flipped it fearlessly. But the weak everyday bulb did not permit the feeling of an all-permitting light. Nothing blazed forth as he had imagined. Then he caught sight of the wonderful blue box with the doors that don't meet, symbol of the workmen's cooperative. In it there would be either a fire hose or a knife switch. The box was freshly painted for the holiday—Lyova smeared his hand blue. There was a knife switch. Resolutely overcoming his shyness of electricity, Lyova threw the switch. A sputter of three blue sparks and the staircase blazed with gala light. Lyova threw his head back—and saw for the first time the chandelier that had always hung there. To the best of his recollection, the staircase has always lain in carved oaken twilight. That means they never switched it on, thought Lyova, triumphantly mounting the staircase, treading the steps like organ keys. The chandelier burst into song. Who'd have guessed! so many and high! thought Lyova. Music played, doors swung open, halls blazed up. He lurched in a dark little corridor, leaned his hand on a random wall—and hit the light switch. The unintentional, unexpected success gave inner corroboration of all this unexpected lightmusic. Without glancing over his shoulder or losing his focus, he walked straight through into the director's office, pressed all the buttons without looking, and flooded it with light. He thrust his hand into his briefcase, immediately felt out the necessary page, and immediately entered into the continuation as if into second wind. Rapidly he wrote note after note . . . He felt he had all the more right to continue at last what had been interrupted, since he himself had lived to have the experience prefigured in his article, he himself was "in the middle of the contrast." The personal motive that once had guided the hand of genius seemed sharp and clear to him—this motive coincided. Lyova became aware of the large and airy space of his body. It was now this whole *house*. Blazing with light, he now sailed in the night like a beautiful ship, slicing through the soundless universal gloom.

The fundamental driving force of his subject was fear. "A choice between humiliations, a fear of the greater humiliation . . . Fear in everything, fear *of* everything; of everything one's own, and now of a movement, a gesture, an intonation, a taste, the weather . . . Something is always reminding us of something . . . Someone's voice speaks another's words, at that moment you are lifting the cup to your mouth in the gesture of a brother who drowned in infancy . . . the weather, like the taste of a cigarette, reminds you of another time of life, another locale, another emotion . . . but you yourself discover you have already *had* this thought, some other time, about the cup and the cigarette. Horror!"

The sobered ending of the sentence offset both the fact that he was lifting no cup right now and that his brother had never drowned—and besides hadn't existed in infancy, because Lyova had no brother—and also the fact that Yevgeny's fear bore no relation whatsoever to his own line of fear, as he perceived it. But he had already raced past the shame and embarrassment of the accidental nature of his running start. He made the leap:

"Completing a series, picking berries—suddenly something falls to the bottom with a clatter: someone's chance face goes clanging down . . . It turns out you've already noted it several times, without remarking it—the series has accumulated. You have already thought this thought, without catching it. Now, suddenly, by chance, you have caught it, never again *not* to think it. The changing of the seasons—for the umpteenth time! Not again! You're sick of this grade-school primer.

"And, confronting the horror of deserved retribution," Lyova wrote finally, "the idiotic Russian idea that we have already *had* happiness, that precisely what we had was happiness. We didn't miss out, they say . . . The suppression of revolt . . ."

Had a darkness fallen, somehow? Lyova had lost the thread. Not exactly lost it, but the tension was growing still higher, still more unbearable, the icy wind was already tinkling the pendants of the chandelier out there on the staircase. And Lyova felt content with his phrase about retribution—the light was failing, his focus dimming. But in reality, too, the room was no longer lighted by anything but the desk lamp. Lyova was sitting in a shaggy ball of light—and all around was gloom. The childish fear of someone else's presence purged his soul completely. He started, his mouth thick with horror; warily, lest he be noticed by that dark someone in the corner, he turned to look. At his shoulder—craning his neck, peering, not breathing, not touching him, hands behind his back—stood Mitishatyev.

"You?" Lyova asked with horror. The voice was coming from him, but he did not recognize it as his own.

"What were you so scared of?" Mitishatyev said, embarrassed. "You turned on every light in the house."

Aha, so Lyova understood about the light: Mitishatyev had put it out. Lyova might have taken private note of Mitishatyev's rare embarrassment, but now he remembered how he had walked along triumphantly turning on the lights, and Mitishatyev, apparently, had sneaked along behind him putting them out. He had extinguished the portholes—the dark ship was going down.

"Were you scared of the policeman, or what? Ha-ha-ha. You thought Gottich had already informed. He's not a stoolie at all. I just said that, for you."

"You *are* a bastard, after all," Lyova said, with a slow, cool quaver in his returning voice.

Mitishatyev straightened up, escaped from his spying pose, and departed headfirst into darkness.

"Is that what you think?" came his voice, also calmly, this time without a trace of embarrassment.

"I used to think you were a decent person," Lyova repeated in a quavery childish voice, "but now I realize you aren't."

"You thought so? Why?" Mitishatyev said with vicious rhythm, spacing his words out, accenting each one and setting it off so that each single word hit Lyova's mistrustful soul, and Lyova gradually became more and more insulted. Especially insulting was the irony of "You—*thought*?" As though he hadn't just been writing words of such a nature! We seem to be least confident where our intellectual capacities are concerned: it's so easy to wound us.

"I did think!" Lyova blazed.

"Why did you ever think I was decent?" Mitishatyev said evenly, and this had a convincing logic to it.

Being a fair person by nature, Lyova could not, for reasons of his own advantage, disagree with something correct. Therefore he was taken aback, and he forgot his hurt feelings.

"How do you mean? What were you pretending to be?"

"Nothing. It was you who took me for something else. No, Lyova, you're a fool, after all. You always think that if a man's a turd he just seems to be one, on purpose, for psychological reasons that have a sociohistorical basis. But he *is* a turd. Want me to give you some advice, Lyova, from the bottom of my heart? Let me suggest a rule, so to speak. Mitishatyev's Right-Hand Rule: 'If a man seems to be a turd, he *is* a turd.' Do you want me—I can't torture a man forever, I admit!—want me to tell you what I really think? Now, isn't it true that you've wanted, all your life, to find out what others really thought— and you can't? And isn't it true that you feel the forces of evil have a special interest in you—isn't that true? I'll tell you: really, it's interesting. Now, how did I get involved with you? I looked, and you weren't a bastard. Damn it, I thought, why isn't he a bastard! He's like a bastard in every way, but not a bastard! Well, I began to test you. Testing, as everyone knows, is a job for *us*, the forces of evil. But you won't be tested. You wriggle out of everything. You find your own explanation for everything, and you feel reassured. But if you aren't reassured, you start to agonize and suffer, with such global reproach that I feel like killing you with my own hands, I hate you so much for making me guilty of your life. Life has no relationship to you! Why do you take it personally? It just is. It doesn't favor you.

You're still lucky, don't you doubt it—you're loved. But you know, there are other people who aren't even loved. Nobody loves them! Have you ever thought about that, about them? How they get along? You think people are unfaithful and betray you? But what can they betray except love! They can't betray unlove, they can only return it with unlove. You think you love? Sure! But you don't consider anyone a person. You don't want to recognize anything in others except fidelity to you. Then you're condescending. Infidelity makes you suffer so much you want to drink a person's blood, suck the traitor dry—therefore, you don't recognize his infidelity, you substitute suffering for recognition. And you smother any revolt! But you don't love the ones you've smothered, either—the minute someone turns blue, you stop loving him. And in fairness at that, for cause, with complete right. But, my God, a conscience is just what you don't have! Because everyone else is petty, base, selfish, calculating, and they know it! They have a conscience! You're above all this. Now, if it were because of your brains . . . I always wanted to figure out, was it your brains? I so wanted to respect you. I wanted to pour myself into that kind of selfless apprenticeship, into service and the altar. But no, you didn't earn your traits, your supremacy, you didn't win by brains—that's the disgraceful thing. You're like that by nature! It's not fair. Breeding? Blood? What does blood amount to! It's incredible. To be given so much for nothing . . . Even if all power over the people were to be concentrated in my hands, I wouldn't be given this superiority—I'll always know who they are, because I am from *them*. I have an abyss under my feet, I'm on the brink, try as I may to scramble out of it. I'm always the outsider, it always belongs to you. After all, why is it we dislike Jews? Because under all circumstances they are Jews. Someone doesn't seem to be Jewish at all anymore, you get friendly, and suddenly—he's still very much a Jew! What we dislike about them is their *belonging*, because we ourselves don't belong. By the way, have you wondered what the Jews like about you? Your belonging. My God, I see and know and understand ten times more about aristocracy than you do, but you don't even need to know! Why bother to pride yourself on it, since it's yours anyway? That's the sum of your famous good relationship with people—no relationship! You didn't even want to recognize my villainy, for example. So, whatever exists for you, that's the norm. Beyond the norm—an ocean of suffering. That's all. Not a chance of any life, other people. Hardly likely that anyone else loves, suffers, feels jealousy. I've said so many times—cautiously, and always watching how you'd answer—'Well, everyone's like that.' And you'd always say, 'Sure, everyone.' As if—this is almost despicable!—as if you even meant that in an extreme case you're like that too, I mean, I am too. I'd invite you to a party. You'd turn around and invite a companion, in order to have a listener. Listen, people, what's happening with a *person*! Find out all about it! How you protect your natural habitat! You think the instinct is strong in primitives—it's strongest in you! You people are the highest form, you're the best adapted! You'll always survive! Everything that's not your own, you'll reject; everything that's your own, you'll accept without gratitude, as your due! It's not that you're conscious of yourselves as higher; we're the ones who know the difference! There lies our strength. But we can't *achieve* anything. There lies our doom. The revolt will be suppressed. That's the meaning of it. And you will implement that meaning, without suspecting it. You're like the Jews, the only way you can be destroyed is physically! But today, at last, I have admired my work. I've had my fun . . ."

"Listen, listen!" Lyova said, deeply moved. "But that's the surprising thing! The surprising thing is that you're saying this to me! What a surprising person you are, Mitishatyev! And what's more, what's more, you remain a person. Where does it come from, this simultaneous frenzy and tenderness in you?" Someone had already said this to him. Lyova burrowed in a corner of his memory, tossing something aside, brushing away a cobweb . . . Grandfather! But Grandfather had said something quite different. About readiness to accept the world into one's scheme. About surpassing the illiteracy of life . . . Strange; the same, and exactly the contrary! What Mitishatyev blamed on aristocracy, Grandfather had blamed on the time. Just when it's absolutely the same, the difference is clear. No, it's not the same. Faina and Grandfather and Mitishatyev and the time, they all wound me at one and the same point—me! That means I am—an existing point of pain! I exist, at the point where they all hit me; it's not that I exist somewhere and happen to be hit by the blows, the unforeseen blows, of a random and alien world! This is the proof of my real existence—that *all* forces apply to me. But it's not a proof of the forces!

So Lyova joyfully explained himself . . .

"Now, you said Christ in the wilderness . . . And you accused me. Not so! All one can do about temptation is wriggle out of it; one can't overcome it. To overcome it is to suffer defeat, because that's admitting it. Not to admit a temptation—that's conquering it! It's true even in Scripture! I never understood," Lyova said, enchanted. "I liked it, but I didn't understand. We have begun to mistake our emotion, when it's aroused, for the content of what aroused the emotion—hence our incapacity to love another. And how differently we've begun to read the Gospel—for pleasure! Otherwise, we'd understand . . . 'To be tempted of the devil,' the Scripture says; not *by* the devil! And Jesus hungered, not from the length of the forty days, but from his final readiness to banish a topic that no longer interested him. He hadn't passed a single test, he didn't want to pass. He rejected them all: to change the stones and to leap on them and to own them. This disregard of temptation—his thrift with strengths that had a purpose, his unwillingness to demonstrate strength—was itself the maturity and strength that now enabled Christ to go to the people, wishing nothing for *himself*. There's no other way of overcoming temptation—the only way is *not* to see it! My Lord, how right you are, Mitishatyev, how right you are!"

"Write that down, write it down!" Mitishatyev said, distraught and angry. "That's a little more interesting than fear, isn't it? Why'd you write about fear if you're not afraid of anything? Does that mean you *do* see temptation, after all? As you yourself say, Christ *became* the Christ, but you've always *been* Lyova. You have possessed—but you will lose it. You're already losing it: you're expounding on fear. After all, I came to you, I followed you, and you yourself turned around, you've already taken a step toward me, on your own . . . Write that down about Christ—it's so fine, write it down—and it will be over, you'll have wriggled out of it again. One has to live and act according to the Word, you know, and something written is itself an act. Why aren't you writing? Do you feel awkward in front of me? Your inspiration will be wasted on me, won't it!"

"Aren't you ashamed, aren't you ashamed!" Lyova said, hurt. "You can't really think that I'm saving it up, that I need something in order to write! I don't write at all anymore, you know. Well—it's my life . . . you can't really reproach a man for living! Anyway, I live. I don't understand, but I live—this matters to me! What can I do, as the witness of my own experience? But still, I don't evade it—"

"But I see the pit! I'll always see the pit beneath me! And always recognize your precedence and hate you! But you'll always fail to notice that I exist! That's how it will be, always! You'll suffer and balk at reality, while I, the servant of your reality, enjoy petty triumphs over you and suffer my congenital defeat. I don't want to go on presenting instructive little scenes of your incorrigibility, your belonging! You'll never speak our language. To this day, you won't string two syllables together. All you do is smile your moronic flustered smile—'What makes you think you're so bad? Why, you're good!'—as if pitying us, as if suffering for us. We're not good! But there are more of us! When will you understand this, when will you digest it and become useful to us? After all, what do we want of you? That you should exist *for us*, since we have recognized you as being above us. But you confuse us, anger us, you try to love us for your own purposes. Don't love us—we'll love you. You'll never understand this, but we'll always understand you. And we'll keep on like this. You'll go to your grave, and what will we have lived for?"

"Mitishatyev, Mitishatyev . . . you're wrong. I never thought I was somehow better or higher than you, why do you . . . Believe me, I didn't know. How can you really call me an egoist. On the contrary, I've always admired you—you're stronger, more vital, more original. Your whole life. You've done everything yourself—achieved everything, thought of everything, all by yourself—after all, what could be more convincing, when a man does it himself!"

"Myself, shit! Self is nothing! The self-made man is shit! We are many, and we're all of us alone: although we know and understand perfectly the mechanisms of life and each other's baseness, we have no strength, and each of us is too few! You people are few, but you're one, and each of you is not one man alone but many: although you don't understand, you are strong! And what you'll never be forgiven is that you yielded to us, deprived us of the right to recognize you. How you betrayed yourselves! Correctly, you should have been killed, liquidated; you disappointed us, you treated us villainously! Stinking humanism . . . What did you want with humanism? Why did you slavishly begin to guess our ideas and pretend you were bringing them to us, why did you convince us that we were people, when it's practically impossible to be a person in your sense—*perpetuum mobile*—you never taught us the art and you've lost it yourselves. That's the true reason I hate you—for my own love, for your betrayal!"

"You're making fun of me," Lyova said, hurt. "Don't you suppose I understood? Oh, why don't you recognize my . . . Sure, there's a lot I don't understand—but not everything! You see, I've changed a lot recently. I've suddenly discovered the people around me. And the strange thing is, just at this moment you attack me. It's all so well timed, though: there's probably some justice in it. But there's no gap in time. Immediately. You've only just understood, and already you can't enjoy the fruits, can't relax and have your high. Retribution for the first moment of understanding, the moment lived in the inertia of the failure (after all, a long failure preceded it—you're in the habit!) to understand. So immediately, so cruelly, so justly, so hard to take, so necessary to live, so impossible to endure understanding! Sinful! That's what I am—sinful! Forgive me, Mitishatyev, forgive me . . ."

That was what they said, each making his own point. The more they revealed themselves and approached the truth—the greater the possibility of understanding what the other meant and what it was all about—the greater the possibility of understanding another person at last—then the less they understood. Drawing near each other, they raced apart. Lyova *remained* Lyova, Mitishatyev *was* Mitishatyev. This phrase should be repeated several times, the emphasis shifting from word to word. Then perhaps it can be understood . . . *Lyova remained an Odoevtsev, a Mitishatyev is a Mitishatyev.*

Was that what they said? Someday, just for fun, we'll write it all over again from the beginning. We'll pulverize the monologues into separate lines, so that one line seems more of an answer to the other— make it plainer, plainer!—delete a word—add a word—could Lyova have used the word "Scripture" instead of "Gospel"—agonize a minute—leave it at that. Agonize a minute longer—and leave the whole thing the way it was. How would something that has already happened get another chance to happen? We'll leave it at that. We'll utter an exclamation and we'll exclaim in a whisper: Not that, of course, that wasn't what they said, but it's what they meant!

"But I was having fun!" Mitishatyev said.

They were flailing their arms, two big shadows on the wall, for Mitishatyev had turned out the light. Soundlessness and bloodlessness. Shadow will persuade shadow: as they struggle, the shadows discover a commonality, so easily do they blend.

"How do you mean, having fun?" Lyova said, taken aback. He went cold. "Are you talking about Gottich again?"

"Have you already forgotten Blank?" Mitishatyev asked demoniacally.

Torment crossed Lyova's face. He distinctly remembered all—but in that case he could not go on living. Horror shackled him.

"What did you tell him!" Lyova cried, clutching him awkwardly by the shirtfront. Mitishatyev purposely did not resist; his clear, indifferent gaze was chilling.

"I didn't tell him anything. Why the panic?"

Lyova immediately felt reassured.

"Forgive me," he said, releasing him.

"Oh, go on." Mitishatyev smirked. He had a split of vodka in his hand.

"Where'd you get that?" Lyova said in astonishment.

"It hardly matters now," Mitishatyev said dryly.

And while they drank . . . while Lyova managed to swallow this bare nucleus of vodka, which leaped and bristled in him as if alive: while Lyova altered space, feeling childishly stupefied by the independence and self-sufficiency of the extraneous life he had taken into him, and while space—which had consisted of a turbid whirlpool of tightly spiraling nausea with mother-of-pearl tints around the edges, striving one minute to swallow him up, the next minute to cast him out centrifugally into the dark upper void—finally stopped and became glaringly bright and transparent, with an optical curvature around the edges, reminiscent of the bulging eye of a deep-water fish, and then became peculiarly, ringingly, tensely quiet, like the bottom of the sea, and then this optical effect dissolved and faded, yielding to a velvety, dusty softness, an absence of scale, where Lyova now cozily settled himself in the farthest distance of the new, outstretched vista, enjoying the immobility, chambered quality, and equilibrium of the small warmth within him—while he thus altered dimensions and abandoned space, that is, while he was dealing with the damned stuff's charming *effect*, which I have just now described a bit more lengthily than is usual, but then again too briefly in proportion to what this effect deserves, for apparently the fact that all mankind is so susceptible to it isn't all that obvious, without achieving the same "effect" by other means . . . While he got drunk and sober, sober and drunk, the far more primitive and severe nausea of his assessment of events kept shifting its angle of approach and raking him with fire from all sides. Because something had happened, something had happened . . . And if something had happened, then there was something that could not and must not exist, ever again, from this moment on. Only—what was it?

Now, all of the day's events still weren't what had finally happened. Even Blank, the inflamed focus of Lyova's treachery—an obvious event—still wasn't what had happened, nor, especially, were those girls, nor even the policeman and the chase . . . it was this conversation with Mitishatyev. But Lyova almost couldn't remember the conversation either, as if he had read someplace sometime something like it—and that was all. The meaning had suddenly evaporated . . . Resiliently and emphatically, the meaning resisted remembrance, and Lyova abandoned this nauseating effort. His memory, habitually and easily, constructed out of the remnants of words and facts a *relationship*, but relationships, as everyone knows, change the lost meaning entirely. And again—the same old Lyova!

Here he sits, with the vodka inside, and thinks about—what? He thinks how strange and impossible it is that Mitishatyev has revealed a "complex" (we do have to use this word, although it explains nothing, because Lyova is thinking with it); the "complex" has always been his monopoly, Lyova's, but things have turned out the other way around, and the "demon" Mitishatyev is full of complexes; nowadays a demon *is* a complex, that's the way times are.

On the other hand, Lyova promptly began to devalue his victorious position: Hadn't he exaggerated it? Maybe Mitishatyev had simply been making fun of him, of his gravity? At this point everything lightly flipped over in place—and now there was no question about it, Mitishatyev had been making fun of Lyova and playing a trick on him, he certainly hadn't exposed himself in his revelations. And what *did* happen between Mitishatyev and Faina? . . . This shadow, glimpsed but once, forever made nonsense of the very possibility of defeating Mitishatyev. All the obvious conclusions Lyova had drawn from Mitishatyev's confessions—his inferiority complex, the envy that was reducing his whole life to ashes, even the social nature of his demonic behavior—all these were dust, for Lyova was jealous of him. Even as he lost, Mitishatyev emerged the victor, because Lyova promptly erected his overthrown enemy above him. How did Lyova manage to do this every time, to be always left vanquished? His riddle, his nature. At this point we can draw but one indisputable conclusion, which Uncle Dickens, in his time, before Lyova was able to appreciate it properly, had formulated so definitively: "Shit is class-distinctive." This bespeaks his exquisite sensitivity to smells. Lyova sniffed, and dozed off . . .

Mitishatyev hovered thoughtfully. And dropped like a stone:

"Why are you so convinced that everything is as you think?"

Lyova opened as easily as a matchbox.

"Oh, I doubt all the time—" he began, immediately trying to justify himself.

"Why are you so convinced that everything is as you doubt?"

Again things flipped over, and it seemed to Lyova that Mitishatyev was making fun of him.

"What do I doubt?" he said, on his guard and rattled.

"Everything: me, yourself, Blank! You've even had time to get comfortable with it. Already you're almost thinking, 'But was Blank here?' He was! Blank was here! And you drove him out!"

"Me!"

"You. Who else? He wouldn't have come to see me, and he wouldn't have left because of me. But he did leave, because of you. You took my side—and he left."

"Wait, wait!" A chill ran down Lyova's spine, and the optics of alcoholic space performed an old childhood trick, the reversed tube: somewhere in the very narrow distance, smirking distinctly, was Mitishatyev's tiny face, his literally tiny face, the size of a child's tiny unwashed fist. "Wait! You can tell me anything you like, my behavior may have been as imprecise, vague, or even cowardly as you like . . . but I could never, never have said to him something that I'm simply incapable of saying! I'm incapable of insulting Blank—he might have construed my behavior, but that's all—"

"But why incapable! You're capable of saying things to me, but not to him. If you were incapable, you wouldn't say them to anyone, you wouldn't have the words, you couldn't listen to my point and support it. Why incapable? You *are* capable! You've said things to me!"

"What have I said to you? What things could I have said to you? And besides, there's a difference: maybe I could say something to you, but that doesn't mean I'd say it to him—"

"Aha! Got you. What is 'it'? And what am I telling you? Why do you say it to me, but not to him? Why should the old man have any illusions about you? You're deceiving him—and that's what I told him."

"Wha-at? What did you tell him!" Lyova was now so terrified that he was unable, and didn't want, to move into a knowledge of what had happened.

"What, what!" Mitishatyev mimicked. "Why, I told him the things we'd been talking about. And you were silent. At first you were still twitching, but then you gave up and smiled, you had a smile like . . . like porridge. You smiled and nodded."

"Nodded?"

"Why do you ask everything twice!" Mitishatyev said, suddenly enraged. "No, you're incorrigible! I demonstrate your villainy to you, and you don't see it. You're no better than I am, not anymore, you're even worse, because this is what I am, but you've betrayed what you were born to be. And you're trying to get out of it again! You're pretending again. Again you've become my equal, but again you don't want to treat me as an equal, again you don't count me as a person, you don't even want to recognize my villainy. Only this time it's not villainy, I've waited for years—now it's justice. What I said to Blank in your name is justice. For once, things have to come to a point! You're a master at hanging on to all the strings, of course . . . but just now you've let go of one. You will never, do you hear, never in your life, succeed in convincing Blank that what happened today was a mistake. At last there's nothing you can correct, iron out, slick down! So answer for it, pay with your soul, like us! We've already paid out ours—we didn't have much in the first place. You wouldn't want to allow yourself everything, and not pay with your soul, would you? In at least one point—a trifle, it won't ruin your life or your general appearance—in at least one point, you're definitive. Blank is a nobody, but he knows you now. He *saw* you! He saw you as I see you!"

"Dear God!" Lyova implored. "This hatred—it's impossible to face! Oh, what have I done to you? I want to understand, please explain—"

"*Not a thing.* You haven't done a thing to me. That's why! Only I don't hate you. There's another word for it. I'd say that I loved you, but it's banal—literature has already destroyed that turn of the plot. We can't live on the same landing—that's what! Maybe this is class instinct?" Mitishatyev guffawed. "Or no, it's probably biology. You think *I* won't give *you* any peace? No, no! You! I can't exist while you do. And you keep on existing, on and on! You're ineradicable. See, I've grown old. Bald. Flabby." Mitishatyev flung himself into the role and hammed it up outrageously on this amateur stage, demonstrating the academic school: pulled up the straggly hair on his head, pulled down the skin under one eye, and stuck out his tongue. "Scared?" He laughed loudly, like Neschastlivtsev. "Sorry, I'm always joking . . . I'm drunk. Drunk, understand? Don't attach any . . . I love you . . . You're all I have. What am I without you? A phan-tom! Atom plus fountain . . . a fan-tasy!"

"I'm going to hit you now," Lyova said at last.

"What for?" Mitishatyev said, with sincere surprise. "But I only wanted . . . What I told you just now is the simple truth, no more. I wanted you not to tangle with them anymore. We need you! You're a prince! You're a Russian man! But you're entangled by them, from head to foot! Notice, you become a very insincere, very deceitful person when you have to show yourself to them. And as what do you show yourself? As what they want from you! They've got you hooked. They see your insincerity—and it's what they need! Then someday when you've swallowed the hook deeper, they'll explain to you. And you'll be theirs!"

"You're crazy!" Lyova said. "I've finally realized. You're crazy. You're a maniac. I won't beat you up. Go along now, go." And he leaned back, eyes shut. The sea of purple nausea licked him up with its very first breaker and began dragging, dragging him in, into darkness.

"Ah, Prince! Despite all, you're a prince! I feel it, in a way that you can't even imagine! No difference—but you're a prince . . . I probably am a maniac; most likely. An aristocratomaniac, is that what it's called? I *love* you! Oh . . ."

With a desperate effort Lyova twisted his head, unlocked his eyes, halted the furious gyroscope that was howling like a child's top—and surfaced, in time to see Mitishatyev, with the little word "Oh," wipe his sleeve across his eye.

"Stop." He felt loathing and a lack of will, flattery's hypnotic spell, which goes beyond the obviousness of fable and proceeds like a nightmare of consciousness, like a disease . . . However, when your boot's been licked, you don't kick.

"Stop . . . well, I got excited, you're drunk, I'm not entangled by anyone, what are you saying, really?"

"Entangled, entangled," Mitishatyev said in an unexpectedly sober new voice. "Even your women are all theirs."

Lyova groaned. Mitishatyev is right, a thousand times right! he exclaimed in despair—but silently. Throw him out! Throw him out on his ear—that's what I've forgotten how to do . . .

"What women?" he groaned weakly.

"Even your wife's a Jew!" Mitishatyev said caressingly, coaxingly.

"What wife, I don't have a wife!" Lyova implored.

"Aha, you see!" Mitishatyev said triumphantly. "You didn't say 'What's the difference!' You do feel the difference, then? But you say you don't have a wife . . . Tsk, tsk . . . What about Faina?" Mitishatyev peeked slyly out of himself.

Lyova had the sensation of a long, wide force. It embraced and lifted him up—into the air for a while, it even seemed—and from there, from above, he looked down at Mitishatyev. Everything was illuminated by such an even, strong, flat, surgical light—Lyova had never come up against this before in his life—such passion, such fury, such anger—blinding!—that it could no longer even be called a sensation, it was an unknown state, which seemed to him a kind of calm.

They fought long, they fought thoroughly and diligently—dirtily and clumsily from an outside viewpoint. It was conscientious work, somewhat boring, unaccustomed and repetitious—so it seemed to Lyova—he felt nothing, only a light lump inside, the lump of a child's peace after sobs—this weightless ball rolled around inside his insensible shell, which consisted of body and suit, and into the same kind of insensibility Lyova sank his empty fists, into wadding and rags, while Mitishatyev tugged and whipped at the rag of Lyova's face . . . Lyova had not a care in the world now—this was almost liberation, almost happiness. In any case, it must not stop, he would have liked to live just this way to the end of his days, live in this, the suddenly emergent—who cared how it looked!—uninterruptedness of his existence. To roll around and hit and maul, feeling nothing but absence, in such a way that the forces, which were already gone, would end utterly, along with him. But . . .

Mitishatyev rolled away into the corner, sobbing like an accordion. Lyova found himself with emptiness and bewilderment in his hands. He got up and dusted himself off, feeling nothing but vexation: Mitishatyev had tricked him just now with his submissiveness, had robbed him and left. Time, just when it was on the point of disappearing, had betrayed him once more. It continued. Lyova looked around.

They had done some damage. An overturned glass display table was lying wrong side up. Lyova lifted it by one edge, saw a book that had fallen face down, and lowered the table again. Nothing perturbed him. He was completely indifferent. But when had they come downstairs to the museum? He couldn't quite remember. They had begun the split of vodka in the director's office—that was right. Lyova took another tour inside himself, like a man in a case, like a mannequin, and felt nothing. He shrugged his shoulders.

"Well, how are you?" he asked Mitishatyev.

"Do you even know what you beat me for?" Mitishatyev asked.

"I know," Lyova said. And, indeed, he did know.

"What for?"

"I won't say"—and now Lyova was rather pleased with himself; now he remembered one more, additional thing that had been in him as he rolled on the floor—and which he had never shouted out. What for. That he remembered: he had been very careful, when he was fighting, not to say. Oh, he hated to admit it, but it was simple as could be—this was no struggle of world views. No. That was something Lyova would never have allowed himself—allowed is the wrong word, he wouldn't have needed to allow himself—could not have done: take advantage of an excuse for active nobility. That was what he had suffered from with Mitishatyev, he could never take advantage of the constant fresh excuses, since he hadn't taken advantage of the very first—but when had that been, the first one? So long ago . . . But at last he had pulled it off, settled it, succeeded—with a totally different excuse. And he had held his tongue. Faina! How simple. The thought was so unbearable: If what *may* have happened back then *did* happen, how does that bastard Mitishatyev dare now . . . That's it. Well done, Lyova thought silently now, pleased with himself.

"You won't say?" came Mitishatyev's voice. He had recovered his breath. "Then I'll tell you what you jumped me for—"

Lyova's eyes went dark, totally dark. He was pinned to the ground by a mucky, turbid force—oh, the exact opposite of being lifted up, before the fight, by the white light of anger.

"I'll kill you," he said hollowly from his new dungeon. "You say it and I'll kill you."

Lyova, what was he rescuing? What was he rescuing now, so confidently, stoutly, and steadfastly? He knew.

"Okay," Mitishatyev said, believing him. "I won't say it."

Lyova was content with this. Now that's what I call an agreement, that's more like it, he thought, unsurprised by life. It's enough for me if he doesn't speak it aloud. We know what: Both of us. I wouldn't have thought it possible . . .

But it was possible.

Mitishatyev rolled a split of vodka out from under a cupboard. Still on all fours, he started rolling the bottle with his nose. Lyova watched him calmly. Even this little bit was enough—winning a fight.

Mitishatyev rolled the bottle onto a rug and sat down beside it, panting. He looked up at Lyova and gave him a ready, open smile. It hurt. He frowned, and licked his split lip; then pulled at it, looked around comically, and smiled again.

"Sit down, my friend!" he said generously, indicating a spot beside him, or rather, beside the bottle.

Charm? Something new.

"You're my nightmare," Lyova said, laughing. "You don't exist."

He sat down on the rug.

"I understand you," Mitishatyev said, when they had taken a brotherly sip, by turns. "I understand you . . ." They sat on the silly little rug as if on a raft, and sailed in the narrow festive night—for no good reason, just because they were on the raft—past now cold relics of the Russian language. They caught a glimpse of Tolstoy's beard in its special little case, heard the clank of the garden shears with which Chekhov trimmed Ionych's gooseberry bushes. A glassed-in, rehabilitated Bunin, without belongings, was smeared flat on the wall.

"You dislike me? I understand you," Mitishatyev said. "I understand very well why you jumped me." Lyova twitched. "Oh, no no, I won't, I won't say it . . . But you jumped me for nothing!"

Lyova's whole being rose to meet happiness. Were Mitishatyev to say that Lyova had been foolishly, unfairly, needlessly jealous, he would fall upon him, smother him with kisses, burst into tears, and—whatever the truth!—he would believe! But Lyova was not allowed to experience that happiness. Mitishatyev disabused him of a different notion:

"What am I, after all? I'm not the cause, you know; I just happened to be at hand. Why choose such an easy target? This is what you hate, not me." Mitishatyev made a sweeping gesture, inviting these walls and these exhibits and this night and this city into the camp of Lyova's enemies. "Why do you punish me unfairly? Are you afraid of them—but not me?"

Lyova frowned. "I'm no upstart intellectual, this logic is opaque to me."

"Well said!" Mitishatyev cried jubilantly. "Listen! Picture this: here we are, sailing along . . ." Lyova even smiled in his pleasure: this Mitishatyev had something, after all! "We're sailing on a ship," Mitishatyev went on. "Well, so next . . . We smash into an iceberg. See, again! It's *them* again!" Mitishatyev chuckled, inviting Lyova to laugh at him. Lyova smiled in spite of himself. "Well, so here's the iceberg—we're drowning. But you've caught a log and I've caught a log, see? You go under, I come up. I drown, you breathe. By turns. We can't see each other. Consequently we don't know, for the time being, that we've got the same log. Oh, and let's say it's night, it's dark, like now. Here"—he offered the bottle to Lyova—"your turn . . . So that's how our voyage goes. The ship may have been large, a superliner; maybe we hadn't even noticed each other yet, we hadn't had time, and we can't see each other here on the log either. We'd get tired on our seesaw and go down—but we're cast up on an island. Uninhabited, of course. Well, we're lying there, lifeless, and the sun comes up. Daylight. Hey, we went to the same school! Like that, see. We're the only two survivors. So we live. Coconuts, fresh water, we've got everything."

"But how could there be icebergs?" Lyova was listening with pleasure. "If there are coconuts?"

"Imagine that, no icebergs on the island either. Just us two. A pure, absolute ethnic majority. You and me."

"Oh, you'd start the same old thing, you'd go and prove I'm really a Jew. You couldn't dispense with that. The two of us would have a Suez incident, Mitishatyev."

"Oh, stop it," Mitishatyev said, brushing him aside. "That's not what I mean. I'm serious about this fairy tale. We're on the island, you understand, the two of us. A day, another day. A week, a month, a year. No ships on the horizon. Gradually we understand that we're here forever. Oh, no perversions, of course. Ethnic hostility is also irrelevant. Will there be conflict? There will. Will you come to hate me? You will. What for? That's what I'm getting at! Now what will you hate first of all: the ship? the iceberg? the ocean? the island? yourself? the reason for the journey? life itself? fate? providence? No! You'll hate me! Do you see why? Because I'm there!"

"Very convincing," Lyova agreed. "But everything's convincing when someone's trying to prove it. Conviction is a matter of time. The only thing is, if I do come to hate you, it won't be because you're there. It'll be because you betray me."

"But to whom—think for yourself—to whom would I betray you, on an uninhabited island?"

"I'm not sure that our island is uninhabited," Lyova said darkly. "There's somebody walking around. I dreamed it. I remembered, I guessed—and there are lots of us. In the final analysis I'm just as unsure that the island is inhabited as I am that we're alone together. But either way, you'll wriggle out of it and betray me."

"Aren't you a . . . a shifty prince. But what am I getting at? Why don't you hate the fact that we were forced to grab hold of the same log, the fact that we were cast up on the same island, berthed on the same ship! Why hate *me* in place of everyone? Here, here!" Mitishatyev jumped up. "These walls here, this banality, these dead men! Whom we, the living, exploit! This age, which forces us to know everything about each other! Because we do know everything! We know so terribly much about each other that—never mind hatred, I can't see why we didn't kill each other, ten, fifteen, twenty years ago! We live on each other, we go to the same latrine, gobble the same corpse of Russian literature and take away the taste of it with the same fixed dinner menu, we use the same monthly ticket to ride the same bus to the same apartment and watch the same TV, drink the same vodka, and use the same newspaper to wrap our solitary herring! Why do you put up with all this, and not with poor little me?"

"I don't notice these things—I had no idea you were so concerned about them. Perhaps you don't have a life of your own, to be looking around you like this! My own life is more than I can handle, I don't notice all these things that you've poured your strength into—"

"No-o! I do *not* have my own life!" Mitishatyev howled, and he kicked the cupboard. The door panel cracked and caved in. He swung

306

his foot again and fanned, kicking air. "And it's a lie that you have one! You don't either! If you did, you wouldn't hate me so—"

"What makes you think I hate you?"

"You're a coward! That's the whole thing! You don't have the guts to agree that you've never done anything real in your whole life, that you're ensconced in your father's footsteps, that the two of you are eating away at your grandpa, that—yes, you do have talent!—you haven't written anything of your own for a long time. I've been waiting, and you don't write! I know! You can't rebel, you've become just as much of a slave as I am. But an exemplary, positivist slave. You don't work for the master out of fear, but in place of conscience! I've always been a slave, I was born a slave, and I see it. But you're still getting used to it, it's something new, you're glad of it: it's working out for you . . . I hate this lawful cowardice! I'm a coward myself, I know. It's better to go to jail than do what we do! Isn't it! Well, come on, I dare you! Am I right, am I? Ah-h-h . . ."

How did this happen? There's been an imperceptible transition here. Ah, yes; when someone tells us to our face what we know perfectly well ourselves, it wakens very strong feelings in us. Besides, it wouldn't take much to provoke Lyova. But still, how did this develop? I didn't notice, I didn't keep track. Forgive me. I was bored. I turned away to the window; the weather outside was pumping up, swelling. Benois had left a scrap of ribbon at sunset: beautiful city! An uneasy sigh . . .

And now what! Lyova had jerked open the cupboard doors and was hurling down fat, dusty folders. Mitishatyev was gleefully catching them and flinging them in the air. Stale dissertations flew around the hall, page after page, free as birds. Glass was crunching underfoot.

"No guts, you say? I'll bet you!" Lyova exclaimed. He pulled over a stepladder to reach the middle shelves. "Here! I do have the guts! Here's your 'Certain Questions,' and here's your 'On the Question,' and here's your 'Basic Underlying Tendencies,' and here's your 'Link between the Bashkir and the Albanian Literatures'! Here, here . . . !"

Fortunately, the stepladder started to wobble. Lyova stood there on one foot, in weightlessness, rotating his arms. Mitishatyev hopped around on the dissertation pages. He was tired of flinging them in the air. The dust! He sneezed, and discovered a new toy. Now Mitishatyev was hopping around with Pushkin's death mask in his hand.

It was too small.

"It won't go on," Mitishatyev said in surprise. "Look—it won't go on! Accelerated growth!" he shouted. "Accelerated growth!"

Lyova leaped down on him, like a hawk.

"Hand it over, you bastard!" he shouted. "Boor! Dumb ox! Put it *down*, you son-of-a-bitch!"

"What's with you?" Mitishatyev hopped away backward. "What's with you?"

Like a bunny. With Pushkin's death mask in his hand.

Again a small skirmish. Lyova tried to take the mask away, Mitishatyev wouldn't hand it over. Not because he didn't want to hand it over, or didn't want to yield to pressure; he just wouldn't, he didn't understand, he was taken aback—and wouldn't hand it over. They wrestled briefly, Mitishatyev stumbled, Lyova gave him a slight push, Mitishatyev swung his arm . . .

Now they stood wordlessly over the broken white shards.

Even Mitishatyev seemed to understand something.

Lyova's long face burned pale and insane.

"Well, that's all."

He did not see Mitishatyev. What stood before him was evil, a geometrical volume of evil.

Mitishatyev might well take fright. He did.

Inconspicuously, he dropped Grigorovich's inkwell into his pocket and held it there at the ready. Lyova did not notice this trick at all. He was insane—that's the right word. His eyes had moved wide apart, they swam on the sides of his face like two cold fish. Stubble had sprouted on his death mask. He suddenly had a lot of hair—tangled curls. His neck had grown thin, and it stuck up loosely from his collar. He was perfectly calm. His hands just dangled, unnecessary.

"I will not forgive you *him*," Lyova said evenly.

"A duel?" Mitishatyev giggled dangerously. He was afraid of Lyova.

"A duel," Lyova agreed.

"With Pushkin's pistols?"

"Any pistols." Lyova was paler and paler.

"It flatters me to duel with you." Mitishatyev grinned. "You're elevating me to your own class."

"We're from the same class," Lyova said expressionlessly. "Five-A, Seven-B, I don't remember exactly."

"Ha-ha," Mitishatyev said. "Bravo! What a sense of humor, on the eve of a duel! Marvelous self-possession."

Lyova frowned in distaste. "Hurry up, let's be done with it."

Mitishatyev glanced at him in surprise.

"Impossible," he said, shocked. "Are you serious?"

"Quite." Lyova was still standing in the same spot; his lips had trouble shaping the Q, and he staggered slightly.

Mitishatyev grinned and dropped his eyes.

"Very well, Prince. But you must remember that a duel implies an equal rival. A duel with me will dishonor you."

"A duel implies just one thing," Lyova muttered evenly, those wide fish of his still seeing nothing before him. "It implies the total impossibility of two particular people being on the same earth."

"Thank God! We've lived to see the day," Mitishatyev said gleefully. "But that, Prince, is not a duel. That is the very fact of which I lately desired to inform you: we live on each other. We cannot have a duel. We can only murder each other."

"Classification is immaterial to me," Lyova said firmly. "The point is that one of us will cease to be."

"Anyway, you haven't lost your sense of logic. I'd even say you've acquired one . . . Very well. Agreed." Mitishatyev went over to the exhibit on Pushkin's death and returned with the pistols. "Here's what I've noticed, it's a curious thing: when you get off in your own world, one way or another—when you used to write, or like today, just off in your own world—which is nowhere to be found but in you, by the way—then you become exactly right, exactly you . . . All day today I've been studying you. Fool or no fool, I thought, you're still a fool! Why on earth does your Faina love you so! I just couldn't understand."

At the word "Faina," Lyova staggered.

"Listen, you look like your own ghost!" Mitishatyev exclaimed.

Lyova ran his hand over his face to check. "I'm here. Give me a pistol."

Mitishatyev looked at Lyova with growing surprise, and his face became strangely bright. "One meaning!" he mumbled obscurely in reply. "One meaning!"

"Listen, Lyova, forgive me!" he said sincerely.

"Give me a pistol."

"To hell with you!" Mitishatyev shuddered. "Here," he said caustically, "take your rod."

He managed to choose the slightly newer pistol for himself, however, and with a smirk he handed Lyova the rusty double-barreled one.

"How do we duel? A barrier? Do we advance toward each other? Do you know how it's done?"

"A coin toss," Lyova said. "By the way, I must explain to you about class, I have realized." He was speaking with slow, transparent effort.

"Different classes—that means an absence of relationships among them. In the sense in which we all have relationships now. Everything's relationships now. To permit relationships with another class is impermissible. If they're permitted, then we're already equal, we are of the same class. A duel is the refusal of a relationship, the cessation of its very possibility. Therefore we are equal, and our duel may take place in keeping with all the rules. This is fair, and fairness has been achieved. That's all."

"You're wonderful," Mitishatyev said. "I surrender."

"No." Lyova was firm.

"I was certain you would not accept my apologies, Prince. I think, sir, you might go over and lean against that cupboard, lest you fall in the event of a slight wound. I'll go over to that one."

Lyova dragged his dignity to the cupboard with the effort of the Commendatore.

"Well, sir, heads or tails?"

"Heads," Lyova said.

"A ruble, the commemorative!" Mitishatyev grinned. "So, the toss!" The ruble clinked dully but sparkled in keeping with all the rules, and was neatly caught by Mitishatyev. He unclenched his fist with the meaningful deliberation of a gambler uncovering the card he has bought in a game of blackjack. The same small-town grimaces. "However, it's tails! Believe me?"

"I believe you," Lyova replied hollowly.

"So, Prince, how will our class contradictions be resolved? What if I should kill you?"

"That is immaterial," Lyova said coldly. "They will be resolved."

"Those are your dying words, Prince!" Mitishatyev made a wry face, slowly lowering his pistol and taking careful aim. "One, two . . ."

Lyova stood there dead, his eyes shut. The double-barreled monstrosity dangled in his hand. His knuckles had gone stiff and white with cramp.

". . . three!" Lyova started . . . For a third time, the author could not bear the shoddy melodrama of life and turned away to the window. A party-cracker shot rang out. There was a slight smell of sulfur. Had Mitishatyev tossed and caught his little ball, perhaps?

A groan, a crunch, an authorial gnashing of teeth. Space went askew behind the author's back. Lost its balance, lurched. The author rushed to catch it—too late—a tinkle of glass rained down. The cupboard gave one more plywood bounce, cracked, and creaked for finality. But Lyova lay motionless, face down, as he had fallen.

Mitishatyev was somewhat puzzled by the effect he had produced. Bewildered, he walked over and examined the cupboard. It was missing a leg. That was the trouble! It had slipped off the brick . . .

"Lyova! Lyova!"

Mitishatyev swallowed convulsively and tried to pull Lyova's crumpled left arm out from under him—and gave up. He tried to extract the pistol from his right hand—it was gripped as in a vise. Frantically, Mitishatyev looked for a pulse—this was a rather strange spectacle, him looking for a pulse in the hand that held the pistol . . . He looked for Lyova's pulse with growing fright, not quite sure that he was doing it properly. His face reflected first despair, then hope, then terror.

"Ah!" he said maliciously, and got to his feet. He lighted a Northland.

After taking several frantic puffs, he had an idea at the window.

Distractedly, he took a thick folder from the table and put it under Lyova's head. He waved a hand. After one more deep and greedy puff, he bent down and stuck his cigarette butt into the barrel of Lyova's pistol.

"Fool!" he said confidently, but with no particular emotion—as a fact.

Smoke drifted from the barrel of the pistol, and Mitishatyev grinned.

His further actions were rapid and final: he put out the light, discovered the inkwell in his pocket, glanced at it with disgust, and hurled it through the window. The glass rained down. After clapping his pockets one last time, Mitishatyev stole out of the hall. The cigarette butt still smoldered red in the darkness.

Now wearing his overcoat, Mitishatyev ran down to the basement. There he found a suitable window and slipped out onto the small lawn in front of the institute. He shut the window carefully behind him, jamming his finger as he did so and cursing foully. He went to the railing and glanced around—there was nobody in this black, vein-swollen Neva night. He vaulted the railing and set off without looking back, rapidly and fugitively, his hands in his pockets. His overcoat was flying open.

"Oh, hell!" He paused suddenly. "Oh, hell!" He clapped himself on the forehead for convincing effect. "I forgot!"

For a moment he thought it was a piece of evidence. His face expressed a habit of suffering, and at that moment it was almost noble.

That was the surprising thing.

THE SHOT

(Epilogue)

Thus I learned the end of the tale whose beginning had once so impressed me.

PUSHKIN, 1830

WE HAVE ALREADY attempted to describe the clean window, the icy sky gaze, that stared straight and unblinking as the crowds came out onto the streets on November 7. Even then, it seemed that this clear sky was no gift, that it must have been extorted by special airplanes. And no gift in the further sense that it would soon have to be paid for.

Indeed, the morning of November 8, 196–, more than confirmed those premonitions. It was awash above the desolated city, amorphously dripping heavy streaks of old Petersburg houses, as if the houses had been penned in dilute inks that were paling with the light of dawn. And while the morning finished penning this letter, which had once been addressed by Peter "to spite his haughty neighbor" but now was addressed to no one and reproached no one, asked nothing—a wind fell upon the city. It fell as flatly and from above as if it had rolled down a smooth curve of sky, gathered speed with uncommon ease, and landed tangent to the earth. It fell, like a certain airplane, when it had had enough of flying. As if that airplane yesterday had expanded and swelled in flight, gobbled all the birds, sucked up the other squadrons, and when bloated on metal and sky-color had plummeted into tangency. A flat wind the color of an airplane glided down on the city. The name of the wind was the childhood word "Gastello."

It touched down on the city streets as on a landing strip, bounced when it hit the ground somewhere on the Spit of Vasily Island, and then raced off, powerfully and noiselessly, between rows of now damp

312

houses, along the exact route of yesterday's march. Having thus verified the city's emptiness and lack of human life, it rolled onto the parade square, swooped up a broad and shallow puddle to smack it against the toy wall of yesterday's grandstands, and then, tickled with the resulting sound, flew through the Revolutionary wicket and took off again, soaring steeply, sweepingly, up and away . . . And if this were a movie, then across the empty square, one of the largest in Europe, the "toss-me, catch-me" that a child had lost yesterday would still be chasing after the wind. Now utterly drenched, it would fall apart, burst open, as if to reveal the wrong side of life: the sad and secret fact that it was made of sawdust . . . But the wind straightened out, soaring and exulting, and high over the city it turned back and streaked away on the loose, once more to glide down on the city somewhere on the Spit, having thus described an inside climbing loop.

It ironed the city flat, and right behind it, over the puddles, dashed a heavy express rain—over the avenues and embankments so well known, over the swollen gelatinous Neva, with its countering, rippling patches of crosscurrent and its mismatched bridges; later we are mindful how it rocked the lifeless barges near the bank, and a certain float with a pile driver . . . The float chafed against the partially driven piles, frazzling the wet wood; across from it stood a house of interest to us, a small palace, now a scientific institute; in that house, on the third floor, a broken window was flapping wide open, and both wind and rain easily flew inside.

The wind flew into a large hall and chased around the floor the handwritten and typewritten pages that were scattered everywhere. Several pages stuck to the puddle under the window. And indeed this whole room (a museum exhibition hall, to judge by the glass-covered texts and photographs hung on the walls, the glass-topped tables with open books in them) was a scene of inexplicable devastation. The tables had been moved from their geometrically suggested correct places to stand here and there, every which way. One had even been tipped wrong side up, in a sprawl of broken glass. A cupboard lay face down with its doors flung open, and beside it, on the scattered pages, his left arm crumpled inertly beneath him, lay a man. A body.

He appeared to be about thirty, if one can even speak of appearances, because his appearance was horrible. Pale as a creature from under a rock—white grass. The blood had clotted in his tangled gray hair and on his temple; mold was growing in the corner of his mouth. Gripped in his right hand was an ancient pistol, the kind seen nowadays only in a museum. A second pistol, double-barreled, with one trigger released and the other cocked, lay at a distance, about two meters away. Inserted in the barrel that had been fired was the butt of a Northland cigarette.

I can't say why, but this death makes me want to laugh. What is to be done? Who should be informed?

A fresh gust of wind slammed the window violently, tearing off a sharp splinter of glass and stabbing it into the windowsill, then crumbling it like a shower of coins into the puddle below. Having done this, the wind dashed away along the embankment. From its own viewpoint, this was not a grave or even a noticeable deed. It dashed onward to whip banners and buntings, to rock river-bus landings, barges, floating restaurants, and the busy little tugboats that were quite alone, this frazzled, lifeless morning, in their flurry of activity around the legendary cruiser sighing quietly at anchor.

The wind dashed on like a thief, its cloak streaming.

The wind dashed away, but we shall return to our hall . . .

At the tinkle of broken glass, a convulsion and a quiver ran over the inert body; there came a sound reminiscent of a moo. The body released the pistol from its hand, with difficulty freed the other hand from under itself, planted both hands on the floor, and tried to raise itself up. But collapsed, with a groan.

After lying helpless a while longer, it finally became aware of its cold and discomfort and raised itself up on its hands more decisively. It twisted its head, mooed, and fixed its still unconscious gaze on the floor in front of it. Before its eyes was a thick folder, which had served as a pillow that night. The man (let us now give our "body" that name) stared long and dully at the folder. On it was pasted a little white square with a precise inscription: *M. M. Mitishatyev*. THE DETECTIVE ELEMENT IN THE RUSSIAN NOVEL OF THE SIXTIES: *Turgenev, Chernyshevsky, Dostoevsky. A Dissertation Submitted for the Degree of Candidate in Philological Sciences* . . .

The man, as though he had finally figured something out, as though something had flown into his consciousness and made the connection between his life and this morning, as though frightened and still unbelieving . . . all of a sudden abruptly turned over and sat up.

Since he has turned his face to us, we can no longer go on pretending that this could be anyone else but Lyova. It was Lyova. Although we may not have been exaggerating that we didn't recognize him immediately. We had never seen him like this.

He was rapidly coming to consciousness (for some reason it's customary to write "gradually" or even "slowly," in such cases). God forbid you should ever have to do this with the same speed. He was coming to consciousness—consciousness was coming to him. They were advancing toward each other, as in a duel. By now it wasn't far to the "barrier." (This is an odd pun, however. It's disagreeable to approach the barrier of consciousness from the beyond, the far side.)

He gazed around the hall. Scattered manuscripts, puddles, trampled plaster, broken glass. His gaze expressed a classical horror, and his face, already pale, paled so deeply that we were frightened he would lose consciousness.

Lyova jumped up and clutched his head with a groan. This was a rescuing pain: it distracted him. He stood fingering his head. There was a terrific bump on it, caused by the cupboard yesterday. Nothing serious, though: he's alive, our hero . . . He glances at the window—the window glances at him.

He approaches the window, which is letting in a terrible draft. He isn't yet quite himself: even from his own point of view, he's still approaching in the third person. He looks out. No, Faina isn't walking there today. The cold wind makes Lyova clearer for us. We breathe on him and rub him with a rag. He is distinct. The poor sad weather, outside the window, has turned utterly demoniacal.

Consciousness has fired its shot. The smoke has cleared. We look at Lyova . . .

Lyova turns around to us. And by now it's he, he's himself. A deadly equanimity on his brow. He has remembered all, it seems. He stares in front of him with unseeing, wide-gaping eyes, with the immobility and apparent calm that reveal to us only a traumatized consciousness. He is cold, but he doesn't notice. However, he is shaken by a cruel chill.

What is to be done! he is probably thinking. What is to be done? And what is to be done?

This is the end, Lyova thinks, not believing it.

(Italics Mine. —A.B.)
Really and truly, this is the end. The author wasn't joking when he tried to kill the hero. The Lev Odoevtsev whom I created was literally left to lie unbreathing in the exhibition hall. The Lev Odoevtsev who woke up doesn't know what is to be done, any more than his author knows what comes next, what will happen to him tomorrow. Childhood, adolescence, youth . . . and now, even yesterday has passed. Morning has come—his and mine. We've sobered up. How quickly we lived our whole lives—as if drunk! Is this the hangover?

315

Time present is ruinous for a hero. Even in life, heroes inhabit only the past, but literary heroes live only in already written books. The pathetic contemporary trolley-car spectacle of a former ace pilot will not prove to us that the hero is still alive. Isn't the attempt to write a second volume (the lame word "dilogy" . . .) every bit as squalid as life after a heroic deed?

Actually, long before the final death of our hero, the reality of his literary existence was beginning to run dry, crowded out by the unsynthesized, formless reality of life—the approach of time present. As soon as we finished with the background at last and proceeded to the plot proper (the anecdote) of the third part, that's just what it turned out to be, an anecdote: "Blank comes to see Prince Odoevtsev, and Mitishatyev is there . . ." That was where the final break in Lyova's fading reality occurred. Only the monstrous constitutions that could withstand such boozing—i.e., only the unreality to which they themselves resorted (intoxication)—enabled the author to make it to the end. I mean to say that what we have now reached began long ago, as far back as we can possibly remember. To use the language of our literary botanists, "shoots of the future, whose roots extend back into the past, have ripened" within the novel. And now we're not supposed to eat of that future fig. With the quick temper of someone not our type, we, too, say, "Dry up!"

Besides, according to the laws by which a literary work is constructed, it really is finished, our novel. We have reached our "Prologue"; that is, we're no longer deceiving the reader with the false promise of a continuation. We have a right to put aside the pen—the reader has even more right to put aside the novel. He's already read it. Let him terminate his impression of the whole right here, and confine himself to that impression. If he's such a friend that he would follow me even further, let him mark out this boundary in his consciousness and draw all his conclusions before he continues. For whether our hero has perished or risen from the dead in the last line is nothing but personal taste and no longer guides the further narrative; the logic of development has been exhausted, all used up. Actually, even this whole useless attempt at a continuation is just an attempt to prove to ourselves that continuation is impossible. It's an attempt at literary criticism rather than literature: the hero is finished, but we've come to feel at home in academe. We'll hang around a while longer and take our time about leaving.

Everything I've written up to now I have written for an imaginary patient reader. But let him bear with me or go to hell. I want a little something too, for myself the unimaginary, for my own explanation, for my own clear conscience. I want to banish the smell of writer's sweat, the effort with which I forced my imaginary reader to experience the novel's events as real. For me this is a matter of honor, you see: an image must be an image. It can be summoned up, but it must not exist in the capacity of reality, clinging to reality. It must not, if only for the reason that reality exists and changes at every second, even the tiniest, while the image once summoned up is frozen, if not forever, then at least for the life of the paper. I do not aspire to power, which I have already gained, you see. And should anyone decide that the image is like me, I have forewarned him. Let him not be angry if it turns out not to be me.

So, Lyova the man woke up. Lyova the literary hero perished. What comes next is Lyova's real existence, and the hero's beyond the grave. Here beyond the grave there is a different logic, or more likely none. The operation of laws is concluded with the inevitable fulfillment of the last one—death. No one knows what is there, in the next world, and no one from the majority has communicated with us, the living minority. We walk in a small procession behind my hero's remains; his existence is exceedingly hypothetical. Here beyond this boundary—beyond which none of us has been, any more than we've been to the future—all is approximate, shaky, optional, accidental, because here the operant laws are not the ones by which we have lived and are writing and reading. The operant laws are ones that we do not know and by which we are living. I don't mean to offend anyone, but what shows very obviously here (in my hero's experience) is that real life is much less real than the life of a literary hero, much less natural, conscious, and complete. Here we enter the zone of Lev Odoevtsev's life where he has ceased to be reason's creation. He has acquired reason himself and doesn't know what to apply it to; i.e., he has become almost as alive as you and I. And that is the highly fantastic working hypothesis of our further narrative—that our own life is the shady, beyond-the-grave life of literary heroes after the book is closed. Then again, such a hypothesis is partially corroborated by the reader himself. Because, if a fascinated reader experiences something written in the past about the past as reality, that is, as the present (and almost as his own, personal present), then can't we assume, in a sophistical way, that he perceives the hero's present as his own future?

The present is indivisible. It is all. We can peer at its pulsing flesh and see that it is alive. This life that it lives apart from us is a final betrayal; for the present has no relationship to us, and yet, by preparing a specimen of our past, we have taught ourselves a sense of belonging.

Continuous, whole, indivisible—the attempt to mirror it is meager in every respect: in our every fresh attempt it's not we who prove something but our attempt that proves something to us. For there is no greater proof of what is than its own existence.

After the hero's entry into a present time coinciding with the author's, all we can do is lackadaisically follow the hero, stupidly spy on him (which is impossible to accomplish in practice, by the way), and describe the sequence of his movements (which lead no one knows where, except to the next instant of the present)—describe at the speed of life itself. This would still be possible, somehow, if the author himself were the hero of his own work and kept a kind of diary. But the author wishes to live his own life, and he doesn't feel very comfortable pursuing the hero so importunately. And then there's the endless waiting while the hero lives long enough for this span of time to turn into the past, so that it can be reported with the speed of coherent narration . . . No, the author is not enticed by such a prospect, we decide at this point. The novel is finished.

But no! While the sentence is written, the instant departs into the past, its light changing the whole past, the whole narrative. Even the last phrase of a novel is exceedingly important. The hero closed his eyes or the hero opened his eyes, he awoke or he fell asleep, he got up or he fell with a thud, he started to speak or he stopped, he remembered or he forgot, he pondered or he gave up, the sun came out or it started to rain, he breathed in or he breathed out—any of these last-phrase actions is an assessment of everything as a whole. Yet we're always so eager to close just on a breath, and in nice weather!

The novel is ended—life continues . . .

VERSION AND
VARIANT
(Epilogue)

WHAT HAVE WE ACHIEVED, though, by merging the author's and the hero's time?

To continue a finished novel is just as impossible a task as for Lyova to wriggle out of his final situation. We had no choice but to ask our editor for an extension, so that Lyova could get everything done.

Thus, by merging the author's and the hero's time in a single present, we have achieved an identity of despair: Lyova's over the situation that has developed, the author's over the blank page. In consequence, the author is better able to appreciate—almost from within, so to speak, like Lyova himself—the difficulty of Lyova's position, as well as his own powerlessness or incapacity to help him.

What can we suggest for him?

Here as nowhere else in the novel are we justified in generating a "version and variant"; that is, a continuation in pure form.

Without any hypothesizing, we can assert that Lyova woke up in a horrible state. He did not remember everything. He remembered only the eight splits of vodka. He remembered practically nothing from the arrival of Blank to the arrival of the girls—only fragments. He shuddered at the memory of Gottich, or rather, at not remembering what he had tried so passionately to persuade him of. He did not remember the walk at all, only the fireworks at the window—and later, being pulled down by the leg from the pseudo-marble beast. The fight with Mitishatyev he remembered well, because of Faina. His last recollections were rather odd: it seemed Mitishatyev and he were sitting on a rug at the seashore. The island was uninhabited, and they were stuffing a note in the neck of a split, with a plea to get them off the rug. After that, he remembered nothing. Lyova racked his brains over the riddle of the double-barreled pistol: a hint of the future lurked in it. Thank you to Mitishatyev, for the Northlands butt! Lyova felt less lonely in the unknown ending of yesterday. They must have been equal co-authors, then, in creating this morning. But just one of them was getting the glory . . . Malice toward Mitishatyev—loneliness no longer.

His head . . . What to tell you about his head? When people say "I have a headache," what do they mean? Surely not this! No. They all, it seems to us, complain of headache merely from envy of other people's complaints. A charming infantilism: "I'm as good as you are!" No one has ever had a headache but Lyova, on the eighth of November, nineteen hundred and sixty-something!

His head has been placed, rather carelessly, on the shaky, melting support of his body. When Lyova takes a step, he seems to walk out from under his head. It stays where it is, a little behind him, and for a while they exist in different spaces, his head and his body.

Therefore, Lyova tries not to make any extra movements. He stands motionless, waits for his head, and thinks:

> *Yesterday was the seventh*
> *tomorrow is the ninth*
> *so today is the eighth . . .*

That's good, that's good. Almost twenty-four hours to go. Almost twenty-four hours before people show up and see all this. Meantime—no one knows anything. Except Mitishatyev. But he's not likely to confess he was here, even to Lyova. No need to worry about him. Of course not, why worry about him? thinks Lyova with a smirk. He got away, as always. But all right, Lyova resolves to himself with fallacious clarity; let's think logically, he proposes to himself. So. No one. Nothing . . . Shouldn't have nodded to himself so decisively and rubbed his hands—no, he shouldn't! Lyova groans and holds his head in his hands.

Standing motionless, Lyova waits for the pain to run ahead a little, and he follows it with his eyes. Then he returns to his thoughts and compiles a mental list:

> *window—one (but panes—two)*
> *cupboard—one (glazier and carpenter)*
> *showcase—one (glazier)*

makes three altogether—not all that much . . . thinks Lyova. He even has a kind of family feeling for the showcase, which he does remember. Lyova looks at the plaster on the floor, cautiously raises his head— the ceiling is unharmed. He picks up a fragment and turns it over in bewilderment. A sideburn!

A leaden fear is smelted within him, rises steadily up his arms, up his legs, surrounds his heart. His heart twitters in the small cavity remaining. Lyova stoops as if paralyzed and picks up a page from the floor: *After the burial of Patroclus, Achilles daily ties Hector's body to his chariot and drags it around the grave of his slain friend. But one night Priam comes to him and begs him to accept a ransom for Hector's body. Priam falls at Achilles' feet, but Achilles takes him by the hand and together they begin to weep over the sorrows of human existence.*

The further course of events, like their beginning, is little touched upon in the poem, since the author assumes that all this is well known to the listener. And so, with the devastation of Troy, the narrative of the poem the Iliad *is brought to a close.*

Of no less interest to us is another poem of Homer's, the Odyssey . . .

What's this? Good God! And now everything comes clear to him: *what* he has done, *where*, and to *whom*. And what *they* are going to do to him for it . . . The fear hardens in his head, in the shape of an outer calm and indifference to what is happening.

Urgently wanted:

> glazier
> carpenter
> scrubwoman
> floor polisher
> sculptor
> aspirin

By the job.

Fee negotiable (double, triple, tenfold . . .).

. . . Now at last we send Lyova out to the people, to see how folks live. He has a slight and very remote conception of this. Remote, first of all, in time—the early postwar years. Then city people still lived in plain view, they were visible in the courtyards and basements. Lyova was attracted to them like a gentleman's son to the servants' hall. He had a friend Misha (Mitishatyev's namesake), the caretaker's son, a "positive" but backward pupil. Lyova helped him with his lessons and loved to eat soup with his family. A standout, that soup! In Lyova's "individual" apartment, where, whatever the amount they had of something, that was the amount they always had, and it stayed there; where the words "quilt cover" or "fiancé" were, if not indecent, never spoken; where such things as forks and spoons, plates, sheets, and pillows were never added or bought (as a grown man, when some newly married classmates dragged him to the store and he was briefly present at their "outfitting," Lyova was very surprised that someone didn't have these things, and that they were sold and bought)—well, in Lyova's apartment, those same soups had neither smell nor taste. Lyova's whole life was lived in this chipped, patched, overlaundered world—but the memory of the *other* soup stayed with him forever. He could not have defined this aftertaste precisely, but it consisted of everything: of words that were not spoken in his family, of "hot pot" and "fries," of a stormy, sensual life with household articles: the picking apart of pillows, the airing of mattresses, the beating of doormats . . . And now, armed with this, the memory of the taste of a soup (unconscious at that—he was in the wrong frame of mind just now for neo-Proustian rambles!), Lyova went out, into this dreadful weather.

And yet he felt better out in the weather! The wind on the bridge blew right through him, battered him, cleansed him, froze him. Shaking way out of control, he was aware of his overcoat as too big, too dangly, and this was almost a pleasant sensation. He was aware of his morning potato cake turning into a *face* under the lash of rain and wind. From a distance he was aware of his face as having suffered much: his eyes grew large, his cheeks adhered thinly. It was getting easier and easier now for Lyova to picture himself organizing everything efficiently.

We won't describe all his rovings. It was an *Odyssey*. We see him next—six hours later—already at Okhta. Because, what had Lyova discovered? That "the people" were gone. Quite possibly, Lyova's ignorance signified an alienation from the people, or a lag behind the time. In any case, it accurately signified a lag behind childhood, when, inescapably, we were in precisely *this* time and *this* world.

There was now no such thing as "the people," as Lyova had imagined them!

The people had moved to the new districts, to individual apartments, and did not want to work. One glance at Lyova told them they could bleed him white—but this awakened no one's greed. The people were not to be had for any kind of money. "You're crazy," they told him. "What's the date today? Who'd work today! Where would you get the glass? . . . Twenty-five rubles, huh? You don't say, friend . . ." So

322

he was told in a tiny short corridor—half of it taken up by a shapeless coatrack with dead quilted work jackets and pants, and boots that stood up without legs—illumined by a naked twenty-watt bulb and the smell of *that* soup at minus twenty years. Lyova stood on the landing of the fifth, top floor, having threaded his way between a baby carriage and a motor scooter; an iron ladder led above, to a black trapdoor into the attic. That was where despair led in dreams . . . and Lyova descended hopelessly to the bottom of the weather, which was more and more dreadful. The swollen Leningrad ceiling hung like a heavy, veined belly. Not rain, not snow—a sort of torn sky-flesh was coming down now, and it plastered the wayfarer in an instant, smothering him like the hateful and nauseating mask of a faint. After the anesthesia, it could do with him as it pleased.

Breathing on each other with the morning-after smell that makes the classes kin:

"I saw you yesterday," the fellow said.

"Impossible," Lyova objected, needlessly. "You couldn't have seen me."

"I didn't, huh! Then who did I see?" The fellow's gaze sharpened slightly with social suspicion: was somebody trying to kid him? But Lyova's rumpled appearance and kindred smell forced him to believe.

"You know our house painter?"

"No, I don't."

The fellow even grunted with vexation: What a dense fool!

Lyova's intellectualism worked against him. How embarrassing, to fall this far short of understanding life's conventionality! After all, what could this look like to people? Mere stupidity. But since he gave the appearance of being a regular guy, it must be some trick, some secret design. Involuntarily, instinctively, it may indeed have been a trick—to find a man and burden him with his own helplessness. As they say, simplicity is worse than thievery.

"What do you mean you don't know him," the fellow lamented, almost angrily. "He may be a house painter, but he can put in glass." He threw Lyova another dubious glance. "Oh, all right, what's to be done with you! Let's see your twenty-five rubles, I'll go try and persuade him. I'll be in apartment 25, in case . . ."

Lyova gladly handed over the money. He waited long and patiently. Thick wet cakes accumulated on his shoulders like epaulettes—he had been promoted to the rank of Great Martyr. But he did not wait to see himself canonized. Maybe his "in case" has finally arrived, Lyova thought with a pathetic, wry grin. Curiously, up to this moment, guarding against the sequential finality of life, he simply had not allowed himself a single healthy suspicion.

A condemned man—merely fulfilling his last formal duties, like trimming his nails or changing his shirt—Lyova emerged from under the snowdrift that had accumulated on him, and knocked at number 25.

He was sure of it now, there couldn't be any house painter living here. Wrong again.

"They left," the wife told him matter-of-factly. "Together. Don't bother to wait."

Bodiless, almost admiring, Lyova descended into the next of Dante's circles. "Think of it, he didn't lie! He didn't lie after all!" he kept exclaiming, in time to his flight. Because in fact he was flying along, caught up by the wind and the flood, on a smooth, conchoidal, glassy breaker, the color of obsidian.

That was at Okhta.

The Neva was overflowing its banks. It had already flooded the romantic steps on which we sit during the white nights, embracing our own jacket on a girl. The Neva beat rhythmically and confidently against the parapet. All that restrained it from surging over the edge, apparently, was the familiar high-school physics principle of surface tension—it had swelled in an unnatural bubble, like a lens. Already the mound of the Neva was almost touching the frightful pendulous belly of the sky, and the only thing preventing them from fusing was imagination's icy lust. Lyova wished he were shorter, so that he couldn't accidentally bump his head on that bloated canopy. One touch and it would . . .

Why bother to put definitive thoughts in our hero's aching head. He wasn't thinking anything.

We have further predictable adventures in store for him in the area of interclass contacts—borrowing money, for example. But enough! He has no other way out; he can still bear this. We can't.

We see this conqueror of difficulties on a famous bridge. The bridge is set squarely on the pillow of the Neva. The city is dead, public transportation not running, streetlights not burning. Lyova is alone on the bridge, right on the hump of it, halfway, in the middle of the contrast—"earth/sky," "hero/author," "left bank/right bank." Lyova must get to the other bank. He has as much chance of getting there as a fly stuck in paste. The weather on the bridge is a thing of just that viscosity and homogeneity. Peter's slop.

Lyova is carrying the glass—three large sheets of it, his arms barely reach. He is twisting under these monstrous sharp sails. On his neck, on a rope, is a package of putty, which gives him the definitive appearance of a suicide. And indeed, in his place, we'd do better to jump in the water, seeing that it's come up so near, right alongside, and we've already got the stone on our neck. But human courage is boundless as despair, and equal to it. It's equal even to this weather, this wind; and beyond this equality there is nothing. Lyova cannot move from the spot. He is twisting, he can't feel his arms, they have grown to the glass—they could be torn from Lyova, but not from the glass. The panes squeak faintly in their slight but·close and wet friction. Large drops run down the glass. Through the glass we see Lyova. The last thing: his face is beautiful! "Marvelous, superhuman music!" Beethoven.

There is no one in this world but the glassed-in, transparent Lyova. Except that at the very rim of the Neva's lens a searchlight is sweeping and a siren hooting. Three desperate black tugboats are bustling around the legendary cruiser, which is icy in the silver of the weather and the beam of searchlights. It has surfaced. It has surfaced for the first time in many long years, torn loose from its roost. The cannon has fired a hollow, muffled shot—no, not the cannon on the ship! The one at Peter and Paul Fortress. It's quite understandable that this empty, vacuum sound could make a drowned man surface, as in olden times . . .

The optimistic will of the author leads Lyova across to the other bank and his institute. It also prevents him from shattering the glass at the end of his heroic journey, as he would surely have done without us. Because we can't bear to continue, the author will concoct a hackwork *success* for Lyova.

No one will help us! For by now we cannot, in good conscience, turn to those who would always help us . . . Mama!

But who loves us?

We have glad news for the reader—Uncle Dickens is still alive! At least, he'll come back to life again and die again, for the sake of the novel. We need him now—no one can take his place. (We do have the excuse that the news of his death, in its time, was included in a chapter by this same tatterdemalion title, "Version and Variant.") Would anyone perhaps prefer that Blank "nobly" notice nothing and return for his bread . . . and the two of them, deeply moved, clasp hands so firmly that their handclasp can never after be broken?

No, the transparent image of Dickens helps us get a glazier and glass, acts as supervisor. He does know how to talk to *them*! He's the one who sees to it that, in this hangover deluging the city, the hungover glazier doesn't cut all the glass down to the size of window vents in his painstakingly wavery range-finding and fitting. Uncle Mitya will always protect against skew.

He inspects and evaluates the devastation.

"Oh, you blockhead . . . what a blockhead! I never expected it of you. Never expected it!" he says. Pleased, he presses Lyova's hand cordially.

Albina, in the meantime, scrubs the floors.

And while she scrubs the floors, Lyova collates the dissertations, page by page, Bashkir literature with Albanian. He comes to know the full sorrow of crushed rebellion.

And everything is transformed! The intact windowpanes shine. Lyova, meticulousness itself, glues the last chip to the cupboard with special BF-2 glue, in exact accordance with the instructions, which are hampering him in his hand . . . to catch a sudden glance from Albina, who is surprised at her own love, as she wrings out the rag, straightens a lock of hair with her elbow . . . a nearsighted floor-scrubbing . . . How lightly we allow ourselves to be noticed! We neglect dignity for the almost-pleasure of safely ignoring those who love us. What else can we exploit, if not the outsider's mechanism of love for us, if not the mechanism of our answering unlove, which paints us with the brown right to belong to our own selves?

You will inquire: And the mask? Mitishatyev brought it—let this be a noble deed performed in his hangover. Besides, he had to get his dissertation . . . Lyova probably needs Mitishatyev again, in order to remember what happened. At this point Mitishatyev has opportunities for power again—and he in turn needs Lyova, in order to make sure of these opportunities . . . Oh no, of course the mask wasn't real! A copy.

And Grigorovich's inkwell? "Here, take this Jewish ashtray," Mitishatyev said darkly. He had found it on the lawn under the window. No, it wasn't broken. They don't make glass like that anymore. Grigorovich did not suffer.

Yet hypothesizing a reconciliation between Lyova and Mitishatyev is so hard, so bad, that we'd better have Albina bring the mask. Either way, the mask—the most irreparable detail, the most frightening to Lyova—will turn out to be exactly the most reparable of all. Albina, graceful, happy to have Lyova dependent on her, foolishly unloved Albina, will say, "Lyovushka, that's nothing! We have lots of them."

And she'll go downstairs to the storeroom, where they lie in stacks, one inside the next. Albina is an experienced linen-keeper. Lyova had no idea of this.

Hypothesizing that he would wriggle out of everything was just as impossible as creating a VARIANT of the present or a VERSION of reality.

Yet he has wriggled out. You don't believe it? I didn't either.

But in actual fact it was I, *I*, who put in the glass for him! By night, like a fairy, I finished weaving the magic canvas.

He has wriggled out of it, and the chapter is written.

THE MORNING
OF THE UNMASKING,
or BRONZE FOLK

(Epilogue)

Yevgeny shuddered. Now his thoughts
Cleared frighteningly.
—The Bronze Horseman, 1833

. . . A FAR SUBURB, homelike in dreams. Quite possibly one like
it has existed in the waking world too, and somewhere still does, but
there isn't a single explicit hint to recognize it by. A spruce-shaded
suburb (Is there something odd about this? Somehow one doesn't think
of a village in a spruce forest), and the five of them, friends and
acquaintances, are renting a house here. The friends' faces, like the
locale, are very familiar and at the same time it's hard to tell whose.
At 5:30 a.m. they are supposed to depart, all of them together, for
Tashkent. To do this, they must leave the house at four-thirty. It's
already late at night, but they are all so afraid of oversleeping that no
one goes to bed. Aimlessly they loaf around the cabin. By three in the
morning they are ready to drop, but for some reason their fear of
oversleeping passes, and they all decide to lie down, just for an hour,
relying on their inner alarm clock. They can't all five of them
oversleep—someone will wake up . . .

Lyova looked at his friends lying on top of the rumpled beds and
suddenly lost all desire to nap with them. He got up off the bed and
went outdoors. Stars. He crossed the road and settled down in the
cabin opposite—no one else was there. Lyova quickly fell asleep.

He woke abruptly, and immediately had a suspicion that he had
overslept. This wasn't a fear that he had been forgotten and left behind,
however; he was afraid the rest had overslept. But his watch showed
four-fifteen, and if they just hurried a little they'd be in plenty of time.
Lyova ran out of the cabin to see how light it had grown. Someone

across the way was driving a cow out, and he became alarmed in earnest. Frantically he put his watch to his ear—it was ticking in good order. He felt reassured. He asked the cowherd what time it was. The reply was horrifying: six-thirty. In his fear, Lyova did not believe it. He raced to the house where his friends were sleeping. The old woman next door was driving her charming flock—a rooster and a little mutt— out of the yard with a switch. The rooster and the mutt were very good friends. The cow barked and charged them, crouching like a dog. Yet the rooster and the mutt were not frightened and didn't run away; tenderly they laid their heads on each other's neck, like horses. Lyova asked the woman what time it was. She looked at her teeny toy watch with its painted hands. Again, six-thirty! Lyova burst in on his friends. They, too, were already awake and in a panic. They checked their watches—everyone's was identical, four-fifteen, everyone's was ticking.

The landlord, a bustling peasant in a Tatar skullcap, was also very upset that they had overslept. He said, "It's because you throwed your coats around the woods that time." (??) Incredible, but a fact—they had overslept! Now they would have to go to Leningrad and turn in their tickets. They would lose thirty percent of the cost, of course . . . $30 \times 5 = \underline{\quad}$. Then again, as Lyova decided on the spot, this was just as well for him personally: he couldn't go anyway, of course, because he had to defend his thesis, and the money would come in very handy to take Faina to a restaurant . . .

With this thought sobering and paling like the early dawn, Lyova scrambled out of his dream and woke up.

He glanced at his watch. It had stopped. Ever since last night, Lyova had been repeating his assignment to himself: Don't oversleep. He must consider everything carefully one more time, collect himself, and prepare for the start of the workday. The most crucial moment was approaching. What had happened here the day before yesterday would come to light, or would not . . . What could this dream mean? Lyova was basically a superstitious person, but he was so uneducated in superstitions that all he knew was that dreams could be interpreted. Exactly how, he had no idea.

"Actually, that's an amusing plot—the collective wrong time." Lyova grinned. The dream was reminiscent of a school arithmetic problem. But how could it have happened, in practice, that all the watches were working and all were wrong? Lyova tried to recall the dream more carefully, to bring it close and examine it in memory in more detail. This was an unpleasant, dizzying effort, and not very successful.

Let's discuss it logically, Lyova told himself, stretching out on the director's couch. Let's assume someone's watch stopped. He noticed and began to wind it, intending to ask someone the time. But there was a conversation going on, and he went ahead and wound it but forgot to reset it. And then—such a coincidence!—someone else's watch stopped, too; he just happened to glance at the first one's watch and set his own by it without asking. And a third person asked the second one for the time and reset his watch by what he said. Then the first person remembered he had to rewind his watch. He asked the third what time it was—and was very surprised that the time matched. That means I wound it exactly when it stopped, he thought, and it didn't have a chance to get slow (that's rare, but it does happen— every one of us has had that silent experience). Or it could have happened another way, Lyova reflected; this would be even shorter and funnier. The first person sets his watch by someone else's watch, which has stopped a little later. That person in turn notices after a while that his watch has stopped, and resets it by the first one's watch, which has gone on ahead . . .

Lyova burst out laughing, remembering how sternly and gravely— importantly, frowning as in the movies before a combat operation— they had said in the dream, before they lay down for just an hour, "Let's synchronize our watches." And everyone turned out to have the exact time. But everyone *already* had the incorrect time. They were already late when they were still just preparing to nap.

Even so, he had failed to interpret the dream. "The collective wrong time"—that was a formulation, of course, but it said nothing about today. What would happen? Lyova turned cold. Oh, good God! Here he was, reasoning about the time, and his own watch had stopped! He didn't know *awake* what time it was!

Lyova jumped up from the couch . . .

We, too, can see no projection in this dream, nothing prophetic, no parable even . . . I have lived for many years under the raised ax of time. This also is vanity. Is not time, like horror, merely our own attitude toward it?

Ah, why marvel at identically incorrect watches, when we already dream common dreams!

Very carefully shaved, like Blank, in a chilling porcelain collar, with his hair impeccably parted, with his hands extremely well (seven times) washed, feeling as ready for execution as for a curtain call and as ready for a curtain call as for execution, long-faced, pale—looking out at Lyova with big suffering eyes was an unknown man, in whom

Lyova recognized himself only by the meticulous, clean little cross on his forehead. A bandage: Albina had put it on, with her very gentle fingers.

Yet he managed to feel glad about his own lack of resemblance. If I'm not recognizable, he reasoned, nothing else will be recognizable. Meaning that it had all been done by that other man, not by this one who didn't look like him, and consequently no complaint could be made against the Lyova reflected in today, since the culprit had vanished . . . His thoughts were coherently tangled.

His extraordinary noticeability, visuality, visibility to all, frightened and embarrassed him. He felt his own irremovability just as keenly as an accidental murderer probably feels the ineradicability of his victim's body: how impossible, how too much to hide are these several kilograms of flesh! And he will sit over them till morning, rocking as if he had a toothache, before the heap of flesh from which life so easily departed and which is so much too much, so impossible, to hide anywhere. He will sit there shocked by the materiality of the world, his first encounter with the insuperability of incarnate categories. People who are agnostic about the material world haven't done anything—it's easy for them to talk. Would they try to act, in their dreamed reality? A criminal is necessarily a materialist: he has done a deed, he has seen cause and effect, "just as plain as the nose on your face." The cause lay prone—the effect kept on going. A materialist is an idealist who has committed a crime.

It's a long time since man lived in the material world. In the material world, only a beast is alive. In the material world, it's so terrifying, so correct, so inevitable! Lyova understood fear.

Lyova was walking back from the barbershop. All the people saw him. They were hurrying about their own petty urgencies, but from the way they all knew all about him, got the point immediately, saw right through him, hid a mental sneer, Lyova could tell that he had become absolutely famous overnight.

He avoided facing passersby, incessantly turned away and covered himself with his handkerchief as if he couldn't stop blowing his nose.

People's faces frightened him with their bareness, nakedness, and frankness—their indecency. Why is it, Lyova wondered, they've always covered the most ordinary, normal things—arms, legs, butt—and bared the most frank and indecent, the face! Everything's backward, Lyova thought. And, in truth, he could not bear the slyness of recognition, the easy malice and curiosity that he discerned in every glance. He was still unaccustomed to fame, his modesty was suffering. Everyone,

everyone had seen him yesterday, when he *didn't remember*! Lyova was gripped by the horror of interrupted existence. This is why we need to remember it all, every step! So that they won't know about us. So that we can always be sole creators of our own version, sole witnesses and interpreters of ourselves. So that we'll be *invisible*. Forget yourself once, and you pass into the possession of men forever. The criminal and sinner is no longer the servant of God but of men. Invisibility—that's the dream, that's the principle! Suddenly, proceeding from nothing but his experience of vindictive childhood notions, Lyova found an easy explanation of all mankind: it lives by hiding. Leaf-colored and bark-textured in the jungles, sand-colored in the desert, imitating transparency in the water. The only thing mankind has tolerated and developed is a mimicry of well-being, health, prosperity, normality, calm, confidence. The most indecent thing, the most ruinous and hopeless, is to become visible, permit interpretation, reveal yourself. You discover that you have lived for a long time, without noticing, in a culture of cannibalism: a man visible in misfortune, in defeat, in illness, in delirium, in crime, that is, a *definitive* man, a man revealed, is the world's prey, its bread. He will dissolve in an instant in the mouth of the crowd, and everyone will run off to his own sequel, clutching in his fist a little thread, holding in his mouth a fading taste, a shred or droplet, of the life force he has snatched on the run from the *defeated* man. A rag will be lying on the pavement . . .

Just don't reveal yourself or what's yours—that is the principle of survival, thought Lyova. Invisibility!

But how very visible Lyova had become! So visible it was impossible to miss him. Only yesterday he had been lying on sharp splinters on the floor, his gaze had pierced holes in the windows, the floor was strewn with thousands of pages that he had spent a whole futile and banal lifetime writing, a snow-white sideburn had fallen off him—he had been the most visible man on earth! His wrath, his passion, his revolt and freedom . . .

And now he was visible in the excessive polish of the floor, in panes of glass cleaner and more intact than before, in the scrawny fresh putty of the windows. Yesterday he had been visible in his deed—today he had become visible in his behavior.

Lyova was astonished by his fear of being noticed. Open space scared him. He remembered a movie: a man was running through a boundless cabbage field, and the field was being raked with fire from all sides, cabbages were exploding under his feet. So he ran in all directions, jerking his legs absurdly, stumbling and falling: it was both impossible to run and inconvenient to fall . . . Those cabbages, like sins, uniform, smooth, synonymous—in all directions, to the horizon. The fruits.

Scenes from another film—his own life—flared up periodically in his mind. The darker and deeper the gaps of forgotten episodes, the brighter the remembered frame between. Here he is, talking with the doorkeeper (she had returned to the institute before anyone else and noticed nothing—the first rehearsal was over, apparently successfully, but the second fear proved greater than the first, and the fact that something, at least, was over made the waiting for what lay ahead even worse . . . She was napping now, tired out by home) . . . Here he is, proving to Gottich that Russia has never existed apart from the classes. "A genius!" Mitishatyev says admiringly . . . Here is Blank: "Why are you silent, Lev Nikolaevich!" (But now another disgrace, mingled with an equally disgraceful reassurance: Blank will never inform) . . . And here is Lyova, passionately proving something to an asymmetrical girl with glass eyes—about Anna Karenina's elbow! Lyova had difficulty suppressing the howl within him—he even kept listening for it to burst out.

The institute was slowly coming to life. People arrived, shook hands, sympathized with Lyova's missed holiday: But then, what did you miss? it was the same old thing, we got drunk and went home, where did the days go? you didn't miss a thing. Someone said that he looked wonderful, Lyova did, and that Tolstoy wasn't the only one to benefit from abstinence.

Lyova wandered the corridors, he was witty, elegant—shadows of corridors, shadows of people, a dream. Much brighter was the reality of the flaring scenes framed by the boundary of forgetfulness. There he went on living, but today was a sluggish dream.

No one noticed a thing!

Something akin to disappointment stirred within him: he had exaggerated his fame. Good Lord, how unobservant people are! he exclaimed mentally. They don't care, and why should they? I felt hounded by the negligence of my secret, the crying obviousness of the evidence . . . But here it is, here, look here! Why don't you notice? You just walked over to the window, why is it all smeared with putty? Fresh, do you see? Unpainted! . . . No, it's none of anyone's business. None at all. I suffered over the shoddiness of my repairs, over the fact that I hadn't achieved the possible, the right, degree of careful fakery, given which I might still—if I was lucky—get away with everything. But no! I've overdone it.

As life returned to normal, Lyova was deeply wounded by the contempt it showed for his defects and oversights. This was the turn of events he had least expected. Life itself was so negligent that Lyova's little rough spots, in this unbroken sea of common negligence, proved to be excess diligence.

Yet this sluggish dream was changing to nightmare! Especially since, in its mildly shifting incorporeality, the dream was turning out to be elusive, unprovable. Can't rouse them, can't wake up . . . The air itself, the gray light itself contained this mild gesture, the cold, puzzled shrug and the return to an interrupted conversation with the full citizens of the dream, refusing to be distracted to the newcomers who were dreaming the dream . . . the dream itself shrugged the shoulders of a shoddily thrown-together space: What are you talking about? . . . I don't understand . . . really now, what do you mean?

Lyova darted about, slipped on the waxed floor, led everyone in turn to the evidence, hinted, interrogated, giggled. No effect! Only a bland smile of embarrassment, an irony—courteous, just in case—in the glance of a well-bred companion, who did not break off the conversation, trying to avoid offending the oddball . . . you know how he is . . . and later go off to his own friends. Lyova thought he was losing his mind.

And here at last is the sum, peak, crescendo-mescendo, apogee, climax, denouement—what else?—the NOTHING; here at last is that critical NOTHING, idol, symbol: a small, smooth, darkly glossy little thing, prolate, fits in the palm of your hands . . . ! now you see it; now you don't! . . . our poet appears before the eyes (or before the eye; we haven't ascertained this, is the other eye glass? or the first eye, why the other?), it had appeared he would and appear he did, our poet, in person, before the single sober and unsleeping eye of this academic dream—the Vice Superintendent for Economic Affairs (the Vice SEA), who was also . . . Does the Vice SEA's glass eye see?

And Lyova thought it *did* see. The Vice SEA as much as touched the little chip glued to the cupboard: well done, good for you, careful job; he was distressed about the putty—my, how spoiled the people are! they don't want to work at all! and they probably charged you a bundle for work like that, too, he really sympathized; but then, the pane that was in two halves—he'd been meaning to replace it for a long time and never could get around to it . . . you know how it goes . . . thanks . . . you really didn't know about the masks? we've got plenty of those things—you needn't have worried so . . . That was funny about the inkwell . . . No, no, Gottich didn't say anything to me . . . Which Gottich?

The Vice SEA gave no sign, perhaps just barely hinted, or maybe not. Shook hands, thanked him, apologized for the circumstances, you know how it goes . . . thanks. You've earned the day off, Lev Nikolaevich. Go out and live it up, have a regular celebration. I praise, I appreciate, my praise is not subject to appeal and has been executed.

Only there's . . . Just a moment, Lev Nikolaevich! Ah, how swiftly Lyova's whole being hurtled to the bottom, but at the same time came alive, as a last hope. How much dignity Lyova managed to put into his obedient "Sir?" or, rather, how much obedience he put into his dignity!

We've got a foreigner here—you know these foreigners!—he's come here to . . . he's interested in . . . you understand . . . in Pushkin. In Alexander Sergeevich (the glass eye, the fricative *g* . . .), in A.S., so to speak . . . Could you perhaps, I urgently recommend, you didn't get to Paris last year but you will, you will! . . . Pleasant for you, and useful to us. A well-known foreigner, by the way, American . . .

Scissors! Someone's been at it with the scissors, cutting and pasting, cutting and pasting an ever more fantastic collage, concocting it from bits and scraps, giggling a little—here's where I'll paste another number, an 88 and a curlicue—and it's done! humor and taste galore . . . contentedly rubbing his hands, fidgeting . . . ah, good! we can call it finished. Which sense are we using when we sense that something more needed doing, something was lacking, but now it's all done—nothing to add, nothing to subtract—the sewing machine and the pince-nez, the brassiere in the desert, the Colt in the cream of wheat, and seven identical busts on the piano . . . And against this background Lyova, with a barely noticeable pin through his chest.

Yes, yes! Everything's in order! thought Lyova, admiring the artistic accuracy of life. NOTHING—and travel abroad as a reward! The in-ephemerality and timelessness of his beloved homeland gladdened him.

Mentally Lyova was already writing a wonderful article. Everyone knows the facts, let's assume, but the angle . . . the perspective . . . what a piercing light! "Journey out of Russia"—that's what I'll call it. "From Poland to China," in parentheses. So dry, strict, academic. The epigraph: . . . *and had never before broken free from the confines of boundless Russia. Gaily I rode into the long-dreamt-of river, and my good steed carried me out on the Turkish bank. But that bank had already been won: I was still in Russia*. Why is it that everyone knows of this, but no one has generalized it? "Pushkin and Travel Abroad"—Lyova could recall no such article . . .

. . . The American was the very writer who subsequently wrote the famous satirical piece "How I Was Hemingway" (but not the man to whom the piece was attributed in our country). Lyova had read his stories some time ago, and hadn't yet devalued them. The surprise, so naïve, of meeting a man who wrote what you read with delight in childhood surpassed Lyova's professional experience; he was astonished to find that good literature is created, not only by the dead, but, lo and behold, specifically by this man here.

He peered at the man's features and saw no resemblance. He might have asked himself where he had expected to see the resemblance—and could not have answered. But most importantly, where was the dusty southern humor hiding? The indifferent, congealed, debauched face, lumpy and red, expressed nothing. Who had done it for him, spun all that brilliance, some spark of which Lyova had inevitably thought to see reflected in his face? An odd type.

They rolled along in a spacious black ZIM, from which Petersburg (because of the foreigner beside him) was so clearly, so newly and fully visible to Lyova. My God! My God, what a city! What a cold brilliant joke! Unbearable! But I belong to it . . . all of me. The city no longer belongs to anyone. But did it ever? How many men—and what men they were!—have tried to associate it with themselves, themselves with it . . . and have merely widened the chasm between the city and Yevgeny, without drawing near the city, merely drawing away from themselves, parting company with their very selves . . . The golden chill running down my spine—that's Petersburg. The pale silver sky, the autumn gold of the spires, the wine-dark ancient water—the weight that pins down the corner of rude Peter's airy pennant, lest it fly away. Since childhood . . . yes, that's just how I've imagined Peter—as the heavy darkness of water under the bridge. Golden Petersburg! Yes, gold—not gray, not blue, not black, and not silver—*gold*! whispered Lyova, surveying his homeland through the eyes with which he vainly endowed the foreigner.

The American wasn't looking around at all. He looked steadily in front of him, and his shortened gaze reflected nothing. This was impossible: his face was the absolute record for immobility! Only his wife could make it liven up a little. Young and pretty, such a bright-eyed little monkey, she kept wrapping her extraordinary coat about her and breathing into the fur, which was from some outlandish animal raised

336

in Siberia for currency. She had a son finishing Oxford, however.

What else? The back of the chauffeur's head, sculpted and cast in flesh. Beside the chauffeur a curly-haired man who looked like the young Bondarchuk. He seemed to have recently learned to smile, and every so often he turned around to try it out. Each time Lyova attempted to tell the story of something, he was thrown off by that smile; then the man would nod encouragingly. "Now, er, this . . ." Lyova would say, inviting them to look out the window, and he himself would turn to look—at the glorious, not-dazzling, not-pure gold of Petersburg.

It was Tuesday everywhere. Tuesday was the day off at the museums. (The employees tacked it onto the holiday weekend—lucky stiffs.) Such ignorance on the part of Intourist surprised Lyova, but "negligence" was the motto of today's reality, and he added this to it. As they scurried around the city from one museum-apartment to another—purposefully, with a smooth soundless swish, from monument to monument—the monuments suddenly became many. Because of the speed, they were standing almost side by side, perhaps shoulder to shoulder. The city was bright and soundless beyond the window, vast, transparent . . . abandoned. And these closely ranked monuments—unexpectedly many, a whole population, the bronze population of the city—were the guides of a blinded time. They had taken Lyova by the hand and led him into today . . .

The museums were closed. Lyova fussed and fumed over this awkwardness: he could not display his commonality with his idol, could not administer communion. The American, however, was unperturbed. Either he had already been surprised by something once and for all, or he had resolved not to be surprised; Lyova was infuriated by his lack of reaction. The American got out of the car, read the plaque, and inspected the lock, vacantly and at length. In the courtyard there was a monument: a tiny standing Pushkin. The American walked around him unhurriedly, inspecting him as he had the lock. A mean little boy with a plastic submachine gun was racing around the monument—rat-a-tat-tat! rat-a-tat-tat!—he raked the foreigner with fire. But the American inspected him, too, as he would a thing. If only his gaze would warm up, if only falsely!

And another event symbolic of that day: they couldn't find the site of Pushkin's duel. (For Lyova, the circle had closed—that frosty visit to Grandfather.) Lyova kept jumping out of the car and asking; people didn't know, they sent him on, kept sending him to the wrong place. Perhaps he would have found it, but at this point Lyova himself did not want to destroy the symbol. Well, so be it, and rightly; let not this sacred place, watered with *his* blood, be seen by those who see not him. He imagined the place: visible only to the initiated, only to the worthy. To the rest, it didn't exist. It had a newsstand, closed for dinner, and that was all. Lyova liked this so much he made no show of persistence. His mission was over, and they went back to the Astoria.

The sun was sinking, and Petersburg still shone like gold. How little, how small it was! How quickly, like the autumn, it had flown past outside the window. Just now the islands—and already St. Isaac's . . .

"And this," Lyova said tediously, without conviction, "is the famous Bronze Horseman, which served as the prototype . . ." Here Lyova flushed agonizingly, then the blood fled swiftly. "My God, what am I saying . . ."

The Neva cast off and sailed away. To the curio house, my friend . . .

To the fatherland let us dedicate . . . It's time, my friend, it's time!
. . . Will outlive my fear . . .

Lyova opened his eyes. The American was fussing over him, unrecognizably revived and transformed. "Curly" was giving him affectionate smiles, encouraging nods. The chauffeur was as implausible and immobile as a plaster cast. The woman was letting Lyova sniff some sort of extremely elegant, unearthly thing; the magical cut glass sparkled in her tiny hand, which peeked out of the fluffy fur like some young, recently awakened creature . . . Lyova was suddenly aware of a shameful unwashedness, which this morning's care over his toilette had not helped—and no amount of care would have helped. Unwashedness in principle.

"Excuse me, I'm sorry, I'll . . . get out . . . take a walk . . . Please—you . . ." Lyova mumbled, climbing over the American hastily and awkwardly. "Later I'll . . . sorry . . ."

"Intelligent, so intelligent," the American said admiringly.

. . . We will leave Lyova taking emphatic deep breaths of the oily air of the Neva. He has leaned his elbows on the parapet and is watching his spit, which is being swallowed up by a little whirlpool. It seems to Lyova that he is happy, that he has finally broken free. He stares at the dirty water, at the iridescent curlicues and various small bits of litter, which seem to him humiliatingly fit for his gaze. For a long time he avoids raising his eyes to the golden and dusty tapestry so dear to him. Worn thin by time, with fine jutting wires of broken dull-gold thread, it seems to have been hung on the other bank to dry. And while the gold of the Petersburg landscape airs on the other bank,

Lyova is thinking that when he does raise his eyes it's perfectly possible that someone will smartly haul up the rope and furl the landscape in a neat little roll. What will he see behind it?

Here is the kind of thought that has already gone through his mind: that it was no accident they didn't unmask him today; that they needed him just as he was, a man who had made an outrageous mess of things and conscientiously eaten it up, licked the bed clean; that there was nothing surprising in the fact they had even condescendingly encouraged him; that he was just the kind of man they could trust . . . that a slave who has suppressed his own revolt by his own strength is both a profitable and a flattering category of slave for the slaveholder: this is precisely how power is recognized, and precisely how it is maintained. "The fact I'm not *theirs*—this they know. But the fact I'm at *their* service—this is what I proved today. And if not *theirs* but at *their* service—what further satisfaction can *they* wish?" All this has already gone through his mind.

And here's what he is thinking while we drift away from him as if on a little river-bus, and before our eyes Lyova begins smoothly rocking, against the background of faded gold with its silhouette of the Bronze Horseman, as though Lyova, like Yevgeny, were about to dance his own pas de deux for us, gracefully expressing his yearning for Parasha (Faina) . . . Here's what he is thinking while we drift away, and until someone jerks up the background behind him: he feels (and the feeling is his thought) that he has *returned*. But from where, and to where? That is what he would like to figure out. The conviction that he has already been at this point in his life, already stood here—but then where has he gadded away the long years, tracing out this dead loop of experience, this long, heavy seine, with which, though he might have caught all the fish in the sea, he has netted nothing but a lot of empty water . . . With this hump on his shoulders, this knapsack of experience, he has returned to his previous place, all stooped and aged, weakened. What is to be done with this hopeless junk, which he has dragged behind him in all his travels and wars? He is tired. Once upon a time, he remembers, he wanted to establish the point from which all had begun, the point at which all had been interrupted—he was already thinking such thoughts—and did not find it.

He stands at this point, he gently rocks, growing smaller against the background, and he sees . . . us rocking on our river-bus.

END OF THE THIRD PART

339

APPENDIX TO
THE THIRD PART

Achilles and the Tortoise

(The Relationship Between Hero and Author)

So he suffered, trembling at the inevitability of the project and at his own indecision.
—The Devils, 1871

. . . REALITY HAD NO ROOM for the novel. Time passed, before I understood the dual nature of the reality surrounding me: it is monolithic and full of holes. Time passed, before I understood that the holes are blocked up the most solidly of all, before I got sick of ramming my head against a hole mended prior to my arrival—before I strode to the wall and freely walked through. Ah, how swiftly I would have dispatched the novel had I known about this! Now I bundle up against the drafty possibilities (always past ones!) that have opened up on all sides, and from habit I detour around the body that used to appear solid. This strange dance circles around the next novel. (*Gambling Fever: An Epilogue-Novel* . . . no, not a continuation, but the kind of novel where . . . how should I put it? . . . there would be no past, only the present . . . as before birth, beyond the grave.)

I seem to remember the author snickering at simpletons who wish to learn what has become of their favorite heroes—snickering at their ignorance of the laws by which a literary work is constructed, their failure to grasp the extent of convention, their lack of literary taste, and so on. For how can a work be continued, after a precisely marked ending? The building is finished, roof and all, people are living in it . . .

Now, scenting an epilogue-novel, the author, too, has begun to be concerned about where heroes go. How is Raskolnikov transformed, for example, after his great chronicler has withdrawn his whole life from him and spent it, over a short span of time, in such a way that no further life is possible, given the findings and the sentence? The sentence has been executed—what

340

slivers and crumbs will the author brush from his table in the epilogue? Read any epilogue, and you will seem to see the cynical grin of its creator: happy family life, triumphs of the spirit . . . he can have anything he wants there. Time in an epilogue is the real, ungoverned present, and the author stops writing not because he has said all but because he lacks the strength to go on, he *cannot* go on. We have already argued that time present, real time, is necessarily the death of the hero; that is why tragic endings are so appropriate. In our unreal time, tragic endings are inappropriate. What awaits the hero, after a death that goes unrecognized as a death? We don't even know whether he's dead, because we count ourselves among the living.

So the naïve desire for a sequel now strikes us as having a more profound, more recondite basis. But no one is likely to want to suffer any further with Lyova. It's painful and too unpromising. At this point we feel a definite guilt toward our hero. It forces us to delay the novel time after time (epilogues —a first, a second, a third . . .), in order to bring on ending after ending, each again unsatisfactory. Day after day we are caught in the misery of the chronicler, who describes, only because no one will do it for him, something he is utterly uncertain about—solely by excluding his own life.

Really now, is it worth it? The writer's sole happiness (for the sake of which, we used to suppose, all is written) is to *coincide completely* with the hero's present, so that his *own* present, being tiresome and unsuccessful, will disappear. This, too, is unattainable. Achilles will never catch up with the tortoise . . . We can't refrain—we append a lemma.

We wander in time present, where each next step is the disappearance of the preceding one, where each, in this sense, is the finale of the whole journey. Therefore, the present of the novel is a chain of finales, the line along which the past rips away from the nonexistent future, tracing out the discontinuity of reality, which has riddled us with holes. Any point in the present is the end of the past, but also the end of the present, because there is no possibility of living on, and yet we live. Actually, there can't even be "any point in the present," the present is itself a point—a point in the mathematical sense— which can be likened only to a sharp little pinprick, and even that is impossible.

And here at the point of this pinprick is located the moral problem—or, if not a problem, then at least the special case—of the mutual relationship between author and hero. We will be told that the hero is immaterial, a phantom, a figment of consciousness and imagination, and therefore the author does not have the same responsibility toward him as toward a live, flesh-and-blood man. Quite the contrary! A live man can resist, reply in kind, hit back. In the end, the law is on his side—and I am very restricted in my behavior toward a man with a body other than mine. But the hero is unprotesting, he's more than a slave, and the author's attitude toward him is a matter of *conscience* to a much greater extent than his relationships with living people. This problem can be, if not likened, then at least compared to the problem of vivisection, which from time immemorial has been considered a moral one. For if there is such a crucial question about our relationship with our lesser brothers stuck on the career ladder of evolution, such as rabbits and mice, then why not raise the question with respect to creatures in our own image? Formally the two problems are extremely similar. Just as a fundamental qualitative boundary exists between the dead and the living, and what one can do with dead material (everything) one cannot do with living—so the boundary between past and present is qualitative, and the hero who, as a result of the narrative, has entered the present, his own time, cannot be treated with the same degree of mercilessness and cruelty as the hero who just recently existed in the past. In some fair land, fairer still than England, one might well find a Society for the Preservation of Literary Heroes from Their Authors. And truly, this mute column of martyrs, incarcerated for all time in cramped little volumes, pale, emaciated to the point of incorporeality, shocked forever by their own crimes against ideals and categories—these guiltless prisoners call for sincere sympathy. All the more so because their torments are only partly their own; to a considerably larger extent, these are the torments of another man, who is cruel and unfair and moreover enjoying the reality and materiality of his own life elsewhere: the author. The patience and indulgence of heroes, and their responsiveness to their creator's torments, are unparalleled and absolute, supremely Christian. Heroes call for sympathy but do not receive it. And they bear without complaint the whole burden of someone else's moral, ethical, civil, social, and what-have-you problems, which writers shift to their incorporeal shoulders as, in its turn, mankind has shifted these same problems to the shoulders of writers. Unquestionably, an author demands more from his heroes than he does from himself in his indulgent practice of life. The laws of retribution and fate operate with considerably greater clarity and effectiveness in respect to heroes than they do in life. For life is everything, but literature is nevertheless something.

Only the past could have been lived in the unique way that has actually happened, and in respect to the past we disclaim any responsibility toward the hero. As for the present, it is unknown and indivisible; and our authorial guile in knowing what *will* happen to the hero can never coexist with a sense of fairness, for the hero doesn't know. Then again, sometimes, toward the end of the work, the hero begins to suspect that certain interested forces of evil, and of someone's authorial will, have selected the artistic details of life's inevitability for him. He begins to grumble a bit, to resist, sometimes he even succeeds (happy, inspired accident!) in foisting something on the author, something small, like a whim . . . but—it's unbelievable, to learn that the implementation of this supreme will rests not with God but in the private hands of some actual author, who, moreover, is quite possibly a rotten person; unbelievable, to learn that an actual person is making decisions along with us, in a setting completely unsuitable and inappropriate to the events under description, by his own hand disrupting his own life and destroying ours; unbelievable that someone, in respect to us, has appropriated to himself both fate and destiny and has seized the power of the Lord. This is the most terrible deprivation of rights we could ever imagine—the lack of a right to God.

It is unbearable to allow a version of the present as a variant of the future. The author's casual attitude flies all to pieces. Lyova got up, Lyova sat down, he took off his hat and squinted—the sun was out. There was a cigarette butt on the ground. Lyova sat waiting for time, which kept not going by. He had: respiration, heartbeat . . . All of this is momentum, for even a mouse without air has momentum, so that we'll be able (have time) to remove the bell jar. The hero alone lives without time, wasting his whole life on being ready for resuscitation: to die at the precise moment when someone will arrive with help.

This novel has been an education for us. We have assimilated the fact that the greatest evil, for us personally, is to live in a ready-made, explained world. This isn't I, you, he, have already lived. It's to live a step away, off the mark, over again, for the nth time, but not one's own life. Here we are up against yet another dark problem in the psychology of creation—the problem of power. We do not, of course, mean that of the government—the superficial first layer of power, which lies in another plane—or the author's relationship with it in the writing process. Needless to say, it exists, that layer, and so does its pressure on the process. We omit any examination of another essential aspect of the problem: the writer's striving for power (honor, influence, money). Let us also omit one other aspect, though it is subtler and concerns us more deeply: an interest in power, a certain contradictory attraction to it, in the very artist who is free. These are already creative problems, this is already a *theme*, too big to . . . we'll devote a future novel to it. Here we have touched upon a very particular aspect of the problem: power over one's own heroes. The extent of this power, its rightfulness and fairness, a feeling for the extent of it in the writing process—this is precisely where we had our difficulties toward the end of the third part . . . We were able to use the floodlights of moral laws to illuminate the hero's dying, his death agony: What is Lyova, we said, after the incident with Blank? After this incident he is irreversibly gone, this time at last he has perished, for what can continue to live in him outside of his soul? But everyone around him is alive: the author, the reader, and the person who will never read this. Can it be that only Lyova is irreversibly gone? We developed a sneaking suspicion that things were somewhat more comfortable for the rest of us, in the dark hall, than for him on his little platform, flooded with the light of conscience for all to see. Therefore, we let up on the pedal. The hero's death has only theoretical interest for us now: how much can be sacrificed in life—and on paper? Has another hero been slaughtered in vain on the altar of fiction? Is this not a ransom?

That's just the point, that if we tell the story of any life with a degree of truthfulness, from an outside viewpoint and at least partially from within, then the picture will be such that the man hasn't the slightest chance of living on. A sequel? Inconceivable! But you live. Only in literature will it really happen: an ending that's the end. By its decency, literature compensates for life's shoddiness and lack of principle.

Everyone already knows what will become of literature if the author behaves there as he does in life: literature will cease to be. It will converge with life, from which it is meant to be separate. And in this ethical discussion, if we may call it that, we find ourselves back at the same point of conclusion: any sequel is impossible.

But let's test this, too. Let's act as shoddily in literature as in life, by utterly breaking down the hero/author distance. Let's allow a confrontation with the hero, let's put this encounter—unprincipled as it is on the author's part—to the test of literary taste.

. . . We recall the bewildered, suspicious glance—the glance of a jealous man who fears to offend the object of his jealousy with a yet unproved suspicion, the glance of an accurate emotion deprived of a voice—the glance of suffering that Lyova threw us on the decadent occasion (true, the only occasion) when our curiosity got the better of us and we went to look at him. That childish glance was impossible to bear, and the author lowered his eyes in embarrassment. In further conversation the author's eyes kept shifting; he was allowed to understand and add to his artistic experience what a shifty-eyed man feels. (Someone who has mastered the shovel of the cause-and-effect connection and feels satisfied with his skill would say that Lyova's glance was suspicious because the author had shifty eyes. I would disagree.) True, we are somewhat justified by the circumstance that we did need to see, at least once, the setting where the novel's action took place. It's effrontery, of course, to describe an institute one has been to only once, but it's even greater effrontery to describe it without having been there even the once . . . Well, but why immediately effrontery? Or perhaps the institute itself is effrontery?*

So far, however, everything matched my descriptions. I banged into three doors before opening the one that was clearly labeled ENTRANCE. Next came the short, wide formal staircase to the main floor; here was the doorkeeper's desk; here was the doorkeeper herself, somewhat other than I had described her, with a touch of the academic manner, like an usherette at the Philharmonic. But her desk was the same, and in the same place: Mitishatyev had sat on it and smoked while Lyova dithered with the keys after escaping from pursuit. The staircase was unlit, the carved oaken twilight was true. Just as Lyova had never noticed the formal chandelier, I forgot to look up and see whether it was there. I made no impression on the doorkeeper, but Lyova's surname did. She tossed her gray perm, stood up partway, told me his extension, checked it for accuracy by finding it on a list under glass, and pushed the telephone over. And while my call was put through, I studied a box that was, well, exactly like the one I described—its doors didn't meet—except that it had a fire hose in it, not a knife switch. I might have introduced myself to Lyova by giving anyone's name—Faina's, Mitishatyev's—but I preferred to give Albina's, in order to avoid making Lyova wonder how much I knew, avoid creating meteorological disturbances, so to speak, in our conversation. I knew that, at the mention of Albina, Lyova's voice would grow bored, eagerly revealing his freedom and independence of her. I was right. Lyova did not keep me waiting; he ran downstairs lightly and carelessly and was just about as I had imagined him, only considerably taller and blonder, which astonished me.

I gazed at his features with peculiar emotion . . . an emotion I can't compare with anything. Except once in a dream, when I saw myself (not in the third person, as one usually does, not in the role of the dream's hero— I was already in the dream, and I/he came in). This was quite terrifying. Or rather it should have been, because my terror was suppressed by another emotion, which had developed simultaneously but at this moment was much stronger—curiosity. It was a hot, voluptuous curiosity, and in the dream I immediately defined it as *feminine* (somehow I was very quick-witted in this dream; that is, I was sleeping with my consciousness switched on, which in

---

* *The novel has changed title several times, reflecting successive authorial encroachments.† Last came* Pushkin House. *It will undoubtedly be criticized, but it's final. I had never been to Pushkin House, the institute, and for that reason (if only that) what I have written here is not about the institute. But I could not disavow the name, the symbol. I am guilty of this "allusion," as it is stylishly called now, and helpless against it. I can only broaden it: both Russian literature and Petersburg (Leningrad) and Russia are all, in one way or another, Pushkin's house, without its curly-haired lodger . . . The academic institute bearing this name is only the latest in the series.*

† A la recherche du destin perdu, *or* Hooligans Wake.

itself is infrequent). I was quick to appreciate the extreme rarity and possible uniqueness of the situation: I had never before seen *myself*, unless you can count reflections in the mirror, and, as I realized then and there, you can't. That is, I was seeing myself *for the first time*. I remember I was perfectly aware that all this was happening in a dream, and I wondered, too, whether it wasn't an early symptom of split personality, but even more clearly I remember being absolutely convinced that this was my authentic double, that I could trust my eyes completely, and that everything I would have time to observe—because what I didn't know was how long the audience would last (i.e., whether I would suddenly wake up)—I must soak up and absorb, like a sponge. This porous, droughty curiosity so possessed me that I didn't even waste strength on hiding it for decency's sake (I remember briefly considering this paradox: that one could be ashamed and try to behave secretively even vis-à-vis one's very self). I stared jealously at myself, as at a rival. So that's what I'm like? That's how others see me? My first impression was satisfying: I looked better than I was accustomed to think. A certain haughtiness (I knew that in this instance it wasn't a function of self-importance) surprised but did not offend me. I even experienced a kind of odd respect for "him/myself," perhaps because "he/I" displayed no such burning interest in "me/me": he seemed to know me already, I just didn't know him. Now I passionately wanted him to start talking, I needed to hear him. "He/I" strolled around the room as if he had come to see someone other than me, and turned to me only when convinced that there was nobody else here. "Well?" he said with a grin. "Excuse me for staring at you this way, but I'm sure you understand," I said. "I suppose so," he said. "One has to be frank about this kind of impression—do you know what my first thought was?" "What?" he asked, out of politeness, obviously knowing what. "Could anyone love me? I mean, would I fall in love with you if I were a woman?" "Have you reassured yourself?" "Generally speaking, yes." "What else would you like to ask me?" "I don't even know . . . What's the most important thing I could pick . . ." Such a strange respect I felt for him! "Well . . . tell me, what am I to do? You know what I mean." "What?" he said, again knowing what. "Why, how am I to go on living?" "The same way," he replied brilliantly. And now he disappeared—either from the dream, or I woke up—but the impression that I had taken part in a real and important event stayed with me for a long time in the waking world . . .

I've digressed by more than a little, because confessions of this sort require nonfiction, and nonfiction is lengthy. That was precisely how I gazed at Lyova's first-time features, and now I don't need to waste energy describing my emotions. He gave me a barely prolonged stare, with his large, somewhat prominent gray eyes, and I looked down. His facial features were devoid of individuality; although his face was unique in its way and fitted no usual type, still—how should I put it?—even though one of a kind, it was typical and did not wholly belong to itself. An expert might have described these features as regular and large, almost "strong," but there was something so hopeless and weak in the sudden downward rush of this sculpted mouth and steep chin that it betrayed, within the Slav, the Aryan with his irresolute courage and secret characterlessness—I would have pictured Mitishatyev thus, rather than Lyova. Perhaps his suspicious glance was what gave him so unexpected a resemblance to his antipode, and in that case it's my fault, because he was right to suspect me. When I violated literary etiquette by turning up in the narrative myself in the capacity of hero, it was as if Lyova's social structure had been shaken for the first time. He had been socially violated, and he glanced at me with Mitishatyev's glance, as Mitishatyev had looked at him. But Lyova was incapable of suspecting anyone whatever of anything whatever (it's not in his social nature to be socially experienced), especially a man he didn't know . . . and his suspicion was all the more agonizing for being unwarranted and unconfirmed, even to him it seemed morbidly apprehensive—and he suspected himself of morbid apprehensiveness. The way he looked at me, he may even have suspected me of a liaison with Faina. Yes, he unerringly sensed and suspected something amiss. How could he help it! This was the conversation that took place between us:

AUTHOR: (What guile! He knows the answers to his questions) *Here's another thing I wanted to ask you. I've heard so much about your paper "Three Prophets." Could you acquaint me with the manuscript?*
LYOVA: *But that article is naïve, it's obsolete, an article out of my childhood. I've become another person. Why would you judge me by that paper? Others I've done are considerably more mature and powerful in every way—"The Middle of the Contrast," for example; "Brilliant Latecomers," or "The I of Pushkin."*
AUTHOR: (Scoundrel!) *Where might I read these papers?*
LYOVA: (Sardonically) *Nowhere. They haven't been published.*
AUTHOR: *Then perhaps you'd let me read them in manuscript?*
LYOVA: (Embarrassed) *You see, they aren't even typed up, I don't think they're quite finished—you'd hardly make sense of the manuscript.* (Confidently) *I'll type them up and give them to you.*
AUTHOR: *But do let me have "Three Prophets." After all, if the article had been published in its own day, you wouldn't be in a position to shield the reader from an acquaintance with it, even if it's youthful and immature—*
LYOVA: (Almost impolitely) *If that one had been published, so would the others. You could have judged and compared.*

347

(Frankly provocative) *But you haven't finished work on the others. How could you* already *have published them?*
LYOVA: (Maliciously) *If wishes were horses . . . In that case, they* would *be finished!*

If we add to this dialogue my shifty eyes and Lyova's just presentiment that I was up to no good, I must have impressed him quite unfavorably. Had he known, he would hardly have entrusted me with his life story.

Meanwhile, we had passed through into the museum, which, as Albina's note made clear, should also be shown to me. (By all means! I very much wanted to check it.) Well, the museum was exactly as I had described it, if you don't count a slight scrambling of the walls and windows. There wasn't a soul in it.

A shadow not unlike a dull, habitual pain crossed Lyova's face when he surveyed the hall.

"Now, er, this . . ." he said sullenly, with a vague wave of his hand. "But I don't have to explain it to you as I would a tour group, do I?"

"No, of course not," I hastened to assure him. I did have some sense of shame.

"It's a while since I've been here myself," Lyova said with relief, benevolently, then and there repenting his "unwarranted" discourtesy to me. "I'll leave you for a short time, you look at everything yourself; anything that especially interests you I can explain later. And don't forget to sign the register, please. We get almost no visitors, and we have orders to record everyone."

Hardly had I released Lyova, hardly had I taken my stance in the middle of the first hall, mentally testing it against the novel and putting checkmarks in the margins beside the inaccuracies . . . when something began to happen in the hall. Something that might have been chalked up to the author's overtired pre-dawn imagination, had it not (like the dream recounted above) been the only documentary fact of the novel.

Into the hall, in full armor and gleaming silver helmet, walked a firefighter. The doorkeeper/usherette ran along behind, fussing. "Well, please, just a minute and I'll go call," she said, sputtering nervously. The fireman peered after her as she retreated: "Got them shoes on? C'mon in, then!" he boomed. One by one, embarrassed, stiff and bristly as crabs, the firemen began to file into the hall, dragging the carcasses of museum slippers on their boots. The hall filled up. They stood wherever they stopped, each stealing glances at what was directly in front of him, and at the ceiling. "Won't be long now, fellas," said the silver one—he was distinguished from everyone here by the elegance of his uniform. A fire god ("Chief of the Fire Brigade": I remembered the appropriate title). He alone had such a helmet, the rest had ordinary gray-green, some sort of tainted metal . . . And in came the tour guide, a graceful, extremely cultured woman with a wise and mocking face. My, what a good thing Lyova had left. This was Albina! It would have been an awkward situation for me.

I could tell by her face how very joyful and rare this was—people in the museum, and such entertaining people. Eagerly, feeling their gaze on her and offering herself up to it, basking in this simple and steady warmth, she walked to the center and rapped her pointer on her graceful, stylish boot top, like a horsewoman or, rather, like an animal tamer. (Or was this her first exhibit? The firemen all looked at her leg.) "Well, what interests you?" she asked, having immediately oriented herself and singled out the silver helmet. "All of it," he barked. She smiled sweetly and nodded with ironic readiness . . . But how strange, I thought, that this woman is Albina, and Lyova the *homme fatal*. Who needs what? Nothing makes sense . . . "All right, then," she said. "We are in . . ." She told us a little about what used to be here, in this building. (I must remember this, I thought—and did not.) Then she said that the first hall gave an overview, as it were, but that even so it had certain relics relating primarily to Count Lev Nikolaevich Tolstoy (that's what she said—"Count"—ah, bold woman!), and here was the portrait by Pasternak, the poet's father, painted at Yasnaya Polyana. She paused for a second, apparently considering her contact with the audience, and at this point the fire god abruptly tossed his head. His helmet flashed blindingly, and he said: "Well, now you understand what valuables they got here. Use of water is forbidden!" The firemen came alive, all at once, and set up a contented buzz. That is the apogee of solicitude toward culture, I thought. But then how do you put out a fire? I looked at Albina and realized that I didn't understand Lyova, I was falling in love. Such light, such promise! The way the laughter broke through her sweet horselike face . . . Recovering, she asked, "What is the purpose of your excursion, actually?" The fire god flushed and said, "Today's our training session, and your objective was targeted." Albina sweetly said goodbye to them, and I soon followed her out, remembering the firemen's faces well, and the exhibits not very well.

I thanked Lyova and regaled him with the story of this ceremonial occasion. He became favorably disposed in spirit. Evidently his moods of wariness and suspicion had been trying to him of late; he shed them gladly, assuming then and there that he had been unjust and that his apprehensiveness was an evil trait (Faina's discipline, she's not a bad operative). But no sooner had the cloud finally slipped from his face—no sooner had he brightened with the simple trusting light of a man warming to his subject—than I began, with evident decisiveness, to say my farewell and depart. Well, I had done my job, my hundred and one percent, it was none of my intention to enter into intimate relations with the hero. (There was also an element of authorial fear for the work already accomplished.)

"I'm keeping you . . ." For him, this simple observation was a penetrating guess, and in proportion as his thought took on a life of its own, his face paled and waned, losing flesh. "Drop in again," he added fussily. "I really am going to give the articles to the typist. 'The Middle of the Contrast,' for a start. It's almost done. Next week . . . ?"

I gave a hasty promise. He did not believe me.

"You're in that much of a hurry?" he said, astonished. "Wait just a second . . . I'll be right back."

He ran off without waiting for my consent. I would have liked to leave—the awkwardness was becoming unbearable—but he returned immediately, out of breath.

"Now these three pages—" I glanced at him, not concealing my surprise. "No, they're not mine." He grinned. "But you were interested in my grand-father's legacy, I know. Drop in next week and return them."

I hesitated slightly.

"You won't drop in?" Lyova guessed. "But what am I saying?" He waved a hand, or almost did. "Take them anyway. You don't have to return them. These are copies."

I thanked him and finally did hurry off, muttering under my arm that yes, of course I would drop in, so long . . .

"Goodbye." Lyova grinned, and I thought I saw in his grin a shade of contempt.

. . . Thus we live, exaggerating others' feelings toward us and underesti-mating our own, and time comes right up close to us. We stand face to face and get away with not seeing at short distances. We are nearsighted in the future, farsighted in the past. Oh, prescribe me some glasses to see with *this instant*! There's no such thing.

And now, having forced the hero into an unnatural confrontation with the author, we no longer have any retreat: our time finally coincides. From this moment on, we live with him in one and the same time, each his own life, and in our everyday space the parallels will never cross. So this brief meeting is a rupture. Actually, any meeting is, sad to say.

It took shape long ago, it happened long ago . . . when the symmetry was completed, and the past, in the mirror of the present, saw the reflection of the future; when the beginning repeated the end and closed up in a ring like a scorpion, and the threat came true in hope; when the novel ended and the author's tyranny over the outstretched, lifeless body began—to leave it slain by an absurd accident (the cupboard) or to resurrect it in accordance with traditions of sobriety and optimism (realism . . .), having punished it by the laws of hangover (retribution . . .)—way back then . . . and ever since (having resurrected it, after all), laboring under the burden of chance and unscru-pulousness, the author has been stealing each subsequent chapter from his own life, writing it by using exclusively the events that had time to happen while the preceding chapter was written. The distance grew shorter, and the close familiarity of his own movements became comical. Achilles stepped on the tortoise, a crunch rang out in the present—and from that moment on . . . we can hardly bear to live, so crushingly, oh, in its loneliness, so heavily did the author's own life come down on him. Scenes of Italy block his view. Ah, what can we say!

We'll take this page to the typist now, and that will be all.

We'll sit quietly while she types: her machine-gun crackle is our last quie-tude. We will rouse ourselves, glance out the window . . .

. . . We will see Lyova for the last time coming out of the entrance across the way. Aha, so that's where he spent the night! He doesn't look as if he slept much. He stops and shivers, somehow bewildered, as if he doesn't recognize where he is or which way to go. He looks at the sky. In the sky he sees a little blue hole . . . What are you smiling at, you sentimental fool? . . . I don't know. He claps his pockets, hunches in a chilly way. What else might happen? Well, he lights a cigarette. Lets out a puff of smoke. Shifts from foot to foot a moment longer. And off he goes!

Bye! So long! We can still lean out and hail him:

"Hey! Hey, wait! Drop in . . . Drop in yourself!"

As he himself, in his time, had wanted to hail Faina . . . We won't hail him, either. We can't, we don't have the . . . We have wronged him.

Where is he off to, striding ever farther away?

We coincide with him in time—and what more do we know of him?

NOTHING

27 October 1971—(November 1964)

THE SPHINX *
(Pages Foisted on Us by the Hero in Parting)
. . . saying, and didn't hear my own words. Didn't even immediately realize that by now I was silent, I had said it *all*. Everyone else was

---

* From a chapter "God Is." M. P. Odoevtsev's last return to his Notes may be dated, by Blok's poem, as no earlier than 1921. —L.O. (Lyova's note. —A.B.)

silent, too. Oh, how long and rapidly I walked toward the exit in that silence!

I came out on the embankment—what a deep breath! By now I had no hatred left. Freedom! Well, that about does it. They won't coddle me any longer. "Got away, the scoundrel! Hey! / Tomorrow you'll get yours, just wait!" By all means . . . Senior Lecturer N., glancing fearfully over his shoulder, darted out after me. Reproached and chided me. "You didn't even need to recant anything. You *knew* that Z. himself would be at the commission meeting! You should have said it was first and foremost a great literary monument, Ecclesiastes was the world's first materialist and dialectician. They'd have calmed down. They had absolutely no desire to destroy you, Modest Platonovich. But you yourself . . ." I comforted the yellow-belly as best I could. We walked as far as the Academy of Arts and said goodbye. He ran back to "put in his time" at the meeting.

I went down to the water by the sphinxes. It was strangely quiet. The Neva was floating, and colorful sharp clouds—as does happen, precisely in gray Petersburg—were drifting across the sky. Drifting above, drifting below . . . and I stood motionless between the sphinxes, in the windlessness and quiet—a sort of farewell feeling . . . as in childhood, when you don't know which train has started, yours or the one opposite. Or perhaps Vasily Island had torn loose and floated away? . . . If we've got sphinxes in Petersburg, what can surprise us? They were identically indifferent to this: they stared with the same gaze—as if into desert wilderness. And truly: didn't the forests grow right up to them in the wilderness, wasn't there a swamp under Petersburg? Strange Petersburg—like a dream . . . As if it no longer existed. A stage set . . . No, it's not the one opposite—it's my train departing.

I'm a riddle to N., you see. Why me, if even these sphinxes are no mystery! Or Petersburg, either! Or Peter, or Pushkin, or Russia . . . They're mysterious only by virtue of their loss of function. The ties have been broken, the secret forever lost . . . a mystery is born! Culture remains only in the form of monuments contoured by destruction. A monument is doomed to eternal life, it is immortal merely because all that surrounded it has perished. In this sense, I'm not worried about our culture—it has already *been*. It's gone. It will exist in my absence, as a meaningless thing, for a good while longer. They will preserve it. Either so that nothing succeeds it, or just on the inexplicable off chance. N. will preserve it. N.—there's the riddle!

Insane liberal! You lament that culture is insufficiently understood, you being the main peddler of misunderstanding. Misunderstanding is your sole cultural role. I kiss you for this on your high little brow! Thanks be to God! After all, to be misunderstood is the sole condition for the existence of culture. You think the goal is recognition, and recognition is confirmation that you've been understood? Blockhead. The goal of life is to fulfill one's function. To be misunderstood, or understood not at all—that is, to go unrecognized—can only protect culture from outright destruction and murder. What has perished in our lifetime has perished forever. But the temple stands! It's still fit to store potatoes—that's a blessing! The great cunning of the alive.

You talk endlessly about the death of Russian culture. On the contrary! It has just emerged. The Revolution won't destroy the past, she'll stop it at her back. All has perished—and in this very hour the great Russian culture has been born, this time forever, because it will not develop in its sequel. And only yesterday we thought it was just barely beginning . . . Now it's hurtling into the past like a rock. Let a short time go by and it will acquire a legendary flavor, like egg yolk in a fresco, lead in brick, silver in glass, the soul of a slave in balsam—a secret! To our descendants, Russian culture will be a sphinx, just as Pushkin was the sphinx of Russian culture. Death is the glory of the alive! It's the boundary between culture and life. It's the genius and keeper of man's history. The People's Artist d'Anthès sculpted Pushkin from his bullet. And now, when we no longer have anyone to shoot at, we sculpt our last bullet in the form of a monument. A million academicians will try to guess its riddle—and fail. Pushkin, how you bamboozled everyone! After you, everyone thought that if you could, he could . . . But you were the only one.

Never mind about Pushkin . . . they don't understand Blok! This same N., full of delight, winking and frothing, slipped me Blok's last poem.

> Pushkin! We have walked together
> And have secret freedom sung . . .
> Give us your hand in this bad weather,
> Our mute struggle is not done.

N.'s so subtle, all he can grasp is the hint. The words he doesn't understand. He's inflamed by the sounds of "secret freedom—bad weather—mute struggle," understanding them as forbidden and yet pronounced aloud. Here again, "We have sung"—that means him, too. The only reason he's not Pushkin, you see, is that they've stopped his mouth. For one thing, nobody's stopped it, and for another, pull out the gag and there'll be an empty hole. Lord forgive me this sorry rage! So these are poems after all, if one can fall as far short of understanding them as N. So these poems will live on, in the manuscript copies of N. and his kind.

This inspires the hope—and precisely nowadays (Blok is king after all, if he can call this merely "bad weather")—that the ties have been chopped forever. Were there a last little thread—what despair!—a bullet through the head. But here: behind is the abyss, ahead is nonexistence, on the left and right they've got you by the elbows . . . and yet the sky overhead is free! *They* won't look at it. They live on the surface, they're not likely to miss anything here, they'll flood every crack with blood . . . And yet, under other conditions, I might never have looked up and learned that I was *free*. I would have roved in all free directions, around Freedom Square, in the freely milling crowd . . .

> *You are king, live alone. Walk the free road*
> *Wherever your free mind shall draw you . . .*

It's not "the road of freedom." But the road is free! The free road—walk it! Walk it—alone! Walk the road that is always free—walk the free road. That is how I understand it, and it's what Blok meant, and Pushkin . . . Far more. Understanding is possible. We have been guaranteed muteness. Its very purpose is that we should have time to understand. Silence—that, too, is a word . . . It is time to keep silence.

Unreality is a condition of life. Everything is shifted and exists a step away, with a purpose other than it was named for. On the level of reality, only God is alive. He is reality. All else is divided, multiplied, canceled out, factored—annihilated. To exist on the honesty of authentic reasons is beyond a man's strength now. It voids his life, since his life exists only through error.

Level judges level. Men ponder God, Pushkinologists Pushkin. Popular experts in nothing *understand* life . . . What a mess! What luck, that it's all so far off the mark!

No need to explain oneself—no one to explain to. Words, too, have lost their function. And no use prophesying—it will come true . . . The last words will fall mute because they knew how to name things with themselves. They jinxed themselves. Only when the thing they fully matched has sunk into oblivion may they have meaning again. Who can say whether they are good enough to survive their own meanings? And especially—recognition. Recognition is retribution, whether for dishonesty or for inaccuracy. That is the "mute struggle." What must a Word be, in order not to wear away its own sound in incorrect use? In order to make all the missiles of false meanings land a step away from its bewitched true sense! . . . But even if a word is accurately pronounced and can survive its own muteness right up to the rebirth of its Phoenix sense, does this mean that anyone will find it in the papery dust, that anyone will even try to find it in a former meaning, let alone its true one—and not simply pronounce it a new way? . . .

TRANSLATOR'S
AFTERWORD
AND NOTES

TRANSLATOR'S AFTERWORD

Pushkin's hold on the Russian heart is unique, not only because of his enormous importance to literature but also because of the poignant details of his life and death. Every Russian, almost before he is old enough to read, knows that Pushkin was Russia's greatest writer, that he was persecuted by the Czar, and that he died very young, defending his wife's honor in a duel. His work is traditionally considered to have laid the foundations for modern Russian literature: indeed, Russian literature has been called the house that Pushkin built.

The inhabitants of this house, the authors and heroes of the ensuing hundred and fifty years of fiction, seem to call back and forth from room to room, echoing the same persistent motifs. Andrei Bitov's *Pushkin House* is rich with overheard conversations of this kind. Through his epigraphs, voices from Russia's great past comment ironically on the text of modern life.

Bitov's method, as he says in his prologue, is to construct a narrative that converges with the reader's daily experience, in such a way that events in the outside world—the kind of thing one reads in the newspaper—seem to be a continuation of the book. Life and literature, historical figures and fictional heroes, are all part of the same scene.

The main action takes place in Pushkin House, a literary institute and museum in Leningrad. The novel opens the morning after an annual holiday celebrating the Revolution of 1917; the city is immobilized by hangover, and the hero's body lies lifeless in a devastated exhibition hall at the museum.

Bitov then recounts the history of his hero, Lyova Odoevtsev.* Like Bitov himself, Lyova was born in 1937, at the height of Stalin's purges. He read "all" of Pushkin in 1949, during a period of renewed Stalinist terror. He finished high school in 1953, the year of Stalin's death. And it is hinted that the fateful events at the museum occurred in 1967, on the fiftieth anniversary of the Revolution. Despite (or perhaps because of) the momentous historical events framing his life, Lyova is preoccupied with the nineteenth century; he is a philologist on the staff of Pushkin House, specializing in Pushkin.

In keeping with Lyova's profession, the book has all the apparatus of scholarly literary criticism. It is divided into "sections," complete with appendices and footnotes. The chapter titles are drawn from literary works familiar to every Russian reader. (At least one academic bookstore, deceived by appearances, has shelved this novel under criticism instead of fiction.) In form, the novel is a parodic "double" of the house that Pushkin built—wittily ornamented, in the postmodern manner, with architectural motifs from the past.

In another sense, however, the novel is indeed an exercise in criticism. Somewhat disingenuously, Bitov questions the validity of realism as a literary method; he experiments with alternative approaches to his hero's life, speculating on their relative truth and reality. But these speculations are profoundly interconnected with Bitov's view of reality itself, where actual events have an air of unreality, and the moral consequences of an act are recognized only in fiction.

So *Pushkin House* is not an academic tour of literary history, or even a sentimental odyssey through the living literature in quest of meaning in present-day Soviet life. It is a double of life itself, in a country where the national literature has always been a focus of the struggle between state and individual. To read this book is to experience the wild paradoxes lived by a contemporary Soviet intellectual.

That experience is shared, in varying degree, by all thinking citizens of the modern world. For this reason, and because Bitov's literary stance is as much a response to Joyce and Nabokov as it is to the traditional Russian classics, the Western reader does not really need to know Russian literature in order to follow the story and understand the deeper levels of *Pushkin House*.

The surface play of wit and irony, however, may be less accessible to Western readers. For those unfamiliar with the clichés of the Russian school curriculum, here is a quick review of the major facts relevant to this novel:

1. The modern Russian state began with Peter the Great (1672–1725), who introduced Western culture and bureaucratic government. These reforms

---

* *Lyova is the ordinary nickname for Lev. The syllable* lyo *is pronounced as in the phrase "all yours."*

set off a philosophical struggle—unresolved even today—between rationalistic "Westernizers" and tradition-loving "Slavophiles."

2. Alexander Pushkin (1799–1837) was the first writer to make sense out of the mélange of linguistic influences resulting from Peter's reforms. He was above all a poet, but he also ushered in a new age of prose with his *Belkin Tales* (1830). His spare prose style and certain of his characterizations were extremely influential in the subsequent development of Russian literature. Bitov's Lyova can claim two of Pushkin's characters as ancestors: the "superfluous man," whose original is the aristocratic hero of Pushkin's *Eugene Onegin*; and the downtrodden "little man," whose prototype is the poor clerk Yevgeny, tyrannized by arrogant authority in Pushkin's *Bronze Horseman*. That both of these heroes were named Yevgeny (Eugene) was no coincidence: as an aristocrat hounded by the Czar, Pushkin identified with both figures. This duality takes absurdly comical form in the life of Bitov's Lyova, but its implications are tragic.

3. The first major elaboration on the theme of the "superfluous man" was Lermontov's romantic novel *A Hero of Our Time* (1840). This hero is an enigmatic, cynical, Byronic figure who has no use for the frivolous society of his day. Nor has he any idea how he might use his life for the betterment of that society. Lermontov's readers were not sure how to respond to the novel.

4. The theme of the "little man" was further developed by Dostoevsky, in two novels about poor clerks oppressed by their jobs: *The Double* and *Humble Folk* (both published in 1846). *The Double* depicts a psychological disorientation brought on by intolerable social pressures; the mad hero is confused by encounters with his own alter ego, people who look like him, and his mirrored reflection. Generations of Russian writers have since been fascinated by this theme. What especially interested the critics of the 1840s, however, was the newly realistic description of poverty in *Humble Folk*. Dostoevsky's realism held promise as an instrument for social change: open discussion of the need for reform was not tolerated, but fiction might be sneaked past the censors.

5. By the time Turgenev wrote *Fathers and Sons* (1862), realistic fiction had become a major battleground in the campaign for public awareness of social issues. This novel depicts a supposedly typical young radical, a nihilist, involved in debate with a family of superfluous men. But the nihilist dies a meaningless death, while the ineffectual aristocrats survive with values intact, making only token concessions to the changing times. Turgenev was violently criticized by both right and left; authors in both camps countered with novels presenting opposite views of reality.

6. One such polemical response, from the left, was Chernyshevsky's *What*

Is to Be Done? (1863). Lenin and Stalin both admired the book, which is still standard reading in Soviet schools. It begins with an apparent suicide, and the reader is playfully led to believe that this will be a novel of love and intrigue. But as Chernyshevsky reconstructs the life of his "dead" hero it becomes apparent that he is setting up a radical as the ideal modern man, urging profound political and social change. The novel was written in prison and published due to a bureaucratic blunder; when the authorities realized what had happened, Chernyshevsky was hustled off to martyrdom in Siberia. The allusion to *What Is to Be Done?* in Bitov's prologue prepares the reader for a mischievous handling of the plot and at the same time recalls the utter seriousness of the issues under discussion.

7. An opposite response to *Fathers and Sons* was Dostoevsky's *The Devils* (1872). His own youthful radicalism had led to ten years in Siberia, a religious awakening, and an about-face in his political views; here he shows the radicals as demons, masquerading in the guise of rationality.

8. Perhaps the greatest of all the realists was Lev Tolstoy (1828–1910). Although excommunicated by the Orthodox Church and harassed by the censors, Tolstoy believed that it was possible to strike a personal, rather than a political, balance between the demands of self and society. His career spanned the entire Age of Realism, and he is a powerful background presence in *Pushkin House*.

9. The turn of the century saw the rise of various competing literary methods. The World of Art movement in Petersburg brought together an eclectic group of modernist painters, philosophers, theater people, and writers, in the pursuit of art for art's sake. Despairing of a political solution to Russia's problems, Symbolist writers such as Alexander Blok (1880–1921) awaited the coming retribution with a mystical horror and reverence.

10. The Revolution of 1917 led to a brief period of vigorous artistic experimentation, but by the 1930s such efforts had virtually ceased. Socialist Realism, as exemplified in the writings of Maxim Gorky (1868–1936), became the officially sanctioned literary method. Writers and critics who could not adapt either emigrated or were silenced; the Western development of modernism as a literary school had no Soviet parallel. Despite an improvement in the literary climate in recent years, Bitov has been unable to publish *Pushkin House* in the Soviet Union.

11. Throughout all these changes, Petersburg (now Leningrad) has stood as a symbol of Russia's problems. Seeking a window to the West, Peter the Great moved his capital from Moscow to a swamp by the Gulf of Finland. The Italianate architecture is gloriously beautiful, but the climate is dank and hostile. Petersburg always presented an oppressive contrast between the pride of empire and the tribulations of the poor. The city's split personality has

been the subject of a long series of explorations, many of them familiar to Western readers: Pushkin's *Bronze Horseman*, Gogol's "Nevsky Prospect," such Dostoevsky works as "White Nights" and *Crime and Punishment*, and the symbolist Andrei Bely's great novel, *Petersburg*. In the latter, the city is not merely the setting but the main character. In Bitov's book, by contrast, the city exists as a letter of intent from Peter, a literary memory, a painting, a stage for illusory events.

The reader who enjoys tracking down quotations will find more detail, along with identification of unfamiliar names and terms, in the notes that follow. One should remember, though, that Bitov's use of this material is generally ironic.

Bitov's style, even for the Russian reader, is often difficult. His complex syntax and unusual word collocations exploit the idiomatic resources of the language to their fullest. Yet both syntax and idiom have the exactness of inevitable choice, often determined by a subtle allusion, a play on words, an intricate sound pattern, or an overriding prose rhythm; the novel is as tightly structured as a lyric poem, its dominant themes and imagery woven into a single unified design. The wordplay and sound patterns, of course, are hardest to sustain in translation, and I keenly regret what has been lost. But since this is a novel, a story, my first concern in translating it has been to follow the curve of Bitov's thought.

I am immensely grateful for the kindness and patience of the many people from whom I have sought advice on troublesome points, especially Professor Michael Connolly of Boston College and my good friends Boris Hoffman and Rima Zolina.

NOTES

PAGE VII / *"Pushkin House! A name apart . . ."* From Alexander Blok's last poem, "To Pushkin House," written for the album of the literary institute and museum attached to the Academy of Sciences in Leningrad.

PAGE 3 / *"On the morning of July 11, 1856 . . ."* The first line of *What Is to Be Done?* by Nikolai Chernyshevsky (1828–89). The hotel staff is upset because a guest has disappeared; he has apparently jumped off a bridge.

November 7 . . . November 8, 196– The Bolshevik Revolution, according to the calendar then in effect in Russia, began on October 25, 1917. The event is now celebrated annually with a two-day holiday on November 7 and 8. The major feature of the observance on the seventh is a great parade, with the general public joining in. In Leningrad, the marchers converge on Palace Square, outside the Hermitage, formerly the Winter Palace. The Bolshevik Revolution began with the storming of this palace; the attackers are said to have approached through the magnificent triumphal gate in the General Staff building opposite it.

"to spite his haughty neighbor"   The phrase is from the opening encomium to Petersburg in Pushkin's *Bronze Horseman.*

Gastello   A Soviet pilot who died heroically in 1941 when he flew his disabled plane into a group of Nazi tanks.

PAGE 5 / *the legendary cruiser*   Now permanently anchored in the Neva River and maintained as a museum, the cruiser *Aurora* fired the shot that signaled the storming of the Winter Palace in 1917.

PAGE 9 / *"Supporting each other . . ."*   From Turgenev's novel *Fathers and Sons* (1862). The son mourned here is the nihilist Bazarov, whom Turgenev portrayed as representing Russia's young intellectuals, in conflict with their fathers' generation. Bazarov achieves symbolic victory by defeating an old aristocrat in a duel, but later meets an accidental death.

PAGE 11 / *Lyova Odoevtsev of the Odoevtsevs*   The hero's surname suggests that of an aristocratic Russian family, the Odoevskys. Outstanding among them was Prince Alexander Odoevsky, a Romantic poet. For his participation in the idealistic Decembrist uprising of 1825, he was sent to Siberia.

"deep into the Siberian mines"   The phrase is adapted from a poem that Pushkin wrote in 1827 to express sympathy and encouragement for exiled members of the Decembrist movement. The poem brought a response from his friend Alexander Odoevsky (see note above).

PAGE 13 / *Pavkas Pavliks*   The allusion is to a genre of Soviet children's stories extolling heroes like Pavel Morozov (1918–32), who as a young teenager denounced his parents to the authorities.

Meresyev   A famous World War II pilot (*b.* 1916). Severely wounded and forced to parachute into a deep forest, he crawled for eighteen days to get back to his unit. Both legs had to be amputated. After mastering the use of prostheses, he returned to active duty and shot down seven more planes. His heroism was the subject of Boris Polevoy's vastly popular *Tale of a Real Man* (1946).

PAGE 14 / *the well-known Benois . . . Liberty silk . . . World of Art stained-glass windows*   The Russian artist Alexander Benois (1870–1960) was a leading figure in Petersburg's World of Art movement at the turn of the century. In addition to promoting a renaissance of Russian art, the group introduced to Russia the avant-garde work of other countries, especially Art Nouveau, which was sometimes known on the continent as the Liberty Style because it had been fostered in its early years by British silk merchant Arthur Liberty.

dating back almost to Elizabeth   The Empress Elizabeth reigned 1741–62.

PAGE 17 / *an Esenin-like purity and doom*   Sergei Esenin (1895–1925) was a gifted poet of peasant origin who welcomed the events of 1917 but later came to believe that he had failed as a poet of the people. He suffered a nervous breakdown and eventually hanged himself.

PAGE 18 / *the* Childhood, Adolescence, Youth *of our hero*   The allusion is to Tolstoy's semiautobiographical trilogy (1852–57).

PAGE 19 / *"Pa, Pa, our nets hauled in a dead man!"*   A line from Pushkin's poem "The Drowned Man" (1828). The fisherman, fearing entanglement with the authorities, decides to throw the drowned man back in the river. The corpse drifts away but returns regularly to knock on the fisherman's window at night.

the Nevsky   That is, Nevsky Prospect, a major avenue in Leningrad.

PAGE 22 / *in the era of* Youth *(the magazine)*   Founded in 1955, Youth *(Yunost)* published many of the best young writers of the sixties, such as Vasili Aksyonov and Yevgeny Yevtushenko.

PAGE 29 / *chifir tea*   Tea brewed so strong that its concentrated tannin and caffeine have a narcotic effect. Uncle Dickens would have acquired a taste for it in prison camp.

PAGE 30 / *Dahl's* Defining Dictionary   Vladimir Dahl (1801–72) was a gifted Russian lexicographer and ethnographer. His four-volume dictionary departed from scholarly tradition to include earthy folk expressions.

PAGE 31 / *Kresty* The popular name of a famous political prison in Petersburg (Leningrad).

PAGE 44 / *the Cult* That is, the "cult of personality" that surrounded Stalin.

PAGE 45 / *"On Brühl Terrace . . . a man of about fifty . . ."* From the epilogue to Turgenev's *Fathers and Sons*. The aging aristocrat Pavel Kirsanov emigrates to Dresden after his unsuccessful duel with the nihilist upstart Bazarov.

PAGE 55 / *he's gone mad, like Hermann* The central figure of Pushkin's tale "The Queen of Spades" (1833) is a young officer named Hermann. He forcibly extracts from an old lady her secret formula for winning at cards, whereupon she dies of fright. He bets the 3 and the 7, as directed, and wins; but when he bets the ace, he comes up with a winking queen of spades. He goes mad and sits in an asylum for the rest of his life, muttering, "Three, seven, ace! Three, seven, queen!"

PAGE 61 / *Rublyov* Andrei Rublyov (c. 1360–1430), a Moscow painter of icons.

PAGE 64 / *from Derzhavin to Blok* Gavrila Derzhavin (1743–1816) and Alexander Blok (1880–1921) were, respectively, the first and last great poets of modern Russian literature (as distinct from literature of the Soviet era).

PAGE 65 / *Tsvetaeva . . . Tyutchev . . . Fet . . . Bunin* All were major poets. Tyutchev and Fet are seen as nineteenth-century precursors of the Symbolist movement. Bunin and Marina Tsvetaeva both emigrated after the Revolution (Tsvetaeva returned to the Soviet Union and eventually committed suicide).

PAGE 68 / *the servant Peter* A kindly treated serf who at first adopts the attitudes of the "new, improved generation" of the 1860s and then settles into bourgeois respectability.

PAGE 77 / *Zero is still intelligent—a grade of 5 is already foolish* In Soviet schools, a 5 is equivalent to an A.

PAGE 85 / *Lermontov . . . Pushkin . . . and Nekrasov . . . chipping in on a half liter* The three maintenance men, who happen to bear the names of nineteenth-century poets, are following a prevalent Soviet custom: because the price of a half liter of vodka stood for many years at about three rubles, it became common for three people to chip in a ruble each and drink together.

PAGE 89 / *"a place to go"* The phrase recalls the drunkard Marmeladov's account of his troubles, in Dostoevsky's *Crime and Punishment*.

PAGE 90 / *the violent pathos and drama of a Gorky play* The plays of Maxim Gorky (1868–1936) are generally about class struggle, especially between effete intellectuals and the proletariat.

PAGE 91 / *Rakhmetov* The ideal modern man described by Chernyshevsky in *What Is to Be Done?*

PAGE 92 / *"given to us only in sensation"* The phrase is a cliché of the Marxist–Leninist philosophy of materialism.

PAGE 99 / *MVD, GPU* Security police, predecessors of the modern-day KGB.

PAGE 122 / *irradiation* In Pavlovian psychology, this term means the elicitation of the conditional response by a stimulus other than the one to which conditioning has been established.

PAGE 123 / *"Yet happiness was so possible, so near . . ."* A familiar line from the end of Pushkin's *Eugene Onegin*.

high and mighty Man (the highwayman) In the Russian original, Bitov makes a clever play on words, combining an old term for a highwayman with Gorky's famous description of Lenin as "a Man with a capital M."

PAGE 127 / *"For a long time I lay . . ."* From *A Hero of Our Time*, by Mikhail Lermontov

(1814–41). The novel draws on Lermontov's own experience as a young army officer serving in the Caucasus.

With a few exceptions noted below, Bitov's epigraphs in Section Two are taken from a chapter called "Princess Mary." The hero, Pechorin, is engaged in a calculated flirtation with the Princess, partly to spite a detested social climber who covets her, and partly to divert attention from his own passion for a married woman. After a duel in which Pechorin kills his rival, he gallops into the mountains in a desperate but unsuccessful attempt to overtake his departing true love. When his horse collapses, he is forced to admit defeat. He returns home and coldly rejects Princess Mary.

PAGE 130 / *a "tie with the past"* This phrase, now a journalistic cliché, is recognized by Russian readers as coming from Shakespeare. Hamlet's line "The time is out of joint" is sometimes rendered in Russian as "The tie with the past is broken."

Shield and Sword A Soviet spy film (1968), based on a novel by Vadim Kozhevnikov.

"Vengeance is mine . . . I will repay" The epigraph to Tolstoy's *Anna Karenina*, taken from Romans 12:19.

PAGE 131 / *The Gospel According to Matthew* A 1964 film by the Italian Marxist director Pier Paolo Pasolini. The only words spoken in it are quotations from the Bible.

"Christ, Mohammed, Napoleon" The phrase is adapted from a famous monologue in Gorky's play *The Lower Depths* (1902).

PAGE 138 / *Solovyov and Karamzin . . .* Short Course *. . . the third questions* The *Short Course* is the standard high-school text on the history of the Soviet Union. The usual history exam includes two questions on Communist Party history and philosophy and one on the rest of Russian history. Mitishatyev, having read only the respected nineteenth-century historians Solovyov and Karamzin, would not know the Party line on Russia's history.

PAGE 159 / *"Like any man, I couldn't talk about love very long standing up"* The Russian version—as remembered by Lyova or by Bitov, or as rendered by a tactful Soviet translator—is softer than Hemingway's original. The line in *A Farewell to Arms* reads: "I was experiencing the masculine difficulty of making love very long standing up."

PAGE 164 / *"You will die today!"* From "The Fatalist," a chapter in Lermontov's *A Hero of Our Time*. The story is about a man who survives a game of Russian roulette, only to die in a grisly accident the same night.

PAGE 171 / *Maxim Maximych* A bluff old soldier, friend to Pechorin, in Lermontov's *A Hero of Our Time*.

PAGE 185 / *Beloved woman, unloved woman, any woman* The name Lyubasha derives from the word for "love" (*lyubov*). Coincidentally, it also suggests a pronoun meaning "anyone" (*lyubaya*).

PAGE 195 / *". . . Pushkin's a black Semite!"* Pushkin's mother was descended from Ibrahim Hannibal, an Abyssinian prince who, as a child, was bought in a Constantinople bazaar and presented to Peter the Great.

PAGE 202 / *Pisarev* The literary critic Dmitri Pisarev (1840–68), who believed that social issues were far more important than aesthetic concerns. He was proud to see his views reflected in Bazarov, hero of Turgenev's *Fathers and Sons*, and he openly praised Chernyshevsky's *What Is to Be Done?* His nihilism brought him frequent trouble with the authorities. His death, perhaps a suicide, was by drowning.

PAGE 207 / *Yevtushenko, Smoktunovsky, Gagarin* Contemporary Soviet celebrities: poet Yevgeny Yevtushenko, stage and screen actor Innokenty Smoktunovsky, and cosmonaut Yuri Gagarin.

PAGE 209 / *Shklovsky* The eminent formalist literary critic Viktor Shklovsky (*b.* 1893).

PAGE 221 / *"I recently learned that Pechorin had died . . ."* From the introduction to "Pechorin's Journal," a chapter in Lermontov's *A Hero of Our Time.*

PAGE 222 / *Levin* As a landowner of liberal outlook and powerful conscience, the character Levin in *Anna Karenina* has much in common with Tolstoy himself. His surname is drawn from Tolstoy's Christian name, Lev.

PAGE 223 / *Mikhail Zoshchenko* A widely loved author of humorous and satirical tales (1895–1958).

PAGE 225 / THREE PROPHETS For a traditionally repressive society, there is special significance in the idea that poets and other serious writers who speak the truth are prophets. The three poets whom Lyova chooses for discussion are nineteenth-century Russia's greatest: Alexander Pushkin (1799–1837), Mikhail Lermontov (1814–41), and Fyodor Tyutchev (1803–73). Pushkin's verse is a varied and highly personal blend of the classical and the romantic; Lermontov's is predominantly romantic; Tyutchev's work in many respects anticipates that of the twentieth-century Symbolists. A Russian, in reading Lyova's essay, would be keenly aware that both Pushkin and Lermontov died in duels.

PAGE 227 / *"With fainting soul athirst for grace . . ."* The first line of Pushkin's famous poem "The Prophet" (1826). The translation is by Maurice Baring (reprinted in *Pushkin,* by D. S. Mirsky [New York: E. P. Dutton, 1963]).

PAGE 228 / *"Since that day when the Lord on high . . ."* Lermontov's poem "The Prophet" (1841), as translated by Eugene M. Kayden (in *The Demon and Other Poems* [Yellow Springs, Ohio: Antioch Press, 1965]).

PAGE 232 / *the 1834* Morning Star The literary review in which Tyutchev's "Madness" first appeared.

d'Anthès The courtier who killed Pushkin in a duel.

PAGE 233–34 / *he was carrying his iron cane* Pushkin, who was something of a dandy, carried an iron cane in imitation of Byron.

PAGE 234 / *Shevyryov and Khomyakov* Both were very minor poets. Shevyryov won Pushkin's passing favor by criticizing one of his enemies. Khomyakov's early work showed some promise, but he was later known chiefly as a religious thinker.

Smirdin The publisher and bookseller A. F. Smirdin (1795–1857), who generated considerable literary excitement by his innovative practice of paying writers a reasonable fee.

the Goncharovs had finally given their consent to his marriage The family of Pushkin's beloved Nathalie Goncharov were at first reluctant to marry her to the roué scribbler. When they finally consented, she was eighteen, he thirty-one.

Boldino Because of a cholera epidemic, Pushkin spent the autumn of 1830 at his estate at Boldino. The forced seclusion led to amazing productivity. In addition to finishing *Eugene Onegin,* he wrote numerous lyrics, *The Belkin Tales,* and his four "little tragedies" (including *Mozart and Salieri*).

PAGE 235 / *the* Contemporary . . . *"Poems Sent from Germany"* The publication of this cycle in Pushkin's literary journal in 1836 brought Tyutchev his first public recognition. He had studied and worked in Germany, and his poems of the period showed the influence of Schelling's *Naturphilosophie.*

"Aged Derzhavin noticed us . . ." From Pushkin's *Eugene Onegin.* The sentence concludes: "and blessed us as he descended to his grave." Gavrila Derzhavin, the grand old man of Russian poetry, once visited the royal lyceum and praised the verse of the youthful student Pushkin.

the recent painting Belinsky and Gogol in the Bed of the Dying Nekrasov All three of these writers—critic Vissarion Belinsky (1811–48), novelist Nikolai Gogol (1809–52), and poet and editor Nikolai Nekrasov (1821–77)—are claimed as forerunners of Socialist Realism by Soviet critics. Lyova's satirical remark exploits the familiar image of Nekrasov on his deathbed as painted by I. N. Kramskoy (1877).

PAGE 236 / *Yuri Tynyanov's article "Pushkin and Tyutchev"* Tynyanov (1894–1943) was a leader of the formalist school of literary criticism. This article, published in 1923, attempts to debunk the legend that Pushkin thought of Tyutchev as his successor.

Raich The poet and translator Semyon Raich (1792–1855) was Tyutchev's tutor for several years.

PAGE 237 / *"Don't let me lose my mind, o God"* Pushkin's poem is given here in Walter Arndt's translation (in *Alexander Pushkin: Collected Narrative and Lyrical Poetry* [Ann Arbor: Ardis, 1984]).

PAGE 243 / *The Humble Horseman* This title is a cross between *The Bronze Horseman* (Pushkin) and *Humble Folk* (Dostoevsky).

The Bronze Horseman is a long poem describing one of Petersburg's recurrent floods. Bitov's epigraph is taken from a passage in which a humble clerk named Yevgeny has mounted a marble lion in front of the Admiralty Building in order to escape the rising water of the Neva. From this perch he can see Falconet's famous statue of Peter the Great—the Bronze Horseman—and beyond it his fiancée's humble home being washed away. Wandering desolate after the flood, Yevgeny mutters a rebellious complaint to the statue. The statue comes to life and furiously pursues Yevgeny through the streets. Yevgeny's body is later found at the site where his fiancée drowned.

The figure of the poor clerk pursued by dehumanized authority became an important literary type. The inarticulate absurdity of such a clerk's life was depicted by Gogol in his story "The Overcoat" (1842); Dostoevsky responded with a heartrendingly realistic portrait in *Humble Folk* (1846; also known as *Poor Folk*). The timid, aging clerk of Dostoevsky's novel loves a poor young girl, with whom he exchanges letters. As the girl introduces him to the writings of Pushkin and Gogol, the clerk begins to find a voice of his own, in both life and literature. The girl finally accepts an offer of marriage from a wealthy suitor, however, leaving the clerk bereft. Bitov's epigraph is the despairing final line of the novel.

A Poem of Petty Hooliganism The word "poem" here means a long poem, such as the *Odyssey* or Dante's *Divine Comedy*. Bitov is not the first to use the word in the subtitle of a prose work: Gogol chose the paradoxical subtitle "A Poem" for *Dead Souls* (1842). He intended the novel as the first part of a modern *Divine Comedy*, a tour of the "Inferno" of the Russian social system. His hero travels around Russia, visiting landowners and buying up ownership rights to serfs who have died since the last census (he hopes to pawn them for enough cash to buy an estate of his own); Gogol makes clear, however, that the true "dead souls" are the landowners and the hero himself.

PAGE 253 / *like Chaliapin* The allusion is to a scene in Mussorgsky's opera *Boris Godunov* (based on Pushkin's verse drama of the same name), as played by the famous basso Chaliapin. Czar Boris is attempting to drive away the ghost of the child he has murdered to gain the throne.

PAGE 258 / *Naryshkin* The surname of a noble Russian family.

PAGE 261 / *Chernomor's March* Chernomor is the sorcerer in Glinka's opera *Ruslan and Ludmilla* (based on Pushkin's poem of the same name). The march is boisterously sinister.

PAGE 267 / *Oktyabr and Novy Mir* Soviet literary magazines (*October* and *New World*).

PAGE 268 / *Chekhov's book on Sakhalin* In *Sakhalin Island* (1893–95), Chekhov described conditions in the imperial penal colony, which he had visited as an independent traveler.

PAGE 270 / *Nathalie was first of all Woman* The discussion is about Pushkin and his young wife, Nathalie. She was very beautiful, immensely successful at court, and surrounded by admirers. Among them was Czar Nicholas himself, as well as a young Frenchman, Baron George d'Anthès. Enraged by persistent gossip linking d'Anthès and Nathalie, Pushkin challenged the Baron to a duel. Pushkin suffered a fatal wound but lived long enough to declare his wife's innocence in the affair. Pushkinologists and the general Russian literary public argued for years about Nathalie's fidelity; in the 1960s, the debate was rekindled by fresh information obtained through study of the Goncharov family archives.

all these poetesses Among those who have written impassioned articles about Pushkin are Anna Akhmatova and Marina Tsvetaeva.

" *'A few days ago, with the help of God'* " From a letter of Pushkin's (1828). The complete line reads: "Why write me about Mme Kern, whom I f—d a few days ago, with the help of God."

PAGE 271 / *Vulf* A friend of Pushkin's, Alexey Vulf (1805–81), whose journal covers the years of Pushkin's courtship.

"Vyazemsky? Baratynsky?" Major poets, lifelong friends of Pushkin: Pyotr Vyazemsky (1792–1878) and Yevgeny Baratynsky (1800–44).

" *'No, I value not riotous pleasure'* " From an intimate poem of Pushkin's, apparently addressed to Nathalie, written in 1831 but unpublished in the poet's lifetime. The gist of it is that he prefers her demure tenderness to the sensual revels of other women.

"She loved Lanskoy" Seven years after Pushkin's death, Nathalie married General P. P. Lanskoy (1799–1877).

PAGE 272 / *Mme Krüdener* Baroness Barbara Juliane von Krüdener (1764–1824), a Pietist mystic, known in aristocratic circles across Europe for both her religious influence and her romantic excesses.

Benckendorff Because of Pushkin's liberal tendencies and literary prominence, all his work had to be passed, not by ordinary censors, but by the Emperor himself and also by the head of the secret police, General A. K. Benckendorff (1783–1844).

Dubbelt After the poet's death, General L. V. Dubbelt (1792–1862) served as Benckendorff's deputy in charge of Pushkin's papers.

" *'Pathetic, filthy, but not like you, villains!'* " A slightly distorted quotation from a letter of 1825, in which Pushkin commented angrily on the public outcry against Byron's morals.

"A lawful c—t" From a letter of 1826 in which Pushkin joked about the marriage of his poet friend Baratynsky.

Khodasevich's "Cupid and Hymen" A quatrain by the émigré poet Vladimir Khodasevich (1886–1939).

PAGE 278 / *Anna Karenina in the role of Doronina* Tatyana Doronina (*b.* 1933) is a Soviet actress of stage and screen.

a Natasha, but in the role of Audrey Hepburn Audrey Hepburn played Natasha in the American film version of Tolstoy's *War and Peace* (1956).

PAGE 281 / *"You're in a fever, I see, prepared to lose all . . ."* From the gambling scene that opens Lermontov's verse drama *Masquerade* (1835).

"Alone I come out to the hi-igh-wa-ay . . ." The first line of a well-known poem by Lermontov (1841). In literal translation, the poem continues: "The sparry path shines through the haze; the night is quiet. The wilderness hearkens to God, and star speaks with star . . ."

PAGE 282 / *a Gogolian exclamation* The allusion is to Nikolai Gogol (1809–52), who frequently intruded on his narratives with comments and lyrical digressions. For the relevance of his novel *Dead Souls*, see note to page 243, "A Poem of Petty Hooliganism."

PAGE 283 / *myrrh-bearer* This term, as used in the Greek and Russian Orthodox churches, refers to the three Marys, who brought balm for Christ's body after he was taken down from the cross.

Benois's perspective   Alexander Benois (see note to page 14) did a remarkable series of illustrations for Pushkin's *Bronze Horseman*, first published in 1904 in Diaghilev's journal *World of Art*.

that it may always be "bright"   An allusion to a phrase in the opening description of Petersburg in *The Bronze Horseman*.

PAGE 286 / *"We fought a duel"*   From a poem called "The Ball," by Yevgeny Baratynsky. Pushkin used the line as the epigraph to his story "The Shot."

"This was at dawn . . ."   From Pushkin's story "The Shot" (in *The Belkin Tales*). In this passage, the hero, Silvio, tells the narrator that his opponent so infuriated him by his insouciant behavior—continuing to eat cherries from his hat while waiting for him to fire—that Silvio broke off the duel, vowing to fire on another occasion. Some years later, Pushkin's narrator happens to meet the opponent and hears the end of the story: when the opponent was finally married, and therefore had reason to value his life, Silvio came to his home and finished the duel in his drawing room—intentionally missing.

" 'Flip the coin,' the captain said ..."   From Lermontov's *A Hero of Our Time*. Grushnitsky has plotted with his seconds to give his rival, Pechorin, an unloaded gun. Aware of the plot, Pechorin manipulates the situation in such a way that Grushnitsky is overcome by conscience and misses his shot. Pechorin then demands a properly loaded gun, offers Grushnitsky a chance to apologize—which Grushnitsky is too proud to do—and kills him.

" 'I will fight in earnest,' Pavel Petrovich repeated . . ."   From Turgenev's *Fathers and Sons*. The duelists here are the aging aristocrat Pavel Petrovich and the young nihilist Bazarov. Bazarov wounds Pavel Petrovich slightly, binds up the wound, and departs to serve mankind.

"Kirillov immediately declared . . ."   From Dostoevsky's novel *The Devils* (also known as *The Possessed*). Although Gaganov has managed to provoke the aristocratic Stavrogin to a duel, Stavrogin remains contemptuous, unwilling to take him seriously. Gaganov is so enraged that he misses all three of his shots; Stavrogin completes his humiliation by repeatedly firing in the air.

PAGE 287 / *"Of all those present, it turned out that . . ."*   From Chekhov's story "The Duel." The coldly rational Von Koren has been challenged to a duel by a "superfluous man" whom he despises as a social parasite. He shoots to kill but misses, distracted by a shout from a horrified priest, who is watching.

" 'I'd like to spit on you,' Peredonov said calmly . . ."   From a grim satirical novel, *The Petty Demon*, by the "decadent" Symbolist Fyodor Sologub (1863–1927). Peredonov is a petty, paranoid, provincial schoolteacher. He lives with the slatternly and jealous Varvara, who is engaged in an intrigue to get him to marry her.

PAGE 290 / *Yevgeny's fear*   The allusion is to the poor clerk in *The Bronze Horseman* and his futile rebellious thoughts in the aftermath of the flood (see note to page 243).

PAGE 301 / *laughed loudly, like Neschastlivtsev*   The hero of a darkly comic play, *The Forest*, by Nikolai Ostrovsky (1823–86), Neschastlivtsev is a tragic actor who has fallen on hard times. Essential to his repertoire is a ferocious loud laugh.

PAGE 304 / *Chekhov trimmed Ionych's gooseberry bushes*   In his drunkenness, Lyova is confusing two Chekhov stories, "Ionych" and "Gooseberries."

A . . . rehabilitated Bunin   Because Bunin emigrated to Paris after the Revolution, his writing has become available to Soviet readers only in recent decades.

PAGE 308 / *Grigorovich's inkwell*   Dmitri Grigorovich (1822–99) was a novelist of Russian peasant life.

PAGE 310 / *with the effort of the Commendatore*   That is, treading heavily, like the avenging statue of Donna Anna's husband. The Don Juan legend, perhaps most familiar to us from Mozart's *Don Giovanni*, is best known to Russian readers through Pushkin's play *The Stone Guest* (1830).

PAGE 312 / *"Thus I learned the end of the tale . . ."*   From Pushkin's "The Shot" (see note to page 286).

PAGE 322 / *Okhta*   A suburb outside Leningrad.

PAGE 325 / *"Marvelous, superhuman music!"*   According to Maxim Gorky, this was Lenin's response to a Beethoven recording.

the cannon . . . at Peter and Paul Fortress   This cannon is fired every day at noon.

PAGE 335 / *". . . and had never before broken free from the confines of boundless Russia"*   From Pushkin's *Journey to Arzrum* (1835), an account of his adventures accompanying the Russian Army on a campaign in the Caucasus. Pushkin repeatedly applied for permission to travel abroad, but it was never granted.

PAGE 337 / *Bondarchuk*   The Soviet film actor and director S. F. Bondarchuk (*b.* 1920).

PAGE 338 / *To the curio house, my friend . . .*   From the fable "The Curious Man," by Ivan Krylov (1769–1844). The man takes note of minor exhibits at the curio house but misses the elephant.

To the fatherland let us dedicate . . . It's time, my friend, it's time! . . . Will outlive my fear . . .   Lines from familiar poems by Pushkin. The last quotation is humorously distorted, with a play on *strakh* ("fear") and *prakh* ("ashes"); what Pushkin wrote was: "My soul, in my cherished lyre, will outlive my ashes."

PAGE 339 / *Parasha*   Yevgeny's fiancée, killed in the Petersburg flood described in *The Bronze Horseman*.

PAGE 340 / *"So he suffered . . ."*   From Dostoevsky's *The Devils*.

Raskolnikov   The hero of Dostoevsky's *Crime and Punishment*. In the epilogue, the imprisoned murderer undergoes a spiritual regeneration.

PAGE 352 / *"Got away, the scoundrel . . ."*   From Alexander Blok's ambiguous poem "The Twelve" (1918). The "twelve" are marauding Red Guardsmen; the Revolution is seen as a mistily feminine Christ-figure, rising out of the destructive storm of events gripping Petersburg.

PAGE 353 / *"Pushkin! We have walked together . . ."*   From Blok's poem "To Pushkin House," written just before his death in 1921.

PAGE 354 / *"You are king, live alone . . ."*   From Pushkin's "To the Poet" (1830).

COMMENTARY

On the momentum of the pen, and proceeding from his relationship with the hero as revealed toward the end of the novel, the author immediately began a commentary, written ostensibly in 1999, ostensibly by the hero—now Academician Lev Nikolaevich Odoevtsev—for the anniversary edition of the novel. This gave the poor hero a chance to get even with the author. Maintaining his academic dignity, he kept calling the author's bluff with well-reasoned arguments; that is, unceremoniously exposing him as an ignoramus. The author defended himself as best he could, trying to pass the commentary off as parody, but the hero had suddenly begun to surpass him in expertise.

And all at once the author wearied, as they said in olden times. His project of extending the author-hero dialogue to the end of the century was never completed. Without noticing, he had become fascinated by a quite different commentary: he had started to annotate, not the specialized things, but the ones that were common knowledge (by the time he finished the novel; that is, by 1971).[*]

The author was suddenly struck that items of common knowledge, on which the contemporary writer has not felt it necessary to dwell at any length—prices, champions, popular songs—are the very things that will vanish into subsequent nonexistence. It would indeed make sense, from this point of view, for Lev Nikolaevich to tell about them in his commentary of 1999. "But I'm afraid he'll feel they

---

[*] His returns to the commentary, however, stretched on until 1978.

aren't academic enough," the author thought. "Or he'll forget." Meanwhile, these subjects may seem quite mysterious, even now, to the foreign reader. From a national standpoint, perception in translation is already perception in a future time.

Naturally, the author could not take a researcher's scrupulous attitude toward his own text; hence a number of incompatibilities with academic protocol.

Page v. CONTENTS

The author feels that a glance at the table of contents should suffice to keep anyone from suspecting him of "elitism," a rebuke now made with great frequency in our literary journals and newspapers (as if we had no other worries). There is no need at all for the reader to know the literature well in order to begin this novel—what he remembers from high school (and a high-school education is compulsory in our country) is more than adequate. The author consciously stays within the limits of the school program. (The same is true of other allusions. See commentary to page 130.)

Page 3. *this clear sky... must have been extorted by special airplanes*

As a rule, the weather on November 7 (October 25, Old Style) is abominable. Such is the season. The festive mood of the thousands of marchers is not enhanced by the wet snow flying in their faces; flags and posters get soaked. More and more often in recent years, however, there has been settled weather—rather clear, if piercing—for the duration of the parade. Such a circumstance is always remarked in the holiday newspapers. Significance is attached to it. According to unverified reports, the weather really has been "settled," and moreover from on high, by combat planes on special holiday assignment. (See commentary to page 5, concerning the weather.)

the childhood word "Gastello"

The foreign beauty of this surname contributed to the fame of the heroic deed and ultimately eclipsed it: everyone is familiar with the hero's name, not everyone with what he did. People do know that he was a pilot. In children of my generation the name Gastello, like the name of the as yet unread *Monte Cristo,* formed a first romantic layer of sediment on the clean walls of memory. (Gastello, Nikolai Frantsevich [1907-1941], Hero of the Soviet Union. Modified Nesterov's feat [see below, *an inside climbing loop*]: perished on the fifth day of the war when he flew his burning plane into a column of German military vehicles and exploded along with them.)

Page 4. *"toss-me, catch-me"*

A cheap bazaar toy sold on the streets, usually by gypsies, during the parades of May 1 and November 7. It is a little ball made of paper, stuffed with sawdust, held together with meridians of thread, on a long thin elastic: when thrown, it comes back to its owner. We used to have a considerably richer assortment of such toys—the "go-away, go-away," the "American resident," the "mother-in-law's tongue," candy cockerels, and many other enticing items. Now the whole repertoire is reduced to little red flags and balloons (the kind that don't fly). One still encounters the "toss-me, catch-me," but less frequently with every year. I suppose there are economic factors at work here, dictating to the private market, but in the meantime the art of making them—these toys—has simply been lost.

an inside climbing loop
Known to us as "Nesterov's loop," after Pyotr Nikolaevich Nesterov (1887-1914), the great Russian pilot who executed it in 1913. He perished when he became the first to employ his airplane as a battering ram.

Page 5. *a Northland cigarette*
A cheap, blue-collar brand. (Red Star was another, but it has been taken out of production.) Smoking a Northland is something of a social characterization: the low price; the feasibility of keeping one in your mouth when your hands are full or dirty; the frequent need to get a light, because they go out easily; and, finally, membership in the specific generation that began to smoke in the war years or before and has remained faithful to its taste—which makes these cigarettes still profitable to produce. But they, too, have something of the "toss-me, catch-me" in them. They, like it, will some day disappear, crowded out by chewing gum, Marlboros, and Pepsi-Cola.

the weather, however, has special importance for us and will play its part in the narrative again
To this day, Leningraders like to reproach Peter for having established his city in a swamp. In addition to the bad weather, they are convinced that there are certain "miasmas" present in the air, which are conducive to colds (people used to say "fevers," but this expressive word has already gone where the "toss-me, catch-me" is going). This is true: chronic illnesses of the ear, nose, and throat are highly prevalent in Leningrad. I can't resist quoting a sample of the style, especially since it dates back to Pushkin's epoch:

> The climate of St. Petersburg—despite its main feature, inconstancy—must be classified as *consistent.*
> *Spring* begins quite late. Not infrequently one sees falling snow in early May. In 1834, it snowed on May 18!
> *Summer* is extremely brief. There are rarely more than six weeks of nice warm weather; other so-called summer days resemble, in every respect, the days of late autumn.
> *Autumn*, often very prolonged, is the least pleasant season in Petersburg, its chief appurtenances being fog, rain, wind, and sometimes snow, which soon disappears at a temperature between -2 and -6 R. The exceeding brevity of the days gives cause for saying that Petersburg, throughout October, November, and December, is covered with gloom, especially for upper-class residents, who, since they wake up late, barely have time to see the daylight, which in November and December disappears at about three o'clock in the afternoon.
>
> Ministry of Internal Affairs, *Statistical Information on Saint Petersburg* (1836).

Pages 4, 5. *the Revolutionary wicket... the legendary cruiser*
In 1819, Karl Rossi undertook to complete the architectural ensemble of the

square in front of Rastrelli's Winter Palace. His skill was manifested with special brilliance in the design of the arch that joined the General Staff building with those of the Ministries. It spanned Lugovaya Millionnaya (now Herzen Street), which had previously approached the square at a tangent. By drastically turning the last segment of the street, Rossi brought it out to the square just opposite the center of the Winter Palace facade—thus fixing the axis of symmetry of the whole ensemble.

Rossi had aimed the muzzle at Rastrelli long in advance, and even though revolutionary sailors belted with machine-gun cartridges didn't really race into Palace Square through the arch of the General Staff building (it's just that Eisenstein's scenes were later given a documentary flavor); even though the corner of the Winter Palace—to this day exhibited by tour guides—did not get knocked off by the shot from the *Aurora*; even though there was no battle for the Winter Palace, and it was guarded not by cadets but by the Women's Battalion; even though the introduction of the New Style blurred not only the fact but also the date, so that we have the October Revolution but the November holidays... though there was neither assault nor salvo nor November... the author does not share this petit-bourgeois triumph. Nothing happened, they say. How do they mean, "nothing"? Then what's all this?

The triumph of Rossi's design.

Page 6. *the great novel* The Three Musketeers
Alexandre Dumas (père, 1802-70), the national genius of France, popular in Russia. In 1858 he made a journey to Russia and described it with his speedy pen: *From Paris to Astrakhan.* Vasily Rozanov, in his article "On the Russian Idea," wrote that any crumbs of experience would suffice a genius to recreate an accurate picture. He was thinking of Gogol, who passed through just once in a kibitka and composed *Chichikov's Journeys (Dead Souls)*; and of Bismarck, who picked up in Russia, not something, but the key word *nichego*—"it's nothing"—which he liked to use in difficult situations after he became the Iron Chancellor. Alexandre Dumas may be included in this series, for it was he who gave Russia the "spreading cranberry tree."

a scrap of newspaper
The author has already been asked, and to forestall such questions I reply: There is no parody here. The scrap is authentic, and I didn't waste a lot of time hunting up a curiosity in a sheaf of newspaper files. I found it where newspapers may be found (in the village of Rybachy in the Kaliningrad Region—the former village of Rossitten in the former East Prussia [the former Bismarck...], in August of 1970), and did not use it for its ultimate purpose. The greatest reproach one could make to the author is that he pinched two snippets off that serendipitous scrap, exclusively for purposes of graphic expressiveness. We may assume that it came from the *Literary Gazette* (one of whose founders was, again, Pushkin).

Page 11. *Lyova was conceived in a "fateful" year*
What can such quotation marks mean? What vague poison did the author wish to inject here?... The author begs the reader to take into account the fact that he began his narrative—even if superficially, even if formally—not with the hero's conception but twenty years before, by driving the relatively perpetual November wind over the march routes of 1917.

"deep into the Siberian mines"
We learned this poem by heart in 1949. Now I take special pleasure in picturing myself in that class, as I feelingly delivered the line:

Russia shall arise from sleep!

There, in class Six-A of Boys' High School No. 213, a fundamental breach was established between emotion and consciousness. Emotion was abstracted as a response to pathos. At recess, however, we fought this corruption in our own way, repeating the lines differently:

Deep in the Siberian pit,
Two peasants sit and shit.

But even in that redaction we understood only the last word. We did not understand that these weren't ordinary peasants but something more specific: a "peasant" was a convict (non-criminal). The folklore of the camps was considerably more widespread than information about them. We knew by heart many such adaptations of famous songs, poems, and fairy tales, without knowing their origin. But then, a Young Pioneer camp is also a camp.
"Keep your proud patience..."

Page 15. *extra-wide tussah slacks*
Before the death of Josef Stalin, trousers ran forty to forty-five centimeters in width; even tailoring them to thirty- five centimeters was forbidden. Soon after he died, the tailors' shops began to make trousers as narrow as thirty, but twenty-two would still get you expelled from college.

Page 16. Health
One of the most popular Soviet magazines (founded in 1955), and a specimen of authentic kitsch. Evidence, again, of the "liberalization": it had become *all right*. It had become all right to read about the existence of abortion, onanism, and even—orgasm!

Page 17. *with an Esenin-like purity and doom in his eyes*
In the year being described, Esenin was forbidden, and popular in the prison camps. Only in the sixties did Sergei Esenin's popularity revive officially and for good, catching up with Hemingway's. These were the first two writers to have their portraits sold at the state newsstands. Hemingway's eyes are smiling; he is

made up to look like the popular actor Yefim Kopelian. Esenin is wearing a hat and holding a pipe and a cane (America!). His eyes and lips have an angelic expression.

Page 19. *might be used to reconstruct the atmosphere of a child's perception of the national drama*

The generation of writers to which the author belongs has extracted a great deal of use from its so-called wartime childhood. The explanation is not only that a person's first memories were of dreadful events, but also that this was the last generation to succeed in jumping on the running board of a great historical event; it closed the series. Revolution, civil war, War Communism, the New Economic Policy, collectivization, industrialization, World War II... To these may perhaps be added the "recovery," but even that ended with the Leader's death. The peace, work, and humdrum life of the ensuing years are devoid of the coloration of heroic belonging. The wartime vein has been exhausted by its immediate participants but continues to be exploited, owing to the growth of the field itself. It is harder and harder to find recognizable shoots of the past in the present: the aging heroines of novels and plays provoke disbelief, they're so well preserved and young-looking. It is harder and harder to meet the girl from whom one was parted by the war, and to love her anew. The adulteries of fresh-faced grandmothers enjoy success only among the performers themselves, who prolong the ingenue role right up to the Veterans' Home, because these actors, too, are of the same generation. The death agony of the theme drags on, postponing the hope that someone will finally undertake life's present time.

Page 20. *Moscow Garment and Leningrad Clothing*

The largest of the ready-to-wear clothing enterprises. As Mandelstam has it:

> I am a man of the Moscow Garment epoch—
> Look how I bristle in my suit!
> Look how I walk and talk...

to get Soviet vodka for the Finns and Finnish polyester for the Soviets

Our border with the Finns is open. In one direction. They come to us without a visa, by presenting their passports. We, however, "process" a passport for foreign travel to a capitalist country. On Saturday and Sunday, Leningrad is flooded with drunken Finns arriving by bus and private car. Either the landscape is dear to their eye, being home; or, after seeing it, they feel like getting even drunker; or Leningrad really is a very beautiful city, such as they don't have. There are three versions of why they drink in our country. One is that they have a dry law; another is that vodka is rationed there, and in short supply; the third is that it's simply cheaper here. Finnish consumer goods, accordingly, although Leningrad isn't exactly inundated with them, are encountered more often here than in other cities. Even fifteen years ago, nylon, Orlon, and polyester seemed to us the height of luxury and elegance. In exchange for a vile nylon blouse, a Finn could stay drunk from morning to night. The author has personally been unable to wear out, since then, a suit and a raincoat of Finnish make—they're eternal. The Finns' freedom to travel here is purchased by one punctiliously fulfilled condition: they do not accept our fugitives. There are two or three legends current in Leningrad about tragic fools who somehow contrived not to know this. One of them is almost humane: A man who has sought political asylum is to be turned over to our embassy, and the Finnish policeman is escorting him there, for some reason on foot. In this patriarchal fashion they walk as far as the ferry to the Swedish shore. Here the policeman asks the fugitive to wait while he buys some cigarettes. The policeman goes around the corner, waits ten minutes, fifteen minutes, and looks out—but the man is still there, staring sadly toward Sweden, waiting for him. "Well, let's go," the policeman says with a sigh, half an hour later.

here came the past,... "shagging along"
Literally, "forcing its way through." In the slang of the fifties, this meant "going for a stroll"—preferably on the *Brod*, or Broadway. Just about every city had its Broadway. The vitality of the idiom was reinforced by the Russian meaning of the word *brod*, "a ford": people dragged their feet slowly, not wrenching their double-thick soles from the asphalt, and really did look as though they were pushing through something more viscid than air, as though crossing a ford. The Broadway in Leningrad, naturally, was Nevsky Prospect—not the whole of it, but a well-defined segment along the left side, from Sadovaya Street to Liteynaya. And back. A rich time!

"Vyatkin..."
Boris Vyatkin (born 1913) was a famous Leningrad circus clown of the late forties and early fifties. He had found the right mask for himself, parodying first the young tough, then the hepcat (in acts called "The Wunderkind's Mama" and "Tarzan"). He would come out with almost no makeup, in a foppish suit, accompanied by his partner Manyuni—a little trained dog.

Page 21. *the Soviet Champagne Shop*
On Nevsky Prospect, between Sadovaya and Malaya Sadovaya Streets. The famous "refined" snack shop, where one could have a Brown Bear (cognac and champagne, one hundred grams each). Regrettably, it was closed in 1970, in yet another anti-alcohol campaign.

Page 22. Youth
A literary journal established in 1954 (first editor: Valentin Kataev). A child of the Thaw, it never did get thoroughly warm. The journal was the origin of "confessional" and "youth" prose, which had a sincere, winning simplicity and enjoyed extraordinary popularity.

the creator of a cosmogonic theory... played tennis
Stalin, like Hitler, had his own cosmogony, not so much scientific as totalitarian (Academicians Shmidt and Fesenkov). The tennis player, however, was Academician Oparin, founder of another total theory—on the origin of life.

379

Page 23. *"the brooks will sing, the rook's on the wing..."*

A popular song from the film *My Love* or *The Hearts of the Four*, as performed by Tselikovskaya or Serova (before the war). These films are of interest now only for their striking resemblance to captured Nazi films.

Page 25. *he was. . . an officer of the czar, but... became a Red officer*

A certain Soviet writer (quite a well-known man, who combined in his creative persona the divergent policies of *Novy Mir* and *Oktyabr* magazines) rebuked the author for this switch, as inescapable evidence of my hero's selfishness and venality. The author heard him out, and deigned to disagree. In the first place, "an officer of the czar" wasn't yet a White. In the second place, at that time people weren't yet armed with modern opinions, which are useful knowledge for all who sit in judgment over people meekly lost in History (he could or could not, understood or did not, cracked or did not...) from a position historically safer and more advantageous.

brought from Germany

Not right, of course. But three items of furniture aren't all that much, compared to what the higher ranks brought out.

Page 26. *a Gillette razor*

In my childhood, this safety razor was a unique reminder of a vanished civilization. My father shaves with it to this day. As he does so, he points out just which part of his design Mr. Gillette patented, so that no one has been able to improve on it for half a century, if not longer, while he rakes in the millions. Actually, my childhood was characterized by an absence of imported goods. Everything we once had had was gone before my time. There remained this razor, which my father preserved as one would perhaps preserve a combat weapon. And for my first shave, I used his razor. When I learned that my future father-in-law had also shaved all his life with a Gillette, my fiancée seemed to become even dearer to me. That ritual—unscrewing it, inserting the blade ("the Martian's visiting card," in Mandelstam's definition), then wiping and blowing into the stem—made me a man. But now... My cheek isn't what it used to be, and the ceremony is missing.

the monogram an N *with the crossbar low*

It would appear that the decanter had belonged to Nicholas I (1825-55), but the author isn't quite sure of this. He has encountered this kind of decanter too often in various houses. Although an auction of palace utensils was held for propaganda purposes after the Revolution, so that many items may have gone to the most unexpected owners, still, there couldn't have been so many of them that every house got a fork or a cup or a chair (more often a tablecloth). The author is no expert and has nobody to consult at the moment, but he wouldn't be surprised if these decanters were found in every tavern before the Revolution, and the monogram symbolized the state monopoly, or the emperor's government, or the tercentenary of the House of Romanov, or the fact that it belonged to the court purveyor. In any case, it's hard to believe that the czar had enough identical items to go around. Not only the czar's utensils but also prerevolutionary consumer goods simply survived in such small number that these things acquired individuality. They were transformed from old to ancient—to antiques.

Page 29. chifir *tea*

Tolstoy, in *The Cossacks,* has the Cossacks drinking moonshine called *chikhir.* In our time, *chifir* is an extremely concentrated tea, the most popular prison-camp narcotic. There are an endless number of secrets for preparing it, to the taste of each preparer. The tea is not steeped but boiled, a whole packet per mug. The result is a thick, brown, opaque infusion, with an iridescent rusty film floating on top. So as not to lose their high, people boil up the tea a second and third time; of course those don't compare with the first. They drink it in small gulps, passing it around the circle (a threesome or foursome), studiously smoking after each gulp. The pulse quickens, the pupils dilate, the blood pressure rises. Sleepiness and fatigue disappear—the *chifir*-drinker is beginning to "fly." They fly until morning, talking at first, later isolated and stuporous. *Chifir* is usually drunk at night, in company with the orderly or in the drying room (wherever there's a stove). It's beautiful, this stillness and darkness, with reddish reflections on the faces... There are recipes for a lethal fortified *chifir,* brewed with tobacco, spirits, vodka, cologne. But in practice they are rarely used, because smoking materials and spirits are harder to obtain than tea, and people prefer to have them in pure form.

Page 30. *a tiny stove*

The handcrafted *burzhuika,* or "bourgeois stove," which can be rapidly fired up with any kind of trash or rubbish, to warm oneself and get a teakettle boiling. There are round ones, square ones, of iron or cast iron or baking sheets—the forms vary with the skill of the craftsman and the material he has available. The pipe is vented directly out the window. Both the stove and its name appeared during the fuel (and other) famine of 1918. It was stoked with furniture and books— hence the déclassé flavor of the new word. The surviving *burzhuika*s saved people during the Second World War as well, thus prolonging the life of this dashing word.

Page 32. *the Hotel Europe*

Along with the Astoria, the most fashionable of the old hotels in Leningrad (1874); located on what used to be Mikhailovskaya Street, which in 1940 was renamed Brodsky Street, in honor of the poet's birth, of course. After the shut-down of the Eastern Restaurant, which had been frequented by Leningrad's black marketeers and Bohemians, many of its orphaned habitues switched to the nearby "roof"—the restaurant on the top floor of the hotel. The establishment is note-worthy for its skylight, a glass roof; it has no ordinary windows. By now the "roof," too, is deteriorating, but you can still go there to dine, unless, of course, all the tables have been reserved for foreigners. But if you're a Finn, or have an in with the hostess, you'll get dinner.

Aphrodite, L'Atlantide, The Green Hat

Only to me, against the background of the Gillette razor (see commentary to page 26), could these novels have seemed "modernist." My grandmother, as a contemporary of Loti and Benoit, had read them when she was young and pretty, without waiting for a translation. Michael Arlen, however, is a bit more contemporary; his dates are exactly the same as Uncle Dickens's (1895-1956). Interestingly, he was an Armenian (Dikran Kouyoumdjian). See commentary to page 115.

Page 33. *a medley of Griboedov waltzes*

Alexander Sergeevich Griboedov (1796-1829) finished the university at sixteen, knew a dozen languages, had a professional involvement with diplomacy and poetry, married the Georgian princess Nina Chavchavadze, and was murdered in Turkey; the coffin with his body was encountered by Pushkin on his journey to Arzrum; a novel was written about him, one of the best, *Death and Diplomacy in Persia*. Moreover, he was a wonderful musician, the composer of several waltzes, which have been performed by professionals (the author hasn't heard them but has questioned some musicologists, who commented favorably). His short life and variety of interests prevented him from devoting himself properly to literature. He is author of but one work of genius, the play *Woe from Wit*.

Pages 38-40. *There was much of the naive and touching in these old traitors*

Here and below, the author leaves unspoken his thoughts on the unmasking of secret agents, informers, and anonymous letter-senders, the zeal for showing people in their true colors—a zeal especially powerful after 1956, when Khrushchev was understood to mean that it was now *all right.* These tendencies did not develop very far and brought small result. One not-so-small result, however, was that it became *public* what many of the unchastised had been involved in. The author is judging only from his own knowledge. Here are two destinies that took opposite shapes, despite the shared nature of their deserts. M. M., a colonel if not a general in the security system, was involved in everything one could possibly be involved in. According to legend, he had served in the Leader's bodyguard (he tasted the soup to see whether it was poisoned). A film dramatist, he collaborated on a great number of scripts (one was made into the best detective movie of the post-war years) and went to prison in 1952 when denounced by his coauthor (who had been a special investigator in 1937). He was released ahead of schedule in 1954, but already as a victim. The first thing he did was go see his coauthor—not to punch him in the face, but to propose working together on a new scenario. As the director of an advanced film institute (marvelous courses!), he taught me how to watch a film, and I owe him a great deal. Y. E., a literary critic, was a man with a rich and dark life story. He went to prison immediately after the Revolution. There he wrote a book praised by an illustrious Commissar of Education. Abandoning literature at the start of the New Economic Policy, he set out to be an entrepreneur, got rich, and flew tulips from Holland for his mistresses (a legend). After his death, my acquaintance U. found among his papers (uncommonly meager, many times sorted and weeded by E. himself) a photograph from the thirties: E. with some typical people in the USA (E. himself had never mentioned this). In 1949 he turned up practically at Beria's side, as an advisor on cultural issues. For some wretched little book, accordingly, he received the Stalin Prize—everyone knows what kind of advice such an advisor gives. In 1957 he was expelled from the Writers Union for his denunciations in '49 (the one and only case!). At the staged meeting, his defense proved brief. "How many writers collaborated with you in those years?" he asked the presiding officers, and sat down. He said nothing more. The general silence vindicated him—he was soon reinstated in the union. He is living out his days as a senior research fellow and has not lost interest in literature or life. I am indebted to him for critical support. Evident in the names that he praises is a literary taste not forfeited in his denunciations. He praises people with the same businesslike cynicism that he must once have shown in damning them.

At the institute where he works, there are two other life stories analogous to the ones I have examined: the director and his first deputy. I knew these men considerably less well. Both had heavy reputations. A reputation is a reputation—it lives its own life, independently of its bearer. I like to put a question to people who spread progressive opinions: "But what did he do, this man of whom you say... ?" What I get in reply is a shift to a whisper, eyes rounded with horrible significance, finger to the lips. Never any information. I found the director likable and impressive. His eyes *looked;* in him, the Soviet swagger was softened, a more appurtenant lordliness. A careerist intoxicated with himself, he assumed that he was on his way to a position in line with his qualities, knowledge, and talent. He was a child: he assumed that everyone was inclined to judge him as he himself did. He would make an attempt to move up, and at this point he would get caught on his lack of distance and fail. By the time he went to prison in 1947, he had entrée at the very top. When he got out (a victim), he received the posts and titles he had missed. But again he began to aspire to a ministry, and here again it was discovered that he *didn't belong.* His route to the top was frozen. Did he know what his sins were, did his conscience suffer?... He had a gravely ill wife, and although he was a very personable man, he persistently, touchingly, and nobly spent time with her. He had a secret program: to publish in Russia the forcibly omitted twentieth-century classics, Kafka, Proust, and Joyce. And he accomplished it, he did publish them, furnishing them with the refined, crooked-mirror reflections of his own prefaces. And all of a sudden he died, without ever realizing, ever being disappointed, that the road to the gleaming summit was forbidden him. Precisely for that reason. As I say, he was a child.

Outwardly, his deputy was not so likable. His reputation had been consolidated in the campaigns of '49. No one had a kind word for him. What was my surprise to hear his praises sung by the widow of the writer who, in my view, had suffered most—Zoshchenko. As it turned out... Symmetrically to the director, he had been the chief intercessor (a real and active one, moreover) for the collected works of Zoshchenko, Platonov, and Bulgakov. He had used his "deserved" reputation as a lever: he could not be suspected from above, and he absolutely stone-walled opinion from below, for he knew by experience where the match is applied. But people who can keep their mouths shut when they have pulled something off—who don't need to justify themselves, when they have quite a lot to justify them as well as a lot to justify—have always seemed to me to be something special. I am not objective here, of course. When Mandelstam was finally published, after fifteen years of fruitless editorial effort, he was provided with a predictable introduction by this deputy. Moreover, his introduction was used in place of a splendid one. The whole thing was as flagrant as if written especially for the naked eye of a liberal. Mandelstam, however, had finally been published, even though in a small edition, even though for hard currency. With the good introduction, he would not have been published... Evident here is the logic of one who intercedes for other people's inheritances. He died immediately after his director, but, unlike the latter, without accomplishing his triad; he was confined to the tainted Mandelstam. Providence must have seen that good deeds are done, after all, by not just any pair of hands.

So, here is a quick schematic correlation.

The director and the director. Both were handsome, imposing, swaggering. Both "suffered" in time to become victims of a departing epoch. Both went no further in their careers. Both maintained their menacing reputations as persecutors and oppressors vis-à-vis those to whom, in their own way, they were benefactors. Both loved their institutions.

The deputy and the deputy. Both were ugly (God marks the scoundrel). Both were stained, finally and irrevocably. Both tried to do good deeds, not merely with unwashed hands, but with the same hands and methods. Neither expected more than he had.

All four had signs of life and, in their own way, "largeness of scale." All four were victims of the rehabilitation rather than the Cult. All four were patrons, benefactors: two to the living, two to the dead. All are correlated by the demagoguery of "real" good deeds, i.e., deeds that have been done. This kind of "atonement" was intuitive, I think, the sins unadmitted to consciousness, swiftly masked by good intentions and a quite sober assessment: Who are my judges? Too many people had been involved in nothing (neither evil nor good), because they were nothing to begin with. All four knew the chasms, had peered down, and could easily imagine the seasickness of the "unstained" liberals, should the latter gain even a fraction of their experience. Here, crudely put, is their logic, even their pathos: Excuse me, but what were *they* worth, those who suffered? If they'd only been good writers! They were dreadful, you know. Dreadfully bad. There was no literature. But what there was... Well, who *really* helped to resurrect them, if not we, alone? Who kept afloat the only three who drifted up, more dead than alive? Who held their heads above our squalid contemporary surface (lest they drown in the—yes, if you will, in the shit)? Me, me. Me, me. A single logic, always the same calculation, patriotic (because democracy was weak) and patriotic no longer (because they lacked conscience and humanity).

Page 40. *something in the Stanislavsky method*

Just as our scholars tried unsuccessfully, for decades, to formulate Socialist Realism, yet that was all we had instead of literature—so, too, no one knew the Stanislavsky method, although that was what we had instead of theater. It was fitting for the summit to stand alone, and this summit always loomed above our territory. Therefore, when a prominent soccer coach was asked what method his team intended to play by in a crucial match, he told the interviewer, not without brilliance, "The Stanislavsky method."

Page 41. *he loved to admire the conciseness, the "definitiveness" of "that Swede's" definitions*

The author of the *Defining Dictionary* was a Dane by origin. Uncle Mitya knew this as well as did the contemporary erudites bent on correcting him.

Page 44. *Father, Papa, the Cult... what other synonyms are there?*

See commentary to pages 11, 16, 22, 38-40, 44, 48, 53, 85, 110, 129, 130, 132, 138, 243, 256, 276, 278, 288, 310, 326, 339.

Page 45. *archives*

Far from every curious reader is privy to the special archive rooms in major libraries. You need an *admittance permit*. The permit is granted upon *petition* of the institution at which you work. Or is not granted. There are permits of varying degrees, according to which materials with different *security classifications* may be given out. There are materials for which each person who has had *access* to them is registered in a special book. The niceties here are doubtless of great interest, but the author not only isn't privy, he isn't even an initiate. Everything is allocated. Including information and knowledge and truth. Indeed, we do not have a society of consumption—we have a society of allocation. It was Kornei Chukovsky, I think, who made the apt remark that the rarest of materials is yesterday's newspaper. Why go so far as George Orwell's contrivances in *Nineteen Eighty Four*, where the Ministry of Truth distorts the information of the last year, when we can simply avoid giving out last year's newspaper. Lest anyone accidentally notice what everyone knows: which friend has become an enemy and which enemy a friend.

Page 48. *would applaud them from the boxes*

The late forties and early fifties brought a flock of biographical films about great Russians, squinting affectionately into the radiant future of today—with a shade of sorrow that they wouldn't get to see it, that they hadn't been born in what was truly their own time, ours—and accomplishing their feats all the more zealously for its benefit, to hasten its approach. Pavlov, Moussorgsky, Przhevalsky Glinka, Popov... This was very much apropos of the campaign against "cosmopolitanism," and the assertion of Russian priority in all areas. These men, though belonging to different epochs and professional fields, had a family resemblance, since they were played by the same actor (Borisov or Cherkasov), and had family ties with the people and with each other... Here are Pushkin and Gogol in a carriage, observing construction work. The people are singing their sledge-hammer song. "Beautiful are the Russian people at labor!" exclaims Pushkin. "But down-trodden, hounded into ignorance and poverty," echoes Gogol, with tears visible to the world, through invisible laughter. "Mikhail!" they both exclaim, having just then caught sight of the great Glinka, who is drinking in the people's melodies, pressing close to the wellspring. "I've been looking for you!" says Glinka. "Today is the premiere of *Ruslan and Ludmilla*." And here is Glinka, conducting. Sitting in a box, suppressing their delight with difficulty, are Pushkin and Gogol, joined by Griboedov, who hasn't been given any lines: he just sits and nods, in his spectacles: "Woe to wit," he is saying... Their life stories, too, were kindred. Here are the obligatory features: (1) They seek advice from the simple folk: a wise, lucid old man tells them a fairy tale, sings an ancient song, and gives them sensible engineering advice. (2) Recognition by the West: Glinka is not tempted by a career as a great Italian composer, and Liszt performs "Chernomor's March" with admiration; Pavlov, huddling by his tiny stove, is offered an institute in California; Marconi tries to slip a million to Popov, and the latter throws him out, delivering an angry speech to the students clustered around him; an English colonel suggests that Przhevalsky discover India. "No!" says Przhevalsky. "China is our brother. It has a great future!" And he pats the head of a bright little Chinese boy who has already understood the compass—the Chinese, too, were the first to discover some things—and the seismograph. (3) An agonizing creative process, in conflict with a Grand Prince or Princess. Usually, at this moment, the creditors are carrying out the piano, the dog with the fistula, or the invented-first apparatus that is giving its first signs of life. (4) A procession down a long strip of carpet. Gray mane, cohort of faithful disciples who never did attain independence. Loud cheers swelling to an ovation. The Grand Prince turns away, and the students come thronging from the gallery, applauding.

There was a man named M. who served with me in the army, a tough-guy and self-styled crook whose ears stuck out in a remarkable way. He was acknowledged to be the comedian of our barracks. He had two top acts: reciting the early Mayakovsky ("I walked into the barber shop and said calmly, 'Be so kind as to scratch my ears'"), and the old revolutionary Stasov in the role of Cherkasov (in a thunderously magnificent nasal voice: "I'm ashamed of you!"). When I recall these films now, inevitably I see them as performed by M., who transported them to the authentic scene of the action.

Page 53. *the image of Thirst*

In 1965 or 1966, I dropped by the Central Literary Club just at opening. Not a soul was there, and as I drank my coffee a man appeared who riveted my attention. His chest was naked under his suit jacket, his feet bare in his shoes; he was lanky and uncommonly shaggy. The waitress, however, received him courteously as someone who belonged. She gave him a large glass of something red—perhaps punch, perhaps wine, perhaps compote. He clambered onto a stool right by the counter, took the glass in both hands, and pressed his lips to it... just as described in the novel.

386

Yuri Dombrovsky's novel *Keeper of Antiquities* came out in 1965. I read it some time after that, about three years later, and became a rapturous admirer. In 1970 I wrote a definitive version of my "Grandfather." In 1973 I took up residence in the Golitsyno "rest home," and there I made the acquaintance of another of its regular inhabitants—Dombrovsky. Whereupon, in addition to the honor of becoming a drinking companion of my favorite writer, I was happily astonished: he was the man from whom I had painted my first portrait of Grandfather. The fact that Dombrovsky was a great man, that his life story included the same ordeals (from 1932 to 1956), that I had had no notion Grandfather was he—all this flattered me.

It is impossible, in our age, not to have had experience of prison camp. If you didn't do time, you had tangencies and intersections: you were close to it yourself, or, instead of you, your near and distant relatives or your future friends and acquaintances dragged out their sentences. The prison-camp way of life has been absorbed everywhere: in the army and the collective farms, at train stations and bathhouses, in schools and Young Pioneer camps, at colleges and in student construction brigades. It is so distinctive that you could fail to recognize it on sight only if you hadn't been in a real camp.

Many of my friends had gone to prison, for short or long terms, three to fifteen years, but "Grandfather" was not among them. (They were nearly of my generation, eight or ten years older.) I fabricated my Grandfather from very slight real premises.

What prompted me to "invent" him was the beginning of the revival of the reputation of literary theorist Mikhail Bakhtin, the first bits of information about him: that Bakhtin had suffered not in 1937 but in 1928; that he had been saved, in his own way; that he had lost a leg; that when money unexpectedly turned up (from the reissue of a book) he hid it in a samovar; that he was afraid to move away from his place of exile in Saransk... Then that image of the thirsty man... And one more fate, known to almost no one even now, though I learned of it in the summer of 1964, soon after the death of its possessor. I relay it as told to me by someone else.

Igor Afanasievich Stin, a count who underwent repression but not rehabilitation, passed away at the age of (approximately) seventy in the village of Syr-Yaga in the Komi ASSR, where he had been a geologist in a prospecting party. My good friend Natasha S. had worked with him. I met her soon after the funeral. Shaken by his death, she could talk about nothing but Stin. She had brought with her a small inheritance: a little amateur photo and a four-reel tape-recording of Stin's novellae, as read by the author. Gazing from the photograph was a gray-haired man, youthfully trim, with a handsome, aristocratic face. He had read his stories at table, and between the novellae one could hear a drunken, half-laudatory roar, as between songs. I listened to the tape just once. Even though the novellae, for my taste, sounded somewhat oversignificant and emotional (possibly because of an inebriated performance—but the voice was pleasant, hoarsely youthful and low), they were of good literary standard. Two or three were absolutely superb and

387

made a strong impression on me. Their material could be divided into two types, prison-camp and "gentry" (recollections of an estate childhood). Prose does not tolerate paraphrase; a miniature, especially, needs to be transmitted word for word. But I am deprived of any possibility of resurrecting the text (Natasha S. has also died), and I am forced... Here is a prison-camp miniature. All week an old convict prepares for a visit from his wife—shaving, bathing, mending, doing laundry—he's as excited as a young man. His comrades empathize with him, but, as later becomes clear, they are looking forward to a good show (the visit is not the first). Finally the day comes. The old man can't stay still. He keeps climbing a post to watch for the old woman. The whole camp (it's Sunday) waits tensely. And here she comes at last, bursting out from behind the hill. Even before, it seems, they had been able to hear her cursing. The old man begins to echo her. They come toward each other as in a duel, making the phrases of their mother-oaths longer and longer, more and more ornate, until, as they draw even, they achieve nightingale virtuosity. The old woman has a heavy basket of eatables, the pies still warm; both her face and his are streaming with tears; their four-letter words flow ever more furiously. An audience of the most expert connoisseurs listens ecstatically. The narrative I have paraphrased is concealed within minimal dimensions; the entire text is a word-for-word recreation of their "duel." Listening to the novella, you will inevitably weep the tears of the old people. (A similar plot, it is true, is encountered in Zoshchenko.) And here is an "estate" story... The elder Stin was severe and extremely cold with his son. Little Igor feared him and, at the same time, yearned childishly for his love (he may have grown up without a mother, I don't remember). One day when his father was gone, the boy ("I" in the novella) stole into the library, which was very strictly forbidden him. Taking down the first book he saw—it was volume P of the encyclopedia—he started to look at it and became fascinated. He did not notice his father come up behind him. The boy was just studying a double-page spread with beautiful bright drawings of the different parrots. There was one in particular he liked, large and improbably variegated. "Well, which do you like best?" the boy heard over his shoulder. He took fright: never before had his father asked him any kind of question, especially so good-naturedly, not punishing him for willfulness. Suddenly he felt that his whole future relationship with his father would depend on his answer. From this moment on, perhaps—"But he's a man," the boy thought, "he can't like the same one I do, just a little boy? I have to guess..." But there were so many parrots! He had them all mixed up in his poor head from trying. "Well?" the father said, more severely now. "This one," the boy said, ready to burst into tears. He pointed to the first parrot he saw, an unprepossessing little gray one. "Strange," the father snorted. "I like this one." And he pointed to the same one, large and variegated, that the little boy had admired. Turning abruptly, he walked out of the library. Never again, it seems, did the boy have such an opportunity to be friends with his father. (In some ways the story recalls Bunin's "The Crow," but Stin could not have known of it, since it belongs to the émigré period of that writer's work.)

These three impressions were the basis for Modest Odoevtsev, made it possible to "invent" him. The author later became acquainted with several similar people and their destinies—with Dombrovsky, for example, as well as O. V. Volkov and C. Amiredzhibi—and read a great deal of prison-camp literature that he hadn't read before. Now there is much he might add in the way of specifics, but he could hardly *write* it.

Page 56. *a good man, Koptelov: he twice* didn't kill *me*
A college friend of mine, from a long line of workingmen, once gave this favorable characterization of his neighbor: "A good man. Twice he almost got me a job." This was said sincerely, with reason. When the good is measured thus, Koptelov's service is immeasurably greater.

dim and invisible as a Japanese ninja
At one time, Soviet popular-science magazines had many articles (reprinted from foreign publications) about this fantastic medieval sect of "invisible beings"—spies and hired killers. Their art was unsurpassed: they could escape from fetters by disjointing themselves, disappear from closed rooms, eavesdrop at an impossible distance by means of flexible tubes of some sort, and dissolve in the air to conceal themselves from pursuit. They wore special shapeless, inconspicuous clothes, making it easy to blend into shadow or twilight. The reality of the existence of invisible beings made a great impression on the immature consciousness of the author (and the popular magazine editors themselves, apparently).

Page 70. *In 1980, you'll read* Ulysses
I don't know that this assertion can be made with the same confidence now, in 1971, fifteen years after Modest Platonovich's prophecies. People are saying that perhaps— and even soon—we will see *Portrait of the Artist as a Young Man*. But people are saying all kinds of things! They even say that the Olympics are certain to be held in Moscow, not this time or next, but time after next. That is, in exactly 1980.

Page 83. *On the dark and empty street, the driver walloped Lyova*
See commentary to page 32, on *Aphrodite, L'Atlantide*.

Page 85. *Syr-Yaga (also known as Voy-Vozh and Knyazh-Pogost)*
Villages in the Komi ASSR (see also commentary to page 53, on Igor Stin). Their names became known chiefly because, in the years of repression, they were the sites of gigantic camps. The author had occasion to make a singular "tour," the derisive meaning of which came through to him much later. At the time, he was merely serving in the Soviet Army, in the military construction detachments. As a four-eyes with no useful specialty, and moreover with some higher education, which embarrassed his superiors (a man with even a secondary education was rarely encountered in the army then), the author was transferred every month or so from one detachment to another, grouped with men similarly unfit, criminal, immature, or sick. Thus I traveled through many former places in Karelia, the

Arkhangelsk Region, and Komi, although I still did not clearly understand to what I was indebted for their abandonment. Our job was logging. We lived in barracks in a compound, with discharged sentries (one time even with some who had not been discharged—under "screws," behind barbed wire: a disciplinary battalion hospitably received our newly organized detachment onto its territory). And we wore prison-camp cottons (the greenish uniform without shoulder straps was introduced only in 1958). True, we did vote in elections for the Soviets. Only many years later did I guess which of History's brackets I had been confined in: 1957-58. The rehabilitation process was coming to an end. Scores of camps had been freed. Someone, however, had to carry on the suddenly interrupted work. The reduction of the armed forces was, in part, an attempt to plug this gap, the point being that the construction detachments didn't count as armed forces. Soldiers divested of shoulder straps were dropped like landing parties onto the territory of the former prison camps. Although none of the soldiers acknowledged himself to be a convict, the uniform offended many (it was hastily changed). But as they breathed the camp air it subconsciously entered their souls. Drunkenness, sabotage, degenerate criminality, gambled uniforms, *chifir*, and tattoos—all of it flourished in luxuriant bloom. Even the threat of a tribunal didn't help much (the circuit court labored without cease during its two-month session).

After finishing this "tour," this light parody of a prison camp, I subsequently read books about the camps not only with a sense of recognition but also with direct recognition.

Pushkin the locksmith

Many have noted the paradoxical genetic poetry in Russian surnames. For example, the prosecutor Kaznin ("Executioner"), the world saber champion Krovopuskov ("Bloodletter"), the ballerina Semenyaka ("Mincing Step"), the wrestler Medved ("Bear"), and so on. The Komsomol ideology instructors whom I encountered in my writing youth, Churbanov, Tupikin, and Pleshkina ("Blockhead," "Dimwit," and "Baldy"), sat in almost the same room and were rather intelligent people, in their own way.

Page 91. *phenomena... which are merely individual now but for which a future has been ordained (Rakhmetov)*

Nikolai Rakhmetov is one of the heroes of Chernyshevsky's novel *What Is to Be Done?*, a revolutionary, the "man of the future." When we studied the novel in school, he was the one who made the greatest impression on the children. In the first place, because he cultivated in himself the "will power" that everyone wanted to have. In the second place, because Chernyshevsky's dreamy imagination had endowed him with incredible physical strength (like Bazarov, he tossed someone into a pond; moreover, he bent five-kopeck pieces and wrestled a bull by the horns). In the third place—something none of us, even the most strong-willed, was capable of (we didn't yet know much about fakirs and yogis, since yoga was a "reactionary, bourgeois religious doctrine")—he slept on nails. It was Rakhmetov who provided the literary critics with grounds for explaining *What Is To Be Done?* as the first work of Socialist Realism in its formulation of the problem of the typical, the problem that had always been the cornerstone of realism (as criticism). Debates on the nature of the typical went exactly like the ones in our novel.

Page 93. *with the whole essence of his plebeianism*

To dispel conclusively any possible suspicion of aristocratic descent, the author takes the opportunity to declare that by his social origin he is a petit bourgeois. His origin is like that of Michel Sinyagin, in Zoshchenko's story of the same name: "He was the son of a noblewoman and a respectable citizen." The author, although he shrinks at the thought, can easily imagine a review or a satirical piece devoted to this novel: "The Michel Sinyagin of Our Day." (Variants: "of the Seventies," "of the Five-Year-Plan for Quality," and the like.)

Page 99. *somewhere in Khakassia, it seems*

The author spent some time in Khakassia in 1964. At a local history museum in Abakan he encountered an archaeology enthusiast, obviously an ex-convict. The strong old man took from the watch pocket of his riding breeches a small black fertility idol, which had given him, at his time of life, a daughter. This remarkable old man was the inspiration for a grandfather of another type (a variant).

Page 103. *the very scene that had to be cut*

There is a curious episode in the Soviet film version of *Othello* (1956). After he strangles Desdemona, Bondarchuk comes out on the seashore. He sits there on a rock, and we see him in a very long shot as he gazes out to sea and weeps. There is enough footage for him to play the entire powerful, fuzzy gamut of feelings prescribed for a great actor. The tears trace two little paths in his makeup, while in the clear Mediterranean sky of Yalta, right where he is gazing with such expressiveness, an airplane flies along, tracing its white thread. The old Moor's surprise knows no bounds.

Page 110. *that he had to take the Komsomol swimming test*

A set of sports norms was introduced by the High Council on Physical Education in 1931. Old people as well as children were expected to pass the tests with enthusiasm, under the motto of a mass movement—"Prepare for Labor and Defense." Passing these norms was compulsory for students at all levels. In many respects this has degenerated into a formality. But if it's not strictly compulsory to fulfill the norms, it's essential that the student pay a respectful *visit*. Otherwise the instructor may not pass him in the test, and this threatens all his studies, regardless of his success in the basic disciplines. In practice, however—not without red tape and humiliation—everyone gets out of the situation. Somehow these norms are passed, somehow everyone meets the standards (in swimming, for example, for those who can't swim). The students fulfill the norms, and their teachers the plan.

Page 113. *a universal quality-control stamp has become visible in DNA*

The quality-control stamp was introduced in 1967. A small pentagon with the inscription "USSR," it is placed on products that have attained world standards in quality. One of the first products to be marked with it was vodka. After public criticism in the press, however, it was decided not to place a high mark on pernicious products—alcoholic beverages and cigarettes. Some enterprises, when required to place a quality mark on something, find themselves at an impasse, and it then appears on very unexpected articles. One would not be surprised to discover it on toilet paper, say, or on large denominations of money.

Page 115. *"On that still and moonlit night, de Saint-Avis killed Morange..."*

See, for comparison, page 83: "On the dark and empty street, the driver walloped Lyova..."

The phrases share a common construction and music. The only writer who had a direct influence on the author was Pierre Benoit (1886-1962). The author denies other, indirect influences. He is exceptionally scrupulous and obtusely honest on this issue: he confesses to everything he can. For more detail on the question of influences, see commentary to pages 178, 345.

Page 129. *for conferring on Pechorin the rank of Hero of Our Time*

The title Hero of the Soviet Union was introduced by resolution of the All-Russian Central Executive Committee in 1934. It is presented along with the Motherland's highest award, the Order of Lenin, and the Gold Star. Literally, it is appropriated: "Appropriate to so-and-so the title..." The destruction of the sense of property apparently led to a change in grammar: it became possible to "appropriate" something to someone else, though not to oneself. An underworld song has the lines:

> Give him a hero's star? But why?
> He's done no heroic thing...

At first the title was swathed in a thick romantic halo. There were few heroes as yet, and the title wasn't easy to earn. After the war, after Stalin's death, it began to be given out much more generously. People were annoyed by this devaluation; they particularly criticized the awarding of the title to the Egyptian leader Nasser. The major factor in their criticism, however, was not the cheapening of the title but the conviction, prevalent among the people, that we were feeding everyone. We ourselves would soon have nothing to eat or to live on, and then they would give us... Popular wisdom in foreign policy.

Page 130. *When we encounter in a newspaper the headline "A Time to Live!" we may confidently say that the author of the item alluded to Remarque, not the Old Testament*

Stalin's death made the first little hole in the curtain. A trickle started to come through, and we all felt as if it were a flood. We watched the first French, Italian, and Polish films, we read the first American, German, and Icelandic books. It didn't matter if these books had been written and published twenty, thirty years ago—they were perceived now. Remarque's *Three Comrades* was a phenomenon of 1956, not 1930. The "Lost" Generation—which had expressed itself in a burst of novels in 1929—that was us (as if there had been no break between the world wars). Just as we were all taught the same literature in school, so we all continued, after we left, to "cover" the same books, simultaneously reading Remarque, Feucht-wanger, Hemingway. "Have you read...? Have you read...?" was the basic mode of getting acquainted and becoming intimate (it wasn't difficult to discover shared tastes). There is an anecdote about some policemen considering what to give their friend for his birthday. "A razor?" "He already has a razor." "A watch?" "He already has a watch." "A camera?" And so on—he already has everything. They see a sign: "The best gift is a book!" "Let's give him a book!" the first one says joyfully. "He already has a book," the second answers in despair... Well, this anecdote yields another meaning, not the policeman's: the "book" means Kafka, Remarque, Hemingway, Pasternak—the book people are chasing after, the one they can't get. "He already has the book" means that he's gotten the latest shortage item (the only copy for everyone). When life's movement becomes visible in History, all the people overtaken by it seem to become one generation (the War Generation, the Khrushchev). They all read one book and are excited by it. But at least they read! When History stands still again, without ever having become a flood, people wearily sort themselves out into tastes and generations and no longer read any-thing, fixing themselves up comfortably in the niche of the layover. Bread hunger gives way to book hunger: to get a book so that one "already has it." The tastes enthusiastically developed by the intellectuals of the departed epoch seep down as merchandise; even our immobile market has adapted to issuing fashionable crusts, "quality" titles, the deadest unreadable books—foreign ones, classics, mon-uments—by now it's all furniture, not spirit. No flood came to us through the lit-tle hole, no one is peering at us through it—it's we who came flooding and got stuck, it's we who are peering at the stage from the auditorium, through the little hole feebly poked by the actors.

Page 131. *We recently saw the film*
See commentary to page 207.

"*Christ, Mohammed, Napoleon*"
Satin's words from the play *The Lower Depths*. Lyova was studying it in school just at the time the following chapter begins.

Page 132. *On March 5, 1953, you-know-who died*
Stalin. Some have disputed this date; it is the official one. But everyone cared far more about having him die officially than factually. Thirty years are no joke! I was born, there was a war, I went to school, I fell in love—all under his rule... But how many people died under his rule! And will never learn that he, too, has died. Yet we know much more about him now than we did then. What did we know,

the children of his school? That he didn't sleep at night, he worked: his window was alight. That he read five hundred pages a day—a great reader!—and here we hadn't gotten through our lesson, three short pages. That Lenin had made (although few) some mistakes (what kind, no one knew), but he had never made a mistake. That he had played a part in the creation of the ZIS-110 luxury sedan, but out of modesty hadn't mentioned his name (the car had received the Stalin Prize—he couldn't have awarded it to himself!). There were also questions never answered (or allowed): Had he been at the front? Did he know foreign languages? Of course he had, but secretly; of course he did, but he didn't like to speak them, just read them (again, those five hundred pages). But he no longer got his hair cut, had his picture taken, gave speeches. When they saw him at last in 1952 in a newsreel (at the Nineteenth Congress), they pitied him: a little old man... A schoolmate of mine, a gentle-faced boy who was active in the ballet club and did pirouettes at recess, told me in a hot, confiding whisper, "Mayakovsky's an enemy." (We were studying the poem "Vladimir Ilyich Lenin.") "No!" I said in fright. "Why, sure: 'Enough of lying around on a bug-infested featherbed, Comrade Secretary! Take that, and that! We request that you immediately register the entire factory in the Communist Party!'" "Well, what of it?" I said blankly. "And *who*," said the vigilant child, sotto voce, "was the Secretary then?"

Page 138. *"of yellow metal," as a detective would put it*
The exactitude of the interrogation report. After all, not having sent the ring for expert analysis, the investigator cannot state with legal certainty which it is, gold or brass. In launching a case, he absolutely must not begin with an investigative error. "Taken from the arrestee [because it hasn't yet been verified that I am Andrei G. Bitov; for the time being, this is just my say-so] were the following: Trousers belt, one. Eyeglasses. Watch, round, of yellow metal ['And if I say later it was gold?' 'Don't give me that, smart aleck!']... of yellow metal. Cash, 006 kopecks. Sign your name! No, not that you don't agree to it! That these were taken from you!"

the Short Course
The *Short Course in the History of the Communist Party (Bolshevik)* was compulsory for all students, along with the book *Stalin: A Short Biography*. People said, with complete conviction (had this been a mistake, it would have been forgivable), that Stalin himself had written them. Why hadn't he signed them? Again, out of modesty. There's no author on the cover, is there? He can't have written his own biography, can he? Well, in any case, he edited it. The cover really did look strange: first *STALIN*, in large letters, as the title of the book, and a bit smaller, as the subtitle, *A Short Biography*. Why couldn't this mean that Stalin was the author, and below him was the title of the book?

Page 146. *They continued to "see each other"*
After the disappearance of the forms for addressing each other, all persons under fifty became "young women" and "young men." As the form of address had

disappeared, so had any intelligible designation for relationships outside of marriage: "to be friends," "to see each other"...

"They used to be friends, but then they began to see each other," a young woman told me, about her girlfriend. I asked her to explain the difference for me. "You understand," the young woman said, blushing.

Page 152. *his glance fell on a trunk*

Where the author may have been hiding. See page 56, and the commentary to *dim and invisible as a Japanese ninja*.

Page 161. *(The footnote)*

The reform of 1961 multiplied the value of money by ten. "Mark my words," the skeptics said, "the bunch of herbs that used to cost ten kopecks will still cost ten kopecks." (Now it's fifteen or twenty.) People all continued to think in the old money while settling accounts in the new. They got mixed up. My mother-in-law made mistakes constantly, multiplying not by ten but by a hundred. "I got cheated again. They took a ruble instead of ten kopecks, but that's ten rubles in new money"—that kind of mistake. The only man I know of who got rich on this reform was my college classmate Z., a poor and very refined young man. He had been amassing copper kopecks (after the war there was a long and persistent rumor that one could get a record-player for forty rubles in kopecks, except that no one had a clear idea where... it's a good thing there's no prison term for holding on to change—apparently they did used to have such a law). By the time of the reform he had accumulated four sacks full, which increased tenfold in value overnight (kopecks were not turned in). Z. is in Canada now.

It appears that the author made the same mistake (multiplying by a hundred) but wasn't up to recalculating.

Page 178. *Rostov (-on-the-Don)*

There is also another Rostov (-Veliki), an ancient Russian town. For some reason, everyone knows that there are two Rostovs, although hardly anyone has occasion to go to Rostov-Veliki. At any rate, in a long-drawn-out game of Cities, when all funds of knowledge are exhausted but the winner still hasn't been established, as a rule, a situation comes up at the letter R: "Rostov!" "It's already been used." "I mean the other Rostov..."

Pages 193-195. *(Mitishatyev's whole conversation about Jews)*

On the substance of this conversation the author can testify as follows: there has been, without doubt, such a conversation. I even suspect it's not too original.

In the winter of 1964, on New Year's Eve of 1965, the author was in Moscow and read chapters from his novel—this chapter in particular—at the home of friends. Everyone liked it. In the audience was the Jewish poet Ovsei Driz, who also liked it. A handsome man he was! Gray-haired, gap-toothed, young... He and I were friends from that day on and met quite often. Now, one time several years later, he leaned toward me confidingly (we were drinking) and said "Do as I ask!" "Anything for you, Ovsei!" "Delete it!" "Delete what?" I said, taken aback. "Why, that conversation." "Which conversation?" I couldn't guess, couldn't remember. "Why, the one you read." "When?" "That time. You remember—" "Oh, that one. But why? After all—" "You promised me." "When?" "Just now." "But why should I delete what I wrote!" I said indignantly. "After all, I didn't mean it like that... I meant just the opposite." "All the same—delete it!" he repeated, adamant. "But I—" "Have I ever asked you for anything? Have I ever said anything amiss? Delete it." "But I—" "I love you and trust you," he said, "and I don't ask this for myself, but for you." We had a long argument, and I felt offended. He was implacable; I promised to think about it, upsetting him by my intractability. We never saw each other again, for he soon died. This had been his will, which I did not carry out. He had told me then, "You must understand! This is such blood! Such blood!" He said it in such a wonderfully beautiful, lisping, gap-toothed way. "You shouldn't touch it... no one should. It's so terrible!" he added. "You can't imagine. It's better you shouldn't know." I said I knew about the pogroms, Majdanek, and so forth. He brushed me aside; that wasn't what he meant. "It's so-o terrible," he repeated in a sing-song voice. Something came close to me—unfathomable, unknown, black as night—I was frightened. I shuddered and burst out laughing. I didn't know what he was talking about. "Maybe it will work out, but maybe not," he said, as if betraying a secret, as if taking a risk (in the face of death, as it turned out), and nevertheless did not finish. "It's such fathomless blood... an abyss... And you don't exist. You can never explain anything, never correct anything..." I didn't fully understand him; I suppressed a vague, unenlightened conjecture. But I believed him. "I'll think about it," I said, upsetting him by my evasiveness.

The conversation (as it is written) no longer pleases me. I may yet...

Page 199. *"Christ-Mohammed-Napoleon"*
It should not be forgotten that Mitishatyev was a schoolmate of Lyova's (see commentary to page 131).

Page 203. *the hand with Pisarev*
Maybe it wasn't Pisarev either...

Page 207. *a showing of a rare film... perhaps a Hitchcock or a Fellini*
A liberal twig, a Khrushchevian offshoot. No one immediately noticed the advanced form of undemocracy in the new liberal concept of the "viewing." One had to *get into* a viewing. To do so one had to exert effort and even passion. The primordial need to be a part of contemporary culture swiftly degenerated into the pure quest for prestige: I saw that, I was there... Right there—at the earliest of the viewings—jeans, suede jackets, and sheepskin coats appeared on people: as though these things had just grown by themselves. Their owners' faces began to develop a peculiar expression of suppressed pride, understood from within as free-dom and naturalness. The question "Where did you get what you have on?" would never have been answered. It would have been unethical, shocking. One's efforts to get into a viewing, obtain jeans, and so forth were removed beyond the brackets of the subconscious: the humiliation was defrayed, with interest, by the

returns from prestige. The viewing hall, in this sense, was not so much the focus and breeding ground of taste, not so much the first harbinger of an imminent expansion of outlook, as the laboratory of the "shortage item"—a concept which by today has completely swallowed up all former liberal aspirations. These people, the first to force their way into a viewing, were the ones who began writing books about directors and films never shown to the people, defending dissertations about never-translated philosophers, and so on. They formed a circle and closed it, deliberately not admitting others to their own opportunities. Trend became privilege, which suited both them and "them." Tightening the screws was to everyone's advantage. No wonder the book has lost its reader now, and the theater its spectator. The book belongs to him who can obtain it; in the theater sit the people who knew how to get in. The chasm naturally dividing the artist from the people has become final. It has formed in an almost natural and, most importantly, a bloodless way. Oh, how bloodless! Admittance permits, passes, and bans could be dispensed with now; nothing will get to anyone, no one will get in anywhere. But this aptly developed relationship must be watched over, so that the shadow of the ban—the image of repression—will never disappear, so that the ideological storm cloud will always hover on the horizon. Otherwise the hall will empty out and be filled by new people, the book will fall into the hands of a reader. Ah, how neatly this has taken shape! Of its own accord. And "they" didn't do it—you did, you! I did.

Page 211. *FAL, LFM, Lyova thought mindlessly*
In Russian naval slang, *fal* means "the end."

Page 218. *Why is it you never see curly-haired people nowadays?*
Curly-haired people are on the decline... My father's hair was never curly, but my mother says it suddenly frizzed up on their honeymoon. In order to determine whether one's hair curls naturally or has been permanent-waved, forensic experts use a simple device—they toss a hair in water. If natural, it straightens out; if artificially curled, it does not. Although this is conjecture on the author's part, it may be that the happy people, rather than the curly-haired, have become fewer.

Pages 221-242. *APPENDIX TO THE SECOND PART*
The chapter "The Hero's Profession" requires too many notes of a specialized nature. A portion of them are available with the chapter as published in *Voprosy literatury*, No. 7, 1976, to which the author refers his unknown reader.

Page 222. *the numerous Proust scholars in the West*
A conversation with L. Y. Ginzburg led the author to these thoughts on the comparison between Lev Tolstoy and Proust.

Page 225. *but he found a third, and the three of them willingly "chipped in"*
The expression "find a third to chip in" originated right after Khrushchev increased the price of vodka. The same song (see commentary to page 129) continues with the lines:

He made the price of vodka high—
It now takes three to buy a drink.

It used to take two. Each would chip in a ruble, scraping the kopecks together somehow. Kopecks don't suffice any more, and the practice today is for three people to chip in a ruble apiece. Although the same bottle that formerly did for two people now does for three, this has not made them drink less, because they've begun to chip in twice. The custom gained international fame thanks to the story "How I Was Hemingway," which describes in detail the Moscow experience of a classic American author (perhaps Steinbeck, perhaps Caldwell).

When this chapter was published in *Voprosy literatury*, the expression was felt to be disrespectful as applied to classical authors. The phrase "chipped in" was replaced with "came together."

Page 243. *THE HUMBLE HORSEMAN*

The author is not prepared to defend this pun, but will take the opportunity to report a cursory observation. The early thirties saw the last prewar edition of Dostoevsky. Other years he wasn't published at all, as an extreme reactionary and bourgeois who had misunderstood, defamed, and so forth. At last in 1954—again, after that death (how many things did it release? The whole country was released by that death, which it had labored over, like a birth, for thirty years)—the first book to come out after the interruption was *Humble Folk* (or *Poor Folk*), with which Dostoevsky had begun his career. In 1955 came *The Insulted and the Injured*. Succeeding volumes appeared in chronological order, as if Dostoevsky were writing them anew. Finally, by 1956, an opportunity suddenly opened up to issue a collection, which even included *The Devils*. The Academy edition begun in commemoration of the author's sesquicentennial rather quickly retraced the ground already covered, and again stopped dead over *The Diary of a Writer*, as over an abyss.

The author is not a bibliophile, but his mismatched library contains a priceless copy of the 1954 *Humble Folk*, with an inscription on the flyleaf:

"To Tanya P—, the champion jumper, grenade-thrower, and runner in all three camp sessions.

Camp Commandant:
Senior Pioneer Leader:
Cultural Workers Union, Pioneer Camp No. 17.

Page 246. *as the poet said of me*
A quatrain by Gleb Gorbovsky.
In the fall of 1968 I signed an agreement with a publisher for this novel. (True, the agreement omitted the epithet Pushkin as unprintable, and all that remained

398

was House.) This meant an advance of 1125 rubles. I arrived home terribly happy. Literally a moment after, Gleb appeared, in a gloomy and exacting mood (at that time he still drank). He would read me a poem, and I should run get a bottle. To my surprise, and delight, this was the quatrain he began with. Although the poem was imbued with a fervid antiprose spirit and concealed an attack, I was stunned by the coincidence, which bordered on the prophetic. A novel! And precisely a *House*. I grilled him: this was the first he had heard of my *House*. We drank. The next day, dropping by to see the publisher (when would the money...), I learned that Gorbovsky had visited the publishing house yesterday, literally a moment after me. He had seen the agreement and inquired whether I was there; on learning that I had just left, he had followed me. The fervidity of the poem came from the fact that if he were not a poet, and wrote novels, he would have a lot of money.

Page 254. *in order to pass the Komsomol fitness test*
See commentary to page 110.

Page 256. *"He's a..." And he rapped expressively on the banister*
Before, when it really was a matter of life and death, people had an unerring instinct for stoolies. You smelled them out and gave them a wide berth. If there was no way to avoid them, you withdrew into yourself. You developed tremendous powers of intuition: what you could say to whom, and when. A person would switch at that very instant, without noticing, and almost without experiencing discomfort. No studies have been done in this area; the dynamic correlation of the tongue has not been described as a phenomenon. In many respects, although it worked with the infallibility of instinct, this reflex atrophied as soon as the immediate threat to life faded. A denunciation now threatens, perhaps, one's career: it may be that a person doesn't go abroad, or is halted on the career ladder, or, in an extreme case, slips down it to a lower rung. At the level of mercantilism, however, the instinct does not work, the accurately divined knowledge is lacking—and imagination cannot replace them. Nowadays it's almost a promotion to suspect that someone is stooling on you; you can boast about it in a loud whisper. At every step you imply the presence of a stoolie: cover the telephone with a pillow, turn on sophisticated music. Your neighbor's success is suspect. Why did they let him out of the country, publish him, give him an exhibit? There's no reason, really. Each person, in proportion to his education and habit of logical thought, has begun to think for the regime, forgetting that it doesn't think—it exists. Either you have no one to suspect, or everyone. If they need to, they'll arrest you. On the way, you'll remember that you forgot to take the pencil out of the telephone dial.

Pages 257-259. *"why is that word so pleasant to pronounce? Pr-i-nce..." (and so forth)*
Mitishatyev catches the essential point crudely, but accurately. In our country a title brings respect, mainly a kind of childish respect learned from reading Dumas. Without prompting, little girls play at princesses and queens: an innate royalism. All this yearning childhood has unexpectedly emerged in the movie the-

ater. With feeling and taste, in a flood of notorious films, actors have begun to play negative characters: Whites, noblemen, officers, princes. The commissars have begun to look increasingly flat and tame. In Central Asian movies, the Basmach counter-revolutionaries are so flagrantly colorful that the spate of anniversary "Easterns" has been aptly dubbed the "Basmach Film."

Page 267. Oktyabr *and* Novy Mir

The sharpness of the contrast between them was the chief cultural victory of the so-called liberal epoch. If the names of the magazines were synonyms at their founding, in progressive minds they had now become antonyms. *Oktyabr* (*October*) was the repudiated past; *Novy Mir* (*New World*) was the future, indistinct but "for the better." The fact we had both signified time. That it was flowing. That it existed. The dialectical difference had finally triumphed and borne fruit—a new double-headed eagle. The brighter burned the difference between the journals, the more they came to need each other; in some sense, neither conscious nor cynical, they began to work together as a pair. In the witty expression of a certain biologist, however, "there is no symbiosis—they are mutual parasites." Difference was supplanted by discord. Practically, it is not known who died first, but then the second died too. Yes, *Novy Mir* was destroyed first, but the triumph of *Oktyabr* proved no less premature: without the New World, October no longer meant anything. The struggle with *Novy Mir* was suicidal for *Oktyabr*. The suicide of its editor, Kochetov, scarcely confirms this. But it's a fact that the need for a contrast had been used up, and History was no longer required; a bitter fact, that the "liberals," and not the "Octobrists," can take special credit for the development of this entropy. I well remember a phrase that signified the death agony: "He gets published in both of them." This was said, not of leftists and rightists, but of "real" writers. The names of these journals are synonyms once more.

Here are one crocodile's tears on the subject:

> The two editors were, I recall,
> enemies fiercely at odds,
> their journals the worthy fields
> of a battle
>   nobly fought.
> Through thunder of steel
>   without fear
> the horses advanced at a trot...
> One man was
>   shrewd in the peasant way,
> the other
>   proletarian-blunt.
> Side by side are their early graves.
> I straighten the roses on the snow.
> Once again, I cannot agree

that personality

        has no great power.

I see the print—

        my flesh crawls.

I remember their eyes—

        my soul warms.

There lived two good writers;

it was interesting on earth.

Page 272. *He even liked the czar*

In 1966, in Wiesbaden, a little boy was born—Alexander von Rintelen, the great-great-great-grandson of Alexander Sergeevich Pushkin and Prince Dolgoruky (of the House of Rurik?); the great-great-grandson of Alexander II (a Romanov) and Prince Nikolau Wilhelm of Nassau; the grandson of Count Georg Nikolau von Merenberg* and von Kövér de Gyergyó-Szent-Miklós.

Also living in the Federal Republic of Germany is his "Aunt" Annie Bessel, the great-great-granddaughter of Pushkin and Dubbelt, chief of the gendarmes. The little boy from Wiesbaden may not have the slightest idea his aunt exists, since her origins are considerably lower, although she has twice as much blood from Pushkin. His blood is just 1.555125% Pushkin's, but that is the only blood that links them—not counting, it is true, the same percentage from Nathalie.

It was Pushkin's younger daughter, Natasha, all by herself, who made these bold rhymes in genealogy. Her first husband was Dubbelt's son (and this was more likely a vindictive attraction to the gendarme's uniform than contempt for her father: she had been deeply in love with Prince Orlov and wanted to marry him, but his father, chief of the gendarmes after Dubbelt, had prevented the misalliance with Pushkin's daughter). Her second was Prince Nikolau Wilhelm of Nassau. One of her daughters by him she gave in marriage to Grand Prince Mikhail Mikhailovich Romanov (which infuriated Alexander III); her youngest son she married to Yurievskaya, née Dolgorukova, daughter of Alexander II (by a morganatic marriage). Strong was her first passion, deep the hurt! Her marriages, her children's, and even her grandchildren's hark back to that first rejection. They resonate with her father's complexes and magnify them—allying Pushkin with two royal houses** and continuing the tradition of linking by blood the poets, the czars, and the police.

Page 274. *"There are seven of them... a hundred of them!"*

From a poem by Velimir Khlebnikov (1885-1922), President of the Earth (1918-22).

---

* Georg Nikolau, grandson of Pushkin and son-in-law of Alexander II, spoke not a word of Russian and died in 1948.

** And even three, since her granddaughter, already a descendant of two royal, albeit morganatic, lines, became the lawful wife of Prince Mountbatten.

Page 276. *". . . in collaboration with Howard Fast"*

In the late forties and early fifties, this writer held the only license for contemporary American literature in the USSR. No one had heard of him in the USA. Vigorously writing over there, meanwhile, were authors whose existence we hadn't heard of—including the man whose portrait ("fishing, wearing shorts") is planned for in every house (see commentary to page 17).

Page 278. *"Unlike Victor Nabutov, my dear,... Vladimir Nabokov is a writer"*

In the days when we had just one of everything, we also had one soccer announcer. At that time Nabutov's voice was well known to each of our two hundred million citizens and convicts. His voice competed with that of Sinyavsky himself (the sports commentator, not to be confused with the writer)—as, in its turn, Sinyavsky's voice was already beating (by reason of peacetime) that of Levitan (the news announcer, whom no one any longer confused with the painter).

He told Natasha how Tolstoy had dreamed about a woman's elbow

The famous story associated with the idea for Anna Karenina. For some reason this story is included—along with Pushkin's excitement over his heroine's marriage ("Oh, Tatyana! What a trick you played!"), and symptoms of poisoning in Flaubert—in the generic triad of popular erudition on "the psychology of creation."

The lock of hair (it wasn't her elbow!) belonged to Maria Gartung, Pushkin's eider daughter.

Page 282. *Here we should have a Gogolian exclamation*

Curiously, although he was the founder of Socialist Realism, Maxim Gorky produced nothing from an artistic point of view—apart from the novel *Mother*—to set a new direction. He contributed a series of mottoes, his own image, and a number of examples of new behavior for writers—no more. For artistic discoveries the young literature went to Lev Tolstoy and, oddly enough, to Gogol—a writer of very distant ideology, to put it mildly. Beginning with Sholokhov and Fadeev, no author could paint a "canvas" without resorting to one or another Tolstoyan intonation. Our contemporary classics, including Konstantin Simonov and even the exile whose name one does not take in vain (in the hypostasis in which, as an artist, he is socially realistic), are powered by Tolstoy's steam. In the era of greatest fact-varnishing, even this epic tone became too objective. Others then resorted to a Gogolian tone, but specifically and solely the romantic one. Open the antique *Hero of the Golden Star* (1949), and you'll be rocked on the Dnepr's wave: "Marvelous is the Dnepr..." Pathos! Great pathos! Greater yet: "Don't you think I know what they pay me for? Pathos!" a man who is now a major émigré figure confessed to me, with sorrow, at the Central Literary Club. "Both abroad," he added, "and here."

Page 284. *A steam band was playing "The Blue Danube"*

The author has a weakness for this music. He likes it before he realizes he likes it—at any rate, not because he *ought* to. Heard suddenly in the open air, it gets into the blood at once, bypassing taste and mind. But marches are even more absolute, even more precise. After them, waltzes are refined sugar, decadence. Marches are primal music, beyond discussion. The snobbery of music-lovers, however, has reached the point where a recording of ancient marches and waltzes has been made for home listening—a wonderful performance by the Combined Military Band, under the direction of a major general, with a colonel as chief conductor. On one side, marches; on the other, waltzes. And here is a curious thing: the marches are conducted by the colonel, the waltzes by the general. (Thus, although the secretaries of the Cinematographers Union advocate contemporary subject matter, they leave it to directors who are still trying to become secretaries, like them, while they themselves make movies of the Russian classics.)

tossed up the white ball and caught it on the black
See commentary to page 4, "toss-me, catch me."

Page 288. *the navy-blue... stomp of the uniform*
The old police uniform—a navy and red combination, of prerevolutionary origin. In 1970 the transition was begun (in the capital first) to a new, nobly diplomatic uniform, of black flecked with gray. Generally speaking, recent years have seen great progress in the field of secondary police characteristics: special cars of foreign make, walkie-talkies, puttees, helmets, stars on the shoulder-straps. All this sort of thing has become handsomer, and there's more of it.

Page 289. *Document-experiment-excrement*
The author's immature mind retained a story told by his brother, a student at Leningrad University, in the very early fifties. The story is typical, and epochally lacking in merit. The university's rector—a forty-year-old mathematician and Academician, Stalin Prize laureate, Expert Sportsman in mountain-climbing, and an alpine skier—caught the starved imagination of the students of those years, not only because of his titles, but also because of the following legend. Reportedly, he was riding on the "sausage" (the bumper of the trolley-car). A policeman blew his whistle, removed him from the "sausage," and demanded his documents. He took out his I.D. as a member of the Academy of Sciences and said, "I'm conducting a scientific experiment." The policeman saluted: "Carry on, Comrade Academician!"
No, I've lived too long after all!

Page 292. "*...Mitishatyev's Right-Hand Rule...*"
These mnemonic rules are a dreadful torment! The author could never cope with either the Right or the Left Hand, let alone the Gimlet. Either he understood the laws, or he memorized the rule. Even now, the author doesn't remember this mnemonic, just the torment associated with it. Here he has found a use for the torment.

Page 305. *"Imagine that, no icebergs on the island either..."*

This joke does not belong to the author (it's not his kind of joke); it doesn't even belong to Mitishatyev, who in this instance is modifying a joke by either Ilf or Petrov.

Pages 307, 310. *How did this happen? There's been an imperceptible transition here... (to the end of the paragraph); A groan, a crunch, an authorial gnashing of teeth... (to the end of the paragraph)*

Authorial euphemism. The author is convinced that every plot is based on a false assumption; otherwise, it wouldn't be self-contained. It would dissolve in life, which, again, has neither line nor theme nor fate—nothing of structure. A man like Raskolnikov, let's say, could not have killed the moneylender (he could have killed Lizaveta, a second victim was natural after the first, but the first was impossible). Dostoevsky was faced with a choice. Crime or punishment? Follow the plot or the hero? Or, take a hero who could kill the moneylender (he would not have killed Lizaveta). But that wouldn't be Raskolnikov—and the novel is Raskolnikov, it is punishment. Dostoevsky preferred his hero over truth of plot. And yet without the plot, although it is based on a false life assumption, the hero would not have reacted as powerfully as Dostoevsky needed. Dostoevsky lied in the plot and won the novel.

One could find other examples as well. The ulcers of the plot's assumptions are always in plain sight; forming on them like pustules are device, omission, glib patter. But without them the book will not gather strength, will not make the leap to the energy level of a great work. I am always embarrassed by this small untruth in large things; although I admire achievements obtained by this means, I could never bring myself to use it for my own work. I understand and accept this in myself, with chagrin, as a lack of strength. But I can't overcome it.

This novel, too, however debilitated its plot, was involved in a metaphorical assumption that did not withstand the test of truth. The hero was supposed to get killed in a duel (extenuating circumstance: a *drunken* duel), by an ancient dueling pistol. Everything went fine as long as this was anticipated (but only because it was anticipated), and everything became absolutely impossible when it approached in earnest. We make the literary soup from the ax, of course (this is literally true in *Crime and Punishment*), but there comes a moment when we have to lick the ax clean in its capacity as marrowbone—and it doesn't taste good. Now we sprinkle in the final spice, colonial commodity: device, trick, grimace, a small authorial voice... The very thing it's all about is always done slapdash.

Page 310. *blackjack. The same small-town grimaces*

Blackjack (twenty-one), as played on the bunks in prison camp, is an intelligent, psychological game of nerves. A man can lose his last ruble, his last pair of pants, his wife, and his life. When he has bought a card, therefore, he must do nothing to betray its worth. The task of not rejoicing and not grieving is too difficult for a man gripped by gambling fever. So the card is turned up slowly, just barely, as if without showing it even to himself—not merely to prevent others from spying, but to preserve his mask. That is how they play on the bunks, and the same style can be seen on the suburban electric trains: either the people who ride them are somewhat marginal types and have seen a lot in their time, or the benches in the car remind them somewhat of the bunks.

Page 316. *the lame word "dilogy"*

In the epoch when increasingly broad "canvases" were unfolding in our literature, everyone began striving to write, not just a great epic novel, but necessarily a trilogy. *Daybreak, Into the Storm, No Rest for the Weary,* let's say. Or *The Gale, Dawn, There Shall Be No Death.* (Usually, by the time the third novel was written, the liberal era had arrived and long titles were in style.) The writers who were late to join in this carpet-weaving—those who couldn't get as far as the third novel, or who had started with the second—brought forth this literary novelty, a genre designation for the unfinished trilogy: the dilogy. For a dilogy, it was already time to receive a prize. Gradually it became clear that the third novel wasn't obligatory. The concept of the "dilogy" was accepted as a new, secretarial genre.

Page 321. *and picks up a page from the floor*

The page is authentic (see commentary to page 85, concerning names). It was found in the same place as the scrap of newspaper (see commentary to page 6), but at a different address (9/11 Rustaveli Street, Moscow—the dormitory of the Gorky Literary Institute).

By the job

Given the absence of competition and unemployment, there are three basic forms of wage: by the hour, by the piece, and by the job. The last is not ideologically encouraged, as a form that leads to rushed work, chiseling, and industrial safety violations and harbors the seeds of capitalist entrepreneurship. The job rate is resorted to in extreme cases (when a thing needs to be done quickly and well). This is a predetermined sum for a set amount of work, without considering the time or the number of workmen (see footnote to commentary to page 345).

Page 322. *There was now no such thing as "the people"*

When nothing is happening, everything is becoming different. After the war, colossal changes occurred in the structure of the city; the intelligentsia learned of them through the impossibility of hiring any kind of help. As soon as the intelligentsia grew somewhat stronger financially, those whom they might have hired also grew stronger. They moved, set up house, and didn't want to "lower" themselves. The fruit of revolutionary change was that nobody wanted to serve anybody else; the society, it seemed, was founded on this. The long and complicated process of alienation from the land, flight from the village, and acquisition of urban status had taken place in a way invisible to the native urbanite. And he discovered, affectedly, that "you can't get help."

405

Page 325. *could make a drowned man surface*

A steamboat sailed down the river and occasionally fired a cannon... A description of this kind of fishing expedition may be found in Mark Twain's *Huckleberry Finn*.

Page 326. *special BF-2 glue*

In the era of the Cult, the birth of a new brand name was a phenomenon. It happened once a year, or even less often. Sugared Cranberries, Rowanberries in Cognac, the Tourist bicycle, the Stalin Motor Works refrigerator, or this: BF-2 glue... They were not objects but concepts, a stirring of life, remarked by all. Everyone glued with this glue; everything that had ever broken was glued; I fought the temptation to break things in order to glue them back together. The Stalin Prize was awarded for the glue, and everyone received this news with great satisfaction. It wouldn't be long now... No, Stalin was doomed. The appearance of BF-2 was one of the signals. The hepcats were another. Their *stirring* is described here in the novel. The *first* things to appear, before his death, were harbingers. Something had begun to appear—in this lay his sentence.

the brown right to belong to our own selves

The author finds it hard to explain this coloration in an understandable way. In any case, he is not alluding to Nazism. But neither can it be said that this is merely the color of shit.

"Here, take this Jewish ashtray"

A curious aspect of anti-Semitism as it develops into persecution mania: people stop recognizing Russians! Either by face or by name. To keep them from doubting you, you have to be towheaded, snub-nosed, and pockmarked, with an unpretentious surname ending in -ov. People have forgotten that Russians have long noses—degeneracy is pursued as a national trait. In any case, Grigorovich was not a Jew.

Page 328. *BRONZE FOLK*

Again without debating the quality of the pun, I refer the reader to the commentary to page 243.

Page 334. *Does the Vice SEA's glass eye see?*

The author lived for some time in the dormitory of the Gorky Literary Institute (see commentary to page 321). Well, the superintendent of this dormitory (the commandant) was the ex-commandant of Butyrsky Prison. He was nicknamed Cyclops because he had one eye. Now he is Vice Superintendent (for Economic Affairs) of the same institute. This does not mean that the author painted from life. An ordinary coincidence, proving the rule.

Page 335. *No, no, Gottich didn't say anything to me... Which Gottich?*

If Gottich really is a stoolie, this Vice Superintendent is the man he would most likely report to.

Page 336. *The American was the very writer*
See commentary to page 225.

Page 339. *pas de deux... gracefully expressing his yearning for Parasha*
Parasha is the heroine of, again, *The Bronze Horseman*. R. M. Glier wrote a ballet based on it, of the same kind as BF-2 glue (see commentary to page 326). I assume it must have a pas de deux.

Page 340. *(The epigraph)*
Given the ever-growing tendency to celebrate anniversaries and dates of all kinds, the author considered dedicating his novel to the centennial of the publication of *The Devils*. Modesty wasn't the only thing that stopped him, however; he also had an inconclusive, ambiguous attitude toward the great novel. To array his own novel with *The Devils*, as if picking up the tradition and carrying on the line, would not only be dangerous, by comparison, but also inaccurate (the latter is more important). The problem is that in some areas, despite all, it remains unclear which comes first: the phenomenon or its reflection? the law or its formulation? the act or the thought? the deed or the word? Yes, Dostoevsky turned the exceptional light of his genius on a phenomenon barely conceived, still insignificant— and illuminated it through and through, like an X ray. But the insignificant is, indeed, insignificant. Did he not also *enlighten* it? Did he not give form to an evil so incapable that it could never have become self-aware, without outside help? It was nothing, yet it had become a phenomenon! Described by a genius! "Isn't this flattering! So we do exist, if someone's writing about us! And look who it is! What a writer!" The fact is, the demons gathered strength when they *found that they existed*, after the novel. It is natural (and accepted) to think that a genius sees the future, that the demons would have developed even without the novel, and that Dostoevsky gave warning. But no one has ever yet heeded the warning of an artist. Literature isn't generally "for use." It isn't a medicine, or any of the other things that aren't literature. Only the devils themselves know how to use it. They can turn anything to their advantage. Uncreative forces are always destructive, even if passive. How can a force that is incapable of creating anything be active? Solely by attracting someone else's creative energy, if only in the form of attention. What can draw greater attention than a great novel? Devils have no pride, no respect, no anything... They exist only in the minds of others; otherwise, they don't exist. To disbelieve that they exist is to subject them to self-annihilation. Did not Dostoevsky breathe life into them? Are we not doing the same now?
So the author thought better of dedicating the novel. It's about something else. It's about the fruits of a relationship, not about forces. To delve into the forces is to summon them to action. No! The author did not dedicate the novel. But he did accept the obligation of finishing it by that significant date—the centennial of the birth of the devils.

Page 341. *we append a lemma*

I had thought I would find the lemma when I was asked about it. But no. As it happens, I haven't yet found the lemma. I've found out what a lemma is, though: a demonstrable truth that has significance only for another, more significant truth, a theorem.

Page 342. *a Society for the Preservation of Literary Heroes from Their Authors*

Such a society would hardly be much less functional than other preservation societies (for nature, for monuments). The literary hero, too, is a natural phenomenon and a monument. At any rate, there are opportunities for symposia and congresses. But what can a preservation society do, except amuse itself on a noble and respectable basis?

An educated friend of mine told me about an important book, *The Rose of the World*, by Daniil Andreev (son of the writer). This is a great systematic spiritual construct, an edifice of Existence—written in prison camp. Its dates are curious: 1949-1958. That is, while we still had the Cult, and later the unmasking of it, while the two epochs were converging and diverging, this man sat calmly between, not in historical time but in the time allotted to him by God, and *did his job*. Well, in his book (as told to me), the world is many-layered. Each layer is real, and one of these layers is populated by—literary heroes! (For the power of an assumption, see commentary to pages 307, 310.) Nikolai Fyodorov, to build his great edifice of the Common Cause, needed the peremptory resurrection of *all* the dead. I am not familiar with the whole of Andreev's construct, but even on its periphery he assumed that literary heroes were alive—not in some figurative sense, as in my book, but in a literal and real sense. Common sense creates nothing: it's a parasite.

Page 345. *I am guilty of this "allusion," as it is stylishly called now*

This has, indeed, become an editorial word; I often hear it. It means (as I gather from its use—I've never learned the dictionary definition) a different perception of the same thing. Suppose you meant to say, and you think you did say, one thing. But you are understood (or could be understood) to have said another, perhaps even the contrary, or in any case not what you would wish. And so on. You intended no innuendo, but it came out as an innuendo; you had no thought of saying anything in opposition, but it... The new life of this word is assured, I think, less by the fact that a remark can have a wealth of meanings than by the fact that it can have *two*. Since we now hold the very polite opinion that an honest man should not be insulted by unwarranted suspicion, and should especially not be accused, this convenient editorial form has arisen—the little word "allusion." Instead of the recent, straightforward: "Why, this will never do, old man! What language! Where do you think you'd be published?" Through the intermediate threat: "Do you realize what you've written!" To the mild form: "You've put down the wrong word. It's not what you had in mind, of course. *I* see what you meant, but, you know, you could easily be understood as saying... You didn't mean that.

You don't mean that, do you? Let's remove it, replace it, change it." Most often the author did mean to say what he said, and the editor understood him perfectly well, and in exactly the right sense, the author's.

By way of evidence, I will cite two or three examples of "pure" allusions from my own experience, when I really hadn't supposed I was writing anything I "shouldn't," but it turned out... In "Journey to a Childhood Friend," for instance, I'm flying to Kamchatka, and I spend a lot of time hanging around in intermediate airports because of bad weather. I needed this device in order to get the story told during the forced layovers. The editor was frightened: "What does this add up to? 'Hellishly bad weather hung over the entire country.' That's what you wrote! Surely you'll be understood to mean..." And he launched into a kind of politics that I really hadn't suspected. I was scared. "But I was thinking only of meteorological conditions, no others! The natural phenomenon." "I believe you," the editor said. We "removed" the phrase.

Weather in general is a dangerous subject. They didn't let me name a book *Life in Windy Weather*. Which climate, where is the weather? From what quarter does the wind blow? In the story "The Wheel," I had a passage about the real place of sporting passions in the world around us. For scale, I got a newspaper and discovered it had three lines—garbled, at that—about a sports event that had filled all my thoughts and emotions. After waxing indignant over this, I took another tack: What if I knew the actual passions, the destinies, that lay behind other transient considerations—for example, the appointment and recall of an ambassador? And the weather, I went on to exclaim, is an altogether cosmic phenomenon. How can we speak of it in a trivial way? —On the whole, an extremely calm and tranquil line of reasoning. At the end of the passage came a seemingly paradoxical question: "Do you know that the fastest motorcycles are now made in Japan? And while we are all afraid of China, the Japanese are going somewhere in a polite and noiseless hurry?" Anticipating that this silly question might call up an allusion, I was prepared to remove China, for that is a name one doesn't take in vain in our country. But I could never, ever have anticipated the way it all turned out. "Quite a job you did. Deft. Well-aimed." "What are you talking about?" I asked, anticipating China. "You're so caustic about the ambassador. Did you have a score to settle?" I was bewildered: "With whom, for pity's sake?" "Oh, come off it! Tolstikov!" "Which Tolstikov?!" Here's what had happened. On the very day I was working with the editor, it had been made public that Tolstikov, who had been first secretary of the party's Leningrad Regional Committee, was being appointed ambassador to China. At the time, there really had been a lot of talk that he had committed some offense, had made people angry, and was going to be removed. No one, of course, expected he would be shipped to China. And now he was removed—would you believe it, on the exact same day "The Wheel" was being edited. He was removed, but so was my paragraph about the ambassador (and about China, of course). I proposed only China. Without it, there wouldn't be any bridge, I said, and no innuendo would arise. I said I had written the paragraph over a year ago, when Tolstikov was very solidly in power. By the time this was published (not tomorrow, after all!), no one would even think of him, and he himself would be far away... Useless! Characteristically, an allusion is in effect at the precise moment of editing, which, at a minimum, is six months distant from the allusions associated with the publication date. No one can anticipate those.

The names of things are the first to be contaminated by an allusion. Here is an example, this time involving *Pushkin House*. Having published separately, in five years of trying, five chapters, mainly from the second part of the novel, I decided to combine them in a book, under the title *A Hero of Our Time*. Each chapter, and the cycle as a whole, had an accompanying epigraph from Lermontov, which made a clear device. Absolutely not! What, and have people think someone like your Odoevtsev is the hero of our time? Argument was useless. The cycle was titled *Young Odoevtsev*. Under the epigraphs it had "Bela," "Pechorin's Diary"—the titles of Lermontov's chapters, but in no case that of the novel from which they were taken. Lermontov was banned, but not Bitov.

The author does not know French, and he hasn't read or seen *Finnegans Wake* (he's not alone). Here I take the opportunity to explain myself on the slippery question of literary influences—a question on which one should never explain himself, lest he inevitably be suspected of the very thing he's disowning.

I recognize full well, of course, that to do a thing the second time is not simply to repeat it; that you can be second even without knowing what you are repeating; that you can catch an influence even from the air, not just from a book you have read; that to invent the integral calculus all over again, out of ignorance, is nevertheless easier and does not require the genius of a Newton; that being first to discover something is a quality, not a registration number. To hear a word or two is more than enough, you don't need to know the context. Mentions of a name, of a book title, are enough to sear you with the heat of discovery. When you know that someone has jumped a height, you won't hope to out-jump the champion by setting the bar a little lower. Knowing that someone else took the risk, and was capable of the feat, is enough to render your independent intention of accomplishing the same thing secondary. Literature, thank God, is not a sport and not a science—accomplishments do not take the form of records and formulas. The same subjects raised by different individuals can have value; closely similar forms can arise independently at the same time or at different times—they will be valuable. But even in literature the first, as a rule, is stronger than the independent birth of the second. With the origination and repetition of new forms, the situation is more complicated: geniuses, as a rule, have not invented new things but have synthesized what was accumulated before their time. In Marlinsky and Odoevsky there are more verbal inventions than in Pushkin, Lermontov, and Gogol, who took advantage of theirs. In Fyodor Sologub we will find poems written "before" Blok. *The Trial*, for all that, is more powerful than *Invitation to a Beheading*; yet what a pity it would be if Nabokov had "read Kafka in time" and failed to undertake his *Invitation*.

The author seems to understand all this... It would be foolish to deny influ-

410

ences. Nevertheless, I would like to answer certain charges of outright imitation, which the author has already heard and hopes to hear again.

The three most substantial are: Dostoevsky, Proust, and Nabokov.

Proust is easiest for me to answer: he is not Russian, this charge doesn't bother me. The possibility cannot be excluded that I had come under his influence when I began the novel, when I was writing "Faina" and "Albina." I had read him for the first time just the year before—I read *Swann in Love,* and it reminded me of many things in myself, I recognized it, it made an impression, and so forth. But even before that, I had finished writing "The Garden," and it seems to me that "Faina" shows much more of this autoinfluence. I hadn't yet moved on from "The Garden." In sum, I don't deny Proust, this doesn't bother me.

It's more complicated with Dostoevsky, whose influence is altogether impossible to deny. But there are two nuances here. First, he is a very "hard-to-remember" writer and would therefore be difficult to imitate directly. Second, Dostoevsky's influence is not necessarily a literary one. He hasn't yet been outlived, he is encountered in life itself, especially in Russian life. Only for a man who recognizes life primarily through literature (as do the critics) will existing reality be contaminated by Dostoevsky's brand. That a phenomenon has been described does not mean it has disappeared from life (although that is what it ought to mean... more on this another time). Precisely because we have forgotten him and emerged from under his influence, it is easy to fall into the Dostoevskian mode—in our lives, our personal experience. Here in Russia people still think, still feel, as they did in Dostoevsky's works, perhaps to an even greater extent than they did in his own time. The same piercing X-ray illumination is manifest here as in the social prophecies of The Devils (see commentary to page 340). So, one may be pushed into "imitating" Dostoevsky, not by Dostoevsky himself, but by the real life that he described yet did not cancel (and even confirmed). Here is a characteristic episode from personal experience... In 1965 I found myself at E.'s funeral repast (without any legitimate purpose—I hadn't even been acquainted with him, hadn't been to the funeral... in the Dostoevskian manner, the Russian manner). A ringleader in the ideological campaigns of 1949, he had a reputation that broke the record for terror. But something, even in him, was not that simple (there wasn't enough black paint, he was supposed to have been so black). Reportedly, toward the end of his life he couldn't read even a line of the literature he had been propagandizing; he became a recluse and read only Chekhov and Dostoevsky; his wife gave herself devoutly to religion and went around in black, like a nun; he associated only with her (she still appeared in public, but he hadn't been seen in years). This was an unexpected twist. He died. I found the funeral repast in full swing. Except for one man, who had invited me, the company was unfamiliar. But within five minutes I had begun to see how diverse and distinctive it was: the people bore a parodic resemblance to Dostoevsky's heroes. Svidrigaylov and Shatov were both here, and a parody of Stavrogin, and a copy of Verkhovensky, and two or three Lebyadkins (I write it this way now—at the time, for some reason, these analogies did not occur to me, perhaps precisely because of the obvious resemblance; afterwards, moreover, I got to know many of them a little better and was convinced in each case individually; still later I connected the scene). They were drinking; Verkhovensky drank nothing, the rest a great deal. They made speeches. One does not speak ill of the dead, and they all began well, noting his scope and talent (besides, even the orators were far from pure). But then, somehow, they would suddenly slide into a deep "but," and, in the effort to scramble out of it, end in outright vilification. So it went with each. There were a lot of people, and most were simply partying—drinking, laughing loudly, and clinking glasses—having frankly forgotten the deceased. Those who were trying to get the company back on the right track (from the best of motives: despite all, it was a death) were themselves industriously reviling E. But they kept on eating and drinking. Never in my life had I imagined such a funeral repast! The loathsomeness of it all sucked you in, and somehow stickily wouldn't let go, as though this spectacle would also, on top of everything else, have to end in such a way that you'd better get out while there was time, but you simply couldn't. And then—the climax. Just as I reached the limit of my endurance and got up to leave, and three others after me—Verkhovensky discovered he had lost thirty rubles. Just what everyone had been waiting for! It had begun! Such sophisticated suggestions and hypotheses. No one leave—search everyone in turn. That proved impossible, however. They unanimously settled on a victim. It turned out to be a very young, pretty (and poor!) girl, whom "Shatov" had brought. She burst into tears and denials. The activists (an instantaneously formed brigade of Young Pioneer do-gooders, a five-man tribunal) undertook to frisk her. They discussed technique and withdrew, dragging her behind them. (Shatov himself, with an expression of adamant exemplariness, gave her a push in the back and an edifying admonition.) Verkhovensky, in his gleeful Komsomol indignation, was in the lead and all over the place. In sum, they undressed her in a specially assigned room—I wasn't there—and found nothing. Again it was proposed that everyone be frisked. I broke out, I don't remember how, carrying this scene in my teeth and trembling over the gift of experience: I would fit this little scene in somewhere, it would not go to waste! And not a word would have to be invented. The whole thing would plop right into a novel, as into a swamp, spattering the chapters... I held it in reserve for several years but never could get myself to write the appropriate novel. And I lost my chance. I reread *Crime and Punishment*, came to Marmeladov's funeral repast—and my eyes popped. Identical! Also an allusion, in its way. And I, too, in hastily describing this episode, have forgotten the main point, the culprit, the death, E. himself, just as all the participants forgot at the moment of the frisking. Is this not a retribution, such a funeral repast? Hence the sole possible toast in the deceased's favor: this meant he had suffered, this meant his seclusion had not been in vain, this meant a little point of conscience had shone in that black hole, if the Lord had managed to chastise him with suffering during his lifetime and with desecration at his funeral, while his soul still saw... After all, the man who escaped a reckoning when he departed bore the final cross: he no longer had a soul to chastise, he was simply no longer on this earth. But this E., perhaps, was already chatting with his friend Chekhov, arm in arm along a cloud, and Chekhov, with no special urgency, was gently chiding him... No, I can't possibly deny the influence of Dostoevsky, either.

Nor do I want to deny Nabokov. Allowing for everything I have said above and below, however, that is what I must do. I first heard his name in 1960 and read him in December of 1970. How I evaded reading him for ten years I can't imagine. Fate. For good or for ill, there would be no *Pushkin House* had I read Nabokov earlier. As for what would have existed instead—I just don't know. At the moment I opened *The Gift*, my novel was in definitive form up to page 337; I had the rest, to the end, in scraps and drafts. I read in succession, albeit in English translation, *The Gift* and *Invitation to a Beheading*—and was silenced. Another six months passed before I recovered from the—I won't say impression—recovered from the blow, and set about finishing the conclusion. From that moment on, I no longer had a right to deny either an aerial influence or a direct one, even though I strove to get back into the groove of what I had written before being disarmed by that reading. Painstakingly I banished each phrase that veered toward Nabokov, except for two (on pages 328 and 337), which I left especially so that people could reproach me for them, because they had already been written on the scraps that ran ahead. Here is what Nabokov himself wrote in the same connection in 1959, in the foreword to the English translation of *Invitation to a Beheading*, where he recalls the circumstances of the book's publication in Russian in 1938:

> Emigré reviewers, who were puzzled but liked it, thought they distinguished in it a "Kafkaesque" strain, not knowing that I had no German, was completely ignorant of modern German literature, and had not yet read any French or English translations of Kafka's works. No doubt, there do exist certain stylistic links between this book and, say, my earlier stories (or my later *Bend Sinister*); but there are none between it and *Le château* or *The Trial.* Spiritual affinities have no place in my concept of literary criticism, but if I did have to choose a kindred soul, it would certainly be that great artist rather than G. H. Orwell or other popular purveyors of illustrated ideas and publicistic fiction. Incidentally, I could never understand why every book of mine invariably sends reviewers scurrying in search of more or less celebrated names for the purpose of passionate comparison.

Then comes a list of twenty mutually exclusive names, embracing five centuries and as many literatures. It includes Charlie Chaplin and the hero of one of Nabokov's novels, a writer by profession.

Imitating him (this time in sound memory), I refer the reader to the commentaries to pages 115 and 178.

One more point. Literature is a continuous and uninterrupted process. If some link is hidden, or omitted, or seems to have fallen out, this doesn't mean that the link doesn't exist, that the chain is broken—for without that link there can be no continuation. It means that we are standing right where the link is missing. This is the end, not a rupture. In order to thread the next (a new) link onto the chain, we will have to discover the lost one again, resurrect it, invent it, reconstruct it from its bones, like Cuvier. Repetitions here—the invention of the bicycle and the discovery of gunpowder—are not so much alarming as inevitable. Nabokov can't help existing in Russian literature, if only for the reason that he does exist. There's no getting away from this. We cannot subtract him, even if we don't know of his existence. Paleontology of this kind is inevitably weaker than the unknown original, but that's another matter. Nabokov is uninterrupted Russian literature, as though nothing had happened to it after his departure; fate had to take a unique zigzag to arrange, for him personally, the phenomenon of extrahistoricity. Nabokov was able to continue *the* literature. As it had been, as it would have been, as it would have become. He prolonged it, he closed it. *The* literature. And yet, wonderful as that literature might have been, prose will still be written. People wrote after the Golden Age of Pushkin, Lermontov, and Gogol—worse, but they wrote. Both the silver and the bronze age have departed. But still to come are the copper, the tin, the wood, the clay, the potato, and finally the cardboard age—and all these will still be literature—before the synthetic age finally arrives, infinite as eternity.

As you see, the author is serious about his own work. He is full of faith. There is yet SOMETHING TO BE DONE.*

1971, 1978

* For example... Page 349. *my hundred and one percent*
This is the minimum amount by which one must "overfulfill" the plan in order to receive the predetermined wage supplements. The figure 101 is so often seen in reports that it can't help raising suspicion. A friend of mine got into a bit of trouble with this. In an essay on whaling ships (which at that time, before the cosmonauts, were in special vogue), he indicated that they overfulfilled their plan by precisely this percentage. I don't know how many this meant—101 whales, or 50.5—but the essay caused a ruckus and was withdrawn in censorship. One may only fulfill, never overfulfill, the plan for whales, it turned out, for the right to this killing is regulated by an international agreement. It can't possibly be overfulfilled. "They" wouldn't understand the hundred and one percent.
Such, too, is this last note. There are now a hundred and one percent of them.

Harvill Paperbacks are published by Collins Harvill,
a Division of the Collins Publishing Group

1. Giuseppe Tomasi di Lampedusa *The Leopard*
2. Boris Pasternak *Doctor Zhivago*
3. Alexander Solzhenitsyn *The Gulag Archipelago 1918-1956*
4. Jonathan Raban *Soft City*
5. Alan Ross *Blindfold Games*
6. Joy Adamson *Queen of Shaba*
7. Vasily Grossman *Forever Flowing*
8. Peter Levi *The Frontiers of Paradise*
9. Ernst Pawel *The Nightmare of Reason*
10. Patrick O'Brian *Joseph Banks*
11. Mikhail Bulgakov *The Master and Margarita*
12. Leonid Borodin *Partings*
13. Salvator Satta *The Day of Judgement*
14. Peter Matthiessen *At Play in the Fields of the Lord*
15. Alexander Solzhenitsyn *The First Circle*
16. Homer, translated by Robert Fitgerald *The Odyssey*
17. George MacDonald Fraser *The Steel Bonnets*
18. Peter Matthiessen *The Cloud Forest*
19. Theodore Zeldin *The French*
20. George Perec *Life A User's Manual*
21. Nicholas Gage *Eleni*
22. Eugenia Ginzburg *Into the Whirlwind*
23. Eugenia Ginzburg *Within the Whirlwind*
24. Mikhail Bulgakov *The Heart of a Dog*
25. Vincent Cronin *Louis and Antoinette*
26. Alan Ross *The Bandit on the Billiard Table*
27. Fyodor Dostoyevsky *The Double*
28. Alan Ross *Time Was Away*
29. Peter Matthiessen *Under the Mountain Wall*
30. Peter Matthiessen *The Snow Leopard*
31. Peter Matthiessen *Far Tortuga*
32. Jorge Amado *Shepherds of the Night*
33. Jorge Amado *The Violent Land*
34. Jorge Amado *Tent of Miracles*
35. Torgny Lindgren *Bathsheba*
36. Antæus *Journals, Notebooks & Diaries*
37. Edmonde Charles-Roux *Chanel*
38. Nadezhda Mandelstam *Hope Against Hope*
39. Nadezhda Mandelstam *Hope Abandoned*
40. Raymond Carver *Elephant and Other Stories*
41. Vincent Cronin *Catherine, Empress of All the Russias*